THEATER
OF THE STARS

ALSO BY N. M. KELBY

In the Company of Angels

THEATER
OF THE STARS

A NOVEL OF PHYSICS AND MEMORY

❧ N . M . K e l b y ❧

An Imprint of Hyperion
NEW YORK

F KELBY

Library of Congress Cataloging-in-Publication Data

Kelby, N. M. (Nicole M.)
    Theater of the stars : a novel of physics and memory / N.M. Kelby.—1st ed.
    p. cm.
    ISBN 0-7868-6858-9
    1. Children of Holocaust survivors—Fiction. 2. Mothers and daughters—Fiction.
3. Suicidal behavior—Fiction. 4. Jewish families—Fiction. 5. Astrophysicists—
Fiction. 6. Paris (France)—Fiction. 7. Jewish women—Fiction. 8. New Mexico—
Fiction. 9. Amnesia—Fiction. I. Title.

PS3561.E382T47 2003
813'.6—dc21   2003044975

FIRST EDITION

10   9   8   7   6   5   4   3   2   1

To my husband, Steven,
who makes all things possible through his love.

In the course of the last four months it has been made probable through the work of Joliot in France as well as Fermi and Szilard in America—that it may become possible to set up a nuclear chain reaction in a large mass of uranium, by which vast amounts of power and large quantities of new radium-like elements would be generated. Now it appears almost certain that this could be achieved in the immediate future.

This new phenomenon would also lead to the construction of bombs, and it is conceivable—though much less certain—that extremely powerful bombs of a new type may thus be constructed.

—Albert Einstein to President Roosevelt in the first of four letters that led to the creation of the Manhattan Project

THEATER
OF THE STARS

"LOVE IS ALL I HAVE EVER WANTED," he told her. They were seated at the café across from his father's fur salon. The café was noisy. Crowded. She leaned in to hear what he was saying. She could not, but nodded as if she did. So he opened the small velvet box. Offered it.

Across the street in front of the salon his father took a photograph of the moment; the ring had been in the family a long time. The father was a romantic. He wanted to have the photo framed and give it to them at the wedding. In the spring of 1940, with the world at war, not many in Paris owned cameras. Not many owned cameras anywhere. The furrier had purchased it on the black market. The photo would have been quite an unusual gift.

But when the picture was developed it just looked like a picture of the street. The father was too far away to capture the moment. The face of his son was unreadable. The woman's long hair cloaked her response.

No matter. There was no wedding.

"I do not see myself as being anyone's wife," the woman said.

"I see," the man said.

Still, his father couldn't bear to throw the photograph away. For him, just knowing his son was capable of love pleased him. He didn't understand that this moment marked the unraveling of everything.

Jacques, the father, died before everything came undone.

OUTSIDE THE HOTEL ROOM, THE PARIS SKY is luminescent as gray pearls. It is nearly sunrise. Light from the street tumbles through the tall narrow windows across Lucienne's bed, the paper of her skin. She is a large woman. No longer that young. Her cotton nightgown is twisted, as is her hair. Tangled like so many copper wires. Her arms are thrown open. From a distance, she looks as if she's in a newspaper photograph. The tornado long gone, she is cast aside, the only thing that remains of what was once a house, a home, a family.

Lucienne is dreaming. Deep in sweat and visions, dreaming of a black hole she's discovered in the Northern Sky. There are several types of black holes, many of them purely mathematical. They can't be seen or measured, absorb all light. Lucienne's black hole is a cannibal, attached to V325Andromedae, a dying star in the

Andromeda constellation, one of the many stars of the "Chained Woman," or so "Andromeda" means. The irony does not escape Lucienne. She's spent the past three years watching this particular part of the Northern Sky. Feels chained to it herself.

But it was worth it, she tells herself and nearly means it. It was the boost her career needed. The black hole Lucienne has found is remarkable. Feeds off the star in a turbulent firestorm. A warped cyclone of ultraviolet rays, spinning this way and that. And she saw it first. Could reasonably prove its identity before anyone else. Ruled out the possibility that it's a quasar, or something other than what she was hoping it was. And so Lucienne had the honor of naming it V325BAndromedae. The "B" stands for black hole.

The name is not very poetic. It's more like a road map, tells you what part of the sky to look in. At least for now. V325BAndromedae is furious and hungry, pulling everything into its swirling path, into its darkness. And now, she finds herself dreaming of it. She doesn't know why these dreams began. What triggered them. Lucienne doesn't usually dream, or at least remember dreaming.

I work too hard, she tells herself. Which is true. Lucienne is the Clare Boothe Luce Assistant Professor of Astronomy at Leeds, a small private college just outside of Boston. It's a prestigious position but, unfortunately, not tenured. Renewable every three years. So Lucienne feels she always has to prove herself. And so she works too hard.

She's come to believe that's why her marriage to Ethan fell apart. One day she discovered they were strangers, had always been strangers. She was just too busy to notice. At least that's what she believes. Tallies up their time together as if it were one of her equations. Ten-hour days at the college. Months away on sabbatical. Weekends working on papers or books, or both. And then there are the public lectures, every Friday night from 9 to 11 P.M. They're more side shows than lectures, multimedia events with fog machines and the heavy-metal music of Metallica, or The Who, or Pink Floyd, depending on the topic. They're not very dignified, but they sell out early and the college needs the money. And so Lucienne does it, and does it well.

But all of it takes time and time adds up.

Sometimes at night, when Lucienne can't sleep, she runs the numbers of her and Ethan's life together, as one would count sheep.

Sixteen years of marriage is approximately 5,838 days, given leap years, she always begins. 140,112 hours. More or less.

Then she calculates the number of hours she's spent away from him. Every time she does this, she remembers a trip she'd forgotten, or a weekend conference. The current total of time she has spent away is 120,400 hours. Which means that in 16 years, Ethan and Lucienne have spent a total of 19,712 hours together, or 821 days, or 27 months. Two years and 3 months is the sum total of their marriage. Give or take a few hours.

What's wrong between Lucienne and Ethan isn't quite as simple as work, and she knows it. But most days it's easier to blame work. Somewhat less painful.

Ethan is also an astrophysicist. Competent, not brilliant, but very charming. They married while they were still students. After graduation, it was difficult to find a university to hire them both. He was offered a part-time position in Gainesville, Florida. Lucienne was presented the fellowship in Boston, a city she loved.

"Just for three years," she promised—and so they went.

That was fifteen years ago.

At first, Ethan tried to find a suitable position so that at the end of the three years they would have another place to go. But it was difficult. His published work was minimal. Academic history, only passable. So after a while, he stopped trying. He began to write Lucienne's grants and to manage her paperwork. Learned to cook well.

"I used up all my ambition in a previous life," Ethan told their friends. He'd been a child star in Israel. Somewhat famous. Somewhat beloved. He worked in both movies and television. In his youth, he had such a sweet face. Black curls like a cherub. But then he grew up.

"Too fast," he'd say, but never elaborate.

The fame of Ethan's youth would have allowed him some cachet in their social circles, but he never would talk about it. When pushed he'd say, "I'm the perfect faculty wife now and that's all that really matters," and through the years he sounded less and less bitter when he said it.

It's often a problem when scientists marry. There just aren't that many jobs. Compromises have to be made. What makes it worse is that astrophysicists often marry one another. It's an occupational hazard of sorts. It isn't easy to date when you spend most of your nights sitting in the dark listening to the stars. And even if you met someone not in your field, what would you have in common?

Science consumes. It's competitive. Intense. After a while it becomes all that you think about. Even if you're not ambitious, even if you don't feel the need to be the first to discover this or that, you're still a public dreamer. Nothing is ever completely taken for granted. Not the sun rising. Not the stars coming out at night. Not the burnished glow of a harvest moon. All of it is a puzzle to be solved.

The nature of the work makes you think in impossible ways, imagine impossible things and then be driven by the need to prove them with equations that sometimes are too large even to be imagined, much less written down and verified.

Family reunions often feel like symposiums.

It's an impossible life. Especially if, like Ethan, you have the sense of wonder, but not the talent.

Lucienne tells her students that if they were born in an earlier time, they'd be populating the asylums.

"Or maybe we are," she says, "and we're just too busy to notice."

The joke always gets a laugh, but on some level she means it.

Still, for a long time, Lucienne felt lucky to be one of the inmates, at least at her particular asylum. It's not difficult to understand why. Leeds College is a well-respected liberal arts school, which, unlike most four-year institutions, pours a good deal of money into its astronomy program. Ivy-walled and nearly postcard perfect, it was named after Julian Leeds, a department store heir with a love of "star gazing," as he called it.

On a brass plaque outside of the observatory there's a quote from the journal of Ralph Waldo Emerson:

This is the road to the stars. Every fixture and instrument in
the building, every nail and pin, has a direct reference to the
Milky Way, the fixed stars, and the nebulae, and we leave
the Americas and history at the door when we come in.

Every time Lucienne passes this plaque she rubs it, as if it were a Buddha, for luck.

The observatory itself is science-grade and features a sixteen-inch reflecting telescope. Baby Kitt, Lucienne calls it, because it's built just like the one at the Kitt Peak National Observatory, and it's nearly as advanced. The telescope is interfaced with software that will automatically locate any object you program it to find, and then capture the image of it with an ultrasensitive CCD camera that will reduce and analyze it.

Serious work can be done here, and is. This past year, thanks to Ethan's grant-writing skills, Lucienne received a $400,000 grant from the National Science Foundation. The money will not only fund her continuing research on the black hole, but underwrite Lucienne's sabbatical so that she can finally have the time to develop a new public lecture series based on her findings, a series devoid of Pink Floyd and fog machines.

The department head is skeptical about its viability, but Lucienne's confident that the series will still sell out. Even without the light show. The concept of black holes is the only scientific theory that Lucienne knows of with groupies and 4,389 Web sites. And conventions. It even has its own conspiracy theories.

"Black holes are the seeds of science fiction," she tells her students. "A ripple in the space-time continuum from which nothing can escape, not even light."

Technically, a black hole is a mass of dense energy that's formed when stars die. Or, at least, that's what's assumed. You really can't see a black hole because no light can escape from one. So, you measure what remains. The gravitational pull. The energy around it. You measure the void, if you can. If it's not too great. It's difficult, though. A black hole pulls everything into it. Swallows it whole.

Just like grief. At least, that's what Lucienne's begun to think. It's an odd thought and she knows it, unscientific, but she can't help thinking it. She misses Ethan, grieves the loss of him, especially those moments that are so difficult to explain. The quiet moments. The grace of them. How they'd lie together before sleep, arms touching, and she'd listen to him breathe, strong and steady. In those moments, she felt connected in a way she never expected to be. Loved.

And now he's gone.

It was her choice, but still, she grieves it. The loss of Ethan has cast a shadow over everything she does. Even her work. She's come to think that the void of a star, like the loss of a loved one, is immeasurable. And dark. So it seems that it's not entirely impossible that there's some connection between stars and people. At least, metaphorically. And that thought always, reluctantly, brings Lucienne back to the M Theory. Which, on some level, still makes her cringe.

The "M" in the theory stands for Magic or Mystery or Mother of All Theories. Or Membrane. Or Matrix. Depends on who you ask. Some believe the "M" is for Maldacena, pronounced mal-dah-SAY-nah, after the Harvard-based theorist Dr. Juan Maldacena, whose work in the theory is well known.

The only thing that can be agreed on is that nobody can agree on what the real name is. But everyone, even the disbelievers, knows it's an ultimate theory. The theory of everything. The M Theory asserts that everything in the world is made up of tiny membranes, or "branes," which vibrate and shimmer in dimensions that you can't even imagine. They're neither matter nor energy, but both. They've been called "God's Tinkertoys." It's a theory so esoteric it can't be proven and may never be. There's no way to measure something that's already been defined as immeasurable.

Before Lucienne discovered the black hole, she always believed that the "M" stood for Mentally Impaired. She once attended a convention and watched in horror as two hundred scientists danced the Macarena, renamed the Maldacena, in honor of a new discovery within the theory. The chorus seemed particularly telling:

> *Who knows what it all means?*
> *I don't, I confess.*
> *Ehhhh! Maldacena!*

There were fourteen verses of this. Lucienne stayed for only two. The rest she read about in *The New York Times*.

Crackpots, Lucienne thought then, but now she's not so sure.

It's the dream that's changed her. The dream of the black hole. V325BAndromedae.

In this dream, Lucienne is not at her observatory with her graduate students, not a doctor of astrophysics at all. In fact, she is not even a woman. In this dream, she exists without form or space. She has no nationality, no family. In this dream, she is all and none. She is a part of some vast being, an intelligence. When Lucienne wakes, she's always unsettled. The dream gives her a headache, a delicate throb at the edge of each temple. And now it's begun to creep into her waking hours.

At first, it was a shadow hovering at the edge of her vision. Something she could sense was there. Then gone. Then back again. Impatient. Waiting. Now, sometimes, if she stands still—doesn't speak, barely breathes—the darkness slips over her again, overtakes her. And she feels calm. And powerful. And at peace. Then the moment passes. Then it comes again. Stays a little longer.

Sometimes, she wants it to stay forever.

Right now, in Paris, in this elegant old hotel, Lucienne is deep in the dream again. She shimmers in perfect pitch. There are others there, too; even though she can't see them, she feels their presence. The essence of them.

Ethan is there. The darkness of his particular beauty. Fresh-cheeked, still, after all these years, but tragic. She can feel his sorrow.

And Marie is there, too. Marie, her neighbor, with her tired hands and gifts of rose-hip jam. Marie, who rises every Sunday at dawn to bake bread and cookies for grandchildren who never seem to find the time to come visit her.

And Josh, the contractor. Josh, who knocked down Lucienne's kitchen wall six months ago then changed his cell phone number and hasn't been back since. Josh is there with his affable smile and winning excuses.

As is her mother. Formidable.

Lucienne feels them all, the core of them, what makes them human, their spark. And she is a part of that. And she is happy.

Lucienne is unaware that her mother, Hélène, lies on the bed beside her, soaking wet and curved into herself like the shoot of a dried fern. Nearly within arms' reach. Hélène, like her daughter, is an astrophysicist. A woman who attempts to chart the darkness. Fails sometimes.

Hélène is dying. It's so unexpected.

That's what everyone will say. Hélène knows that. This was to be a time of great celebration. The Institut d'Astrophysique de Paris was planning to honor her daughter, Lucienne, with a citation for her discovery of the black hole. Hélène was invited to present the award. The committee was overjoyed at her acceptance and now will feel somehow responsible.

"It will be wonderful," they had said. "One generation honoring the next. We will honor the future while remembering the past."

But the past is something Hélène wants to forget.

Some call her a victim. Others wonder aloud if she was not a traitor during the war, a collaborator with the Germans. But one thing that can be agreed upon, Hélène has had a remarkable career. As a young woman, she worked with Frédéric Joliot-Curie, the Nobel laureate and son-in-law to Madame Curie.

"If you can imagine it," Frédéric told her when they first met, "it can be."

"I can imagine a great deal," Hélène replied. And could. Her student work, though merely speculative, was focused on a process by which one could harness energy through neutron bombardment. Something Frédéric had been working on himself.

"I'm making my own sun," she told him when they first met. And she was, indeed. It was also the perfect bomb. Whether she knew it or not is still a matter of public debate.

Her career, however, was overshadowed by the war. Shortly after the Germans invaded Paris, Hélène disappeared. One day she was working with Frédéric, attempting to explore the feasibility of nuclear power. The next day she was gone.

Many years passed before she finally reappeared. In America. At a small new observatory in New Mexico with an infant daughter, Lucienne. The observatory was looking for a receptionist. Hélène told them she knew how to answer a phone. Two months later, when she was caught at 3 A.M. adjusting the telescope, baby in one arm, she told them she knew how to do a few other things, too. Then she mentioned her work with Frédéric. So they let her stay.

"But no unscheduled research," the director told her, and

shook his finger at Hélène as if she were a child. For a moment it looked as if she would slap him. Or say something. But she didn't.

"Thank you" was all she said.

"Thank you" was all she could say. It was 1957. There was only a handful of jobs for women in science in America. She seemed to have limited credentials. She couldn't explain why she came to New Mexico. Or how she knew the area so well. That was all classified information. So she just said, "thank you," and considered herself lucky, even though the job required her to wear proper attire, no skirts shorter than three inches below the knee. No smoking. White gloves at all times.

So, Hélène answered phones in the daytime and when the telescope was free, she spent her nights balancing Lucienne on one hip while searching the bruised heavens until dawn.

No one knew exactly what Hélène was looking for. Every week the focus of her research seemed to change. One week she'd look for an unusual pattern in a set of wavelengths near Saturn. The next, she was searching for traces of boron in the shadow of a particular star at a particular coordinate. The only thing that remained a constant was that when observed, her methods seemed impeccable and exacting and she was determined to find what she was looking for. She was unrelenting and often went weeks without proper sleep. She made notes she would share with no one.

Still, there was something about her devotion that touched the director. The single-mindedness of it. And so, a year after she arrived, he found a new receptionist and gave Hélène her own office and a small salary.

Soon, the mystery that surrounded Hélène inspired curiosity. Several former French colleagues attempted to trace her journey to America, but could not. As far as anyone could tell, Hélène had just appeared one day. But, while the exact nature of where she'd been for fifteen years and what happened to her remained a secret, it was clear that something had happened. Something violent. Scars bore witness. One, a starburst, is still visible on her left shin. The other, on her scalp, feels like a bump. Underneath the flesh, a bit of something remains imbedded. These scars are the ones that can be seen with the naked eye. The rest run deeper.

Before the doctors discovered the right combination of small white pills, Hélène would slip back to that moment in Paris when her life began to unravel and, without notice, the shelling would begin again. In a car, or on a sidewalk, or sometimes at the grocery store, a noise, a look, a gesture would take her back into the past, the shrill skies and the shards of what once was. The Germans would arrive and conquer over and over again.

Lucienne, her daughter, was raised in the shadow of this war.

There was no choice. Lucienne had no father of record. No relatives to call. No place to go, except to strangers. So during these moments when time became fluid and Hélène spoke to those who were not there, screamed at bombs that were not falling, Lucienne stood alone, mute. Waiting for the moment to pass. Her hands would sweat. Her heart sped, beat with fury. She wanted to join her mother's secret world. Wondered what it looked like on the other side.

Don't go, she thought. But, of course, Hélène did go. And one day she did not return.

It happened when Lucienne was ten years old. August 9, 1967. Hélène usually spent nights working, but not that night. That night the weather was bad. An unstable front promised to bring a series of electrical storms to the sand hills. There was too much static to work, so Hélène sent the baby-sitter home and she and Lucienne waited for the storms to arrive.

Together the mother and daughter stood on the cool stone of the adobe porch and watched the thunderclouds roll in. Despite the fact that it was early evening, nearly sunset, waves of heat washed over them, unrelenting. Lightning illuminated the desert floor, like strobes. Snakes jumped. Hissed. The air was filled with the smell of coming rain, the pressure of storm clouds.

Behind them, inside the small adobe house, an old recording of Caruso vibrated the curtains, the smooth walls. The music was loud but the tenor's voice sounded tinny. The record snapped and popped. Lucienne could feel it in her bones.

They stood like that for quite some time, watching. Watching the red sun, the red mesas, and the red storm sky.

As the storm pressed closer and closer, Lucienne counted the seconds between flash and boom.

"One thousand one. One thousand two. One thousand three. Thousand four. Thousand five."

Hélène put her arm around her. Held her close for a moment.

"I'm not afraid," Lucienne said.

"I know."

Then Hélène did something she hadn't done in a long time, hadn't done since Lucienne was a baby. She picked her daughter up in her arms and held her, balanced her on the edge of her hipbone. Lucienne was half as tall as her mother and skinny, all elastic arms and lopsided legs. She dangled there a moment, unsure, uneasy.

"It's okay," Hélène whispered. "I've got you." Then she kissed the salt of Lucienne's forehead.

"I won't let you go. Ever."

Lucienne relaxed for a moment. Then wrapped her legs around her mother's waist and held on. Held on tight.

"I'm not afraid," she said again, her face buried in her mother's hair. Hélène nodded. And they remained like that for a moment. Calm. The waves of the storm breaking all around them.

If you saw them from a distance, from the ridge of the canyon or the edge of the dirt road that wound its way into the small desert town, you couldn't tell where the mother ended and the child began. In that dying light, all you could see was a veil of red, the red of their skin, their hair, the small adobe house, and the mesas. All you could see was the ripe angry sky, dark and low. And lightning.

"One thousand one."

Lots and lots of lightning.

"Thousand two."

Then the air went tight.

A bolt slid down the porch beam.

The ground shifted.

Boom, Lucienne thought, then felt her body rattle.

Hélène and Lucienne were thrown backward through the open door, into the house. The stone roof bounced. Windows bowed, then shattered. Hélène was caught in the spray. And then, a siren. A fire in the distance. A fire truck, its piercing wail. Hélène covered her ears. The wail of the siren grew louder, wrapped itself around her. She may have screamed, it's hard to tell. The siren is the last thing she told the doctor she remembered.

Lucienne crawled through the glass to her.

"Mama?"

The very last thing.

At that moment, if you could have looked closely into Hélène's eyes, you would have seen them move back and forth, rapid, as if she were in a dream state, REM taking hold.

The tenor, his crackling aria, sang of fickle women. *La Donna è Mobile.* False altogether. An ambulance joined in. Twin wails.

Outside the house, straight line winds carried away the neighbor's aluminum chairs, the grate from a Japanese grill, and a stray cat who screeched with fear, then surprise, then joy, at the suddenness of flight, the secret pleasure of birds.

Lucienne slammed the front door.

Then lightning. Again.

Caruso fell silent.

This time a bolt hit the roof, slid down the television antenna, down the wires, and into the set. For a moment the TV lit up as if turned on. Light flooded into it, hurt Lucienne's eyes. The glass tube exploded. Thousands of bits of mercury shot out all over the floor, like hail, like silver, but hot. It danced.

Flames crawled up the pleats of the beige linen drapes and melted the tiny hooks that had held them so neatly. Then the fire wrapped itself around the tan couch, spilled onto the floor, and rolled in great waves toward them.

For Hélène time slowed. Then stopped. Then rearranged itself. Logic shifted. She looked at her daughter and saw a stranger. Then saw her daughter again. Reality was fluid.

"Mama!" Lucienne screamed, and pulled Hélène deeper into the house, away from the fire through the kitchen to the back door and outside into a Paris street that only Hélène could see, where there was chaos and screaming and snipers everywhere.

"Keep your head down," Hélène screamed.

When the fire truck finally arrived, then the ambulance, smoke surrounded the house, thick as thunderheads.

Hélène and Lucienne were in the garden hiding beneath a wheelbarrow. Their arms and legs stuck out.

"Mama?"

"Shh. We cannot let them find us," she said, and pulled Lucienne closer. "We must be quiet."

Lucienne could feel her mother's heart beating as if it were her own. Don't go, she thought.

All around them, people were shouting. Firemen were shouting. Policemen were shouting. Mrs. Jensen, the neighbor, was shouting. Her daughter, Erica, with her dishwater pigtails and tiny pink sneakers, was shouting. Everywhere there was shouting. People standing in the fading light of the fire, standing in the hail and rain, shouting. Shrill chimes. The ambulance siren spun like a tornado.

Lucienne didn't mean to cry but she couldn't help it. "Shh," her mother said, but Lucienne couldn't stop.

Hélène looked at her daughter with flint eyes. Then wrapped her hands around Lucienne's neck.

"Oh," Lucienne said and nothing more. Her mouth grew numb. Then her face. Her arms and legs felt as if they were turning to straw.

I love you, Lucienne thought. Her small nails scratched her mother's arms but couldn't loosen the grip.

"I'm sorry," Hélène whispered, "but we cannot be found." Hélène's eyes were filled with tears. She kissed her daughter's forehead. Her breath was sour. "I'm so sorry."

There was something in her voice that seemed to Lucienne as if she were speaking from another room, through a door, thick and locked. Lucienne could feel her lungs slowly close, fold into themselves like sails in still air. I love you, she thought.

"Over here," someone shouted, and threw back the wheelbarrow. All Lucienne could see were many flashlights and shoes covered in mud: black boots, brown shoes, blue terry-cloth slippers with rosebuds, and tiny pink sneakers, all wicking the dirt and rain. A fireman picked Lucienne up in his arms. He smelled of stale coffee and smoke. She reached back for her mother but Hélène looked away.

"It's okay," he said softly. "It's okay now."

But Lucienne knew it wasn't.

In the back of the ambulance the world was pure sun and sponge words.

"You are fine now. Just fine. I have a daughter your age. Such a good girl."

"We'll take you where it's safe," someone said.

But all Lucienne wanted was her mother. The handprints on her neck turned from red to purple to black. She could still feel her mother's hands, but not around her neck. They felt as if they were around her heart.

"Shh," everyone told her. "Don't cry."

And so Lucienne stopped. Stopped crying for a very long time.

And after that, Hélène spent the next few years in and out of private clinics and hospitals. It was all court ordered and very discreet. In between, in a series of halfway houses, Hélène chainsmoked and furiously wrote a labyrinth of theories that were scattered in so many areas, it seemed as if each was a part of some larger conclusion that she hinted at, but would tell no one. And they were published. The journals had no choice. While Hélène was quite mad in person, on the page she was brilliant and lucid. Unerringly so.

During this time, Lucienne learned how to live with people she did not know, sleep in beds that were not hers, and make herself as small as dust. She always made it a point not to unpack her suitcase. "My mother's coming for me soon," she'd explain, and when she said this she sometimes sounded happy, sometimes fearful. Occasionally, a foster mother wanting to help would hang Lucienne's dresses in the empty space of a closet and fold her blue jeans into a dresser drawer, but Lucienne would quietly repack. Then tape the suitcase shut.

"Profoundly withdrawn," the caseworker wrote in her file.

In six years of foster care, Lucienne lived with eight families. Went to five different schools. She told herself it was temporary and tried not to learn anyone's name: not her foster parents' or their children's or her teachers' or the other kids' at school. But she did learn astronomy, the language of her mother. She learned about the great vacuum of space, where stars erupt and burn and re-create their lives without shame. She learned that numbers can be trusted to reveal truth; and that truth is simple, and beautiful, and will not hurt you. Unlike love. Love is impossible. And dangerous. She never let anyone get too close.

When Lucienne turned seventeen, she was allowed to live with her mother again. For weeks after she moved in Lucienne dreamt of that night on the Mesa, of her mother's hands on her neck. She would wake sobbing, inconsolable.

"The past is unimportant," Hélène would tell her, to reassure her, to reassure them both, but they knew it wasn't true. So, they ate their meals in silence with the sun rising and setting and so much going on within their hearts, at times, it made them both want to weep. But they didn't. Silence settled on them like fine, gray dust.

Now, tonight in Paris, the silence is all that is left.

The waiting is nearly over, Hélène thinks. She'd grown tired of waiting. Back home, in Boston, in a tall thin brownstone, just down the street from Lucienne's, Hélène spends every day waiting. She waits until her housekeeper brings her breakfast. Then, after breakfast, she waits for lunch, usually soup or a salad. Then, after lunch, for supper. Then dusk.

At dusk, slowly, very slowly, Hélène climbs the narrow winding stairs to the fourth floor, the observatory. In the center of the room there is a skylight that can be opened in good weather. Underneath it, a telescope. A housewarming gift from her son-in-law. "It's important to keep up," he said. And all these years later it sits unused. These days, most work is done on computers. The data can be collected from observatories all over the world, then downloaded and analyzed. Direct feeds from telescopes and satellites can be accessed with a click of a mouse. All you need is the vision to imagine a world without limitations. And, despite everything, Hélène can still imagine a great deal.

So, every evening at six o'clock a program turns on the computer. It goes on-line to an observatory Web site and, even without her, searches. Downloads the heavens. Hélène doesn't need to be there for it to happen. She's programmed the computer with the specifics of what she's looking for, even though she still refuses to tell anyone else. If it finds it, and she's not there, it doesn't matter. The computer is programmed to lock in the coordinates. And the next night, again, it will turn itself on, set itself to these coordinates, and download. Once it zeros in, it will track her request through the heavens until it's told not to. Unlike research assistants.

Hélène knows she doesn't need to be there all night long, watching. But she is. She's always there. Year in and year out. Waiting, until, exhausted, she falls asleep in her desk chair, head cocked to one side, and dreams of shooting stars: their fire, their grace.

It doesn't have to be this way. Hélène knows she could go with her daughter to art museums, concerts, or even to the new planetarium in New York. They were invited to the grand opening celebration, but she didn't go. She couldn't. The waiting was all she had left.

In the past few months, however, her body's grown frail, weaker than she'd ever imagined it could be. Small strokes, like fireworks, come and go within her brain. No one notices. Not even Lucienne, who tries to visit every Sunday and tell her mother the gossip of their world—who might discover what, whose grant was denied. Lucienne, who brings her mother unfiltered Gitanes despite the doctor's orders, and mint teas from the Arabian market, and dozens of lace handkerchiefs from Belgium, which she buys at import stores and flea markets. Not even Lucienne, who attempts to tend to her mother's every need, has noticed the change in Hélène. At least, not allowed herself to notice it. Now, it's too late. Now, Hélène lies at her daughter's side. Tomorrow, the citation will not be given.

The waiting is nearly over, she thinks. Rain from her coat soaks through the fine linens. It didn't have to be this way, but it is.

Hélène has her own room that connects with Lucienne's, her own bed that is just as grand. The silk brocade headboard. The Belgian lace canopy. In the next room, the streetlight also streams in through the tall, thin windows. The dust dances silver in the darkness there, too. All in all, it is a very nice room. Nearly identical to Lucienne's. A mirror image.

But it's a lonely place to die, in another room.

So she must be quiet. Hélène knows that if her daughter were awake now, she would call for the hotel doctor, order warm milk from the kitchen staff, and force her to vomit. She would take the thick towels from the heated rack in the bathroom, rub her small body, hoping for a spark, and then wrap her in the soft bathrobes of this place, its emblem embroidered in gold over her heart. Hélène knows that would happen. And, while waiting for the hotel doctor, Lucienne would fill the tub, steam hot, and pour her Chanel #5 bath oil into the steady flow. Clouds of vanilla and sandalwood and rose would surround them, remind them of a summer's day. "Don't go," Lucienne would say. "This is what you'd miss." Hélène knows Lucienne would say and do all these things, if she were awake. So, Hélène must remain very still.

As Hélène feels her body grow numb, she counts backward from one hundred. First in French, the language she still thinks in, even though she spent so much of her life never wanting to think of Paris again. Then, in German, a language with too many memories to bear.

As her breath slows, Hélène reaches out to touch her child, but Lucienne is too far away. Her hand falls, unnoticed. Wake up, Hélène thinks, then lets this dark dull sleep wash over her. Her fingers grow cold. After a time she knows blood will no longer reach them.

There was a moment when Hélène first slid into the bed, shoes and all, the rain rolling off her black wool coat, there was a moment then, when in Lucienne's dream rain appeared. When she could smell the hot sewer smell of Paris in September, the slick streets.

Lucienne could have awakened then, saved her mother, but the moment quickly passed. She rubbed her nose by rote. The dream moved on, changed rhythm and logic.

Things did not have to be this way, but unfortunately, now, they cannot be undone.

As Hélène's breath grows shallow, her mind runs like ink and the world becomes filled with the fragrance of chestnuts, that rich oil scent, that familiar smell. Sometimes it would come to her when she least expected it. Typing a letter. Filing a report. And sometimes, during testing, when the flash of light still hurt the backs of her eyes, made the hairs on her arms stand straight up, she remembered the smell of chestnuts, dark and sweet. It was the smell of his skin.

The rest of the details: the heavy salt air, the snakes that wrapped themselves in the cool branches of the trees and the rain, the permanent steady rain of a Paris winter, she does not remember as clearly.

And her parents. Her father the butcher, his anger and violence. And shame. Her French mother, bird-boned and always homesick for Paris. All she can remember of them is their hands waving as she boarded the train to Paris, their savings sewn into the lining of her coat. She doesn't remember that she was on the last train out of Prague. Doesn't remember that the Germans were closing in on the city. Hélène doesn't remember this at all. But the smell of chestnuts, always. She remembers that clearly. And of course, his hands. Not so much the feel of them, but the luminescent prints they left on her coat, her blouse, and the zipper of her skirt. They were radioactive.

Hélène knew it all along. And so did he. And that was the one thing she had not remembered until now.

AIR RAIDS WERE HARD TO RESIST. THE planes fly low, shake you. The surprise of light and heat is remarkable. And Hélène was cold, so cold she feared she'd never be warm again. There was no coal left in Paris anymore. No wood. Rain soaked every floorboard and every bone. No relief.

The only thing left to burn in Paris was the buildings, stray bits of furniture, leaves and twigs that are found in the streets. Hélène took home whatever she could find. Broke it down into tiny pieces and burned it in a flowerpot. The fire filled her small attic room with smoke and soot. Ash covered everything. Everything was stained—her clothes, her hands, the phonograph, the mattress on which she slept—and still there was no warmth.

So the air raids drew her in. In the weak light of dawn, she watched as the bombs fell along the edge of the city. They hissed, then hit. Then heat.

Heat is the one thing she missed so very much. And so Hélène would not go to the shelter. She never did.

They didn't bomb often. Paris, for the most part, remained intact. Still, it was a war. On that day, the bombs hit closer. The ground heaved under her feet and she tumbled, rolled and ran toward the flames. She wanted to roll inside of them. Have the heat of the fire wrap around her like so many hands.

But she didn't. At least not that day. There was no time. She was going to the opera.

The raid was mercifully short. And so, life continued. It was Paris, after all. The only concession that Paris was willing to make to the war was that time had been reversed.

At the Place Pigalle they danced in the light of day with curtains pulled back, windows open. The sun and its jaded eye. Under the glare, everything lost its illusion. Shadow and ambiguity was not possible.

Still, the theaters, the cinemas, the cabarets in Montmartre were full, in spite of the early hour, the air raids, the rationing, in spite of everything.

The opera house was also filled. And massive. Glittering. *Opéra de Paris* was designed by Garnier for Napoleon III. The grand belle époque style at its most monumental. Nymphs and cherubs. Velvet and crystal. An island of gilt. There is such abundance, the walls seem to be made of butter cream and gold leaf. It is unapologetic for its beauty, even in times of war.

Without electricity, thousands of candles lit the stage, the aisles, teetered precariously in the hands of actors. They illuminated the sweat that ran down their faces, the streaks of their makeup, and their eyes wild within the moment of the scene.

In the audience, sophisticated women made fashion a point of national pride. With bits of wood and kitchen knives they carved high heels for shoes. Some covered their legs with a flour paste to give the impression of silk stockings, then traced a darker line to imitate the seam. Hair and hats were high and wrapped in tulle scaffoldings with real flowers and feathers taken from nests.

Hélène's thick hair was piled on top of her head, wrapped in the pearl strands of a rosary she had found in the street. Jesus on his cross was safely tucked into her crown. She was wearing a black silk dress she carefully folded in tissue paper after each use, her only good pair of heels. Uniforms were everywhere; she didn't expect that. Made her heart race. There were Germans in all three balconies and in the stalls, but in the warm candlelight, Hélène could see only faces. Faces that looked much like her own.

A man leaned over to her. "*La Bohème* today," he said, reading the playbill mimeographed on cheap pink paper. "When is it not *La Bohème* these days?"

He laughed. Smelled like sour wine. She moved away slightly. Acted as if she didn't hear. The overture began. On stage were Puccini's bohemians. They are hungry, they sang. They are cold.

"Who isn't?" the man said, much too loud. Heads turned.

Hélène wanted to change seats but she was meeting someone, an old friend. At least, that's how she's come to think of Vincent. It had been several months since they'd spoken, since she told him she couldn't be his wife, but she asked him to meet her. She needed money. And he has so very much, she thought, and hoped he still loved her. Enough, at least, for a few hundred francs.

But he's late. He's always late. She knew she should have waited for him in the lobby, that would have been the polite thing to do, the smart thing, but she was tired and hadn't slept for days. If he can't make his way in the dark to the seats, she knows she'll find him at intermission. She has to. Tomorrow she leaves Paris. Maybe forever.

Two days ago the Germans raided the laboratory, but Frédéric was prepared. He'd sent Hélène to bury their work and notes in a bunker outside the city. She buried it deep. When the Germans arrived, they demanded to see the experiments, demanded all the heavy water and uranium Frédéric had been working with. He shook his head. "There is nothing," he said. "You are mistaken."

But they knew better and were intimate with the details of his staff. "Where is the girl from Prague?" they asked.

"I don't know," he said, but they didn't believe him and barred him from the lab. Left a student in charge. A German. Wolfgang Getner. That was their mistake. They didn't know Getner was anti-Nazi. That night, he met Hélène and Frédéric at a student café. He explained to Hélène how the Underground worked, the danger she now faced, and her chances.

"Not good, I'm afraid," he said. "The Germans know who you are and what you know."

"I'm so sorry," Frédéric said, and under the shaky table, handed her two letters. One from himself, a letter of introduction. The second was to Frédéric from a colleague, Enrico Fermi, the young Nobel laureate. Fermi was hoping to set up a team to work on the first controlled self-sustaining nuclear chain reaction. An experiment based on the work of Frédéric and his wife. In America.

"A power like no other," Fermi wrote.

The power of the sun, Hélène thought. She and the Joliot-

Curies had recently split uranium themselves. Frédéric had received several patents on the project and the results of the experiment, even though it was on a very small scale, were amazing and unwieldy. Difficult to control. A chain reaction with a force that seemed to multiply exponentially. Hélène knew that to be able to control nuclear power, as Fermi intended, would be a major accomplishment. And impossible to achieve in Paris without the Germans' knowing. To continue the work, Hélène knew she had to travel to America, and the letter from Fermi asked the Joliot-Curies to join him and bring along any of his students whom they felt would be of help.

"By the end of this project," Fermi wrote, "we will need all the world's greatest minds gathered in one place."

Frédéric explained that he had already told Fermi he couldn't go. His wife's tuberculosis had worsened and she was confined to a nursing home. And even if she weren't, his elderly mother would be left unprotected. Besides, Frédéric knew that he was safe in Paris. He was too valuable for the Germans to kill, and too well loved for them to torture. The Germans just couldn't risk it. The invasion wasn't going well. Even though they'd captured Paris, they had not truly defeated the French. Many of the people were defiant and angry. The cunning among them had guns, and the rest threw rocks at the soldiers, poisoned them when they could.

So, it was clear that the Germans couldn't risk any harm coming to the Joliot-Curie family. They were, after all, considered one of France's national treasures.

"So," Frédéric told Hélène, "you must be the hero for us all."

She felt a rush of excitement, then fear. Then Hélène looked at the date of the letter. It was written a few months earlier. Her heart sank. She knew that the Joliot-Curies had recently fallen out of favor within the scientific community for publishing the results of their work in fission. It was feared the Germans could use their findings to create their bomb. So, while loved in France, the Joliot-Curies were now considered traitors by many of their peers, including Fermi.

"Do you think he'll accept me?" Hélène asked.

Getner shrugged. "That's the least of your worries," he said.

"He will welcome you I'm sure," Frédéric said, but sounded otherwise. "You are, after all, a fellow scientist in need."

Hélène wanted to believe him. The idea of working on such a large-scale project, of containing such an incredible force, was intoxicating. And the plan sounded simple enough. She would leave Paris and travel to the Belgian Congo.

"The Belgians are shipping all the remaining uranium to America from the Congo. You can accompany it. The letters will grant your safe passage."

"Or Morocco, if you can manage it," Getner told her. "There's talk the British are planning a strike there. If they're successful, they'll set up base with the Americans. You could catch a plane from there."

"If they're not successful?"

He shrugged.

And so, the choices were simple and impossible at the same time. Get to the Congo and the Americans will take you to Fermi. Or go to Morocco and wait, and if you're lucky, the Americans will take you to Fermi.

Unless somebody shoots you first, she thought. She doesn't even want to think about the possibility that she could get all the way to America and Fermi would deny her access.

In a sense, it didn't matter. She had to leave, to take the chance.

The Germans had already been to her apartment. And probably, she imagined, those of her friends.

Maybe that's why Vincent's late, she thought.

She pushed the thought away and thought about leaving. How she would miss it all. Maybe not Paris so much, but the nights spent working in the laboratory. The beakers, radioactive, glow an iridescent blue. Small moons. So beautiful. She wondered how much access Fermi would give her. She was still a student after all. And a woman. That was always a problem. But Hélène had no choice and knew it. So, she waited for Vincent, and all his money, to ask for enough to travel with. The letters, and her identification papers, sewn into the hem of her dress. But he's late, she thought. So late.

Onstage, the actors stood very close together, held candles to their faces, and sang. The force of their voices made the flames flicker, threatened to extinguish them. From where Hélène was sitting, just two rows back, all she could see were teeth and tongues illuminated by the flames. The rest of the stage was murky. The faces floated in the dark, the peeled paper skin, wet coal eyes. In the orchestra pit, there were small pools of light. Like fireflies. Candles clipped to music stands. Instead of a baton, the conductor gingerly waved two white tapers. His movements were small, gentle. Still, wax sprayed the first violinist, over and over again. Burned his cheek, his forehead.

Onstage, Rodolfo, the poet, began to sing. He is so poor, he says, he must burn his life's work, his book of poems, to keep warm. The man next to Hélène whispered, "Lucky man. I have nothing left to burn. I eat dirt to trick my stomach into thinking it's filled."

Hélène turned toward him, took his hand in hers for a moment. She squeezed it lightly. She's not sure why she did this. It was just an impulse. His hand felt coarse and rough. He turned to her in the half light and she could see the watery blue of his eyes, the old man shock-blue of them.

"Dandelions," she whispered, "they work better than dirt. Grass, too."

"Crows," he said. "That's what we have become."

The soldier in front of them cleared his throat. We're too loud, Hélène thought. He wants to hear Puccini.

At that moment, Puccini seemed more beautiful than ever. The poet's lament was not maudlin, as it had been in some productions Hélène had seen, but true. The tone of his voice was clear with a purity that was remarkable. He was not asking for pity, but simply acknowledging what had become a way of life for him. She looked around her and many were leaning forward in their seats, their mouths slightly open, rapt. Even the soldiers.

The poet, still holding a candle in one hand, raised his book into the air. It was difficult for him to see, the stage was so dark. By accident, he brushed the book against the candle. The book flared like a torch, but the actor didn't put it out. Instead, he wept, as the poet would, exhausted by misery and fear and hunger.

The audience was stunned. And some, embarrassed. But all were unable to look away. Or run.

The actor dropped the burning book and it tumbled through the candle smoke and darkness, landed on a rug. Fire spread quickly along the floor of the stage, but no one was moving. Flames leapt, unencumbered, toward the leg of a chair, slipped onto the velvet curtains, and began to wind their way up the wall toward the gilt ceiling, like an elegant snake.

The orchestra continued to play. The actors still sang.

Finally, when the velvet curtain was engulfed in flames and fell onto the stage, smothering an actor, someone in the orchestra pit shouted, "Fire!"

Jolted, the audience crowded into the aisles, their voices suddenly rising in panic. There was a great breathless push toward the door. All around Hélène there was shouting. The fire slipped down the stage and onto the first row of seats. Smoke cascaded behind it like a wave. Hélène's hair unwound. The rosary fell down around her neck.

All she could see were the backs of people's heads, beads of sweat. The crowd was packed so tightly together they breathed one breath and it was shallow and quick. Hélène was pushed down the aisle, out the side door, and into the bright sun of morning. The world radiated. For a moment, she was blinded. Then pushed up against a wall. She didn't even see the sniper who fired into the crowd. He was aiming at the soldiers, but she was hit. First in her shin. Then the top of her head.

✎ 4 ✎

THE DOCTOR FROM THE EMERGENCY ROOM OFFERS a chair for
Lucienne to sit in. "It's quiet here," he says softly. "Please." His
English is cautious. Precise. She sits. He's a large man but moves
with the well-practiced grace of an athlete past his prime. Like
most of the hospital staff, he is dressed in somber black. Black silk
shirt. No tie. Black jeans. Jacket. Serene and competent. Every time
Lucienne looks at him, she sees him pulling her mother back into
this life; hears the hum of the defibrillator; sees him leaning over
Hélène, paddles in both hands; hears the clap of them against her
mother's chest; feels the electricity run though her own heart.

The doctor closes his office door gently behind them. It clicks
shut, a metallic sound. The hospital is small and very near the
hotel. Modern, as is this room. Bleached wood desk. Birch wood
chairs. No pictures, no diplomas on the wall. Modern and cool to

the touch. The chair Lucienne sits in is of some vague industrial Danish design. Her body aches. One floor above, her mother is comatose in the intensive care unit.

"There is a pulse," the doctor has told her, "but it's faint."

A neurologist is with Hélène now, running tests. Soon, a specialist will be assigned to the case.

"But that's later," the doctor told Lucienne, "when we know what we're dealing with." Right now, all Lucienne can do is wait.

"Still dizzy?" the doctor asks. She can't remember his name. He had found her leaning against a wall. She shakes her head.

"I'm fine," she says, although the world seems to slip in and out of focus.

"Let me see," he says, and tilts her chin toward him, shines a small penlight into her eyes. First the right. Then left.

He's looking for signs of shock; she knows that. Pupils dilated. Shallow breath. Knows he'll find them.

"I'm fine," she wants to say again, to insist, but doesn't. She's not sure she is. The light hurts her eyes but she doesn't blink. It all feels so dreamlike. The moment. The doctor. Her mother. Lucienne hardly remembers what happened. How she came here. Only bits and pieces. She studies the doctor's face. He seems ageless. Not too old, not young. His hair is dark, gray in odd places. His face is elegantly etched.

"Would you like some coffee?" he asks, but doesn't wait for an answer. He leans across the desk, dials the phone, and asks for two coffees and, perhaps, a sandwich, if there are any available.

At least that's what Lucienne thinks he said, her French is very bad. On the phone, the doctor speaks expansively. In his own language, he seems to be a different man. Not as cautious as he is in English. Not reserved. He seems to be a man she has not met yet.

Language changes everything, she thinks. Revises people.

"A few minutes," he says. Hangs up and sits.

He takes cigarettes from his top drawer and offers her one. "It helps sometimes. Relaxes," he says. Lucienne shakes her head. The match sparks and flares, fills the moment with the acid smell of sulfur and smoke. He takes a long pull on the cigarette. Then looks at it gently, as if seeing it for the first time.

"Are you sure? They're very good. Moroccan tobacco. Fragrant, like chestnuts," he says.

She shakes her head.

"Does the smoke bother you?" he asks.

"No. My mother smokes." Then corrects. "Smoked." Lucienne closes her eyes for a moment. The doctor looks away, uncomfortable.

"It is never easy," he says.

I'm not ready for this, she thinks.

Blue smoke slides between the shades toward the air vents and quietly slips away, outside, into the courtyard. Lucienne and the doctor watch the smoke escape, not wanting to look at each other. Not wanting to speak. The difficulty of language, its nuance, is too much to overcome at a moment like this. They both know it. It's clear. So they settle into the silence. The doctor puts out his cigarette.

"Comas are very complicated," he says quietly, as if talking to himself. "There is always damage, you must prepare for that, but sometimes when the patient wakes they are nearly the same as before. Maybe a slowness of response. Or loss of short term memory. I had a patient once when I was an intern who had lost his sense of taste—"

Lucienne stops listening, feels the room tilt and spin. Hélène is dying and Lucienne knows it, feels it in her bones, but it's so difficult for her to believe. Like this. In a strange place. It's not what she had imagined would happen. She had always hoped that when the time came her mother would die peacefully, perhaps in her sleep. Not suicide. So violent and tragic. A desperate act. Impossible.

How can you do this to me? she thinks, and feels abandoned again. Angry as she was as a child, taping shut her suitcase, unwilling to unpack, left alone in a cold room listening for comfort in the voices of strangers.

"Let me check on the coffee," the doctor says, and stands. "I'll be right back."

Lucienne doesn't want coffee or sandwiches, but says nothing. She's too numb to speak. All she really wants is to be able to understand why her mother would do such a thing. It just doesn't make sense. She's made every effort to see that her mother was taken care of. Every need anticipated. She and Ethan bought Hélène a brownstone down the street from theirs. Found her a housekeeper to watch over her. Took out an insurance policy so that if Hélène could no longer be cared for at home, she would be able to go to a nursing home. Someplace nice, though. Lucienne would insist upon it. And expensive.

Despite it all, Lucienne feels responsible for her mother's attempt at suicide. Perhaps, she thinks, I just never loved her enough. And it feels true.

In the beginning, Lucienne took care of her mother only because she felt it was her obligation. She'd never quite forgiven, or understood, that night on the Mesa. Hélène's hands around her neck. Never quite trusted her mother since then. Never quite felt safe around her. Never loved her the way Lucienne thought a daughter should love.

Still, after a time, Lucienne began to look forward to the Sunday visits and to holiday dinners, with watered-down cocktails and an opulent table filled with food that's old-fashioned and deadly. Sweetbreads in cognac. Foie gras baked in brioche. A saddle of hare to "jump start" the new year. And champagne. Always champagne.

"You're going to kill us, Mother," Lucienne would say.

"Do you know a better way to die?"

And then Hélène would smile, pleased with herself and the feast. Eventually, Lucienne had to admit that she knew no better way to die than sitting at her mother's table with a fine glass of champagne in hand, tucking into the remains of a *Bûche de Nöel*, the Yule log, with its mocha–butter cream icing. Which she knows is made with at least two cups of cream and God knows how many eggs. And love.

"We are French, after all. Are we not?" Hélène would say.

"We are French," Lucienne would answer, but would still calculate the calories, carbohydrates, and fat grams in her head.

Now, outside the hospital window, Lucienne can hear children playing, their joyous screams. They are French, she thinks. Not me. And that makes her feel more isolated, more alone. A woman's voice joins in. Their mother. Together the voices jangle and swoop. Lucienne thinks again of her own mother, Hélène, of her hand lying on the silk bedspread, curved toward her. A slice of a moon, cold and too distant to reach.

Don't go, she thought. Thinks now. I don't even know you.

Lucienne runs a hand through her hair. She hasn't combed it since last night. It smells of her perfume, of musk and spice, and of sweat. The doctor walks back into the room and hands her a chocolate bar.

"Eat this," he says. "The coffee is on the way."

Lucienne takes the candy and puts it down on the corner of the desk, pushes it away from her.

"It's from Normandy," he says. "They make very good chocolate."

"What time is it?" she asks, and is surprised by the sound of her own voice. So hoarse, it cracks. The doctor looks at his watch.

"Half past."

Half past what? she wonders. It's hard to tell. Lucienne imagines it's sometime in the late afternoon, but time feels as if it has stopped. The window shades are linen, diffuse the light, and reduce everything to a shade the color of resin, luminous and deeply yellow, as if she and the moment are captured in it. It's felt that way since morning, since she crawled down to the end of the bed and gently shook her mother's shoulder. "Wake up," she said. Took her mother's body in her arms. Cradled it like a child.

That's all Lucienne remembers. She's not sure how long she sat like that, holding her mother in her arms. All she remembers is that she studied the lines in her face. So many of them were like her own it amazed her that she'd never noticed that before. Never looked that closely. Never really noticed the deep furrows that ran from her mother's nose to her mouth. The lines around the corners of her eyes, and the eyes themselves. Just like hers.

The doctor picks up the chocolate bar and unwraps it. Her stomach growls. The chocolate is dark and fragrant. He takes a piece and puts it in his mouth and holds it there for a moment. Chews it slowly.

"It's very good. Here," he says, and hands her a piece.

She looks at it in her hand, slightly melting. "Coffee, cigarettes, chocolate," she says. "What kind of a doctor are you?"

"Popular. Now, put it in your mouth."

Reluctantly, she does. At first, it's like a red wine, spicy with tannins, and then there's a lush note of vanilla. And a coffee bean. Deep-roasted. It crunches.

"Nice?" he asks. "Those are espresso beans."

She nods and can feel the caffeine creep into her system.

"Have another piece. Doctor's orders. The caffeine will help clear your head."

Lucienne takes another. It is lovely, she thinks. The chocolate makes her hands feel slightly warmer.

"You have to take care of yourself," he says. "Be careful you don't get run down. Drink plenty of fluids."

"It all feels so surreal."

"You've had a bad shock."

"I just don't understand why she'd do this."

He shrugs. "It's hard to tell. I did have a question though. You mentioned that you and your mother were both in town for a conference at Institut d'Astrophysique de Paris."

She nods.

"But your hotel is so far away from the Institut and so very close to this hospital."

"My mother chose it. Why?"

"Perhaps it's nothing," he says, and opens his desk drawer, takes out a file folder. Hélène's name is typed along the edge. Inside, there's a small white envelope with black trim. It's old. Very old. Smells of Chanel, and mothballs.

"They found this in her pocket. The envelope is very traditional, usually reserved for notices of death."

Lucienne picks up the envelope; she's never seen it before.

Inside there's a photograph of a Paris street. The doctor leans across the desk and turns it over for her. On the back there's a date written in script, small rounded letters.

Lucienne can see it's the type of handwriting her mother has, the type she associates with the French, but she can tell it's not her mother's writing. The letters all lean a little too far to the left.

"Spring 1940," he reads. "The Germans invaded June 1940. When did your mother leave Paris?"

"I'm not sure. She won't talk about it."

She runs a finger along the letters on the back of the photograph. The black ink is not faded. The caption seems recent.

"The writing's new?" she asks.

He nods. "But what I find the most odd is that this street, this café, is very close to the hotel, very close to here."

"You're sure?"

"I grew up across the street, in an apartment above the furrier's salon." He points to where the salon would be. "It looks to me as if someone took this photo standing in front of my building. It's such an odd coincidence, don't you think?"

Lucienne nods and looks at the photograph again, remembers seeing the café. The awnings are different but the name remains the same.

"Do you think she could have gone to the café last night?" he asks. "I know she had her coat and boots on when she was brought in."

"I don't know," Lucienne says. More secrets, she thinks, and closes her eyes for a moment. The world seems to be spinning again. She thinks about the things she knows for sure. Facts. No mystery. No secrets.

Darkness is a total state.

Nothing can escape the gravitational field of darkness.

Darkness collapses everything into itself.

And then she realizes she's thinking about the black hole again. The properties of a black hole.

And grief.

Overwhelmed, she feels the pull of her mother like a star that has burned itself out.

"Your father," the doctor says, "have you had a chance to telephone him? I assume he's in America?"

Lucienne looks down at her hands. "Dead," she says, even though she's not sure that's true. She has no idea if he's dead or alive. Or who he even is.

A look of sorrow passes over the doctor's face. "I see," he says, and it feels to Lucienne as if there's something else. Something he's not saying. Something he's hiding. More secrets, she thinks, and feels the chocolate go sour in her stomach.

There's a knock at the door and it gives them both a start. An orderly is there holding a tray with two china cups, a metal coffeepot, and cream in a small pitcher. Everything is lovely, like a still life, but the room suddenly feels too close. Lucienne slips the photograph into her pocket. "Look, I have to go," she says, and pushes past the orderly quickly. A bit of coffee splashes the sandwiches, the perfect lace doily. She's not sure why she's leaving or where she's going. This doctor, whose name she can't even remember, may be the key to her mother's past. Or her past. May help her find her father. But she shuts the door behind her. The lock clicks and echoes down the cool hallway, as does the click of the heels of her perfect Italian pumps. Nothing can escape the gravitational field of darkness, she thinks over and over again. The world feels as if it's spinning out of control. The tapping of her heels sound like a heartbeat. Nothing can escape the gravitational field of darkness. It's the one thing Lucienne knows to be true and she can feel herself being pulled into it. And so she runs.

∽ 5 ∾

THE TAXI SHAKES WITH MUSIC. RHYTHMIC SINGING and the down-beat of drums. Something vaguely Middle Eastern, Lucienne thinks. The driver has a large tape recorder in the front seat. The cheap speakers vibrate. The sound is muddy, too much bass.

Outside the taxi a soft rain falls, inky and hot. Steams the window as it makes contact. Even though it's September, it's unseasonably warm. And still. The air feels close. The street is a panorama of speed and sound. Men and women whisper in cafés. Drivers bark. Car horns and radios build toward some unknowable crescendo. The street is narrow, uneven. The taxi takes the corner just a little too sharply. The tape recorder warbles. The taxi was a mistake. Lucienne realizes this as the cab runs up onto the curb and nearly hits a couple trying to cross the street. The young man grabs his lover's hand and pulls her back toward him.

The angry man shouts at the cab. Embraces the woman.

"Sorry," Lucienne says, but not loud enough.

She studies her mother's photograph with its unknown street and the lovers sitting at the café. The street is long and narrow, flanked by apartment buildings and the small café at the bottom of one. There's nothing remarkable about this street. It looks like so many others in Paris. The cobblestones. The narrow sidewalks.

She searches the women's faces for her mother's but they're too small. It's difficult to distinguish one from another. The picture's slightly out of focus. Everyone seems cloudlike.

But still, Lucienne searches. There is one woman in the photo who seems more in focus than the rest, with hair worn long to the waist. And there's something else. Something about the nature of her. It's an intangible thing, but distinctive. There's a seriousness that Lucienne recognizes. The woman has her back to the camera. She's leaning across the table talking to a man in a dark sweater. Their heads are very close together, as if sharing a secret. It has to be her. The man seems rapt. The woman's posture is perfect. Ankles crossed. In one hand she holds a cigarette, as if she were offering it to him. An intimate gesture. She sits like a beautiful woman and one can see that the man leans into her like a man enthralled.

It must be her, Lucienne thinks, but as soon as she does, she realizes how absurd that idea is. Her mother is not beautiful in that kind of way. Yes, there is something about her, that's true. A charisma, but it's tempered by drive. An iron will. And she would never be sitting idle in a café, she thinks. Lingering somewhere. Smoking. It's just not her nature.

Lucienne feels a migraine coming on. A series of tiny lights flash at the edges of her vision. Too much stress. The driver changes lanes abruptly. Lucienne jerks forward. He looks at her through the rearview mirror but says nothing. The contents of her purse fall to the floor. A Cross pen. Her planning calendar. Her billfold fans open. There is one credit card in the plastic pockets, where photos should be. The rest are empty.

It is then that Lucienne realizes that if her mother is not in this photograph, she has no pictures of her. Not even one. Not at home or her office or anywhere. If Hélène is not the woman in this photo, the only photographic evidence of her life is in the official things that document her, label her. Her driver's license. Passport.

The cab bounces, picks up speed. Lucienne puts her mother's photograph back in her purse. Zips it shut. The cab takes another sharp turn. Lucienne hits her knee on the metal ashtray. Not hard, just enough to make it feel bruised and hot.

"*Excusez-moi,*" the driver shouts over the music. The drumming has become frantic. The beat, like a stone tossed in water, moves out to her, then through her, then beyond. "*Excusez-moi.*"

A French tutor once told Lucienne that the phrase "excuse me" is good for any situation, whether you've stepped on someone's foot or hit him with your car. "In French, there are few degrees in the request for forgiveness," he said. "You desire forgiveness. That, in itself, is most important."

Now, she looks at the cab driver in the rearview mirror. Can't tell if he really wants to be forgiven or not. His eyes are shadows. He slams on the brakes. The traffic ahead is stalled.

"*Excusez-moi,*" he says again.

"*Oui,*" she says, although it's not exactly the correct response. He smiles. Sizes her up as an American, an awful tourist who isn't polite enough to learn the language. He watches her in the rearview mirror. The cab smells stale. She opens the window, even though it's still raining. The air outside is not much better. The sidewalks steam and smell of wet paper and dogs. The cab starts up again. Her cream blouse is wrinkled. Sticks to her back.

A hot bath, she thinks. Some wine.

The cab turns down another street. This one is small and winding. Rue something. She can't make out the name. Rain from the open window wets the side of her face, her blouse, and her black cotton skirt. They turn another corner sharply. She recognizes the street. The hotel is near. There's a florist's shop she remembers seeing with its windows filled entirely with black roses. Next door, a shop known for its elaborate chocolates. Dark chocolate bars, postcard size, painted to resemble Monet's garden series. Just yesterday her mother had pointed them out to her.

"I'd never eat such a beautiful thing," she said.

Yesterday seems so long ago.

"My brother is singing this song," the cab driver says loudly, as if he wants Lucienne to acknowledge it, look at him. "He's an American now."

Lucienne doesn't want to make eye contact. She's just too tired. She looks out the window and nods. He pulls over the taxi in front of the hotel. She hands him the fare quickly.

"America," he says to her, "home of the brave."

She doesn't reply. Slams the car door by accident.

"Home of the brave," he says again, and pulls away and waves. She watches him for a moment making his way down the narrow street. As he drives away, the brother's voice, distant and wavering, comes to her as if across the ocean.

Inside the hotel, the night manager is waiting to greet her.

"We understand you will be with us for a while," he says, and slips a key, the size and shape of a plastic credit card, into her hand. "I have taken the liberty to find you a more suitable room."

She stares at the card for a moment.

Of course, she thinks.

"Shall I escort you?" he says.

She can see he's anxious, as if he were somehow concerned that she would cry or shout or make some sort of scene that would alarm the other guests—or perhaps him. She shakes her head and hands him a few francs for his trouble. He smiles, clearly relieved. "You have many messages on your voice mail," he whispers.

Lucienne takes the elevator to the third floor. Room 314. Two floors down from the old one. The room smells hotel-clean. She opens the closet. Someone has hung her silk blouses ranging in shade from light to dark. In the dresser, her cotton underwear and brassieres are neatly arranged, as one would see in a department store. It reminds her of foster care and the mothers who tried so hard to make her feel part of a family. She tries to remember their names and faces, the sound of their voices. Tries not to think of the room just two floors above her, the memory of her mother's dying there. Tries very hard not to think of it at all.

It's nearly 5 P.M. Seventeen hundred hours, she thinks. On the dresser the manager had placed a plate of figs and cheese and a small bottle of red wine. It's the same vintage she and her mother had ordered the night before in the hotel dining room.

"For you," his note read. No need to mention why.

The room is cool and dark. And quiet, so quiet. A bite of fig, the gentle caramel sweetness. A sip of wine. She sits down on the bed, looks at the television, and sees her own image reflected in the gray glass. She turns it on. Mutes the sound. The light turns every-thing a comforting blue.

She doesn't remember when she fell asleep but it's nearly mid-night when the telephone rings. Not exactly a ring, more like a jin-gle, hushed and elegant.

"Bonjour, Lucienne—"

She is asleep when she answers. Lost in a deep dreamless sleep. No black hole. Just darkness. "Wrong number," she says and hangs up. It takes her a moment to realize that the voice sounded like that of the doctor. She runs a hand though her hair by habit. He'll call back, if it's him, she thinks. But she isn't too sure. Every-thing feels blurred.

How long have I been asleep?

Her cream blouse sticks to her. Nylons bind her legs. Her con-tacts are so dry they make her eyes feel raw. Disgusted, she takes everything off—her clothes, her contact lenses—and throws them into a heap at the side of the bed.

Blindness is better, she thinks, rubbing her eyes, and then won-ders if it really is. Without her contacts, the world has gone too soft. It takes a moment for her eyes to readjust to the light of the television, the room, the flashing of the phone that indicates she's forgotten to collect her messages. The last time she saw her glasses they were in the bathroom of her former room, two flights above her, with the rest of her contacts in their neat disposable packages. So, where are they now?

Lucienne turns on a light by the side of the bed and her eyes begin to water profusely. She snaps it off again. That was stupid, she thinks, and stands up. The bathroom has to be in the same place as it was in the other room. She tries to feel her way over to it. Hits the edge of the nightstand. A bruise begins to spread. That's the second bruise today. Outside it's still raining, harder than before. The wind kicks up, rattles the small windowpanes. The noise makes her jump. For a moment, standing naked and bruised and blind in the unfamiliar room, she feels vulnerable, as if she's being watched, as if someone is standing behind the thick curtains, just waiting.

Her body begins to shake, mostly from the cold.

She looks over at the television. It's still on. There's video of people running in clouds of smoke down narrow streets. Some sort of news. CNN. The clouds catch up, engulf the people entirely. She can barely make it out without her glasses. She pats the bed to find the remote to turn on the sound. It's not there. It must have fallen on the floor.

The phone rings again. The ring seems louder this time. Startles her.

"Hello?" she says, and nearly knocks it over. On the mute television screen a large airplane banks. She can see that, even without her glasses. She knows it's going to hit. Where are my glasses?

"Your mother has started breathing on her own," the doctor says. "The nurse went to adjust the tube and noticed it. She's still in a coma, but it's a good sign."

On the television, the footage is shown again. This time from a different angle. This time, the enormity of it sinks in. She can hardly breathe.

"If one were to believe in God," the doctor continues on, "this could be called a miracle."

On the television there is a wide shot. Then slow motion.

"Lucienne? Are you there?"

"I'll be right there," she says, or thinks she does. Hangs up the phone.

Fifteen minutes later, she's showered and changed. New contacts. She can see clearly again. Everything's back in focus. The airplane hits the building. And she can see it. Clearly. Over and over again. It banks and turns.

The night manager has sent for a car to take her to the hospital. "Half an hour," he says, though she wants to leave sooner.

"Too dangerous for taxi," he says. "Too late."

Lucienne turns up the sound on the television. It's difficult not to watch. In one shot, she notices something odd. A moment before the second tower folds in on itself, she sees what seems to be a flock of birds, wingless, escape out the windows.

Oh, Lucienne thinks, not birds. She cannot imagine the choice. Lucienne turns off the television. Checks her watch. Ten more minutes before the car arrives.

The flashing red light of the phone reminds her of Ethan. He's probably called. She'd like to call him back, just to talk. But talking, just talking, is a habit she knows she'll have to break. Soon, he'll find someone else to talk to even though he says, "We'll always be close," and seems to mean it. Lucienne knows that won't be true. Not always. She also knows that the separation didn't have to happen. She could have just let things go on the way they were. In many ways, their marriage was perfect. Ethan was the outgoing, charming one. She was quiet and reserved. At parties, he worked the room. She watched. They completed each other, but too much went unsaid and, finally, it chipped away at them.

A couple of years ago, they were in a cab coming home from a fund-raiser for the planetarium. They both had had too much wine, and it was too late, and they were too tired, and Ethan had spent the night flirting unashamedly with everyone's wife.

"Do you consider yourself happily married?" she asked.

"I think that's a stupid question," he said, and never answered it. All Lucienne wanted him to say was that he was happy with her most of the time, or some of the time, or even every now and then, but he didn't. He changed the subject, so she never asked again.

After that night, Lucienne began to question her life with Ethan, and to not live it. She shut down. Started running the numbers of their lives together. How many hours making love? How many talking? The calculations were elaborate and she eventually came to the conclusion that the marriage would fail, it was inevitable, no matter how hard she tried. In a way it was true, but not for the reasons she thought. Lucienne had always mistrusted Ethan. He was too handsome, too affable. There were too many women in his past whom he still considered "friends," still took to lunch or went to the museum with. And there were parts of his life that he never talked about, especially his days as a child actor, and that always bothered her.

"It must have been difficult to be a star and to be a real kid," she said to him when they first met.

"It was just a job, like a paper route," he'd say and nothing more.

At first, Lucienne thought he was just being modest. Then, she imagined the worst, that Ethan was somehow traumatized by his experience. Maybe his parents had pushed him too hard. Abused him somehow.

Soon Lucienne began to fantasize that Ethan's father was cold and demanding and that his mother was a shrew who lived out her fantasies through her son's career. But none of it was true. When Lucienne and Ethan became engaged, and the Segals came from Palm Beach to visit, Millie and Howie were warm and funny.

Loved sophisticated food and fine wines, and, most important, they loved Lucienne.

"Our little shiksa," they called her, and kissed her on both cheeks. Only mentioned conversion once or twice. Acquiesced gracefully when Lucienne announced that they were having a justice of the peace perform the ceremony. For ten days, Millie's "Love that Red" lipstick was the only blush Lucienne needed. And that was fine with her. Millie and Howie were the family Lucienne had always wanted. They were both mathematicians, so cocktail hours could be spent knee-deep in theory. Even Hélène seemed to like them.

"I think they're too tan, though," she said. "Makes them look indolent."

The only thing odd about Millie and Howie is that they, like Ethan, refused to talk about his acting career.

"He's a grown man now," Howie said, seeming uncomfortable. "A good man. A good citizen. That's more important."

And it was, until this summer.

The summer started out badly. School had been out for about two weeks when Lucienne discovered that a team at Palomar Observatory was trying to disprove that V325BAndromedae was indeed a black hole.

"I could have missed something," she told Ethan, and he could see that she was going to wind herself up over it. Spend days and nights rerunning the numbers. Worrying. Not eating.

"If you were wrong, there's nothing you can do about it," he said. "Do us all a favor and go clean the attic. Work the stress off."

So, she did. And that was the mistake. In the back of the attic, there was a cardboard box marked "ETHAN'S." It was old. Forgotten. The tape cracked. Must have been here since the move, she thought. So she opened it. She's still not sure why. She tells herself it was more of an innocent impulse, and as soon as she ripped off the tape, she felt embarrassed. It was Ethan's, after all. His name was on it as if to somehow separate these things from their things. It felt private. And it was.

There were things inside she had never seen before. Most of them, quite sweet. His baby teeth. A picture of his parents at an awards ceremony. A ragged bean-bag frog with only one eye.

And then an article about a shooting: "Child Actor on Rampage." It claimed that Ethan was seventeen years old and drunk. Enraged. The man killed was his best friend. Lucienne's hands shook while she read it. This boy didn't sound like Ethan at all. Through the floorboards she could hear him below, in the kitchen, making dinner. Ethan loved to cook and took great pride in it. She imagined him chopping the carrots, onions, and celery, just so. Placing them into neat piles. Left to right across the cutting board. Just as he always did. The thought made her cry.

Lucienne knew that if she said anything, there would be no going back. No more glasses of wine while dinner cooks. No more nights falling asleep listening to his sure, steady breath. It would all be over. Or at least shifted somehow. But she had to ask him. Just couldn't let it go.

When she opened the kitchen door, Ethan didn't turn around, he kept on chopping.

"I'm making lobster gumbo," he said. "I promised chicken, but lobsters are so cheap right now. Couldn't help myself. Let me get you a glass of wine."

A timer ticked. A large pot of water was boiling. She could see claws hanging over the rim. When Lucienne finally found her voice she asked, "How could you keep this from me?"

Ethan stopped pouring the wine. Turned around. He was oddly calm. Controlled. It was as if he'd always expected this moment. "It happened a long time ago," he said. He was wearing a ripped pair of shorts, his old college T-shirt. Well-loved and faded. On the front it read, "The top reason I became an astrophysicist . . ." And on the back: ". . . so I can tell liberal arts majors, 'Yes, I would like fries with that.' "

Lucienne had seen that shirt a hundred times over the years. Never noticed how faded the letters had become. And the sentiment. He should have thrown it away long ago. She handed him the article. He put it down on the counter and stepped away from it, as if to distance himself.

Then he did something he always did. Something, after all those years of marriage, Lucienne does now, too. He ran a hand through his hair. It's his tic. A habit. The gesture always shows off the black curls, still thick and beautiful, a part of the movie-star quality that never seems to fade.

He looks so innocent when he does that, she thought. A beautiful child.

And suddenly, that angered her. Ethan had run his hands through his hair thousands of times since they met. Hundreds of times she'd had that same thought—how innocent—but now the gesture seemed deliberate. Like something he once learned. Did on cue. He was an actor after all.

"Much-loved," the article stated.

"You're just upset about work," he said.

V325BAndromedae, she thought, and knew he was right, but

there was more to it than that. She felt betrayed. Unsafe. He had, after all, killed someone.

"It's the past," he said. "Not important anymore."

Then she remembered what her mother had always told her. The past is unimportant.

And remembered her mother's hands around her neck.

And she couldn't breathe.

"You have to leave," she told him, and Ethan didn't argue.

"I'll always love you whether you believe it or not" was all he said. Then left. That was four months ago.

Now, Lucienne runs a hand through her own hair. It's still damp. A few strands fall in her lap. Gray.

When did I get this old? she thinks, but she's only forty-three. Not that old at all, she hopes. Still, not that young.

She sits down on the bed and closes her eyes. So tired. And then she feels it: the black hole. Feels as if she is falling into it, as if she is a huge wingless bird, and all around her there are the others. Ethan and Josh. Marie. Her mother. And those from the tower.

But they do not shimmer in harmony, a perfect pitch.

They scream.

THINGS MIGHT HAVE TURNED OUT DIFFERENTLY IF Vincent had found someone to love, someone other than Hélène. He was not unattractive. He had a kind face. Inviting. Handsome, in the way one would say a racehorse is handsome: sturdy and well shaped. Beautiful hands. Nails like blanched almonds.

But he was a small man, just over five feet. Delicate bones. This, of course, was his curse. Some women shunned him. Some felt protective and treated him like a pet. Some found themselves willing to share secrets, and yet, nothing more.

Vincent was well educated, interested in many fields. He enjoyed the company of academics and hoped to be a doctor some-day. But in the winter of 1937, when he turned twenty, Vincent enlisted in the army as a medical assistant in Morocco.

"To cure a broken heart," his father told everyone.

"To fulfill my duty as a Frenchman," Vincent said.

Morocco was the last place anyone expected Vincent to go. Even Vincent himself, but he had no choice and thought everyone would understand that. He was too small a man to be drafted, and it was well known that in Morocco men were needed, especially men who had studied medicine, which he had done. At least slightly. Six months to be exact, but the army could not afford to refuse him. So he lied about his experience and signed on.

Colonization is never easy and for the French in Morocco it was almost impossible, a long and bloody battle that was passed from one generation to the next.

In 1904, France signed a secret treaty with Spain in which the two countries divided Morocco and agreed not to oppose the British in Egypt. The Moroccans had little to say in the matter. That was the beginning of the end. The end of peace. And colonization. Dissent became a way of life until the Spanish Civil War began, both in Spain and in Spanish-held Morocco. Soldier rose up against soldier and the French had no choice but to be sucked into it.

The event was, in some sense, predictable. As war always is. There was one uprising. Then another. Then the next. Then people were taken hostage. Then there were body counts. Then battles that were named and recorded. Then attempts at compromise, of course. Diplomatic gestures. Moments of peace. Or at least, reprieve. And there were heroes who surpassed everyone with their bold-faced courage. And there were their families who cared little for the fame of heroes and would trade it all for just one last kiss, salty and sweet.

All countries are built on bags of bones. It was the same for Morocco.

By the time Vincent arrived there in 1937, the French had been fighting small bands of the Berber tribe in the Atlas Mountains for nearly a decade without much success. There was talk of an organized national revolt. Every man was needed, even the ones, Vincent thought, who seemed smaller than most.

"Heroes come in all sizes," he said.

The recruitment officer had seen the bravado of youth before, the foolish logic, and looked askance. "It is difficult to civilize a nation," he told him. "No matter how large a man you are. Or how large a fool."

Once in Morocco, Vincent soon understood what the officer meant. It was a place of wild extremes. There was Marrakesh, noisy and hot. Rhythmic. Unrelenting. Its narrow streets filled with beggars and their singsong "Money for rice. Money for rice," and merchants who hawked hay, sweet hay, and carrots and potatoes and cumin and cayenne and smooth dates and sweet blood oranges and goats, both dead and alive. Every part of the goat was for sale there. Intestines and heads. Eyes like dice. "Every part. Every, every part," the merchants sang.

Every street had its own song: "Try good. Try like. Try good. Try like."

And every street had its cool rooms where one could eat stewed goat with couscous. And had its dark places, where the golden hashish, called kif, perfumed the air, encouraged forgetting.

And, underneath it all, there was the music of greeting, a plea for peace. *Salaam aleikum. Aleikum asalaam.* And thanks for God. *Al humdul'allah.* This was the music of Marrakesh.

Once outside the city, however, the world grew silent. The heat gave way to the mountains, snow-capped and treacherous. When Vincent arrived in late winter, blizzards swooped over the razor peaks without warning, howled through the canvas of his tent and his clothes. Filled his pores with snow and sand. In the mountains, there seemed no difference between day and night. The snow, the stars, the pale sun cast everything in shadows. Dusk and dawn, and the hours in between, were indecipherable. Battles were fought in the shadows. The Berbers knew each crevice and canyon of the mountain range as one does his own home. There was no place to hide. No strategies to employ. No way to outmaneuver. The French were forced to wait for the enemy to find them. And they did find them. With great efficiency.

Wrapped in the white fur of goats, the nomads could stand so quietly that one thought they were part of a snow drift. Only if one looked closely could their eyes be seen, like the heat of a flame. And then, of course, it was too late.

The losses were staggering. The soldiers of one regiment brought to Vincent's tent were nearly cut in two, bones ragged and torn. He'd never seen such pain and suffering, such total devastation. Vincent quickly discovered that he was alone and unprepared. He had only just begun his medical training at the university and understood the body in a general way. He knew how to treat mild ailments, such as colic and gout. He'd assumed that, as a medical assistant, he would assist someone more skilled. But in the Atlas Mountains doctors were an unheard of luxury. On the very first day, Vincent found himself holding a man's heart in his hand as if it were a helpless bird.

Still, even the most experienced surgeon would have been of little help. Supplies were limited and Vincent had orders to help only those who had a good chance of surviving, which were few. So he used the morphine on himself. Just a bit at first, to take the edge off. Just a bit won't hurt. And then kif, which he bought from travelers. And other soldiers. The incense of its smoke, so sweet and floral, would sometimes bring him to tears.

It all helped. All made each day meld into the next. And after a time, Vincent began to believe that the only thing he could do was give comfort.

"What is the place you want to see again?" he would ask each soldier, softly, and if the man could reply, then Vincent would say, "I will take you there."

And in a low driving voice, a voice that did not seem to be his own, Vincent would tell the most intricate tales about places and things he could only imagine. The brothels of Morocco where the women's eyes were dark with kohl and their skin perfumed with the oil of cloves. The secret gardens of Kyoto where geisha flowered in the moonlight. Or a simple country wedding where a promise that was made could be kept.

Vincent was a gifted storyteller, a trait he inherited from his mother, Katherine. When he spun these stories, he thought of her and her voice and the mesmerizing stories she could weave and how, even though they were all lies, they were somehow truer than any fact he ever knew.

"The day is calm," he would always begin. In Vincent's stories, as in his mother's, the days were always calm and the air was sweeter than ever before.

On the other nights, the nights in which all the dying were gone, one way or another, carried down the mountain or buried on it, Vincent wrote his father long letters. Not because he missed him, or wanted to talk to him. He wrote his father because he had no one else to write to. On these nights, and there were many, Vincent would sit in his tent and write until morning. When he began, he never knew what he was going to say and often surprised himself with the depth and frankness of his feeling. Sometimes, it was as if there were another person living inside of him, someone bolder and braver and more understanding of the world, someone who had been to the brothels and teahouses and who understood a country wedding with a trembling bride. It was someone he did not recognize. Someone who was not a small man.

"I am still in the thick of this," he wrote as the snow piled around the tent and the endless wind pushed this way and that. He wasn't sure what he meant by that sentence. Wasn't sure if he was saying that he was still in the thick of battle, or of snow. Both were true. And, in his mind, he imagined them both to be the same. Imagined that soon the snow and the battle would take him over completely. And, like the mountains that surrounded him, he would become blinding and dangerous.

"Part of me will always remain here," he wrote. "Perhaps the only part worth saving."

Despite these circumstances, the act of writing itself was never frantic or hurried. The words did not come tumbling out, pushing their way to the surface. Quite the opposite. Much to Vincent's surprise, he found himself to be methodical when it came to these letters. Everything had to be perfect before he could begin. The expensive linen writing paper his father gave him was always placed exactly in the center of the old field desk. The ink well to his right, just so. A sense of order was crucial. And so, with everything in its place, Vincent began to write. Slowly. He took his time. Unlike the careless writing of his school days, with badly looped letters nearly leaning against one another, here, near the top of the world, knee-deep in the dying of others, his penmanship was perfect. The wind piled foot upon foot of snow above him, around him, caused the pole of the tent to creak and sway, and yet every word was unhurried. Every vowel and consonant was as well formed as one would expect from an educated man.

Still, despite his best efforts, his careful preparation, and slow but deliberate work, Vincent's letters were difficult to read. The beautifully formed words and commas and periods, the architecture of the elegant paragraphs, all bled off the scalloped edges of his father's fine linen stationery. It could not be helped. When Vincent wrote, tears rolled down his cheeks and mixed with the ink.

It wasn't the kif or the morphine. He took neither when he wrote. And, despite his childlike stature, he wasn't a man given to tears, or even to much emotion. But there was something about the act of writing, the release of it, that touched him. It was as if when he wrote he could be the man who was trapped inside of him. And so he wept and could not stop.

When later asked about the blurred ink of his letters, he told his father that the smoke of the oil lamp made his eyes water. He didn't care if his father believed him or not. The writing was all that really mattered to him.

His father, Jacques, read his son's letters with great interest. Jacques Laloux was a furrier who came from a family of furriers. Very good ones, at that. He was born a man of more than modest means and high aspirations, as his father was and his father was.

"To me," he wrote to his son, "fur is the ultimate sign of a civilized society. It is proof that we can conquer a beast and make it into a thing of beauty."

Vincent might have disagreed if he had had the chance to read the letter. Might have told his father of the savage Berbers hiding in the fur of goats. But he never read the letter. He never knew what his father's reply was, and frankly didn't care. Vincent burned that letter unopened. Burned every letter unopened. He never wrote expecting a response and when one arrived, he found it to be inconvenient, at best. And so, Vincent had no choice but to burn them all. Which was a great pity, because the letters Vincent's father sent were filled with pride for his son. And love.

The old man was overjoyed to receive each and every letter his son wrote and reciprocated in a way that could be described, at the very least, as effusive. Perhaps he has finally found a place in his heart for me, Jacques thought when the first one arrived. Time softens, he told himself. Jacques was a romantic. He carried his son's letters with him everywhere he went.

"News from Morocco," he would say, waving them like a flag. With great enthusiasm he would read them to customers, his seamstress, and the old man who ran the café down the street. He'd read his son's letters to anyone he met who was willing to listen. And even those who were not so willing.

"My son has become a good and dutiful man," he would say. And as the stack of letters grew fat, many believed this to be true.

"He must love you very much," the seamstress said.

Jacques hoped it was true. Vincent's mother left when he was just a boy. He was too young to understand what happens between people who love too much, or badly. Or both. But not too young to remember the details of the event. So, every time Vincent thought of that night, thought of her, his mother, he was again the eight-year-old. He felt the same sick feeling, the helplessness. Felt his parents fight all over again, as they often did, but this time their anger twisted around itself. Clockwise. Then counterclockwise. Chairs. Plates. Vincent. Everything was pulled into it.

And then the door slammed.

"Bring her back," Vincent screamed. His face swollen. His small fists pounded his father's chest.

Vincent's memory of the event stopped there. What he didn't recall was that his mother had left before. Many times. And not because of the fighting. She left because it was her habit.

At the moment that Jacques raised his hand to slap his son away, the boy cowed. And in that moment Jacques saw all that was Katherine in his son—her hair, her beautiful hands, the dead look in her eyes whenever she saw him—and he was sorry for what they had become. Jacques felt his entire life slip away from him. Everything he valued, his home, his wife, his only child. So, he reached out and caught his son's fist in his hand. Held it gently, as if it were made of blown glass.

"She'll be back soon," he said. "You'll see."

But Vincent would have none of it. He jerked away, all sour heat.

"She won't!" he screamed, defiant. "She left her key."

Jacques turned and saw Katherine's key hanging on its nail by the door in the kitchen.

"She can't get in without her key," the boy said.

And Jacques knew it was true.

She is never coming back again, Jacques thought.

So he did something that he had never done before. He picked up his son and held him in his arms. Squeezed him hard. Kissed him.

"We'll leave the door unlocked then," he said. But the boy would not stop crying.

"She's not coming back, ever."

And then Jacques said the one thing he regretted.

"She'll come back," he said. "She's your mother."

Then he put his son down, turned away from him. Left Vincent standing in the middle of the kitchen, red-faced, no dinner, no milk poured, everything turning sour around the small boy. Jacques had no choice. He couldn't face his son anymore, the bits of Katherine in him, the lies he knew he needed to tell to lull his son to sleep. So, he closed his bedroom door and lay on the bed, hoping to dream of nothing. But that was impossible. Katherine was everywhere. Her scent on the sheets. The empty arms of the hangers that once held her dresses, her many furs. He closed his eyes but she was there, too. The soft of her neck. The sweet cream of her breasts. After a while, there was a hollow knock at the door. Jacques opened his eyes, but did not move. His body was too heavy. He shouted at the ceiling, "Go to bed now, boy. Stop crying. She'll be back soon. She'll be back."

So, Vincent did what any other child would have done. He waited. He stood by the front door and waited for the knob to turn. He stood there until he could no longer stand. Then he sat. Then laid across the threshold, staring up at the brass doorknob as if it were the waning moon. He waited all night. And the next night. And most nights after that. Every night, Vincent slept curled by the door like a dog, until his father carried him back to his bed.

"The floor is no place for the son of a furrier," he scolded, but every night the small boy returned to the same spot.

"You have to sleep," Jacques would say, but he could see that Vincent didn't care. The boy was determined to wait for her as long as need be. So, it became their ritual. Every night, Jacques would put Vincent to bed in the boy's small bed. It was soft and warm with too many pillows and a stuffed brown dog that Vincent once said he loved more than anything. And every morning,

Jacques woke to discover the small boy, cold and exhausted, in the foyer, leaning against the front door of their apartment, his well-worn dog keeping watch.

"How long is 'soon'?" Vincent finally asked.

The next day Jacques bought a large leather chair and placed it by the door. It was overstuffed and there was a footstool to match. Brass upholstery nails kept the leather in place. It looked as if it belonged in a men's club. It didn't match anything in the room but it was big enough for a growing boy to curl into and sleep comfortably. And so that's what Vincent began to do. After a time, however, things changed. Vincent eventually began to sleep in his own bed.

That's always the way with grief. It shifts.

Six months after his mother left, he couldn't remember the sound of her laughter. A year later, when Madame Assam, the housekeeper, *femme de ménage*, arrived with her kind arms, it was difficult for Vincent to recall if his mother's eyes were more blue than green or more green than blue. Soon, the sorrow no longer burned in him but became more like a parasite, small and quiet, hidden near his heart. He felt himself grow smaller with each passing week.

Sometimes, on his birthday or on Christmas, Vincent would still sleep in the overstuffed chair by the door, an unread book open in his lap. Waiting. No one ever told him to go back to his own bed, not even Madame Assam, whose job it was to keep the boy safe. Not even her son, Basheer, who looked on the boy as if he were his own brother. No one ever spoke of the waiting. There was no need. The habit of sorrow is a difficult one to break. At least, for a boy who is willing to wait.

Unlike his son, Jacques never waited for Katherine's return.

His sorrow did not erode him. The moment he saw her key still hanging on the hook, he knew she was not coming back.

"Katherine is one of the great mysteries of the world," he told his customers when they asked after her. He didn't know what else to say. It was true. She was like no one he had ever met. She had the eyes of a fallen angel. Hair, wild as wind. She walked into his shop one day and said, "I am lost."

Jacques knew the moment he saw her that he was lost, too. Katherine was a Gypsy who traveled in the countryside reading fortunes. She was a painter's model but had to leave Milan when the painter was killed by his jealous wife. She was a pirate who sailed along the Tropic of Cancer. Arched the equator. She was all of these things and none of them. That's all Jacques knew for sure and he wanted her all the more because of it. He wanted the mystery of her. They could have courted, as others do. Quiet dinners. Walks along the river. But they didn't. The only place they ever went was the workroom. It was cold. It smelled of hide and dirt. It was a world that belonged to just the two of them.

She'd pull him into her arms, the shoals of her lips. "We are on an island," she would say, "and the island has a name but no one can remember it because the island is so beautiful, the name has become unimportant. All that is important is that you are there and I am there and the air is sweeter than ever before." The pelts were rough against their skin. Rubbed their flesh raw.

For their wedding, Jacques made her an ankle-length coat of tiger skins. "Your true skin," he said, and for the first time in his life, he found himself happy. And also rich. As rich as his grandfather and father had always hoped they would become. Katherine and her gifts as a storyteller had proven to be quite an asset in business. Jacques's customers were lonely. Katherine would often invite them for champagne and sweets and end up selling them wildly expensive coats that had enchanting, although not wholly accurate, histories.

"They know me to be a wonderful liar," she once told her son, "which is a priceless skill they are willing to pay for." Vincent understood. He often sat in the salon and watched his mother at work. By the second glass of champagne, the third tart, a special coat would be offered from the back room.

"Just for you," she'd say in a schoolgirl whisper and begin to weave the tale. A coat could be made from the rare white minks that roamed the uncharted islands off Borneo or from the snow leopards of India that were skinned by the son of Rudyard Kipling himself. It all depended on the likes and dislikes of the client. And, of course, the level of their wealth. The fact that the coat was actually rabbit fur made absolutely no difference at all.

"Everything is as true as one needs it to be," Vincent's mother told him. And he hoped she was right.

❧ 7 ❧

WHEN LUCIENNE ARRIVES AT THE HOSPITAL, IT'S nearly 1 A.M. and everything is hushed. The lights in the hallways are dimmed. The nurses are whispering at the station. Hélène has been moved from the Intensive Care Unit to a private room. When Lucienne opens the door, it feels as if she's intruding. Hélène is not alone. The emergency-room doctor sits by her side, holding her hand. Leaning into her. The scene is so intimate, for a moment Lucienne thinks she's in the wrong room. The room is dark, lit by banks of monitors. Green lines. Yellow waves. Red spikes that travel up and down like fountains. It's a private room. Just Hélène in a single bed. It feels like a secret place. The machines hum, softly beep. The light from the hallway makes the doctor squint.

"This is the difficult part," he says. "She's made some progress but she's still unresponsive to light and touch."

He gently places Hélène's hand back under the thin blanket. Smooths the sheets and whispers something Lucienne can't make out. She notices he's shaved. Changed his shirt. This one's newly starched, quite white, stiff around the collar. Professionally pressed. He smells of soap, antiseptic and clean. Lucienne imagines he's going home, his shift is over.

"I came to say good-bye," he says. "Once a patient is moved up here, they're assigned to someone else. Dr. Belliard will take over now. She's very good. Very thorough."

"I see," Lucienne says, and suddenly feels abandoned. She tells herself she's glad she doesn't remember his name. But isn't.

"Well," he says, but says nothing else. There's nothing left to say. They sit for a moment in this odd twilight.

Lucienne stares at the machines, their wires and tubes. A highway of technology. Outside, a truck rumbles by. Backfires. The honk of a horn. She trembles slightly. Hélène seems so small now, diminished, swaddled in the bleached sheets. Her hands are crooked as rivers. Her face is so white, it's nearly invisible. Lucienne looks at her mother. Then away. The room suddenly feels too cold.

"You look pale," he says.

"Tired. That's all."

Carefully, Lucienne sits down on the edge of her mother's bed. The added weight makes the IV pull a bit. Lucienne sees it. Feels a sharp pain in her own arm.

"It's all right," the doctor says. "It's safe."

Lucienne sits.

"It's late," he says. "I should go." But he doesn't move. It's clear he wants to say something else.

Lucienne can feel the mattress beneath her rise and fall with each soft breath her mother takes. Breathing. Still breathing. There's comfort in that. The tick of it. The metronome of her mother's heart keeps panic at bay.

"Look," he finally says, "if you need anything—"

"I'm fine," Lucienne says, but her voice cracks.

He opens the drawer in the nightstand next to him. It's empty. "Do you have a piece of paper?" he asks. "Something to write on?"

Lucienne shakes her head.

"This will have to do then," he says, and takes her hand, pulls out a cheap ballpoint pen, and begins to write his phone number on her palm.

"What are you doing?" Lucienne says, and pulls away.

"I'm out of business cards."

"That's my hand."

"I know," he says, and takes it back, continues writing. "We studied that in medical school."

"Look, I'm really fine—"

"You're really not. I lost my own mother to suicide. I know how difficult it is."

The words suddenly make the room feel even colder. Lucienne looks at the phone number and then at him. In the darkened room, he looks much younger than before. And kind. An odd angel of mercy.

"I know you're alone in Paris," he says softly. "And while Dr. Belliard is very good, she makes it a practice to keep a professional distance. Doesn't get too involved if she can help it. I, on the other hand, am totally unprofessional. So, if you find you need to talk, call me."

Lucienne nods, but wonders if she will.

The doctor moves past her gently. "Be well," he says, and opens the door to leave.

"What was her name?" Lucienne asks.

"Belliard," he says.

"No," Lucienne says. "Your mother."

The doctor seems wary. "Why?"

She shrugs. "I don't know. I just suddenly wanted to know somehow. It's stupid. I'm sorry. Forget it."

The doctor is holding the door open with one hand. The white uniforms of nurses blur behind him. It's difficult to see him clearly, the hallway is now filled with hard light. Lucienne moves toward him. Shades her eyes. She can still smell his skin. See the grief on his face.

"Really, I'm sorry," she says, fumbling for the right words. "I have no idea why I even wanted to know—"

"Manon," he says, and says it so sadly, it's as if even the word itself is unbearable to hear. For a moment, Lucienne and the doctor stand together, half in and half out of light.

"Manon is a beautiful name," she says gently.

"*Bonjour*, Dr. Assam," a nurse says as she passes.

"*Bonjour,*" he says.

That's when they hear it. An odd sound. A single note. Not quite middle C. Its vibrato rattles. It's coming from the room. Hélène is turned toward them. Humming. The note grows louder, more shaky. Her eyes are open but unfocused. Milk glass.

"Nurse!" the doctor shouts, pushes past Lucienne. Hélène's humming quivers as it grows louder. Then whoops and whirls. Her arms flail. A cup of water falls over onto the floor, rolls under the bed. She is like a windup doll. Everything moves. Hands and arms. Feet kick.

"Mother, can you hear me?"

The nurse arrives with a small tray. A delicate needle.

Hélène's frail hand swings toward the doctor and scratches his cheek by accident. A thin line of blood rises to the surface. He doesn't react. He taps Hélène's arm. A blood vessel rises. Lucienne can't look.

Suddenly, Hélène speaks. "I'm so sorry," she says frantically. Her body still thrashing. Breath labored. "I never—"

Lucienne moves to the side of the bed. "Mother?"

"I never meant—"

The words are exhaled, not spoken.

Lucienne feels as if the blood has drained from her heart. It beats tin. Clangs.

"Mother, it's me," she says. "Lucienne."

But Hélène stays focused on the doctor alone. Her body seems to move of its own will. Tears rim her red eyes, splash onto the bleached white sheets. She bites her lower lip. Her head shakes back and forth. Words stagger.

"I never—"

A look of horror passes over Dr. Assam's face. He steps away slightly. Then leans in again. He seems to be both repulsed and drawn into the moment. "Shh. Shh," he says. Taps the vein again. Pushes the plunger. Hélène's body jerks.

"It is forgiven," he whispers.

The words, or the drug, take effect. It's difficult to tell which. Hélène's body relaxes. Eyes close. Then sleep.

The room breathes.

"What's going on?" Lucienne says. "What just happened here?"

"It's good, now. Better," Dr. Assam says to no one in particular; his eyes are on Hélène. He checks the monitors. Their rhythm is back to normal. The rise and fall. "The pulse is good again," he says.

The nurse picks up the tray, the spent needle. A single drop of liquid falls from the point onto the metal. "We'll call Dr. Belliard at home," she says to Lucienne. "I'll need you to go out to the waiting room for a while."

"I'm staying," she says.

"She's resting now," Dr. Assam says. "She needs to rest."

Lucienne picks up her mother's hand and holds it. It's cold. She rubs it. "I'll wait until Dr. Belliard comes."

"Outside might be better," Dr. Assam says. "They'll need to run some more tests right now."

Lucienne moves away from him. "She spoke to you," she says.

"People in comas sometimes seem lucid, but they're not," he says, but he doesn't sound convinced.

"Then why did you tell her she's forgiven?"

Lucienne looks at the thin cut on his face. There's a small bit of blood. He moves away slightly. She moves in closer. Just a bit. It suddenly feels as if there's something he's holding back. Something he knows. A secret.

The nurse taps Lucienne on the arm. "Madame, please, you must wait outside."

"Perhaps we should take a walk," Dr. Assam says.

"Perhaps we should," says Lucienne.

~ 8 ~

VINCENT AND HÉLÈNE MET AT AN OPEN house at the home of Frédéric and Irène Joliot-Curie on a crisp September day in 1938. Vincent had just come home from Morocco. Discharged, dishonorably, for the use of drugs. He was still gaunt and too thin, despite his father's best efforts. Still smelled of kif, every now and then. The day threatened rain. No matter, spirits were high. The event was a ritual of the household. A salon, of sorts. Twenty people fit around the kitchen table, and so twenty were invited. The guest list always changed. As did the topic of conversation.

The only constant was that every Sunday at one o'clock a handful of strangers, family, and a few old friends gathered at the long wooden table set with garden flowers and wine, as much as could be found or afforded, and ate. Usually stew. Not Frédéric's favorite, but it was the best Irène could do. Her health had been poor for more than a decade. So, certainly, the meal itself was the least important aspect of these dinners. And so was ill health.

"Illness is a great waste of time," Irène would often say. Didn't believe in wasting time. And so, with their children playing at their feet, she and Frédéric would host these weekly rambling conversations with guests that would include Nobel Prize winners and goat-cheese makers sitting side by side. The only real requirement was that one could tell a story. And, at least this was a requirement of Irène's, each guest must have read at least one novel by Colette or Kipling, or her very favorite book, *Gone with the Wind*.

Irène loved popular novels and read them whenever she could find the time. In fact, this is how she and Vincent met. Both were trying to buy the same copy of *Captains Courageous* from a book-stall. At first glance, Irène seemed so pale, Vincent imagined her to be a sickly mother of seven, with little money for children's books. So he offered to buy it for her. An act of kindness, but she took offense. Introduced herself.

"I can well afford a book," she said.

"The scientist?" he asked.

She nodded.

"I am greatly honored," Vincent said, and meant it. In medical school, he'd read of her courage during the Great War when, at the age of seventeen, Irène traveled with her mother, Marie, along the front lines to X-ray the wounded. But he also knew of the rumors surrounding her marriage and felt great pity for her. Frédéric Joliot was a handsome and charming scientist of average ability who worked as an assistant to Madame Curie. Irène was gifted but gangly and awkward. Frédéric wooed and married her within a year. Added her famous name to his.

"Opportunist," people called him. And still did. Even after they won the Nobel. Even after more than a decade of marriage.

"I can always get another copy," Vincent said. "The Kiplings are friends of my family; his son provides us furs from rare white tigers." Then he handed Irène a card, which she did not take or even look at.

"John Kipling?"

Vincent nodded, though he was unsure. It was just a story after all. Kipling's son, that's all he knew. He never knew the son's name. No one ever asked. It was just a story, he wanted to say.

"Yes, John Kipling," is what he said.

Irène frowned, brushed her billowing sleeves as if they were suddenly covered by dirt.

"John Kipling died in the war," she said. "Nineteen-seventeen, I believe. How can you make coats from furs supplied by a dead man?"

Vincent didn't even take a breath. "Because," he said, "at Laloux and Sons, we are quite skilled as furriers and liars."

Irène laughed. It was difficult not to. It isn't often one hears a statement that is embarrassingly true. And the laughter sent her into a coughing fit. Tubercular, Vincent thought. Everyone in Paris knew about that, too. He rubbed her back gently until the fit passed.

When she finally caught her breath she said, "You are quite an honest man for a liar. Come to our house on Sunday and we will eat like pigs and lie to each other until the sun sets."

So, on that cool September Sunday, Vincent was seated next to Hélène at the long wooden table. A bottle of wine between them. He noticed that her hair was the color of wet leaves, smoky, piled high on her head. But he didn't know how to tell her that, or anything else.

Hélène was not like the girls Vincent paid for, their slightly acid smell. Thin and brittle. Legs always parted as if by habit, or efficiency. Hélène seemed to be sculpted from marble. Cool and perfect. Lush. But dark, too. Like the smoke of her hair. Smoldering. Vincent couldn't imagine speaking to her. So, he kept on drinking until he could.

Hélène, on the other hand, was not as smitten. She could feel Vincent watching her. The heat of him. A furrier's son, she was told. She imagined he was a dandy who thought himself to be charming and she hated men like that. Especially those given to staring. And, of course, drinking too much. He'd already had two glasses of wine. She was counting. Then the stew was passed. Then one glass more. And he's such a small man, she thought. Only slightly taller than me. She imagined him falling over stone drunk, at any moment. But he didn't. After the third glass was finished, he was still watching her every move. She was unnerved. By the time the fourth glass was poured, she'd had enough of this man. His silent desire.

"Madame Irène tells me that you read Kipling," she said. "Children's tales, aren't they? Like Mowgli in *The Jungle Book*?" Her voice was sharper than Vincent expected. A bit cruel, which he often liked in a woman.

"Who cannot relate to being a boy raised by wolves?" he said, and meant it as a joke, but Hélène didn't laugh.

"Madame also tells me that you're quite a fascinating liar." Then drank the rest of her wine in one indelicate swallow.

"Madame is correct," Vincent said. At this, everyone turned

slightly. Frédéric, who was sitting across from them, stopped talking to his mother. His mother turned her good ear toward Hélène.

Vincent poured Hélène more wine, splashing a bit on the table. It was her third glass. He was counting. He expected her to fall drunk into her stew at any moment.

"I hate liars," she said. The words a bit slurred.

The aged, slightly deaf Madame Joliot turned to her son. "She hates liars," she said cheerfully. "This is wonderful! These dinners are always so interesting."

Frédéric laughed. "Yes, Mother. Quite lively. These are the moments Irène revels in."

At the head of the table sat Irène. Weak, but smiling. She was hoping that Vincent, whom she characterized as a small man with a large heart and an even larger imagination, would find love with her husband's assistant, Hélène, a bright young woman who was too serious and too lonely for her own good.

"I'm worried about her, Frédéric," Irène said. "Hélène has no outside interests. No friends. It's not healthy."

Frédéric understood. Sometimes he'd find Hélène sobbing for no reason. Or wild-eyed and sleepless. All he knew of her personal life is that her mother was from Paris and married while on holiday in Prague. That's all Hélène would say about her family. Frédéric didn't even know if she was an only child, or one of thirteen. And of Prague, "It is a city like most cities," she said.

Hélène was secretive and intense but something about her made Frédéric feel protective. Perhaps, he often thought, it was as simple as the fact that his own daughter was named Hélène. And was also delicate and thin. And just as stubborn. Neither would ever take his advice.

Vincent picked up the bottle of wine, nearly empty, and poured a bit more in his own glass. "There is nothing more noble than a lie," he said. "Or liars."

Hélène's head wobbled a little to the left. "What?" she said. Incredulous. All around the long wooden table the undercurrent of conversation stopped entirely. Everyone was staring at the two young people, both a little drunk, both leaning to the left. A moment passed. Then another. Irène finally leaned in. "Tell us more, Vincent."

Vincent felt his face color. The wine, he thought. Too much. Too much. He looked down at his stew, now cold. He could look nowhere else, for all eyes were on him. So he watched the perfect cubes of veal float. The small wild mushrooms. Then took a deep breath. This was not how he expected things to go. Vincent had hoped to be charming, but failed badly. Now, more than anything, he just wanted to eat. Say nothing. Lean into Hélène and sit in the shadow of her perfect beauty and eat. But everyone was waiting. Wanting to hear what he would have to say for himself. So he cleared his throat.

"You see, lies are the only way some truths can be told," he said. "The real truth is often too difficult to speak. So, in that sense, to lie is a noble and brave act."

"It's a riddle!" Madame Joliot said. "How can a lie be truer than truth?"

"You're drunk," Hélène said to Vincent.

"No," he said, then thought better of it. "Well, yes. I am drunk. But that makes no difference. I'm also correct. Sometimes you hear a lie and you resonate, as if you were a bell. It feels truer than truth itself."

Irène picked up her glass of water and took a long sip. "I never thought of that before. It makes sense though."

"Absurd," Hélène said ruefully and turned to Vincent. "Tell me something that's true but is a lie. I would like to resonate, as you say, like a bell."

Vincent paused for a moment and looked into Hélène's eyes. Could see the pain she tried to hide there, the anger, then said, "When Madame Joliot-Curie and I met at the bookstore we were both reaching for a copy of *Captains Courageous,* did she mention that?"

Hélène nodded.

"Well, it's not Kipling's best, by any means, but it's my favorite. Would you all agree that a book, such as *Captains Courageous,* is a lie?"

"Well," Irène said. "A lie of sorts, yes. A fiction is always a lie, by its nature."

"An entertaining lie," Frédéric added.

Hélène said nothing.

"Good," Vincent said. "Then we are all agreed?" he asked, and searched Hélène's face. Reluctantly, she nodded.

"Good," he said again, then he looked at everyone seated around the table, waiting for him to speak. Madame Joliot, still dressed in widow's black for a husband long gone. Frédéric, her son, tall and elegant, blessed with good looks and intelligence. Irène, sitting patiently at the head of the table, ghostlike, her children climbing onto her lap. And all the others whose names he did not remember. The red-faced parish priest. The squinting mathematician from America. They were all watching him. Waiting. As was Hélène.

It overwhelmed him. All these people.

"Reconsidering?" Hélène asked roughly.

Vincent shook his head, continued on. "As you know, the hero of the book is set adrift at sea. I know that boy," he said gently. "When I read his tale, I know it is true. My heart tremors at the truth of it."

Around the table, some nodded.

"I see what you mean," the mathematician said. Took his glasses off and cleaned them on his coat sleeve. "Interesting."

Hélène leaned in closer, filled with disdain. "And how do you know this boy?" she said. "He's a lie. The product of an overactive imagination, such as yours."

Vincent's face turned red. In a low, dark voice he answered, "My mother left when I was that age. I know what it's like to be set adrift."

The words took Hélène's breath away.

Irène jumped to her feet, baffling the children. "Coffee?" she asked, and filled everyone's cups without waiting for a response.

After dinner they all sat on the lawn in clusters of twos and threes, finishing the pear and almond tart. Hélène sat next to Vincent and said nothing, she just played with the children. Someone took photographs and everyone smiled the best they could. And they all watched the sun set and the stars spark one by one like fireflies. After a time, Hélène leaned into Vincent and quietly said, "Sometimes, I feel I am adrift and drowning, too."

And so, after that, they went to the opera. And on picnics. And dancing with the Joliot-Curies, when Irène was well enough. Much to Vincent's surprise, the older couple was most supportive of the relationship. They seemed to understand how love is not always obvious to the outside observer.

For a time, it seemed as if Hélène and Vincent could be happy, but gradually Vincent grew more and more distant. Eventually she will pity me, he told himself, they always pity me.

He'd seen it in the others, the cool-eyed look once the wine wore off, or the sun rose. He couldn't bear to see it in Hélène. So, after a time, he would forget a dinner, or a picnic. Disappear for days without an excuse. Slowly, the other things in Vincent's life pulled at him. The brittle girls he paid for. The hashish that made them seem sweeter, made him seem a different man. It all pulled at him, but he never stopped seeing her face in every girl. Never stopped loving her. But, the more he loved her, the more he feared losing her and the more he ran from her.

Vincent and Hélène saw each other on and off for almost two years before Hélène decided to end it. It was a warm clear night. They were walking along the river. There were couples all around them holding hands, laughing. Kissing. Vincent and Hélène walked without touching.

"It feels as if you are already gone," she said, "and that distracts me, keeps me from my work. I can't have that."

Vincent watched as Hélène walked away, blending into the crowd of lovers. He watched until he lost sight of her completely. Until she seemed as if she were a dream he once had, not real. The next day, he tried to imagine what his life would be like without ever seeing her face again. But he couldn't. What a coward I've been, he thought, and a week later, proposed.

"I am sorry," she told him.

In a way, he was not surprised. He always knew it would end badly. He was, after all, a small man. So much in the world was beyond his reach.

❧ 9 ❧

ONCE OUTSIDE THE HOSPITAL DR. ASSAM ASKS, "Would you like my jacket?" and puts it around Lucienne before she can answer. He has a habit of caretaking, she can see that. The leather jacket is warm from the heat of his body and smells like him, like chestnuts, like the small brown cigarettes he smokes.

They are walking to the café in the photograph. The night air is damp, soft against the skin.

"Warm now?" he asks. She nods but feels a chill. Pulls the jacket around her tightly. Damp air, she thinks. Or maybe it's just the moment, the surprise of it. It's difficult to tell. All Lucienne knows is that she's not sure what to expect. Of this Dr. Assam. Of this walk.

"I think my mother committed suicide in 1941," he says. "At least, that's what I've been told; I was just a baby when it happened. There doesn't seem to be a death certificate on record. It was, however, during the war. . . ." His voice trails off. He kicks a stone down the sidewalk. It rattles.

Lucienne takes her mother's photograph from her purse. "The inscription reads 'Spring, 1940,' " she says.

"That's why it caught my attention," he says. "I wondered if she knew my family." He takes the photograph from her hand, looks at it closely under the streetlight. "You see," he says, "I know very little about them. My father died before I was born. His second cousin, Basheer, was enlisted by the family to marry my mother and give me a name. And he did. But when the war began, Basheer met a woman and left us. I assume that's why my mother killed herself, but it's difficult to tell."

"And you think my mother may know something about that?"

"I don't know," he says. "Maybe our mothers were friends." He points at the picture. "Right here, there are two women talking, having some sort of meal together. Maybe it was them. I was hoping you might know."

Lucienne looks at the photo closely. The two women are slightly out of focus but, indeed, sitting together. Talking.

"Does this look like your mother?" she asks.

"I don't know," he says. "There are no photos of her. All I know is that she was small and dark. A Basque."

"And Basheer? Did you ever hear from him again?"

Dr. Assam shakes his head. "No. He never tried to find me after the war. I was raised by a friend of his, Vincent, who took me in after my mother's death. Raised me like his own son."

"That's hard."

"It used to be. When I was younger, I was angry, inconsolable. But now, I've been a doctor for so long and have seen so much, I wake up every morning and know I am oddly blessed. My former wife, Emily, is still, miraculously, thankfully, my good friend. Her new husband and I often play bridge together and smoke cigars. Gossip about her bad habits. Very Freudian, but interesting. And through the years, my son, Philippe, has forgiven my transgressions and learned to love me. As does his too-thin wife, Lucia."

"But still—"

"No. No. It is a very good life. On Sundays, I go to my son's house for dinner. Lucia is a vegan, no animal products, and not a very good cook. We eat plates of raw things, carrots and lettuce. We eat like rabbits, but Philippe loves me so I go. And sometimes, he even invites women for me to meet. And sometimes I bring a woman I am fond of. And we always invite Vincent so that he can play the role of Grand-père and sit at the head of the table and portion out our bunny food with the gravity that only a man who is feeding the starving can muster.

"I am a man who is loved. And happy. I tell myself this every day."

"And do you believe it?"

He takes a deep breath and pauses, then says, "I've come to believe it."

"But?"

"Well," he says. "If I am to be honest, I would have to say that I still long to know my father. And my mother, of course, is always here in my heart."

"And Basheer?"

Lucienne can see the sorrow return to his face.

"I still have this dream," he says, "where I'm enraged and beat him senseless, but when his body falls to the ground, I see his face as my face and I wake up, sweating and sick to my stomach."

"I'm sorry," she says.

He shrugs. "It is what it is," he says. "And you? Do you think of yourself as happy?"

"I don't know," she says. "Sometimes I think I'm too neurotic to be happy," and she thinks about Ethan and Sundays. When they were first married, Ethan would often bring her breakfast in bed on Sundays. A warm croissant with apricot jam and freshly ground coffee from the bakery down the street.

"They roast their own beans there," he would tell her. Sumatran. Guatemalan. Sulawesi. Tazania Peaberry. Ethiopia Harrar. The choices changed every week. "Depending on the season," he'd say, speaking as if he were lecturing students. "The monsoon season is important for coffee, it gives the beans a dark nose. Fruity."

Lucienne could not believe that there are seasons for coffee and that intelligent people like Ethan know that and know exactly what season it currently is and what the "nose" of the coffee will be because of it. And care about it, too. To her, coffee was, and is, something that comes sealed in a can and smells a little like potting soil.

She'd always end up moving the tray off the bed. Sit on a chair and eat. "Crumbs," she'd say. There was something indolent about breakfast in bed that made Lucienne uncomfortable. It felt too intimate.

"I'm just trying to make you happy," Ethan once told her, and she wanted to explain that she didn't trust happiness. It's lazy and fat and feels like a trap. A diversion from real life. But she didn't. After a while, he stopped bringing her breakfast.

"I've come to believe that being happy is a choice you make," Dr. Assam says. "Maybe you just haven't been ready to make it yet."

"Maybe," she says, and wonders if that's true. The two fall silent, walk along the narrow sidewalk. It's nearly 3 A.M. Above their heads, the moon is new. The sky is beginning its slow turn from ultramarine to eye-blue. Every now and then, Lucienne catches the sight of a star, or two, undimmed by city lights. *Miza, Zeta Ursae Majoris.* Lucienne thinks of the hum of it. The particular hum of that star and of the moon, and all the other stars she sees around them. The orchestration of this part of the sky. Its music. The pitch and coo of the radio telescope as it scans. How pure and beautiful a sound it is. The sound of mystery.

When they turn the final corner, "Here," he says, and Lucienne is amazed. The street is not what she expected but it is, indeed, the same street in the photograph. The café is still in the center of the block. She can see the awning, but everything else seems different.

Over the years, it appears as if the street has become some sort of a nightclub district. Neon signs. The sound of music is everywhere, a banging argument of notes and noise. Lots of noise. So much noise it feels like heat. Despite the fact that it's so late, there are people everywhere. Talking. Dancing. Waiting to dance. Holding one another without dancing at all.

The street is an odd mix of blight and boom, old and new. Many of the apartments seem abandoned. Broken windows. Shredded curtains move in and out with the breeze. But the shops have found new lives. The café is now a cyber café. A neon sign, written in English, announces "TWELVE TERMINALS ON-LINE. 24/7/365." It's crowded, though not as Lucienne imagined. There are couples, yes, but they hardly look like lovers. Once inside the Art Nouveau doors, a classic example, the doctor offers, she can see that the small marble tables are covered with documents.

Paperwork. Despite the early hour, everyone seems to be doing some sort of business. Cell phones. PDAs. Laptops.

"It's nearly lunchtime in Tokyo," Dr. Assam says. "The brave new world never sleeps."

"Wait a minute," Lucienne says. "You lived across the street in 1940? How is that possible?"

"I'll be sixty-one."

"You look forty-eight."

"I'd like to think I look thirty-seven."

"That's a joke, right?" she says.

"It is now," he says, and smirks. "Maybe we should ask someone if your mother was here in the last few days."

At the espresso machine the woman listens carefully. She shakes her head and dozens of earrings rattle like wind chimes.

Outside, next to the café, Lucienne notices a tattoo shop where the milliner had been. The top hat sign remains. "TATTOO YOU," it reads. Across the street, the bakery is a nightclub.

"Let's try there," she says.

La Fille du Boulanger, The Baker's Daughter, is an after-hours club. Small and hot. Cases for pastry and tarts now hold mix tapes from DJs and T-shirts. It's a tourist club. Everything's written in English and Japanese. There's a dance floor where the ovens once were. It's crowded with a global tribe in leather, tattooed and young. The room riffs with the techno trance of Brazil and Africa, the pulse of musicians who came to Paris and stayed.

"I know the owner," the doctor shouts in her ear, "but he probably left long ago. He's ancient, like us," he says and smiles. Lucienne yawns out of reflex.

These kids, she thinks, they're young enough to be my grandchildren. Which she knows is an exaggeration, but it depresses her nonetheless.

"Come on," Dr. Assam mouths over the driving sound. It's quieter outside, but not by much.

"That's the building I told you about. Where I grew up," he says. "My son, Philippe, rents it now."

The building next door is indeed beautiful. Stately and unusual. Unlike the rest of the block, it's only three stories high. Statues of marble women protect a narrow courtyard, balance the arch of a portal on the top of their heads. It seems to be another club, but it's in better shape than the others. Each window has glass and opaque curtains. The music is just as loud, but there is no one outside waiting. The brass stairways look newly polished.

A man steps out from the darkness of the doorway. Looks like a bouncer. Or pirate. Long hair. A gold hoop in one ear.

"Inside," he says, and waves them in. "They are all inside."

He holds open the door for Lucienne and the doctor and rings a buzzer. Inside, there's a foyer with a series of skylights above. Winding stairs lead up to three levels. There's a small plaque that explains that the building once housed members of an equestrian circus. Then a furrier.

The furrier's sign is still there. At least, somewhat. The lettering is faded and hard to read. There are a series of business cards taped over the gold-and-red leopard logo of Laloux and Sons. Lucienne can see they belong to Internet companies. "Militaria.com," "Global.net." It's more like a bulletin board than a sign.

"For only three hundred thousand dollars you can buy us a real sign," says a voice in the dark, and there's the sound of someone running down the staircase.

Dr. Assam looks pleased. "Philippe. I thought you were still in America."

"Well, I thought you were from Chase, so we're even."

"At three A.M.?" Dr. Assam asks.

"A man can hope, can't he?" Philippe says and laughs. The two men hug. Philippe is somewhere in his late twenties and has his father's elegant face but is the size of a football player. Linebacker. Tall, soft around the middle. His English is American. He turns to Lucienne.

"Just in case you're from Chase, for six hundred thousand dollars we could get our own entrance, too. With an elevator."

"What is this place?" she asks.

"Club Med for geeks. The Silicon Valley of Paris. Every room in this building, as with most of the apartments above the clubs, is filled with geeks like me who are dreaming in code."

"A think tank?"

"Not that organized. We just ended up here because it was cheap. Mostly abandoned. Some of us are squatters. Some, like me, have a kind landlord who doesn't mind when the rent is late."

"Well," Dr. Assam says, "let's just say, I don't mind too much."

Philippe grimaces, turns to Lucienne.

"So, if this isn't business, why do you have my father out at this hour? He's a bad, bad boy but don't let him fool you. He's old and needs his sleep."

Dr. Assam puts his arm around his son. "Philippe," he says. "Was there an older woman here last night? Late? Almost morning?"

"Last night? Yes, I spoke to her. I thought she was from

Chase." Then he turns to Lucienne. "I think everyone is from Chase these days. We're trying to IPO in America. I'm obsessed."

"That was my mother," she says. "She tried to kill herself last night. Anything you can remember her saying may be important."

Philippe looks stunned. Turns to his father, who nods.

"It's very sad," Dr. Assam says.

"I'm sorry," Philippe says. "Let's go to the café where we can talk. It's too noisy in here."

The three walk across the street in silence. Settle at a small table. While they wait to order, Philippe explains that he's trying to create a gatekeeper that would shut out those with a history of surfing the hate and sex sites of the Net.

"I call it Perv-Gate," he says, "but, for obvious reasons, Chase would like a better name."

They order coffees. "My mother?" Lucienne asks.

"I'm sorry. Yes," he says. "She asked for Grand-père. Thought he still lived in the building. I assumed she was an old client of his."

The doctor looks uneasy. "That's odd. I spoke to him yesterday when I first saw the photo. He said he didn't know Dr. Kundera."

"Maybe he forgot," Philippe says. "It was more than fifty years ago, after all."

Or, Lucienne thinks, maybe he knows something.

Dr. Assam suddenly looks worried. Checks his watch. "I need to make a call," he says. "I'll be right back."

Philippe and Lucienne watch as he makes his way through the crowded café toward the public phone. The doctor nods at tables as he passes. Seems to know quite a few people, even though the crowd is mostly young, like Philippe.

"I'm sure Grand-père just forgot," Philippe says. "Has your mother ever spoken of him?"

Lucienne shakes her head. "No. Not a thing. I know she couldn't have been a client, though. She doesn't believe in fur. Thinks it's barbaric."

"Maybe they were neighbors then."

"I don't know. Could be. The only thing I know is that before the war, when she lived in Paris, she worked with Frédéric Joliot-Curie, Marie Curie's son-in-law."

"That's odd," he says. "Grand-père has these stories about the Joliot-Curies. Wild stories. Quite charming, though total fabrications. He's quite the storyteller."

"Maybe there's a connection."

"Maybe, although I should warn you that he also tells us long and convoluted tales about Kipling's son and tiger furs. And the time the queen of England came to buy a hat."

Lucienne suddenly feels tired, feverish. She wants to lie down. Two days without a good night's sleep, she thinks, and feels uneasy. Philippe seems like such a nice kid. And his father, the doctor, seems loving and kind. She hates the thought the old man may have lied to them. Hates to think what that might mean for them. And her.

"I should go," she says.

"Wait," Philippe says, and scribbles an address on a paper napkin. "I gave your mother this. It's Vincent's new place. Maybe somebody saw her last night. It was late, but you never know. Do you know how to get there?"

Lucienne looks at the address. Shakes her head.

"It's easy. It's near Palais Royal. You go in through the garden. West. You can walk from here if you know where you're going. Do you know where you're going? I could show you."

"I'll find it."

"You know," he says, "Grand-père is a good man. An artful liar, but a good man. He didn't have to raise my father, but he did. I'm sure he has nothing to do with your mother's suicide. It seems so unlikely."

"You're probably right," Lucienne says, and hopes he is. Philippe obviously loves his grandfather very much. She opens her purse, takes out a business card, and borrows the pen.

"If you think of anything else," she says, "here's the hotel I'm staying at. Give me a call."

"I'm really sorry about your mother," he says. "I can't imagine it. Do you have anyone in Paris? Family?"

Lucienne shakes her head. "Not that I know of."

"Your husband then—"

"No, I'm—"

"Then why don't you come to dinner on Sunday?" he asks. "It's just a family thing. The food is awful, my wife can't cook, but Grand-père will be there. You can talk then. Save you a trip to the salon."

"That's very kind," she says. "But—"

"You shouldn't be by yourself right now," Philippe says. "Besides, I'm sure Father would enjoy your company."

Lucienne looks at the doctor who's still on the phone. His back is to them. She takes off his leather jacket. Looks at her watch. 3:30 A.M. A chill runs through her. Maybe he's talking to Vincent, she thinks. It's possible. She knows her own mother is often sleepless at this hour.

"Tell your father thanks for the jacket," she says, and suddenly wants to talk to Vincent, too.

"Sunday?"

"Depends on how my mother's doing."

"Of course," Philippe says. "I'll give you a call."

He flips the card over, studies it for a moment. "Boston?" he smiles. "I did my graduate work at MIT a few years ago. That's where I met my wife."

Lucienne doesn't hear. She's already out the door.

⟊ IO ⟊

VINCENT HAD SEEN THE WOUNDED BEFORE, OF course, but not since Morocco. Blood appeared foreign now, a dark river whose currents he could no longer navigate. He felt panic for a moment. Wondered how much blood Hélène had actually lost. He'd carried her three blocks, maybe four, to the salon. She was heavy, but he had no choice. His clothes and hands were wet where he had held her close.

"I'm so sorry. This is my fault. If I'd been there this wouldn't have happened."

Vincent was late, again, of course, but this time he had a good reason. He'd stopped to open the safe and take out the small velvet box. It was clear, after all, Hélène had changed her mind about his proposal, about loving him. Why else would she want to see him after all this time?

It was January 1941. Nearly a year had passed since they'd seen each other.

Once inside his workroom, Vincent laid Hélène down on the cement floor, elevated her head on a packing crate, and wrapped her leg wound with a bit of torn silk. The bleeding had slowed. He took out the morphine. Since the war, he always kept a few vials close by.

"You'll be fine," he said to her. When the needle hit Hélène's vein, her body relaxed. For a moment, she seemed to be back again. In her own skin, he thought. Felt her forehead. Hot.

"I'll get you some water," he said. Didn't know what else to do. He poured her a glass from the sink. When he came back, her mouth opened slightly. "Just swallow," he said, and poured a bit into her mouth, but it streamed down her lips, down the silk of her black dress. It was then that he noticed the rosary around her neck. The cross covered in blood. How odd, he thought, and put it in the glass. Watched it float there for a moment, then dried it on his coat sleeve. That's when the panic finally eased into him. *What next?*

He sat on the cold floor next to Hélène. Her skin was nearly colorless.

"I've missed you," he said. Then he tapped his own vein. A new one. In the fat of his palm, near the lifeline. Eased in the needle. The heat of the morphine made him sweat. But he was used to it. Very used to it.

When Vincent came home from the military, Jacques was taken aback by his son's frailty. Told himself it was understandable that Vincent had returned a different man. Sleepless, forgetful, and coughing up blood. War does that. He didn't know about the dishonorable discharge. Didn't ask about the series of small bruises on his arms, the backs of his legs. The odd smell of incense that seemed to follow him everywhere.

Vincent refused to go to the family doctor. So Jacques called for Dr. Calaferte, an old client who had given up practice more than a decade before. Now eighty-six and nearly blind, he recommended bed rest and warm milk toast with cinnamon. Vincent felt like a colicky baby at the mercy of dusty old men.

"This is absurd," he told his father, although the sweet milk made him sleep, dreamless and deep.

"We have only each other," Jacques said, and clucked as he applied a mustard plaster to Vincent's small bony chest.

The sharp smell and heat made Vincent sneeze uncontrollably but he knew there was no argument that could be made to stop his father and his unnecessary doting. I am being smothered, he thought, but grew stronger. After two weeks, the color returned to his face. The coughing stopped. The morphine began to seem unnecessary. Just a bit, every now and then. To ease.

By the time Vincent had met Hélène on that day in September the mountains seemed like a nightmare that belonged to someone else. With Hélène his life seemed normal. At peace. Some evenings they went out like other couples. Some, they just lay on the bed in her narrow room, in the candlelight, drank wine, and talked about nothing in particular. Or played records, mostly jazz, the Belgian Gypsy Django Reinhardt with his smoky swing, or Josephine Baker, stormy and filled with wanting.

Outside the room, there was the ever present smell of cooking, that sharp garlic smell, and child after child crying, exhausted by colic or teething or little sleep. And, of course, the war was a soot that covered it all. But inside Hélène's room, in the waxy light, the world seemed a different place. Quiet. Kind. Safe. And eventually one kiss turned to another and another and then, one night, her hand found him hard and wanting. And he panicked. Left her lying alone in the narrow bed, legs slightly open like the girls he'd paid for.

The next evening they met at the café across the street from the salon. They met there often. It was convenient for them both. They didn't speak of what had happened the night before. They ordered some soup, vichyssoise, which was all that was available that night. And waited in silence for it to arrive.

It is finished between us, he thought.

The café owner had a radio playing. Earlier that week, there'd been a shooting at the German embassy. A seventeen-year-old boy, a Polish Jew, an exile whom the French had tried to deport, shot a diplomat. In the abdomen. Twice. The man, Ernst vom Rath, had just died. When arrested, the boy, a Herschel Grynszpan, told French police, "I have a right to live and the Jewish people have a right to exist on this earth. Wherever I have been I have been chased like an animal."

The radio news announcer explained that the boy had received a postcard from his family in Poland that prompted the act. They needed money. They had been taken by train to the countryside and were starving. But the boy was penniless and was starving, too. "It was a foolish act of revenge toward an innocent man who happened to be German," the announcer said. "A lashing out."

And now the German minister Joseph Goebbels called for Germans everywhere to "rise in bloody vengeance against the Jews." Even in Paris.

When Vincent and Hélène first heard of *Kristallnacht,* it was several weeks later on Sunday at one o'clock. They were seated at the long kitchen table in the house of Joliot-Curie. There were no flowers. The wine was bitter. The stew, thin. The children did not squirm in their mother's lap, but sat straight in the chairs usually reserved for adults. The adults spoke in whispers.

"So much was destroyed," Irène said. "The streets in Germany were filled with glass, deep drifts, as if a blizzard had come."

"They blame it on the boy," Frédéric said sadly, "that Herschel Grynszpan. He shot one man and now tens of thousands are being arrested in revenge. It's madness." Frédéric pulled his young daughter close to him. Kissed her forehead. Held her. She was just a few years younger than Herschel.

"I can't imagine it," Frédéric said. "It all seems unreal."

Irène, coughing and pale, turned to Vincent and said, "If you love your Hélène, do not hesitate to tell her. The world has gone insane. Who knows if we'll even be here tomorrow?"

That night, Vincent and Hélène went back to her narrow room. "No lights," he said. She pulled back the curtains. Through the dusty window, the Paris moon looked molted, yellowed. He took off his shirt. She held her breasts, one in each hand, as if an offering. Leaned in and kissed him gently.

"I'm afraid to touch you," he said.

"I know," she said, and was amazed at how frail he looked. The lines of bruises on his arms and legs. The chest smooth as a young boy's. She thought of the boy who killed the German diplomat.

"Would you kill a man for your father?" she asked. "Like the boy? Would you start the world on fire for him?"

"No," Vincent said. "But, I would for you."

And tears began to roll down his cheeks onto her breasts.

And at that moment, Hélène loved him more than she ever thought possible. So, she told him what she would tell no other. Told him the true story of her life.

"My mother met my father on holiday in Prague . . ."

Hélène spoke soft and low until she got to the part she couldn't put into words, the part about her father, the butcher, his rough mouth on hers, and his hands, the dried blood still beneath the fingernails. And the smell of his skin, like sour wine. And then the pain of him inside of her.

Then afterward, his tears, his shame, how it hurt her even more.

"Just hold me," she said, her voice cracking. So Vincent held her in the dark until she fell asleep. Then quietly left before morning light. They went on like that for over a year, nearly two.

Now, all this time later, he took her in his arms again. The arms she once sought shelter in. Gently, he thought. So much blood.

"Hélène?"

Her eyes opened a bit.

"You came. I was afraid you were still angry," she said.

"Of course not," he said, felt the small velvet box like a fist in his pants pocket.

"I've been shot?"

He nodded.

"It burns."

"Shh—"

Vincent felt her heart pounding, as if it were his own.

"I know things. The Germans want me. It's not safe—"

"Shh—"

"I have to get to the Congo," she said. "But it's a secret."

"I know. I know," Vincent cooed as if talking to a child. Doesn't believe her. She's hallucinating, he thought.

"I need money, that's why I came to you," she said. "I have to leave or they'll kill me."

Morphine, he thought. It gives one such fantastic dreams.

11

LUCIENNE IS LOST. SHE KNOWS THAT FOR sure. She doesn't remember having passed the Opéra on the way from the hospital. Even I would have remembered this, she thinks.

It is a place one would definitely remember. Massive and lovingly overdone. Lucienne had read in the in-flight magazine that a river runs underneath the Opéra Garnier. Inspired the legend of the phantom, which eventually became the musical that Lucienne loathed but her mother loved and wanted to see over and over again. And here it is. But where is the hotel?

Lucienne's so tired, she feels sick to her stomach. It's nearly 7 A.M. She's been lost for hours. Wandering the wet streets alone. She'd planned to go back to the hotel, get some sleep, then stop by the salon and talk to Vincent, get it over with, then go back to the hospital. Stay with her mother as long as she could, as long as they'd let her. But now, she's lost. People bump past her from both directions. Which way is west? she thinks. I'm supposed to be going west.

Lucienne looks to the sky for the sun, an old scouting trick, but the day is now overcast. She opens her purse, a large bag, to rummage again for the map the concierge gave her.

"It's small and easy to use," he promised, and she'd love to have the chance to prove him right, but she can't find it. She's looked three times. She remembers putting it in her bag, but no luck. She found a missing checkbook, a bill she forgot to mail. But no map.

The idea of asking for directions makes her feel queasy. She hates to ask directions in America, she's certainly not interested in doing it in France, in a language that, on her best days, makes her head hurt. Besides, who would I ask? The street is filled with so many people she could be in Boston or New York. The longer she stands there, the faster they seem to go. They hum.

Lucienne steps out of the fray for a moment, stands against a wall, and closes her eyes. Just for a moment. She concentrates on the hum of them, as if the frequency were originating from a black hole. There's something similar, she thinks, the particular sound of the moment. It's somehow the same. Beautiful. The beep and static of morning. The sound of people as they make their way some-where, by foot, by car. So beautiful. Like radio waves. Lucienne feels the hum of all these people run through her as if she were a tuning fork. It's the same sensation she has when she loops through the black hole. Maps it. And when she dreams of it. And now, these days, when she thinks of it.

"Excuse me," a man says. He's French. Seventy or so. And round. "You are American?"

She nods.

"You are afraid?"

The question confuses her. Afraid of what? But then she remembers what she'd seen on TV. First one plane. Then the next.

"The terror," he says. *"Nous sommes tous Américains."* Then translates. "Today we are all Americans."

He covers his heart with his hand. "That is what *Le Monde* wrote. That is what I feel."

She doesn't know what to say. She thinks of the pictures of people walking down the street, dazed, covered with soot. Like Pompeii. It was impossible to tell if they were black or white, brown or yellow, or French or American or Japanese or German. They just were.

She feels afraid. The man embraces her for a moment, as if she were his lost child.

"I am so sorry for us all," he whispers.

Suddenly, Lucienne finds herself weeping. It is the first time in many years. The tears roll down her face. She can't speak.

"Let me take you where you need to go," he says, and they leave the shadow of the Opéra Garnier and walk along the street where so many years ago Hélène was shot and found and the mystery of her journey began.

Now Lucienne's begins here, too.

12

VINCENT HAD BEEN SLOWLY UNRAVELING FOR QUITE some time. Kif and morphine helped, of course. Then the Germans arrived and his business was more or less closed. Food was rationed. Lights out at dusk. But what made it all worse is that he was alone. Two months after he and Hélène parted, Jacques, his father, died.

It was all very sudden. Jacques hadn't been sick. More tired than usual, perhaps, but nothing to cause alarm. To Vincent, everything seemed to be as it had always been. There were the nightly arguments over the tablespoon of paregoric and steaming bowls of milk toast and cinnamon served as a bedtime snack. Nothing seemed amiss.

But one morning, Vincent awoke with a start. Felt uneasy. He'd had a dream of his father. He never dreamt of him at all, at least not in a memorable way, but in this dream Jacques was sitting at the end of Vincent's bed dressed in his finest suit. His legs elegantly crossed. Hands cupped over the knees. "Stay warm" is all he said. Then Vincent awoke. Covered in sweat, as if a fever had broken. It was late morning, his room was filled with sunlight. He'd overslept. His mouth was dry. The dream was so vivid that he felt he was still a part of it.

"Father?"

Vincent wanted to go back to sleep. To re-dream the dream. Shift it somehow. Instead, he found his father sitting at the breakfast table. His coffee was cold. The cream, tiny islands. Jacques's head was drooped to one side. Almost as if sleeping, Vincent thought. One hand was draped over the arm of the chair. His fingers reaching. A book, fallen to the floor.

The funeral was long and as grand as Jacques would have wanted it to be, as elaborate as the war allowed.

"Not bad for a tailor," he would have said, and winked.

The day was properly overcast. The church service was filled with many social clients. Some even wept a bit, remembering fondly the days before the rationing, days spent in Jacques's showroom drinking good champagne and feeling as if anything in the world could be bought for the right price. A white dove was released and, theatrically, flew into the dark clouds never to be seen again.

"Beautiful," the matrons said to each other.

Inside the casket, Jacques lay dressed in his finest suit, his "dream suit," as Vincent had come to think of it.

"Keep warm," Vincent said when he saw his father lying there. Then he placed his mother's full-length coat of tiger skin, the coat that Jacques had given her on the occasion of their marriage, around his father's shoulders like a blanket. When the casket was closed, Vincent thought he could still smell a faint trace of his mother's perfume seeping through the brass hinges, the finely crafted locks.

The day after his father was buried, Vincent had nothing to do. The funeral was over. His father's clothes had been given to the poor. There was no one left to visit, or who would visit him. Everyone had been seen, notified, consoled, and paid. Out of respect, the shop was closed for the entire month. For mourning. Although, because of the war, they had not sold a coat in a very long time. Or even made one. And so, Vincent sat in the leather chair by the door and waited. He wasn't sure why. Or for what. Hélène was certainly not coming back to him. And he'd long since given up the idea of his mother's ever coming back. But still, he found himself unable to leave the chair. Its cracked leather. Its familiar smell, a combination of hair tonic made from crushed violets and smoke. It was his father's smell, though Vincent didn't recognize it as that. To him, it was just the smell of home.

Soon, morning turned into night. Then a day passed. At one point, Vincent thought he heard a scratching at the kitchen door, but he remained seated and the sound soon faded. He knew he should have stood up to see if someone was there, but he didn't. At one point, he thought he might be hungry, his stomach felt empty and sour, but he couldn't bring himself to eat. After a time he did sleep, however. Odd, fitful dreams. Bits and pieces of his life floating by like ash.

Finally, at the end of the second day, there was a timid knock at the front door. Vincent sat perfectly still. At first, he wasn't sure he heard it at all.

"Vincent?"

It was Basheer, the son of their housekeeper. Vincent recognized his voice right away. They had grown up together, like brothers. At least, that's what Vincent believed Basheer told his friends, though Vincent would not admit that to members of his own circle. Basheer was, after all, an Arab. That's all that needed to be said. To Vincent, the word separated them forever.

Vincent was never sure how Basheer and his mother, who was always known as Madame Assam, came to move into the large room behind the kitchen. He never heard the story of how his father found them, even though he'd asked several times. The reply was always the same.

"It was a miracle," Jacques would say.

It did seem like one. Or, at the very least, a blessing. In the months after his mother left, it became quite clear that Vincent and his father knew nothing about housekeeping, or laundry, or the preparation of even the simplest meal. So, the women of the neighborhood would come often, out of pity, and take in some laundry or send over a bit of ham. But their mercy would only go so far. It was clear that Jacques needed someone to take over the household.

"Just a housekeeper," Vincent overheard one of the women tell his father. "Until Katherine comes home."

"Yes," he said sadly. "Until then."

The next day Vincent came home from school to find a tall dark woman with hair that rolled like waves down her back and a round plum of a boy named Basheer. She told him her name was Madame Assam, and he liked the way her name sounded, the music of it.

"Where did you come from?" he asked her. She was dressed in yards of rich fabric, carefully draped and folded.

"From everywhere," she said, her son peering from around her long robes, "and nowhere." The boy whispered something to his mother. Madame Assam laughed.

"My son," she said, "would like to touch you. You are so pale, he thinks you may be made of smoke." Vincent held out his hand.

"I'm not sure if I am or not," he whispered.

Soon, Vincent's world was filled with the orderly smell of ammonia and the deep fragrance of saffron rice and chicken baked with preserved lemons and almonds. Instead of soured milk and cold coffee left on a counter, mornings began with mugs of cocoa and sweet apricot bread.

Before school, Madame Assam would sit with the boys in the dining room and review their lessons. Vincent would sit very close to her. To him, she smelled like velvet and saffron threads and cardamom and everything that was warm and comfortable. Sometimes, Jacques would join them for breakfast, insisting that Madame Assam and her son stay at the table and eat with them.

"You and Basheer are members of this household," he would say, but Madame Assam would resist.

"We are more comfortable in the kitchen. The light is better there," she would say.

On the occasions that Jacques would insist, the mother and son would always sit with their chairs pushed slightly away from the table. It was as if they were part of the family, but not quite. After dinner, when darkness fell, the boys would climb onto the roof together and watch the stars come out one by one and talk about everything and nothing much at all. Basheer always led the way, since he was stronger and more powerful.

Basheer and Madame Assam stayed with them until Vincent enlisted and left for his mountains. Their mountains. Morocco.

"It's too difficult for me to remain," read the note she left behind for Vincent's father. "Your son is killing my people."

So Vincent was quite surprised to see his old friend at the front door.

"I am sorry," Basheer said. "I am sorry for your father's passing." Vincent gestured for him to come in. Basheer paused, looked into the kitchen, the door there. "I knocked yesterday. At the back."

He seemed uncomfortable, hesitated in the doorway. It was then that Vincent realized Basheer had never entered the apartment through the front door. They'd lived together for more than a decade and he always came in through the back. The servants' entrance.

"Please," Vincent said. "Come in."

Basheer didn't move. "I only came to give you this," he said and handed Vincent an envelope filled with francs across the threshold.

"I don't understand."

"Your father's money. He paid for my schooling and I've been saving to pay him back. There's not much there, but I thought you might want it to help bury him."

It had been just a few years since they'd seen each other. Basheer had grown from a plump boy to a large balding bulldog of a man with kind eyes.

"How old are you now?" Vincent asked.

"Still a year younger," he said, and laughed. Ran a squat hand through what remained of his hair. "Though my hair thinks otherwise."

"Come in," Vincent said, and they sat at the kitchen table. Basheer, out of habit, pushed his chair away slightly, as he and his mother had always done.

"Your mother? How is she?" Vincent asked.

"Madame Assam is fine. Arthritic but still blessed with the fire of youth."

"That's good," Vincent said. "I still think of her fondly. I hope she still feels the same about me."

Basheer seemed even more uncomfortable.

"What is it?"

He hesitated.

"Tell me."

"I am sorry, Vincent," he said. "I would like to say Madame Assam sends her regards, but I am afraid that is not possible."

Vincent let the words seep in. He remembered the note she'd left. Your son is killing my people.

"I understand," he said. But he didn't. It was difficult for Vincent to understand how Madame Assam, who always made sure he knew he was loved, at least by her, how this Madame Assam no longer wished him well. It was impossible to understand.

"I did not come to make you uncomfortable," Basheer said. "I came to bring you this. I'm sorry."

He pushed the envelope back toward Vincent. "I should go."

"There's no need to repay anything," Vincent said.

Basheer shook his head. "There is to me. Jacques was not my father."

The words sounded more sad than defiant. The two men sat for a moment just looking at each other, searching each other's faces for the boys they once were. But Vincent could see only the faces of all the wounded French soldiers that he could not save. And Basheer could only see a man who went willingly to kill his people. The envelope of francs remained on the table between them.

How can this be happening? Vincent thought. How can boys

grow into men who sit in the kitchen with their history stuck in their throats?

"I think, sometimes," Vincent said, "my father forgot we were not family."

Basheer nodded. "Sometimes, I forgot, too."

The words pained him. Vincent suddenly felt an overwhelming need to explain duty, the importance of it, but didn't. Basheer stood and took Vincent into his bulldog arms and squeezed him for just a moment, as a brother would. Kissed him on both cheeks. Vincent held him tight. Remembered the part of himself that loved him.

Soon after, Vincent found himself frequenting the Arab Quarter, as it was unofficially called. "Looking. Just looking," he'd say. At first, he asked after Basheer, but no one seemed to know a Basheer Assam. Or a Madame Assam, even though Vincent described both in vivid detail. One day, Basheer found him instead.

"What are you looking for?"

"I don't know," he said.

"Then, go home," Basheer told him. "Nothing you have lost is here. You are looking in the wrong place."

Soon after that, Basheer started coming to Vincent's apartment on Wednesdays and the two men played cards and smoked and talked until the late hours. During these times, Vincent learned some things about Basheer, but not much. He always seemed to hold a part of himself back. Answered in general ways. When asked about work, he said he sold fruit, but never mentioned where or what the people were like who bought it.

One day he told Vincent he was married with a son.

"He is Basheer, son of Basheer. Some think that it is bad luck to name after the living. But I do not trust luck, good or bad." And that was all he ever said about him.

Still, Vincent looked forward to these evenings, when he would win and lose the same ten francs and talk or not talk depending on need and desire. Eventually, he found himself again in the Arab Quarter. Looking. Just looking. What he looked for changed from night to night. Sometimes it would be a young girl, not more than eleven or twelve years old, whose breasts were hard as the pits of apricots and twice as bitter in his mouth. Sometimes, he would go down to the baths and sit in clouds of steam and listen to the hiss of stones and laughter of a language he could not speak well. And sometimes, he went to the unmarked cafés. No alcohol allowed. No food. Either sweet thick tea or coffee, only a few chairs. Mostly pillows on the floor. In these places, no one paid him any attention. He could sit in the smoke of kif and simply be. Known and not known, at the same time. Invisible.

And so, bit by bit, Vincent unraveled. Until he came to this point, where he was so drugged all he could do was sit in his work-room and watch Hélène slowly bleed to death. Think of her beauty, and how fantastic her stories were of Frédéric and the Germans and the Underground.

"I have always liked stories of intrigue," he told her. And Hélène wept with the little strength she had.

"Shh. Shh," he said.

And the night turned into day and into night again, but it was hard for Vincent to tell. The morphine had him in its delicate grip. He didn't even remember it was Wednesday, the night Basheer always came for cards, until he knocked.

"Not now," Vincent said softly in Arabic, but knew Basheer couldn't hear him.

From where he was sitting he could see Basheer's face was pressed against the front window. On the stoop there were drops of Hélène's blood. Basheer pounded harder.

"Vincent?"

Vincent shook his head and said to himself, "Not now, old friend."

But Basheer continued to pound on the door until the glass panes shook.

When Vincent finally opened the door, "Please" was all he said, all he could say. The drugs had slowed his mind. Language failed him. Basheer pushed his way into the room, followed the trail of blood to Hélène, who glistened with sweat.

Basheer was horrified. He stopped a moment and prayed for himself, and for the man he once called friend. Then he took a cloth and wet it. Cleaned her wounds, gently. She was unconscious. Drugged, he thought. All around there were spent vials of morphine. The needle lay dry.

Vincent stood by the door watching Basheer. "She loves me," Vincent told him.

She is lucky, Basheer thought, but not in love. She was lucky to be alive. He could see that Hélène's head wound was minimal. The bullet must have shattered before striking her. Maybe struck something else first. There was just a fragment of metal left. Hopefully, he thought, it's just under the skin. No deeper. Will work its way out. The leg was worse. The bullet went right through it. Chipped the shin bone. "Why isn't she in the hospital?" Basheer asked.

Vincent pondered this question as if it required deep thought.

"Never mind," Basheer said. Pathetic, he thought. He always

knew one day something awful would happen to Vincent. Too many drugs. Too much time alone. It had all done him in. He was not surprised, but sorry. So sorry. He'd always hoped their friendship could make a difference, help Vincent not to feel so alone.

But it didn't, Basheer thought. And now, here we are.

"Vincent," he said loudly. "Who is she?"

"Mine," Vincent said, as a child would, as if Hélène were a doll he was fighting over.

There was blood all over Vincent's hands, his white shirt. Blood streaked across his face, as if he had rubbed his eye, then his nose. For a moment, Basheer wondered if Vincent had shot her himself, but he didn't see a gun anywhere and the amount of blood on the floor and outside the door made him think that Vincent probably carried her from somewhere else. Why? That would have to wait.

"She loves me," Vincent said again.

Basheer could bear it no longer. He pulled back the sleeves of Vincent's pressed shirt. Shook his arms, bruised from needles.

"This is what loves you," he said roughly. "The morphine. Not this woman."

Vincent shook his head and whispered. "No. No. She loves me."

"Stop it," Basheer said, and slapped him. He knew the situation was out of control. Vincent was an addict, he thought. This woman, whoever she is, could bleed to death if left in his care.

"Did you do this to her?"

"No."

He looked at Vincent carefully. Vincent looked afraid, like a little boy. Not violent. Not capable of violence.

"All right," Basheer said. "I believe you."

Then he turned his attention back to Hélène.

"Can you hear me?" he asked. No response. He looked at her arms. Needle marks. But just a few, not like Vincent.

"Did you do this?" he asked Vincent.

Vincent nodded. "For pain."

Basheer put her arms back under the blanket and felt her forehead. Her eyes fluttered. She seemed to be responsive.

"It will be all right," he told her. "The wounds are not so bad."

"It burns," she said.

"Who are you?"

"Hélène." Then she slipped back into sleep.

Basheer looked around the workroom carefully. The morphine seemed to be gone. There was just a handful of empty vials. Vincent was pale, exhausted and helpless.

"Go upstairs and lie down," Basheer said to him. "Lock the door behind me and then go upstairs and lie down."

"I'm tired," Vincent said, as if he were going to cry.

"I know," Basheer said, and wet the cloth again. He wiped the blood from his friend's face, gently. "I know."

So sad, Basheer thought, and he was glad Jacques was dead, not able to witness what had become of his beloved son. He smoothed the fair hair back away from Vincent's handsome face, his dull eyes.

"Madame Assam," Basheer said. "I will go and get Madame Assam. She will help care for the girl."

Vincent nodded.

"I want nothing to happen to her when I am gone," Basheer said, sternly.

"I saved her."

"Then keep her safe."

"She loves me."

This is impossible, Basheer thought. "I will be back within the hour," he said. "Let her sleep."

Then he left.

Not much time, Vincent thought and locked the door. Pulled the curtains closed. An hour wasn't long at all. He had to hurry. He ran upstairs to his room for more morphine. Then back down the stairs two at a time. The needle went into his vein easily. The morphine felt hot and welcome. It coursed through his heart. For pain. For courage.

"Can you hear me?" he asked Hélène, and shook her until she slowly nodded.

"Good," he said. "What is the place you want to see?"

He leaned in close and she whispered, "Belgian Congo. I need money for the Congo."

"Good," he said. "I will take you there."

AND SO VINCENT BEGAN HIS STORY.

"The day is calm," he said. "The air is sweeter than ever before."

But it's not, Hélène thought. Nothing feels calm or sweet at all.

The dock swayed under her feet. The sun was high. She wasn't quite sure how long she'd been waiting. Everything shimmered, dreamlike. The rickety town with its dirt roads and low cement buildings. The barge she had just left. Even the ocean shimmered from heat. The air was thick with salt and diesel. She looked into the water. There were dead fish, belly-up and bloating.

Welcome to the colonies.

The captain passed her, nearly pushed her out of the way. His skin was darker than any blindness. He was a native, he told her that.

"Lebu," he said, "the tribe you colonized along with Dakar."

"I'm a scientist," she told him.

"Colonization is a science, Madame. An exact science."

As he passed her he didn't stop to greet her or even tip his hat. She couldn't remember if she'd offended him. Or even exactly how they met. Or anything about the journey.

The heat seemed to blot everything else out. All she remembered was that she knew he was Lebu from Dakar. And that Dakar was in West Africa. And that she was in the Belgian Congo. Or was supposed to be. On a tip of a town near the Atlantic Ocean. But she couldn't remember the name of the town she was in. Or how she got there.

All she remembered was standing here on this dock. Nothing before.

"Where are the boys to take my bags?" she said.

Her voice was shrill. She didn't care. She felt tired. Her body burned. It had been a long journey, she thought, but wasn't sure why. It will be a longer one to America. All she wanted to do was to get settled in to start work. As soon as she could. That's the one thing she was sure of.

"I need help," she said, but the captain didn't turn around. It didn't seem to matter to him. He just kept walking. "You don't understand. Someone is coming to meet me," she said. "I need to have the boys take my bags from the dock to the road."

He turned his head slightly. "If someone is coming for you," he said, "then I suggest you find some shade."

His white uniform radiated in the sun.

Impertinent, she thought.

"Try the hotel," he said. "Everyone waits at the hotel."

Hélène scanned the horizon and saw nothing. No hotel. Nothing that would even pass for a hotel. She was told that the Belgian Congo was a beautiful but primitive place. Wild and lush. Huge and dangerous. Huts, not houses. The port on the Atlantic wasn't even supposed to be a town. But from the dock, she could see there were streets lined with buildings squat and fat and concrete.

There are supposed to be trees, she thought. It's a jungle. With volcanoes and molten rivers of lava. And gorillas. And snakes.

"Where is this hotel?" she shouted. "I was not told there was a hotel. Just a few scattered houses in the jungle."

It was hot. Very hot. The sun was high. Everything was so bright, it was nearly incandescent. The heat wrapped itself around her. Squeezed. The captain was still walking, seemed to fade away. He dissolved into the wavering sky. But that didn't make sense. This time of the year, it should be temperate, at least for central Africa. December should bring mild summer-wet heat. Not this baking, unforgiving sun.

"Where is the damn hotel?"

Hélène suddenly felt dizzy. And cold. Heatstroke, she thought. She was wearing her black dress, and it wicked the sun. Her head felt dull. There was a pain in her shin. She felt her skin redden. The back of her neck already felt sunburned. And, most troubling of all, she seemed to be wearing a rosary around her neck, like a string of pearls. The rosary looked familiar, she remembered finding it, but not putting it on.

She looked at her watch: 13:00 hours. Paris time. If there's a town, she thought, there has to be a taxi somewhere.

The streets, however, seemed deserted. She'd been told that the Africans stay indoors in the early afternoon. No one seemed to be anywhere. The harbor master's door was closed. The shades pulled down. Everything was quiet. The only sound was that of the ocean lapping up against the dock, an occasional bastard gull laughed overhead. The captain was now nearly out of sight. Sweat was rolling down her face and into her mouth.

"Tell me where the hotel is. Please."

The captain stopped and turned around abruptly. She couldn't make out the look on his face. He was too far away. His entire body seemed absorbed by the heat and glowing. He pointed to the sea. Then turned around again and continued to walk.

Hélène looked again toward the sea. This time, she saw a hotel, a large hotel, the color of crushed roses, take shape in the wavering heat. It was difficult to tell how far away it was. Maybe a few blocks. Maybe a mile. It just seemed to be somewhere fairly close, close enough to walk to. It straddled the coast. It was mammoth, six or seven stories. Moorish in design with two bell towers. So odd she didn't notice it at first. Of course, everything about this place seemed odd. She turned back and saw the barge she'd come in on. It looked like all the rest. Rusted and bobbing. The name of it had faded away.

There was no place to go except to the hotel. So she walked along the shore toward it. But the longer she walked, the farther away the hotel appeared to be. At one point, she stopped by a group of concrete pilings that seemed to have once been the foundation of a pier. They jutted into the ocean. She waded into the green water alongside of the remains. A school of stingray, with their stealth elegance, glided by. On the abandoned pilings mussels set forth a colony, grew one on top of another, a honeycomb of blue-black shells.

She tried to pull one off, cut herself instead. She raised her hand to inspect the wound and blood rolled down her arm into the water. Spread. A lot of blood, more than she'd ever seen. More than a shell from a mussel should cause, she thought. It ran down her arm and leg. She touched her face. There was blood there too.

This is not real, she thought.

"We could cook those for you in wine."

She looked up. On the shore was a man in a white linen shirt. Open collar. No shoes. Beautifully tan. He looked familiar to her somehow. Like someone she knew, but couldn't place. His face was handsome. Even features. Balanced and sturdy. Behind him was the hotel. She'd somehow come upon it and hadn't even noticed. Heatstroke, she thought. It was the only explanation. Up close, the hotel looked more like a palace than ever. An expansive staircase opened out to the sea. Gulls swooped and cawed around her.

"Mussels in wine are very good," he said. "Garlic. Parsley. Just a heel of bread with it. A feast. Sometimes the British like them in curry," he said, and laughed. "Of course, the English will curry anything."

There's something about his laugh that she thought she remembered, as if they had already met. This is wrong, she thought. All this is wrong. I know him. This doesn't make sense.

"We have a lovely room for you facing the ocean," he said. "I'll send the boy around to get your trunk."

"This hotel is not supposed to be here," she said.

"Of course it is. Where else would it be?"

Next to the hotel was what seemed to be some sort of a market. She pointed. "What is that place?"

"For the fishermen. They bring in their catch to sell and trade."

She could see rows of stalls with bolts of fabric and small brass bracelets and wooden carvings of natives and boats. There were fish, too. So many fish, of all colors, shapes, and sizes, in straw baskets and barrels. The market was filled with people. Beautiful. Graceful. Regal in bearing. Their skin was the color of charred wood. In the full African sun they glistened. Kings, Hélène thought. Some wore a labyrinth of fabric, elaborate and lavish with embroidery. Some wore gowns dyed in a sunset of colors, beautiful but fading.

"Later I will take you to the market," he said, and offered his hand to her. His hands are beautiful, she thought. Well formed and elegant.

She took his hand hesitantly. It felt as if she were in a movie. Everything felt heightened. The smell of crisp salt air. The caw of gulls. It was all unnerving, extreme. And then the man. It felt as if she knew him from another life. Some place other than the island. She felt as if she should be terrified, but wasn't. She felt numb.

"Am I dreaming?" she asked.

"It is like a dream," he said. "It is always like a dream."

And then he did something Hélène didn't expect. He pulled her into his arms and the arms became her father's. Her father's butcher arms. They smelled of blood and rotting flesh. And of sorrow. And the moment shifted. Became savage.

Hélène screamed but no one could hear, except for Vincent. And he would never forget the sound.

"Shh. Shh," he told Hélène. Then he remembered what Irène told him that last night at her long table and Vincent repeated it to Hélène.

"We have so little time left," he said. "The world is burning around us."

But Hélène could hear only her father's voice and she felt his butcher's hands on her breasts. And so she screamed until she grew hoarse.

≈ 14 ≈

THREE HOURS PASSED. THEN FOUR. FINALLY BASHEER arrived, Madame Assam behind him. "There were so many soldiers it was difficult to come," he said. And then he fell silent. The air was brined with sweat.

Madame Assam pushed past her son.

"She was clothed when I left," Basheer said.

Vincent wouldn't look at either of them.

"Women are not animals," Madame Assam said, "to be skinned and laid bare." She covered Hélène's body with the pelts that had been thrown to the floor.

"Leave us," she said. There were tears in her eyes.

Vincent and Basheer went into the salon and sat at the small round table on the tufted silk chairs and said nothing. Basheer was so filled with anger, he was beyond words. Vincent, beyond shame.

It is not as it looks, Vincent thought over and over again until he nearly believed it himself.

From the workroom, they could hear Madame Assam running water. Then praying. Vincent imagined that she was washing Hélène. Bathing her gently, as if she were a child. He felt a certain tenderness toward Madame Assam for that. And relief. Give comfort, he thought. Comfort is what you give so well.

After a time, Basheer spoke. "Where is your heart?" he asked.

Vincent thought about the question. Then answered. "In your mountains," he said. "Buried under sand and snow."

BY THE TIME LUCIENNE ARRIVES AT LALOUX and Sons, it's mid-morning, but the salon is closed. No posted hours. She can see through the window that it's well-appointed. The walls are burnished gold. There are tufted chairs in somber tones. Everything about the salon says "old money," but it's closed, unlike the other equally elegant shops in this arcade, which are open and doing business in hushed tones. Seems odd, she thinks.

The Palais Royal itself is striking. Once the private theater of Cardinal Richelieu, it's now filled with shops and modern sculpture and lush public gardens. Contemporary and ancient. Complicated and elegant. Whimsical. Accessible. And not. Not the Paris Lucienne expected. None of it is. Makes her feel worse that she never learned the language. That her mother never told her of this place. Its beauty. Its lavish joy.

Next to the fur salon is a *parfumerie*. They must know something about the furrier, Lucienne thinks, opens the door and is overwhelmed by the exotic air, complex layers of myrrh and musk, of orange blossoms and cedar. An elegant young man in a somber gray suit offers a strip of paper, a *mouillette,* he says, of "Rahå Loukoum. Bitter almond, musk and heliotrope."

It's rich and subtle. Yet somehow filled with sorrow. Lucienne doesn't know what to say. Doesn't wear perfume. Never knew it was so complex.

He pulls out another. "Santal de Mysore. The purest of all sandalwood."

"Opulent," she says, and means the moment. The fragrance, the elegant young man, and the room, which is rich in tones of purple, from the deep stillness of sunset to the silk of orchids.

"Try one or two," he says. "Wear them for a while. Fragrance cannot be rushed. We must choose wisely."

"This is fine," she says, and suddenly feels embarrassed. Doesn't want to take up his time. Just wanted to ask a few questions about the furrier and his shop. "The sandalwood is very beautiful," she says.

"It is," he says, "but let us see." He holds her wrist for a moment. Holds the paper against it gently and then releases. Breathes deeply. Evaluates with a clinical air.

"No. I'm sorry," he says. "It does not fit you. We must find the fragrance that is you and willing to be you."

She wants to explain that she merely came in for information, that she's not a customer, but it's difficult. The fragrances are overwhelmingly beautiful and he is kind. So she sniffs each of the tiny strips of paper, one after the other.

"The furrier," she says finally. "I see he's closed."

"It's appointment only," he says, and pulls out another glass bottle. Dips another bit of paper.

Of course, she thinks. It's not a department store.

"This may be what we are looking for," he says. "Iris Silver Mist, named for Botticelli's muse, Simonetta Vespucci. She had the blood of the explorer running through her and was the *Birth of Venus* in all its glory."

I should go, she thinks, but holds out her wrist and he brushes the fragrance along thin blue veins.

"This," he says, "is absolute grace."

"I'm not sure I'm absolute grace," she says.

"Ah," he says, knowingly, as if perfume is some sort of diviner of nature. "Try it for one day and then tell me if I am wrong."

She raises her wrist to her face. The fragrance is, indeed, beautiful.

"I'll be back," she says, and thinks she probably will be. Steps into the cool marble air of the arcade. The garden that surrounds it is serene. Perfectly manicured grass. She raises her wrist close to her face again. She doesn't notice that someone is watching her. Has been watching her ever since she approached the *parfumerie*. The pillars of the atrium obscured him. He knew they would. He understands watching. Through the years, he's practically made a science of it.

He is a small man, his hands still elegant. His body slower, but still fit. His hair is still full, but ashen. His clothes, tailor made. He walks with a slight stoop. A silver headed cane for balance.

"I believe you have been looking for me," he says.

Lucienne is startled, but not entirely. He is smaller than she imagined and more refined. She nods.

Vincent unlocks the door to his salon.

"Come in then," he says, and locks the door behind them.

❧ 16 ❧

SOMETIMES HÉLÈNE WOULD BE CALM. SOMETIMES SHE would be back at the pink hotel. Seagulls cawed. Hands pulled at her. She would scream. Not loud, but muffled, like a cough. This was how the first day passed.

On the second day, fever ran through Hélène like a current. One moment, she soaked through the blankets. Her skin glistened. The next, she was chilled. Her body shook. Sleep gave her no rest. When she closed her eyes, all she could see was the betrayal of her father, and of Vincent, and their faces filled with shame.

Madame Assam had never seen anyone in such misery. She prayed to God and Allah and Buddha. She prayed to everything holy she had ever known, had ever evoked, had ever abandoned. And prayed to the demons, too.

When Madame Assam wasn't praying, she wondered what

type of woman this poor wounded lamb was. Young, yes. Beyond that it was difficult to tell. Married, more than likely. She was of that age, and not unattractive. Madame Assam imagined the faces of children waiting. A family of young children all wondering where their mother was. This made her pray even harder. For the girl, her imaginary children, and for herself. Why am I here? she thought, but knew the answer. Tigers and goddesses.

Jacques had told her about India and the place called Assam, the name she took from a tea. He told her how beautiful it was.

"Tigers and goddesses," he said. "Goddesses like you. Worth dying for."

And so, Madame Assam could no longer sit with Jacques at the table.

"Too busy," she'd say.

She had to. She found herself falling in love with him, which would only complicate matters. She was still married to Karim, her husband, who would still be her husband until the day she died. No matter how many wives he took. No matter how much that hurt her.

Still, she never forgot tigers and goddesses.

She came in Jacques's memory to make things right. But once she arrived, she knew what was wrong could not be fixed with cocoa and cardamom, or even love.

Vincent took some money from the safe.

"Where are you going?" Basheer asked.

"I'm not a monster," he said. "Please tell Hélène that."

"I'm not sure she'll believe me."

"Tell her it was all a dream, then. A fever."

"Will you return?"

"Eventually. There is no place for a man like me to go."

That night Basheer watched Hélène while Madame Assam slept. He would have liked to have taken Hélène to the hospital, but she didn't seem to have her identification papers and that was a problem. Without papers, the hospital would not admit her and she would be left unattended until she was identified. Or died. Or she could be arrested and taken to jail and left to die there. Basheer didn't know the papers were sewn into the hem of her dress. And she was too sick to tell him. So, he sat with her. Watched her. Waited.

The moon, sheer silk, streamed through the skylight, illuminated Hélène's skin. Incandescent.

"How can a woman be so pale?" he wondered, and thought of his own wife, Manon, her clove skin. He imagined her asleep in their bed, her infant son beside her, sleeping, cradled in the elegant branch of her arm. He longed to be home and longed for her, for the way her lips were smoky and sweet. Longed to have her kiss him, for once, out of love, not duty.

The Found Woman, as Basheer began to think of Hélène, was all angles and sharp lines. The first sight of her filled him with anger. Then worry. Then fear. The Found Woman, he knew, was trouble. Colorless as a demon, but there was something oddly familiar about her. As if he knew her from somewhere.

Perhaps the market, he thought and tried to imagine her buying small black raspberries, but it was impossible. So he fell asleep wondering and awoke in the middle of the night. She was watching him. It took him a moment to realize that. She must have been watching him sleep for a long time.

"He loved me once," she said.

Basheer felt his face get hot. She knew him, he thought, I was horribly wrong.

"It is the morphine that changed him—" he tried to explain, but Hélène didn't hear. Drifted back into the brutal sleep.

⫷ 17 ⫸

"ALL I CAN OFFER YOU IS CHAMPAGNE," Vincent says. "There's not much else. We always have it on hand for clients. Helps the sale along."

"I'm fine really."

He opens the bottle anyway, as if he doesn't hear her. The pop of the cork is discreet. Hushed and throaty. The glasses are hollow-stemmed and delicate. The salon is elaborate in a way that is old-fashioned, yet timeless. Thick velvet drapes, rose red. Matching silk cushions on all the chairs. The mahogany settee. Thick carpet. It all says beauty, but fading beauty. There's a slight musty smell.

"It's too early for me," she says. It's not even eleven o'clock. Vincent begins to pour, as if she has not said a word. He must be hard of hearing, she thinks.

"I'm eighty-six," he says. "Difficult to believe, is it not? The key to my health is champagne every day, work every day, and a swim at the Ritz on the Place Vendôme. They have a club there that people can join. Do you know it? There are mermaids in mosaic at the bottom of the pool. Very beautiful. Mythic."

He wraps a linen towel around the neck of the bottle. Lucienne covers a glass with her hand. "I'm fine," she says loudly, slowly. "None for me."

Vincent looks at her as if she's been quite rude.

"Shouting is not necessary," he says quietly. "I understand what you have said. I also know why you are here. Basheer explained the situation to me. He called me early this morning, which is fine, I never seem to sleep anymore. He told me you may be coming by today."

"And?"

"And I am not heartless. I know your mother is in a coma. Her vital signs are strong, though. And for that we should be happy. We should drink in her honor."

Lucienne looks at Vincent closely. It's clear to see that he is an old man and his life has been difficult. And it's nearly over. But it's an odd juxtaposition. His clothes are stylish and cut for someone much younger. The top two buttons of his silk shirt are open. She can see he wears a chain around his neck with a gold fist dangling from it. An amulet for love, she thinks. Or maybe luck. She isn't sure.

He pours the champagne again with practiced precision. The perfect bubbles break against the crystal. Then re-form. He places a tall glass in front of her. The fragrance of the wine, like the perfume on her wrist, is golden.

"To your mother," he says, and raises his glass. His eyes are like the ocean, seemingly clear but fathomless.

Lucienne's glass remains untouched. "What did you say to her last night?"

"Nothing. She stayed only a moment, then left."

"That's difficult to believe."

He shrugs. "I'm sorry, it is true."

Lucienne can smell that acid edge of sweat that one acquires with age. The body erodes, she thinks. No matter what. She tries to imagine what he looked like as a young man.

"Then why did you lie to Dr. Assam about seeing her?"

"I didn't want to upset him."

"Because my mother knew his? Why would he be upset over that?"

Vincent's face colors. "Let us just say that your mother knew the family and leave it at that," he says.

It is then Lucienne remembers that Basheer left his wife for another woman, remembers her mother's plea for forgiveness. Her stomach goes sour.

"Basheer? She was the one who left with Basheer?"

Vincent hesitates, then nods, and Lucienne feels a chill. It only makes sense, of course. Her mother never returned to Paris. She never spoke about her life during the war. All those secrets. Shame explains them. To be the cause of someone's death must be overwhelming, Lucienne thinks. Then suddenly realizes that Dr. Assam must have suspected that her mother was the other woman but never mentioned it. An act of kindness, perhaps. Or maybe something else.

Vincent takes another sip of champagne. His hand shakes. She can tell he's hiding something.

"Did she ever speak of me?" he asks.

Lucienne shakes her head.

"Never?"

"No."

"Well," he says, more like a sigh. "I had hoped otherwise."

He loved her, she thinks, and is sad for all the pain her mother seems to have caused. There feels as if there's some mistake though, her mother doesn't seem to be the kind of person who would do this kind of thing.

"What was she like, my mother? I've never met anyone who knew her before the war."

He smiles. "Much like you," he says. "Beautiful. Intelligent. But sad, always sad. Sometimes it seemed as if sorrow ran through her veins."

Lucienne can see tears welling in his eyes. He wipes them away quickly.

"It is time for my swim," he says, and his voice cracks. He clears his throat and taps his watch. "If you'll excuse me, I must go."

She reaches out and touches his forearm.

"Do you know where they went?" she asks gently.

"What do you mean?"

"Do you know where Basheer and my mother went. If you know where they were going, I may be able to piece together what happened."

"How?"

"I can search Internet databases for refugee centers. Or the prison camps. Most everything is public record now."

"Everything can be traced?" he asks, and suddenly looks quite pale. In the corner of the room, Lucienne sees he has a computer. It's discreet, hidden in faux-marble casing.

"Yes. It's amazing what you can find if you know where to

look," she says. "That's the key, though. You have to know where to look."

"But it was your mother's past. She wants to keep it private. You should respect that."

"I can't. I'm trying to find my father," she says. "At least know who he is."

"She won't tell you? She must have good reason."

"I don't know if she does or not. All she'll say is that he was one of her assistants."

"But your birth certificate—"

"All it says is that I was born in Taos, New Mexico. Given the year I was born, and when she came to the United States, I have to assume that she knew my father here, in Europe, before she came over. But it's difficult to trace without knowing where she was during the war."

"I'm sorry. I can't help you."

"Can't or won't?"

He ignores the question. Taps his watch again. "I'll be late for my swim."

"I'm just asking where they went. Or where you think they went. You knew them. You must have an idea," she says. "I just want to run a search."

He opens the door for Lucienne to leave.

"You are searching for ghosts," he says. "Now please, I'll be late."

She hesitates.

"Please," he says again. It's clear the conversation is over.

He locks the door behind her. Between the blinds, she can see him turn on the computer. Pick up a phone. Obviously, his swim can wait.

✽ 18 ✽

THE NEXT NIGHT VINCENT STILL HAD NOT returned. Madame Assam was asleep in the other room and Basheer found himself talking to the Found Woman. Talking about himself. About Madame Assam. About anything he could think of. He was nervous. Hélène told him that the Germans were looking for her, and why, and that she had to get to America. To build the bomb first. Her story made his hands cold. His mouth dry. And he couldn't stop talking. He rubbed his hands together as he spoke and told her about everything in his life. Even about Manon and how they came to marry.

"Figs," he said. "That's how it started. She was the widow of my cousin and my aunt wanted me to marry her, to give the child a name. I wasn't so sure, but Madame Assam told me, 'Meet her. What harm would it do to meet her? I've been told she's charming.'

"And so I did. And she was. She sells fruit by the university. Every day, I would buy a single fig. She would talk to me. Small things at first.

"They were lovely figs," he said. "Very delicate."

While Basheer spoke he watched the Found Woman as she stared at the skylight. The reluctant moon. She said nothing. He talked even more. He told her about his life as a student. He wanted, he said, to learn more about the stars. "I have a theory that each star is a soul," he said. Hélène still did not speak. He lit a cigarette. One of the last he had left. The smell of chestnuts warmed him. "Think of it this way," he said, "what are the stars made of?"

Hélène turned toward him for the first time. She was wearing Madame Assam's sweater. Olive wool. Threadbare. It made her seem paler then she actually was. She reached out a shaky hand and took the cigarette from him. Basheer could see that she was weak, but better. The bleeding had stopped. The fever lessened. She closed her eyes. Smoke curled around her head. She inhaled deeply.

"Dust," he said. "The stars are made from dust. And what are we made of?"

She exhaled.

"Dust," he said. "When our bodies decompose we are dust. So we are dust and the stars are dust."

Her hand, the cigarette, went lax, brushed against Madame Assam's sweater. Tiny bits of thread flared. He took the cigarette from her hand. "I think it's very possible," he said, brushing the ash from her shoulder. "It's very possible that we and the stars are dust. If that is indeed true, then it is entirely possible that there are souls in the sky. Maybe that's how the idea of heaven came about."

She coughed.

"Get some rest," he said, and covered her again with the blanket, as if she were a child, like his own son. Small and helpless. And that opened his heart to her, just a bit. Then he thought of Manon.

"When will you be back?" Manon asked. Her voice was bitter.

"Soon," he told her, and she walked away from him without saying a word.

"Sleep," he told Hélène, and she turned to him. Full-eyed as the moon.

Outside life had turned into a newsreel. Everything now separated into black and white. The SS in uniform. Blackbirds. Not just at the opera, or patrolling the streets, but dining in cafés. Everywhere. And some of them were looking for Hélène.

It was early the next morning when an Opel Admiral, black and newly polished, pulled up. The driver, in full uniform, came to the door. Knocked.

Basheer had been upstairs in the apartment scavenging for food in the cupboards. He ran to the front window. From that angle, straight above, all he could see was a slice of a black hat. The low, growling car.

Each knock made Basheer's heart beat faster. He wanted to warn Madame Assam, but was trapped. There was no way to get down the stairs without being seen. All he could do was pray, pray that Madame Assam had not heard the knock. Pray that if she had, she understood not to answer.

Basheer held his breath for no good reason and prayed for them all.

Soon, the driver stopped knocking. He walked over to the

front window of the showroom and tried to look through the gap of the curtains, the narrow slit of light. Basheer's mouth turned sour. He remembered he'd left Hélène's bloody clothes on the floor in the front room. He didn't know what to do with them. He was afraid to throw them away. They could be seen. The driver seemed to linger by the window.

Basheer could hear his own breath, shallow and quick. I could shout, he thought. Divert attention. Save them, at least. He opened the apartment window. His heart felt squeezed. Wait. The driver stepped away.

Basheer held his breath. Moved back behind the curtain. The driver walked back to the car, then turned and looked at the building, looked again for signs of life.

The car window rolled down.

Quick, Basheer thought, ran down the stairs two at a time. He didn't stop to think what he was doing. All he could think of was that the women were in danger, needed him. And so he ran.

Madame Assam heard him. Opened the workroom door.

"Shh," she said. "You run like thunder."

Hélène was huddled in a corner of the room. She held her knees to her chest, as if she were a child afraid of storms.

"They're still outside," Basheer said.

Madame Assam nodded. "Shh."

The rumble of the car's engine was loud. They all kept still. Outside, someone coughed. For a moment, Basheer imagined that Vincent had returned. Told the driver about Hélène. He imagined it all in slow motion, frame by frame. But the front door remained closed. The driver slid a calling card into the jamb. Pushed it until it fell on the stone floor.

On the front of the card it read Department of Research, with an address. On the back, there was a note addressed to Vincent. A date and time. "Do not be late" was printed in small block letters.

It was a long time before anyone spoke.

Finally Basheer said, "She'll have to be moved. I've heard of a man who is in Marseilles. He's had luck getting people out."

"But how will you get to Marseilles?"

"The train," he said. "We will all take the train. The Germans are allowing Algerians and Moroccans to go home. They will grant us safe passage."

Madame Assam sat down hard on the tufted chair usually reserved for customers.

"But we are home," she said. "Paris is our home. Surely there's a place she can hide here. This war will not last forever."

Basheer shook his head. "There are no places to hide in Paris. The Germans are everywhere. They will find her."

"But it's not our problem. It's Vincent's," Madame Assam said.

Basheer held up the calling card. "And you think Vincent will go to this meeting and not mention our names?"

A pained look crossed Madame Assam's face.

"Besides," Basheer said, "Paris is not our real home. I would like to go to Morocco. To be one of the many, instead of one of the few. I would like to raise my son as he should be raised. With his people."

Madame Assam said nothing. She had no idea Basheer had any feelings about Morocco, this way or that. He had never spoken of it before. She couldn't imagine his thinking about it as home. She knew she couldn't go back. She'd run away from Karim, Basheer's father. Runaway wives are usually stoned.

"I've been thinking about it a lot, Mother," Basheer said. "This war is not our war. Why should we suffer?"

"But your son is French. As is his mother. The birthright passes from mother to son. And you have taken the flag, you are now a French citizen. Morocco is not your home."

"But it is my father's home," he said.

The words stung Madame Assam, although Basheer didn't mean them to. He knew his mother left because she felt betrayed by his father's multiple marriages. Karim had promised her that she would be his only love, even though that was not the custom in his family. And she believed him and loved him for it. Until he met Selua.

"I can't go back," she told Basheer.

"How do you know?" he asked. "Perhaps he has many wives, but only one love. Perhaps he has always loved only you. Don't you think it's time you found out?"

Madame Assam closed her eyes a moment. Said a prayer for them all.

"Perhaps," she said. But she couldn't imagine it. That's not the way the world works, she wanted to say, but she could see how happy Basheer was at the possibility of seeing his father again and knew she couldn't disappoint him.

Two days later, Hélène was well enough to travel but still refused to speak more than a word or two.

And Vincent had returned.

"And me?" he said. "Will I come, too?"

He was loud and drunk and smelled as if he'd been drunk for a long time. Madame Assam wouldn't even look at him. Locked the door to the workroom behind her. Hélène covered her head with a pillow. Hummed until she could hear only the tone of her own voice, flat and wavering. She couldn't bear to hear Vincent's voice again.

"Am I to stay behind?" Vincent asked, this time louder. Even more angry.

Basheer said nothing, pulled a chair in front of the workroom door. Crossed his legs. Wouldn't let Vincent pass.

"She doesn't want to talk to you."

"She loves me."

"She came to you for money. That is all."

When Basheer said this, Vincent was struck. The truth of it resonates, he thought, as he once said, like a bell.

"It's not true," he said, but finally knew it was and was propelled by anger and shame. The money. That's all.

"Maybe you should go upstairs and sleep," Basheer said, his voice condescending. "You look tired."

"I want to say good-bye, then," he said. "Let me at least say good-bye to her. You can be in the room."

"That would not be wise."

"You ask her if she'll talk to me. She will."

"She's sleeping," Basheer said.

"Then wake her."

"You need some sleep yourself."

"She loved me once."

The alcohol, drugs, the moment, the lack of sleep converged. Wore a hole in Vincent. The money is all she wants now. He was holding the card that the driver left behind. A swastika embossed in the corner of it. He'd missed the appointment already. Three hours late. Vincent knew what he had to do. Besides, he thought, she came back only for the money. Not love.

"I'm going for a walk," he said. His red spider eyes hidden.

And in that moment Basheer understood that he and Madame Assam and the Found Woman would have to leave. Right now. And hurry.

After all, Vincent was already three hours late.

LUCIENNE DOESN'T WANT TO TAKE ANOTHER TAXI and she's too tired to walk. The Métro is everywhere. Every block. So she goes underground. Buys a ticket and waits. She is going back to the hospital to sit with her mother and wait again. Waiting seems to be the only thing she can do now.

The train should arrive in ten minutes, she hopes. The maps and signs are confusing. The Métro station, however, is very clean, cleaner than the T in Boston. It's pleasant and well lit and smells oddly like flowers. She checks her wrist to be sure it's not the perfume.

No, it's the air, she thinks. Some sort of air freshener. She's read they do this in Japan, too.

Nearby, there's a blond woman with dreadlocks drumming the *Boléro* on a series of trash can lids. "MONEY FOR BO," a sign reads, neatly written in five languages. The suitcase below it is filled with coins and bills. And there are tourists, lots of tourists, guidebooks in hand. One man is wearing a cheap beret and a T-shirt that says "Paris," as if he needs to remember where he is.

But, in the corner of the fray, sitting on a bench, there is a woman who is writing in a notebook. She's bent over, knees nearly touching her forehead. An odd sight. She's in her eighties, at least, Lucienne thinks. Her mother's age, more or less. The woman's fingertips bleed blue ink. She doesn't look up. She's dirty. She smells. Her pen scratches at the paper, enraged, inconsolable. Around her neck is a chain, a small Star of David swings back and forth.

Lucienne is fascinated. She sits down next to her. The woman doesn't look up. Keeps on writing. Ignores the lines on the paper. Piles words over words. Big block letters. Childlike. It's one sentence, Lucienne can see that. When the old woman turns the page, she can make it out clearly.

"Pardonne, n'oublie pas."

The little French she remembers comes back to Lucienne.

"Forgive," it reads, "but do not forget."

Ghosts, she thinks, are everywhere.

~ 20 ~

WHAT LATER SURPRISED ALL INVOLVED WAS THAT Vincent knew
where Basheer lived. He'd known for a long time, but never mentioned it. Vincent always enjoyed knowing something he wasn't
supposed to. It was thrilling. Although the secret life of Basheer
really wasn't that difficult to figure out. Vincent simply followed
him home one evening. Then waited the next morning and followed him again.

   Basheer didn't live in the Arab Quarter at all. That's where
Vincent had originally made his mistake. He lived in a neighborhood known more for students and artists, quite near the university. That surprised Vincent. He never thought of his old friend as
being an academic, but every day for a week Vincent followed
Basheer and watched him take his seat in the large lecture halls. He

seemed to be a good student. Kept his head down. Never stopped taking notes.

Vincent also followed Basheer's wife, Manon. She'd never met Vincent, so that was easier. He watched her open the series of locks on the small fruit stand and she paid no attention. That made it even more thrilling. Vincent watched Manon for nearly a month. The minutiae of her life became addictive to him, unlike Basheer's well-worn path from his apartment to the classroom to the library and back again. The wife was less predictable. Vincent never knew what she had planned. Some days she would take the child with her to work. Some days Madame Assam would come early in the morning, before Basheer left, and spend the day watching him. Some days Manon left the baby with a neighbor, a fishmonger's wife, who seemed to look after many of the neighborhood children.

"Be good, Basheer," she'd say, and Vincent stood so close he could hear her and watch her as she handed her child to the red-faced woman.

"I love you," she'd whisper in the baby's ear.

He could hear that, too.

Manon never noticed Vincent following her at all. After a time, it became a game of sorts. Vincent watched Manon as she opened the small stand. Took deliveries. Gossiped. She never noticed. He could walk right up to her, put a plum in his mouth, run away, and she would just shout after him, "Crazy boy," and not think twice.

I'm not a boy, he'd think. Not at all.

The next time he'd steal a pear. Or a perfect white peach.

According to the fishmonger's wife, who was often very lonely during the day and very talkative, the stall had been Manon's dead husband's. Now hers. Now Basheer's. "Manon is ten years older at least," she told Vincent. "And not Arab. Dark, though. Basque maybe."

The fishmonger's wife was French and had been raised in Algiers. Unsure about Arabs. "I'd never marry one," she said. "Can't trust them. Stab you in the back. The Basque will marry anyone, though."

But Manon did not seem to be Basque, at least not to Vincent. She reminded him of the paintings of Gauguin. The women of Tahiti. Bronzed. Small-boned and delicate as a fish. She was not the kind of woman Vincent expected Basheer to marry. Even out of duty. She was too fragile. It was all so unexpected. Everything. Basheer as a student. A soft tiny son. And the wife, delicate and older. But then Basheer always had a way of surprising him. So, it was only fair that Vincent had turned the tables.

He is not my brother, Vincent thought.

He is not my brother, thought Basheer while he watched Vincent walk past the café, the SS officer's card in his hand. It was very clear where Vincent was going and that he was willing to betray them. Basheer could see it in his face. The cool vacant eyes. Bitter. So, Basheer told his mother to run, run all the way to tell Manon and his son they were all leaving.

"But what if she chooses to stay?" Madame Assam asked.

"Reason with her. There is little fruit to sell now," he said. "If the Germans are willing to let us go home to Morocco, we should. We can start over there."

So Madame Assam ran, knowing all along that she would not go to Morocco. Once in Marseilles, she planned to stay there until the war was over. Maybe even find her sister Nor there. When the Germans first took Paris, Nor, like thousands of others, fled on foot. Some of them made it. Some of them were shot running. Madame Assam stays up nights wondering if Nor was one of the lucky ones. Now, in Marseilles, she can know. It's the place everyone escapes to. The only way out of France.

So she ran all the way to the fruit stall, to gather up her daughter-in-law and grandchild. But Madame Assam was an old woman, not used to running. And, unfortunately, they were already there.

"Basheer!" she cried out.

And the men all thought she meant Basheer, her son, the one who was hiding the girl from Prague that they had been looking for. The one whom they assumed was being arrested at that moment across the city.

Not Basheer, the infant, whom she had no idea that Vincent was picking up from the fishmonger's wife at that very moment. The woman had seen the long black car pull up to the fruit stall. Had heard screaming. "What should I do with this?" she said to Vincent and shook the baby as if it were a doll. "I don't want the Germans to think I'm involved in whatever the Arab was doing."

"I'll take the child," he told her, "and I'll never tell anyone that you and the Arab were friends." Then he paid the red-faced woman handsomely to ease any future misgivings and left.

The men knew nothing about that Basheer, the Basheer that Vincent held in his arms. And that Basheer, the infant, was as Vincent expected. A bright sun that would be a comfort to a man in his old age. He held the tiny baby so tightly to his chest, the boy cried out in pain.

"A SEARCH ENGINE IS EASY TO USE," Philippe explained to Vincent. "And difficult, too."

After nearly an hour at the computer, Vincent understood what he meant. When he typed in Basheer's name, there were forty-eight mentions. Two were about a presentation Basheer gave at a medical convention last year. But nothing about Basheer the father. And Hélène's name was even worse. There were thousands of Web sites featuring papers by her, about her, or referencing her. Criticizing her.

This is impossible, he thought. Then tried one more name. A name too difficult for Vincent to say.

Just two hits.

The first was a list of the names at the Memorial of Deportation, the names of those who were taken by the Germans to camps, and killed.

The second was unlikely. A photo of a place in Morocco.

He'd found the ghosts Lucienne was looking for. The ones Vincent had always wanted to forget.

$\backsim$ 22 $\backsim$

THERE WASN'T MUCH TIME. THAT WAS CLEAR when Vincent left. Basheer took the last box of morphine he found hiding under Vincent's bed and the rest of the money from the safe, which was a considerable amount. Too much even to count, so he took it all. It was good that Madame Assam remembered the combination.

It was decided that they would all meet in Marseilles. Madame Assam had taken several hundred francs and was to gather Manon and Basheer and take the next train to the city. The trains left frequently. Basheer told her, "In just a few hours we will all be together. And safe."

Basheer had known a few artists, neighbors of his, who'd escaped this way. He'd been told that the trains were watched by police, but the check point at Marseilles was easily avoided by going through a service exit at the station's restaurant. "If anyone asks," he was told, "you just tell them you are making a phone call or washing your hands."

It seemed easy.

"We will meet at the foot of the station stairs," Basheer told Madame Assam. "I have been told that is the best way."

It all felt lucky to Basheer, and he never trusted luck.

Hélène's fever had suddenly returned, made her languid, wanting to sleep. The letters Frédéric had written her, which she'd sewn into her dress along with her own ID papers, were streaked with her blood but still somewhat legible.

"These will do," Basheer said. "But since the Germans are looking for you, best to keep these hidden. In Marseilles, we'll get you a new ID, a different name. One that draws less attention. In Marseilles, anything can be bought."

"Quick, quick," Madame Assam said, and showed Hélène how to wear one of her gowns and wrap the scarf around her head, so she would be properly covered from head to foot. It had been nearly twenty years since Madame Assam had worn it. The dark fabric smelled musty and had been eaten away in places by moths.

Madame Assam kissed Hélène on both cheeks, as was the custom in France, the country that she had grown to love.

"Soon," Hélène said. "We will see each other again soon." Hélène held her tightly, felt her small bones against hers.

Basheer kissed his mother. "Go without fear," he said, the Muslim farewell. He squeezed her so hard she could feel her ribs bruise one after the other. But she didn't cry. That surprised her. Madame Assam didn't cry until much later, until the moment the soldier grew angry and beat her daughter-in-law. Didn't cry until Manon folded onto the floor like a sheet. Madame Assam cried then, but not for herself. She cried for her son Basheer and everything he had ever loved in his life, for Manon and her grandchild. And then she cried for Jacques and for Vincent, the boy she worried would never grow. And didn't.

Then the angry soldier turned to Madame Assam. The gun was raised. Her tears stopped. He took aim. Madame Assam heard Basheer's voice again, his sweet deep voice. "Go without fear," he'd told her.

My son, she thought.

And knew it was the last thing she would ever remember of this world. And for that, she was happy.

AT THE HOSPITAL ALL IS IN ORDER. The smell of antiseptic is reassuring. Dr. Belliard, Hélène's new doctor, is primly blond and nearly sixty. Coolly competent. She says that Hélène is doing as well as can be expected.

"If the coma lifts," she says, "then we shall see what we are dealing with."

"If not?"

"Then decisions must be made."

Decisions, Lucienne thinks. It still seemed so unreal.

Dr. Assam had not returned to his office. His nurse explained that it was his day off.

"Would you like to make an appointment?" she asked.

Lucienne shook her head. "It can wait," she said, but didn't mean it. The more she thinks about Vincent and how he lied about knowing Hélène, the more uncomfortable she becomes.

Visiting hours are almost over. The hospital is generous, family members can stay all day and into the early evening, but not overnight. Only until it's time for the supper trays to be delivered. Lucienne has been sitting in a wooden chair for over twelve hours. She's seen all French television has to offer. Mostly American cartoons, at least on one station. The Roadrunner still beats the coyote and that's comforting. Beep, beep, she thinks. A little bit of home. But not too much. She avoids the news. Too much. Too much.

For most of the day, Lucienne has sat by her mother's bedside alone. The doctors and nurses make themselves scarce, since they're not needed anymore. The coma is on auto-pilot, she thinks. Machines monitor its progress. At this point, waiting is the only thing that can be done. She takes her mother's hand. Hélène's fingers do not move. Lucienne squeezes it hard. Again, nothing. The rhythm of her mother's breath, once a source of comfort, now drives her fears. Not dead. Not alive, either.

"I know you can hear me. People in comas can hear everything. You're just being stubborn. Squeeze my hand. Move a finger. Something."

Hélène's hand feels cold and heavy.

Lucienne remembers the fire in the Mesa long ago. Her mother's hair burning. The sweet nut smell. And her mother's hand, this hand, around her neck. Lucienne feels her throat tighten.

"You are loved," she says. Forgiven.

She places her mother's hand back under the thin blanket and closes the door gently behind her.

✒ 24 ✑

MARSEILLES PROMISED FREEDOM, DESPITE THE VICHY. ANYTHING could be bought there, and was, including visas. Which, of course, was key. The country of origination didn't matter. Spain was a popular choice, but difficult to obtain. China was easier. For the right price, a visa could be bought from a minor official at the Chinese consulate. However, when translated, they read, "This person shall not, under any circumstances, be allowed to enter China."

But that was fine. No one could translate Chinese and a visa of any sort was good enough for a person to use to cross into freedom. And so they came. They all came. The watchers and the watched.

In Marseilles there were refugees of every kind. Writers, artists, painters, politicians, scientists. Thousands of Jews. And there were also soldiers, too. They were there to keep the peace. There were men from every branch of every army, French and otherwise. A coalition. The colonials with their red fezzes. Zouaves in the full sails of their Turkish trousers. The Senegalese with their proud white turbans, a single gilt star keeping it all in place. The Alpine chasseurs, dusty in green, with enormous berets set rakishly low over their left ears.

There were soldiers in helmets and soldiers in tunics and soldiers in dove-gray riding pants. Soldiers in velour caps that made them seem more like scholars than warriors. And Vichy police who smelled of cheap cognac. And the ordinary soldiers, the infantrymen. Tens of thousands of them. Complete, utter confusion. That's what it was. Of course, it was inevitable that this would happen, this convergence. In Marseilles, freedom could be bought. It was simple. You paid for the papers you needed and waited. It was civilized. At least, at first. And if you were rich and not a Jew the waiting was simple. Most waited in cafés. Overflowed them. The playing of jazz and dancing of any kind were forbidden by the Vichy but people still ate and smoked and drank. And laughed. The laughter was the most amazing thing about Marseilles. It had been such a long time since Basheer had heard an adult laugh, he would sometimes stop and just listen to it, let it wash over him. He'd think about his own son's laugh, the high peal of joy that a baby makes. The soft gurgle, the coo of it.

Things were different in Marseilles. Just as in Paris, there was the grinding sense of war and a resignation to it that filled the air and every conversation. But, unlike Paris, no one was starving. No one was cold. And there were still newspapers. They were only two to four pages long, but they did report some news and sold classified ads to families trying to reunite.

"Father seeks only son, Pierre, age seven, lost on the road just outside of Tours."

"Woman seeks sister, Magdalene, gone missing at train station in Lyon."

Everyday Basheer searched these ads. Looked for his name.

"Any luck?" Hélène would ask.

"I don't trust luck."

When Hélène and Basheer first arrived at the train station they waited until dark for Madame Assam, Manon, and Basheer. But once night came, so came the rain, and they were told that the only rooms available were at the Hotel Suisse, a family hotel. The rooms were small, noisy, and cold, with bed sheets that smelled of mold.

There was only one room to let, so they took it. Basheer volunteered to sleep on the floor. "We have no choice," he said.

The most important feature of the Hotel Suisse was that it was directly across the street from the Gare St. Charles, the main railway station. From their window they could watch the people swarm in and out, search the crowd. It was a perfect vantage point.

"It's only temporary," Basheer said. "They will be here soon."

And he said little else.

He didn't know what else to say. Basheer and Hélène were officially strangers. They had nothing in common, except for the fact that he had saved her, and he was not even sure why he did it. He could have just walked away. Left her there. It was, he thought, Vincent's problem after all.

But Basheer was caught up in the moment. He wanted to be a hero, a savior, though he knew that never works. It was the same with Manon. He thought he was her hero and that she loved him for it. But, on their wedding night, she explained the truth of the matter.

"But what of love?" he asked, and placed his hand on her belly and felt the child kick in her womb.

"I am a practical woman," she said, "I'm not sure I believe in love."

Basheer spent the night watching her sleep. I saved you, he thought, and longed for her, her round belly, the plump curve of her breast, but her dreams were unfathomable and deep, and held her tightly within their grip. By the time morning came, Basheer realized that he would always be known as a man bound by duty. Not husband. Or father. Manon and Basheer were his and not his.

So, he was resigned to living his life in that in-between world, because he was, indeed, a man bound by duty. But still, he missed them.

I should have gone back and gotten them myself, he thought. I should try to go back now.

He told himself this over and over again but knew it was impossible to go back to Paris. A foolish gesture, at best. Basheer's exit papers stated that he was returning to Morocco. When they were stamped at the checkpoint, he was warned that to travel back to Paris would mean arrest. Maybe death.

So he had to wait. He knew that. And he was willing to wait for as long as it took. But, in his darkest moments, he thought Manon had abandoned him. It was entirely possible. The fruit stand was now hers. Her son had a name. Basheer knew he was no longer needed. She was, after all, a practical woman.

But still, Basheer waited. He had to. He loved her. And sometimes believed that she loved him, too. He thought of the nights they would lie in bed with the boy between them and watch him until he fell asleep. His small perfect feet. The dark curls of his hair. And sometimes Basheer would shed a tear, not in sorrow, but in awe of such beauty. And Manon softened to him. Kissed his tears away. So Basheer waited. Waited as long as possible. But he expected that soon, he'd be waiting alone.

Hélène's wounds were healing quickly. Basheer could see that even on the train. He was surprised at how well she managed the station, the wait, the long ride without a complaint, though he heard her labored breath.

Of course, he was also surprised how well his plan had worked. In his mother's clothes Hélène was invisible. No one paid any attention to her at all. The police never asked for her papers. They didn't even stop her. She moved through crowds as if she were an afterthought. He felt lucky and that made his hands sweat.

Once inside the hotel, Hélène slept for nearly a day and then ate an entire baguette and all of the dried apricots Basheer had bought for both of them at the market. Later he brought her wine that made her face turn red. She laughed too loudly and he went to sleep knowing she would survive.

"I'm fine," she said the next morning, and she appeared to be. It had become clear that the fragment lodged in her scalp would prove to be an ongoing nuisance. It was a dull pain that sometimes itched, and if she scratched it, sometimes bled down her face in an alarming manner. So she tried not to scratch. At least not in public. As for her leg wound, it took more than a week before she could walk with some level of comfort. She could stand only for short periods of time. Limped slightly. But overall Hélène seemed to be well. Sturdy, even.

At least that's what Basheer thought. He couldn't see the fissures that first began when Vincent took her, as her father had done. That was something they never spoke of. To Basheer, Hélène seemed to be a woman who needed no one's help to survive. Strong, like his mother. Strong-willed, like Manon. Hélène sat by the window with him and waited, searched the faces of the people who flowed down the stairs and into the busy street. And while they waited for his family to arrive, they passed the time talking. Hélène smoked and cursed and talked to him about the world of science and the politics of it.

"No one studies science for the beauty anymore," she said. "It's all about the official science of governments. What they need to know, not what the soul needs to understand."

There were no chairs in the room, just the bed. So they sat on the floor, covered in blankets to keep out the chill. Watching. Watching.

"Still," she said, "to work in science is like being inside the mind of God, rattling around for his secrets."

Basheer lit another cigarette. They had been sitting in the stale room watching for nearly a week. "Sometimes," he said, "I think it's more important to be in God's heart than in his mind."

After the first week, Hélène wanted to go outside. To sit in the small park next to the station and watch from there. "That way we get some sunlight," she said. "The mold is settling in my lungs."

Basheer agreed, even though he knew that from the park their view was limited. He'd begun to feel that the room was too intimate. Improper. The bidet in the center, an embarrassment. The bed with its musty sheets. Not easy to ignore. And worst of all, he sometimes went for hours without thinking of Manon, or of his son's small fist clutching his finger.

So, Hélène and Basheer spent the next week sitting in the small park watching the people flood down the enormous winding stairs of the station. They made an odd sight. She was covered from head to foot. A mystery. Basheer, on the other hand, seemed to be exactly what he was. A student from Paris, as clean shaven as possible. He was dressed in the typical baggy wool trousers and too formal jacket, both of which seemed to need a good airing. They spent their days deep in conversation about one theory or another. The superiority of science over philosophy. About Darwin. And Buddha. They smoked and watched the men stop at the single *pissotière*. Watched every squirrel and bird and every face that came within view.

"I'm glad we did this," Hélène said. "I think better in the sunlight." And so did Basheer. In the warmth of the coastal sun, he would tell himself that there were many reasons why his family had not arrived yet. Good reasons.

It was safer to wait a week.

Basheer has colic.

Madame Assam had twisted her ankle and could not travel until it healed.

He would run these scenarios over and over in his head and always come to the same conclusion.

But all is better now, he would think, and they will be here on the next train.

But the next train always came and went.

Little by little, sitting in the warm sun, talking and talking, afraid to be silent, Basheer came to realize that he was alone. His son, his mother, his wife and her clove skin, all gone. Perhaps alive, but gone to him.

The idea frightened him at first, but somehow didn't surprise him. He recognized that he risked his life, his family, for someone he did not know. He said nothing of this to Hélène. What could he say? It wasn't her fault he'd been a fool, caught up in the moment. A false hero. He understood that completely now. And now, he was alone. Not lying in his wife's bed, with their son between them, but curled like a dog in the corner of a stale room, with his mother's olive sweater underneath his head, listening to the breath of a woman who had no use for him any longer.

When the third week began, Basheer had given up watching the train station. He understood they weren't coming. Not now. Not ever. He began to feel like a sleepwalker. Awake but not. Living in dreams. One morning before dawn, he left the moldy room without Hélène. Left her sleeping. Wandered the streets. Even at that early hour in the dark, Marseilles was filled with people waiting, just like him. Waiting for visas and passports, waiting for any scheme or opportunity to escape. Their shadows clustered in groups. Whispering from this corner to that.

He walked through them without speaking. He had nothing to say.

When Hélène awoke and found that Basheer was gone, she suspected he'd finally given up. She had known they weren't coming a long time ago, though she found it difficult to admit. Ever since Madame Assam kissed her cheeks, she felt it. A premonition, she thought, but ignored it. She was buoyed by Basheer's hope. And now that was gone, so she wept for him. And herself. Without his hope, she felt rudderless.

That night, well after curfew, nearly midnight, Basheer returned dazed and sweating. Silent. Hélène could see the shadow of him at the window, looking out toward the train station, deserted at that hour, just looking. She put her arms around his waist. Her head against his back.

"I will always be indebted to you," she said. "You saved my life."

And he turned to her in the darkness. So much taller. A cedar. The moon, a shy crescent, shone though the window.

"But who will save mine?"

❧ 25 ❧

HOUSEKEEPING HAS FORGOTTEN TO TURN OFF THE TV.

That's the first thing Lucienne thinks when she walks into the room. The smoke from the towers seems to have slowed, but now the streets are filled with men and women holding pictures of loved ones. The missing. The pictures are incongruous. A wedding photo. A father with his newborn. A birthday cake with too many candles. Moments of simple joy captured forever. Now, forever linked to this moment. On the TV, those who are left behind crowd the camera. Try not to push and shove but it's difficult. There's a sense of urgency. And panic.

"I've been looking for him since the moment it fell," one woman says. She's pretty. Dark-haired. "He's a trader. North Tower. 102."

She holds a wedding picture to the camera.

Lucienne turns off the TV. She just can't take it anymore. Too much sorrow. She feels as if she's drowning in it. Her body aches. The red light is still flashing on the telephone. Lucienne hasn't picked up messages in four days, ever since she and her mother arrived. So she dials. A recorded voice, a woman's, explains how to use the hotel's mail system. Her instructions are clear. Precise. And in French. But the cadence is universal.

Lucienne presses one to listen.

"It's Ethan. Give me a call."

He left this the first night, she thinks. He doesn't sound panicked or upset. She plays his message again. Then saves it. Can't erase it. There's something uncomplicated about his voice—simple and straightforward. Makes her feel safe. She presses one again.

"Lucienne. Ethan. Call."

There's an edge now. And one more message. At first, there's no sound. Just a pause. Then a breath exhaled.

"Please."

Ethan's voice sounds so small. Far away. Forgotten. She calls him. The phone rings only once.

"Hello?"

He'd been sleeping, she can tell that. He's hoarse.

"I'm afraid," she says.

"I know."

Then she tells him the story of her mother and the street where something has happened and, she suspects, is happening. And Vincent, but not about Dr. Assam.

And he tells her about the hijackers, how they think one of them lived in Boston, not too far from her mother's brownstone. And theirs, she thinks, but Ethan doesn't mention that. He says the man was seen on a weekly basis buying a *TV Guide* and a pint of Ben and Jerry's.

"It's strange," Ethan says. "All these details that may or may not show up in the history books. The manager said the guy seemed like a regular guy. Liked Wavy Gravy."

As Ethan talks, Lucienne cradles the phone with both hands. Closes her eyes. Imagines him sleepy, lying on his bed with pillows tossed on the floor. Top sheet twisted. Cold coffee on the night stand. Newspapers still on the floor where he left them, where he always leaves them.

And then he says something she doesn't expect.

"Don't do the divorce."

She doesn't know what to say, so she says nothing. Thinks back to the way it used to be when they met. They were students. Hopeful. Listening to the darkness together, not needing to speak or define anything. Floating. That was so long ago, she thinks. It now seems irrelevant. Just like searching for someone whom you know is dead.

"You still there?" she asks after a time.

"I'll always be here," he says.

His voice is more sad than angry. He hangs up the phone.

Lucienne listens to the static of the dead line for a long time, first out of surprise, then for the pure sound of it, as one listens in the lab, listens for sounds of life.

BASHEER AND HÉLÈNE HAD BEEN IN MARSEILLES for over a month. The hotel was expensive.

"We can't stay here forever," Hélène said.

But Basheer said nothing. Pushed his soup back and forth with his spoon.

It was early evening. March 1941. They were sitting in the café across from the harbor having a bowl of fish soup and watching the circus of the street. The sun, blood orange, slipped into the dark water. She'd fixed her hair. Swept it up in a way that covered the wound on her head. Secured it with hairpins. She'd made an effort. She was wearing the dress he'd bought for her at a shop around the corner. Slate-blue.

"Like the night sky," he said.

It suited her. And him. It had become difficult for Basheer to watch Hélène wearing his mother's clothes. Even though they both knew it was safer for her. Attracted less attention. Now, he regretted buying her that dress. As a Muslim woman, she had to travel with him. Needed him. As a French woman, she could go anywhere she wanted without him now. No matter how dangerous, he thought.

"I'm sorry," she said.

A gull swooped low and took the last piece of bread from the plate between them.

"Scavenger," Basheer said, angry. Hélène wasn't sure if he meant the bird. Or her.

"I'm sorry," she said again. "It was the first name that came into my head."

He asked the waiter for more bread.

"I wasn't thinking," she said.

When the bread came, Basheer threw it, tear by tear, to the gulls. They cried. Cawed. Wanted more. She wasn't thinking, that was true. But he didn't care. She had no right.

And she didn't. She knew that. When Hélène bought the identity card and the matching passport, she didn't think at all. She needed new papers to cross through Spain, into Africa, they both knew that. And false papers were dangerous to get. So she went alone. She'd already put him in enough danger.

It was still dark when she left Basheer sleeping in the corner of the room. Madame Assam's sweater, the empty arms, his blanket. She was wearing the dress Basheer had given her. Her long dark hair wrapped into a bun covered the wound on the top of her head. She took extra hairpins, just to make sure. I'm ready, she thought, but felt shaky. She hadn't been anywhere without Basheer for over a month. He had become a part of her. Not just the man who saved her, but something more. Something she found difficult to admit. But as soon as Hélène closed the door behind her, gently, she missed him. Missed the shadow of him. Wanted to wake him, but didn't.

Out on the street, there were people everywhere. People rushing up the stairs into the train station. People waiting for the shops to open. People walking. Running. A policeman taking pictures. She covered her face with her arm.

Basheer said that one had to arrive at the shop before sunrise. The door was only open for a few minutes. Hélène knew the address wasn't that far away, just two blocks, but there were so many, too many, people. She felt her chest go tight. And the world shift, off center.

Suddenly, it felt as if she were at the opera again, the fire, being carried away in the sea of people. The dangerous current. It was all there. The tremor of it. The sky above her was turning from gray to blue. Nearly sunrise. No time. A flock of seagulls banked left then right. Elbows and arms bruised her. She pushed harder. Pushed a man into his child. The little boy fell. The father grabbed Hélène by the arm. Shook her. Her long hair uncoiled, exposed the shaved spot on her head, the fragment.

"Go back" is what she heard him say.

"Be careful" is what he said.

Hélène quickly wrapped her long hair back into a bun, over the wound. Secured it on the top of her head. It was sloppy. Loose.

It was then that Hélène felt someone watching her. Following her. She looked around. Looked for the policeman, but he wasn't there. Just a flash in the distance. No one who seemed to pay any attention to her at all. Not the police. Not the soldiers. Not the women with straw baskets filled with bread. Or the children laughing, running through the crowd.

"Vincent?" she called out.

She could feel him, even though he wasn't there. His thorn eyes.

The sun was rising. Hélène was close. She knew that. She could see a woman herding people into the shop. Quiet as cattle.

"Wait!" Hélène screamed.

The woman was closing the door.

"Not today. No more," she said under her breath, but Hélène pushed past her. The woman shrugged. Locked the door behind her.

It took a moment for Hélène's eyes to adjust to the hushed room. Shutters over the front windows. No air. The shelves were empty. People milled around. Wordless. Waiting. There were no chairs, so they just circled each other, gray-faced as sharks. Every now and then a man, thin and cranelike, would appear from the back room. Choose someone. Go back again.

Hélène had to wait a long time. Her leg throbbed. Her skin felt as if it were peeling away, layer by layer. She wanted to bathe. But she had to wait.

After a time, she began to pick at the itch of her scalp. The bit of metal moved. She felt as though she was teetering. Swaying this way and that. When the man finally came for Hélène, he led her back into the storeroom by her elbow. He didn't look at her. She paid in American dollars, as was the custom. She laid out the bills. One dollar for every forty francs. The dollars were guaranteed to be real, she told him that, and he examined them closely. Sniffed them.

"The real ones smell like skin."

Then he asked her the name for the passport.

"Pick any name," he said, "any name you like."

"Manon," she said.

Hélène wasn't thinking at all. She tried to correct herself. But the man raised his hand to her lips. "One name is as good as another," he said, and he took out his special typewriter, the one with the Arabic characters, and began to work.

When Basheer saw the passport he turned away from her. Shook.

Now, hours later, they were sitting at the café, their café. Not speaking. It didn't seem right.

"I meant no harm," she said, and felt herself teetering. "It was the first name I thought of. It was a stupid mistake."

This is not how Hélène wanted the evening to be. Toward the end of their month in Marseilles, it had become their habit to sit here and drink wine. Eat a bowl of soup. Watch the people flow by, watch the tide rise and fall. And to talk about things. Dust and stars. The theories of the world. She wanted that again, one last time. But it was not to be.

Basheer thought of each in turn, his mother, his wife, and his child, in exquisite detail, until the wine dulled him. He remembered small things; his son's soft gums, pink, waiting for teeth. Every part of his family Basheer remembered, still felt in his arms. His heart was filled and leaking.

Now, the bread was gone. The seagulls had left.

"We have to go," Hélène said. "We really can't stay here any longer."

Basheer was quietly drunk. He was watching a couple at the next table. They were older, much older. Married. The man reached over and kissed his wife's hand. She began to cry.

Hélène was watching them, too. They reminded her of

Frédéric and Irène. The tenderness. She looked at Basheer. There were tears in his eyes. She wasn't sure if he was crying for himself or the couple or just the world at large, but it touched her and she suddenly felt that she didn't want to leave him alone. Not after all he'd done for her.

"The Belgian Congo is so very far away," she said. "And Morocco so close. I could wait there with you for the Americans to arrive. I've been thinking about it. We could wait together in Morocco."

She remembered what Getner had said that night in the café with Frédéric: "If they're successful, you could catch a plane from there."

Morocco felt like such a large risk back then, but now it was one she was willing to take. Basheer, after all, had saved her. She couldn't leave him like this.

Basheer acted as if he didn't hear her. "A toast," he said. "*Vive Pétain!*"

Hélène lifted her glass.

"*Vive Pétain,*" she said sadly. The wine was thin. Burned her throat.

And then she said, "We will place an ad in the newspaper for Madame Assam to meet us."

And the words fell. Bottomless.

It was a lie they both understood.

So they sat silent for a long time, thinking. The café closed around them and one by one, the stars revealed themselves. And they watched.

"Dust," Hélène finally said, "and stars and souls."

She reached across the table and took his hand. A lifeline.

You saved me, she thought, and whispered, "They will never be far from us. Your family. They will always be with us wherever we go. Every soul is a star, is that not right? And the stars are always in the heavens watching."

Basheer said nothing, but she could see him wavering in the candlelight. Tears ran down his face onto his thick bulldog hands.

"We will place an ad in the newspaper. Tell them to meet us," he said quietly.

He knew it was time for them to go.

WHEN PHILIPPE CALLED, LUCIENNE WAS STILL ASLEEP. It was early afternoon. About 2 P.M. She could hear housekeeping knocking on neighboring doors. The whine of a vacuum cleaner. She could barely hear him.

"I'm at the café," he said. "You should come. It's important."

And then he said something else but she didn't catch it. Too much static.

"Are you on a cell phone?"

He laughed. "Are you breathing air?"

"Mostly."

"Just come."

"I'm not dressed."

"Then I'll come to you. We need to talk. Ten minutes."

PASSING THROUGH SPAIN WAS SIMPLE. BASHEER AND Hélène, dressed in Madame Assam's clothes, her face neatly covered, reported to the first checkpoint. Showed their papers and moved on. From there they took the ferry to Morocco.

"Going home," Basheer told the soldiers when they stopped him, then let him pass.

"Go without fear," Basheer said to them and they nodded. It was all very simple. As the ferry neared the shoreline, Basheer could see the dusky outline of Morocco. The plum of sunset. Home, he thought. Basheer could barely imagine being back again. He was just a boy when he left, but still remembered many things, even though he wasn't sure how many of them were true. Or how many were just the imaginings of a child.

He remembered his father's house was a castle. The endless

hills of sand. Candy made of rosewater. Pigeon pies. The smell of camels, that burnt earth smell. And his father, Karim. Or at least, Basheer remembered the way his father was always in the shadows, watching. Watching every part of Basheer's life.

Basheer could still feel him watching. He imagined his father's praise and disapproval at every turn, although he remembered little of the man himself, his likes and dislikes. He didn't even remember how he looked. Or the smell of him. Or his strength. So when Basheer thought of his father he imagined him to be a man quite like himself. Fat, yes, he often thought, probably fat, as I am fat.

But all about Karim was not forgotten. Basheer did remember one thing very clearly. His laugh. The surprise of it. Loud. Always. Like an explosion. He remembered how it made him shake.

The last time Basheer saw his father, or remembers seeing him, Karim was sitting on the side of Basheer's bed. It was late. Karim woke him. Pressed a domino into his hand. "Your fortune can be made with this," he said. Basheer could still hear the slow ticking of a fan overhead. Could still see the blades behind his father's head. A halo.

And then his father said, "But remember there is no such thing as luck. Skill, not luck."

Karim ran a gaming house outside of the city in an oasis, on the way to the dunes of Erg Chebbi. Pink as a palace, and nearly as grand, it was built by a prince who needed a home for his concubines. Like many grand houses it was designed with a courtyard in the center, a place to call all to prayer five times a day. But the courtyard of this house was designed for amusement, not worship. It was tiled in different shades of blue. Iridescent. The tiles shimmered in the sunlight with a sunken pool in the center for bathing.

The effect was stunning. If you looked out into the courtyard, the water and the iridescent tiles seemed to be one, seemed to be a small blue sea, so blue it shamed the sky. Circling this iridescent sea was an irrigated garden of orange trees, perfectly shaped and usually blooming. In the middle of the desert.

The house was called the Water of the Moon.

When the last concubine died, the grandson of the prince inherited the house. The grandson was a man who believed in luck. Swore by it. Boasted of it. Told everyone he was the luckiest gambler on Earth. Unbeatable. He even told Karim, who smiled and then smiled again when the house became his.

Robber baron, that's how Basheer imagined his father. A robber baron living in an oasis, floating in the Water of the Moon, waiting for travelers, or new concubines, to come his way. And Basheer envied him. Or at least told himself that he did. Basheer always wore the domino his father gave him around his neck on a leather cord as a keepsake.

What will my own son remember of me? Basheer wondered as the ferry drew closer. In Marrakesh, things were not as Basheer expected. The Vichy was everywhere and there was noise, constant noise. Fat transports choked the sky, lumbered toward Algiers. And fighter planes, shrill, screamed day and night. And the explosions. So many explosions. Like feet stomping. And there was smoke everywhere. It seemed as if the desert surrounding the city was on fire. Cars and truck and motorcycles in clouds of smoke and sand.

"Rommel," everyone said, and nodded as if that one word was both the question and answer. Rommel was in the desert. Not far. Circling low.

"The Americans obviously have not arrived yet," Hélène said.

"Then we should go to my father's house," Basheer said, and the words made him sweat.

They found a guide easily enough. Despite the danger, there were many who wanted to go out into the desert. There was money to be made on both sides of the battle. Working for the Germans. And against.

"Rommel," the guide said, and opened both palms, "he brings us wonderful opportunity. Wonderful money. Like water falling."

ᔥ 29 ᔥ

PHILIPPE ARRIVED IN TWENTY MINUTES, NOT TEN. The maids had just finished cleaning. Lucienne had just finished her shower. Dried her hair and dressed.

"Grand-père called me yesterday," he says, "asked how to do a search. He wouldn't tell me what he was looking for. So I assumed it was about your mother. Thought I would take a look myself."

"He wouldn't tell you?"

"Naw. He gets weird like that sometimes. Clams up."

The boy seems guileless. He reminds Lucienne of a dog she and Ethan once had, a cocker spaniel and golden retriever mix. Smart, big, and under the mistaken assumption that he was a lap dog, he was seventy pounds of insistent love that never quite understood the meaning of "Down" or "Heel" or "No."

Lucienne opens the curtains wide. Lets the sunlight, garish and unforgiving, flood the room. She looks at Philippe's computer screen. It seems blank. She closes the curtains slightly. The words on the screen reappear.

"Anyway, I looked up your mother. Ran her name through a few search engines. Not too flattering," he says. "Now, your mother worked with the Curie family, so I began there. Narrowed it down quite a bit. The public files are limited, but I remembered a friend who has access to some personal stuff."

Lucienne leans over and looks at the computer screen. There's an e-mail with a photo attachment. It's from a Suzanne at Archives de Paris. A picture begins to take shape on the screen. "I don't know if you've seen this," he says.

The attachment seems to be a page from a family album. The Curie family. It's a photo of what appears to be a picnic. People are sitting on the grass, well dressed. Drinking wine. Eating tarts. The women wear hats. Ankles crossed. In this photo, Irène Joliot-Curie has the kind of beauty one sees in cameos, the elegant outline, sharp but sad eyes. Her daughter sits on her lap, perfect as a new doll. Frédéric, the father, looks haggard. The camera captures him not quite posed, sly eyes, running a hand through his hair.

And then there's Hélène, unmistakably Hélène, tickling a small boy. Lucienne can see that her mother is radiant and laughing. She feels a pang of jealousy. She's never known her mother to be like that with her. Happy.

Then she looks closely. There's someone who's just out of the frame, reaching in as if to rescue the toddler. He's wearing a suit, too. You can see the edge of his jacket. The thin pinstripe of the pant leg. At the bottom of the page someone has written a single sentence. The print is so small Lucienne can hardly make it out.

With Hélène Kundera. Fall 1938.

"That's all Suzanne could find in the papers," Philippe says. "But take a look at the man's hands. The one reaching into the frame."

Lucienne looks closely. "They're distinctive, aren't they?" he asks. "Elegant. Beautiful nails. They're Grand-père's. No doubt about it."

Lucienne nods. "Did you show this to your father?" she asks.

Philippe shakes his head. "He's not picking up. I left a message.

"So, here's what I'm thinking," he says. "Tomorrow you come to my house for dinner. It's Sunday. We can all talk. I just called Grand-père before I came. Told him about the picture. He did know your mother. He was just trying to protect us. He sounded so sad. I think she broke his heart."

"He agreed to talk?"

Philippe nods. "Says he'll tell us anything we want. A regular Q and A. Wants to clear the air. I think that's really healthy. About time, too."

Lucienne wonders what Dr. Assam thinks. All those years of being lied to. Maybe that's why he's not answering his phone.

"Did Vincent tell you I saw him yesterday morning?" Lucienne asks. "Right before he called you?"

"No," Philippe says, surprised. "But he was busy when I called. We didn't talk that long."

"You'd think he would have mentioned it, though."

"I'm sure we'll talk about all this tomorrow."

"And the search? Did he tell you if he found what he was looking for?"

He shakes his head. "He told me that everything would be clear tomorrow. I guess we have to wait."

Philippe writes out his address on the hotel stationery for her. "I'm sure it's nothing sinister," he says. "Sounds more like some sort of a love triangle. It's kind of sad, really."

"It is," she says.

He hands her the address. "Here you go."

She looks at it for a moment. Knows she will not go. "I was wondering," she says. "What did Vincent say exactly when you told him about the picture at the Joliet-Curies'?"

"Nothing much," Philippe says. Then rethinks. "Oh yeah, wait. He said something about Kipling. *The Jungle Book*. When I told him about the picture he said, 'That was the day Mowgli joined the human world.' I didn't remember it as a quote from the book, but maybe it is."

"I have no idea," she says.

"We'll find out tomorrow, I guess. By the way," he says, "you should probably eat before you come. My wife has to be the worst cook in all of Paris."

⚘ 30 ⚘

FLAT. FLAT. FLAT. WITH SMALL BLACK STONES. Seas of stones, not sand, but stones. Round and smooth. No sand. Just stones. In the distance, far away in the distance, the Erg Chebbi. A thin mountain of sand, slicing the sky. But that was in the distance. Far away. Barely visible. Underneath the camels' twin toes there were round stones. Black. Blinding. Tricking the eye. Their nails clicked. Everything seemed dark, but it was early morning. The camels, their doe eyes, rocked back and forth. Hélène was seasick and dizzy.

Basheer prayed. Under his breath. Not out of fear, but awe. He was overwhelmed by the sight of the black blanket of stones, the tall sand mountain in the distance. He'd dreamt of these things for so many years, he came to believe that they did not exist. And here they were. Basheer had not prayed in his native tongue for so long, tears ran down his face. Allah. I am home.

Soon, like a mirage, like a memory, like a dream, wavering, the Water of the Moon began to take shape on the horizon.

"Ahead. Ahead," the guide barked, and slapped the sides of each camel with a whip. They snorted, huffed, and trotted just a little faster.

As they came closer, Basheer could see that the pink walls were now worn white. But the oasis was still there, still winding its way along the edge of it all. Still verdant. Still blindingly green. But it was now, also, a junkyard of sorts. At the foot of the waterfall, a burned jeep. A dozen or more tents, still rolled, tossed like stones. And nose down, leaning against the garden wall, was an airplane, a U.S. Army Recon, painted the color of sand. Above it all palm trees stood still as a witness.

"Welcome to the war," the guide said.

And then they heard it. Rhythmic. Hypnotizing. The sound of men singing. Tone upon tone, spinning out across the sea of black rocks. Spinning out in praise, in love. Spinning out and back again.

The camels stopped outside the gates. The sound made them afraid. They refused to go any farther. "Ata Allah, God's gift," the guide said to them lovingly, and stroked the rough necks, the coconut hides, but they wouldn't move.

Basheer and Hélène were forced to walk the last few feet alone. He helped Hélène down and held her, his hands on her shoulders, for a moment, afraid to let go. She could see it in his eyes. "You are home," she said.

"I think I may be."

Inside the gates of the grand house, in the blue of the courtyard, the walls and water were still intense. More blue than the sky. Around the brilliant pool, men, a dozen or more in black robes, were spinning like tops. Slowly, at first. To the right. To the right. Their hats, tall and white, like pillars of salt. Their black robes, black as the tomb, unfurled like storms, then fell to the ground. One by one. Underneath, they wore dresses of pure white, voluminous skirts.

"Dervishes," Basheer whispered.

It was as if they were lotus blossoms spinning in the deep blue of the sea. Hélène was amazed at the beauty of it. In the corner of the courtyard, there were two musicians sitting cross-legged under the blooming orange trees, their delicate air. One man kept the rhythm with a drum. A heartbeat, too fast. Then too slow. One played a reed flute. Thin and eerie. Hélène found herself pulled into the moment, the rhythm of the music, the chants, men spinning faster and faster. Their ecstasy. Still seasick, she leaned into Basheer.

"Dervish means 'doorway,'" he said. "They are the gatekeepers of paradise."

"Well done," a voice behind them said. Booming and dark. And they turned.

"Even the sacred must find shelter in war. Rommel and the British have scattered these priests across the desert."

Karim, she thought. The likeness was unmistakable. Barrel-chested, but not fat. A bulldog of a man.

A look of surprise, then joy, came over the old man's face. He took Basheer into his massive arms. Kissed both cheeks.

"I am sorry, my son, for what has separated us," he said.

My son, Basheer thought, and the words sounded so strange. He had not been someone's son in such a long time.

"My son is gone," Basheer said, and for the first time, he understood what his father had gone though. The pain of losing a son, even if he is not your blood, is deep and immeasurable. The small fist of his hand around your finger is not easily forgotten.

And so, the two men held each other for a long time. Weeping.

31

AFTER PHILIPPE LEFT, LUCIENNE CALLED THE SALON. Vincent didn't sound surprised to hear her voice.

"This evening we can meet behind Notre Dame," he said. "There's a garden there. A memorial garden. On the east end of the Île de la Cité. Do you know where that is?"

"Why can't we just meet at the salon?"

"Too many people working late. Holiday orders."

In the background she can hear what sounds like dozens of sewing machines. The whir and hum of them.

"Where is this place?" she asks.

"Take the Métro at Saint-Michel or Cité, on the island itself; or as I do, from the Métro at the Hôtel de Ville—crossing the place and the Pont d'Arcole. It's very simple. I live nearby. Just go to

Notre Dame and you can find it. It closes at seventeen hundred hours. I'll be there slightly before."

"Isn't there a restaurant somewhere? I'd rather meet in a restaurant," she says, uneasy, but he's already hung up.

32

AT SUNSET, BASHEER AND HIS FATHER PRAYED together in the courtyard. Kneeling. They were wearing traditional robes, sand-colored and full, which caught the cool evening breezes like sails. The iridescent blue sea of tiles, like shimmering water, surrounded them. From the balcony of the apartment, Hélène could hear the music of their voices. A harmony. The call and reply of faith. She had never seen Basheer pray before. It made her feel even more alone.

Home, she thought. He is finally home.

In the distance she could see the sun slip over the Erg Chebbi and cast the dune in the color of blood. She could hear the roar of Rommel. The growling, low and dark. But that was in the distance. All around her, the heat of the day was quickly fading. She felt cold. Stepped from the balcony into the large bedroom, reserved for guests. The canopy of the bed was silk. And the sheets. It was difficult not to feel like one of the prince's concubines. Her skin smelled of almond oil. As did her hair. Selua, the oldest of Karim's three wives, had oiled her long hair into a waterfall of waves.

A convoy of planes rumbled overhead.

Selua was a creased woman of uncertain age. Slow. Hunched. She spoke no French and went about her work with the silence of a monk. She covered the wound on the top of Hélène's head with a lock of hair. Held it in place with an ivory comb. Laid out a caftan for Hélène to wear. It was the color of apricots. Embroidered around the neck and arms. A matching scarf for her head. They were both silk and elegant, but old. Fragile.

Selua had helped Hélène dress. Fastened thick gold earrings to each ear. Around her neck, Selua placed a matching neckpiece inlaid with topaz, the color of clarified butter. It was beautiful. And heavy. When she was finished, she placed the silk scarf around Hélène's head. It covered everything. The jewels. Her beautiful hair. The ivory comb.

"No," Hélène said, "I don't need to hide anymore," even though she knew Selua did not speak French. Then Hélène unwrapped the silk scarf, and shook her hair until it cascaded down her back again.

Selua slammed the door behind her.

When the bells rang for dinner, Hélène decided that she didn't want to eat with Selua and the other women. Selua was sullen. Karim's other wives were thin and wound around each other like snakes. Not one of the women spoke French. They laughed only to themselves. So, Hélène decided to eat with Basheer and his father.

In the dining room. It wasn't until she arrived that she understood what a mistake she had made. She was not expected. Or, perhaps, even allowed.

The room was filled with men. A dozen or more sitting along a plank table and the rest were cross-legged in clusters on the floor. When she walked in, she heard a great clatter of voices and laughter. Then all fell silent. Completely silent. It took a moment for Hélène's eyes to adjust. She could see Basheer and Karim at the end of the long table. Both dressed in ornate robes. They looked like sultans, she thought. Hair oiled perfectly. Eyes shining. Bookends. They were watching her. The other men, too. Some hissed. Some just looked shocked. Without the scarf on her head, she was naked to them. It was a sign of disrespect. Madame Assam had told her that, but she'd forgotten.

"I'm sorry," she said, though no one seemed to understand.

Karim stood and took her hand. "In the desert we do things differently," he chided, but didn't seem angry, just concerned. Then said something in Arabic to the men and they went back to their eating.

"What did you say?" she asked.

"I reminded them that all is allowed in the desert as long as we are under the roof," he pointed to the ceiling. It was painted with clouds. "As long as Allah does not see."

"I'm sorry," she said.

"Sit. Sit," he said, graciously. "Tonight, you will be our queen."

He poured her a cup of mint tea, never took his eyes off her. Then filled Basheer's cup and poured his own. Karim watched her so closely, she felt uneasy. Then he took her hand in his.

"We are cosmopolitan here. Welcoming of those who do not know our customs," he said. "I often entertain the French, at least before Rommel came. Now, the Germans. The Italians. All come and all are welcome."

His hand was hot. She felt herself begin to shake apart again. She couldn't stop thinking about the moment she walked into the room. The men all staring at her. Hélène pulled back her hand away from Karim and wiped it on her gown. It didn't feel clean.

"Forgive me," Karim said. "Forgive me my rudeness. You see with your hair oiled. And her jewels. And her gown. I cannot see you for the memory of her."

Madame Assam, she thought.

"I am sorry if I have made you uncomfortable. It was not my intent."

His French was perfect. Courtly. Basheer, dressed in his father's robes, offered Hélène a plate filled with a salad of sliced oranges and cracked olives.

"You should eat something," he said. "You look pale."

Hélène looked from father to son and back again. The resemblance was remarkable.

"I'd like a cigarette instead," she said, and left the room.

A few minutes later, Basheer found her in the courtyard by the pool washing her hand over and over again in the cool water. The silk of the old gown was wet and heavy. It looked golden in the moonlight.

"Do you have a cigarette?" she asked.

He took one out and lit it for her. "He's gone, Hélène. Vincent is gone."

She didn't answer. Basheer put a hand on her shoulder. She was shaking. "You're cold."

She took a long drag on the cigarette. She felt herself shake even harder. Above, the stars and planets hung low like ripe fruit. Venus. Then the blue-white Regulus, "the heart of the lion," as it is sometimes called, the brightest star in the constellation Leo. On that night it shone so clear, like a bowl of diamonds, she thought. But the slender crescent moon was the most brilliant of all sights. Cradled in the thin hook of it, there was a ghostly outline of a full moon. It was a trick of the light, of course. It was the Earth reflecting sunlight, fooling the eye. But it was still very beautiful. The new moon and the old seemingly joined together for just a moment in time.

Basheer said, "You are not this woman. You are not a woman who is afraid."

But she ignored the comment.

"Do you see this overhead?" she asked. "The stars? The moon?"

He looked above him at the stars, so brilliant and low, and the crescent moon. "Amazing," he said. "It looks as if an old moon is cradled in the new moon's arms."

Basheer sat down next to her on the edge of the iridescent pool. For a long time they said nothing, just held each other's hands shyly and did not speak.

I am home, he thought.

I will miss you, she thought.

❧ 33 ❧

LUCIENNE ENTERS HER MOTHER'S ROOM. THE VENTILATOR is back, taped into her mouth.

"Another stroke," Dr. Belliard says. The tests have also come back, she explains. The CAT scans show a long history of damage. "Months of strokes."

A vegetative state. That's the diagnosis. Lucienne says nothing. There's really no reason to speak. Words rust.

"I'll leave you alone," the doctor says. The door swings shut. It takes a moment for Lucienne to realize that she is standing perfectly still. Not running. Her heart beats as if she is running. She's breathing hard and shallow, as if. She sweats, as if. But she is not. I am standing perfectly still, she thinks, but doesn't believe it.

Outside in the hall, she can hear the soft shoes of nurses. The metal wheels of a cart. She can hear it, muffled, through the closed door. Then it fades. It all fades away.

Vegetative, she thinks. Everything around her seems to slowly blur.

And then she feels it. The darkness. Again. Familiar. The black hole. It's not like a dream this time, or a vision, or madness. She feels it for what it is, a void left by a dying star; swallowing her and everything in her world.

A void, not in space, but in her own heart.

Lucienne pulls back the bleached blanket and climbs into the bed next to Hélène. She puts her head in the crook of her mother's arm. The arm is cold. Doesn't matter. Lucienne buries her head in her mother's neck as she had always done as a child, before her mother went away. She gently wraps a leg across her mother's small frail body. The ventilator hisses. The monitors beep and hum. She pulls the blanket back over them both. She can feel her mother's heartbeat.

Lucienne closes her eyes. Wants to remember what it was like being suspended, floating in the darkness of her mother's womb. Her heartbeat, thunderous. The rest of the world, a murmur, as if behind a door. But can't. She feels tired, so tired.

"I'm not afraid," she says, and kisses her mother's neck, as she once did on the Mesa when she was a girl and they watched the storm, angry and red, roll in. Lucienne gently lifts her mother's long hair from around the pillow, places it over the two of them, a shroud. It no longer smells of Chanel and cigarettes, but of Betadine.

"I'm not afraid."

She holds her mother closer, until they are both tangled in the wires and tubes. And cries.

❧ 34 ❧

WHEN THE AMERICANS FINALLY CAME TO NORTH Africa it was well after the fall of Paris. The Vichy government had already been set in place in all the French colonies. Field Marshal Erwin Rommel had already arrived. The Desert Fox, as he was known, was a brilliant tactician. His Deutsches Afrikakorps were a deadly, elite group.

Slowly, very slowly, the Americans came to Africa in 1941. To evaluate. To consider. To weigh the chances of the Allied Forces winning a desert war against the Fox. At first, they arrived, just a few at a time, in lumbering planes the color of sand. They flew only in the hours before dawn. Flew low, so low that if they passed overhead the night sky would suddenly seem as if it were filled with dark clouds churning. Thunder waiting for spark. Then all would be clear.

They came in planes like the Nighthawk. Long range, low flying, with a glass-enclosed cockpit that looked more like a hothouse than it did the nose of a plane. On some, there was painted a small emblem of a skeleton wearing a tuxedo and silk hat. He was riding in an open cockpit. Smoking a cigar. Twirling a revolver.

Just a little bit of home.

When the Americans finally came, they came John Wayne silent. Needed remote locations where they could land and take off without being seen. The Water of the Moon was perfect. Isolated. Far away from any city of any size. And for a price, Karim welcomed all. It became a destination of sorts.

A few days before Basheer and Hélène had arrived an Army Recon tried to land at the Water of the Moon in the thick of a sandstorm. The plane was out of fuel and luck. The pilot miscalculated and slammed into the desert. Nose first. Howling.

When the storm was over, Karim looked for survivors, but there were none. The airplane's nose had folded in on itself. The pilot was crushed upon impact. The cargo seemed to be an odd mix of things. A few bags of mail. Cases of American cigarettes. And a machine that made dry ice.

The day after Basheer and Hélène arrived, Karim gave them a tour of the wreckage.

"What would they want with dry ice in the desert?" he asked his son. Basheer shrugged.

"Probably seeding clouds to make rain," Hélène said. "Rain in the desert would give the Allies an interesting advantage against the Germans."

"Does that work?" Karim asked.

"In theory," Hélène said. "Everything works in theory."

Two days later, Lieutenant Buddy Fisher landed his Nighthawk alongside the Water of the Moon. The lieutenant was part of the "look see," as he called the intelligence effort. He had a farm-bred freckled face, too fair for the desert sun. Tall and thin. Eyes like the prairie, open and endless.

Even though he didn't know the pilot, the downed plane had been under his command. The lieutenant came as soon as the storm let up, but knew in his heart he'd be too late. And he was. Everything in the airplane was already gone. The cigarettes. The mail. The dry ice machine. Even the watch on the dead man's wrist. Karim had been very busy.

Lieutenant Buddy Fisher wasn't surprised. He knew things had a way of disappearing in the desert. And he also figured the pilot was dead. The lieutenant had heard the mayday call; the boy's last words were, "I'm spinning into the mouth of hell."

So, all the lieutenant expected to find at the Water of the Moon was a set of dog tags to send home to the boy's parents and a body that needed to be buried. He didn't expect to find Hélène.

She was dressed in a caftan, her head covered. She spoke little English. "To America," she said, and tapped herself on the chest. "Please."

The lieutenant had no idea what Hélène was talking about. He spoke no French. But when she showed him the packet of letters that Frédéric gave her, the name Curie caught his eye.

"X rays? Right?"

Hélène took the scarf from around her head and nodded.

"You know anything about radar?" he asked.

"Radiation, yes?"

"You bet. Loads of it."

She let the silk scarf fall to the ground.

Thirty hours later, Hélène, wearing the night-blue dress

Basheer gave her, climbed aboard Lieutenant Buddy Fisher's Nighthawk. She was going to South Africa, to the military outpost on Robben Island, to help work the radar and wait until it was safe to travel out of Africa.

Radar uses microwave radiation to detect objects. Hélène understood how it worked. The lieutenant was relieved that she agreed to come. The radar outpost worried him. The South African Special Signals Services Unit had just recently come into being and was still in the process of setting up a series of coastal stations with radar sets. The unit was seriously understaffed and had been forced to recruit local college women to operate the facilities. If anything broke down, it stayed down for quite a while. It was dangerous.

When Hélène said she thought she could help, he almost kissed her.

"You can stay in Cape Town until we get your security clearance," he told her. "Shouldn't take long. We've got some AT&T fellows in a special unit laying down land lines for phones. The lines scatter transmissions over an entire block of the spectrum. Germans can't figure it out. We'll have a secure line to Washington by the end of the week."

"*Sprechen Sie Deutsches?*" he asked tentatively.

Hélène smiled and nodded, relieved. She spoke German quite well. Most in Prague did, since Germany was so close and the language so similar.

"That's good," he said in German. "Seems like it's the only language we have in common these days. Know your enemy and smoke him out."

Then he radioed ahead to Robben Island.

When Hélène told Basheer she was leaving, he didn't seem to be surprised, just saddened.

"I'll miss you," he said simply. It was not a plea for her to stay, just a statement of fact. But it was true and she could feel it.

"I know," she said.

They were standing in the concrete outbuilding where Karim had hidden the dry-ice machine. The gas generator whined and filled the air with thick smoke.

"Let me show you why I have to leave," she said and she took a hammer and smashed an iridescent tile from the courtyard into a dozen pieces. "It's radioactive. That's why it shines. Cobalt glass, some pottery, the faces of watches. All radioactive."

She'd asked Basheer to assemble the rest of the needed equipment. Alcohol from the medical kit. An old glass jar. A bit of velvet.

"Now, watch this," she said, and poured alcohol into the jar. Shook. Drained it. Then added the broken bits of blue tile. Stretched the velvet across the lid. Turned it all upside down in a pan filled with dry ice.

"You have to be careful of the ice, it burns," she said, and suddenly a fog of vapor began to billow from the tray, mix with the exhaust from the generator. The room was soon filled with gray clouds.

"We'll asphyxiate ourselves," Basheer said.

Hélène laughed. "Put your hand on the jar. It's called a cloud chamber. You like stars, don't you?"

"I like them in the sky. In my hand, I'm not so sure."

"Just watch," she said, and put her hand over his.

Hélène and Basheer stood like that, quite still, for five, then ten minutes, watching the jar intently. It was difficult to see. The room was filled with clouds. Then suddenly it happened. A spark. First one. Then another. Soon, it seemed as if the room were filled with stars. Shooting stars. The fury of alpha particles, relatively heavy, spun past them in dense straight trails. Beta particles, too light, left trails that spun, wispy, like locks of hair, curling and uncurling in sharp winds. It was as if Hélène and Basheer were standing inside of clouds, dodging falling stars.

"Uranium fission," she said. "Frédéric once said it was the most beautiful phenomenon in the world."

The stars spun around her head. Through her hair.

"Beautiful," Basheer said. "But not the most beautiful."

And then he leaned across the jar and kissed her. And she leaned into it.

The next morning, Hélène was gone.

❧ 35 ❧

THE GARDEN BEHIND NOTRE DAME IS NOT difficult to find. Nor, for that matter, is Notre Dame. But the garden is not what Lucienne expected. It's not a garden in the usual sense.

Its formal name is the Memorial of the Deportation, that much she can tell from the sign. A memorial garden. There's also a plaque in French that's difficult for Lucienne to translate:

> *Pour que vivent les souvenirs des deux cent mille Français sombrés dans la nuit et le brouillard exterminés dans les camps Nazis.*

Something about those who were caught up in the same "night and fog" as the French. She knows the word "fog" by heart now. From the newspaper. It seems to be a constant in the recent weather report. And then, of course, there's the word "Nazi." Such an odd word, she thinks. Nazi. So much memory associated with it that no one wants to hear it spoken. It leaves a metallic taste on the tongue.

Lucienne doesn't want to go through the gate, but she does. He's waiting. He may have already left. Her sides hurt from running. She's been running flat out since she left the Métro. The back of her shirt is wet. She's breathing hard. Her sensible shoes have rubbed her feet raw.

The nurse found her sleeping in her mother's arms.

"It is very difficult to let go," she whispered to Lucienne. Pulled her gently from the bed as one does a sleeping child.

And so Lucienne ran, and kept on running. To the Métro. From the Métro to here. And now that she's here, she wants to run again. She didn't expect this at all. The garden is a courtyard made of low concrete walls. Grim. No fountain. No flowers. A trellis of black iron that looks like barbed wire. A long, narrow stairway, going down. No one else seems to be around except for a guard who watches her closely.

"Go," he says, and gestures to the stairs. He's clean shaven as stone.

The steps are narrow. Squeezed and dark. Claustrophobic. Lucienne takes them carefully. All she can see is a small concrete chamber in front of her and the sky above.

"Vincent?"

The coo of pigeons overhead. Then ruffling. An echo.

She looks behind her, up the stairs. Nothing. Not Vincent. Not the guard. The walls seem to converge. It's difficult for Lucienne to keep her balance. The thin stairway is damp and slick. One foot slips slightly. Then the other. Her heart beats in her neck. Above her she can see that the sky is growing dark. The sun must be setting. She runs her hands along the walls. They're rough, grate her skin. There are two flights of this. Walls burrowing into the earth. She feels as if she's buried in a history she knows nothing about.

When she finally reaches the bottom of the stairs, the sky is dark above her. There's a round plaque in the floor. She thinks it says something like, "They went into the mouth of the earth and did not return."

Ahead, there's a long tunnel of crystals, lit from behind. Thousands of crystals. Tunneled into the earth. A heaven's worth, she thinks and then notices that the walls that surround her are covered in names, lists of names. Organized. She runs her finger down the lists. There are thousands of names, as many as there are lights, she thinks. Looks for the name Assam, like the tea. And it's there.

Manon Assam.

Not suicide at all, she thinks, and suddenly knows Vincent's not coming. Knows where he is. Knows it too late, but still she runs.

✤ 36 ✤

IN JULY, THE WHALES CAME TO ROBBEN Island by the hundreds, churning the water with graceful fury. It was always the same kind of whale, the Southern Right. *Eubalaena australis*. Ancient and huge, not sleek. Mottled. Their fat bodies leapt out of the ocean. Perfect arches, seeming to defy gravity. Then they did it again. Slapped the water with their tails, blew.

That first July, there were 264 whales. At least, that's what Hélène counted. Two hundred sixty-four who, at night, would moan in chorus, low and trembling. It made the walls vibrate. Chipped the china.

Hélène didn't complain, though. The whales' noisy migration made it nearly impossible to think about anything else. During whale season, she hardly ever thought about how hopeless the war seemed. How underfunded and understaffed the base on the island was. How brutal the weather: violent and gray. She never thought about the sharks, either. How schools of sharks always circled the island, all teeth and misery. Never thought of the jagged shoreline with the small white crosses bearing the names of loved ones who got too close.

Hélène never thought of any of these things during whale season. She just stood on the cliff and watched the whales, their enormous ballet. Watched the winds, constant and high, carry the small white crosses out to sea where the memory of love turned to salt.

And, of course, during whale season she never really thought about Basheer. Not really. Never really thought about his theory of dust and the souls of stars. Never thought about the shadow of him, the comfort. She liked whale season best of all.

In May 1941, Robben Island was a small jutting rock on the Cape of Storms overrun with seals and deer, ostrich and rabbits, and penguins who paced up and down the shoreline, aimless and hungry, squawking.

And there were also lightning storms as furious as any madness.

There was a town of sorts, surrounded by the broken teeth of the houses that belonged to natives who still lived on the island. And a stone fortress that had been part of the old leper colony, in its basement a makeshift dormitory with blacked-out windows where Hélène and the others slept in thin bunk beds. The island also had a lighthouse, not in service because of the war. And an old church with peeling paint that flaked like snow in high winds. And the radar building, camouflaged in gray and moss to blend in with the cliffs.

And that was all. No schools. No cafés. Nothing.

"Everything eventually gets swept into the sea," the commander of the radar group told Hélène when she first arrived. She could see it was true. It seemed to be the only reason why one was sent to Robben Island. To be swept away. Out of sight. Since the Dutch came to South Africa, the island had been a prison of one sort or another. Home to dissenters, then lunatics, then lepers.

No one came to the island for pleasure. There was no reason. Most of the year, it was dangerous and bleak. The few natives who lived there were the children of guards and lepers. They, like everyone else, worked for the war effort. Spent their days perched on cliffs, searching the skies for the enemy.

When Hélène arrived on Robben Island in 1941, radar was still primitive, used two cathode-ray tubes. That's all. One for distance. A second to pinpoint the direction. Both were inaccurate. So, whenever it looked as if a plane was approaching the coastline, someone would have to run outside and "take a visual" to determine if the plane was actually approaching and if, indeed, it was an enemy craft.

It made for long stressful days. Longer nights. If they were wrong and misidentified a plane or frigate or destroyer—or missed one altogether—lives could be lost. Including their own.

Commander Adam Wilkenson headed up the radar group. He was an academic who had no military experience; the title was honorary. His field was science. Tall and fatherly, he was fond of saying, "It is very important to me that my girls should be happy." He made sure his "girls" always had butter, something that was difficult to find on the mainland, and games, like Chinese checkers, and plenty of American movie magazines with glamorous stars in USO poses.

"Anything to relieve the grind," he'd say, and try his best to make them all happy with regular weekend passes to Cape Town, weather permitting, for co-ed dances at the Services Club with big band music and American Coca-Cola. But none of it interested Hélène.

Even though she was about the same age as the other women who worked the radar, she made no close friends. Barely spoke to any of them. To her, these women of the Special Signals Services Unit, these college girls, seemed much younger, frivolous, more interested in their clothes and men and the impossibility of army-issue underwear, which they called "passion killers," than the work of war.

So she kept her distance. Dreamt of fission. Tried not to think of Basheer at all. After a time, she found herself becoming increasingly afraid. Easily startled. Worn down.

The enemy. That's what it was. The enemy wore her down. In the months, then years, since the war began Hélène had gradually become consumed by the idea of the enemy. Not Hitler. Or the SS. Or the "Desert Rat" Rommel. When Hélène thought of the enemy, she thought again of those faces in the Paris Opéra. They were all watching *La Bohème*, Puccini's bohemians, as she was. Those faces so much like hers.

Then she'd think of her father. Then Vincent. How they were the enemy, at least to her. She'd think of how quickly their love turned to violence. How deep the violence was. How dark. How is it possible? she wondered over and over again. Tried to make sense of it, to find logic in violence, a cause, a root, but couldn't.

The more Hélène thought about it, the more the thought possessed her. She began to search everywhere for the enemy, just to see his face. To examine it closely. Look for clues. She wandered the cliffs at night. The caves at low tide. The beaches where the tiny crosses were planted. She worked days without sleep, wild-eyed, her heart beating furiously and trapped. It became all she thought of. The focus of her life.

In December 1943, more than two years after Hélène arrived, Lieutenant Buddy Fisher, now Lieutenant Colonel Buddy Fisher, took the tiny ferry, the *Issy,* from Cape Town to the island for a "look see," as he still called it. Commander Wilkenson had asked him to come. Wanted to talk about the new radar system Hélène had set up. Wanted to talk about Hélène, too. The lieutenant colonel had left her in Wilkenson's care and promised to return for her when passage from Africa was secure. Two years ago. I can't believe I forgot, Fisher thought when he heard her name again.

Thin as air, he thought when he first saw her. She was in the radar room working. Leaning over a map. Mumbling something to herself. Her hands shook a bit. She didn't even notice when he walked into the room. The change in Hélène was striking, especially in contrast to the other women around her who were perfectly military, sat upright in their crisp uniforms, with regulation length hair. Their shoes were brightly polished. Their brass buttons shone.

Hélène, on the other hand, looked like what she was. A refugee from war. Her long dark hair hung limp to her waist. Her night-blue dress had faded to dusty gray.

"How are you?" he asked, and touched her shoulder lightly. "It's me. Buddy Fisher. Lieutenant Colonel—"

Hélène kept on working. Didn't look up.

"Busy," she said.

"I don't know if you remember me—"

"I do. Go away."

He went away confused.

"We're all a little under pressure," Commander Wilkenson

later told him, and had nothing but praise for Hélène's work. She'd modified the tracking process with the addition of more tubes and an elaborate rigging system.

"Quite a boon," he said. Then looked uneasy.

"But?"

"Well, some of the girls are afraid of her. She doesn't fit in too well."

Early the next morning, before dawn, Fisher found Hélène standing watch on the cliffs overlooking the harbor. The port was filled with a large convoy of Allied ships at anchor.

"You can leave tomorrow," he told her. "We can finally get you out, it's safe enough. I've arranged for passage on the convoy. In a month or two, you'll be with Fermi and the rest in America."

"Sorry it took so long," he said.

He was amazed at how easy it was to make the arrangements. The army seemed very eager to have her come. Anxious, almost.

"That is," he said, "if you still want to go."

Hélène said nothing, watched the ships intently. There were two dozen or more, their decks filled with hundreds of soldiers, all leaning over the rails, smoking, watching the sunrise. All the men leaned the same way, toward the leeward side. The ships leaned, too. Guns at the ready.

"You all right?" the lieutenant colonel asked.

Hélène turned and looked at him closely. His face was deeply burned. Cracked. No longer farm-freckled, but eroded. His green eyes clouded, not clear.

"Are you?" she asked.

The question surprised him. He thought about it a moment. "Probably not," he finally said.

Behind them, over the mountains, they could hear the faint

sound of children singing. A dozen or more voices, sweet and pure. They were too far away to hear clearly, the words were difficult to understand, but the melody was joyous. Infectious.

"What's that?" he asked.

"Natives," she said. "Children of the lepers. They stand watch during the day on these cliffs."

"It's a beautiful song," he said.

"They sing it all the time."

Hélène and the lieutenant colonel listened for a moment to the children's singing. The air was cool. The morning, calm. The sun rose slowly through a sky streaked with rose and amber and the delicate pink of a shell. Below them, in the harbor, hundreds of men stood in battle dress, watching. They were all leaning toward the sun.

"Have you ever wondered who the enemy really is?" Hélène asked. "If they're really any different from us?"

"No," he said sadly. "I just shoot who they tell me to."

And the voices grew closer. "What are they singing?" he asked. "It's Zulu, isn't it?"

She nodded. "We are all one," she said. "All one."

The sunrise was fading. The men below in the harbor turned, one by one, back to their duties. The ships righted themselves.

On the cliff, Fisher and Hélène could see the children clearly now. Some of them were dark as smooth stones. Some pink as the sunrise. Some without fingers. Some without toes. Some as perfect as porcelain.

"One heart," they sang. "One soul."

The next day Hélène left the island with the song still running through her head.

37

THE NURSES ARE ALL BUSY WITH DINNER trays. Vincent remembers their routine from the times he came to meet Basheer after work. That's why he chose this time. Saline feeds the comatose. So there is no dinner tray for Hélène. He knew he'd be safe. He could slip into her room unnoticed. So he does.

He is surprised to see how much she has changed in just three nights. Not even a week. How much smaller she seems. Her face is now child-sweet, beautiful in a way he has never seen. No threats. No anger.

His hands sweat.

"Can you hear me?" he asks, leaning over her. Doesn't expect an answer. The ventilator is still taped to her mouth.

"I'm sorry," he says, and takes her hand, an awkward stranger. Kisses it tenderly. His face feels hot.

"I only wanted to sit with you again. To hold you. To see your face once more."

When he read that she was coming to appear at the Institut, he sent her the photograph his father had taken of them. No return address. He wanted it to be a mystery. He knew Hélène always loved a good mystery. As all scientists do.

Vincent wanted to say he was sorry for the past, but he didn't know how. It all felt too enormous. So, he sent the photo to Hélène in care of the Institut, and hoped she would find him and that when they saw each other again, he'd know what to say. Perhaps, the spark between them would return. All would be forgiven.

But when Vincent saw Hélène standing outside the salon, the lights of the courtyard illuminating her from behind like a Madonna, like an apparition, like a dream, he found himself speechless. It was difficult to believe that she was really there. After all those years. She had come back to him.

The small hollow taps of her knock nearly made his heart stop.

"I have never stopped loving you," he said.

Hélène hadn't even taken off her coat. He quickly poured two glasses of champagne, just as he had planned. His hands trembled.

"It's a lovely wine," he said, and noticed that her skin had the texture of dried roses. Its faded hue, still beautiful in its own right. Perhaps even more so, he thought. Turned delicate by age.

But the glasses sat on the table, untouched. Her face was white with anger.

"You told the Germans—" she said.

"I had no choice—"

"Manon. Madame Assam. They had even less—"

This was not what Vincent expected at all.

Think. Think. Think.

He snapped off the lights.

"What are you doing?" she said.

"You loved me once."

"I loved who I thought you were. The man who loved Kipling because he was a boy raised by wolves. A boy swept into the sea."

It was then that Vincent realized the one thing that would change her mind about him. The one thing Hélène would understand.

"A boy swept away, like Basheer?" he said, nearly whispering. "Basheer the son, not the father."

She took a sharp breath. He knew she was listening.

"He is alive. I raised him as my own. Loved him as if he were my own son. And he loves me."

In the darkened room, Vincent could hear Hélène's breathing, quick and shallow as a bird.

"He's a good man," he said quietly. Had her attention. "He's the doctor I always wanted to be. Respected. Runs the emergency room at the hospital near the café.

"You remember the café, don't you?" he asked, and hoped for at least a moment that she remembered it as their café. Would remember it fondly. But Hélène said nothing.

"I am not an evil man," he said. "Not everyone can be a hero. Please tell me you forgive me."

She remained silent.

At first Vincent thought, perhaps, she didn't hear him. Or didn't understand. But she did. Hélène had thought the boy Basheer was dead long ago. As soon as she heard his name, she imagined he'd grown up to be a man quite like the Basheer she knew. His kind heart. His faithful love. The memory of it made her dizzy. She held her head in her hands for a moment. It was at that moment that Hélène decided. I'm too tired, she thought. Too tired to remember anymore. Too tired for everything.

Vincent slapped on the lights. The sight of Hélène, head down, sobbing, made his stomach turn. "I'm sorry," he said, and was sorry for it all. For losing her. For what he did to Basheer. "I was a different man than I am now. Being a father changed me. I've learned courage from my son. And compassion. And love, real love."

Hélène looked up at Vincent; his once handsome face was now deeply etched by time and longing. The boy had been alive all these years, she thought. Could have been with his father. And mother. If not for me.

It overwhelmed her.

"Could I have a glass of water?" she said, and felt so tired.

"There's champagne," he said. Please forgive me, he thought.

She shook her head. "It's so late." The clock behind her read nearly midnight. "Just a cup of water. I'm very thirsty."

"Of course," he said, and went into the workroom.

Hélène opened up her purse and took out a bottle of sleeping pills. I'm sorry, Basheer, she thought and thought of them in the horrible hotel in Marseilles waiting for Manon and Madame Assam, who were probably already dead. Hélène poured half the pills into her hand. Then placed them in her mouth.

I am too tired, she thought, and drank the champagne. Then swallowed the rest of the pills. Made sure she took them all.

When Vincent returned with the water, Hélène was gone. The bottle of pills lay empty on the table. She'd run down the street. It was raining hard. He tried to run after her, but couldn't see her in the foggy night. Taxis hovered for tourists. She jumped into the first one that came along.

Not much time. All she had was twenty minutes, more or less. She knew that. Only twenty minutes before she would slip into unconsciousness.

Now, outside of Hélène's room, Vincent hears the voices of nurses.

"I'm sorry," he whispers.

The squeaking wheels of the food cart. The lid lifted off a plate. The door opens a crack. Light pushes its way in. He blinks. Doesn't move. Doesn't breathe.

"*Non*," he hears one say. "This one is dying. IV."

Dying, he thinks. The word sounds so peaceful. The door closes again.

Vincent sits down on the bed next to Hélène. Kisses her forehead. Watches her face for a reaction. Nothing. Her eyes are closed. Perfectly still. Everything about her is perfectly still, except for her chest, which moves ever so slightly up and down. "A vegetative state," Basheer had told him.

He knows he can't leave her like this. Half in and half out of the world. He can't because he still loves her. Always has. He leans over her again. Kisses her cheek. First the left. Then the right. As is the custom when one says good-bye.

Then gently pulls the tape from around her mouth.

First one strip.

Then the other.

A slight tug.

"We loved each other so much," he says. And then, gently, very gently, he removes the respirator from her mouth. Puts it in his pocket.

"I've never forgotten. Even if you have."

Her heart stops beating.

He opens the window. An alarm goes off. Shrill and screaming. But he is calm. The night air is cool. Sweeter than ever before.

A nurse, Dr. Belliard, who was leaving for the night, and Dr. Assam, who was just about to start his shift, rush in.

And Vincent jumps.

38

LOS ALAMOS WASN'T AT ALL WHAT HÉLÈNE had expected. She was only twenty-four years old when she arrived on the top of the Mesa, thirty-five miles from Santa Fe, not far from the muddy Rio Grande. It was April 1944. The view was breathtaking. Behind her were the Sangre de Cristo Mountains. At sunset, they were awash in violet light. Ahead, the settlement. Fifty-three thousand acres. A makeshift city devoted to metallurgical research, at least that's what Enrico Fermi had called it. That's what he told the two hundred scientists he brought to the site. They were going to do research for the war effort. Make feasible a new power source. The word "bomb" was never used.

The word "gadget," however, was a particular favorite.

Once past the heavily guarded gate, inside the barbed-wire fence, Los Alamos was more like a prison than a city. There was a seemingly endless series of corrugated metal tubes, or "hutmets" as they were called, metal huts, living quarters, stuck in the mud. A few rickety houses with tar-paper siding. A handful of apartment buildings that seemed lopsided, sunk under their own weight. Dormitories, squat and squalid. Rusty trailers. Laundry hung on clotheslines everywhere. No gardens. Just dogs running in circles. Trash cans overflowing.

At the center of the enormous site was the old Los Alamos Ranch School complex. Lovely and ramshackle. Calm and orderly. A different world. The school had been converted into elegant living quarters for the famous physicists and high-ranking military officials of the project. The building itself had an odd history. The school was founded in 1917 by Ashley Pond, the delicate son of a wealthy Detroit businessman. Pond had enlisted with Teddy Roosevelt and the Rough Riders to fight in the Spanish Civil War but collapsed from exhaustion before he saw any action. So, in the middle of the Depression, instead of fighting a war, Pond began a school where wealthy boys could "regain their heritage of outdoor wisdom" for only $2,400 a year, plus $380 for a riding outfit that included a neckerchief. Many of the graduates grew up to run the Manhattan Project.

Surrounding the school were a handful of beautiful houses made of logs and stone, complete with manicured lawns and trees. And bathtubs. These houses had the only bathtubs on the entire site, so it became known as "Bathtub Row." For many at Los Alamos, the Ranch School and the adjoining Bathtub Row seemed to be indicative of the elitism of the project itself. The famous slept in comfortable surroundings. Took baths. The rest slept in mud.

To Hélène, Los Alamos looked as dilapidated as any tenement she had seen in her train ride across America. As bad as any in

Washington, New York, or Chicago. It was not what she had expected at all. But she was happy to finally arrive and so exhausted that all she could do was cry.

It was a long journey. Four months total. Much longer than she had expected and much more difficult. Fisher had arranged military transportation. So she was never alone, escorted from one place to the next, seated on the jump seat of bombers, then search planes, then transport planes, until the whine of the engines made her shake for no reason. Then, the endless waiting between connections. Sometimes, a week or more. No route was direct. It seemed odd to her that it took so long, but whenever she asked she was told, "Things slow down in times of war." And that made sense.

But, once in America, there were the trains. Lots and lots of trains, whose views gave Hélène the impression that the United States was made of a handful of decaying cities and garbage dumps and too many mountains.

She seemed to crisscross the nation. "No direct routes," she was told whenever she asked. And at every station there was always a man from "G-5" sent to meet her. Take her safely to the next train. The men seemed all the same. Average height. Average weight. Made no eye contact. Always stayed and watched the train as it pulled from the station.

When Hélène finally arrived in Santa Fe, the G-5 there took her directly to 109 East Palace, the Los Alamos "information center." The address was in the historic section of town, and easy to find. Outside the ancient adobe building, there were dogs tied on leashes. Children played tag. Delivery trucks. Soldiers stood watch. Inside, it was crowded with people, most of them exhausted. Men in wrinkled suits. Young mothers with wailing babies. The phones never stopped ringing. Secretaries ran from one room to the next to answer them. Every now and then, one of the women would shout, "Whoever's new needs to sign in."

When Hélène's name was finally called, four hours after she arrived, a tall, thin woman with glasses dangling around her neck on a pearl chain told her she'd have to wait.

"How long?" Hélène asked.

The woman shrugged. "Hopefully, not too long, dear," she said, and patted Hélène on the back. Then she took her passport and put it in a folder.

"I need that," Hélène said.

"We'll keep it safe," the woman said, and answered the phone.

The idea of being without her passport, her official papers, made Hélène uneasy. She did, of course, have papers and a passport in Manon's name. The forged ones from Marseilles. The ones no one knew about. But still.

"When can I get that back?" she asked when the woman hung up the phone.

"I'm not sure," she said kindly. "Security says they need it. And whatever Security needs they get. By the way," she added, "do you have any money? You'll need a place to stay."

Hélène shook her head. "Maybe enough for a week or two. That's all."

The woman made a note on her file. "I'll tell them," she said. "They wanted to know."

Hélène was told that everyone, even those with letters of introduction, were subject to massive security checks and the waiting for clearance to take the bus up to "the Hill," as it was known to the locals, was difficult. Santa Fe had very few hotels and rooms were scarce. Some of the scientists bought tents and pitched them outside the city. Some slept in their cars. Hélène, nearly out of money, spent her nights as many of the city's homeless did, sleeping on the church floor of Santuario de Guadalupe.

Our Lady of Guadalupe, her hands outstretched, her eyes toward heaven, welcomed all. And even though the floors were cold, and the deep drunken snores made it hard to sleep, for the first time in a long time, Hélène felt safe. The war seemed distant. The enemy far away. She felt herself relax. The world suddenly seemed filled with possibilities. The past became unimportant. Every morning, she would walk to 109 East Palace, clean herself in the bathroom there and sit on the government-issue furniture and wait. Happy. Expectant. Anxious to get back to work.

The women who ran the office were kind to those who waited. They often brought in plates of cookies from home. Or cold fried chicken. Or tamale pies that were spicy and made Hélène sneeze.

Whenever Hélène asked, "It shouldn't be too long," they said.

At the end of the second week, a security officer called Hélène into an office. He was well-pressed and balding. In a low Texas drawl, he explained that there didn't really seem to be any room for her to work as a researcher. What he didn't say was that of the 1,700 physicists employed, only 100 or so were women, and most of them were working below their capabilities, as secretaries or assistants.

It didn't matter. The real reason she couldn't be hired to do research was much more complicated than that. It was the same reason the army had decided she should spend the rest of the war at Los Alamos, where they could keep an eye on her.

"I do have a job for you, though," he said.

"But not in research?"

He shook his head.

"But I'm a scientist."

The officer looked uncomfortable. "These days, you're actually kind of an errand girl. Just running errands. You'll be paid though. Have a nice place to live until the war is over. It's a sweet deal."

"But I can't work in the laboratory?"

"No. But you can drive a stick shift. Not many women get to do that."

"What about my passport?"

"You don't need that right now," he said. "Once you go up the Hill, you can't travel more than two hundred miles from here. Nobody can. Part of the rules. No exceptions. So you won't need this passport for a long time."

Hélène suddenly felt like a prisoner.

"But what if I decide not to go up the Hill?" she asked.

"I'll walk you to the bus," he said, and took her by the arm.

Hélène thought about running away but didn't know where to go. She was in the middle of the desert. In a strange country. Even if she could figure out a way to get back to Paris, or even Morocco, if the Germans found her she'd be killed. And she had no money.

So she got on the bus. And, as soon as it pulled away, she found herself shaking. Cold, in the heat of midday.

❧39❧

IT'S NOT FAST, THIS FALLING. THAT SURPRISES Vincent. Eight floors. That's not very high, he thinks. This should have been over by now. But it's not. At least, it still feels as if he's falling. But it's not that high. But it feels like it. I may be dead already. Perhaps this is just a trick of the mind. Vincent feels as if he's falling in slow motion. He opens and closes his hands, his beautiful hands, several times. His life does not flash before his eyes, like a movie, as it is sometimes said. Or unpeel like ripe fruit. A clementine or sour orange.

Instead, all he can think of is the ground below him. The uneven cobblestones of the street. For a moment he thinks he hears Basheer's voice calling out. Thinks he hears him say, "Father," and that touches Vincent. He'd always hoped the boy would be a comfort to him in his old age. He raises his hands to the voice, as if to catch it in his hands, his beautiful hands, as if to hold on to it. Cling to it.

Father, he thinks. It's such a lovely word.

SALLY RYDER, A TALL ALL-AMERICAN BLONDE, WHO usually went by the name of Sal, was a graduate student in physics at the University of Wisconsin before she came to Los Alamos. She came for two reasons. First, she was asked. Second, she had no choice. The university's Physics Department was being dismantled around her.

Los Alamos needed people and equipment, so they borrowed them from the universities. Berkeley. Chicago. Purdue. And, of course, the University of Wisconsin. At first, Sal noticed that the lab was disappearing bit by bit. Samples went missing. The accelerator disappeared. No one seemed concerned. Soon, her fellow graduate students vanished one by one. Then her teachers.

By the time the offer to work at Los Alamos arrived, Sal was nearly alone in the department and none of the administration could tell her why. It was all very confusing. The project was described as top secret, part of the war effort. Sal had never been to New Mexico, so she went to the library to find a book on the state. On the borrowers' card, she noticed the names of her fellow students and teachers. So, Sal signed on.

She worked as an assistant on reactor design and construction and was granted limited security access. She was told very little. She played a mean fiddle and twitched. Never stopped moving. She was twenty-four when she came to Los Alamos, just like Hélène. She was just as passionate for the work, the beauty of fission, and just as cavalier about the danger.

They met one night after dinner, at a Tech Center Safety Orientation Meeting. A party, really. No talk of safety. Just men and women flirting and dancing until the generators failed and the electricity went out or the Military Police broke it up and sent them all back to their own beds alone. There were regulations against sex for unmarried couples. Women could be jailed. Men, fined. It seemed as if the District intended to re-create the boarding-school life of Ashley Pond's Ranch School. A hothouse of healthy competition and wholesome fun. There were activities like cleaning contests—"Men Versus Women; May the Best House-keepers Win!"—and contests featuring interior decorating for hutmets.

The safety meetings, like safety valves, were designed to blow off steam. Staff driven. Army disapproved.

Everyone around Sal and Hélène was drunk and slurring.

"They must think I'm a Communist," Hélène said.

"Can't be that. I'm a Communist. This place is crawling with Communists," Sal laughed. "And those who aren't Communists are Martians, at least that's what Grandpa Joe thinks. The Martians are everywhere. Isn't that right?"

"Grandpa Joe" was Enrico Fermi. In Los Alamos, everybody had another name. A code name that changed at whim. Real names were forbidden. The word "physicist" was never used.

Fermi was deep in conversation with a group of men when Sal interrupted him.

"Coffee, Sal," he said. "You need coffee."

"I'm not drunk," she said. "Just indignant."

Sal laughed even louder, harder. It was Saturday night. They were at Fuller Lodge, leaning up against the large stone fireplace. The air was heavy with wood smoke. The fire snapped and sparked. Some were trying to dance to a jazz trio made up of other scientists. Some were just whispering in corners.

Enrico Fermi was holding court. Hawk-eyed and charismatic, he was the heart of Los Alamos, the entire project was based on his work. In 1938, he'd won the Nobel Prize in Physics for discovering nuclear fission. In 1942, he was the first person to create a controlled, self-sustaining nuclear chain reaction—which he did under the stands of a squash court. He nearly blew up most of the University of Chicago doing it. And most of Chicago, too.

"The Italian explorer has landed in the New World!" Fermi cabled his superiors. So President Roosevelt approved the creation of Los Alamos, a secret place to create a nuclear reaction on a massive scale that was not only controlled, but deadly.

Fermi knew more about nuclear power than any man alive and, at forty-five, he was one of the oldest members of the project.

And he really did believe in Martians. He often searched the night sky looking for them, could sometimes be found screaming, "Where are you? Show yourselves!"

Sal wagged her finger at Grandpa Joe and said, "Communism is no reason to have Frédéric Joliot-Curie's assistant running sandwiches from the commissary."

Grandpa Joe looked closely at Hélène, then at her blue ID badge.

"You two haven't met?" Sal said.

"I have to go," he said abruptly.

"Wait," Hélène said. "Frédéric said—"

"I'm sorry but we are not to speak," Fermi told Hélène, then picked up his drink and started to walk away.

Frantic, Hélène grabbed him by the arm. "I've come all this way to work for you."

"Then bring me my sandwiches and ask me no questions." He pulled away from her. A bit of red wine splashed on her hand.

"Sal? Are you coming?"

Sal looked at her mentor, then back at Hélène. "I guess I better be going, too," she said. "See you tomorrow, kid."

Hélène, a little drunk, shouted after him, "Why am I a prisoner here?"

Fermi turned, lowered his voice. "The truth is," he said, "on some level, we're all prisoners."

"Then why can't I work for you?"

"You worked for Frédéric and he's a collaborator."

"That's not true."

"He joined the French Communist Party," Fermi said. "He's officially the enemy now."

The words stunned her. "How can Frédéric be the enemy?"

Fermi said nothing. Turned and walked away.

Sal put her arm around Hélène's shoulders for a moment. Squeezed. "Sorry, kid," she said.

"But you're a Communist," Hélène said.

"I've come to think that's why I'm here. I suspect that's why you're here, too," she said. "They pick our brains and keep an eye on us at the same time."

41

"I DON'T KNOW."

Lucienne is quickly losing count of the number of times she has said this.

"I just don't know."

Lucienne has been at the police station for over three hours. The investigator is a woman. Not young or thin. But well dressed, with a tight skirt. Nails perfectly manicured.

"Would you like to fix yourself before we go any further?" she asks Lucienne. "Clean your face or something?"

Lucienne shakes her head. Imagines she looks horrible, but doesn't have the energy to do anything about it. She's been running on adrenaline and it's quickly fading. She can't stop thinking of Vincent lying on the sidewalk. The glass canopy shattered around him. A thin line of blood.

And then Dr. Assam, Basheer. Dazed. "My father," he told the police. "It's my father."

She looks at her hand, his phone number is still written in her palm but the numbers are faded. She suddenly feels queasy, throws up in the investigator's wastebasket.

"Maybe you should go," the woman says, and is clearly annoyed as she calls for the janitor.

A policeman drives Lucienne back to the hotel. He makes her sit in the backseat with the windows open.

"Just in case," he says.

At the hotel, there are several arrangements of flowers in her room. The hospital sent them over. They were for Hélène. They are all very beautiful. There's one, Japanese in style, with a single spray of white orchids and an engraved card with the hotel's monogram.

"The staff," it reads.

Another is a large bouquet of white roses and lilies with a card that reads, "Get better soon." It's from the Institut.

Lucienne turns on the shower, hot, until it steams.

On the phone, the red light blinks. There is a message. Only one. She plays it back. The hospital needs to know where the body should be sent. As if her mother is a letter. She feels nauseated again. Lucienne had no idea what to do with her mother's body. Travel between Paris and the United States is halted and it might be some time before she can safely get back to Boston.

So much work to do at home, she thinks. But then again home means Ethan, which feels complicated. On one hand, she wants him to hold her. On the other, she isn't sure if she should.

If there was one secret, she thinks, how many more?

She imagines the wire services have already asked him for a comment. Already written their leads. Already sent the news out across the world. She hasn't had the chance to call him herself. He's heard it from strangers.

She steps into the shower. Turns up the water. Too hot. It nearly burns her skin.

Downstairs, the manager at the front desk did not stop the doctor. Nor did the bell captain. Basheer knows what room Lucienne is staying in, and so he knocks until she hears him.

When she opens the door she's still wet. Her hair, bare feet, bathrobe.

"We should talk," he says.

"I don't know what to say," she says quietly.

"Neither do I."

So she lets him in. He puts his arms around her. To comfort, she thinks. He smells of chestnuts and smoke. There's something different about him. Worn. She rests her head on his chest and closes her eyes. His breath is irregular. He's crying, she thinks, and cries, too.

It's not clear how long they stand like this, or who found whose lips first, but soon the moment turns from comfort to passion.

This should not be happening, she thinks. But it is.

Lucienne is amazed how beautiful he is. She never noticed that before. How beautiful his skin is. Polished like rosewood.

This is wrong, they both think.

Neither cares.

42

HÉLÈNE NEVER DELIVERED SANDWICHES, OR MUCH OF anything. Sal made sure of that. "I can get my own damn sandwiches," she told Security. She pushed to make Hélène an "unofficial consultant." After all, Sal argued, she'd worked on the French atomic effort with Joliot-Curie. Unlike Sal, Hélène had actually worked in the field, not in a classroom. She understood from experience how unstable nuclear energy could be, and how dangerous. Sal knew that Hélène could provide valuable advice on matters of design. And Sal needed help. Desperately. Even though she was brilliant, her "progressive leanings," as cited in her background check, gave her limited access to the classified information she needed to create a bomb that would explode when she wanted it to. Instead of just exploding at will. Which, she explained to Security, was inconvenient at best.

Sal was building blind.

"And nobody's that brilliant," she said. "I promise I won't let Hélène out of my sight."

So it was agreed and Sal and Hélène became inseparable.

"I was a farm student until I walked into a chemistry class in high school," Sal told her. "They had a cloud chamber up and running and I opened the door and saw this room filled with sub-atomic fireworks and that was it for me. Turned out I had a knack for it, so I left pig husbandry behind and didn't look back."

And Hélène told her about Basheer's theory of stars and dust. And how she's never stopped thinking of it.

"It's biblical in its implications," Sal said. "From dust to dust. But how do you prove it?"

"Oppenheimer," Hélène said.

"The Hallowed One?"

"Before the war, he was working on a theory about stars. He speculated that when massive stars die they create these dense spinning bodies that no light can escape from. They pull everything into their neutron cores. Feed on it, in a sense."

"Like a 'gadget,'" Sal said.

Hélène nodded. "So, if the stars are made of atoms and we are made of atoms, then it could be possible to trace a person's atomic signature."

Sal laughed. "So what you're saying is that after I kick, you'll be able to find me orbiting Pluto?"

"The key is to determine if each person has a unique atomic signature."

"And if they do? The Universe is a pretty big place. You could look your entire life for someone and never find him."

"But it would be worth the effort," Hélène said.

"Well, if you look for me," Sal said, "start by Pluto. I like a planet that has a dog named after it." Then she laughed and Hélène laughed too.

Hélène flourished at Los Alamos. For the first time in her life she was happy. The work, and Sal's friendship, kept her madness at bay.

In the summer of 1945, the "gadgets" were ready to test. But it seemed, at least to some, that they had become less necessary. The war was nearly over. The Allied forces had the upper hand. At least it seemed that way.

In February, an air raid on Dresden, Germany, created a series of firestorms. Fifty thousand people were killed.

In March, it was Tokyo. Nearly four hundred B-29s fire-bombed the city. Sixteen square miles of the city burned. One million, five hundred thousand people were left homeless. More than 100,000 dead.

In May, the German forces surrendered. American planes still continued to bomb Tokyo. The death toll continued. By the end of the war, half the population of the city would be dead. And yet the Japanese did not surrender. Although it was rumored that surrender was close at hand.

"How can this war not be over yet?" Hélène said, but she wasn't sure where she'd go when it was. She'd come to love American jazz and beer. The crushed velvet sunsets of the mountains. And tamale pie. And Sal. Hélène had never had a friend before. She'd miss Sal, she knew that.

Sometimes they'd steal a jeep and ride along the mountains at night, the cool dry desert wind though their hair. The stars low and ripe.

Sometimes they'd spend the day hiking the ocher cliffs, come across clusters of adobe houses, the flat roofs strung with ears of drying corn for masa. Yellow, blue, and red, like so many wind chimes. Ropes of chili peppers, the color of dried blood.

And then the work. She'd miss the work, clearly.

The Canyon Group, as they were called, worked in the canyon far away from the main laboratory, just in case there was an accident, in case things "went critical." It was a wise precaution. Without knowing the exact amount of control Fermi had gained over nuclear reactions, it was difficult to understand how to accurately design and control rods. How to vent and cool things down. And when one needed to. So they guessed.

Things very easily could have gone critical, if it wasn't for Hélène. The Joliot-Curie effort in France was much more advanced than the American attempt. Before the war broke out, they weren't quite able to control the chain reaction themselves, but they certainly understood how it was done. And what the end result could be.

Hélène quickly became an important member of the team, although never completely trusted. Always watched. And she knew it. Which made it difficult to sleep at night.

Most nights, after Sal left her at the dorm, Hélène went back to the laboratory. The guard always watched at his post nearby, but she didn't care. She didn't touch a thing, just watched the beakers, radioactive, glow an iridescent blue. And thought of Basheer, the warmth of his lips, his brave heart, and the Water of the Moon until she was calm enough to sleep. Or until morning came.

Although the actual date of the test was top secret, the closer it came the more life unraveled. Water was scarce or undrinkable, either yellowed from chlorine or filled with vermilion worms. Electricity was inconsistent at best. There was not enough food. Sewage was backing up everywhere. Typhoid was common. There was even a polio scare. And rabies. Oppenheimer, himself, had contracted chicken pox and was working with a temperature of 105 degrees. He was blotchy, gaunt, and unshaven. His eyes were glossy and unfocused. He looked quite mad.

Worst of all, a petition was being circulated protesting the use of the bomb. Sixty-nine physicists signed, but Fermi and Oppenheimer refused. They instead wrote a letter that urged the bombing of Japan. "We see no acceptable alternative to direct military use," they wrote.

The letter was forwarded to President Truman himself.

The world of Los Alamos was coming undone.

Then, on July 16, everything changed.

The rumor was that the test was scheduled for midnight. Sal and Hélène stole a motorcycle and drove into the middle of the desert, to a spot twenty-five miles outside of Alamogordo, the Trinity test site. At least, that was the rumor.

So, they lay in the desert on their army-issue blankets and watched the stars and waited. Midnight passed. The air grew cold. They talked about nothing in particular. Dozed on and off.

At 5:29 A.M. the gadget exploded. It was remarkable.

It began with calm. An odd stillness. No sound. Not hawk or coyote. Not wind. The hairs on Hélène's arms stood straight up. Then there was light. Burning brighter than any sun. It curled around them like a wave, pulling them into its vortex. Then turned violet. Then blue. Then red, dark red. And rumbled. And the mountains rumbled, too. And the earth beneath them. And the dawn broke.

Glorious, Hélène thought.

In the control room, Oppenheimer turned to the technician and quoted the *Bhagavadgītā*.

"I am become death, shatterer of worlds," he said.

And someone else said, "Now we're all bastards."

That night, in spite of the mixed feelings, the lack of water and electricity and rampant illness, spirits were high. There were endless parties, some formal. Black tie and ball gowns. Some more casual. Just a few couples drinking beer and vodka on the Mesa until they could no longer stand. After all, everyone always worked hard and played hard and after nearly three years, they had succeeded.

The world would never be the same again.

After dinner, in the lodge, there had been a concert. Sal and some of the others in the Canyon Group formed a quartet and had practiced a medley of Italian operas in honor of Fermi. The tenor was quite good. He was an army nurse who had been assigned recently to help at the hospital. He had sung in choirs, his voice was clear and fragile. Striking.

But Fermi sneaked out the side door before it began. Five minutes later, so did Oppenheimer, with Hélène close behind.

"I have this theory I've been working on," she said, and picked up pace alongside of Oppenheimer. "I believe that everything in the world is part of the same fabric, not just atoms, but some ultimate—"

He kept walking. "Based on the neutron?" he said.

She nodded.

"Then you've read my work?"

"Berkeley papers 1938–39—"

"You don't need to impress me. Tell me what you want."

"I was just wondering if you think it's possible. The gadget, this neutron bomb, the stars—"

Oppenheimer stopped and turned to her.

"It's not only possible, it's probable," he said. "There are incredible powers dormant inside of all atoms. This gadget, as we call it, is not just a bomb. It is the violence within ourselves."

On the top of the hill they could see a small man in the moonlight. Arms outstretched.

"Fermi is looking for his Martians again," he said.

They could hear him shouting in Italian. They could also hear the faint sounds of singing. Sal's quartet was still playing at the lodge. The tenor, his clear pure voice. *La Donna è mobile,* he sang. Above, the sky rumbled in fitful sleep.

"Remember this moment," Oppenheimer said to Hélène. "It is all here—violence of the world, the madness, and beauty. And it is all within us, too."

Then he turned and left her standing alone. Watching.

When Hélène first heard that America had dropped the bomb on Japan, she and Sal were on a bus back from Taos. It was Hélène's twenty-sixth birthday. In town, they'd celebrated with tamales and Mexican beer. Sal had bought her a parchment with a Chinese proverb written on it.

"Understand that you are another world in miniature, and that you are the Sun, the Moon, and also the Stars," it read.

"Don't forget to look for me left of Pluto," Sal said, and cackled.

When the bus arrived at Los Alamos, a security officer boarded it. "I have an announcement to make," he said, and everyone fell silent. The moment felt ominous.

"Hiroshima was bombed at 08:16:45."

People sat in disbelief. Some cried. What the officer didn't say was that 140,000 civilian citizens were killed.

"Bastards," Sal said.

Hélène was too shocked to speak. She had never really expected the government to drop the bomb on civilians. She, like Sal and some of the others, were all just hoping it would be fired off in Tokyo Harbor, a warning shot as it were.

That night, Hélène and Sal went back to Alamogordo. They stood in the crater and gathered handfuls of blackened glass that was formed by the explosion; the heat had fused sand and rock and bits of the bomb. It was Sal's plan to mail pieces to the leaders of the world. Enclose a note that read, "Work for peace. Don't let it happen again."

Hélène knew it was a childish thing to do, but went along with it anyway. She didn't know what else to do. The world felt as if it were slipping out of control. And it was. On August 9 at 11:02:00, seventy thousand civilians were killed in Nagasaki. Two weeks later, Harry Daughlin, a fellow researcher, became the first American victim of a nuclear accident.

And after that, Hélène began to unravel again.

LUCIENNE WATCHES BASHEER DRESS. BEHIND HIM, THE flowers from her mother's hospital room, the white roses and lilies, seem incongruent in their innocence. She thinks about her mother alone with Vincent. Dying at his hand. Feels the panic rise in her again. She reaches out to touch Basheer's chest, to feel the warmth of his skin again for just a moment. He backs away slightly. Shy now. Everything feels awkward.

He keeps on dressing. She notices he's meticulous about himself. His laundered shirt is, for the most part, still neatly pressed. His suit well cut. Unwrinkled. His shoes polished with great care. He takes an envelope from his suit pocket. It has both their names on it.

"The police found this in Vincent's things at the office. I thought you might want to see it."

She opens it. Unfolds the papers. It's a download from a Web site for a bed-and-breakfast in Morocco. It's a beautiful place. There's a color photograph. The center courtyard has iridescent tiles and a reflecting pool.

"Philippe says that Vincent asked him how to use a search engine right before he died. He thinks this is what he found," he says.

"The Water of the Moon. That's lovely."

The doctor turns to the last page for her. "Our History," it reads. The Web site looks rather amateurish, with odd lettering. She imagines it's supposed to be Moroccan, but it is just hard to read. So she skims it. It says something about a prince and his concubines and then a gambler whose son built an observatory for his wife.

"When the gambler's son died in 1956, his wife disappeared. Some say they haunt the observatory. Some say their cries can be heard at night."

The year before I was born, Lucienne thinks.

"Take a look at the photos," he says.

She looks closely. There are quite a few pictures. There's a bad reproduction of an oil portrait of the prince. A smiling Englishman and his pleasant-looking wife who now operate the B&B.

And then she sees it.

It's grainy, black and white, and smaller than the others, but clearly it's a photo of her mother standing next to a seated man. The pose is very formal. Hélène is wearing tailored pants and a man's shirt. Her hair is swept up. She looks a little like Katharine Hepburn, Lucienne thinks. The man is in traditional Moroccan dress. There's a kindness about him that's unmistakable. Both smile at the camera.

The caption reads, "Basheer and Manon Assam. Our ghosts."

Lucienne doesn't know what to say.

The doctor is looking out the window into the small narrow street. It's raining again. He opens the window slightly. The smell of rain and traffic and the cold night air fill the room. Bits of rain splatter his perfect jacket.

Lucienne feels a chill. She picks up her bathrobe from the floor where she left it. Pulls it on. It smells like his skin.

Shame. Sorrow. Desire. She feels it all.

"I wonder what it was like," he says. "Falling. I wonder what it was like for Vincent. Eight floors. The feeling itself. The release. Then impact. The snap."

Lucienne thinks of CNN, the twin towers. Huge wingless birds. The choice.

It is then he turns to her. His face is wet. It's difficult to tell if it is rain or not.

Vincent was the only father he ever knew, she thinks.

The doctor sits down next to Lucienne on the bed and she looks at him closely, wonders how much he is like Basheer. How much she is like Hélène. She feels as if she's in her mother's skin, just for a moment. It's not where she wants to be, but it feels too late to change it.

And then she remembers Manon. Remembers the garden behind Notre Dame where Vincent sent her. Directed her. He must have known Manon's name would be listed there as a prisoner of war, she thinks. Maybe he found that on the Web, too. It would be easy, if you knew where to look.

It's clear to Lucienne that Manon didn't commit suicide over Basheer's leaving. And Vincent knew all along, but he lied to Basheer. Made up that story. And now, he's leaving us clues to our past, she thinks. A giant puzzle to solve. Secrets to unlock one by one.

"We have to talk," Lucienne says, and when she's finished telling Basheer everything she knows, he looks drained.

"I loved him" is all he can say, and she holds him in her arms for a long time.

"I know," she says. "I know."

❦ 44 ❧

HÉLÈNE WATCHED HARRY DIE INCH BY INCH. She didn't even know him well, just in passing. But he wanted to be photographed extensively, so everyone could learn about the effects of radiation, and no one would do it. Except her. So Harry gave her his Brownie camera, and a few rolls of film, and she became the only witness to his disintegration.

Sal couldn't believe Hélène could do such a thing. "I couldn't," she said. "I don't have the stomach for it."

But Hélène did. It was like watching the death of a star.

Harry was a large man, tall, with wire-rimmed glasses and a mop of curly hair. All Hélène knew about him was that he always seemed to be working and that he had studied at Purdue. He shouldn't have been in the laboratory alone. Still, for some unknown reason, Harry traveled back to the lab to run a test by himself. It was against the rules. But he went anyway.

Some speculated that he was just trying to cement the case that Los Alamos should be kept open after the war, to continue the work to develop atomic power as a safe energy source. Some said the decision had already been made and Harry was just being a cowboy, like one of the Ranch School boys, in touch with his nature as lone wolf.

There was a flash of light. That's all anyone knew for sure. A sphere of plutonium turned blue. And Harry connected the current of energy. The arch of it ran through him. He was so hot, the Geiger counters jammed.

Harry's total-body radiation exposure was estimated to be 480 roentgens of soft X rays and 110 roentgens of gamma rays. But there was the additional complication arising from the non-uniform distribution of radiation exposure, particularly to the upper body and, especially, to the hands. The right hand was particularly bad.

Sal and Hélène had just driven up to the lab and saw the flash. "I don't think it's too bad," Harry said, but his hand was swollen and numb. So they took him to the hospital. Ninety minutes later, the nausea began. Then dry heaves, nearly continuous. The second day, the nausea persisted cojoined with hiccups.

Then he got better. He was even hungry. But a small blister on his right hand appeared thirty-six hours after exposure and his nails turned blue. Still, he could eat. And even though the doctors suspected his circulation was impaired, they were hopeful. He could, after all, eat, they said. And they had never treated a case of radiation sickness before.

Harry Daughlin was the first they had ever seen. When Hélène ran out of film, they gave her more. She knew he was dying. She could see it in the way his eyes began to cloud. Every hour she took one or two photographs. His peeling fingers, the handfuls of hair that fell on the floor.

She even photographed him at night. No flash necessary. His hands glowed blue. And soon, his whole body radiated, iridescent. Beautiful. She couldn't stop watching even if she had wanted to. She was pulled into it, drawn. But had to be careful not to get too close. He was, after all, radioactive.

On the third day, Harry's right hand became blistered. The palm. Between the fingers. The blisters grew quickly and his hand soon became so swollen that it couldn't be touched. Then the skin of his left hand and abdomen turned red. The doctors of Los Alamos didn't know what to do. They gave him anesthetics, cut the damaged skin from his hands, and coated them in Vaseline gauze and a pressure dressing. But the flesh would soon blister again and turn a blue-purple, again, showing the lack of oxygen. The pain continued.

Harry was lucid through most of it, at least in the beginning. On the tenth day, he knew he was dying. And he was. His body had again begun to reject food. On the fifteenth day, after receiving a blood transfusion and intravenous fluids, he suddenly became pale and clammy. Had a temperature of 105. When he went into cardiac arrest, Hélène shot off the rest of the roll. It was over. They couldn't save him.

By the time Harry died, he was nearly all peeled away. Just flesh and bone. In a coma. He'd survived almost twenty-six days. Four hundred eighty photographs.

Hélène had stopped speaking on the twenty-fourth day, but nobody noticed.

In *The New York Times* it was reported that, according to Los Alamos officials, Harry Daughlin died from "chemical burns," rather than from the results of radiation-induced injuries.

Hélène was sitting in the dining hall when she read this. Everyone else was having breakfast with real eggs. Not powdered. The war was over. But she couldn't stomach it. Harry's accident made the laboratory off limits. Radioactive. There was no place for her to work, even if she wanted to, or could. And Sal was missing. Someone said she'd hot-wired a jeep and gone into the mountains to think.

So, at least for that moment, Hélène planned to read the entire *New York Times* and sit as long as she could. She was comforted by the sound of other voices. The familiar chatter of gossip. It felt, somehow, normal.

Farther down the page there was an article about three doctors, Avery, MacLeod, and McCarty, who in 1944, were researching pneumonia when they discovered something completely different. Something they called "DNA," a threadlike fiber present in all cells that the three had come to believe was the carrier of hereditary information.

The article went on to explain that "no two bits of DNA are alike except for those found in identical twins." The doctors were now looking for practical applications for their discovery.

A unique signature, Hélène thought, that could be traced in the heavens, that could find Sal orbiting Pluto.

Of course, Hélène knew Sal was right. It could take a lifetime to prove Basheer's theory. So Hélène left on the next bus. Security still had her passport, but it didn't matter. She'd kept Manon's all this time. It was all she really needed. The only regret she had was not saying good-bye to Sal, but it felt like there just wasn't time. She had wasted five years already.

～45～

LUCIENNE ISN'T SURPRISED THAT VINCENT HAD MET with his lawyer before he took his own life. What surprised her was that she was included in the reading of his will.

"I'll pick you up," Basheer tells her when he calls. "It's at the salon. Vincent wanted it that way."

When they meet in the hotel lobby, he kisses her on both cheeks like an old friend, not a lover. It was three days since they last spoke, since he left her hotel room in the middle of the night. Lucienne feels shy. Basheer is dressed in a well-cut suit. Black. In mourning. As she is.

"You don't need to come, if it's too difficult," he says.

"No. No. I'm fine."

"Shall we walk? It's not too far."

The night is cool and dry. September is almost over. They walk in silence. After a time, Basheer takes her hand in his.

"I'm starting to feel like I live here," she says.

Lucienne has been in Paris for nearly two weeks now. Air travel has resumed between Europe and the States, but shipments, such as bodies, are still prohibited. She is planning to have her mother cremated tomorrow and to apply for a permit to take the ashes home. Since the terror attacks, everything is suspect.

"When do you leave?" he asks.

"I don't know," she says. "I'm on sabbatical this year. I'm supposed to be developing a presentation on a black hole."

"You could do that from anywhere, you know."

"I could," she says.

The windows of Laloux and Sons are draped in black velvet. A small, tasteful sign is in the window, an explanation. No furs are on display. A black wreath is over the door. Basheer opens it for Lucienne and she steps into a room filled with people she doesn't know and wonders, again, what she is doing here.

Philippe comes from the back room, talking to a waiter who is balancing a tray of champagne. He seems happy to see Lucienne. Kisses her on both cheeks and hands her a glass. Takes one for himself.

"To difficult love," he says quietly, and she can see that he's speaking of his grandfather. There are tears in Philippe's eyes. He loves him no matter what, she thinks, and remembers Vincent lying on the sidewalk. The delicate bones piled in a heap. Then thinks of her own mother, and her secrets, and the father whose name she may never know, and she's angry and yet still filled with love for her mother, filled with sorrow that she will never see her face again.

"To difficult love," Lucienne says, and a tear runs down her face.

"You okay?" Basheer asks, wiping the tear away with his finger.

"Yes," she says. "Just a little overwhelmed."

"Come sit," Philippe says. "It's nearly time to eat."

The table is long and wooden. Looks like it belongs in a farm-house. Seats about twenty people.

"Grand-père bought it at an estate auction and gave it to us as a wedding present," Philippe explains. "He told us it once belonged to Madame Curie, which at the time we thought was just another story." He shrugs, looks a little like a spoiled boy. "I'm afraid we never believed him. Of course now," he says. "You never really know about stories, do you? Never know how true they really are."

The table is beautifully set. Crystal and lace. Small vases filled with jasmine at each setting. And, at each setting, a box, like a Christmas gift, wrapped in gold paper with iridescent ribbons. Everyone is slightly nervous, talking a little too loud. At the head of the table is Basheer; Lucienne sits to his right. Next to her is Lucia, Philippe's wife. She's so thin, she's sinewy, but has a warm smile and a soft Boston accent.

She introduces herself and says, "Philippe and I met running numbers at MIT. Not gambling, but nearly."

Philippe smiles and sits to the left of his father. The rest of the group are business associates and employees. Vincent's designer. The head seamstress. The housekeeper. The office manager. No actual friends. No one who knew him well. The lawyer, white haired and pin-striped, taps a water glass with a knife.

"In front of each person is a box Vincent wished to leave you with."

Lucienne is almost afraid to open hers, but does. Inside, there's a copy of the photograph of the café, enlarged and framed, a rosary, and a note.

"The rosary was your mother's," it read. "The photograph is of the day I proposed. She loved me once, but when I could finally love her back it was too late."

Enlarged, the photo is grainy but now she can clearly see that the woman is her mother. Lucienne finds herself crying. Basheer reaches out and takes her hand, squeezes it gently.

"Can I get you something? Water?"

She shakes her head. "It's them, right here." She shows him the photograph. Vincent's back is to the camera.

"I think my box goes with yours."

Inside Basheer's box is another box, black velvet. An engagement ring. Old-fashioned. Square cut. Large.

"This is yours, too," he says.

In his pocket, there's the note from Vincent. "If you think you could love her, give her this," it reads. "She is so much like her mother, but stronger. Treat her well."

"It's very beautiful," she says, slips it on her finger out of reflex. It fits.

"Then you should keep it," Basheer says and thinks how impossible love is. Or seems to be. At least for him.

"Thank you," she says and there are tears in her eyes.

He wants to kiss her, but doesn't feel as if he should. But he wants to. And not out of grief, or need. And that surprises him.

When all the boxes are opened, the lawyer stands. Clears his throat. Taps the glass again. "There is one final box," he says.

The box is addressed to Basheer and Lucienne. Inside are two airplane tickets to Morocco with open dates. A photo copy of the Web site for the B&B. And a note.

"We should all face our ghosts," it reads. The handwriting is nearly perfect. Each letter well-formed. But the ink ran in places.

❧ 46 ❧

WHEN HÉLÈNE ARRIVED AT THE WATER OF the Moon, Basheer was still there. Karim had died the year before.

"Weak heart," Basheer explained.

Selua, the eldest wife, and the two others went back to their families. But Basheer was still there. Still at his father's home. The iridescent blue of the tiles was still beautiful. Still radioactive, she thought.

"I waited," he said, "for a very long time."

Hélène wasn't sure if he was talking about her, or his wife and child. "Let's talk about your dust," she said, and hoped he'd been waiting for her.

"Will you stay?" he asked.

With the pool behind him, Basheer seemed as if he were floating, still floating. Adrift in the Water of the Moon. She felt calm again, safe.

"I'd like to," she said. "I'd like that very much."

AT ORLY AN AIRPORT SECURITY OFFICER PULLS Lucienne aside.

"You are traveling with that man of your own free will?" she asks. "Not coerced?"

Lucienne looks at Basheer. His skin. His eyes. So different from Lucienne's.

"Yes," she says.

The officer makes a note. "Is there anything else you'd like to tell me?"

Lucienne shakes her head.

"You should know," the officer says, "that his people just released a statement. They say they are praying to Allah for 'the destruction of the United States of America' and for 'the destruction of the Jewish people and state.' You might want to ask him about it."

"His people are French," Lucienne says.

The guard says nothing and lets her pass.

Basheer is strip-searched. He's the enemy now, Lucienne thinks, but can't imagine it.

In Morocco, a yellow Hummer is waiting at the airport. "WATER OF THE MOON" is painted across the doors. McAllen, the innkeeper, is a jolly man who doesn't seem to breathe when he speaks. He's English and has a red bushy beard. "Part Irish," he says. McAllen is in his late forties and he's wearing a caftan that's the color of the Hummer. Too bright. Too shiny. It clangs.

"Bloody hot," he says to Basheer as a way of welcome. Shakes his hand like a well pump.

Lucienne is surrounded by children dressed in cast-off shirts that read "Just Do It" and "I ♡ NYC." They press tiny tokens in her hands, origami-style camels made of dried palm fronds. "One dollar. One dollar," they shout.

McAllen shoos them away like so many ants.

"Do you like my outfit?" he asks Lucienne. She can see that he's serious, or seems to be. He models it for her. Turns and poses. Turns again.

To her he looks like a giant hibiscus. His head, a stem.

"I'll take that horrified look on your face to mean it's not exactly brilliant on me," he says. "Not my best foot forward."

"Well," she says.

"Duly noted." He nods. "Wife wants me to match the car. Some promotional rip she's onto. Bloody hell, I just look like a wayward bumblebee."

He laughs but Lucienne doesn't. She feels the heat seeping through every pore.

McAllen revs up the Hummer. Slaps the air-conditioning on high.

"That good?" he asks Lucienne. "Just want you to be comfortable. Never driven the children of ghosts before. Ever been to Morocco?"

She shakes her head.

"Well then," he says, "there's a trick you should know. Play deaf. That's what I tell everyone. In Morocco, everyone will offer to give you a tour of the desert. Don't do it. All the tours, from the bellboy's tour to the chef's tour to the maid's sister's tour will end up with you drinking mint tea at their brother's or cousin's or nephew's house and the bloke will always have the best prices on rugs and free shipping. Always free shipping. And they will hound you and shame you into buying. Mark my words."

He looks at the doctor in the rearview mirror.

"I've got nothing against them, mind you," McAllen says, tries to soften the moment. "I know some who do, but not me. I think they're lovely people. Just poor. But lovely. Desperate sometimes, though."

Basheer says nothing. He hasn't said much since they were pulled aside at Orly.

"Awful bit of business, that," McAllen says. "The hijacking. Those towers. Two weeks later, still tough to believe."

Basheer looks out the window. And so McAllen turns to Lucienne.

"It's mostly safe here," he says, and pats her hand. "Just don't go out alone."

The bee-bright Hummer crawls though ancient alleys, down the narrow winding streets, and children begin to follow it. They slap the doors with their hands and shout. Begging. Lucienne tries not to look at them. They beg in several languages. Italian, she thinks. English. And French, for sure. Maybe German.

Every now and then, McAllen throws coins when they get too thick. The children scurry. The Hummer inches forward. More children step up and try their luck. The air is warm and filled with the fragrance of olive oil and spice. Every corner seems to have a communal bakery.

They're in what's called the old town. Ancient and worn. There's a spice souk on one corner that takes credit cards. Visa. American Express. A handmade sign in the window reads "OPIUM."

McAllen laughs. "Don't you love it?" he asks. "It's just poppy perfume. I drive the tourists by here. Show them the sign."

Finally, the small streets open out into the desert. Lucienne can see that the city is surrounded by olive groves. It looks calm in the rearview mirror. The road ends but there are dozens of minivans and tour buses, Jeeps and Land Cruisers and Hummers all heading the same way. Converging from different parts of the city to form a caravan of sorts in the desert. McAllen speeds up: 85, 90 mph. He kicks up huge walls of sand.

Basheer points out the window. "What's that?" he asks. "Some sort of motor race?"

"That's the way to Erg Chebbi," McAllen says. "Largest sand dune in this part of the world. It's a little to the left of where we're going, and about six hours away, but if you like I can give you a tour of it later on."

He says the word "tour" with a wink and a nudge. "I have a brother/cousin/uncle in the rug trade. Don't worry," he says. "It'll be a brilliant tour. I know sign language."

And then he laughs so hard he spits and the car speeds up. Kicking waterfalls of sand, on its way to the Water of the Moon.

48

AS MANON ASSAM, HÉLÈNE COULD WORK WITHOUT question. Live without question. Which is what she and Basheer did for over a decade. Lived and worked side by side. Like Frédéric and Irène. Like husband and wife. And Hélène was happy. And careful. And made Basheer be careful, too. But still, accidents happen.

When Hélène realized that she was pregnant, thirty-six years old and pregnant, she could hardly believe it. It was dangerous and impossible. Especially, she told herself, after so many years of exposure to radiation. The chance of a healthy baby being born, she knew, was limited. Given the statistics, either she or the baby would die.

So Hélène told Basheer that she'd heard that there was a doctor, an expatriate, a tax evader, who opened up a practice in Tangier. Expensive, but reliable. He was a specialist in such things. An abortionist.

Basheer said nothing for a long time. And then:

"You would kill our child?"

There were tears in his eyes.

Tenderhearted, so tenderhearted, she thought.

Injured birds. A dog gone blind. The sorrow of the world touched Basheer. Affected him deeply.

"It's not that simple," she said, and tried to explain the life the child would have. "If it is born a Mongoloid, its head would not support a brain."

Basheer was trembling. "Stop," he said, and stood. "If my child was born a stone, I would still love it. Still hold it in my arms."

"What about our work? We couldn't possibly care for a child and continue our work. Even if the baby was healthy, you can't raise a child in a laboratory," Hélène said. "This child was a mistake—"

He cut her off. "No child is ever a mistake," he said, and thought of the boy he left behind, the baby Basheer. His sweet, soft skin. The way his small fingers reached for him. And that made him even angrier and he began to shout, "To you, the world is all about your science. Your stars. Your neutrons. You have taken everything from me. My wife. My son. And now you take this child, that is my own flesh? I have known you for over a decade," Basheer said, his face drained and trembling. "I loved you and now I see I have loved a monster."

And he stormed away into the desert.

And so Hélène left, too. He'll calm down and see I'm right, she thought. He'll come around.

She was gone two weeks. Not long, but long enough.

The details of the accident were sketchy. She and Basheer had been doing some experiments with high-grade uranium before she left. It was dangerous, but she wanted to create a nuclear reaction to study the effects of radiation on DNA, to see how it changed the signature. "That could be the key," she told Basheer. So, they took the risk even though their lab was not set up for such a sophisticated experiment.

"Fermi created the first sustainable nuclear reaction under the grandstands at the University of Chicago," she reasoned. "I think you just have to improvise. And be very careful."

Basheer was by himself when it happened. Alone in the lab. There was a flash of blue light, that's all the servants could agree upon. When she heard that, she thought of Harry Daughlin at Los Alamos, and began to shake uncontrollably. She had to be sedated. Her madness now rushed over her like a wave. Over, then back again.

Intellectually, Hélène knew Basheer's death was quicker and, perhaps, less painful. The uranium was more concentrated. The point of impact, closer. By the time Hélène returned, Basheer was already dead. His ashes scattered in the desert. Still, she couldn't help thinking about Harry and all the photos she'd taken. A month's worth. Hundreds of photos. Every time she thought of them, she saw Basheer's face, not Harry's. And she had to be sedated again. And then restrained. They tied her down with bedsheets until the madness passed. Or seemed to.

The servants, the doctor, the lawyer who came to sort out Basheer's will—everyone kept a close eye on Hélène. They had to. She wanted to go into the laboratory, to see for herself what had happened, but she couldn't. It was dangerous. Not so much for her, but the baby. Their baby. The baby she couldn't let die.

"I have become like you, so tenderhearted," she shouted to the stars over and over again, and hoped Basheer could hear her.

49

LUCIENNE KNOWS THEY SHOULDN'T BE IN THE room. They've already been told that.

"The only place off-limits," McAllen said.

But they couldn't help it. It was their room, their parents'. It feels as if it belongs to them.

Everything glows an eerie blue.

"It's beautiful," Lucienne says.

It's also radioactive.

McAllen's father didn't know that when he bought the place.

"Apparently, your parents were working on some sort of an experiment. Difficult to tell. There was an accident and the room was hot. Of course, back then nobody knew how to clean it up. My dad had no idea about radioactivity. He used to go in there and sit at night and look at the stars. Probably killed him in the end," McAllen said, with only a trace of bitterness. "I've had it cleaned, but it's still on the hot side. Apparently, it's the best they can do. The technician told me that Madame Curie's labs still glow. It is beautiful, though. You can still see their handprints. That's how we got the idea for the ghost story. It's like watching ghosts."

And so Lucienne and Basheer are there. Watching the ghosts. Lucienne finds a clean print on a beaker, puts her own hand over it. The match is perfect. Basheer finds a larger print. It's very close.

"It's amazing," he says.

And it is. Blue handprints are everywhere, overlapping, glowing. "It's like we can still feel them."

There're an open skylight and a telescope. It's very large and primitive compared to today's standards, but Lucienne recognizes the brand. Her mother has one just like it in her brownstone. And, like everything else in the room, it glows.

"Can you focus it?" Basheer asks. "I want to see what they saw."

"The sky changes, you know," Lucienne says. "We really have no idea if this was the last thing they saw or if they even saw this at all."

She looks through the eyepiece and the sky is so clear, it's as if she could reach up and pick a star. A small ripe fruit.

"You try," she says.

"What should I be looking for?"

"I don't know. The North Star is traditional. It's the one that'll always lead you home."

When she says the word "home" her voice breaks. She feels confused, unsure where her own home is now. Boston without Ethan hardly feels like home.

"Home," he says. "That's a difficult word."

And Lucienne finds herself crying. It's suddenly clear to her that she's alone. Completely alone.

Basheer gently kisses the tears from each cheek. "I did not try to make you sad, I'm sorry," he says. Then he kisses her lips.

The room is radioactive, Lucienne thinks. We shouldn't be in here, but she kisses his hands, each finger, slowly, one by one.

"Don't go back," he says. "Stay, at least for a while."

"I can't," she says, but isn't sure that's true.

Basheer takes her hand and gently pulls her onto the wooden table. And she lets him. Kisses him slowly, sadly, in the shadows of the blue hands, the hands that once held them as children. Once cradled them. Seem to hold them once more.

In Boston, in her mother's brownstone, Hélène's computer is on, locked into a new coordinate. It's been that way for more than a week. Downloading the heavens. Hélène would have been pleased. It's finally found what she's been looking for all these years. The culmination of more than fifty years of research. All this mystery for such a simple thing, so small it would go unnoticed.

DNA. DNA in the heavens.

Basheer's DNA.

Stars and dust and souls.

Basheer was right and finally Hélène proved it. But it doesn't matter anymore. She's found him again. The waiting is over.

✐ Author's Note ✎

DESPITE THE FACT THAT THIS IS A work of fiction it took a great deal of research to write. I am very grateful to all who helped me, including Lucia Barrett, a sharp-eyed reader and patient friend, and fellow writers Marcia Bartusiak, *Einstein's Unfinished Symphony*, and Stephen Maran, Ph.D., *Astronomy for Dummies*. I would also like to thank the scientists who made time to answer my questions, Kim Venn, Ph.D. from Macalester College, and Alyssa A. Goodman, Ph.D. from the Harvard Smithsonian Center for Astrophysics.

Funding for my research was provided by the Minnesota State Arts Board, made possible by an appropriation from the Minnesota State Legislature with additional funding from the National Endowment for the Arts. I also am grateful to have received a Jerome Foundation Travel and Study Grant, supported by the General Mills and Jerome Foundations, Target Stores, Marshall

Field's, and Mervyns's, with support from the Target Foundation, and a grant from the Howard B. Brin Jewish Arts Endowment, a designated endowment of the Jewish Community Foundation of the Minneapolis Jewish Federation.

Finally, my sincere gratitude goes to my agent, Lisa Bankoff at International Creative Management, for her good humor and honesty and to my editor, Peternelle van Arsdale, for her diligence and wisdom.

Making America

Making

THE SOCIETY & CULTURE

America

OF THE UNITED STATES

Edited by Luther S. Luedtke

THE UNIVERSITY OF NORTH CAROLINA PRESS

CHAPEL HILL & LONDON

Library of Congress Cataloging-in-
Publication Data
Making America : the society and culture of
the United States / edited by Luther S.
Luedtke.
    p. cm.
Includes bibliographical references (p.) and
index.
ISBN 0-8078-2030-X —
ISBN 0-8078-4370-9 (pbk.)
1. United States—Civilization.   2. National
characteristics, American.   I. Luedtke,
Luther S.
E169.1.M23   1992
973—dc20   91-50786
                    CIP

Earlier versions of Nathan Glazer's chapter,
"Individualism and Equality in the United
States," have appeared in Bruce A. Lohof,
ed., *Through the Eyes of the World*
(Hyderabad, India, 1978), and Herbert J.
Gans, Nathan Glazer, Joseph R. Gusfield, and
Christopher Jencks, eds., *On the Making of
Americans: Essays in Honor of David Riesman.*
Copyright © 1979 by the University of
Pennsylvania Press.

The chapter by Jane Sherron De Hart and
Linda K. Kerber, "Gender and Equality in
the American Experience," was published in
significantly different form in *Women's
America: Refocusing the Past.* Third Edition,
edited by Linda K. Kerber and Jane Sherron
De Hart. Copyright © 1982, 1987, 1991 by
Oxford University Press, Inc. Reprinted by
permission.

Contents

Preface

The controversies over cultural literacy, canon, core curriculum, and multiculturalism that are raging in our universities, government chambers, and the press have made Americans of every class and ideology more self-conscious today about how their society came into being, where our culture is taking us, who sets the national agenda, and what it all means. Clearly no one political point of view or single academic discipline can answer these questions of identity and purpose. To many scholars and America watchers the terms of debate do not seem entirely original, however, nor the "new historicism" particularly new. It has always been axiomatic to the practitioner of American Studies that the most important questions require the most democratic vistas.

Alexis de Tocqueville's classic *Democracy in America* (1835–40) continues to challenge our imagination a century and a half later not only because of its formulations on equality, individualism, and the American character but also for the magisterial way Tocqueville synthesized observation and theory and for his synoptic treatment of the customs, races, political institutions, commerce, family life, sexual relations, literature, oratory, arts, religion, and philosophy of the new nation. When the American Studies movement began in earnest in the United States amid the deep self-analysis of the 1930s, it fought for a similar breadth of understanding against the reigning specializations and ideologies of the academy. An enlightened general education was one of its goals. The simultaneous appearance in 1949 of *American Heritage* magazine and the journal *American Quarterly* signaled a healthy interest by the reading public as well as scholars in seeing the life of the United States both whole and in significant detail.

A half century of interdisciplinary and cultural work has given us a cornucopia of literary and social histories, document collections and anthologies, essays in political sociology, community studies, and explorations of representative myths, ideas, themes, values, and figures. General readers and university audiences can choose today between many excellent narrative histories of the United States and anthologies of American literature. But there is almost nowhere to turn for a comprehensive and multidisciplinary account of the American experience. The purpose of *Making America: The Society and Culture of the United States* is at once simple and formidable: to give a critical and historical account of the United States that will both excite the public interest and provide a text for college and university courses in American Studies and related fields; to do so in one volume; to address its audiences in accessible language and rich detail; to point the way to further reading across the fields represented.

A few comments on nomenclature might be appropriate at the outset. As its title suggests, this book approaches America as an ongoing process—an active construction of human design as well as natural and historical forces. *Society* and *culture* are perhaps the most encompassing terms we have for "a way of life," including its signifying systems, and they appear in the subtitle with all the breadth social scientists and humanists give them, if not always with the same precision. The *America* meant here is the *United States*—its peoples, resources, and histories. No satisfactory neologism has appeared to distinguish this *America* from *North America* or *the Americas*, and so, with cordial regards to our hemispheric partners—at the quincentennial of Columbus's first voyage, and on the eve of a North American free-trade zone—the authors usually follow the worldwide practice of referring to the natives, colonial forebears, and citizens of the United States simply as *Americans*.

The twenty-eight critics and scholars who have come together to create this book represent a wide cross section of disciplines, personal histories, institutions, regions, and political points of view. Seven of the twelve "cultural regions" described in Raymond Gastil's chapter now are home to the authors, many of whom, like the nation's population at large, have migrated westward during their careers. The political diversity of the authors is immediately apparent by some of the journals they edit: the *Nation*, the *Public Interest*, *Christian Century*, the *Journal of Family History*. A quick comparison of Richard Lehan's and William Goetzmann's views of Jacques Derrida, Jean Baudrillard, and the latest French pundits on America will show how distinctive the authors' voices and styles remain. But all write with the authority of long research and publication at the leading edge of their fields. And within the space available to them, all have set out to provide extensive information on their subjects, pursue developments through time, and apply critical points of view.

The organization of the volume reflects a concern both for social and cultural processes and for the specific institutions, modes of behavior, and faiths that have grown out of the American experience. Following my introductory essay on "The Search for American Character," part 1 charts the drama of landscape, immigration, settlement, and adaptation from which characteristically American forms of citizenship, frontier and urban life, and regional cultures have emerged. Part 2 traces cultural expressions through manners, art, architecture, literature, the mass media, and sports. Part 3 is concerned principally with the individual as a member of society and the impact of social forces on behavior and values. Part 4 explores the life of the mind in America—in religion, scientific discovery, philosophy, and social and political thought. The book thus progresses generally from historical to cultural to sociological to critical-philosophical modes of discussion. The individual chapters in each part are more fully introduced at the beginning of each section. In their search for the roots and the branches, the historical developments and the contemporary forms of American life, the authors weave a pattern of connecting themes: experimentation, a sense of uniqueness and historical purpose, a federalism of peoples and cultural styles, national pride and self-criticism, the dilemmas of racial and social inequality, and especially what William Chafe called in a recent book "the unfinished journey."

This text cannot tell quite everything, of course, that one would like to know about the United States. A longer work might have emphasized agriculture, the social welfare system, work and the workplace, the organization of business, political parties, America at war, American music, as well as other subjects. But even though such topics and themes are not featured individually, it is hoped that the book will provide sufficient contexts and starting points so that they can be more meaningfully addressed.

Readers who take up the chapters in their dynamic sequence will experience the still-evolving society and deepening culture of the American people. Many, no doubt, will use the book in a more selective fashion, pursuing individual interests and comparing personal perspectives with, say, Arthur Mann in "From Immigration to Acculturation," Norman Corwin in "Entertainment and the Mass Media," Nathan Glazer in "Individualism and Equality in the United States," Tamara Hareven in "Continuity and Change in American Family Life," or Martin Marty in "Religion in America."

Whether as the basic text or supplemental readings, *Making America* offers a flexible and creative resource for courses in history, literature, society, politics, rhetoric and composition, and American Studies. The recommendations for "Further Reading" will be a valuable aid for librarians and directors of research and teaching centers when filling out their collections, for instructors designing new courses and preparing syllabi and lectures, and for students developing research topics and preparing bibliographies. Above all, this book is addressed to anyone seeking a vivid explanation of "who we are."

In an earlier form *Making America* already has established itself as a principal text for students, scholars, and observers of America around the world. The book originally was commissioned by the Division for the Study of the United States, of the United States Information Agency, and appeared in the USIA's Forum Series in 1987. The USIA edition has gone through many reprintings in English and has been translated into Arabic, Chinese, Korean,

Portuguese, and Spanish. It is not, however, available in the United States. For this new domestic edition published by the University of North Carolina Press four chapters have been added, and the remaining essays all have been updated and revised, often substantially.

Over the course of its development this book has benefited from the advice of friends and critics, both in the United States and abroad, who are too numerous to acknowledge here. I do want, however, to thank the USIA's Merrill Miller, Leslie High, C. William LaSalle, Barry Ballow, William Bate, and Perry Frank for first giving shape and life to this complex undertaking. I am further grateful now to the University of North Carolina Press for making the book a part of its distinguished American Studies list—especially to Iris Tillman Hill and Lewis Bateman, who embraced the need and timeliness of the work and underwrote the many substantial changes; to managing editor Sandra Eisdorfer, who has generously but firmly kept us on track; and to Paula Wald, whose intelligent and meticulous copyediting has sharpened and polished the text at every turn. My thanks also to Kaye Watson at the University of Southern California for many hours of typing. All have worked with confidence that *Making America* is a timely and rewarding contribution to our national self-understanding.

Luther S. Luedtke
Los Angeles, 1991

Making America

The Search for American Character

Luther S. Luedtke

I speak of the American in the singular, as if there were not millions of them, north and south, east and west, of both sexes, of all ages, and of various races, professions, and religions. Of course the one American I speak of is mythical; but to speak in parables is inevitable in such a subject, and it is perhaps as well to do so frankly. . . . As it happens, the symbolic American can be made largely adequate to the facts; because, if there are immense differences between individual Americans . . . yet there is a great uniformity in their environment, customs, temper, and thoughts. They have all been uprooted from their several soils and ancestries and plunged together into one vortex, whirling irresistibly in a space otherwise quite empty. To be an American is of itself almost a moral condition, an education, and a career.
—George Santayana,
   Character and Opinion in the United States (1920)

It is a commonplace to state that whatever one may come to consider a truly American trait can be shown to have its equally characteristic opposite. This, one suspects, is true of all "national characters," or (as I would prefer to call them) national identities—so true, in fact, that one may begin rather than end with the proposition that a nation's identity is derived from the ways in which history has, as it were, counterpointed certain opposite personalities; the ways in which it lifts this counterpoint to a unique style of civilization, or lets it disintegrate into mere contradiction.
—Erik H. Erikson, *Childhood and Society* (1950)

For the past decade and a half the American people have been enmeshed in rituals of reflection about their character, purpose, and destiny. At the close of the "American century" a series of occasions has arisen for soul-searching and prophecy. The bicentennial of the Declaration of Independence in 1976 soon gave way to anniversary celebrations of the new nation (1983), the Constitution (1987), and ratification of the Bill of Rights (1991). The quincentennial of Columbus's first voyage, in 1992, has pushed American memory further backward through its frontier, Enlightenment, and Puritan heritages to Old World designs and indigenous New World cultures.

Among these opportunities for national stocktaking, the bicentennial of the U.S. Census in 1990 holds a distinguished place. While the constitutional government of the United States is relatively unchanged after two hundred years, the composition of the American people has evolved dramatically since the first census in 1790 counted a population of 3.9 million persons with its midpoint twenty-three miles east of Baltimore. Centennials are often occasions for unbridled celebration; bicentennials tend to be more sober affairs. Up to the census of 1890, immigration had not changed fundamentally the Northern European, Protestant consensus of the United States—although the director of the 1890 census declared the frontier officially "closed" because of pervasive settlement in the western territories, and this *fin de siècle* act provoked Frederick Jackson Turner to write his seminal essay "The Significance of the Frontier in American History." Even the most farsighted census-taker in 1890 could not have projected the fourfold increase of our population over the past hundred years, or its extraordinary diversity, or the fact that now a mere five million Americans farm our lands.

In September 1990 the National Park Service and a coalition of corporate and private benefactors completed a $156 million restoration of Ellis Island, the largest amount ever spent restoring an American shrine. Half of the structure is dedicated to a Museum of Immigration. Since 40 percent of Americans today are descended from immigrants who passed before the Statue of Liberty and through the gates of Ellis Island, the potent symbol seems worth the cost.

☆ ☆ ☆ Citizenship and National Identity

Immigration to the United States is so commonplace as to be scarcely newsworthy anymore. An article headlined "6,000 Line up for U.S. Citizen Oath" got only a picture and three short columns in an interior section of the *Los Angeles Times* on 29 June 1984. The immigrants gathered at the

Shrine Auditorium to swear allegiance to their new nation and pick up citizenship documents. The largest number, nearly a thousand, had come from the Philippines. They were followed closely by groups from Mexico (890) and Vietnam (704). There were 110 from Lebanon, 126 from the United Kingdom, 62 from Israel, and a few from Lithuania, Zimbabwe, and Tanzania. In the auditorium foyer, where League of Women Voters members handed out voter registration forms, one new citizen asked Rosemary Fitzpatrick if she was a Democrat or a Republican. "I want to do it right," the man said. Fitzpatrick explained that he would have to make up his own mind.

This event, so routine and inevitable, holds the keys to a process by which American character has been formed for over two hundred years. It typifies the American experience in at least three ways.

First is the continual ingathering of races and peoples—driven or drawn by religious, political, and economic forces—that have chosen to make the United States their home. Whether perceived through the now somewhat tarnished metaphor of the melting pot or through ethnic pluralism, America has assimilated and set its seal on an extraordinary diversity of peoples. Struggling to define the essence of the new land at the time of the American Revolution, the French immigrant J. Hector St. John de Crèvecoeur posed the classic question of American nationality in his *Letters from an American Farmer* (1782):

> What then is the American, this new man? He is either an European, or the descendant of an European, hence that strange mixture of blood, which you will find in no other country. I could point out to you a family whose grandfather was an Englishman, whose wife was Dutch, whose son married a French woman, and whose present four sons have now four wives of different nations. *He* is an American, who leaving behind him all his ancient prejudices and manners, receives new ones from the new mode of life he has embraced, the new government he obeys, and the new rank he holds. He becomes an American by being received in the broad lap of our great *Alma Mater*. Here individuals of all nations are melted into a new race of men, whose labours and prosperity will one day cause great changes in the world.

After two hundred years the sources and genres of the "new race of men" have expanded far beyond Europe, but the process of uprooting, transplantation, adaptation, and renewal continues.

Although the massive waves of migration that added some 37 million foreign-born to the population from the 1820s to the 1920s are unlikely to recur in the same scale, during the last two decades the United States has become a haven for millions of economic and political refugees and advantage seekers, principally from Latin America and Asia. The nation is growing by some 6,300 persons daily, of which 2,000 are immigrants. During the 1980s 2.1 million of the newcomers became naturalized citizens, a 50 percent increase from the previous decade. Results of the 1990 census have indicated a total national population of 248.7 million. Thirty million (12 percent) of these were black, 22.4 million (9 percent) Hispanic, almost 2 million (.8 percent) Native American, and 7.3 million (2.9 percent) Asian or Pacific Islanders. To speak of these as minority populations is misleading, for the nation has no clear ethnic majority. The largest identifiable ethnic group, that of British ancestry, accounted for only 15 percent of the population at the 1980 census, as compared to 13 percent of German ancestry, and 8 percent Irish. The United States already has the fifth-largest Spanish-speaking population in the world, and it is assumed that Hispanics soon will be the largest single ethnic group in the United States. In the county of Los Angeles—the "new Ellis Island"—non-Hispanic whites comprise only 40.8 percent of the population; Hispanics provide 37.8 percent, non-Hispanic blacks 10.5 percent, and Asians and Pacific Islanders 10.8 percent. As the population of California as a whole grew 26.1 percent during the 1980s, the number of whites increased by only 13.8 percent and blacks by 21.4 percent, while the number of persons of Hispanic origin climbed 69.2 percent and Asians and Pacific Islanders 127 percent (on top of a 140 percent increase during the 1970s). The heartland city of Fresno experienced a phenomenal 626 percent increase in its Asian population, and its Hispanic population more than doubled. A similar phenomenon is occurring from Texas and New Mexico to Missouri, Illinois, and New York.

A second key to the national experience that can be read from the *Los Angeles Times* report concerns the intentionality of American citizenship. The modern concept of citizenship derives from the American and French revolutions, which repudiated rule by monarchy and over time established the right of the individual to choose his or her own citizenship. Following the adoption of the Fourteenth Amendment to the Constitution in 1868, Congress formally declared the right of the citizen to change allegiance at will. Citizenship in the United States is conferred not indelibly by blood or culture, but by birth within the Union or by free choice. It is a matter of both covenant and achievement.

The persons taken into citizenship at the ceremony in Los Angeles had satisfied residence requirements, been found morally fit, passed simple literacy requirements, and demonstrated a basic understanding of the U.S. Constitution. Each had declared, "on oath, that I absolutely and entirely renounce and abjure all allegiance and fidelity to any foreign prince, potentate, state, or sovereignty of whom or which I have heretofore been a subject or citizen; that I will support and defend the Constitution and laws of the United States against all enemies, foreign and domestic; that I will bear true faith and allegiance to the same . . . so help me God." The majority of Americans will never attend citizenship training classes or pass through the ritual of citizenship so self-consciously as the quarter million immigrants who are "naturalized" each year, but the civics instruction and pledges of allegiance that suffuse our educational system and public observances habituate Americans to consider their citizenship a personal obligation.

The third key is closely related to the second, namely, the ideological core of the American commitment. In undertaking to "support and defend the Constitution and laws of the United States," the new Americans gave their allegiance to a national polity rooted in concepts of justice, equality, the unalienable rights of the individual, and government by and for the people. "Natural and subconscious forces have generally contributed to the process of a nation's coming into being more than free human decisions," noted Hans Kohn. "Not so with the Anglo-Americans. They established themselves as a nation without the support of any of those elements that are generally supposed to constitute a separate nation"—such as common descent, a common religion, a historically defined territory, cultural uniqueness, or a distinctive language, law, or literature. The mixed origins of the American colonists, the newness of their culture, and their constant mobility precluded any such organic solidarity. The tie that united the colonies, and at the same time separated them from all other nations, was founded "on an idea which singled out the new nation among the nations of the earth."

This idea, expressed in the Constitution and the Bill of Rights, has continued to define what it means to be an American. The English tradition of liberty flourished in North America unhampered by feudalism or monarchy, encouraged by favorable geography and abundant natural resources. In a trenchant and prophetic discourse called *Barbarian Sentiments: How the American Century Ends* (1989), which appeared just before the reunification of Germany and the latest ethnic schisms in Yugoslavia, William Pfaff recently wrote: "The fate of the American, unlike that of the European, is inevitably a political fate. In this, the United States is unique. . . . The nation today rests upon a political compact or treaty among people of increasingly diverse origin and religious belief, or lack of belief, but who have in common a political vocabulary and constitutional system: and it is that which justifies the national existence. . . . If that Constitution should be abrogated, or if the political system that it established should fail or be overturned, then there would be no point to the United States." Walt Whitman was in essential agreement when he called attention in his *Democratic Vistas* (1871) to John Stuart Mill's essay *On Liberty* (1859) and to the two constituents Mill demanded "for a truly grand nationality—1st, a large variety of character—and 2nd, full play for human nature to expand itself in numberless and even conflicting directions." But he went beyond social covenant by then declaring: "The true nationality of the States, the genuine union, when we come to a mortal crisis, is, and is to be, after all, neither the written law, nor (as is generally supposed) either self-interest, or common pecuniary or material objects—but the fervid and tremendous Idea, melting everything else with resistless heat, and solving all lesser and definite distinctions in vast, indefinite, spiritual, emotional power."

Merely to remind ourselves of its ideological core, of course, hardly does justice to the colorful skein of American life today or the complex and manifold ways in which the American nation has evolved. Skeptics, indeed, will ask whether it is not futile to seek commonality among a population so large and ethnically diverse as that of the United States, spread across fifty states, six time zones, and tens of thousands of local communities, with neither a centralized educational system nor a ministry of culture. Since the 1960s scholars, journalists, and community leaders often have been more eager to feature the neglected experience of particular races, classes, and genders in the United States than to look for unity. While the public has celebrated a succession of national anniversaries, our cultural politics have moved from mainstream to margin, from hegemony to deconstruction. Yet there is no intrinsic reason why focuses on individual, group, and nation cannot be both synoptic and synchronic.

Whether Americans perceive themselves as more diverse or more alike depends chiefly on point of view and one's purpose in posing the question. Weighing the relative diversities or unity of the United States in the 1880s, Lord James Bryce remarked: "Scotchmen and Irishmen are more unlike Englishmen, the native of Normandy more unlike the native of Provence, the Pomeranian more unlike the Wurtemberger, the Piedmontese more unlike the Neapolitan, the Basque more unlike the Andalusian, than the American from any part of the country is to the American from any other. . . . It is rather more difficult to take any assemblage of attributes in any of these European countries and call it the national type than it is to do the like in the United States." The same can be said today notwithstanding America's polyglot immigration or the European Economic Community. Gunnar Myrdal later made Lord Bryce's point in sociological language: "*Most Americans have most variations in common* though they are arranged differently in the sphere of valuations of different individuals and groups and bear different intensity coefficients."

For over a century and a half observers of the United States—the seasoned and scholarly as well as the transient and impressionistic—have written a catalog of American traits and remarked on its coherence. This catalog is, as Clyde Kluckhohn claimed, "based upon stubborn and irreducible facts of repeated observations that have amazing continuity over time." Lately, the forces of instant nationwide communications, constant mobility, a homogenizing popular culture, and the standardization inherent in mass production and a technological culture have steadily reduced the margins of idiosyncratic behavior in the United States.

The foundation of a people's character forms far earlier than their self-consciousness about it. The question of a distinctive American character was moot for the first hundred years and more following the settlements of the early seventeenth century. The early settlers saw themselves as colonists and an extension of British and European empires. Not until the eighteenth century did their nurture and patrimonial stake in the new land, combined with a spatial, commercial, and emotional distance from Europe, evoke the sense of a separate, distinctive society determined to be free. As Robert Frost saw in his poem "The Gift Outright":

> The land was ours before we were the land's.
> She was our land more than a hundred years
> Before we were her people. She was ours
> In Massachusetts, in Virginia,
> But we were England's, still colonials.

There were premonitions of difference from the outset, however, even before the first settlements. As Howard Mumford Jones vividly portrayed in *O Strange New World!* (1964), America inherited a legacy of medieval and Renaissance dreams and romantic visions. "The concept that the New World is the peculiar abode of felicity lingered for centuries in the European imagination and, like the youth of America, is one of its oldest traditions." Goethe's declaration *"Amerika, du hast es besser / Als unser Continent, das Alte"* was a late expression of a well-established sentiment. Over time, the Old World's pastoral visions collided with New World realities of wilderness and frontier. But after the vision of America as Eden came Exotic America, God's New Israel, Republican America, Immigrant America, and the Pax Americana. Each of these encounters of Old and New Worlds, people and environment, has ingrained itself in the American character.

☆ ☆ ☆ The Study of American Character

American character is only one in a populous field of terms used today for generalizations about the United States. In the quotation above Erik Erikson equated *national character* with *national identity*. Other common equivalents range from *typical personalities* and *cultural patterns* to *value system*, *worldview*, and *way of life*. The currency of *national character* has slipped somewhat in the recent past, both out of wariness about its authoritarian overtones and because of new work in culture studies. Historically and functionally, however, *American character* still best suggests the nation's preoccupation with defining itself and "who we are."

The purpose of this introductory essay is to discuss the search for reasonable and valid generalizations about the character of the American people. While it is impossible to cover the historical and scientific literature on American national character, it will be useful to identify some of the major directions the study of American character has taken, periods of special activity, and the current state of the field, especially the treatment of contradiction and paradox. The suggestions for "Further Reading" at the end of the essay indicate the next levels of exploration.

Professional study of American character began shortly before the turn of the century, principally through the influence of two historians. According to Michael McGiffert, the first historian "to take cognizance of the national character as a legitimate subject for investigation" was Henry Adams (1838–1918), who challenged the reigning preoccupation with political and diplomatic history, called for a comprehensive cultural approach, and declared that "of all historical problems, the nature of a national character is the most difficult and the most important." For all Adams's voluminous histories, essays, works of fiction, and biographies, however, no statement has had a more enduring impact on both scholarly and popular conceptions of the American character than the paper "The Significance of the Frontier in American History" read by his contemporary, Frederick Jackson Turner, at a historical congress held in conjunction with the 1893 World's Columbian Exposition.

☆ ☆ ☆ Between the World Wars

The social and psychological milieu in the United States between the First and Second world wars did not lend itself to an impartial study of the American character. The devastation of World War I and the ensuing return to "normalcy" introduced a decade of general skepticism, intolerance, and conservatism. Nativists pointed with alarm at prewar immigrants ghettoed in American cities and, playing on the fear of foreign ideologies, the Red Scare, and a general spirit of isolationism, closed the doors of asylum with the exclusionary legislation of the 1920s. The apparent values of the decade were its materialism, conformity, and provincialism; its representative man was Sinclair Lewis's George Babbitt. Many of America's intellectuals and artists expatriated to Europe and explored the ideas of Freud and Marx.

Historians, too, reflected the spiritual bifurcation of the times. The nativists tended to exaggerate the virtues of agrarianism and the frontier—individualism, self-reliance, independence—and to portray the essential American as immune to the artistic and industrial qualities of the city, which was the typical venue of the new immigrants. They "asserted that the distinctive qualities of the American, produced by racial inheritance and the selective influences of colonization and the frontier, were not well suited to industrial and urban life," Thomas Hartshorne noted, and they blamed the immigrant for the decline of America from its early idealism to a state of crass materialism. The antinativists, on their side, argued that the real danger lay with the established Americans, who had begun to take liberty for granted, and that the new immigrant, with a deep idealistic devotion to freedom, could redeem the American character from commercialism and materialism. Amid this fervid debate on Americanization, assimilation, and immigrant heritage, Horace Kallen advanced his manifesto of "cultural pluralism" as a means for preserving liberty and diversity in the face of numbing uniformity. Like Van Wyck Brooks and George Santayana, Kallen depicted the American as arrested—unhappily divided between a desiccated intellectual, Puritan culture on the one hand and a utilitarian, anti-intellectual pioneer culture on the other. In their *Middletown* studies of 1929 and 1937 Robert and Helen Lynd found the American caught in a tension between the individualizing experience of the frontier past and the social demands of the present. Americans strove for monetary success, the Lynds believed, in order to overcome the confusion and contradictions in their pursuits.

To some observers the stock market crash of 1929 and the onset of the Great Depression were a natural judgment upon the reactionary and self-satisfied twenties. With all the deep schisms and internal problems of the 1930s, the national character was not a primary focus of attention. Emphasis shifted from the national and abstract to the local and particular as politicians, anthropologists, journalists, and artists joined in a process of diagnosis and repair. Encouraged by Washington, they drafted town histories and state guidebooks, recorded folk songs and painted murals in public buildings, photographed the Okies, planted greenbelts, and planned model communities and regional projects like the Tennessee Valley Authority. Digging down to the bedrock of American culture, however, they also laid the foundations for a healthy new federalism—one based on variety, regionalism, and the people.

During the 1930s a number of forces gathered in preparation for the study and celebration of American character in the following decades. Important advances were made in immigration, labor, and urban history. Under the impetus of John and Alan Lomax and Constance Rourke, American folklore, humor, and lifeways gained scholarly attention. Ruth Benedict broke ground in the field of cultural anthropology by characterizing the psychological coherence of cultures, and Edward Sapir, Margaret Mead, and Clyde Kluckhohn, following psychoanalytic perspectives, laid the foundation for the study of personality and culture. The 1930s were a period of transition from eclectic writings on American character by journalists, historians, philosophers, and humanists to the emergence of a self-conscious field of inquiry in the social sciences, particularly in sociology, anthropology, psychology, and social history. Questioning the utility of the "typical individual" for studying modern heterogeneous societies, scholars developed new cultural approaches and explored value analysis as a defensible basis for generalization.

☆ ☆ ☆ World War II and the Incentive for Character Study

The groundwork laid during the 1930s was dramatically extended by the events of World War II. Here was a clear moral and ideological confrontation that, unlike the internal complexities of the 1930s or the ambiguities of World War I, the nation knew how to address. Both wartime and postwar conditions evoked the conviction that America, indeed, was endowed with a special mission and that American spirit and character, as much as its organizational skills, technological know-how, and material wealth, had redeemed the world from fascism. As Great Britain handed over the reigns of world power to the United States and statesmen declared the "American century," a new imperative emerged for explaining the American national character—to the world and to Americans themselves.

Work in the social sciences and humanities reflected the enlarged sense of purpose and a desire to understand America's character and culture in relation to both her allies and her enemies. Manifestos like Margaret Mead's *And Keep Your Powder Dry* (1942)—with its schematic essay "We Are All Third Generation"—explicitly applied the tools of the field anthropologist to an appreciation of American behavior and values. Mead wrote at the behest of the U.S. government and later reflected: "In the United States, the study of national character as the application of anthropological and psychological methods to contemporary modern societies developed during World War II. It was the wartime situation—in which the United States was faced with the problem of waging a total war, including psychological warfare, against little-known and inaccessible enemies—which stimulated this special scientific development." While Mead was analyzing the Americans, Ruth Benedict was investigating the Japanese national character and writing her landmark *The Chrysanthemum and the Sword: Patterns of Japanese Culture* (1946).

Social and institutional history saw bold new writings like Oscar Handlin's *Boston's Immigrants* (1941) and Alice Felt Tyler's *Freedom's Ferment* (1944). The expression of American uniqueness was also marked in literary history and criticism. F. O. Matthiessen defined the great tradition in *American Renaissance* (1941), and a battalion of scholars collaborated in writing *The Literary History of the United States* (1946), whose editors acknowledged: "The disruptions of the war and postwar eras, far from presenting handicaps, have stimulated interest by emphasizing the need for cultural redefinition." A new standard of intellectual history was set by works like Ralph Henry Gabriel's *The Course of American Democratic Thought* (1940), Perry Miller's *The New England Mind* (1939, 1953), and Louis Hartz's *The Liberal Tradition in America* (1955), which found the key to the American creed in the playing out of Lockean liberalism in a politically and socially new continent. Calling the 1930s and 1940s the "heroic age" in the development of American intellectual history, John Higham noted that the 1950s were dominated by intellectual historians and general historians wielding new cultural interpretations. "The most exciting, as well as the most controversial, single achievement of intellectual historians in the 1950s," Higham wrote, "was a fresh vision of the meaning of America. . . . According to this approach, a unifying framework of ideas and values had created a distinctive American people. It explained the durability of their society and institutions. The crucial task of historians was to define the matrix of beliefs and attitudes that shaped American history. Intellectual history gave the bite of scholarship to a broad quest for the American character."

Driven by the new confidence of American intellectual, cultural, and literary history, American Studies programs proliferated across the country in the 1940s and 1950s, many of them, significantly, insisting on the title "American Civilization." Scholars committed to a unifying knowledge of the national experience organized the American Studies Association in 1951. Similar associations soon came into existence in Great Britain, Germany, Japan, and other nations touched by the United States' presence in World War II. The Fulbright program, launched in 1946, stimulated American Studies around the globe.

Nothing provokes a nation's self-consciousness about unity and values more quickly than external threats and confrontations with alien ideologies. This was conspicuously true at the time of the American Revolution and again in World War II. "Foreign policy is the face a nation wears to the world," Arthur Schlesinger, Jr., wrote in his essay "Foreign Policy and the American Character" (1983), and the world provides the mirror in which a nation composes its face. During the Cold War of the 1950s J. Robert Oppenheimer noted that the conflict with the Soviet Union threw a harsh light on "our inability to give an account of our national purpose, intentions, and hopes that is at once honest and inspiring." The lack of a clear ideological imperative or strategic objectives during the Vietnam War plainly contributed to the fading interest in intellectual history, consensus, and national character studies in the later 1960s and early 1970s and to a surge of community studies and urban anthropology.

During the 1980s, however, the pendulum of interest began to swing back toward political theory and assertions of American uniqueness in academic as well as public discourse. Fading memories of the Vietnam War, the holding of American hostages by the fundamentalist regime in Iran in 1978–79, and a torrent of asylum-seekers from Eastern Europe, Southeast Asia, and Central America all spurred renewed interest in American institutions and character, however grim the nation's internal problems might have seemed. The swift and sure prosecution of the Persian Gulf War in 1990–91 loosed an outpouring of patriotism and homage, at home and around the world, such as had not been seen since 1945. To many Americans, divine guidance, republicanism, frontier savvy, and technological-scientific acumen all appeared alive and well once again in the "redeemer nation."

☆ ☆ ☆ Social, Behavioral, and Political Sciences

The engagement of the social and behavioral sciences in the study of national character has followed generally the same pattern as literary and historical studies—tilling and seeding in the 1930s, a harvest of works during the war and postwar decades, reconsideration in the 1960s and 1970s. Over the last half century anthropology, psychology, and sociology have brought to the arena their respective expertise with culture, personality, and social structure. The curve of their interest has reflected both the internal development of the disciplines and the public exigencies of the times.

By the mid-1930s the field of anthropology was moving from description of social norms to investigating personality as an expression of culture, that is, the ways in which individuals internalize cultural values and learn appropriate behavior. As Alex Inkeles and Daniel Levinson pointed out in *The Handbook of Social Psychology* (1968), Ruth Benedict "went beyond the mere behavioral description of the individual as a product of his culture, to characterization of the *psychological coherence* of the culture as a whole." In linking sociocultural and personality systems, Benedict motivated other anthropologists to study the relations of culture and personality and to explore the basic personality structure of Americans. During the war and its immediate aftermath national character became a major field of study for anthropologists and allied behavioral scientists interested in the psychology and character of nations. "The decade from 1935 to 1945," according to Inkeles and Levinson, "bracketed by Benedict's *Patterns of Culture* (1934) and Kardiner's *Psychological Frontiers of Society* (1945), was the seminal period of development. The period that followed was one of self-confident affirmation as the results of wartime research and new field work poured in." By the early 1950s, however, anthropology had largely withdrawn from personality and culture research and from national character studies in general.

Social psychologists remained aloof from personality theory and national character research through the 1920s and 1930s, both because of their commitment to experimental techniques and the way generalizations about group character were associated with race theory and stereotyping. Beginning in the late 1930s, however, psychoanalysis and new methods of clinical research stimulated psychologists' interest in personality and culture studies. "It was not," Inkeles and Levinson wrote, "merely that anthropologists turned to psychoanalysis. What was equally important, a number of creative psychoanalysts turned to anthropology and other social sciences." An inclusive psychosocial approach was envisioned in the fertile intellectual environment of the 1930s and 1940s. By the mid-1950s the study of personality in a societal perspective had been accepted as an appropriate concern for academic psychology.

Sociologists made little effort to study personality as a factor of social organization before the 1950s, but then began to recognize the importance of the motives and means of adaptation possessed by members of the group. David Riesman's *The Lonely Crowd* (1950) particularly enhanced the study of social character. Reflecting the general postwar concern with autonomy and conformity in a mass society, Riesman depicted a shift in the character and values of middle-class Americans from an "inner-directed" type (whose values were inculcated by parental instruction and example) to an "other-directed" type (shaped by peer-group pressure).

The anthropologists, psychologists, and sociologists who took up national character studies in this era illuminated a dynamic interaction of individual, social group, and historical contexts. Their attention to personality structures, nurture and child rearing, and functional adjustment to the values demanded by society gave a new theoretical integrity to the discussion of national character and established new uses for impressionistic accounts of daily life like those provided by nineteenth-century travelers to the United States. Throughout the 1950s the exploration of the American character was promoted by such theses as David Potter's *People of Plenty* (1954), which claimed the influence of abundance in shaping American character, especially in child rearing, and William Whyte's *The Organization Man* (1956), which advanced the thesis that the Protestant ethic of work, thrift, and deferred gratification had been replaced by socialization and conformity. The status of national character studies in the contemporary social sciences has been summarized by Inkeles and Levinson in these terms:

> The concept of national character is an important but problematic one in the social sciences. It has been strongly rejected in the hereditarian or racist forms in which it was couched by earlier writers. Seen in more modern perspective, however, it poses fundamental problems for social-scientific theory and research: To what extent do the patterned conditions of life in a particular society give rise to certain distinctive patterns in the personalities of its members? To what extent, that is, does the socio-cultural system produce its distinctive forms of "social character," "basic personality structure," or "modal personality"? Further, what are the consequences, if any, of this patterning in personality for stability or change in the societal order?

The global warfare of 1939–45, followed by the dismantling of European empires and a multiplication of independent new nations, also elicited a vigorous concern for national identity among political scientists, whose work has not yet received sufficient attention in American culture studies. Super Power alliances in the postwar era and the traumas of modernization among developing nations called attention to the complex nature of nationalism and the forces that integrate peoples at subnational, national, and supranational levels. The new emphasis on "nation building"—a self-conscious process marked by objective indicators and thus susceptible to quantitative analysis—has brought more scientific precision to previously organicist and subjective explanations of national character by political historians. In formulating criteria for national mobilization and assimilation, political scientists have erected matrices of ethnicity, language, caste, education, religion, economics, and individual will and given weight to communication processes and the symbolic content of messages exchanged within groups of people. The methodologies they have developed for charting the conditions, course, and rate of consolidation in the new nations are useful, after the fact, for tracing American national consciousness through its formative years. Conversely, the experience of the United States—the first modern nation to break away successfully from colonial rule through revolution—offers a model for twentieth-century nation builders. As is true for the new nations of the post–World War II era, nationality within the United States has been a twin process both of protest and secession from a larger empire and of internal unification.

The study of nationalism is especially indebted to Hans Kohn, who did his work when the "problem of nationalism" was becoming most apparent. Kohn's *The Idea of Nationalism* (1944) is essentially a survey of nationalism's "long period of incubation from Ancient times to the French Revolution." In his *American Nationalism: An Interpretive Essay* (1957), Kohn then examined the ideological origins of the American nation and, from a comparative perspective, the forces that unified and gave a distinctive style to the American people.

At this same time Karl Deutsch, like Kohn an émigré from Prague, Czechoslovakia, was laying foundations for the study of national development and international community. Where Kohn's interest in nationalism was largely historical, Deutsch and his associates proposed experimental tests to measure "the extent of complementarity among members of one people in matters of social communication" and "quantitative concepts which could be applied to social, educational, political, and economic statistics for the prediction of national assimilation or differentiation of mixed populations in a given territory." In *Nationalism and Social Communication: An Inquiry into the Foundations of Nationality* (1953) and elsewhere, Deutsch set forth his theory of "a people as a community of social communication" and his concern for the persistence of nationality in mobile and competitive industrial societies.

Richard Merritt is one of many political scientists who have been influenced by Deutsch's theoretical and applied work. In *Symbols of American Community, 1735–1775* (1966), Merritt used content analysis to attack questions of when the colonists began to consider themselves "Americans" rather than British subjects, what process brought the isolated colonies into integrated political community, and whether American community awareness preceded or followed formal political integration. In order to gauge the colonial outlook as British, American, regional, or local, Merritt quantified the frequency and distribution of geographic place names appearing in colonial newspapers over a forty-year period and substantiated that the shift from colonial to American national consciousness was well advanced before the colonists undertook to revolt against the mother country.

Perhaps the most influential study in this area is Seymour Martin Lipset's *The First New Nation: The United States in Historical and Comparative Perspective* (1963), which addresses the social and ideological development of the United States in light of problems faced by emerging nations. The dialectically opposed values of equality and achievement that Lipset saw enacted throughout American history will be mentioned again. The inspiration for the book and its title, however, was Lipset's belief that America's experience in establishing national authority and formulating a national identity would be of value to other nations seeking stable democratic institutions, a view that certainly has been supported by the constant emulation of the Constitution of the United States.

The psychological consequences of social mobilization, extended communications, and nation building have been well articulated by Lipset's colleague at Stanford University, sociologist Alex Inkeles. In *Becoming Modern: Individual Change in Six Developing Countries* (1974), Inkeles and David M. Smith reported the results of a sophisticated program of interviews in two South Asian, two African, and two South American nations and assessed the personal traits called forth by modernity. In contrast to the "traditional" person, who is locally oriented and suspicious of authority and education, the "modern" personality evoked by urban industrialism is an active citizen, open to new ideas, educated, and committed to individual and social planning—traits necessary for the development of social democracies.

Such work in political sociology and social psychology not only highlights the internal difficulties confronting new nations but also increases our appreciation for the times in which American nationhood and identity were forged. America's political institutions were created in conditions of relative well-being among a people who already had achieved levels of literacy, education, communication, and assimilation that were supportive of nationality.

☆ ☆ ☆ National Character: Modal Personality Structure or Ethnography?

In his methodological essays, Inkeles has pointed out three traditional perspectives for regarding national character: as a nation's typical institutional patterns (political, social, economic); as a history of behavior and actions; and as cultural themes (values, religions, ethos, the arts). For a modern and scientifically feasible alternative he has proposed that national character "be equated with modal personality structure; that is, it should refer to the mode or modes of the distribution of personality variants within a given society." The quantitative and empirical requirements of this approach are facilitated by the development in modern behavioral sciences of "measures for recording individual opinion, habit, belief, behavior, and psychological disposition. These permit us to base our assessment of the American national character on the direct study of representative samples of the population of the United States." Opinion polling that cuts across class and ethnic lines should be able to define commonly held proclivities. Inkeles has concluded that not only is such a method a conceptually valid basis for generalization, but also that "it can be shown that on the most fundamental values, and in the more basic psychological dispositions, minorities such as blacks and Catholics share the general American national character."

Among the continuities that Inkeles has marked are the conviction of America as a promised land, based particularly on pride in American government and political institutions; independence and self-reliance, accompanied by the imperatives of persistence, hard work, and initiative; commitment to communal action, voluntarism, and "organizational democracy"; trust and respect for the mutual rights of others; optimism; authoritarianism; equality; and a "restless energy, pragmatism, a tendency toward brashness or boastfulness, this-worldliness, a preference for the concrete, and a certain discomfort in coping with aesthetic and emotional expression." All "can be documented by recent empirical psychosocial tests still to be part of that syndrome that makes up the modal personality pattern of the current population of the United States."

In explaining how the masses of American immigrants possibly could have acquired the attitudes and values that typify the American character structure, Inkeles grants some validity to the theory of selective and differential recruitment of immigrants but ascribes more importance to "the responsiveness of government, the experience of equality, the active practice of democracy, and the relative abundance of the material means of existence." He also gives large credit to the modern public school system, which by its nature instills such elements of the American national character as "a sense of personal efficacy and of openness to new experience, a sense of self-reliance, and striving for independence from traditional authority."

Other modal approaches to national character also have been introduced. In *The Civic Culture* (1963), for example, Gabriel Almond and Sidney Verba examined modal political attitudes in population samples from five democratic nations, preparing the way for further research in "political culture."

Although given new scientific credentials, the results of such inquiry often do not differ greatly from the "typical" American drawn by Tocqueville or canvassed by other nineteenth-century observers. Lord Bryce, too, knew the relationship of character and opinion, observing in *The American Common-wealth* (1888) that "the public opinion of a people is even more directly than its political institutions the reflection and expression of its character." Bryce found the American people overall to be good-natured, hopeful, educated, moral, religious but unreverential, commercial, associative but unsettled, changeful, and conservative.

In *Democratic Vistas*, Walt Whitman probed "the important question of character, of an American stock-personality, with literatures and arts for outlets and return-expressions." Neither the bardic generality of Whitman's "stock-personality" nor the abstraction of the "modal personality structure," however, has been satisfying to all scholars. Anthropologist Theodore Schwartz of the University of California at San Diego has proposed a more dynamic model for studying the interaction between individual and culture—one that does not reduce him to "a *typical* American" (who must he represent but himself?), nor lump him into a social class (which is "so cross-cut by other differentials . . . that its effects are buffered, muted, and greatly weakened"), but rather respects his irreducible individuality within a "common identity as an American."

In a new essay entitled "The Structure of National Cultures," Schwartz moves through "unitary, segmental, and distributive" models of culture to focus particularly on the *idioverse*. "The personalities of individuals," Schwartz writes, "are the distributive locus of culture and that culture is the set of personalities of the members of a culture. . . . This common part is its set of intersects with all other personalities in the population." The structure of culture and the shape of its complexities are to be found in those factors that differentiate or assimilate "the experience of individuals." Schwartz proposes as a goal for teaching and research "the cumulative development of an ethnography of our culture," an ethnographic grid that displays the intersections of personal experience. Such a model repudiates neither commonality nor generalization, for the idioverse, the local identities Americans assume "as they migrate or transfer around the country," and their common identity as Americans are linked by "a multiplicity of bridging institutions like the overpasses at the intersection of major freeways." Although they succeed only partially in standardizing the national experience, "schooling, military service, sports, popular culture and the mass media all are sources of unifying experience." The lines of our cultural complexity are the locus of struggle and politics but also of emulation.

Seeking a "mid-level of description and understanding" that recognizes both diversity and unity, Schwartz suggests that if there are "core characteristics of American culture, one of them would be the cultural, social, and political adaptation to diversity." National culture is partly "self-recognition after the fact of historical differentiation, partly a will to separate identity—a *construction*." Even marginal differences may be more perceptible than the massive similarity, but worldwide "the cultural *big bang* has reversed itself in increasing convergence" since the age of Columbus.

☆ ☆ ☆ Value Analysis

The new social science approaches to national character, with their negotiations of individual personality and the social group, have given a high degree of prominence to value analysis. The search for a dominant and endur-ing value system as the index to national character makes particularly good sense for a heterogeneous society in an age of mass communication. "Formerly regarded as supplemental to the study of personality traits, behavioral pat-terns, and institutional structures," Michael McGiffert pointed out, "the ex-amination of values has now been widely accepted as a coordinate approach in national character analysis; many scholars have found in it a key to aspects of the American character which are less accessible by other avenues of investiga-tion." These scholars tend to divide into two camps: those who emphasize consensus and the "core" values by which the society is defined and unified and those who stress diversity, pluralism, and tensions in American values.

Definitions of *value* vary from Robin Williams's "criteria for selection in action" to Ralph Henry Gabriel's "an ideal, a paradigm setting forth a desired and esteemed possible social reality." Concurring that they "are by definition criteria, that is, ideals, goals, norms, and standards," Ethel Albert cautioned that values, known chiefly through verbal behavior, should not be mistaken for the actualities of conduct. Furthermore, cultures tend to maintain two orders of value: "high-level ideals [that] are not intended for universal, literal realization" and the secondary values that are the practical guides to behavior. The contrast between its ideal and realistic values—as between its standards and achievements—helps define the characteristic tensions of a society. Tra-cing those tensions has become a major task for modern American historians and social scientists.

Many inventories have been made of America's traditional core values, some of which have been cited above. In the early 1960s, Albert and Williams drew particular attention to these features:

• An activist approach to life, based on mastery rather than passive accep-tance of events

• Emphasis on achievement and success, understood largely as material prosperity

- A moral character, oriented to such Puritan virtues as duty, industry, and sobriety
- Religious faith
- Science and secular rationality, encouraged by a view of the universe as orderly, knowable, and benign, and emphasizing an external rather than inward view of the world
- A progressive rather than traditionalist or static view of history, governed by optimism, confidence in the future, and a belief that progress can be achieved by effort
- Equality, with a horizontal or equalitarian rather than hierarchical view of social relations
- High evaluation of individual personality, rather than collective identity or responsibility
- Self-reliance
- Humanitarianism
- External conformity
- Tolerance of diversity
- Efficiency and practicality
- Freedom
- Democracy
- Nationalism and patriotism
- Idealism and perfectionism
- Mobility and change

Even a cursory view of these and other attributed values will turn up seeming contradictions and tensions. Can a people, for instance, be simultaneously idealistic and materialistic? Conformist and individualistic? Law-abiding and violent? Dedicated to both work and leisure? Religion and science? Agrarianism and industrialism? Competition and love? It would be convenient to suppose that in a nation of a quarter billion people the putative values and traits of Americans are parceled out in internally consistent packages to separate groups within the culture. But while there will be saliences of value in various groups and regions, we know not only that the personality of Americans contains such apparent antitheses as those enumerated above, but also that most Americans hold them in some form of characteristic suspension. Walt Whitman observed for the American people of the nineteenth century:

> Do I contradict myself?
> Very well then I contradict myself,
> (I am large, I contain multitudes.)

Just how the American contradicts himself or herself may be our most important question. Explaining the multitudinous character of Americans has produced a school of scholarship in the last years occupied with contradiction, dilemma, and paradox.

☆ ☆ ☆ Contradiction, Dilemma, and Paradox

Perhaps the most agonizing contradiction in American culture has been the long coexistence of an official creed of individual freedom, equality, opportunity, and justice and the de facto, when not de jure, discrimination against African Americans. Gunnar Myrdal posed this problem in his momentous study, *An American Dilemma: The Negro Problem and Modern Democracy* (1944), but also conceded that belief in the "American Creed" has been a major factor in changing the position of the African American for the better. Three decades later, Daniel Bell focused on a distinctively modern fault line in the American character in *The Cultural Contradictions of Capitalism* (1976). According to Bell, America is a deeply schizophrenic nation today; its culture is drifting toward hedonism and consumerism even while its societal structure stands on the old virtues of thrift, hard work, self-denial, and efficiency.

While some critics in the 1970s portrayed a nation bewildered and schizophrenic, others saw the dualities in American life as typical—a dialectic that has long characterized the nation. In his *People of Paradox* (1972), Michael Kammen cited a few of the single-factor explanations that have been ventured to account for the American character but also noted the dualities that have struck prominent observers of the American scene: Alexis de Tocqueville commenting that individualism and idealism were as characteristic of America as conformity and materialism; Van Wyck Brooks describing two main currents running through the American mind, the transcendentalism of Jonathan Edwards and Ralph Waldo Emerson and the practicality that Benjamin Franklin turned into a philosophy of common sense. From the very beginnings of the nation, Kammen wrote, "there has been contention over the meaning of America. Was it to be a conglomeration of individuals, each going his own way, or a well-ordered society of generally co-operative groups. The very vastness of the landscape made the former almost inevitable, but the latter nearly a necessity." Kammen sought a means of getting beyond both monocausal explanations and conflict-versus-consensus arguments by calling attention not to deformities or uniformities but to *biformities* in American life. "What finally matters," he offered, "is the particular configuration of tensions within a national setting, as well as the behavioral, intellectual, and emotional consequences of that configuration."

One way to reconcile the host of explanations for American character is to demonstrate a style of mind attuned to function in the presence of deeply felt antitheses. Considering the alternatives facing most Americans, psychoanalyst Erik Erikson claimed: "Thus the functioning American, as the heir of a history of extreme contrasts and abrupt changes, bases his final ego identity on some tentative combination of dynamic polarities such as migratory and sedentary, individualistic and standardized, competitive and cooperative, pious and free-thinking, responsible and cynical, etc." As Kammen observed, "The United States may very well be the first large-scale society to have built innovation and change into its culture as a constant variable, so that a kind of 'creative destruction' continually alters the face of American life."

Robert Wiebe has advanced a similar thesis in *The Segmented Society: An Introduction to the Meaning of America* (1975). Eschewing the notion that historical and social continuity implies uniformity, Wiebe perceived America as a persistently segmented—not fragmented—society, "a configuration of small social units—primary circles of identity, values, associations, goals— that have sufficient authority to dominate the terms of their most important relationships with the world outside." The social segments may be based on kinship, work, locality, religion, community, or ethnicity, but they recognize the individual's role within a self-contained system while interlinking with other segments. This is a society brought about by cultural diversity, open land, and material abundance. Along the "lines of tension" the Americans have built a web of "remarkably tough societies" that derive their characteristic beliefs, behavior, and cohesion from their very segmentation.

More recently, in *American Politics: The Promise of Disharmony* (1981), Samuel Huntington has argued that America is fated to disharmony, with intermittent periods of political passion, because of the inevitable gap between its noble historical creed of liberty, equality, democracy, and constitutionalism and the realities of political institutions.

☆ ☆ ☆ Polarities and Reconciliations

Working together, historians and social scientists have woven a pattern of character from the warp of core values in America and the woof of individual experience. As their culture evolves across the intersections of unity and diversity, scholars have been pressed to develop strategies for reconciling the apparent contradictions in American values. In chapter 14 Nathan Glazer considers the inherent conflict between equality and individualism and between two forms of individualism in the United States. Four other polarities in American life that have received widespread popular and scholarly attention are: individualism and conformity, idealism and materialism, equality and achievement, individualism and commitment.

In his essay "The Quest for the National Character," David Potter observed that in the long history of thought about American character, from Thomas Jefferson and Alexis de Tocqueville to David Riesman, there have been, at bottom, two basic explanations around which almost all other interpretations can be grouped. "The most disconcerting fact about these two composite images of the American," Potter claimed, "is that they are strikingly dissimilar and seemingly about as inconsistent with one another as two interpretations of the same phenomenon could possibly be. One depicts the American primarily as an individualist and an idealist, while the other makes him out as a conformist and a materialist."

To unlock these contradictions, Potter turned to the American commitment to equality, which Tocqueville called "the fundamental fact from which all others seem to be derived." Following the logic of equality of opportunity, one encounters an individual obligated, in competition with his fellow Americans, to earn the rewards that skill and talent can bring. So compelling is this competitive race that everyone has an almost sacred duty to succeed and to manifest the tangible results of his success. "Here, certainly, an equalitarian doctrine fostered materialism, and if aggressiveness and competitiveness are individualistic qualities, then it fostered individualism also." To account for the American idealist praised by Jefferson as well as the conformist discovered by Tocqueville, Potter turned to that "strand of equalitarianism which stresses the universal dignity of all men," and which hates rank as a "violation of dignity." The American commitment to progress, based on a prior belief in human perfectibility, is idealistic. Yet "American idealism has often framed its most altruistic goals in materialistic terms—for instance of raising the standard of living as a means to a better life." The American, in George Santayana's classic epigram, has been "an idealist working on matter."

While Potter sought in equalitarianism a key to reconciling polarities of individualism and conformity, idealism and materialism, Seymour Lipset has regarded equality itself as one side of a pair of core values that have determined American behavior and institutions. Before the doctrine of equality was enunciated in the revolutionary period, the Protestant ethic of work and individual achievement had set its imprint on American life. These two cultural themes—equality and achievement—according to Lipset, established a dynamic interaction that has continued to shape the national experience. They may be mutually supportive, inasmuch as "the ideal of equal opportunity institutionalized the notion that success should be the goal of *all*, without reference to accidents of birth or class or color." On the other hand, "the equalitarian ethos of the American Revolution and the achievement orientation of the Protestant ethic . . . also involve normative conflict." Variations in personal talent and skill inevitably lead to different rates of success, to material inequality, and to the emergence of a stratified society that, nevertheless, "has been checked by the recurrent victories of the forces of equality in the political order." American society, Lipset claims, has exhibited a high level of continuity as it perpetually realizes the significance of the two basic values to which it is committed.

The two supposed conversions in American character that have had the widest celebrity are a sacrifice of individualism for conformity and the demise of the achievement ethic. Yet even these notions may be evoked more by idealization of the past than by present-day realities. The mirror that foreign commentary holds up to America reflected essentially the same traits in the 1830s and 1840s as in the 1970s and 1980s. Readers of Tocqueville should remember his remark: "I know of no country in which there is so little independence of mind and real freedom of discussion as in America." Harriet Martineau was also quick to note the hesitancy of Americans to speak their own minds on politics out of concern about the opinions of others. Populism is nothing new. Clyde Kluckhohn observed that, in matter of fact, "today's kind of 'conformity' may actually be a step toward more genuine individualism in the United States"—not the exhibitionism of the nineteenth-century individualist, but a public acceptance of the conventions of one's group by which "one may have greater psychic energy to develop and fulfill one's private potentialities as a unique person." The vigorous exercise of press freedoms and the intellectual autonomy of the nation's universities have sanctuaried and institutionalized the critical process. Similarly, there is little reason to believe that the aspiration level of Americans is in general decline. The personal sacrifices, savings, and work habits of new immigrants to the United States, the professional aspirations of college students, and the cultural life of the nation as a whole reflect no more passivity in the latter half of the twentieth century than in earlier periods.

One of the newest formulations of American life, true to the idiom of its time, has featured a dialectic of individualism and commitment. Taking their title, purpose, and technique directly from Tocqueville's *Democracy in America*, University of California sociologist Robert Bellah and his coauthors meditated in *Habits of the Heart* (1985) upon their experience and conversations with a cross section of white middle-class Americans in the 1980s. While Tocqueville considered equality to be the "fundamental fact," Bellah and his colleagues, including two other sociologists, a philosopher, and a theologian, believed that "individualism lies at the very core of American culture." Individualism is not a monolithic code of conduct: there is "a biblical individualism and a civic individualism as well as a utilitarian and an expressive individualism." But in its diverse and often contradictory manifestations, they contended, American individualism has become a sacred and a moral obligation. It is bound to "our highest and noblest aspirations, not only for ourselves, but for those we care about, for our society and for the world." It is also closely linked to problems of personal intimacy, community, and commitment in the social, civic, and religious areas of life. The contradictions and paradoxes contained within American individualism, according to the authors, are bases of the collective identity but also forces threatening to destroy from within.

☆ ☆ ☆ Hope and Fear

As justification for surveying middle-class Americans only, the authors of *Habits of the Heart* pointed to the importance of this class in republican theory and to the Americans' habit of thinking "in middle-class categories, even when they are inappropriate." In a recent book, *Fear of Falling: The Inner Life of the Middle Class* (1989), Barbara Ehrenreich first laments the concentration by American cultural theorists on "a bland and neutral mainstream—from which every other group or class is ultimately a kind of deviation"—and then addresses the same population. The professional, mostly white middle class may constitute a form of elite in American society, Ehrenreich claims, but it is "an insecure and deeply anxious one"—fearful of the downward slide that any misfortune might induce; fearful also "of inner weakness, of growing soft, of failing to strive, of losing discipline and will," fearful "of hedonism and self-indulgence," fearful, "always, of falling."

Ehrenreich's book and Rupert Wilkinson's *The Pursuit of American Character*, which appeared a year earlier, suggest a final dialectic that has exercised Americans, and America watchers, for generations: the polarities of optimism and pessimism, hope and fear. Wilkinson, a British scholar trained in America, had explored contradictions and internal tensions in an earlier study of popular culture called *American Tough: The Tough-Guy Tradition and American Character* (1984). In the new work he reviews interpretations of American character since the 1940s, weighing Americans' constant efforts to pin down a national identity and offering a scheme of "four fears" in explanation: "the fear of *being owned*," "the fear of *falling apart*," "the fear of *winding down*," and "the fear of *falling away* from a past virtue and promise."

Wilkinson's four fears might strike one at first as a sly inversion of Franklin Delano Roosevelt's four freedoms (the last of which was "freedom from fear") or perhaps a grievance that the scepter of authority passed from Britain to the United States in 1941. But his survey of American self-analysis and self-criticism, and his quickness to see "fear" as a source of strength as well as weakness, are a healthy reminder that the anxieties many contemporary critics see as acute are, in fact, through the longer lens of history, both chronic and characteristic. Who could read *Death of a Salesman* or *The Great Gatsby*, *The Rise of Silas Lapham* or *Home as Found*, for instance, and not be keenly aware of republican dreams and middle-class anxieties? The "howling wilderness" and a fear of backsliding motivated colonial Christians; Thomas Paine rebuked "the summer soldier and the sunshine patriot"; *neurasthenia* entered the national vocabulary late in the nineteenth century. Walt Whitman was as clear about the tension of individualism and conformity as today's pundits. "I say we had best look our times and lands searching in the face," Whitman wrote in 1871, "like a physician diagnosing some deep disease. Never was there, perhaps, more hollowness at heart than at present, and here in the United States." He recognized a contradiction, too, between the "mass, or lump character," and "the singleness of man, individualism," and declared, "our task is to reconcile them." What the authors of *Habits of the Heart* call *commitment*, Whitman referred to simply as *amativeness*.

While the 8 July 1991 issue of *U.S. News and World Report* featured "America before Columbus: The Untold Story," *Time* magazine's cover story on the same day wondered "Who Are We?"—and then debated issues of "commonality" and "multiculturalism" that are pulsating through the American educational system. Two months earlier, on 5 May 1991, the *Los Angeles Times* had published a special report on "America and the New Immigrant Experience" that began with a pair of articles entitled "Coming Together" and "Coming Apart." These are the yin and yang of the American experience. Erik Erikson's proposition that a nation's identity is the way it counterpoints opposite personalities—"the ways in which it lifts this counterpoint to a unique style of civilization, or lets it disintegrate into mere contradiction"—suggests that in America's diversity *is* its unity.

Like the Mississippi River, American character is a network combining tributaries, confluences, margins, and mainstream, overflowing dikes and levees, carrying tourists and commerce, fertilizing but also destroying the land, in constant change and process, enduring. Like the much-prophesied silting up of the Mississippi Delta, the decline of the American character, too, has been greatly exaggerated.

FURTHER READING

Every student of American national character sooner or later draws on observations of foreign travelers and visitors to the United States. J. Hector St. John de Crèvecoeur's *Letters from an American Farmer* (1782), Alexis de Tocqueville's *Democracy in America* (1835–40), Harriet Martineau's *Society in America* (1837), and Lord James Bryce's *The American Commonwealth* (1888), all fundamental, are available in many editions. A wide range of commentary has been anthologized in Henry Steele Commager, ed., *America in Perspective: The United States through Foreign Eyes in Thirty-Five Essays* (New York, 1947), and Marc Pachter, ed., *Travelers to the New Nation, 1776–1914* (Washington, D.C., 1982). Arthur M. Schlesinger listed the traits "most frequently noted" by foreign visitors in "What Then Is the American, This New Man?" *American Historical Review* 48 (January 1943). See also Gerald E. Stearns, ed., *Broken Image: Foreign Critiques of America* (New York, 1972), a collection of critical assaults, and Peter Conrad, *Imagining America* (New York, 1980), an appraisal of British writers who journeyed to America.

Recent British critiques, fond and otherwise, include Anthony Bailey, *America, Lost and Found* (New York, 1980); Jonathan Raban, *Old Glory: An American Voyage* (New York, 1981); Edmund Fawcett and Tony Thomas, *The American Condition* (New York, 1982); and Alan Whicker, *Whicker's New World: America through the Eyes and Lives of Resident Brits* (London, 1985). The British response has been analyzed by Richard Rapson in *Britons View America: Travel Commentary, 1860–1935* (Seattle, 1971) and for the years since 1935 by Barbara Bennett Peterson in *America in British Eyes* (Honolulu, 1988). French reactions at the time of Crèvecoeur are sampled by William Pencak in "In Search of the American Character: French Travellers in Eighteenth-Century Pennsylvania," *Pennsylvania History* 55 (January 1988). Contemporary French writings on America range from hopeful to sardonic, as in Jean-François Revel, *Without Marx or Jesus: The New American Revolution Has Begun* (New York, 1971), and Jean Baudrillard, *America* (New York, 1988), respectively.

Americans, too, are perennially crisscrossing the land "in search of" America. Thomas Jefferson's *Notes on the State of Virginia* (London, 1785), which began as a statistical inquiry into the boundaries, climate, resources, and institutions of the then-vast state of Virginia, is unequaled as an exposition of the "empire of liberty." The quest for meaning, customs, mores, and idioms continues today in works like

John Steinbeck, *Travels with Charley: In Search of America* (New York, 1962); Studs Terkel, *American Dreams: Lost and Found* (New York, 1980); Charles Kuralt, *Dateline America* (New York, 1982); William Least Heat Moon, *Blue Highways: A Journey into America* (Boston, 1983); and Richard Reeves, *American Journey: Traveling with Tocqueville in Search of Democracy in America* (New York, 1982). In further response to Tocqueville, see Robert H. Bellah et al., *Habits of the Heart: Individualism and Commitment in American Life* (Berkeley, Calif., 1985). *The American Commonwealth*, ed. Nathan Glazer and Irving Kristol (New York, 1976), is a neoconservative appraisal along the lines of Lord Bryce.

American nationalism is still well approached through Hans Kohn's books *The Idea of Nationalism: A Study in Its Origin and Background* (New York, 1944), *American Nationalism: An Interpretive Essay* (New York, 1957), and *The Age of Nationalism: The First Era of Global History* (New York, 1962). On global community, modeling, power alliances, and communications, see Karl W. Deutsch's *Nationalism and Social Communication: An Inquiry into the Foundations of Nationality* (Cambridge, Mass., 1953) and *Nationalism and Its Alternatives* (New York, 1969). See also Deutsch and Richard L. Merritt, *Nationalism and National Development: An Interdisciplinary Bibliography* (Cambridge, Mass., 1970), and Deutsch and William J. Foltz, eds., *Nation-Building* (New York, 1966), especially the bibliography, Hermann Weilmann's essay "The Interlocking of Nation and Personality Structure," and Richard L. Merritt's essay "Nation-Building in America: The Colonial Years." Merritt's *Symbols of American Community, 1735–1775* (New Haven, Conn., 1966) and Wilbur Zelinsky's splendid *Nation into State: The Shifting Symbolic Foundations of American Nationalism* (Chapel Hill, N.C., 1989) demonstrate quantitative techniques for charting national consciousness from political, social, and cultural data. For multinational studies of "political culture" based on survey research, see Gabriel A. Almond and Sidney Verba, *The Civic Culture: Political Attitudes and Democracy in Five Nations* (Princeton, N.J., 1963); Almond and Verba, eds., *The Civic Culture Revisited* (Boston, 1980); and Verba et al., *Participation and Political Equality: A Seven-Nation Comparison* (Chicago, 1987). An important application of survey research domestically is Joseph Veroff, Elizabeth Douvan, and Richard A. Kulka's *The Inner American: A Self-Portrait from 1957 to 1976* (New York, 1981).

The constitutional roots of American national identity and the relation of American character to foreign policy are treated in Leslie Berlowitz, Denis Donoghue, and Louis Menand, eds., *America in Theory* (New York, 1988); Arthur Schlesinger, Jr., "Foreign Policy and the American Character," *Foreign Affairs* 62 (Fall 1983); Michael P. Hamilton, ed., *American Character and Foreign Policy* (Grand Rapids, Mich., 1986); and William Pfaff, *Barbarian Sentiments: How the American Century Ends* (New York, 1989).

Louis Hartz, *The Liberal Tradition in America* (New York, 1955), emphasizes the ideological legacy of the Revolution, utopianism, chosenness, the flight from Europe, and characteristic American tensions. The melding of religious calling and manifest destiny ("civil religion") is studied in Ernest Lee Tuveson, *Redeemer Nation: The Idea of America's Millennial Role* (Chicago, 1968), and John F. Wilson, *Public Religion in American Culture* (Philadelphia, 1979). In this context, see also Daniel Bell's essay "The End of American Exceptionalism," in *The American Commonwealth*, ed. Glazer and Kristol.

Howard Mumford Jones tells of the marriage of Old World myths and traditions to New World conditions in *O Strange New World!: American Culture, the Formative Years* (New York, 1964). James Oliver Robinson continues the story in *American Myth—American Reality* (New York, 1980). In *The Quest for Nationality: An American Literary Campaign* (Syracuse, N.Y., 1957), Benjamin T. Spencer traces the effort to foster a national literature from the seventeenth through the nineteenth centuries. C. Vann Woodward, ed., *The Comparative Approach to American History* (New York, 1968), studies two dozen movements of U.S. history in international perspective.

After first considering Frederick Jackson Turner's *The Frontier in American History* (New York, 1920), which contains his famous essay "The Significance of the Frontier in American History" (1893), students of America's natural and social frontiers might move on to Ray A. Billington, *America's Frontier Heritage* (New York, 1966), and Billington, ed., *The Frontier Thesis: Valid Interpretation of American History?* (New York, 1966). The standard text is Billington and Martin Ridge, *Westward Expansion: A History of the American Frontier*, 5th ed. (New York, 1982). For other expressions of the frontier ethos, see Henry Nash Smith, *Virgin Land: The American West as Symbol and Myth* (Cambridge, Mass., 1950); Harold P. Simonson, *The Closed Frontier: Studies in American Literary Tragedy* (New York, 1970); John William Ward, *Andrew Jackson: Symbol for an Age* (New York, 1962); Leo Marx, *The Machine in the Garden: Technology and the Pastoral Ideal in America* (New York, 1964); Billington, *Land of Savagery, Land of Promise: The European Image of the American Frontier in the Nineteenth Century* (New York, 1980); and Richard S. Slotkin, *Regeneration through Violence: The Mythology of the American Frontier, 1600–1860* (Middletown, Conn., 1973), and *The Fatal Environment: The Myth of the Frontier in the Age of Industrialization, 1800–1890* (New York, 1985). In *The Moving American* (New York, 1973), George W. Pierson shifted the focus from geographical frontiers to the "M-Factor" of migration and mobility. The "new Western history" can be sampled in Patricia N. Limerick, *The Legacy of Conquest: The Unbroken Past of the American West* (New York, 1987).

Two landmark analyses motivated by wartime patriotism are Margaret Mead's *And Keep Your Powder Dry: An Anthropologist Looks at America* (New York, 1942), and Denis W. Brogan's *The American Character* (London, 1944), a friendly effort to explain American attitudes and principles to the British. British anthropologist

Geoffrey Gorer gave a nettlesome, "psychocultural" portrait in *The American People: A Study in National Character* (New York, 1948). See also Geoffrey Bateson, "Morale and National Character," in *Civilian Morale*, ed. Bateson (Boston, 1942), and Margaret Mead and Muriel Brown, eds., *The Study of Culture at a Distance* (Chicago, 1953), a manual describing strategies, methods, and objectives for national character study, with extensive bibliography.

Robert S. Lynd and Helen M. Lynd's *Middletown: A Study in Contemporary American Culture* (New York, 1929) and *Middletown in Transition: A Study in Cultural Conflicts* (New York, 1937) are essential background, but compare the more recent accounts of Hervé Varenne, *Americans Together: Structured Diversity in a Midwestern Town* (New York, 1977), and Peter Davis, *Hometown* (New York, 1982). The 1950s brought seminal theses like David Riesman with Nathan Glazer and Reuel Denney, *The Lonely Crowd: A Study in the Changing American Character* (New Haven, Conn., 1952); William H. Whyte, Jr., *The Organization Man* (New York, 1956); and David M. Potter, *People of Plenty: Economic Abundance and the American Character* (Chicago, 1954). For other writings by Potter, including "Abundance and the Turner Thesis," "Is America a Civilization?," "The Quest for the National Character," and "American Individualism in the Twentieth Century," see *History and American Society: Essays of David M. Potter* (New York, 1973) and *Freedom and Its Limitations in American Life* (Stanford, Calif., 1976), both edited by Don E. Fehrenbacher. Michael Barton, "The Lonely Crowd in Minnesota: A Psychometric Approach to the Study of the Modern American Character," *Prospects: The Annual of American Cultural Studies* 7 (1982), suggests that Riesman's hypotheses can be verified by standard psychological testing.

The 1950s saw a growing methodological interest among social scientists. Elting E. Morison, ed., *The American Style: Essays in Value and Performance* (New York, 1958), contains Clyde Kluckhohn's "Have There Been Discernible Shifts in American Values during the Past Generation?," Robert Oppenheimer's "Theory Versus Practice in American Values and Performance," and other important essays. The *American Anthropologist* 57 (December 1955) featured a series of articles on American national character. Michael McGiffert inventoried the new scholarship on American character, and culture and personality, through the 1960s in two excellent bibliographies: "Selected Writings on American National Character," *American Quarterly* 15 (Summer 1963), and "Selected Writings on American National Character and Related Subjects to 1969," *American Quarterly* 21 (Summer 1969). McGiffert's gathering of thirty historical and scientific essays, *The Character of Americans*, rev. ed. (Homewood, Ill., 1970), is still a useful reader on American identity, character, values, and behavior. It reprints, among other commentaries quoted in this chapter, Robin M. Williams, Jr., "Changing Value Orientations and Beliefs on the American Scene," and Ethel M. Albert, "Conflict and Change in American Values: A Cultural-Historical Approach."

Ralph Henry Gabriel's United Nations Educational, Scientific, and Cultural Organization (UNESCO) paper "Traditional Values in American Life" (1960), reprinted in Gabriel, *American Values: Continuity and Change* (Westport, Conn., 1974), is an excellent directory of American values in law, religion, education, science, economics, art, society, and international relations. Francis Hsu's "American Core Value and National Character," in *Psychological Anthropology*, ed. Hsu, rev. ed. (Cambridge, Mass., 1972), represents the contradictory values noted by behavioral scientists as manifestations of a single core value, self-reliance, which expresses itself psychologically as fear of dependence. A special issue of *Daedalus*, entitled *A New America?*, 107 (Winter 1978), offers eighteen essays on relative change and continuity in American values and institutions during the 1960s and 1970s.

For state-of-the-discipline reports on character and culture, see George A. De Vos, "National Character," *International Encyclopedia of the Social Sciences*, vol. 2 (New York, 1968), emphasizing modal psychological structures and personality and culture, and H. C. J. Duijker and N. H. Frijda, *National Character and National Stereotypes: A Trend Report Prepared for the International Union of Scientific Psychology* (Amsterdam, 1960), an extensive treatment with bibliography on the concepts, methods, and prospects of national character study. Walter P. Metzger, "Generalizations about National Character: An Analytic Essay," in *Generalization in the Writing of History*, ed. Louis Gottschalk (Chicago, 1963), proposes a "dramaturgical model" for the analysis of national character. See also Robin J. Williams, Jr., "Individual and Group Values," *Annals of the American Academy of Political and Social Sciences* 371 (May 1967); Anthony F. C. Wallace, *Culture and Personality* (New York, 1961); and Daniel Bell, "National Character Revisited: A Proposal for Renegotiating the Concept," in *The Study of Personality: An Interdisciplinary Appraisal*, ed. Edward Norbeck et al. (New York, 1968). Theory and methods of culture study are much influenced today by Raymond Williams's *The Sociology of Culture* (New York, 1982) and Clifford Geertz's *The Interpretation of Cultures: Selected Essays* (New York, 1973), beginning with his essay "Thick Description: Toward an Interpretive Theory of Culture."

For excellent historiographies of American character, see Thomas L. Hartshorne, *The Distorted Image: Changing Conceptions of the American Character since Turner* (Cleveland, 1968), and his follow-up article, "Recent Interpretations of the American Character," *American Studies International* 14 (Winter 1975); and Rupert Wilkinson, "American Character Revisited," *Journal of American Studies* 17 (August 1983), and *The Pursuit of American Character* (New York, 1988). See also Emmett B. Field's overview, "Another Look at the American Character," *Soundings* 65 (1982). John A. Hague, ed., *American Character and Culture in a Changing World* (Westport, Conn., 1979), offers an array of relevant essays, especially in the sections "Special Groups" and "Personality and Culture."

Gunnar Myrdal gives a classic definition of the "American Creed" in *An American Dilemma: The Negro Problem and Modern Democracy*, 2 vols. (New York, 1944). See Myrdal's first chapter, "American Ideals and the American Conscience." Philip Gleason weighs the ethnic factor in "American Identity and Americanization," in *Harvard Encyclopedia of American Ethnic Groups*, ed. Stephan Thernstrom (Cambridge, Mass., 1980).

The effort to establish *character* as a legitimate field of social science inquiry, with polling, quantification, and empirical verification, owes much to Alex Inkeles. Especially relevant here are Inkeles and Daniel J. Levinson, "National Character: The Study of Modal Personality and Sociocultural Systems," in *The Handbook of Social Psychology*, ed. Gardner Lindzey and Elliot Aronson, 2d ed., vol. 4 (Reading, Mass., 1968), and Inkeles, "National Character and Modern Political Systems," in *Psychological Anthropology*, ed. Francis L. K. Hsu (Cambridge, Mass., 1972), where Inkeles proposes more effective means of delineating the "democratic character." Inkeles has adapted and extended his earlier work in "National Character: A Key to Understanding the USA," in *Understanding the USA: A Cross-Cultural Perspective*, ed. Peter Funke (Tübingen, 1989), where his concept of "modal personality" stands head-to-head with the "ethnographic" model proposed in Theodore Schwartz's essay "The Structure of National Cultures." See also by Schwartz, "Where Is the Culture? Personality as the Distributive Locus of Culture," in *The Making of Psychological Anthropology*, ed. George Spindler (Berkeley, Calif., 1978), and "The Size and Shape of a Culture," in *Scale and Social Organization*, ed. Fredrik Barth (Oslo, 1978).

Seymour Martin Lipset, *The First New Nation: The United States in Historical and Comparative Perspective* (New York, 1963), pursues themes of American exceptionalism and the conditions for stable democracy in a world of "revolutionary equalitarian and populist values." The chapter "A Changing American Character?" traces the tension in America's two core values—"equality and achievement"— back to the nation's revolutionary origins. See also Lipset, *Continental Divide: The Values and Institutions of the United States and Canada* (Washington, D.C., 1990). The exploration of American character through contradictions and difference continues in Robert H. Wiebe, *The Segmented Society: An Introduction to the Meaning of America* (New York, 1975); Michael Kammen, *People of Paradox: An Inquiry Concerning the Origins of American Civilization* (New York, 1972); and Samuel P. Huntington, *American Politics: The Promise of Disharmony* (Cambridge, Mass., 1981). See Huntington's chapter "The American Creed and National Identity."

Ominous fault lines in American character have appeared in Daniel Bell's *The Cultural Contradictions of Capitalism* (New York, 1976); Christopher Lasch's *The Culture of Narcissism: American Life in an Age of Diminishing Expectations* (New York, 1979); and Barbara Ehrenreich's *Fear of Falling: The Inner Life of the Middle*

Class (New York, 1989). Widely different scenarios are described for end-of-the-century America in works like Andrew Hacker, *The End of the American Era* (New York, 1970); Steven Schlossstein, *The End of the American Century* (New York, 1989); James M. Fallows, *More Like Us: Making America Great Again* (Boston, 1989); and Henry Nau, *The Myth of America's Decline: Leading the World Economy into the 1990s* (New York, 1990).

For further historical discussion of unity and dissent, order and disorder, in American society, see Robert H. Wiebe, *The Search for Order, 1877–1920* (New York, 1967); Rowland Berthoff, *An Unsettled People: Social Order and Disorder in American History* (New York, 1971); and Bernard Sternsher, *Consensus, Conflict, and American Historians* (Bloomington, Ind., 1975), a historiographical treatment. The sophisticated essays in John Higham and Paul K. Conkin, eds., *New Directions in American Intellectual History* (Baltimore, 1979), weigh the impact of the new social history on the history of ideas in America.

The American Studies movement, which has had a major stake in formulations of the national character, can be traced through Tremaine McDowell, *American Studies* (Minneapolis, 1948); Sigmund Skard, *American Studies in Europe: Their History and Present Organization*, 2 vols. (Philadelphia, 1958); Robert Walker, *American Studies in the United States* (Baton Rouge, La., 1958); Robert Merideth, ed., *American Studies: Essays on Theory and Method* (Columbus, Ohio, 1968); Cecil F. Tate, *The Search for a Method in American Studies* (Minneapolis, 1973); Luther S. Luedtke, ed., *The Study of American Culture* (De Land, Fla., 1977); and a special section, "The American Studies Movement: A Thirty-Year Retrospective," ed. Gene Wise, in the Bibliography Issue of *American Quarterly* 31 (1979).

PART

ONE

Building a

Nation

In his *Letters from an American Farmer*, written at the dawn of the Republic, J. Hector St. John de Crèvecoeur took an environmentalist view of the American people. "Men are like plants," he wrote; "the goodness and flavour of the fruit proceeds from the peculiar soil and exposition in which they grow. We are nothing but what we derive from the air we breathe, the climate we inhabit, the government we obey, the system of religion we profess, and the nature of our employment."

Without doubt the character and values, the society and politics of America have been vitally connected to the natural resources and benign climatic position of the country. The experience of gradually occupying an accessible, sparsely populated, and richly endowed continent instilled some of our most commanding habits of thought. The "City upon a Hill," "Novus Ordo Seclorum," "Manifest Destiny," "American Dream"—these and other credos have codified a drama of landscape, migration, settlement, and nation building. Whether the natural abundance of the New World was precisely a blessing, a trust, a challenge, or even a curse, however, was less certain. Did the "Errand into the Wilderness" lead to a "promised land" as anticipated by the first Puritans or to a depleted "valley of ashes" as warned by F. Scott Fitzgerald's *The Great Gatsby*?

How nature would set its mark on those in the New World has been a matter of curiosity for both foreign observers and American settlers from the beginning. Renaissance maps of the Americas were decorated with mythical beasts waiting just beyond the pale of man's exploration. Laboring under the belief that all forms of life necessarily would be attenuated with distance from the core of culture and civilization in Europe, the eighteenth-century French naturalist Count de Buffon claimed in his *Histoire naturelle générale et particulière* (1749–1804) that animal life in the New World, including the Native American, was diminished in variety, size, reproductive power, feelings, and courage. The Abbé Raynal pursued this thesis in his *Histoire philosophique et politique* (1770), declaring that "America has not yet produced one good poet, one able mathematician, one man of genius in a single art or a single science" and prophesying that both animals and humans would progressively degenerate on the American soil.

The condescension of Buffon and Raynal drove Thomas Jefferson to extended refutation in his *Notes on the State of Virginia* (1785), where he documented that the New World was at least as conducive to size, health, and civility as the old except perhaps under extreme, transient wilderness conditions. At a dinner in France, Benjamin Franklin took a more humorous revenge. He invited the company to stand, whereupon it was evident that the Americans were large in stature and the Abbé "a mere shrimp" of a man, as Franklin later told Jefferson. Crèvecoeur, while respectfully dedicating his *Letters from an American Farmer* to Raynal, asked whether the propertyless, starving wretch of Europe could "call England or any other kingdom his country" and then answered: "No! Urged by a variety of motives, here they came. Every thing has tended to regenerate them; new laws, a new mode of living, a new social system; here they are become men: in Europe they were as so many useless plants, wanting vegetative mould, and refreshing showers; they withered, and were mowed down by want, hunger, and war; but now by the power of transplantation, like all other plants they have taken root and flourished!"

In the first of the following chapters, Peirce Lewis maps the natural landscape that beckoned, challenged, often shattered, but finally rewarded the settlers who came westward and eastward and northward to America's shores. The composition of these migrant waves and the process of Americanization are then described by Arthur Mann. From the millions of discrete episodes of migration and transplantation Lillian Schlissel has taken a case study of "The Frontier Family: Dislocation and the American Experience" that reveals behind our western myths the heartbreak, perversity, and pain that often awaited the migrants. Next Richard Lingeman and Carl Abbott trace the evolution of small towns and complex urban systems to the point where today only 2 percent of the national population lives on farms. Raymond Gastil's chapter surveys the end product, the cultural geography of the United States, showing the nation to be a network of "cultural regions" far more distinctive than the bland and monolithic portraits that sometimes are drawn.

Students of American character and institutions are continually drawn to the momentous era of expansion following the Louisiana Purchase in 1803 and Andrew Jackson's defeat of the British forces at New Orleans in 1815. For the balance of the nineteenth century, notwithstanding the schism of civil war, the nation reaped the benefits of its natural riches, bought or taken in war, as territories were settled, towns plotted, states created, canals dug, telegraphs and transcontinental railroads laid, millions of migrants sought and absorbed, industry established, and iron, coal, and precious metals extracted from the earth until the entire continent from the Atlantic to the Pacific was a patchwork of settlements. The effects of this *Völkerwanderung* were charted with awe and trepidation by a succession of foreign visitors, American journalists, politicians, and writers (from Washington Irving and James Fenimore Cooper to Mark Twain and William Dean Howells) and by the community of historians (from George Bancroft and Francis Parkman to Theodore Roosevelt and Frederick Jackson Turner). It is important to recognize here the role in American development usually attributed to the westward-moving frontier.

The culminating statement on character and national development in the nineteenth century was Frederick Jackson Turner's 1893 essay, "The Significance of the Frontier in American History." Turner, a young University of Wisconsin professor, was stirred by the findings of the 1890 census that settlement had so thoroughly permeated all areas of the West that it was no longer possible to mark a frontier line separating the inhabited from the wilderness areas of the nation. The virgin spaces that waited the simple farmers of Crèvecoeur and their nineteenth-century successors were closing, and with their passing a historical process of discovery and adaptation was coming to an end. Looking backward at the waves of settlement and a succession of frontiers since the early colonies at Plymouth and Jamestown, Turner invited his audience to "stand at Cumberland Gap and watch the process of civilization, marching single file—the buffalo following the trail to the salt springs, the Indian, the fur-trader and hunter, the cattle-raiser, the pioneer farmer—and the frontier has passed by. Stand at South Pass in the Rockies a century later and see the same procession with wider intervals between." After the farmer came the small town, the industry, and the large cities of America.

Turner argued that the true point of view for understanding the history of the United States was the great West and the frontier: the meeting point of savagery and civilization, "the line of most rapid and effective Americanization." He surmised that the United States had developed not along a single line but through a series of evolutions as man was precipitated into primitive conditions and continually began again the course of social development. "This perennial rebirth, this fluidity of American life, the expansion westward with its new opportunities, its continuous touch with the simplicity of primitive society," Turner claimed, gave Americans their composite nationality, shaped their political institutions, molded the national character, and promoted democracy and individualism. "The result is that to the frontier the American intellect owes its striking characteristics. That coarseness and strength combined with acuteness and inquisitiveness . . . that masterful grasp of material things, lacking in the artistic but powerful to effect great ends; that restless, nervous energy; that dominant individualism, working for good and for evil, and withal that buoyancy and exuberance which comes with freedom." While gradually transforming the wilderness, the pioneer American also was transformed by it.

Turner's thesis was not entirely original, of course. James Fenimore Cooper had dramatized both the barbaric and the noble character of the frontier individual in his Leatherstocking novels, and Henry David Thoreau captured the spirit of his time when he said: "Eastward I go only by force; but westward I go free." A few years before Turner, Lord James Bryce remarked more soberly, "The West may be called the most distinctly American part of America because the points in which it differs from the East are the points in which America as a whole differs from Europe." But Turner's landmark thesis has permanently affected students of nation building and American exceptionalism. "It is generally recognized," Hans Kohn wrote, that

> the American frontier was a unifying element in American nationalism because it peopled the vast lands with Americans originating from the various states and sections of the nation; it melted them in this process into something new, and fitted all Americans with pride in their common venture of empire building. But of equal importance was the fact that this westward movement contributed much to the illusion that the United States was something fundamentally different and remote from Europe. . . . The United States turned its back upon the Atlantic and set its face toward the Pacific.

Influenced by the depression of the 1930s and the nagging inequalities of urban America at mid-century, a later generation of historians has challenged the frontier thesis as novelistic and myopic about both the persistence of Old World traits and the roles that ideology, race, class, industry, and urbanism have played throughout the colonial and national history of the United States. The "new western historians" today are trying to separate historical understanding from the myth of the West by focusing on conquest and the environment, women on the frontier, Native Americans, Mexican-American and Asian-American populations, and western regionalism. Lillian Schlissel's depiction of the "carnivalesque" frontier experience of the George and Abigail Malick family and William Goetzmann's treatment, in a later section, of government-sponsored exploration of the West represent the new social and intellectual approaches to western history.

Nonetheless, while under review, the weight Turner gave to the encounter with nature along a succession of frontiers remains illuminating and provocative. David Potter's thesis in *People of Plenty* (1954) that the American character has been shaped by economic abundance found support in the links Turner forged between individualism, egalitarianism, and the opportunities provided by available land. Likewise, George Pierson's "M-Factor" as a determinant of national character—"the factor of movement, migration, mobility"—simultaneously extended and limited Turner's thesis. Pierson argued that Americans have been a people on the move away from as well as to the frontier, "from farm to town, from region to region, from city to city." Movement means change, and "in all this," Pierson claimed, "the frontier played an important but limited part." Still, the midpoint of the nation's population has traveled westward with every census since 1790, crossing the Mississippi River for the first time in 1990.

The self-determination, ingenuity, idealism, and institution building that have been attributed to the frontier found a clear voice in the utopian communities that sprouted along the frontier lines from Massachusetts to California during the nineteenth century. Moved by the same teleological spirit, Walt Whitman said to America in his poem "Passage to India" in 1871:

> Lo, soul, seest thou not God's purpose from the first?
> The earth to be spann'd, connected by network,
> The races, neighbors, to marry and be given in marriage,
> The oceans to be cross'd, the distant brought near,
> The lands to be welded together.

Together, the essays in this first section portray an intricately patterned nation standing between East and West, between the "valley of ashes" and what F. Scott Fitzgerald also spoke of as the "fresh, green breast of the new world."

Landform outline map of the
UNITED STATES
with adjacent parts of Canada and Mexico

by Erwin Raisz

Scale 0   300 Miles
Copyright 1954 by Erwin Raisz

Map 1.1 Erwin Raisz, Landforms of the United States (excluding Alaska and Hawaii).

I ☆ America's

☆ Natural

☆ Landscapes

☆ Peirce Lewis

Before we present you the matters of fact, it is fit to offer to your view the Stage whereon they were acted, for as Geography without History seemeth a carkasse without motion, so History without Geography wandereth as a Vagrant without a certaine habitation.
—John Smith,
   The Generall Historie of Virginia,
   New England, and the Summer Isles (1624)

The Geographic Dimension in American History

One of the great themes of American history emerges from the epochal story of Americans confronting and coming to terms with a huge wild country. Quite unlike the Old World, where people had occupied the land for as long as history could recall, and where adjustment to environment came so gradually as to be almost imperceptible, Americans' encounter with their land was abrupt and often violent, consuming much of the nation's energies and powerfully gripping its collective imagination. It has been said that America is a nation with an abundance of geography but a shortage of history, and there is some truth in both statements. It took less than four hundred years to subdue more than three million square miles of territory; in fact, Americans occupied the bulk of their national domain within the last century and a half. Even today much of the United States remains only semipopulated and semitamed. It is no wonder that the struggle to conquer America's physical geography looms so large in the nation's memory. Just as Americans have reshaped the face of their land, the people themselves have been shaped and reshaped by constant intimate encounters with that land.

Most of the time the settlers of America lacked any kind of detailed geographic knowledge, but their expectations were usually optimistic. Except for Africans who were brought to the country as slaves, most migrants came to America of their own free will, hoping for a better life than they had previously known. Quite naturally they were predisposed to think well of the new land, even when they knew little about it. More often than not, their expectations were met—and met handsomely. Very often American history has been a tale based on geographic superlatives.

Even at the most general level the country was geographically fortunate. Two large oceans insulated the United States from political threats in Europe and Asia, and for most of the nation's history those oceanic buffers spared America the need to maintain expensive and potentially mischievous military machines. The vast expanse of national territory contained a wealth of environments, which allowed the nation to become self-sufficient in agriculture and most basic minerals. And a magnificent system of natural waterways hooked this territory together, so that travel was cheap both for goods and people—making possible a degree of mobility (both geographic and social) unknown in most parts of the world.

Over the course of time the American land yielded a geographic bounty whose reputation spread around the globe and helped provoke a flood of migrants that shows no sign of diminishing even today. To be sure, the reports of that bounty were often overblown, especially by land speculators and travel agents with financial interests in promoting migration, and more than a few people have been enticed to America through promises of paradise on earth and cities with streets paved with gold. In spite of overstatements, however, the geographic truth was still formidable. Long before the accounts had been totaled, America was known to be a very rich land.

Like so many things in human history, America's geographic good fortune seems more obvious in retrospect than it did during the actual course of events. Settlement of the American land was often a painful process, for territory was usually settled before it was well known. ("The land was ours before we were the land's," Robert Frost remarked.) Few of the settlers possessed accurate maps of the land they would occupy, and most of them had no systematic knowledge at all of the natural processes that shaped the country that would become their home. America's physical geography had to be learned by trial and error, from the hard experience of innumerable settlers who discovered particular necessary facts as they went along and left grand patterns for their descendants to reveal. But we can see those patterns today, and a knowledge of them sheds considerable light on the way the nation's history unfolded.

The natural landscape of the United States has two fundamental dimensions, like landscapes anywhere in the world. One dimension results from *geologic* processes in the crust of the earth, which determine the main patterns of landforms, drainage, and minerals and influence the fertility of soils to a considerable degree. The other dimension is determined by *meteorological* processes in the atmosphere, which dictate the nature of weather and climate and in large measure the geographic distribution of vegetation and soils. While geology and meteorology are not entirely independent of each other, both produce patterns on a map that differ so greatly that they constitute two separate geographies (compare maps 1.2 and 1.3). In any particular place or region, the landscape is a composite of these two patterns, but they are best understood if they are first seen separately.

☆ ☆ ☆ Patterns of Landforms: The Main Framework

America's geologic and topographic framework is built around a huge interior lowland that has yielded some of America's greatest agricultural and mineral wealth, contains a large bulk of its population, and is the heart of what politicians like to call "middle America." The region is drained by the Mississippi River and its great tributaries, one of the largest navigable river systems in the world. The Mississippi is not merely a useful river; it also serves as a potent geographic symbol—the traditional dividing line in America between "East" and "West." This great lowland rises toward the north, where it butts sharply against the wilderness bulwark of the Canadian Shield. To the south, the lowland opens almost imperceptibly to a broad coastal plain that fringes the Gulf of Mexico. To the east and west, the land rises gradually and then abruptly to mountain ranges that flank the lowland on either side and separate it from the Atlantic and Pacific oceans.

The mountain ranges, however, differ substantially from each other. The Appalachians to the east stretch almost unbroken from Alabama to the Canadian border and beyond. They are much-eroded old mountains (the highest elevation is less than seven thousand feet) and are set back from the Atlantic by a broad belt of coastal lowland. While this coastal region contains no very remarkable scenery nor much in the way of mineral wealth, it was here that the American nation was planted and took root in the seventeenth century. The original thirteen colonies were all located in this narrow belt, and almost half of America's history has been played out here. It was not until the Revolution (1775–81) that significant numbers of American settlers began to spill westward across the Appalachians into the interior lowlands.

To the west of the interior basin lies the mighty system of mountains that

Landform Regions of the United States

Atlantic Plain
Appalachian Mountain System
Interior Lowlands and upland fringes
Western Cordillera and Intermontane Region

Spanish explorers named the "Cordillera"—a collective term for all the high rough country of the western third of the United States. The Cordillera is part of a global mountain system that encircles the Pacific Basin; it is geologically young and contains great geologic and topographic variety. Quite unlike the East, the western United States has almost no coastal plain, and the mountains along the Pacific coast drop abruptly and often spectacularly into the sea. This western country is both complicated and varied, containing some of the highest mountains in North America but also a vast expanse of intermontane basins, plateaus, and isolated ranges. Taken together, America's mountainous West is a peculiar and portentous place—a land of impressive scenery, considerable environmental variety, and great mineral wealth. It is hardly surprising that much of this western country was settled by adventurous folk in search of quick riches or freedom from the conventions and traditions of the crowded, long-settled East. Its picturesque scenery and history have caused many Americans to see the West as a wild eccentric kind of place—a view reinforced by novelists, artists, newspaper writers, and filmmakers who have painted the American West in bright uncomplicated colors.

In sum, geographers recognize four first-order topographic regions of the United States. From east to west (in the order that Europeans found them), they are the Atlantic and Gulf Coastal Plain, the Appalachians and their foothills, the Interior Lowlands, and the Cordillera, which includes both the main mountain ranges and a variety of intermontane valleys, basins, and plateaus.

Each of these large regions, however, contains a good deal of internal variety.

The Coastal Plain

European settlers first set foot in the territory that would become the United States and found a plain, facing the Atlantic, which in general outline seemed very similar to the Europe they had left. The settlers quickly learned, however, that America's Atlantic plain was unlike Europe's, and that it was far from homogeneous.

South and west of the mouth of the Hudson River, now the site of New York City, stretches a widening band of coastal plain, which extends unbroken to the Mexican border at the Rio Grande. The Coastal Plain is more than simply a lowland that happens to lie next to the sea. Like such regions in other parts of the world, the character of the shoreline and the plain itself is determined by elementary geologic facts: that the region is underlain by young sedimentary rocks, recently deposited by the ocean and by the streams flowing directly into the ocean—mostly uncemented sand, gravel, silt, and marl. The surface slopes very gently beneath the sea, where it forms the Continental Shelf, a region that is merely the submarine equivalent of the Coastal Plain. (Thus, the fabulously rich oil and gas fields of east Texas and south Louisiana extend offshore into the Gulf of Mexico, differing in location but geologically identical.)

The combination of weak bedrock materials and gentle surface slope has produced a kind of physical geography that has caused settlers of the Coastal Plain a good deal of trouble from earliest days. The problems were evident even before Europeans had set foot on American soil. Offshore the water is shallow—an easy place to drill for oil in recent times but a dangerous place for sailors, especially in bad weather. To make matters worse, the action of waves has carved the malleable shoreline into a profusion of barrier islands, spits, and offshore shoals, all of which shift unpredictably under the attack of Atlantic storms. Much of the coast is fronted with wide sandy beaches, popular spots for America's urban population to besport itself on hot summer weekends but a bad place for a sailor in colonial times approaching the shore in search of a sheltered deep-water anchorage.

In a few places there are gaps in the coastal barrier, and these gaps are as important as they are rare. As it commonly does, geologic history helps explain present-day physical geography. During glacial times a large volume of ocean water was locked up in continental ice sheets, and sea level consequently dropped—perhaps as much as two hundred feet. Rivers flowing to the sea quickly accommodated themselves to the new sea level and cut deep, wide valleys into the sandy materials of the Coastal Plain. Then, when the glaciers melted and sea level rose again, those valleys were flooded to form large ragged bays, some of which reached deeply inland. The convoluted shore of Chesapeake Bay, actually the drowned mouth of the Susquehanna River, created the famous Tidewater country of Maryland and Virginia, one of the earliest concentrations of population in colonial America. In the same way, the great indentation of Delaware Bay gave ocean ships direct access to fertile agricultural country in southeastern Pennsylvania, and the city of Philadelphia grew up naturally at the point farthest inland on the bay. In fact, from New York southward all of the nation's big coastal towns were necessarily located at or inside one of those rare breaks in the barrier bars; it was simply not possible to bring ocean ships ashore anywhere else. Norfolk, New York, Charleston, Savannah, and Jacksonville are among the most obvious examples—and the scarcity of such breaks helps explain why much of the American South is largely lacking in big coastal cities.

Coastal Plain soils have also played an important role in American history, for they nourished the plantation agriculture that made slavery profitable in the American South. Those soils were among the best in colonial North America, partly because they were easy to work, partly because they contained large volumes of forest humus. Once the forests were cut, however, that humus was not renewed, and the fragile soils were exposed to erosion. During the heyday of cotton and tobacco cultivation of the eighteenth and nineteenth centuries, profits were so large that planters paid little attention to soil conservation. Decades of abuse ruined the soil over much of the Coastal Plain. Some of the nation's richest agricultural land during colonial and early national times is now gone, so impoverished that it has been abandoned as farmland and allowed to revert to scrub or pine forest. It was from exactly such country over the last century that poor blacks and whites migrated, leaving their worn-out plots to go north in search of a better life.

Today the Coastal Plain does not seem a very remarkable place, with its low relief and cover of scrubby pine forests, but it was the stage set for major events in the history of the American confrontation with the physical environment. It was the place where Americans first ventured into large-scale commercial agriculture—and made huge profits by doing so. The Coastal Plain was also the place where Americans first learned the bad habit of plundering fragile environments for immediate profit and then, when the land was exhausted, throwing it away and moving on to repeat the process elsewhere. That precedent would be repeated many times in the process of settling the American continent. It was not until the twentieth century—when it finally became obvious that the supply of land was not infinite—that there were serious efforts to break those exploitative habits in the United States.

The Appalachian Mountains

Like the Coastal Plain, the Appalachian Mountain system has played a role in American history that is far out of proportion to its area. This is not because the Appalachians are high or spectacular, but rather because they helped steer American development in early periods, when many national habits were still being created.

Geologically the Appalachians are the oldest system of important mountains in the United States. For millions of years there has been no major geologic deformation of Appalachian rocks. As a result, the present mountains are fairly low and represent the worn-down skeleton of a much higher mountain system of ancient times. Thus Appalachian topography is entirely the result of erosion, and it follows that internal differences in Appalachian topography faithfully mirror the differences in underlying geologic structure.

A glance at any good map of American landforms (see map 1.1) reveals that the Appalachians are not a single homogeneous range but rather four parallel belts, each differing in geology—and therefore in topography as well (compare map 1.2).

The oldest and most complicated rocks occur closest to the ocean, where they have produced the two eastern belts of the Appalachians—the Piedmont and the Blue Ridge. (This was the main axis of Appalachian mountain-building activity and therefore the place where rocks are most intensively deformed.) The Piedmont is underlain by fairly nonresistant crystalline rocks that have been worn down to a gently rolling plain. From Pennsylvania southward into the Carolinas and Georgia, this Piedmont plain is covered with deep layers of weathered material that have yielded the best soils in eastern North America. North of New York City, however, this weathered layer was scrubbed and removed by glaciers, which then withdrew, strewing the surface with boulders, sand, and gravel. This is lowland New England, which colonial settlers farmed and cursed and promptly abandoned as soon as more fertile country opened up for migrants to the west.

Glaciation affected more than just soils. The enormous weight of the ice sheet gradually depressed the entire surface of New England, so that the lowest elevations were drowned below the sea. Although the land is once more rising, it still is much lower than it was. Thus New England has no coastal plain, and the ocean beats directly against the ancient Appalachian rocks to form a convoluted, picturesque coastline, abundantly provided with deep water and sheltered anchorages. If New Englanders found agriculture difficult, there were few problems in going to sea—as fishermen, whalers, and commercial traders. Thus, glaciation helps explain New England's rich maritime tradition, in sharp contrast with the unglaciated South, with its productive farmland but formidable shoreline. It also explains why nearly all the farms in New England have been abandoned and most of the land covered with woods.

Farther west, Appalachian crystalline rocks are much more resistant to erosion, a circumstance that yields the highest and most rugged country in the eastern United States. South of the glacial boundary in northern Pennsylvania, this belt of mountains is called the Blue Ridge, a region that few settlers even tried to farm and that was generally shunned by westerly-trekking migrants. A handful of early Anglo-Saxon settlers penetrated some of the isolated valleys, and their descendants have remained there in poverty-stricken isolation, preserving a rich variety of old folk cultures that are only now beginning to break down under the onslaught of modern technology and the curiosity of tourists. New England has a geologic version of the Blue Ridge in the White Mountains of New Hampshire, whose ice-scrubbed crags have attracted tourists since eighteenth-century Bostonians first visited the region and began to proclaim its scenic virtues.

Farther west from the Blue Ridge/White Mountain belt the intensity of geologic deformation drops off rapidly. The original sedimentary rocks were subjected only to moderate pressure during the main period of Appalachian mountain building so that they were "folded"—much as a rug is crumpled into folds if it slides across a slippery floor and collides with a piece of furniture. These folded sedimentary rocks vary greatly in resistance to erosion. While the whole region has been reduced to an elevation that rarely exceeds three thousand feet, the alternation of weak and resistant rocks has been eroded into a series of long linear ridges and valleys, which from aloft look as if some monstrous rake had been pulled the length of the Appalachians, all the way from Alabama to northern Vermont. In this Ridge-and-Valley terrain, none of the ridges are very high, but since they were arrayed at right angles to the main direction of westward migration, they posed a major barrier to travel, especially before the building of railroads and superhighways. Wherever possible, migration routes followed the long valleys, and the occasional "water-gaps" that cut through the ridges thus came to play important roles in funneling migrants through a very few places.

The westernmost belt of the Appalachians is called the Appalachian Plateau, actually a transition zone between the mountains and the interior lowland. The Plateau was formed by thick layers of sedimentary rocks that were uplifted during the late episodes of Appalachian mountain building but were otherwise undeformed. Subsequently, long periods of erosion have etched this tableland into an intricate system of knobs and low mountains, none very high, but very difficult to farm and a serious barrier to transportation.

Altogether, the Appalachians do not seem very impressive, especially compared to the mountains of the American West. But they influenced American history in two crucial ways—through their topography and through their minerals.

Appalachian topography was hard to cross, especially by horse or wagon. Early travelers either circumvented the ridges entirely or followed one of two well-defined routes across them. One of those routes led through Pennsylvania from the Atlantic at Philadelphia to the head of the Ohio River at Pittsburgh, and it helped convert two medium-sized eighteenth-century towns into booming nineteenth-century cities.

The second route was easier and even more important, connecting the Atlantic at New York with the east end of the upper Great Lakes at Buffalo. The Erie Canal came this way, wedged in a narrow trough between the

Appalachian Plateau and the Adirondacks. It was the subject of endless legend—a triumph of engineering and the main artery that connected the interior of America with the Atlantic Ocean. Only the Mississippi River was its
equal in fact or in myth.

Minerals were just as important, for the Appalachians contain some of the
world's largest deposits of coal. Anthracite for making steam and heating
houses came from eastern Pennsylvania, and bituminous, used for coking and
steel making, is found in a great geologic basin that stretches from Pittsburgh
to Birmingham, Alabama. It is ironic that America's early settlers thought
themselves unlucky because they never found the silver and gold that the
Spanish discovered in such abundance in Mexico and Peru. The difference
between Anglo-America and Hispanic America is partly a difference between
Aztec gold and Appalachian coal. Gold yielded riches beyond the dreams of
Croesus—but ultimately produced very little. Coal was dirty and unglamor-
ous, but it fueled an economic revolution that helped to convert the United
States from a modest agrarian society into the greatest industrial power on
earth.

The Interior Lowlands and Their Upland Fringes

Andrew Jackson supposedly remarked that America begins at the Appalachians, by which he meant that it was only west of the mountains in the
great interior lowlands that Americans could break loose from the European
links of the Atlantic seaboard and become truly independent. Although one
can argue whether or not the Interior Lowland forms the cultural core of the
country, there is no argument that it forms the continent's physical core.

Geologically this huge region rests on a low and much-eroded platform of
very old and very resistant crystalline rocks, undisturbed by major geologic
events for over a billion years. Over most of the central United States that
ancient platform is buried in deep blankets of sedimentary rocks, but the older
basement rocks rise to the surface and crop out along the nation's northern
borders, where they form significant uplands—the Adirondack Mountains of
upstate New York and the Superior Uplands of northern Michigan, Wisconsin, and Minnesota. These two regions, however, are merely southerly penin-
sulas of the Canadian Shield, a forbidding expanse of ice-scoured wilderness
that stretches north to the Arctic Ocean. In Canada, where the Shield makes
up about a third of the national territory, it is a ubiquitous brooding presence,
described by one Canadian prime minister as "the single most important fact
in Canadian history." It is the permanent northern frontier of major settlement
both in Canada and wherever it appears in the United States. Both the
Adirondacks and the Superior Uplands are very sparsely populated, and most

of the inhabitants depend on seasonal tourism, forestry, or mining—all fairly undependable sources of income. The region's minerals, however, are legendary. One of America's first large-scale ventures into metal mining began in the 1840s in the copper country of Michigan's Keweenaw Peninsula, and the iron mines of Minnesota's Mesabi Range were literally fabulous, providing America with about four-fifths of all the iron it has ever used. From the mid-nineteenth century onward, it was the combination of Minnesota iron and Pennsylvania coal that built the foundations of the American industrial revolution.

From the edge of the Shield southward to the Coastal Plain those ancient crystalline rocks are buried by sediments; as a result, the landscape is totally different. This enormous lowland region, which stretches all the way from the Rockies to the Appalachians, contains some of America's richest territory.

At the center of this national heartland is the so-called Central Lowland, itself a sizable expanse. Visitors often complain that its landscape is dull, for elevations rarely exceed two thousand feet, and much of the land is farmed. There is considerable variety, however, largely due to recent glaciation. The ice advanced southward roughly to a line described by the Ohio and Missouri rivers, and the valleys of both rivers were carved by meltwater that ran along the edge of the ice. North of the glacial margin the advance and readvance of ice over the last million years have left an intricate mosaic of landforms and surface materials, so that soil quality and topography can vary radically within short distances. The ice wiped out preglacial drainage patterns and left behind a chaos of lakes and stream channels—some abandoned, some still extant. The Great Lakes are only the biggest of a very large assortment. Thus, whatever else the glaciers did, they left behind a system of cheap water transportation in the central part of the United States. Any nation would have been lucky to have either of those two magnificent waterway systems—the Great Lakes or the Mississippi River system. But America had both, and as it turned out, they were easily connected by canals following the course of abandoned glacial drainage channels—which were in turn reinforced by railroads and highways built alongside the old canals.

Glaciers were friendly to Americans in another way. As the ice withdrew, meltwaters spread huge deposits of finely ground rock materials across the land in front of the ice; some of that fine material was picked up by the wind and redeposited in the form of *loess*, or wind-borne silt. The loess extended in a wide belt from Nebraska to Ohio, and from Minnesota to Mississippi, covering glacial and nonglacial country alike, sometimes to great depths. This blanket of loess did two things to middle America: it smoothed the preglacial surface to the point where parts of the American heartland seem almost mathematically flat—boring to travelers, but delightful to farmers—and it produced soils of astonishing fertility. If Mesabi iron and Appalachian coal were the foundations of America's industrial wealth, America's agricultural abundance springs from midwestern loess. As if the American midland were not rich enough, its wealth is linked together by the superb inland waterway system, also carved by glacial meltwater. When Americans total their geographic balance sheets, they have reason to be grateful to the gods of melting glaciers.

In shape the Central Lowland resembles a great open saucer, rising gradually toward its fringes. Southward and eastward, the sedimentary rocks are warped upward to form low plateaus, separated by the bulk of the Mississippi River Valley: the Ozarks of Missouri to the west and the Interior Low Plateaus of Kentucky and Tennessee to the east. In both of these regions, only the Kentucky Bluegrass region and the Nashville Basin contain very good farmland; otherwise, most of the territory is hardscrabble hill country, with thin sandy soil and scanty mineral wealth.

West of the Central Lowland lie the Great Plains. For as long as Americans have known the plains, the region has loomed large in the national imagination, for it symbolizes the beginning of the West: a vast, intractable land that thrusts its bulk across the path of all cross-country travelers—five hundred miles wide and spanning the entire distance from the forty-ninth parallel to the Rio Grande.

The Great Plains are often described as flat; in fact their surface slopes upward toward the west, in testimony to their geologic origin. The plains were formed as a huge apron of alluvial debris—gravel, sand, and silt eroded from the western mountains and swept eastward by streams flowing toward the Mississippi and Missouri rivers. The eastward slope is simply the original gradient of those streams. These alluvial deposits have been reworked by the wind over large areas so that loess and sand dunes are common features. As elsewhere, loess makes fertile soil, but—since most of the area is quite dry—overgrazing and careless plowing have exposed much of the land to wind erosion, especially in drought years.

In the whole lowland expanse between the Appalachians and the Rockies, mineral resources derive mainly from fossil fuels, as is usually true in regions of sedimentary rocks. Large deposits of high-quality coking coal occur in structural basins in the Midwest, and lignite is extensively strip-mined in the northern Great Plains. While oil and gas have been found in some quantity in almost every part of the Interior Lowlands, the midcontinent fields of Kansas, Oklahoma, and Texas are the biggest, satisfying an important part of America's demand for energy.

The Western Cordillera and Its Intermontane Basins

Just as the eastern and central United States are mostly lowland, much of the West is mountainous, and even where elevations are not high, the country is commonly rugged and often picturesque. Unlike the Appalachian Mountains of the East, however, this great western mountain system—the Cordillera—is not a continuous chain, but a rather sprawling assemblage of ranges separated by large plateaus, basins, and trenches. The geology varies greatly from place to place, and so, consequently, does the topography.

In its grand geographic outline the Cordillera is framed by two high mountain systems along its eastern and western borders. On the east are the Rockies, on the west the Coast Ranges and Sierra Nevada–Cascade mountain ranges. Together, they contain some of the highest and most spectacular country in the United States. Paradoxically, the Cordillera offered less of an obstacle to transcontinental travel than did the much lower Appalachians. For example, the Rockies are almost three miles high, and seen from the neighborhood of Denver, they are an awesome spectacle, rising from the Great Plains like a mighty rampart. But the Rockies are broken into several discrete units, and the gaps between them are so large that a traveler by way of the Union Pacific Railroad in Wyoming or the Southern Pacific in New Mexico could cross the country without ever seeing the Rocky Mountains.

The western ranges of the Cordillera are bigger and more complicated, arranged in an echelon parallel to the seacoast. Along the Pacific, the low but almost unbroken Coast Ranges rise abruptly from the ocean so that the California and Oregon coasts have a deserved reputation for rugged beauty. The loftiest mountains of the West, however, are set back from the coast: the Sierra Nevada of California and the Cascade Mountains of Oregon and Washington. The two ranges form an almost unbroken line of high mountains from southern California behind Los Angeles to the Canadian border near Vancouver. The Sierra Nevada and Cascade mountains differ greatly, however. The Sierra Nevada Mountains are a great fault block, tilted upward on the east, where they confront the Nevada desert with a wall of granite almost fifteen thousand feet high. At higher elevations the Sierra granites have been severely scoured by ice, producing scenery that Americans have admired ardently since the mid-nineteenth century. The Yosemite Valley, for example, has been turned into one of America's most popular national parks, and various attempts to exploit its scenery for commercial (and even industrial) purposes have produced stormy political battles—major landmarks in American environmental history. The Cascades, by contrast, have a tamer kind of scenery and history. They consist mainly of dark basalt that poured out in great flat seas of lava, which, after they cooled, warped upward to elevations that rarely exceed seven thousand feet. That rather subdued range, however, is studded with a row of high and handsome volcanoes, capped with snow, some of them dangerously active.

Between the Coastal Ranges and the Sierra Nevada–Cascade line is a discontinuous but very deep trench—part of a global furrow that appears in various locations along the eastern Pacific from the Vale of Chile to the Gulf of Alaska. These troughs are not large in area, but they have played inordinately important parts in western history, for they contain some of the richest farmland and some of the largest concentrations of population in the western states. The Wilamette Valley of Oregon is part of the trench, a flat-floored temperate place whose reputation as a sort of agricultural New Jerusalem provoked the "Oregon fever" of the 1840s and the first large-scale settlement of the West Coast by Americans. California's version is the Central Valley, where the trench is filled with debris carried down from the Sierra Nevada by the tributaries of the Sacramento and San Joaquin rivers, leaving the largest and richest piece of commercial farmland in the entire West. The Imperial Valley of extreme southern California is yet another part of the trench, where the delta of the Colorado River has dammed the Gulf of California and created an exotic bit of land below sea level that produces a large part of America's winter vegetables. In Washington the same trench was glaciated and depressed by the weight of glacial ice, thus producing Puget Sound.

Although the Cordillera's Pacific coast is scenically handsome, there are only four gaps that offer easy connections between the ocean and the continental interior. Those gaps are consequently important, the focus of vital transportation lines and the site of the West Coast's biggest cities. The Los Angeles Basin is one such place—one of the rare bits of lowland on the Pacific coast. In northern California, the main break is the Golden Gate, leading by way of San Francisco Bay into the Central Valley. Farther north the Columbia River cuts through the Coast Ranges, connecting the ocean with Portland and the Wilamette Valley. And along the Canadian border the Strait of Juan de Fuca links the ocean to Puget Sound and the metropolitan corridor that stretches from Olympia and Tacoma, past Seattle, and across the Canadian border to Vancouver.

Much of the Cordilleran region, however, is by no means mountainous. Between the Rockies and the Sierra Nevada–Cascade line lies a very large area that early explorers named the "Great Basin"—a name that can still be found on some archaic maps. That basin, in fact, contains three sizable regions, each with its own peculiar topography and thus its own special geographic personality.

The largest is the so-called Basin-and-Range region, covering all of Nevada and a considerable territory in adjacent states. Rocks of the earth's crust have been faulted into blocks, commonly a few miles across and several dozen miles long, then tumbled, eroded, and partly buried in erosional debris. These eroded blocks now form long linear mountain ranges, mostly aligned north to south and isolated from adjacent blocks by broad basins filled with sand, gravel, and dried salt. On a map they resemble nothing else in North America, and Clarence Dutton, the pioneer geologist, remarked that a map of the Basin-and-Range looked for all the world like "an army of caterpillars crawling northward from Mexico."

Over the northern part of the Great Basin recent lava flows have buried most of eastern Washington and Oregon, as well as the valley of the Snake River in southern Idaho, to form the region known as the Columbia Basin. Where the lava is still new and uneroded—as in southern Idaho—the terrain is fairly level, although the largest rivers like the Snake and Columbia have cut deep canyons into the blackish-brown basalt.

The southern margin of the basin is the Colorado Plateau, remarkable if only because it stands as an island of tranquility in a sea of geologic activity. Throughout the Colorado Plateau deep layers of nearly flat-lying sedimentary rocks have been uplifted and subsequently eroded by the Colorado River and its tributaries. While the geologic history is unremarkable, the scenery is not. Since the region has been uplifted more than a mile in some areas, rivers have cut awesome canyons into the sedimentary rocks, and the whole plateau is intricately carved into isolated mesas and buttes, typically with flat tops and clifflike margins. The rocks are commonly very colorful—reds, yellows, or-anges, browns, and even occasionally greens and blues. In an arid climate like the American Southwest, these gaudy shapes and colors are fully exposed to view, and most Americans would agree that the canyon lands of the Colorado Plateau contain some of the most picturesque physical landscapes in the entire country. (The Grand Canyon of Arizona is merely the biggest and most famous example.) A considerable part of the region has been set aside in national parks, monuments, and similar public preserves.

A wide variety of minerals has been found throughout the Cordilleran region—not an unusual circumstance in a large area with such a tumultuous geologic history. Those minerals have played a dominant role in much of the Cordillera's human history. Much of the region, after all, is sparsely populated, and settlement is precarious, so that in many places mineral discoveries were responsible for drawing the bulk of the population from outside, especially in early times. Thus gold from the Sierra Nevada caused the mass stampede of 1849 that brought California enough people in one year to allow it to qualify for statehood in 1850. Gold rushes and silver rushes produced the first major migration of Americans to both Colorado and Nevada, and baser minerals like copper and lead have influenced the economy and politics of places as far apart as Arizona and Idaho. Only the Columbia Basin with its blankets of barren lava is lacking in major mineral wealth. But despite the romance of gold and silver mining, the Cordillera's main mineral wealth comes from fossil fuels— oil and natural gas in California and extensive deposits of coal in the Colorado Plateau and the intermontane basins of the Rockies.

☆ ☆ ☆ Climate and Its Consequences

European settlers arriving on the western shores of the Atlantic found a climatic and biotic environment that was a mixture of familiar and unfamiliar elements. As settlement spread inland, however—across the Appalachians, across the Mississippi, and onward across the plains toward the mountains and the Pacific—it became increasingly and painfully clear that the European climatic experience would not be a very satisfactory guide for survival in America. That was especially true in the subtropical South and the arid West, regions that provided unexpected opportunities but also posed obstacles for which there were no obvious analogies in the Old World. In many ways, Europeans learned to become Americans in the process of learning to cope with this variety of unfamiliar climates and vegetations.

The Humid East

The first Europeans in British North America landed in a region that today's climatologists call "the humid East," a region that includes almost half of the present-day United States (see map 1.3). Throughout the whole region drought is a rare occurrence—and in that respect eastern America closely resembles northwestern Europe.

But temperatures are different, and significantly so. The climate of northwestern Europe is strongly influenced by westerly winds that bring mild moist air from over the Atlantic. Summers are warm but rarely very hot, and winters are cool but seldom extremely cold. Europeans expected America to be much the same, and some enthusiasts suggested that it would probably be even better. After all, they said, America faced the Atlantic, just like Europe. Perhaps it might be even a bit warmer. Was not New York at the same latitude as Spain—and London to the north of everything in America?

The truth, alas, was quite different. American weather comes from the west, just as in Europe. America's western air comes not from the ocean, however, but from the continental interior—extremely cold in the winter, ovenlike in

Bioclimatic Regions of the United States

THE HUMID EAST

Tropical

Northern Forest

Midlatitude Mixed Forest

Subtropical Forest

HUMID-ARID TRANSITION

Semi-Arid

MOUNTAIN

THE DRY WEST CLIMATE

True Desert

Marine West Coast

Mediterranean

HUMID PACIFIC COAST

Miles

0 100 300 500

Kilometers

0 200 500 800

Map 1.3. Bioclimatic Regions of the United States (excluding Alaska and Hawaii). *(Generalized in part from maps by C. Warren Thornthwaite, 1948, and A. W. Küchler, 1949.)*

the summer. Later on climatologists would give technical names to that difference between European and American climate. Europe, with its mild oceanic temperatures, would be said to have a "marine West Coast" climate; Americans would eventually encounter similar conditions in their own Pacific Northwest, a region that strongly resembles Britain and western France. The climate of eastern and central America, with its great seasonal extremes of temperature, would be called "continental."

The settlers also discovered major differences in climate within the humid East, and those differences were also dictated by temperature. Eventually they came to recognize four major climate subregions that stretch westward from the Atlantic in broad swaths (see map 1.3). Climatically, those regions differ in the length of growing season and in the intensity of winter cold. The consequences were crucially important, for they dictated differences in natural vegetation, in the kinds of crops that could be grown, and ultimately in the whole way of life.

The northernmost zone, adjacent to the Canadian border, is a region of northern forest that stretches from Maine across northern New England and the upper Great Lakes. The growing season is very short, and the winters long and fiercely cold. For farmers it has always been miserable country, and without a rural population base there has been little reason for a network of roads and towns to develop. Most of the region is now covered with second-growth coniferous woods since the original forest was cut for lumber in the late nineteenth century to build houses for the nation's booming industrial and commercial cities. Today most of the population depends for a scant living on mining or forestry and increasingly on recreation. Most of it remains poor country and sparsely populated.

Southward the temperature moderates, with far-reaching impact on human settlement. With a longer growing season, milder winters, and hot summers, this environment encountered by the Europeans would presently make America famous as a land of plenty. It was a region of "midlatitude mixed forest"— needleleaf and broadleaf trees, many of them valuable for buildings and for cabinetwork. Settlers discovered to their delight that they could grow most of the crops they had known in the Old World and a variety of New World crops as well. Because American summers were considerably hotter and longer than in Europe, American crops often yielded more bountifully. Especially in colonial and early national times, when land was still cheap and plentiful, it was the kind of place where a farmer, if he worked hard and was reasonably lucky, could make a comfortable life for his family—and might even make himself rich. It was here, in America's rural North, that European peasants turned themselves first into yeoman farmers and eventually into American agribusinessmen. It was they who cut down the original forest, not so much for lumber, but to make new farmland—and to make their fortunes. It was here that America first developed its reputation abroad as a kind of agricultural New Jerusalem. Over two centuries, millions of Europeans migrated to America to make new lives for themselves in this region. Many failed, but enough succeeded so that the flood of migration continued long after the best land had all been taken.

Still farther southward one crosses an invisible but crucial line, the northern boundary of America's most distinctive region. Ecologists call it a "humid subtropical forest" region because of its short cool winters and long hot summers. To historians, human geographers, and most Americans, however, this is simply "the South." And it was climate that made the South distinctively southern.

The crucial facts of the southern climate are hot, humid summers and a long growing season: everywhere within the South the frost-free period exceeds 180 days—long enough for a variety of valuable subtropical crops to be grown, such as indigo, rice, and cotton. During most of the seventeenth and eighteenth centuries the American South supplied Europe with subtropical agricultural products it could get nowhere else. But it was cotton in the nineteenth century that imprinted the South with its peculiar and distinctive personality. Until the early twentieth century the South had a virtual monopoly on the world cotton trade. Since most of the world's inexpensive cloth was made of cotton, the demand was enormous—and so were profits. That fact had far-reaching consequences. Those who owned cotton land grew rich and formed a small self-appointed aristocracy dedicated to maintaining the status quo—economically, politically, and socially. The whole system rested on slavery, for until the invention of mechanical cultivators and pickers, cotton remained a very labor-intensive crop. African slaves were imported and bred in such numbers that blacks far outnumbered whites in much of the cotton-growing South.

Furthermore, the semifeudal plantation system that accompanied cotton growing tended to discourage the growth of cities and towns so that the South remained an overwhelmingly rural region. Correspondingly, the existence of a large slave-labor force discouraged the immigration of free white labor that had begun to arrive in large numbers in the North, and the white southern population remained largely Anglo-Saxon in ethnic ancestry. Throughout, the profits from cotton were so alluring that cotton was grown wherever it would grow, and in many places where it should not have grown. As long as "cotton was king," erosion control and crop rotation were virtually unknown, and much excellent farmland was irretrievably ruined. Cotton remained king, however, only as long as the American South had a monopoly on cotton growing, and that monopoly came to an end in the early twentieth century as a result of new competition from Indian and Egyptian cotton and an infestation by the boll weevil. Much of the South went bankrupt, becoming a rural area with impoverished soil and impoverished people. Beginning around World War I many of those poor people, most of them black, began moving to northern cities to find work in what became one of the largest internal migrations in American history. Meantime most of the old cotton country reverted to piney woods, although more recently some of the land has been turned into pasture to support a considerable cattle industry. Despite new urbanization and new migration into the South, the region remains the poorest in the nation.

The southernmost climatic region of the humid East is the only genuinely tropical part of the United States aside from Hawaii. In a small part of coastal south Florida freezing temperatures are almost unknown. But the land is low and swampy and remote from the nation's main centers of population. It was not until the twentieth century that significant numbers of Americans moved into the area. The two primary economic activities stem directly from climatic circumstances: a flourishing winter tourist industry and a very intensive form of specialized agriculture that supplies most of the United States with the bulk of its winter vegetables.

The Arid West

From earliest times Europeans and Americans knew that the western part of America was dry—a very different sort of place from the well-watered shores of the Atlantic. The Spanish, who had come north from Mexico to explore the American Southwest, were well acquainted with arid climates and knew the techniques of coping with such places. Americans from the humid East had no such knowledge, however, and for a long time their map showed a great blank void with the sinister label "Great American Desert." From time to time that label covered a good share of the western United States, reflecting an imperfect knowledge of western geography but also the belief that civilized humans could not be expected to settle such territory. As it turned out, of course, that bleak generalization was untrue—as today's booming population of the Southwest clearly demonstrates. But the first American settlers of the West headed directly for the humid fringes of the Pacific coast, crossing the drylands much as a mariner might sail across a stormy sea; they crossed it because they had to, but there was little thought of permanent settlement. That would come later as Americans began to understand the dynamics of drylands, to gather the special technology that would allow settlement to occur, and above all to learn that there were important regional differences within the arid West. Most of the West was dry, to be sure, but it was not all the same.

The Desert

The dry core of the arid West is a belt of desert that lies in the rainshadow of the Sierra Nevada and Cascade ranges and stretches north from the Sonoran Desert of Mexico across Arizona, New Mexico, and Nevada into southern Oregon. Rainfall is both scarce and undependable, and the only important human settlement occurs in irrigated oases. Most of the oases—conspicuously the Imperial Valley of California—support significant agriculture, and a few— like the Salt River valley of Arizona—are seats of major cities. (Phoenix was counted by the 1990 census as the ninth largest city in the United States.) But life depends on water, and outside the oases the desert is almost empty. Vegetation, of course, is sparse, ranging from nothing at all (a rare circumstance mainly confined to sand dunes and salt pans) to a scattered cover of gnarled scrub and short-lived annuals that spring into flamboyant bloom after the infrequent rains. As for soil, in much of the desert it is virtually nonexistent, since wind erosion tends to remove fine materials from the surface, leaving behind a veneer of broken rock that geologists call "desert pavement." Even under the best of circumstances, it is a hostile place.

The Humid-Arid Transition

Paradoxically, it was not the true desert that posed the greatest difficulty for American settlers. The desert, after all, offered a clear uncompromising choice: with irrigation the land could be made to bloom luxuriantly; without irrigation it was uninhabitable.

The challenge was more subtle in the great zone of transition between the humid East and the arid West. In the beginning it all seemed very obvious: as one moved out from the green East, across the Midwest into the Great Plains, the country became gradually drier. The settlers were prepared for that. All along, the vegetation had advertised that gradual change, as the eastern forest opened up and gave way to the tall-grass prairies of the Midwest. (In Illinois and Indiana much of the prairie was man-made, the result of Indian burnings, so that American migrants concluded incorrectly that there was no relationship between vegetation and rainfall.) It was fine farmland—some of the nation's best—with deep black prairie soils formed of humus and loess. Farmers adjusted to this new environment by abandoning their traditional mixture of crops and dairy cows and going over to grains. Wheat was the favorite, and it seemed a reasonable choice. Wheat, after all, is a grass—just like the native vegetation. What the settlers did not understand was a simple but deadly law of climatology: as total rainfall decreases, the reliability of rainfall also decreases. In practical terms, settlers had moved into a region where the climate is defined by its erratic rainfall—where years of surplus rainfall routinely give way to years of rainfall deficit.

The native grasses, of course, had adapted nicely to these routine fluctuations. In dry years, they simply stayed brown and dormant, storing moisture in their roots. In moist years, the grass turned green and luxuriant. If the farmers had been all-wise and all-logical, the land would have been left in grass. It had been fine grazing land for native buffalo, and it could have been used the same way for domestic cattle. It was not cattlemen, however, but farmers who came from the humid East to settle this transition zone in the mid-nineteenth century. Overwhelmingly they preferred to grow wheat, a much more profitable venture than cattle raising. In moist years, of course, the land produced bumper crops. But in dry years the seeded wheat refused to germinate, or else the young plants sprouted and then withered in the scorching summer heat of this continental interior. Unlike the native prairie, whose soil was protected by a dense veneer of turf, plowing exposed the desiccated soil to the wind, and it blew away in dust storms that darkened the midday sky. Inexperienced pioneer farmers borrowed money in moist years to invest in new land and machinery, but in the lean dry years they lacked money to pay off the loans. Thousands went bankrupt in the decades that followed initial settlement.

More recently, things have gotten better. A good deal of research has gone into inventing techniques for conserving soil moisture by reducing evaporation from plowed land. These techniques now allow most of the land to be planted in wheat and other small grains, but much less intensively than in earlier days.

The Semiarid West

Further west, in the semiarid region of short grass where farms ended and cattle ranches began, the situation was even more precarious. In years when rains were plentiful, the steppe grasses grew "stirrup-high," tempting cattlemen to enlarge their herds and to expand pastureland into marginal areas. When the drought arrived, inevitably but unpredictably, the larger herds starved and died. Continental temperature extremes added to the woes. Blazing summer heat dried up what little moisture was available, and in winter arctic temperatures combined with howling blizzards to make life miserable at best, deadly at worst.

There were periods of plentiful rainfall when the grass was high and green, and land speculators persuaded eastern farmers that western Kansas could be plowed and planted just like Ohio. It was a deadly trap. Most of those farmers stayed long enough to watch their land blow away during the next year's drought. It was not until much later that the weather bureau would warn farmers and ranchers that years of "average" rainfall were not average in regions of semiarid climate. Meantime farmers and ranchers had to learn climatic laws the hard way, over a series of years that alternated between feast and famine. In the process, a good deal of land was ruined, and a good many lives were ruined too.

Starting as early as the 1870s the American government sought ways to learn how dryland environments worked and then persuade farmers and ranchers (not to mention salesmen and politicians) to moderate their demands on the land—to leave land in grass instead of plowing it, reducing the size of herds to avoid overgrazing. But it was only in the 1930s, when a series of ruinous drought years turned the western Great Plains into a Dust Bowl and provoked a desperate mass migration from the region, that conservation programs began to meet with much success. For the first time problems of the semiarid West attracted wide public attention, stimulated in part by government publicity but in large part by John Steinbeck's epic tragedy, *The Grapes of Wrath*, which told the story of an Oklahoma family that flees to California in the face of drought and poverty.

Most of the abandoned land ultimately reverted to the federal government, today the largest landowner in much of the American West, and it has been government policy to lease land only to those who practice conservation in farming and ranching. Sometimes the policy has worked; often it has not. In most western states the hottest political debates are chronically waged between those who want to relax government regulations on the use of federal land and those who want to extend and tighten restrictions. It seems doubtful that the question will be settled soon, especially in the semiarid parts of the West where Americans are still in the process of learning the limits of their own environment.

The Humid Pacific Coast

The only substantial humid region in the western United States is wedged into a narrow strip between the Pacific coast and the Sierra Nevada–Cascade ridge line, extending south from British Columbia through western Washington and Oregon into central California. Seen from the East, that distant edge of the continent has long appeared as a kind of oasis, a land so favored that Americans were willing to make a thousand-mile trek across the arid interior in order to occupy and settle it. It was only much later that they returned to undertake settlement of the arid interior.

The humid West, however, differs radically from its eastern counterpart—and not merely in size. Unlike the East, with its continental extremes of summer and winter temperatures, West Coast temperatures are moderated all year long by westerly winds from the ocean so that the entire littoral from Canada to Mexico enjoys cool summers and mild winters, a fact much touted by chambers of commerce from Seattle to San Diego. Inland from the ocean, however, it is a different story, and only a short distance inland summers are routinely blistering. Wherever that hot interior can be irrigated, however, it can be luxuriantly productive, and the Central Valley of California and the Wilamette Valley of Oregon contain some of America's most valuable farmland.

West Coast rainfall patterns also differed from those in the East, and those differences impart a special personality to the Pacific Coast climates. In the humid East rainfall is taken for granted since most places get plenty of rain at all times of the year. That is not true in the West, where rainfall differs significantly from place to place and from season to season.

To begin with, rainfall diminishes gradually from north to south. Thus western Washington and Oregon receive enough rain to support forests of tall, straight, fast-growing evergreens—the spruce and fir that produce the bulk of America's lumber. By contrast, central California is noticeably drier, with low gnarled trees and open grasslands that are well adapted to drought. By the time one reaches southern California, the climate is technically defined as semiarid, and true desert lies not far beyond the city limits of Los Angeles and San Diego.

West Coast rainfall, furthermore, is markedly seasonal. Winter is the rainiest time everywhere, and summers almost everywhere are bone dry. In the moist northern end of the coastal strip—the part of Oregon and Washington that climatologists call "marine West Coast"—the dry season is short and of little consequence. Thus visitors to western Washington will remark about the "nice" summer weather with clear blue skies, but will hardly notice a summer drought. Toward the south, however, the summer dry season begins earlier and lasts longer, and from about San Francisco Bay to the Mexican border the drought lasts so long that much of California becomes a genuine desert in the summertime.

The regime of winter rain and summer drought is what climatologists term a "Mediterranean climate"—named after its analogue in Western Europe. Ecologists apply the same word to central California vegetation—a scrubby woodland of scattered drought-resistant trees interspersed with grassland.

Plants necessarily do all of their growing in the cool moist winters, and spring is the season of maturation, a flowery time much beloved by tourists. In summer, however, grass turns brown and growth stops. By autumn the whole landscape is sere and desiccated, save in irrigated patches. Under natural conditions brushfires were part of the normal ecological cycle, and periodic burning kept brush down and grasslands open. In the hilly suburbs of large California cities, fire is naturally discouraged, so that brushy undergrowth grows more luxuriantly than it did a century ago. Thus when fires do get started—and it is impossible to prevent them all—they can be devastating, as wealthy Los Angeles suburbanites annually rediscover to their sorrow.

Despite drought and fire Americans have found California's Mediterranean climatic zone a peculiarly alluring place. (Oregon and Washington are held in similar esteem, although to a lesser degree.) Near the coast summers are cool and pleasant, and even the mild rainy winter is often not very rainy, except in the far north. The combination has attracted both tourists and permanent residents from less delicious climes in the North and East, a fact that helps explain why California has recently become the most populous of the fifty American states. The unusual combination of wet winters and dry summers, moreover, makes it possible to grow crops that will not mature anywhere else in the country, with the result that California has the most lucrative agricultural industry in America.

The Mountain Climates

Perhaps the commonest feature of America's western climates, however, is the enormous variation to be found within very short distances. Mountainous terrain causes most of the variety since both temperature and rainfall are strongly affected by elevation and the direction in which slopes are faced. The west side of the Cascades in Washington is covered with luxuriant rain forest; the east, only a few miles away, is sagebrush desert. Similarly, basins in the Nevada desert are bone-dry and crusted with salt, while nearby mountain slopes are forested with pine and cedar, and the highest peaks rise above timberline into a zone of arctic tundra. Indeed, the highest mountains are capped with snow, most conspicuously the volcanoes of the Cascades and the rugged mountains of southern Alaska, where enormous snowfalls accumulate to produce large and spectacular alpine glaciers. Much of the mountainous West contains such enormous variety within such small distance that it is broken into a mosaic of microclimatic regions. It is the despair of mapmakers, who throw up their hands and noncommittally designate the ruggedest part of the West simply as "mountain climates" (see map 1.3).

☆ ☆ ☆ Retrospect: Geography and American History

Any simple explanation of great historic events is likely to be wrong or at least seriously misleading. That is certainly true when one tries to explain the rise of America to world power. But no account of that portentous event can ever be complete unless it recognizes that America's economic and political strength rests on very solid geographic foundations.

Geography alone cannot explain the American success story, of course. If different groups of people had settled America—people with different tools and ambitions and values and memories—the story surely would have come out differently.

But certain things seem obvious. America's wealth of resources certainly made the job of settling America easier than it would otherwise have been, and the large variety of geographic environments guaranteed that Americans would find both opportunities and challenges that would be denied to people in less-favored parts of the earth. If the country's riches rewarded luck and hard work, its geographic variety rewarded those who were capable of adapting to new circumstances. That same geography punished failure too—and ruthlessly. Thus if American history is a catalog of human success, it is also a catalog of shattered hopes. But the very size and diversity of American territory encouraged optimism: if one failed in one place, there were always other kinds of places where one might start anew. So it is no accident that the greatest works of American literature—such novels as *Moby-Dick* and *Adventures of Huckleberry Finn*—tell stories not so much of our confrontation with each other, or even with God—but rather of our confrontation with a rich and varied and powerful Nature. It is a story that underlies the whole American experience.

FURTHER READING

Although there is a large scholarly literature on the separate aspects of American physical geography, there is no single definitive book on the subject. The closest approximation is Charles B. Hunt's *Natural Regions of the United States and Canada* (San Francisco, 1973). The first three chapters of J. Wreford Watson's *North America: Its Countries and Its Regions* (New York, 1967) also serve as a useful summary.

The individual topics of landforms, climate, and vegetation, however, have received much better treatment. The most recent authoritative treatment of American landforms is William Thornbury's evenhanded and well-documented *Regional Geomorphology of the United States* (New York, 1967). Older but still useful are Wallace W. Atwood, *The Physiographic Provinces of North America* (Boston, 1940), and Nevin Fenneman's monumental *Physiography of Western United States* and *Physiography of Eastern United States* (New York, 1931, 1938).

Maps, of course, are indispensable in the study of landforms and their geologic foundations. The best and most elegant depiction of America's natural landscape is Erwin Raisz's cartographic tour de force, *Map of the Landforms of the United States* (Boston, 1957). (A simplified version of Raisz's map is included as map 1.1 of this chapter, but the magnificent original is available at a much larger scale and is exquisitely detailed.) The most comprehensive geologic maps have been published by the U.S. Geological Survey and are summarized at reduced scale in *The National Atlas of the United States of America* (Washington, D.C., 1970). Individual maps also have been published separately. Two are really basic: the *Geologic Map of the United States* (Washington, D.C., 1974) and the *Tectonic Map of the United States* (Washington, D.C., 1989). The Geological Survey also publishes two other important maps of surface deposits associated with Pleistocene glaciation: *Pleistocene Eolian Deposits of the United States, Alaska, and Parts of Canada* and *Glacial Map of the U.S. East of the Rocky Mountains* (Washington, D.C., 1952, 1959).

The subject of American climate has never been treated better than in the U.S. Department of Agriculture's classic *Yearbook of Agriculture—1941, Climate and Man* (Washington, D.C., 1941), a collection of authoritative essays on the nature, causes, and effects of climate in America, as well as monthly rainfall and temperature data for a fine network of U.S. weather stations. More recently, the U.S. Environmental Data Service (a branch of the Department of Commerce) has published an inexpensive and useful collection of climatic maps: *Climatic Atlas of the United States* (Washington, D.C., 1968). Overwhelmingly the most comprehensive collection of detailed climatic data for the United States is Frederick L. Wernstedt's *North American Climatic Data* (Lemont, Pa., 1984), a volume that contains a large variety of monthly statistics for 470 American weather stations.

The regional geography of American vegetation is also the subject of a large literature. A fine readable summary is Henry A. Gleason and Arthur Cronquist's *The Natural Geography of Plants* (New York, 1964), which contains well-illustrated descriptions of America's main plant communities. The best medium-scale map of American vegetation is A. W. Küchler's authoritative "Natural Vegetation of the United States," published in E. G. Espenshade, ed., *Goode's World Atlas* (Chicago, 1984).

The relationship between climate and natural vegetation is obvious but far from simple. The most ambitious recent attempt to correlate them is Robert G. Bailey's map, *Ecoregions of the United States* (Washington, D.C., 1976), sponsored by the U.S. Forest Service. Bailey has written a succinct monograph to explain the map, *Description of Ecoregions of the United States* (Ogden, Utah, 1980), which contains a good bibliography of American regional ecology, as well as related literature across the broader field of regional physical geography.

2 ☆ From

☆ Immigration

☆ to

Acculturation

☆ Arthur Mann

In the two centuries after the founding of the American Republic, a population already multiethnic became fantastically more so. Territorial expansion through conquest, purchase, and annexation added to the original diversity, but the primary source flowed from a massive infusion of immigrants from almost everywhere. Their acculturation sheds light on the national character. At issue is what it has meant to be an American in a land whose history has denied its people the bond of a common paternity.

J. Hector St. John de Crèvecoeur had such considerations in mind when he asked in 1782: "What then is the American, this new man?" The War of Independence was drawing to a close, and Crèvecoeur—a French immigrant married to a native New Yorker of English descent—perceived that his adopted country, peopled by diverse stocks from across the Atlantic, contained a "strange mixture of blood, which you will find in no other country." What therefore did the Americans have in common other than the fact that they sprang from different ancestors?

The question called attention to a matter that was to be of lasting concern, namely, the interplay between ethnic diversity and national unity. It lasted because the more immigration continued to change the ethnic and religious composition of the population, the more Americans felt compelled to articulate who they were as a whole. But before turning to the character of that articulation, which one observer has called a "patriotism of reflection" and another a "creed," we must first grasp the magnitude, continuity, dispersion, and variety of immigration since Crèvecoeur's time.

☆ ☆ ☆ Statistical Overview

It is easy enough to cite the statistic that over fifty million immigrants have arrived since that time in the United States, but it is something else for the human mind to take in the immensity of the figure. The total number of inhabitants at the beginning of the War of Independence was scarcely one-twentieth that amount, and a century would have to pass before it reached the fifty million mark. Today the population of many a good-sized country—including Poland and Thailand—falls below that mark. It exceeds the combined populations of Sweden, Norway, Denmark, Ireland, Israel, Austria, and Czechoslovakia. More relevant to the point at hand, the volume of immigration to the United States thus far has surpassed that of all other major immigrant-receiving countries taken together.

Although heavier at some times than others, the stream of newcomers has been continuous. Of the thirty-eight million to arrive between the end of the Napoleonic Wars and the onset of the Great Depression in 1929, half came before 1900. Some five million entered prior to the beginning of the Civil War in 1861, with the result that by 1860 Boston's population was 36 percent foreign-born, Brooklyn's 39 percent, and New York's 48 percent. After the war, in the peak decade of the 1880s, the United States admitted 5,246,000 immigrants. By then the census-takers were enumerating not only immigrants but their native-born children as well and calling the two groups foreign stock. In 1890 that stock accounted for 68 percent of the people living in Boston, 71 percent in Brooklyn, and 80 percent in New York.

Restrictive legislation in the 1920s, immediately followed by the Great Depression and World War II, slowed immigration to a trickle. The flow resumed after the war, aided by special congressional acts and then by the repeal of the 1920s laws. Although the proportion of admissions to the American population since 1950 has been lower than the proportion before 1930, the figure is by no means inconsequential. By 1980 it totaled more than ten million, exclusive of many Puerto Rican migrants to the mainland, who as U.S. citizens are not listed in the official statistics as immigrants.

Far from putting down roots only in the East, as is sometimes supposed, immigrants dispersed throughout most of the country. In 1890, as in many cities on the Atlantic seaboard, the proportion of foreign stock in San Francisco was 78 percent, in Salt Lake City 65 percent, in St. Louis 67 percent, in Duluth 75 percent, in Chicago 78 percent, and in Milwaukee 86 percent. Nor was immigration merely a big-city phenomenon. Immigrants and their children at the end of the nineteenth century constituted a majority in the still heavily rural and small-town states of Minnesota, the Dakotas, Montana, Arizona, Wyoming, Utah, Nevada, and California.

The story was much the same in the next century. According to the 1920 census, Utah's foreign stock was roughly equal to Pennsylvania's, and Minnesota's was higher than New Jersey's. The state in 1920 with the greatest proportion of foreign stock to its total population was not, as one might guess, Rhode Island, Massachusetts, New York, or some other eastern industrial state. It was North Dakota, where no more than one person out of three had been born in America of native-born parents. Only the race-torn South failed to attract a substantial portion of nineteenth- and twentieth-century immigrants.

Seven decades after Crèvecoeur called attention to the varied roots of his contemporaries, the novelist Herman Melville exclaimed: "You cannot spill a drop of American blood without spilling the blood of the whole world." Many migrations later, according to government statisticians just before World War I, some sixty different ethnic groups lived all over the United States. There are at present over a hundred of them.

Europe is no longer the United States' chief supplier of immigrants. The lead passed to Asia and Latin America in the 1960s, and by the next decade their arrivals were outnumbering those from the Old World by four to one. Nationwide they still comprise a small minority in a quarter-billion population, yet they have changed the ethnic mix of a half dozen and more major metropolitan centers.

Although an extreme case, Greater Los Angeles by the 1980s exemplified the forces at work. Its Hispanic population increased threefold and its Asian tenfold in twenty-five years. As a result, the city and its environs contained over 2,000,000 Mexicans; 600,000 Iranians, Armenians, Arabs, and Israelis; close to 500,000 Chinese, Japanese, and Koreans; 250,000 Salvadorans and Guatemalans; 150,000 Filipinos; 60,000 Samoans; 40,000 Vietnamese; plus smaller but visible numbers of Thais and Indians and many other stocks. In the homes of one-fifth of Los Angeles' schoolchildren, English was second to 104 different ancestral languages.

To go on with this statistical and demographic review would be tedious. It is enough to say that more immigrants, and more different kinds of immigrants, have entered the United States than any other country in modern history. The conditions that caused them to leave their native homelands varied: overpopulation, contracting economic opportunities, famine, drought, war, religious persecution, political oppression. Whatever the push that set them in motion, the pull that lured them to America was the promise of a fresh start. Much the same reasons explain why newcomers are still coming, between four and five million in the last decade, not counting an unknown but doubtlessly large number of illegal entrants.

But why, in the first instance, did the United States open its doors to strangers? And how was it supposed that they and the host people could form a common American nationality? Both questions require that we return to Crèvecoeur's generation, for it was this group that laid the foundations of the national identity and initiated the country's immigration and naturalization policies.

☆ ☆ ☆ Kinship through Citizenship

The founders of the Republic had no way of knowing the degree to which immigration would transform the population, but they had no doubt about the means to absorb ("acculturate" is the favored term nowadays) the foreign-born. A uniform naturalization procedure was authorized by the Constitution and written into law by the first Congress in 1790. A revised version of that statute passed in 1802 still remains in force.

The law defines the terms by which newcomers with a bewildering variety of backgrounds are able to join the host people as citizens of a republic. Over the objections of a minority of lawmakers who wanted a long probationary period, the 1802 act set a five-year residence requirement, which was judged sufficient for immigrants to familiarize themselves with American life, to show intent to remain here, and to demonstrate "good moral character." If the process was meant to be quick and hospitable, it was also demanding. Not only did prospective citizens have to swear to "support the constitution," they had to prove to the satisfaction of a presiding magistrate that they were "attached to the principles of the constitution." The test for citizenship was so exacting that an aristocratic candidate for naturalization had to "make an express renunciation of his title or order of nobility."

No other country at the time had a law like the act of 1802. In England, whose jurisprudence the Americans knew well, naturalization was not a popular right administered by the nearest court but an occasional gift from the monarch bestowed through special parliamentary act. The proceedings were expensive, there was no residence requirement, and the only persons eligible were Protestants who would take the sacraments in the Church of England. Above all and beyond everything else, naturalization did not make one a citizen. All Englishmen, the native-born and the naturalized alike, were subjects of the monarch.

Other European powers were no more inclined than England to receive immigrants. The United States was the first nation in modern history to do so. Hardheaded reason lay behind the decision. America's vast expanse was underpopulated; immigrants would help to fill it. America's boundless resources were unexploited; immigrant manpower and skills and capital would contribute to developing them. In plainer words, immigration promised to make the United States more populous, more wealthy, more powerful.

To leave the story there, however, would leave out a substantial part of it. The lawmakers of 1802 were governed by ideals, not only by reasons of state, in uniting the foreign-born with the host people through a common citizenship. It is therefore necessary to discuss what the founders thought their nation building meant.

The American War of Independence was the first successful anticolonial war in modern history. Yet the victors set up a nation without the then-usual prerequisites for nationhood. Unlike the older states in Europe, the United States could not say that it had natural territorial boundaries and a long history or that its people belonged to the same church, shared an ancient folklore, or descended from a common stock.

That the English were the most numerous group in the United States goes without saying. They were also the most influential, and it would be hard to overstate the importance, then or now, of the English language, English law, English religious ideas, and English political ideals and institutions. All the same, the English were not—nor were they destined to be—the parent stock of the American people as a whole.

The evidence is clear in regard to that point. Of the 3,929,000 men, women, and children enumerated in the first census in 1790, the English and their descendants constituted just under half the population. The next largest group—from Africa—accounted for close to 20 percent. The remaining third comprised persons of Scotch-Irish, German, Scottish, French, Irish, Swiss, Spanish, Dutch, and still other origins. Small wonder that Crèvecoeur asked wherein lay the Americanness of the Americans?

The founders' answer was ideological. Even Crèvecoeur, although opposed to the movement for independence, described the American as a new man because he acted "upon new principles . . . new ideas . . . new opinions." Revolutionary leaders made the same point in one way or another. In a long work published just after the adoption of the Constitution, Joel Barlow argues that what Americans think is what Americans are. An ideological answer was the only sort possible to the then-youngest country in the world. Americans could not claim to be distinctive for reasons of territory, history, church, folklore, or folk.

The process of self-definition began in the 1760s with the struggle against the mother country and continued through the 1790s with the establishment of the new nation and its justification. In the end the argument evolved that, unlike the Old World, which the founders homogenized into a bundle of evils, the United States stood for liberty, opportunity, religious pluralism, a balanced and representative government, widespread property ownership, and a better tomorrow for everyone. Nor was it necessary on this side of the Atlantic, as it was on the other, to rely on such historic props of authority as monarchy, aristocracy, and established clergy. A free people were themselves a sufficient source of authority.

Stated differently, the American Republic rested on its citizens. Their recently won status from England legitimated, in the founders' eyes, both the War of Independence and the foundations of the American experiment. Not only did the American experiment deny the principle, in which even Whigs believed, that the sovereign power resided in the throne; more profoundly, it rejected the whole hierarchical view of society. In the Old World even "dukes and earls are creatures of kings," explained a South Carolinian revolutionary of Scottish immigrant parents, whereas "citizens possess in their own right original sovereignty."

Clearly, the important thing about Americans was what they believed in, not the origins of their ancestors. The United States was an ideal, the embodiment of the values for which the Enlightenment stood. Excepting a minority of doubters, the revolutionary generation was so confident of the appeal of its ideal that it was unafraid to share it with immigrants. The sole condition was that they link their individual futures to the future of a nation that had inaugurated, in the words of the Great Seal of the United States, "a new order of the ages" (Novus Ordo Seclorum).

The next year, in 1783, George Washington wrote: "The bosom of America is open to receive not only the Opulent and respectable Stranger, but the oppressed and persecuted of all Nations and Religions." All nations? Not quite, in the beginning. Like the act of 1790, that of 1802 confined naturalization to any "alien, being a free white person." The exclusion of blacks did not survive the Civil War. After three constitutional amendments to free the slaves and make them citizens and voters, Congress in 1870 extended the law of naturalization to "aliens of African nativity, and to persons of African descent." The latter phrase cleared the way for numerous candidates from the West Indies.

Thereafter the color line followed an erratic course. Special measures conferred citizenship on the native Indians from Mexico but not from Canada; on Hawaiian Chinese but not on Chinese immigrants to the mainland; on Puerto Ricans but not on Filipinos (except for those who served in World War I). For years legal opinion divided over the "whiteness" of Parsis, Hindus, Koreans, and Japanese until, finally, the higher courts agreed that none of the four was white. All the while, in a cruel irony, the Fourteenth Amendment raised American-born children over their proscribed immigrant parents.

By World War II America's racial preferences, a marvel in whimsicality, turned into an unbearable embarrassment. To cement the Roosevelt administration's "good-neighbor policy," the Nationality Act of 1940 permitted the naturalization of indigenous persons from the entire Western hemisphere. After Pearl Harbor, mindful of the need for military allies in Asia, Congress dropped the bars against naturalizing Filipinos, Chinese, and peoples from the Indian subcontinent. But not until the ensuing Cold War, during which America competed against Communist countries for the loyalty of emerging nations in the nonwhite world, did the law dating from 1790 become fully color-blind. Congress stated in 1952 that the "right of a person to become a naturalized citizen of the United States shall not be denied or abridged because of race."

☆ ☆ ☆ Discord

From this brief legal history of naturalization it is apparent that, for a long stretch of time, color prejudice set limits to the universality of the American creed. In moments of crisis, moreover, the country was torn by ethnic and religious discord. The anti-Catholic flare-up just before the Civil War, the anti-German-American hysteria of World War I, the Ku Klux Klan obscenities of the tribalistic 1920s, the internment of Japanese-Americans during World War II—these and still other bouts of bigotry accompanied America's ingathering of the peoples of the world.

Insofar as immigration policy was concerned, a movement began in the last decade of the nineteenth century to persuade Congress to close the doors. Led by Yankee blue bloods, southern white supremacists, trade-union officials, academics, and disillusioned reformers, the restrictionists publicized their views for some three decades in books, pamphlets, magazines, newspapers, and a forty-two-volume government report. More than anything else, they argued their case in terms of Anglo-Saxon superiority.

The emergence of that doctrine coincided with the founding of history and the social sciences as academic disciplines in the United States. Many leaders in those fields were obsessed with what was then called race. The conventional wisdom of their day, influenced by the theory of evolution, sanctioned the classification of human beings by relative fitness. Accordingly, scholars arranged America's ancestral groups in hierarchical order, placing Anglo-Saxons and their Nordic cousins from Northern and Western Europe at the top and Southern and Eastern Europeans, Orientals, and blacks at the bottom. The ranking was grounded in the then-scientific understanding that moral and intellectual characteristics, not just physical ones, were inherited from generation to generation. For that reason, contended Anglo-Saxonists, some nations progressed while others fell behind into "the beaten men of beaten races."

Such notions were eventually to be congenial to a society that, in the half century after 1880, was transformed by urbanization, industrialization, and immigration. In 1896 newcomers from Southern and Eastern Europe surpassed, for the first time, arrivals from Northern and Western Europe. The gap between the two streams widened with the passing of years. By 1907, for every person entering from the old areas, four were being admitted from the new. A quarter century earlier, when the first signs appeared that a major demographic shift was in the making, the ratio had been just the reverse.

The more the population changed, according to Anglo-Saxonists, the more the American landscape spoiled. Were it not for the influx of inferior types, the explanation went, the country would be free of slums, poverty, strikes, radicalism, broken homes, drunkenness, crime, prostitution, gambling, illiteracy, and corrupt political machines. What made the picture uglier still was the nostalgic view that no serious social problems had existed when, earlier, an essentially small-town and rural America drew its people from Nordic Europe. The conclusion followed that only through racially selective laws of admission could the country escape further deterioration.

Congress came around to that point of view in the Johnson-Reed Act of 1924, which went into effect five years later. Reducing immigration to a trickle and classifying newcomers by national origin, the law shut out all Asians and assigned meager quotas of admission to Southern and Eastern European countries, larger ones to Western and Northern Europe, and the largest to Britain and Northern Ireland. More plainly, the law stated that the dominant group preferred that future citizens be more like their Anglo-Saxon Protestant selves.

That preference had been expressed time and again since the closing years of the previous century. How is it that not until the 1920s did it receive official sanction? The answer lies in the xenophobic fears of that decade. As a result of the disillusionment with the outcome of World War I, Congress was afraid to entangle the United States in the affairs of the League of Nations and the World Court. The country also felt threatened by bolshevism, changes in moral standards, the decline in religious orthodoxy, the violence growing out of the failure of Prohibition—all of which were blamed on foreigners. As confidence had supported a policy of unrestricted immigration, so loss of confidence led to its rejection.

For the next two decades there was silence. The greatest folk migration in recorded history came to an almost dead stop, and almost no one seemed to care. As a result of the Great Depression and World War II, few Americans considered immigration a relevant issue. Then the McCarran-Walter Act of 1952, which codified existing legislation except for amendments assigning quotas to Asian countries, aroused a nationwide movement to repeal the exclusiveness that marred the statute books.

The demand reflected profound changes that had taken place since the 1920s. For one thing, the descendants of the new immigrants were strong enough to speak up in their own behalf and to put pressure on their Democratic party. For another, a new generation of scholars discredited the formerly accepted proofs for the doctrine of Anglo-Saxon supremacy. Also, America was no longer isolationist and had to show an unprejudiced face to the world. Above all and beyond everything else, Nazi Germany had demonstrated the appalling consequences of equating superiority with a particular race.

What finally cleared the way was the election in 1960 of the country's first Irish-Catholic president. While still a junior senator from Massachusetts, John F. Kennedy took up the fight for repeal of exclusionary immigration laws. He entered the White House with that pledge but died before carrying it out. The triumph of reversing the racist legislation of the 1920s fell to his Texas-born successor. Congress in 1965 wrote a new act to admit immigrants according to their skills and to reunite families. President Lyndon Johnson signed the bill at the Statue of Liberty. The Anglo-Saxonist-inspired national origins system "has been un-American in the highest sense," he said, "because it has been untrue to the faith that brought thousands to these shores even before we were a country. Today, with my signature, this system is abolished." Officially America stood, once again, for a nationality based on democratic belief. There, at present, the matter rests.

☆ ☆ ☆ Assimilation and Ethnicity

And yet, there is more to say. The repeal of the national origins plan would seem to suggest that the people of the United States consider themselves Americans and nothing else. That is in fact the case for many persons, but not for all. Numerous others identify themselves as both Americans and members of an ethnic group.

The founders of the Republic were aware that this phenomenon existed in their own time. Some liked it, others did not, and still others left no opinion to posterity. In any case, none of them thought it a subject for government intervention. The state stood aside, silently acknowledging that ethnic affiliation, like religious affiliation, to which it was usually allied, was a matter of individual choice.

Thus, as before the establishment of the United States, each new incoming group formed its own associations. That process is still occurring and can be seen among recent immigrants who have not yet built their institutions. Conversely, the once-potent institutions of other groups such as the Manx and Scotch-Irish have disappeared. Plainly, every ethnic group has had a history of its own in America, shaped by place of origin, area of settlement, time, circumstances, and relations to others.

Nevertheless, it is possible to make generalizations. First, America's ethnic groups are unlike their seeming counterparts in, say, the Soviet Union, Czechoslovakia, or Yugoslavia. Such countries have been, in one degree or another, federations of nationalities. The United States is not. There is no legal recognition of ethnic groups; no group lives in a historic homeland of its own; and most groups no longer speak their original languages.

Things might have been different had it not been for public policy. In a precedent-making refusal in 1818 to approve a petition from the Irish Societies of New York and Philadelphia for a western land grant, Congress established the principle that the federal government would assist no overseas group to create a homeland in America. Were the Irish permitted to do so, it was thought, the Germans might be next, followed by other groups. The result would transform the federal Union into a union of nationalities.

Another generalization that can be made is that ethnic groups aided their members in acculturating to America through varied institutions. Immigrant banks provided capital to persons going into business; building and loan associations offered mortgages to potential home owners; mutual benefit societies insured families against illness, accidents, and death. Meanwhile, the foreign-language press informed its readers about what was going on in the United States; and however corrupt at times, political bosses introduced newcomers in their own groups to the power of the vote, a power that seldom existed in the old country.

The church also played a major role. Everyone in America was supposed to have some kind of religion; the immigrants fit in by almost immediately transplanting the religion they brought with them. Many of them had belonged to the established church in their native country; here they learned the advantages of sustaining the ancestral faith through their own efforts. By so doing, they discovered the value that Americans placed on voluntarism and pluralism.

This is not to say that the ethnic group was the sole agent of acculturation. Far from it. For every parochial institution, save the church itself, there was a competing public one, from schools to banks. Then, too, great public events, including wars, drew immigrants into American life. Beyond everything else, outside pressures quickened the process of learning English. Yet the fact remains that even from within each ethnic group, itself an American artifact, immigrants took important steps toward becoming Americans. Crèvecoeur saw as much in 1782.

In coming back to Crèvecoeur, we come back to the question: Who are we? Is the American a product of the melting pot? Yes, to the extent that hardly anyone of any descent is the same as his or her original ancestors in this country. When the melting-pot idea caught the public fancy before World War I, however, it was predicted that intermarriage would result in a single American stock. That fusion has yet to take place, notwithstanding a great deal of intermarriage.

According to a U.S. Bureau of Census survey of 1979, eighty-three million Americans reported that they descended from "multiple ancestry groups," and ninety-six million from a "single ancestry group." The returns broke down, respectively, to 38 and 45 percent. An additional 6 percent, totaling between thirteen and fourteen million persons, most of them living in the South, considered themselves American in origin and nothing else. What is less clear from the survey is why roughly twenty-three million (11 percent) chose not to answer the question about their ancestry.

In any case, it is incorrect to state flatly, as have two celebrated students of the subject, that the "point about the melting pot . . . is that it did not happen." Millions of men and women have testified that it did happen, and is still happening, to themselves and their families. What is more, in recent years the rate of intermarriage has become considerable in groups where once it had been minuscule. In the last decade, for example, the rate for Jews was 30 percent. It ran as high as 40 percent for Mexican-Americans and 60 percent for Japanese-Americans.

But although it is applicable to many individuals, the melting pot is a misleading figure of speech for America as a whole. It ignores the persistence of ethnicity. It denies the legitimacy, and value, of ancestral groups. It under-estimates the strength of family, religious, ethnic, and racial constraints against intermarriage. It deprecates marrying inside the group. Were mixed ancestry the sole measure, President John Fitzgerald Kennedy, a fourth-generation Bostonian of unmixed Irish-Catholic parentage, would have been an inadmissible American type.

Nor does the currently favored theory of cultural pluralism provide an adequate answer to the question first posed in 1782. Although the United States is indeed pluralist, it is not the "commonwealth or federation of national cultures" that the father of cultural pluralism, Horace Kallen, hoped it would become. Like Israel Zangwill, who popularized the metaphor of the melting pot, Kallen claimed too much for his metaphor of the United States as a harmonious orchestra of foreign-language groups.

Except in scattered pockets, no major group of the past managed to transmit its language to a sizable number of descendants beyond the second generation. Today's Hispanic newcomers, particularly from neighboring Mexico, hope to succeed where others have failed. Easy and frequent travel between the United States and Mexico favors that ambition. Also, in 1968 the federal government sanctioned, for the first time in American history, bilingual education in the public schools.

What remains to be seen is the degree to which Spanish will challenge the hegemony of English. Already a reaction has set in. Ten years after the passage of the 1968 law, it was amended to stipulate that bilingual education was being funded not as an end in itself, but as a means to teach English to foreign language–speaking children. Congress acted on a widely held belief in the country that although no federal statute ever declared English official, it is in fact the language of the United States. As for the intergenerational continuity of various ancestral tongues, that is a matter for voluntary effort by interested parties, not state intervention.

Perhaps no summing up, metaphorical or otherwise, can do justice to the complex interplay between immigration and the national character. However, the ethnic identification among individuals can be classified now as in the past. Beyond the affiliation that others might ascribe to them, immigrants and their descendants fall into one of four categories:

Total identifiers live out their lives entirely within the ethnic group. They reside with members of their group, go to school with them, work with them, pray with them, eat their food, relax with them, marry them, and vote and campaign for them. The persons who do so willingly constitute a tiny fraction of the population. More commonly, total identifiers are recent immigrants who, for reasons of poverty or prejudice, have no choice but to live completely by themselves.

Partial identifiers take their ethnicity in measured and selected doses. It is usually most important to them in primary associations, but they are apt to define themselves in nonethnic terms at work, in the community, or at college. The more such individuals play autonomous roles, the more they see themselves as being more than solely ethnic. They constitute a majority of Americans who retain ties to their ancestry.

Disaffiliates grew up in ethnic or ethnoreligious neighborhoods but cannot go home again because they have chosen not to. They are most often found in the worlds of academia, the media, and the arts. They are intellectuals, in a word. One critic has written that they are the same as ethnic groups. That they constitute a tribe of their own is true. They have their own values, rituals, heroes, fears, ways of bringing up children, and so on. Yet, unlike members of ethnic groups, disaffiliates are not tied together by common ancestry. They number in the many millions and are likely to remain numerous considering the extraordinarily high percentage of Americans who go to college.

Hybrids cannot identify themselves with a single stock. They are of mixed ancestry and come from families that have intermarried for generations. In a course at the University of Chicago recently on ethnic factors in American history, students with that background had difficulty grasping the concept of ethnicity. A few resented it, thinking it a form of bigotry to sort people according to their origins. Such Americans are literal products of the melting pot.

Each of these categories calls for refinements. It is extremely hard to classify individuals in a fluid society and for individuals to classify themselves in it. Perhaps that is why the United States engenders more alienation than societies where everyone knows exactly where he or she fits. Such were the lands, however, from which the masses of immigrants were uprooted and set in motion. In adjusting to their adopted country they, and later their progeny, fashioned ties of belonging appropriate to their changing conditions. The process is likely to continue, for where boundaries are loose there is freedom to choose.

It remains to say that a good part of the civilized world now subscribes to the proposition, first enunciated by the United States, that expatriation is a basic human right. In taking the lead, the United States served its needs as the world's leading receiver of immigrants, yet it also released a liberating idea for humankind—the idea that nationalities are changeable rather than irrevocable. Like so many other aspects of the American experience, the welcome to newcomers symbolizes a fresh start, the chance to begin anew.

At the same time, the terms for becoming a naturalized citizen do not require immigrants to give up their religions, languages, memories, customs, music, food, or whatever else they care to preserve in the folk culture. The process of acculturation, therefore, leaves room for different antecedents and ethnic affiliations while upholding the values of a common civic culture. Like every human contrivance, this one has had its ups and downs. Yet even the downs serve as a reminder that the national identity, first articulated by the founders of the Republic, rests on the faith that unity and diversity are not only mutually compatible but supportive of liberty.

FURTHER READING

For an annotated bibliography prepared for college students, see John D. Buenker and Nicholas C. Burckel, *Immigration and Ethnicity: A Guide to Information Sources* (Detroit, 1977). In his *American Immigration* (Chicago, 1960), Maldwyn Allen Jones provides a thoughtful historical survey down to the date of its publication. Compare it to a later effort by Thomas J. Archdeacon, *Becoming American* (New York, 1983). There is a wealth of information and insight, representing the most recent scholarship, in Stephan Thernstrom, ed., *Harvard Encyclopedia of American Ethnic Groups* (Cambridge, Mass., 1980). A helpful visual companion to that superb work can be found in James Paul Allen and Eugene James Turner, *We the People: An Atlas of America's Ethnic Diversity* (New York, 1988). No student, however, should miss two works by the major founder of immigration history, Marcus L. Hansen, both posthumously published: *The Atlantic Migration, 1607–1860* (Cambridge, Mass., 1940) and *The Immigrant in American History* (Cambridge, Mass., 1940). The most imaginative and perceptive synthesis remains Oscar Handlin's *The Uprooted* (Boston, 1951).

The national identity stands out all the more sharply when seen in comparative context. Hans Kohn took that approach in *The Idea of Nationalism* (New York, 1944) and again in *American Nationalism* (New York, 1957). The same is true of Henry Steele Commager's *The Empire of Reason*, aptly subtitled *How Europe Imagined and America Realized the Enlightenment* (New York, 1977). For a different emphasis, see J. G. A. Pocock's *The Machiavellian Moment: Florentine Political Thought and the Atlantic Republican Tradition* (Princeton, N.J., 1975). In his splendid *The Creation of the American Republic, 1776–1787* (Chapel Hill, N.C., 1969), Gordon S. Wood picks up the story where Bernard Bailyn left it in his brilliant *The Ideological Origins of the American Revolution* (Cambridge, Mass., 1967). The best account of the relationship of the national identity and citizenship is by James H. Kettner, *The Development of American Citizenship* (Chapel Hill, N.C., 1978).

Three excellent works trace the shift in attitudes toward immigration that led to restrictive legislation: Oscar Handlin, "Concerning the Background of the National-Origin System," in President's Commission on Immigration and Naturalization, *Hearings before the President's Commission on Immigration and Naturalization* (Washington, D.C., 1952); John Higham, *Strangers in the Land* (New Brunswick, N.J., 1955); and Barbara Miller Solomon, *Ancestors and Immigrants* (Cambridge, Mass., 1956). There are also revealing insights in Mark H. Haller, *Eugenics: Hereditarian Attitudes in American Thought* (New Brunswick, N.J., 1963), and in Thomas F. Gossett, *Race: The History of an Idea in American Thought* (Dallas, Tex., 1964).

Hardly any immigrant group of size has escaped the attention of historians. The most penetrating studies thus far have been local studies. Hence Oscar Handlin's *Boston's Immigrants* (Cambridge, Mass., 1941), mostly about the Irish; Kathleen Neils Conzen's *Immigrant Milwaukee* (Cambridge, Mass., 1976), mostly about the Germans; Moses Rischin's *The Promised City* (Cambridge, Mass., 1962), almost entirely about New York City's Jews; Humbert S. Nelli's *The Italians in Chicago* (New York, 1970); and Edward R. Kantowicz's *Polish-American Politics in Chicago* (Chicago, 1975). For a rich history that treats several immigrant groups in the same locale, see Melvin G. Holli and Peter d'A. Jones, eds., *Ethnic Chicago* (Grand Rapids, Mich., 1984). In *Strangers from a Different Shore* (Boston, 1989), Ronald T. Takaki attempts a history of all immigrant groups from Asia.

It has been more common for sociologists than for historians to formulate bold generalizations about ethnicity in the United States. The most influential books of that sort are Nathan Glazer and Daniel Patrick Moynihan, *Beyond the Melting Pot* (Cambridge, Mass., 1963), and Milton M. Gordon, *Assimilation in American Life* (New York, 1964). Largely in response to the post-1960s ethnic revival, however, some historians have attempted to translate monographic research into conceptual guides for understanding the interplay between ethnic diversity and national unity. See, for example, John Higham, *Send These to Me* (New York, 1975); Arthur Mann, *The One and the Many* (Chicago, 1979); and Philip Gleason, "American Identity and Americanization," in *Harvard Encyclopedia of American Ethnic Groups*, ed. Thernstrom.

3 ☆ The

☆ Frontier Family

☆ *Dislocation and the*

☆ *American Experience*

☆ Lillian Schlissel

The outermost edge of the westering adventure for Americans was the frontier. From the Appalachians to the Pacific slope, frontier was the changing face of the land. It could mean deep forests or grasslands stretching for a thousand miles; it could mean red dirt flats or outcroppings of rock surging up against the sky. The only quality frontiers shared was that, however different, each would disappear within a generation, wilderness transformed into settlement in less than twenty years.

But in the brief experience of living beyond the precincts of society, Americans found the quintessential values of their culture. Frontier was the seedbed of national character and political egalitarianism. The frontier set its imprint upon American manners, economics, and society.

☆ ☆ ☆ The Frontier and the Family

In the Homestead Act of 1862, the U.S. Congress provided for the distribution of public lands to heads of households, giving formal recognition to the fact that since the seventeenth century families had been the irrepressible units of American westward expansion. In a young and impatient nation that mistrusted both church and state, a Christian family was sufficient expression of political and social order.

Families took up the challenge of western lands in a variety of ways. Some families moved west in loosely organized groups made up of kin or neighbors or simply those who happened to be traveling in the same direction. They drew up constitutions and chose leaders and generally applied the democratic process to the journey west. The federal government, for its part, provided little help—no maps or transportation, no tools or agricultural information, no medical services and little protection. Beyond the westward-running rivers there was no road until wagons rutted the way so that one could see a trail—or until enough wagons became lost and doubled back to warn others against their mistakes. Nonetheless, the lure of "free land" was irresistible. One way or another, with a wagon train or alone, a family packed its belongings and its livestock and set off toward the next "empty" space.

Cycles of "boom and bust" intensified or slowed the westward movement. In 1837 depression in the Midwest brought the price of wheat to ten cents a bushel, and corn was given away. Steamboats along the Missouri River were burning grain for fuel, and farmers looked to escape from their economic woes. The migration that began to take form in the 1840s, however, was different from anything that had gone before. The "new country" this time was the Pacific Northwest, eighteen hundred miles away from the "jumping-off" places in Kansas and Missouri. In 1841 a few hundred families managed to cross the continent in wagons smaller than Columbus's ships. Within twenty years the overland migration swelled to more than a quarter of a million men, women, and children crossing a distance as wide as the Atlantic and as treacherous.

The audacity—and the magnitude—of that migration captured the historical imagination from the start. We know the routes of each wagon party and each "cut-off" as it was discovered. We know the mishaps and the encounters with Indians. We know the discoveries and the triumphs over the land. The westward journey has been the national epic, the story of heroic men and women. On the frontier, Americans found an agenda for greatness.

But if we are to come to terms with the realities of the past, and with the lives of the ordinary folk who lived by day-to-day chores and accidents, we need to find another dimension in which to retell the story. This chapter is an attempt to write one aspect of western history by reconstructing the lives of a single pioneer family from their letters, discovered at the Beinecke Library at Yale University. Their history unfolds dramatically. The microcosm of their private lives shows how often frontier families veered into eccentric directions, yet these very anomalies bring us closer to understanding what migration and life on the western frontier were all about.

☆ ☆ ☆ A Family Seeks the "American Dream"

George and Abigail Malick came from Pennsylvania. They were of German Lutheran descent and were typical of their neighbors and of rural families in terms of family size, social class, education, religious affiliation, and economic status. From Pennsylvania they migrated to Illinois, where their eldest daughter married and started her own family. In the summer of 1848 the Malicks headed west again with three sons and three daughters, leaving their eldest daughter and her family behind.

The Malicks weighed the advantages and disadvantages of moving west and thought they were making a reasonable choice for milder winters and for free land. Clearly, they uprooted in order to better themselves. Yet once they were on that journey, the conduct of their affairs was seldom in their control. They could not know how treacherous the journey would be, or how unpredictable the far western frontier.

Seventeen-year-old Hiram wrote exuberantly of preparations to get under way: "Mother is agoin' to make the wagon covor to morrow and I want you to wright to us just as quick as you get this be cause I want to hear from you before I go." Stoutly he told his sister, "I must [tell] you that I dont ever expect to com [to Illinois] again. . . . I like the far west." How could he or anyone else know that he would die on the journey? Eighteen months after their arrival in Oregon Territory, Abigail wrote to her daughter: "Hiram is dead. . . . He swam Acrost the river and the Watter run very fast and he could not rach the Shore. . . . The other boys Cald to him and said O hiram O swim and he said O My god I cannot eney More they said he went down in the watter seven or eight times before he drounded and then he said O My god O Lord Jesus receve my Soal for I am no More." His mother wrote, "It has Al most kild Me but I have to bar it And if we are good per hapes then we can meet him in heven."

☆ ☆ ☆ The "New Country"

Arriving in Oregon in 1848, George and Abigail claimed 640 acres—one mile square—of good land under the Donation Act, which provided equal shares for husband and wife. They were skillful farmers and used to hard work. Within a few months of their arrival, news of gold in northern California exploded through the territory, and every able-bodied man in the region set off to find a fortune. George Malick and his eldest son Charles went to the goldfields and came back with five thousand dollars, and then Charles went back alone. At first there was no word from Charles; then came conflicting stories that he had been set upon and robbed and that he had died of "brain fever." Abigail wrote, "Charles was on his way home and got in to green wood valley And was Robed [of seven thousand dollars] and that was the Caus of his death. . . . It hurt him so much that he took the brain fevor And died."

As if to make up for the deaths of two sons in a year's time, Abigail begged her married daughter to join them in Oregon: "[Th]ares a plenty of money hare . . . and A very pleasant Place to live. . . . We have Made a bout two hundred dollars on the claim. . . . You could make APlenty of Money heare and if you did not wish to stay heare you could leve your family with us and go to the Gold Mines and get all that you ever would want. . . . We have a Plente wheat and it is Agreat Country for weat and the pretist wheat that ever I seen." The Malicks raised potatoes, oats, barley, and peas. Day labor for men who had the time brought between five and ten dollars. "Fir tres are very tall and o they make a most butiful lumber." The Columbia River, close by their claim, held more salmon than one could eat. Their homestead grew: "We have got a new clock . . . and a very handsom looking glas to set on a beaurough and it caust fourteen dollars . . . and a half a dozen Chairs they Cost seven Dollars." George built a porch around the entire house. "My o dere children I wish that you were heare."

In 1852 Rachel Malick became engaged to a young man named John Biles from the family's home state of Pennsylvania. The bride was seventeen and "in snaird in love." Her mother sent swatches of the wedding dress and some wedding cake back to Illinois. Rachel gave birth to a son in little more than a year and was soon pregnant again. This time she carried twins, who at her confinement presented in breach position. Beyond medical help, Rachel died in childbirth at nineteen. The Malicks cared for her surviving child for four years until his father remarried. In 1854, only six years after arriving in "the new country," George Malick died and Abigail was left to carry on with what was left of her family—two young daughters and one errant son.

Shindel Malick was never cut out to be a farmer. He would neither go to school nor help cut the wood nor plow the fields. He preferred gambling and racing horses with the soldiers of Fort Vancouver to his mother's call that he help with the chores. Father dead, two brothers dead, his older sister dead, Shin had little sense of family obligation and too much of the "frontier spirit" to heed words about work and duty. Abigail wrote to Illinois, "After your Father died Everything was Left on My hands and Shin would go off to town and Stay away when i would have anything to do." Abigail tried to hire Indians or other settlers to cut wood or do the planting, but most of the time she did all the work alone. "This winter I had to go and Chop Wood My Self . . . for I could not get a man to do it."

Schooling was important to Abigail, who paid for each of her younger children to attend schools when schools were available. But teenagers on the western frontier set their own course, and Abigail's children were no exceptions. In time, thirteen-year-old Jane was courted by a lieutenant from nearby

Fort Vancouver. He was ten years older than she, raced blooded horses, and cut a handsome figure, but Abigail was suspicious: "I thought he had no business to notice a little school girl." Jane's liaison with Henry Pearson, against everything her mother could do or say, proved a disaster.

It seems probable that Jane was pregnant when Abigail arranged a hasty wedding performed by a justice of the peace. The child that was born soon died and the handsome lieutenant squandered Jane's dowry. Jane herself came home subject to seizures of madness.

> We should Have had to of Sent Her to Stockton to the Mad house or the Insane Ascilum And that Would have Bin Very Hard for her and us for they whip them Every Morning or when they do Eney thing so I am told And get Hardley eney thing to eat. . . . Before [Jane] came to her sences she went out to the Well and drew eighteen buckets full of Watter and Threw Watter All over her self and Striped Her Self down to her Wast and took a Black Ball Brush and some Sand and Scoured her head and Hear Cloathes and Her Body All over and scoured the Well curb . . . and the ground. . . . She Climed upon the Top of the House and Farley tore the Hool Roof Al of and then she Tore the top of the Chimney down and then we Cald her to Come down But she would not. . . . She Came to her sences Againe O I have had An Abundance of trouble with Jane.

Abigail tried to hide her troubles, but she wrote to Illinois that she had had "to tak [Jane's] Babe and Not Let Her See it for two and three Dayes at a time and Tie Her down on a Bed and It took three of us to do it."

Susan, the youngest daughter, eloped when she was fifteen, was brought back home, and then married against her mother's objections. When her husband threatened to kill her, she obtained a divorce, but instead of coming home, she joined a troupe of traveling actors. Against all the misadventures of her children, Abigail put on a good "face." She wrote, "Susan is an Actress in a Fine Theater Group She will Be gone A Bout three Months. . . . They give Susan Twenty Three dollars a Weak Clear of al Expenses and Take good care of Her. . . . They are All Very Nice." Coming closer to the truth, Abigail confessed in another letter that the frontier was just not a good place to raise children. "I have so Mutch trouble with the Children. They are Not like Children raised in the States. They have no Father and They will Not Mind Me."

Whatever else they learned on the frontier, the Malick children understood the powerful impulse of personal independence, and each of them in turn fled the constraints of family. Their rejections of the farm and of their parents' life-style is one of the characteristics of this particular family history. Finding employment in small businesses and in the mines, the three younger Malick children shifted class and economic affiliation. Without the children, the land Abigail and George farmed and loved was sold, and virtually no records remain of the family's stay.

But the Malicks were not unusual. The Clark County census shows forty-four families living on claims in 1850, but only nine of those original families were still there a decade later. Like the Malicks, 80 percent of the families of the first settlement had broken apart or moved on. Where one might expect that the hardships of the overland journey would have anchored settlers for generations to come, census data contradict expectations. Emigrant families continued to move. They searched for that final geography, that ultimate configuration of land that would make them rich, and so many roads beckoned that uprooting itself became a way of life.

☆ ☆ ☆ A Precarious Life on the Frontier

Although the national folklore portrays pioneers as figures of strength and hardiness, the Malick history shows them to have led the most fragile kind of existence. They worked hard, made judicious choices, and yet they were subject to all the accidents of chance and of fate. The frontier was a volatile environment in which the lives of men, women, and children were precariously balanced. The question for the historian is how much of the instability was common to the frontier condition and how much the experience of one particular family. Some conclusions can be drawn:

1. In leaving their daughter and her family in Illinois, the Malicks were typical of emigrant families. Separations from family and loneliness were the most common emigrant experiences. Abigail's letters to her daughter represent a decade of devotion. She filled her letters with the tangibles of everyday life. She sent swatches of dresses and bonnets, gold pieces and rings, fancy stamps and pieces of cake, flower and vegetable seeds, spears of grass, newspaper clippings, photographs. She passed along even the smallest economic facts of life: the prices of land, cows, pigs, timber, wheat, chickens, eggs, potatoes. She told how much it cost to buy and sell land, how much they had managed to save, the amount of taxes they paid for schools and roads. And she pleaded for more letters and more news, for photographs of her grandchildren and seeds from "home." Abigail's longing for her eldest daughter was a wound that never healed. In a sample of 103 diaries of women who made the same journey, 63 percent told of similar separations from parents, from siblings, and from children. There is no theme more poignant in all pioneer diaries and letters than the longing for family left behind.

2. Eleven percent of this sample of diaries tell of the deaths of fathers, husbands, and brothers in drownings, and another 8 percent tell of men and boys in neighboring wagon parties who died in similar fashion. Exertion and accidents took their toll. The work of moving heavy wagons across a raw continent, hauling them up and down mountain ranges by winches and pulleys, leading oxen and then wagons through swollen rivers—all of these "ordinary" mishaps of the road exacted a toll that far exceeded any that can be attributed to the Indians. Dysentery and typhoid were rampant, and cholera in epidemic proportions swept the trail from 1849 through 1853. Nowhere could it have been more dismal to die, far from friends and family, than on that road or in the tents and shacks along the riverbanks and rocky gorges of the "rag towns" where men looked for gold. The deaths of the Malicks' sons were commonplace experiences of the frontier where accident and disease took the lives of young men who set out upon adventure.

3. Young women too were at risk. The census seldom enumerates the deaths of women in childbirth, and stillbirths, miscarriages, and abortions are not recorded at all. Yet evidence drawn from personal narratives suggests that at least one in five pregnancies "failed" and that at least the same number of infants died before their fifth year. The birth rate in the Oregon Territory in 1850, however, surpassed the national average by more than 50 percent, and there are estimates that during this period in the Northwest Territory the ratio of infants to women was almost double that of India in 1961. Somewhere within that high fertility ratio lies the suggestion of a large number of maternal deaths in childbirth. Rachel Malick's death is a reminder that complications in pregnancy or in delivery could be fatal even to women who were young and strong and hardy.

4. In the matter of divorce the Malicks highlight a characteristic pattern, for Washington, Montana, Colorado, Arkansas, Texas, Oregon, Wyoming, Indiana, Idaho, and Oklahoma had the highest divorce rates in the nation. In 1858–59 the Oregon legislature convened a "memorable Divorce session" in which thirty couples were divorced and ten other requests were turned aside as too late for action. The ratio between the sexes in the early years of settlement gave women every reason to look for a new match if the first proved unsatisfactory. There were men enough, and frontier pragmatism encouraged one to "try again."

5. One would suspect, finally, that insanity should have been the least representative factor in the Malick family history. Yet between 1850 and 1870 there were no fewer than three institutions for the insane in the Northwest, one in northern California at Stockton and two in Oregon at Salem and Portland. The *Reports of the Insane Asylum of Portland, Oregon,* from between

1870 and 1890, show that the total number of patients treated in that hospital increased from 260 in 1870–72 to 411 in 1876–78, rising to 734 in 1884– 86. Of this number, the ratio of female to male patients begins at approximately one-third and increases within one decade to one-half. The frontier conditions generated their share of emotional tensions and instabilities. Insanity was not an example of the random misadventures of one family but a condition sufficiently present in the larger community to draw purposeful response.

The sense that permeates the family letters is that their frontier condition generated instability so diffuse that it could not be contained. Accident and sudden death, childbirth trauma, insanity, marital breakdown and violence, financial misadventures and insolvency, transient relationships and shifting populations—each aspect of everyday life was uncontrollable.

Given the volatile character of the frontier, family was the only bulwark against disorder. In the years 1848–67 the Malick household provided an astonishing range of services to family members in an effort to maintain family coherence. It provided care of the temporarily indigent and of orphaned children, living quarters for widowers, shelter for divorced and deserted wives, hospice for transients, medical care of the sick, nursing for the convalescent, and, ultimately, home care for the insane ("I have to tie her down to her bed"). Survival on the frontier may have been the triumph of individual perseverance and strength, but it was also built upon the care that sprang from households where women like Abigail Malick sustained the family's weakest members.

☆ ☆ ☆ Reassessment: The Frontier as Garden, Carnival, and Perversity

Thomas Jefferson imagined the frontier as a garden, the home of the yeoman farmer where man and earth are bound to each other in the benediction of fruitful labor. The image of the garden holds family and land and inheritance in balance. Generations are joined together here in a sedate and orderly progression. The idea of the garden moved the Malicks from Pennsylvania to Illinois and then to the Oregon Territory. The classic vision that empowered Ma Joad in Steinbeck's *The Grapes of Wrath* still shapes political ideology with compelling memories of pioneers and sober family farms. It is what the poet Wendell Berry calls "the gift of good land," a dream of order and blessing that resonates down through American history.

But frontiers never have been just as they were imagined. The outlying rim of settlements also has been the place for breaking bounds. Amid disorder the unexpected came to pass. The frontier was a "fool's day" where hunger, desperate effort, and fear could be transformed by hilarity. In this carnival, this Mardi Gras, one wore different faces and lived different lives that needed no accounting. The carnival frontier was the place of high stakes and low jokes, a place for buffoonery and swagger, where cowboys and Indians played deadly games with breakneck courage. This was the place of "striking it rich," and Abigail's children lived on such a frontier. Shindel saw his misfortunes as merely one of the "hands" in a game of cards; Jane married men her mother considered shiftless, "mean," and "dirty"; and Susan's attachment to the traveling players proclaimed her view of the frontier as a place for comedy.

Frontiers have also worn aspects of heartbreak. Walter Prescott Webb said in 1957 that western history is "brief and it is bizarre." It is "full of negatives and short on positives." Under all the promise there is something of the perverse, something that distorts human effort. Such landscapes inspired the black humor of Mark Twain's *The Mysterious Stranger* and *Pudd'nhead Wilson*. Such thoughts were set down in Melville's *Pierre* and *The Confidence Man*. Those who survive on Gothic frontiers, like the protagonist in Hemingway's *The Old Man and the Sea*, retrieve a trophy that is only a skeleton.

These frontiers transcend geography but are nonetheless real. One man prospers; another dies. Abigail's vision of sober Christian order on the western frontier was as clear and as palpable as the vision of children who follow a piper in a hat with clamoring bells.

☆ ☆ ☆ The Family "Dis-Assembled"

Given the character of frontier experience, its instability and its hardship, why have Americans ventured again and again into that disordered space? What is there in the core of American history that has drawn so many westward in such endless pursuit?

Henry David Thoreau witnessed the breaking apart of generations when he wrote: "The old have no very important advice to give the young. Their own experience has been so partial, and their lives have been such miserable failures." Although Thoreau's "West" was Walden Pond, he perceived that family rebellions are powerful and they are real. Shindel rejected his mother's life with defiant passion when he left the farm to work in the mines. After him Susan eloped, married and divorced her husband, and then joined a company of traveling players—all before she was sixteen. Even the stalwart John Biles had run away from home to join the army when he was seventeen. His parents did not know for twenty months where he was. The frontier players cut themselves free from family with savage intensity and tolerated few other boundaries on their lives.

The dramatic gestures of the Malick children were absorbed by the frontier around them. Shindel's departure from the farm did not seem extraordinary in a region where parental obligations seldom governed young men. Even Susan's eloping at fifteen and her theatrical adventure were unremarkable when other young women were flying the flag of romantic love in order to break free from the family. She went on, as Mrs. Levant Molton (until her new husband was killed in an accident), as though nothing extraordinary had occurred. Jane's "insainity" was not so unusual that she could not remarry and settle down to being a wife and mother. Frontiers absorbed the erratic; they gave wide berth to idiosyncrasy and dissipated the passions that exploded within families.

Abigail, the bulwark of stability, herself became a study in contradictions. Through all her letters filled with pleas for news, for photographs, for seeds, for scraps of clothing to keep the fragile ties of family alive—through everything Abigail maintained a stubborn refusal to live with her own children. She refused to go back to the family in Illinois in her old age. She died where she wanted to be, in her own house, on her own land—among strangers. She yearned for family, but she resisted them too, preferring the lonely bastion of her frontier solitude. The frontier family was "dis-assembled" by distance, by change, and by time.

☆ ☆ ☆ Homecoming and the Frontier Legacy

In a nation where the frontier defines the future, in a culture that rewards mobility and "newness," the continuities, interdependencies, and compromises of family are subversive of all that we are taught to desire. Given our traditions, it must be something of a miracle that families have survived at all. In three and a half centuries of frontiering, we have continued to transplant families with abandon. Set a family down however one will, wherever one will, and it will grow. But families also come apart. As Americans tumbled across the continent in makeshift wagons, jalopies, vans, pick-up trucks, later on trains and jets, they left a sister or a brother along the way, a father or a mother stayed behind, a child set off in its own separate direction. With each move, the fabric of affections is torn loose and some part of ourselves is left behind—a story touchingly told in the novels of Ole Rölvaag and Wright Morris as well as in the plays of Sam Shepard.

The "dis-assembled" family is an American accommodation, over time, to frontiers. We have grown comfortable with separation. We seldom grow to maturity within the circle of our grandchildren; the network of kinship has narrowed. We have learned to want empty space on which to construct our own lives, beyond the limitations that come with generations that touch. Family and frontier are, in the end, magnets cleverly charged so that they force each other apart. The family gathered at the Thanksgiving table is swiftly caught in the eye of the Instamatic camera before the figures break apart into the "frontiers" of their separate lives.

The Navajo call themselves a wandering people. They imagine they are completing a circle that reflects the universe, and they find blessing in unifying all things in an ordered world. Unlike the Navajo, our journeys do not yield the benedictions of return. However much we yearn to come within the circle of home, we are also determined, like the Malicks, to escape.

FURTHER READING

Historians of the family have focused upon different periods, applied varied perspectives, and used diverse research methodologies ranging from study of diaries and personal papers to statistically sophisticated analyses of census data. Many of the recent studies have concentrated on families in nonelite groups. Among the most significant works are the following: William N. Stephens, *The Family in Cross-Cultural Perspective* (New York, 1963); Philip J. Greven, Jr., *Four Generations: Population, Land, and Family in Colonial Andover, Massachusetts* (Ithaca, N.Y., 1970); John Demos, *The Little Commonwealth: Family Life in Plymouth Colony* (New York, 1970); Charles E. Rosenberg, ed., *The Family in History* (Philadelphia, 1975); James R. McGovern, *Yankee Family* (New Haven, Conn., 1975); Lawrence Stone, *The Family, Sex, and Marriage in England, 1500–1800* (New York, 1977); Herbert G. Gutman, *The Black Family in Slavery and Freedom, 1750–1925* (New York, 1976); Bernard Farber, *Guardians of Virtue: Salem Families in 1800* (New York, 1972); Tamara K. Hareven, ed., *Family and Kin in Urban Communities, 1700–1930* (New York, 1977); Carl N. Degler, *At Odds: Women and the Family in America from the Revolution to the Present* (New York, 1980); and John M. Faragher, *Sugar Creek: Life on the Illinois Prairie* (New Haven, Conn., 1986).

The historiography of women on the western frontiers recently has attracted considerable interest. Major works in this area are John M. Faragher, *Women and Men on the Overland Trail* (New Haven, Conn., 1979); Glenda Riley, *Frontierswomen: The Iowa Experience* (Ames, Iowa, 1981), and *The Female Frontier: A Comparative View of Women on the Prairie and the Plains* (Lawrence, Kans., 1988); Julie Roy Jeffrey, *Frontier Women: The Trans-Mississippi West, 1840–1880* (New

York, 1979); Joanna Stratton, *Pioneer Women: Voices from the Kansas Frontier* (New York, 1981); Elizabeth Hampsten, *Read This Only to Yourself: The Private Writings of Mid-western Women, 1880–1910* (Bloomington, Ind., 1982); Christiane Fischer, *Let Them Speak for Themselves: Women in the American West, 1849–1900* (Hamden, Conn., 1977); Fred Lockley, *Conversations with Pioneer Women*, ed. Mike Helm (Eugene, Oreg., 1981); Cathy Luchetti and Carol Olwell, *Women of the West* (St. George, Utah, 1982); Joan Jensen, *With These Hands: Women Working on the Land* (New York, 1981); Teresa Jordan, *Cowgirl: Women of the American West, An Oral History* (New York, 1982); Kenneth L. Homes, *Covered Wagon Women: Diaries and Letters from the Western Trails, 1840–1890* (Glendale, Calif., 1983); and Sandra Myres, *Westering Women and the Frontier Experience* (Albuquerque, N.Mex., 1982).

The historiography of children is a small but valuable adjunct to the fields described above. See Elliott West, *Growing up with the Country: Children on the Far Western Frontier* (Albuquerque, N.Mex., 1989); Joseph M. Hawes and N. Ray Hiner, eds., *American Childhood: A Research Guide and Historical Handbook* (Westport, Conn., 1985); and Bernard Wishey, *The Child and the Republic: The Dawn of Modern Child Nurture* (Philadelphia, 1968). The literature is rich in individual accounts and periodical essays.

The history of the Malick family in this chapter is taken from a collection of manuscript letters in the Beinecke Library at Yale University. Their full story is told in Lillian Schlissel, Byrd Gibbens, and Elizabeth Hampsten, *Far from Home: Families of the Westward Journey* (New York, 1989). For a sampling of 103 diaries, see Schlissel, *Women's Diaries of the Westward Journey* (New York, 1982).

A

Consonance

of

Towns

☆ Richard Lingeman

A dissonance of parts and people, we are a consonance of Towns. Like a man grown fat in everything but heart, we overlabor; our outlook never really urban, never rural either, we enlarge and linger at the same time, as Alice both changed and remained in her story.
—William Gass, *In the Heart of the Heart of the Country* (1968)

Confronted by what the seventeenth-century Puritan preachers liked to call "the howling wilderness," the earliest settlers in America lived in towns or villages. Huddling together for protection amid a hostile environment is an instinctive animal reaction, but more than instinct was involved. After all, many English writers called the New World the "American Eden"—that is, a benign place.

Captain Morton and his band of escaped bond servants at Merry Mount, near the first Pilgrim settlement at Plymouth, probably leaned toward such a view, which led to their undoing. The Pilgrims claimed to have sound reasons for sending a band of soldiers under Miles Standish to arrest Morton and his men, accusing them of selling firearms and liquor to the Indians. Their carnal trafficking with Indian maids also had something to do with it.

"Outlivers," the English Puritans in the Massachusetts Bay Colony would contemptuously call the people who did not dwell in the prescribed orderly villages. The conflict between the Pilgrims and the Merry Mounters in 1628 was an emblematic one, the earliest example of the tension between community and individual, society and nonconformists, that has continued to pulse, like an alternating current, throughout American history. Towns and villages have played a historical and generative role in the idea of community in American society—beyond their pragmatic role as habitations, as transit points and supply depots in the western migration, and as seats of government, social control, religion, and education in the newly organized territories.

From the beginning, the settlement of America divided into two cultural streams, one in the South and the other in New England, that in turn shaped the nature of the towns and to a degree the character of the people. We can observe these two rivers of people, which flowed from a common source in England, divide and take on new and distinctive characteristics from their separate channels.

☆ ☆ ☆ The Virginia Plantations and Decentralization

The first stream flowed through the southern part of the vast uncharted area on the eastern seaboard granted to the Virginia Company. The "planters" dispatched by the investors ("adventurers") in London were adjured to found "handsome towns," but as reports of harsh realities trickled back, the principals in London soon scaled their charge down to the more realistic "compact and orderly villages." The reasons behind both injunctions were the same, however. The principals in England wanted to make certain their men would work collectively at extracting the putative riches of the New World, providing mutual assistance and also watching one another, checking any tendencies to theft and immorality, or reversion to savagery.

The investors' vision of neat orderly towns flowering in the Virginia garden soon shattered against the harsh conditions that existed there. The first settlement, Jamestown, founded in 1607, was sited in a marshy area. Malaria wiped out large numbers of planters; fires and Indian assaults did the rest. After being resupplied, reinforced, and rebuilt several times, Jamestown was abandoned in 1676 after it was burned during Bacon's Rebellion. Other early settlements, planted farther up the river during the next decade, never amounted to much.

After decades of failure, the Virginia colonists began the cultivation of *Nicotiana tabacum*. Tobacco was their salvation, the first viable cash crop of the New World. The colonists were otherwise indifferent farmers, and they continued to import the bulk of their supplies from England. Tobacco could be grown on large plantations, and the wealthier of the planters—many of them second or third sons of noble houses disinherited under the law of primogeniture—bought large tracts of land or acquired them through influence at court.

Poor whites toiled for them as indentured servants, while a sprinkling of the middle order cultivated smaller farms. Each year the planters brought their crops to "ports"—small settlements at the heads of the numerous creeks, inlets, bays, and estuaries that formed natural harbors along the coastline of tidewater Virginia and the neighboring colony of Maryland's Chesapeake Bay. In his *Notes on the State of Virginia*, published in 1785, Thomas Jefferson explained why Virginia was still a region of plantations and farms: "We have no townships. Our country being much intersected with navigable waters, and trade brought generally to our doors . . . has probably been one of the causes why we have no towns of consequence."

Many travelers from England, finding the early society of Virginia a primitive, lawless one, blamed the lack of fixed communities. An aristocratic sojourner, John Aubery, came upon some squatters living in the inland regions, most of them probably indentured servants who had served their time. "Mean people," he sniffed, "who live lawless, nobody to govern them, they came for nobody, having no dependence on anybody."

This was by no means true of all Virginians, however. A certain rural society, loosely patterned after country society in England, had evolved by the end of the seventeenth century. The Virginia gentry on their plantations aped as best they could the lords of the manors in England. They made their plantations self-sufficient economic units, with their own stores and artisans. The smaller farmers formed a loose society of "neighborhoods," networks of people who lived far from one another yet close enough so that each might practice some specialized trade—blacksmithing, doctoring, coopering, and the like—that the others needed.

In sum, the Virginia planters improvised a decentralized society held together by slender strands of interdependence. Law was dispensed at county courthouses located centrally in the countryside and standing in splendid isolation. When court was in session, those with legal business came from miles away and stayed in an adjacent inn. Similarly, the churches were sited, not in a village, as in England, but in widely scattered parishes.

The governmental, religious, and trading centers of Virginia did not grow into towns, at least in the early stages of settlement. The plantation economy retarded urban development in the South for many years. Periodically the English authorities complained about the situation. Each new contingent of immigrants was provided with elaborate town plans, but they remained on paper. Robert Beverley could write in 1704 that the people of the colony "have not any place of cohabitation among them that may reasonably bear the name of town."

☆ ☆ ☆ New England and the Concept of Community

In contrast, the Massachusetts Bay Colony to the north, where the Pilgrims and Puritans first set foot slightly more than a decade after the founding of Jamestown, boasted more than one hundred towns by the year 1717. The explanations for this disparity may be found in the usual determinants of geography and economics, but also in the different backgrounds of the colonists. The New England settlers were largely religious dissenters who had been subjected to state persecution, which annealed them into tight little bands of believers.

By the time the Pilgrims reached Plymouth in 1620, all the passengers aboard the *Mayflower* had signed a governing compact by which they agreed to obey society's laws and the church's ordinances. The Pilgrims were a cohesive group, but there were nonbelievers among them, and it was thought best to take out this civil insurance policy. Other Puritan settlers drew up similar covenants. The Puritans regarded town and congregation as coterminous. Godly people, they believed, must live under the constant surveillance of their neighbors if they were to stay godly. They regarded humankind as incorrigibly sinful. The pastor was "watchman in this place," and the townspeople spies of God assisting him in rooting out secret transgressions.

Congregations were self-governing, but at their head was a group of elders. These "visible saints" corresponded to the "elect" of Calvinistic theology, that is, those persons secretly chosen by God to prosper on earth and in the afterlife. It was a short step from holding meetings to deal with church affairs to assembling at regular intervals to discuss secular ones—dividing common land, fencing fields against stray animals, erecting bridges, building roads.

Whereas Virginia's only representative assembly, its House of Burgesses, developed into a scintillating political club, in the colonies of Massachusetts, New Hampshire, Vermont, and Connecticut the town meetings were the basic cells of the body politic. They were truly independent, while the colonial legislatures at least nominally answered to a governor appointed by the king. The significance of the town meetings would become clear by the mid-1700s, when the countryside rang with the voices of rebellion. As Alexis de Tocqueville wrote, "The doctrine of the sovereignty of the people came out of the townships and took possession of the states." The town meetings were the local incubators of an embryonic democracy. The process of town founding by a congregation was institutionalized in colony law. A group of people who wished to establish a town would draw up a covenant, apply for a land grant, and settle on it. They divided the land, giving the largest tracts to those with the biggest families or the most property—that is, to those who were best able to farm it. Inevitably, they recapitulated the immemorial form of the agricultural village they had known in England, which the American anthropologist Robert Redfield has called "the very predominant form of human living throughout the history of mankind." (Tocqueville wrote that it was the "only association so perfectly natural that wherever a number of men are collected it seems to constitute itself.")

As in the mother country, each New England village was a parallel row of houses along a single street with long narrow strips of fields extending out behind them. Each man's holdings were scattered about, and at first villagers worked the land communally. In time, however, the hardest workers resented sharing with the lazier ones. Communal farming was abandoned and the plots were worked individually. Families continued to live in the village, however, or within a few hours' travel of it so they could attend the required all-day Sunday services at the church-cum-meetinghouse located on the village's highest ground, with the distinctive green common nearby.

The ideal New England village was a peaceable, orderly place. The reality was more robust. Living in such close proximity to one's neighbors and subject to their censorious reports, many of these villagers seethed with suppressed tensions and spites. Venomous gossip erupted into quarrels and congealed into feuds. When disputes got out of hand, the preacher intervened, or the church mediated. The unregenerately antisocial might be punished with "churching," or excommunication, the Puritan's ultimate sanction, which branded the culprit an eternal outliver from God.

The Puritans had a deep respect for the literal word of the Bible. Their preachers delivered scholarly sermons, lasting for hours, and an alert minority on the hard benches were always keen to criticize. Theological disputes frequently broke out that divided the congregation into opposing groups, or a faction might form in protest against the minister's interpretation of Scripture. "Contention" was the Puritan's greatest enemy for it contradicted the ideal of a harmonious town-church with a docile, pious citizenry. Eventually either the dissenters would take over or, more commonly, they would secede and found a new town. Their desire to live outside the ambit of the main church posed a serious dilemma to town authorities, for every person was supposed to "belong" to the town as he or she belonged to the church.

Another source of contention was land. As the first generation of settlers died off, the parcels were divided up among the sons. A father's plot was usually large enough so that he could leave an ample tract to each of his sons—and most men had many, for families of a dozen or more were the rule. By the time the third generation came of age, however, the inherited plots were too small to support a family. This created population pressures on the available land, with the inevitable result that the younger generation moved away.

Even before the third generation came forward to claim its legacy, there were always some men who yearned for better lands beyond the town boundaries or wanted to consolidate their holdings into a single plot in the interests of more efficient farming. The New England town was, as mentioned, a pressure cooker, and the heavy lid of Puritanism needed escape valves to let off the accumulated steam.

Fortunately there was plenty of land to be had in the north and to the west. Thus, contrary to the Puritan-English ideal of small compact villages in which a succession of generations lived out their lives, individuals and families moved away. Often they went in groups—a dissenting congregation being the frequent example. "Hiving off," it was called. At first, they might only move to an outlying area, but as the land filled up, they headed to more distant frontiers, into northern Massachusetts and New York. The Pilgrim leader William Bradford noted this tendency among his flock early on: "No man thought he could live, except he had cattle and a great deal of ground to keep them; all striving to increase their stock. . . . Some were still for staying togeather in this place, alledging men might here live, if they would be contente with their condition, and that it was not for wante or necessitie so much that they removed, as for the enriching of them selves."

☆ ☆ ☆ Convergence in the West

Following the American Revolution and the opening of the Old Northwest Territory, the two streams that had risen on the North American littoral began flowing westward. The emigrants from the South characteristically came as individuals or small armed parties, while those from New England traveled in organized groups, either as congregations or as shareholders in a stock company that owned the land on which they would plant their town.

At the end of the journey west the two strains converged: the individualistic southerners, superb woodsmen who tended to be outlivers and to move on when they saw smoke from a neighbor's fire; and the communal, orderly New Englanders. To this mix were added the inhabitants of the Middle Atlantic states, with their secular governing institutions.

One of the first acts of the earliest town planters in the Old Northwest, the revolutionary war veterans who settled Marietta in southern Ohio in 1788, was to promulgate a code of criminal laws—by nailing them to a tree. While the Congregationalist meetinghouse had been the emblematic institution of New England and the plantation the dominant one in Virginia, in the Old Northwest it was the courthouse, which was an architectural amalgam of meetinghouse and Virginia county court.

The Puritan theocracy with its democratic town meeting did not take in the West. There were too many other ambitious sects now, and the Methodist and Baptist circuit-riding preachers were busy among the pioneers. The chief concern of the majority of the people, once the Indians had been defeated in war and separated from their lands at the peace conference, was establishing legal institutions. In the early days a jail, a log blockhouse usually, was the first public structure to be erected. The territorial legislatures would designate a "seat of government" as the counties, the fundamental geographical-governmental units, were surveyed. The bumptious pioneer towns vied fiercely with one another to become county seats, for with that designation came a modest package of patronage, legal business, and a greater likelihood of becoming the trading center of the area. County-seat "wars" between rivals were common, some of them marked by violence, others by chicanery and bluffing and bribes to state legislators.

Of course every town needed some kind of economic base if it was to survive. The mortality rate among new places was high. The earliest function of the pioneer towns was to serve as a trading center for the settlers in the immediate area; many of them grew up around a gristmill, to which farmers brought their grain to be ground into flour. They would keep a portion for use on their own tables while bartering the surplus for supplies.

Towns also sprouted at crossroads taverns, along wilderness trails, at ferry landings, on the site of forts built during the Indian wars. A few sprang up near deposits of coal and iron ore and carried on a rudimentary form of manufacturing. The villages at all those sites attracted a variety of specialized artisans and traders to service the rural population. If settlement proceeded at a slow pace, or crops were bad, the early town merchants would scatter to more promising places, leaving the abandoned town behind them. From the beginning the relationship between town and countryside was symbiotic, with the farmers producing for a local market and trading and bartering with merchants, who extended them credit. At first merchants were part-time farmers themselves, but as the economic interests of town and country began to diverge, they became specialized entrepreneurs.

☆ ☆ ☆ Speculation as the Basis of Settlement

As settlements spread westward into Indiana, Illinois, Michigan, Wisconsin, and Minnesota, speculation in town sites became a thriving local industry. Land was the primary basis of wealth in the West. Ever since Congress opened up the public domain to purchasers of large tracts after the Revolution, the speculator in real estate had been a figure of consequence. As a founder of towns, he first appeared in New England, despite the Puritans' attempt to regulate town founding by law and confine it to church congregations. In such speculative towns, buyers were linked in an economic nexus rather than bound by a religious covenant.

Farther west, this system became the rule and the Puritan style of town faded into history, although along the Western Reserve the New England heritage was memorialized by the white spires of Congregationalist churches, central village squares or greens, and "blue laws" proscribing certain pleasures. The older system did not accord with the individualistic pragmatic temperament of the new settlers.

As speculators bought up tracts of the best land across the Middle West, their handbills appeared at ferry landings, river fords, taverns, and wherever else the stream of settlers passed. A typical one from 1817 read:

The subscriber is laying out a NEW TOWN, on the waters of Wakatomica Creek, of the town of Clarksville, and will offer about sixty of the lots at Public Auction, on the ground, on the 20th of March next. . . .

The site of the town possesses nearly as many advantages as the most flourishing town of the state of Ohio . . . and will, probably, before long become a county seat.

Like Clark and his Clarksville, many of these early speculators were farmers who had purchased more land than they could farm, hoping to make some money by creating a town. As time went on real estate speculation became a full-time, if precarious, profession. The rutted muddy streets of the raw young city of Chicago were crowded in the 1830s with a raucous throng of these town jobbers, brandishing their plats (maps) of future thriving cities. Passing through Ohio twenty years before, the English philosopher Morris Birbeck had observed the wild speculation in that state: "Gain! Gain! Gain! Gain! Gain! is the beginning, the middle and the end, the *alpha* and *omega* of the founders of American towns."

Some of the gaudier speculations, like Gallipolis, Ohio, and Cairo, Illinois, lured European settlers and investors. Many a bubble of prosperity burst when the town did not "take." Cairo was the horrible example that stood for many.

Located at the confluence of the Ohio and Mississippi rivers, on what was considered a prime site, it never lived up to the exaggerated promises of its promoters. Perhaps the town jobber had chosen a bad site, or lost the battle for the county seat. Whatever the reasons, many towns that were born trailing clouds of promised glory as future metropolises vanished into the mists. "Every day has its town and every town its day," observed a cynical newspaper editor.

Their common origins as real estate speculations left a stamp on middle-western towns. Such origins instilled in them a compulsion to grow, to succeed, to run faster just to stay in the same place. Urban critics of the small town, from Thorstein Veblen, the radical economist, to Sinclair Lewis (in his novels *Main Street* and *Babbitt*) noted this psychology. It promoted a ludicrous rivalry among towns and a "booster" mentality—a provincial chauvinism that required the stalwarts of each place to trumpet "Our Town" as the liveliest little burg in the state of Winnemac. So brayed the hustling businessmen whose economic health depended on steadily rising land values. To quieter folk, however, the town provided a pride in place.

The most stable towns were those founded by the New England groups, who brought a sense of community with them. But the homogeneous New England–style town could not accommodate the heterogeneous tide of immigrants that flowed into the Middle West, both native-born Americans of other faiths and foreigners with clashing cultural values (who sometimes founded their own towns). The speculative town was open to all who had the price of a lot, and it tolerated variety better than the New England towns could.

The speculators' towns were for the most part laid out functionally, in the gridiron or checkerboard pattern that became ubiquitous in the Middle West and that was so well adapted to the sale of individual lots. The heart of town was either a square or simply a junction of Main Street and Main Cross. Here the business district (sometimes called the "business heart") was located, along with a governmental building, perhaps an imposing county courthouse. The juxtaposition of law and commerce symbolized the main functions of the middle-western town.

☆ ☆ ☆ Tensions between Town and Country

Its financial root structure extended out into the countryside, drawing pecuniary nourishment from the surrounding farms. If the farmers were prosperous, the town merchants were too—only a bit more so, for the farmers were a captive market and the merchants charged whatever their customers could pay. Not all merchants were so venal as Thorstein Veblen portrayed them in his classic essay "The Country Town" (1923), but such practices engendered the tensions between town and countryside in the late nineteenth century.

Relations improved somewhat in the 1900s as farmers grew more prosperous. Still, many a small town—inhabited by what the people in the growing cities, most of whom hailed from just such places, would call "rubes" or "jays"—was a glittering Baghdad to farm boys and girls. On Saturdays the farmers came to town to do their trading, and that excursion was to them "the sweet reward of the long week's labor," wrote novelist Glenway Westcott. "It is their opera, drama, their trip to Zanzibar." At the same time, to the young men idling on every street corner on Saturday night, ogling the girls, sneering at the farmers, it was the dullest place on God's footstool. They yearned to sample the superior pleasures of city life. Like the big fish who swallows the little fish, only in turn to be swallowed by a bigger one, the country towns first swallowed the boys and girls from the farms, educated them, and made them more "urbane." The cities then ingested the graduates of the town's high schools, the most restless and ambitious youths, who had no entrée by inheritance into the tight little local business community. Because of this social food chain, America never developed a peasant class like Europe's. The rural American set his sights on the town, and the small-town American set his on the city.

☆ ☆ ☆   Instability of Communities in the West

Eventually there was no longer a frontier out there to beckon the youths of rural America. In 1890 that invisible watermark of "manifest destiny" was officially pronounced closed. According to the director of the Bureau of the Census at that time, "The unsettled area has been so broken into by isolated bodies of settlement that there can hardly be said to be a frontier line."

Yet much of the Far West was only thinly settled. In those vast empty regions people depended on the railroads to connect them with the markets and civilization back east and with one another. The first transcontinental railroads had snaked across the country after the Civil War, linking it from coast to coast. The conquest would have been a hollow one if no people followed.

So the railroads went into the business of town promotion. Towns were formed along the tracks like beads of rain on a telephone wire. When the main lines extruded trunk lines, other towns clung to them, and towns that were bypassed quickly evaporated.

Like the county seat wars of old, which continued in the Far West, towns vied with one another for a railroad line, raising by subscription the money the railroad company demanded to lay the connecting track. Because of the fickleness of the railroads, the sparseness of settlement, and the difficult farming conditions, the mortality rate for the towns was notably high in the West. Even in Iowa, a fertile farming state, 2,205 towns, villages, and hamlets were abandoned between the 1840s and the 1930s, an average of twenty-two a year. America was a country of disposable towns. By the turn of the century some farm towns were courting outside industries, which on their side were attracted to a pool of cheap, nonunion labor (some of it displaced farmers) imbued with the Protestant "work ethic" and a reluctance to strike.

Even more disposable were the mining towns of the Far West, which popped up like mushrooms after a spring rain wherever gold was found and vanished when it was played out. Beginning with the California gold rush of 1849, men—and women too—regularly headed west seeking their fortunes. Prospectors chased rumors of gold up and down the state, across the Rocky Mountains, north to Oregon, and as far south as Arizona. The Forty-Niners started a tradition of distinctive "communities," which, although they consisted mostly of tents, a store or two, and several shacks optimistically denominated saloons, had their own rudimentary form of government and legal system. Eventually the regular courts would recognize miner's law, with its established ways of awarding claims and adjudicating disputes. Many mining camps had their own courts, which prevented quarrels from escalating into violence or, when they did, meted out punishment to the offenders. Although only a step above lynch law, the miners' courts kept order and belied the western image of pervasive lawlessness.

Similarly, the notorious cow towns of the High Plains, with names known to every reader of western romances—Dodge City, Abilene—and their pantheon of tarnished heroes—Wyatt Earp, Bat Masterson, Doc Holliday—were considerably less violent than the dime-novel chronicles portrayed them. To be sure, they were regularly overrun by swarms of cowboys who had spent long months on the trail driving herds of ill-tempered longhorn steers from Texas and who were ready for rest and recuperation. But Dodge City and the others worked out a system of quarantining the hell-raisers. They located all their saloons, bordellos, and gambling dens on one side of the railroad tracks that cut through the town's midsection, while the respectable folk lived in peace on the other. A study of homicides in the five most important Kansas cattle towns (Abilene, Dodge City, Ellsworth, Wichita, and Caldwell) during the years 1870–85 found a total of forty-five murders, an average of only three a year. Dodge had five killings one year, which was considerable for a town of about two thousand but moderate in view of its large and armed population of transients in a mood to raise hell. Most years there were far fewer or none at all.

The cow towns had their churches, libraries, schools, and hospitals. The majority of their citizens lived humdrum lives, undisturbed by the hullabaloo across the tracks. The town merchants, who fattened off the cowboy trade, were loath to expel the "boys" or crack down on them too harshly, so the two elements coexisted in a state of uneasy truce until cattle drives eventually were stopped by the farmers who covered the open range with their farms and fences.

Thus the two streams of settlement, which rose from a common English source and were fed by tributaries of other peoples, flowed behind the moving frontier. The communal stream of the Puritans with its utopian vision of founding "a city upon a hill" seemed to have run dry in the Ohio Territory, but it merely went underground, to emerge from time to time in varying guises: the religious communities of the Rappites, the Mormons, the Shakers, and other sects.

☆ ☆ ☆ Mobility and the "American Dream"

Complementing and clashing with the communal tradition was the frontier psychology of mobility and disposability. There was a strong impulse to seek the better place just over the next hill. Morris Birbeck, among others, noted this trait. "The American," he wrote in 1818, "has always something better in his eye, further west; he therefore lives and dies on hope, a mere gypsy in this particular." Americans kept moving until there was no frontier left, and then they made the city the frontier. The 1920 census was a watershed: it reported that more than half of the people lived in towns or cities. Thereafter the urban side of the scale grew heavier.

In our own day, another redistribution is taking place. According to the 1980 census, for the first time since the founding of the Republic the rural areas registered greater population gains than the cities. In part at least this trend was grounded in the traditionalist side of the national character, which yearns for roots, community, stability. The new pioneers said they were not seeking economic betterment but rather intangible values that could be lumped together under the rubric "quality of life." Some of them were half-searching for the utopian community that Americans have always sought, while others, like the outlivers of old, wanted to live free with a buffer of land between them and their neighbors. Many inhabited the scattered clusters and developments, the so-called "low-density towns" and "liner suburbs," that have become ubiquitous in the countryside. The traditional social distance between town and country has closed. We are a nation that is neither rural nor urban, but "rurban."

By the mid-1980s the "rural renaissance" had slowed. The smallest farm towns of the Middle West and the Plains states are dying off at a faster rate than ever as bankrupt farmers leave the land. Footloose corporations come and go, first exacting their tribute in the form of tax concessions and infrastructure improvement, until the lure of even cheaper labor pulls them to Mexico or Taiwan and they leave behind a weakened town. The small town of the 1990s finds that it must compete in the global economy or go under. Slumping oil prices have ravaged the rural Southwest. Merchants competing with Wal-Marts and K-Marts in shopping centers try to fight back by restoring their central business districts. Some assume astonishing guises with restored downtown streets lined with boutiques and tourist restaurants. Most small towns, however, are as slow to change as they ever were, their downtown areas quietly peeling and flaking as the commercial action moves to the "stripvilles" on their peripheries, where the automobile dealers, the motels, the fast-food restaurants, and the pornographic movie theaters are located.

☆ ☆ ☆ Nostalgia for What Never Was

Is there any other country where the concept of "hometown" has such emotional resonance—where so many people anchor their beings in some small town they or their parents fled long ago? Even if the small town has been absorbed by a mass society, as some sociologists hold—the national government usurping local functions, big corporations taking over local businesses, freeways and jet planes and radio and television binding people together in a mass consciousness—we Americans still cling to the small-town myth, and the same mass media glorify it. Grown men and women secretly harbor a nostalgia for their home place, even though they once thought it suffocating and conformist and lacking in opportunity. "Everyone knows everything about you there" is a stock description of the small town, but the other side of the coin of small-town nosiness and gossip is neighborly concern and an escape from the awful loneliness of the human condition. So we come full circle to the primal American town, the Pilgrims' Plymouth. There, too, men and women were moved to depart and seek "the enriching of themselves," leaving a few thoughtful people behind to lament, as did the Pilgrim leader, William Bradford: "And thus was this poore church left, like an anciente mother, grown old, and forsaken of her children (though not in their affections). . . . Her anciente members being most of them worne away by death; and these of later time being like children translated into other families, and she like a widow left only to trust in God. Thus she that had made many rich became herself poore."

FURTHER READING

Direct treatments of the role of the small town in American history and culture are few and far between. Two excellent studies are Page Smith, *As a City upon a Hill: The Town in American History* (New York, 1966), which argues for the importance of the New England "covenanted town" in American life, and Lewis Atherton, *Main Street on the Middle Border* (Chicago, 1966), a social history of daily life in the Middle West from, roughly, the 1880s through the 1980s. In his interdisciplinary *From Main Street to State Street* (Port Washington, N.Y., 1977), Park Dixon Goist draws together portrayals of the American town, city, and community. The first volume of Max Lerner's *America as Civilization* (New York, 1957) has a good chapter on the small town. Carole Rifkind, *Main Street: The Face of Urban America* (New York, 1977), approaches the American town from the point of view of its core street. See also Richard Lingeman, *Small Town America: A Narrative History, 1620–the Present* (New York, 1980).

Historical treatments of town development in the South are rare, but Blaine A. Brownell and David R. Goldfield, eds., *The City in Southern History* (Port Washington, N.Y., 1975), is a good introduction. New England's colonial towns, by contrast, have attracted thorough scrutiny. Among the most valuable are Richard C. Bushman, *From Puritan to Yankee: Character and the Social Order in Connecticut, 1690–1765* (New York, 1967); John Demos, *A Little Commonwealth: Family Life in Plymouth Colony* (New York, 1970); Philip J. Greven, *Four Generations: Population, Land, and Family in Colonial Andover, Massachusetts* (New York, 1970); Michael Zuckerman, *Peaceable Kingdoms: New England Towns in the Eighteenth Century* (New York, 1970); and Kenneth A. Lockridge, *A New England Town the First Hundred Years: Dedham, Massachusetts, 1636–1736* (New York, 1985). Far-western towns are cogently studied in *The Cattle Towns* by Robert R. Dykstra (New York, 1976). A classic but dated work on gold-rush towns is Charles Howard Shinn's *Mining Camps* (New York, 1884). Michael Lesy, *Wisconsin Death Trip* (New York, 1973), challenges the popular nostalgia for agrarian America by documenting actualities of rural and small-town Wisconsin life at the end of the nineteenth century.

Sociologists have made the American small town a laboratory. The classic studies include Robert S. Lynd and Helen M. Lynd, *Middletown: A Study in*

Contemporary American Culture (New York, 1929), and *Middletown in Transition: A Study in Cultural Conflicts* (New York, 1937); Theodore Caplow et al., *Middletown Families* (Minneapolis, 1982); William Lloyd Warner, ed., *Yankee City* (New Haven, Conn., 1963); and John Dollard, *Caste and Class in a Southern Town* (Garden City, N.Y., 1957). Also informative are Albert Blumenthal, *Small-Town Stuff* (Chicago, 1932); Angie Debo, *Prairie City* (New York, 1944); James West, *Plainville, U.S.A.* (New York, 1945); and Herman R. Lantz, *People of Coal Town* (New York, 1958). Of the more recent studies, Arthur I. Vidich and Joseph Bensman, *Small Town in Mass Society* (Princeton, N.J., 1968), and Hervé Varenne, *Americans Together: Structured Diversity in a Midwestern Town* (New York, 1977) are excellent. Also worthy of note are Richard Critchfield, *Villages* (New York, 1981); Tony Parker, *Bird, Kansas* (New York, 1989); Osha G. Davidson, *Broken Heartland: The Rise of America's Rural Ghetto* (New York, 1990); and Ron Powers, *Far from Home: Life and Loss in Two American Towns* (New York, 1991).

In *The Little Community* (Chicago, 1956), social anthropologist Robert Redfield presents conceptual schemes for studying the community. Anthony Channell Hilfer's *The Revolt from the Village, 1915–1930* (Chapel Hill, N.C., 1969) offers a thorough discussion of the American small town in literature.

5 ☆ Urban America

☆ Carl Abbott

Cities have been the pioneers of American growth. From the beginnings of European exploration and conquest, towns and cities were the staging points for the settlement of successive resource frontiers. Boston and Santa Fe in the seventeenth century, Philadelphia and San Antonio in the eighteenth century, Cincinnati and Denver in the nineteenth century, Anchorage and Miami in the twentieth century: all played similar roles in organizing and supporting the production of raw materials for national and world markets. It has been city-based bankers, merchants, and journalists who have linked individual resource hinterlands into a single national economy.

The reality of the "urban frontier" clashes with the deeply ingrained myth of American pioneers as rugged individualists. In his famous 1893 essay "The Significance of the Frontier in American History," Frederick Jackson Turner asked his readers to take an imaginative stance over the Cumberland Gap between Virginia and Kentucky to watch the "procession of civilization . . . the Indian, the fur-trader and hunter, the cattle raiser, the pioneer farmer." City-makers by implication trailed so far to the rear as to be lost from sight. From James Fenimore Cooper's novels and Theodore Roosevelt's *Winning of the West* to Paul Bunyan stories and John Wayne movies, there is little place for the bustling levees of New Orleans, the surging crowds of Broadway, or the smoky cacophony of Pittsburgh steel mills.

A comparison of U.S. urbanization to the rest of the world contradicts a second part of the national image. Americans have always prided themselves on their youth as a nation, born free of the shackles of the feudal past. They have happily quoted Goethe's lines about America's superiority to the old, tired Europe. They have agreed with J. Hector St. John de Crèvecoeur that "here everything is modern. . . . [The] imagination, instead of submitting to the painful and useless retrospect of revolution, desolations, and plagues, would, on the contrary, wisely spring forward to the anticipated fields of future cultivation and improvement, to the future extent of those generations which are to replenish and embellish their boundless continent."

In sober fact the United States was also a pioneer among urbanizing nations. Along with Britain, France, Belgium, and the Netherlands, it was among the very first to feel the effects of the urban-industrial revolution. The history of American cities is substantially a story of frantic invention of new institutions and technologies to cope with massive nineteenth-century urbanization. We were able to learn on occasion from the London Metropolitan Police, French engineers, or German housing programs. Far more often, the American experience has been copied in Latin America, Asia, Africa, and even in Europe.

☆ ☆ ☆ Stages of Urban Growth

The making of an urban America has followed the same demographic pattern found in every urbanizing society for the last two centuries. The term *urbanization* refers to an increase in the proportion of national or regional population living in cities. For the first six thousand years of urban life no society was able to maintain an urban ratio greater than 5–10 percent. Starting in late eighteenth-century England, however, one nation after another has experienced an accelerating shift from rural to urban population. After several generations of rapid urbanization, the process tends to level off toward a new equilibrium in which about three-quarters of the population live in cities and many of the rest pursue city-related activities in smaller towns. The result when the urban proportion of a population is graphed against time is an "s-shaped" curve that turns up sharply and then tapers off.

Urban growth in the United States has clearly followed these three stages of gradual growth, explosive takeoff, and maturity. The era of colonial or premodern cities stretched from the seventeenth century to the 1810s. Then the rise of the industrial city dominated a century of rapid urbanization from 1820 to 1920. The third era of the "modern" city runs from 1920 to the present.

The first century of British and Dutch colonization along the Atlantic seaboard depended directly on the founding of new cities, from New Amsterdam (1625) and Boston (1630) to Providence (1636), Charleston (1672), Norfolk (1682), Philadelphia (1682), and Savannah (1733). These colonial towns resembled the provincial market centers in the British Isles. Compact in size and small in population, they linked the farms, fisheries, and forests of New England, the Middle Colonies, and the South to markets in Europe and the Caribbean. With populations that ranged from fifteen to thirty thousand at the time of the American Revolution, the four largest cities dominated the commerce of regional hinterlands. Portsmouth, Salem, Springfield, and Providence looked to Boston; Albany traded via New York; Philadelphia took its profits from the rich farms of the Delaware and Susquehanna valleys; Charleston centralized the trade of Savannah, Wilmington, and New Bern.

All of these colonial capitals looked to the sea. William Penn's Philadelphia was designed to march inland from the Delaware River, but the economic life of the port drew settlement north and south along the river. Charleston faced the Cooper River and the Atlantic beyond its barrier islands. New York similarly faced its harbor on the East River. Taverns and warehouses lined the wharves. Merchants crowded the coffeehouses to share the latest shipping news and arrange for their next cargoes. The upper crust built near the governor's residence on lower Broadway to enjoy the fresh air off the Hudson River and a relaxing view of the green New Jersey shore.

Taken together, the twenty-four recognized cities with 2,500 people or more at the first census of 1790 accounted for only 5 percent of the national population. A generation later, after the disruptions of the War of 1812, with its British attacks on Washington, Baltimore, and New Orleans, and the panic of 1819, the 1820 census still counted only 700,000 urban Americans—a scant 7 percent of the national total. A century later, the 1920 census found a nation that was 51 percent urban, giving 1920 as much symbolic meaning for American history as the supposed closing of the frontier in 1890.

Nineteenth-century urbanization meant more cities and bigger cities. From 1820 to 1920 New York expanded from 124,000 people on the lower end of Manhattan Island to 7,910,000 spread across fourteen counties. Philadelphia grew from 64,000 to 2,407,000. Over the same period the number of cities from the Mississippi River to the Pacific Ocean increased from a handful of settlements—St. Louis, St. Genevieve, San Antonio—to 864 cities, topped by San Francisco and Los Angeles.

New city people came from farms and small towns on both sides of the Atlantic. Whether it involved a transatlantic voyage from Liverpool or Hamburg or a fifty-mile train ride into Indianapolis, migration from farm to city was the other great population movement in nineteenth-century America. It simultaneously balanced and was part of the westward movement across the continent. The physical construction of cities—houses, bridges, sewers, streets, offices, factories—was a complementary process of capital formation that, likewise, balanced the development of farms and their supporting railroads.

American cities by the end of the nineteenth century fell into two categories. The nation's industrial core stretched from Boston and Baltimore westward to St. Louis and St. Paul, accounting for the overwhelming majority of manufacturing production and wealth. Many of these cities were specialized as huge factories—textile towns, steel towns, shoemaking towns, pottery towns. Their industrial labor force drew from the millions of European immigrants and their children who made up more than two-thirds of the population of cities like Detroit, Chicago, Milwaukee, Pittsburgh, and New York. Cities in the South, the Great Plains, and the Far West were the suppliers and cus-tomers. They funneled raw materials to the industrial belt—cotton from Mobile, lumber from Norfolk, metals from Denver, cattle from Kansas City. In return they distributed the manufactured goods of the Northeast.

Chicago was the great exemplar of the growing industrial city. It did everything big and everything fast. Between 1880 and 1920 historians have estimated that 605,000 foreign immigrants and 790,000 native-born Ameri-cans moved into the city. Chicagoans lifted their entire city ten feet to improve its drainage. They built the world's first skyscrapers and some of its first grain elevators. They remade American taste with the World's Columbian Exposi-tion of 1893. They competed with Odessa as a grain port, with Pittsburgh as a steel city, with Cincinnati as a meat packer, with London and Paris as a national railroad center.

Looking back over thirty-five years of growth, a local journalist in 1868 proclaimed that Chicago was "pre-eminently the wonder of the nineteenth century. . . . The history of centuries is crowded into half an ordinary lifetime, and her forward march is still so rapid that it is scarcely permitted to us to ponder on the achievements of to-day, ere they are swept out of the memory by the still grander conquests of tomorrow." Outsiders tended to agree. Bostonian Charles Francis Adams agreed that "the young city of the West has instinctively . . . flung herself, heart, soul, and body, into the movement of her time. She has realized the great fact that steam has revolutionized the world, and she has bound her whole existence up in the great power of modern times."

The most recent period of urban growth has revolved around the adapta-tion of American cities to "twentieth-century" technologies of personalized transportation and rapid communication. The 1910s and 1920s brought modern art, modern music, and modern architecture to Berlin, Paris, and New York. The same decade also brought full electric wiring and self-starting automobiles to the middle-class home. George F. Babbitt, the hero of Sinclair Lewis's 1922 best-seller, lived in a thoroughly modern Dutch Colonial house in the bright new subdivision of Floral Heights in the up-to-date city of Zenith. He awakened each morning to "the best of nationally advertised and quantitatively produced alarm clocks, with all modern attachments." His bathroom was glazed tile and silvered metal. His business was real estate, and his god was "Modern Appliances."

The metropolis that Babbitt and millions of real automobile owners began to shape in the 1920s broke the physical bounds of the nineteenth-century industrial city. In 1910 the Census Bureau devised the classification "metro-politan district" to collect information about the suburban communities that had begun to ring the central city. By the 1980s the federal government recognized more than three hundred metropolitan areas with a total population of 170,000,000. The metro areas of middle-sized cities like Atlanta, St. Louis, Minneapolis–St. Paul, and Houston all stretch for more than one hundred miles from one suburban margin to the other.

The cities of post–World War II America have had the greatest ethnic variety in national history. They have been destinations for a massive "northward movement." Rural southerners of both races moved north (and west) to cities and jobs. Starting with the Great Migration of 1917–18, the African American experience became an urban experience, creating centers of black culture like Harlem in the 1920s and feeling the bitter effects of ghettoization by the 1930s and 1940s. During the Great Depression and World War II Appalachian whites joined black workers in middle-western cities like Cincinnati and Detroit. Okies and Arkies left their depressed cotton farms in Oklahoma and Arkansas for new lives in Bakersfield and Los Angeles, incidentally making southern California a new center for country music.

The northward movement has also crossed oceans and borders. Puerto Rican immigrants after World War II remade the social fabric of New York and adjacent cities. Half a million Cubans had an even more obvious impact on Miami after the Cuban Revolution of 1959. The Puerto Ricans and Cubans have been followed to eastern cities by Haitians, Jamaicans, Colombians, Hondurans, and others from the countries surrounding the Caribbean. Mexicans constitute the largest immigrant group in the cities of Texas, Arizona, Colorado, and California. Temporary workers, shoppers, visitors, legal migrants, and illegal migrants fill neighborhood after neighborhood in El Paso, San Antonio, San Diego, and Los Angeles, creating bilingual labor markets and downtowns.

By the 1970s and 1980s Asia matched Latin America as the source of 40 percent of documented immigrants. Asians have concentrated in the cities along the Pacific coast and in New York. Los Angeles counts new ethnic neighborhoods for Vietnamese, Chinese, Japanese, Koreans, and Samoans. Honolulu looks for business and tourism to Asia as well as to the continental United States. A new generation of migrants has revitalized fading Chinatowns in New York, Chicago, Seattle, and Los Angeles.

The rise of Latin American and Asian immigration is part of a rebalancing of the American urban system. What journalists in the 1970s identified as the rise of the Sunbelt is part of a long-term shift of urban growth from the industrial Northeast toward the regional centers of the South and West—from Detroit, Buffalo, and Chicago to Los Angeles, Dallas, and Atlanta. The causes include the concentration of defense spending and the aerospace industry since the

1940s, the growth of a leisure economy, the expansion of domestic energy production, and the capture of "sunrise" industries. The result has been booming cities along the South Atlantic coast from Washington to Miami, through the greater Southwest from Houston to Denver, and along the Pacific coast from San Diego to Seattle.

☆ ☆ ☆ Cities and American Values

These basic facts about the integral relationship between urban growth and American continental expansion have clashed repeatedly with the American mythology of national uniqueness and pioneering individualism. Urbanization in the United States lagged behind Great Britain and a handful of nations in Northwest Europe, but it led the rest of the world. One result has been an ambivalent response in which Americans have praised cities with one voice and shunned them with another. Recent public-opinion polls show that most Americans would prefer to live in a small town. A few extra questions reveal, however, that they are just as certain that they want easy access to the medical specialists, cultural facilities, and business opportunities that are found only in cities. Over the years the American debate about the value of cities previewed many of the current arguments about the net impact of urbanization and modernization in the developing world.

Thomas Jefferson set the tone for American antiurbanism with the strident warning that cities were dangerous to democracy. At the time of Philadelphia's deadly yellow fever epidemic of 1800, Jefferson wrote to a friend that "when great evils happen, I am in the habit of looking out for what good may arise from them as consolations. . . . The yellow fever will discourage the growth of great cities in our nation, and I view great cities as pestilential to the morals, the health, and the liberties of man." In part Jefferson feared that American cities would inevitably grow into facsimiles of the London of the 1770s or the Paris of the 1780s as sinks of poverty, scenes of unemployment, and breeders of riotous mobs. He also feared that because city dwellers were dependent on others for their livelihoods, their votes were at the disposal of the rich. Only in a nation of independent farmers could government remain virtuous. If Americans became "piled upon one another in large cities, as in Europe," he believed, they would become "corrupt as in Europe."

If Jefferson feared first for the health of the Republic, many of the antiurban writers who followed feared instead for the morals of the individual. A genre of sensationalist exposés developed the typical comment in Chicago's *Prairie Farmer* that "city life crushes, enslaves, and ruins so many thousands of our young men, who are insensibly made the victims of dissipation, of reckless speculation, and of ultimate crime." George Foster drew the stark contrasts between rich and poor in *New York in Slices, by an Experienced Carver* (1849) and *New York by Gaslight* (1850). Books like *Female Depravity, or the House of Death* (1852) and *The Gamblers' League, or the Trials of a Country Maid* (1857), detailing the corruption of innocent country girls in the dangerous metropolis, were little more than pornography wrapped in moralizing covers.

Far more serious were religiously based indictments of city life as corrupting of both rich and poor. In *The Dangerous Classes of New York* (1872), Charles Loring Brace warned of the threat posed by the abject poor, the homeless, and the unemployed. With no stake in society, they were a riot waiting to happen and a responsibility for more comfortable citizens. Jacob Riis used words and photographs to tell the middle class about the poor of New York in *How the Other Half Lives* (1890). A few years later W. T. Stead used the wonderful title *If Christ Came to Chicago* (1894) to indict the big city as unchristian because it destroyed the lives of its inhabitants.

The first generation of urban sociologists wrote in the same vein in the 1920s and 1930s. Teaching at the University of Chicago, Robert Park worked out a theory of urban life that blamed cities for substituting impersonal connections for close personal ties. As summarized by Louis Wirth in "Urbanism as a Way of Life" (1940), the indictment dressed up Thomas Jefferson in the language of social science. Wirth's city is the scene of transitory and superficial relationships, frantic status seeking, impersonal laws, and cultural institutions pandering to the lowest common denominator of a heterogeneous society.

The attack on city living was counterbalanced by sheer excitement about the pace of growth. By the 1830s large numbers of Americans had come to look on cities as tokens of American progress. Booster pamphlets and histories of instant cities drenched their pages in statistics of growth. *Pittsburgh As It Is* (1857) offered statistics on coal mining, railroads, real estate values, population, employment, boat building, and banks and a "progressional ratio" comparing the growth of Pittsburgh to the rest of the nation. Boosters counted churches, schools, newspapers, charities, and fraternal organizations as further evidence of economic and social progress. One Chicago editor wrote before the Civil War that "facts and figures . . . if carefully pondered, become more interesting and astonishing than the wildest vision of the most vagrant imagination." His words echoed seventy years later as George Babbitt sang the praises of "the famous Zenith spirit . . . that has made the little old Zip City celebrated in every land and clime, wherever condensed milk and pasteboard cartons are known."

Urban advocates in the twentieth century have extended the economic argument to point out the value of concentrating a variety of businesses in one location. The key is external economies—the ability of individual firms to buy and sell to each other and to share the services of bankers, insurance specialists, accountants, advertising agencies, mass media, and other specialists. In *Cities and the Wealth of Nations* (1984), Jane Jacobs argued that cities and hinterlands form the natural economic units whose vitality transcends the artificial boundaries of states and nations.

American writers and critics since the time of Ralph Waldo Emerson and Walt Whitman have acknowledged cities as sources of creativity. Henry David Thoreau may have taken to the woods at Walden Pond, but his mentor Emerson argued the merits of cities as centers of intellectual life. "We can ill spare the commanding social benefits of cities," he wrote in his essay "Young America" in 1844. Nathaniel Hawthorne allowed his protagonist in *The Blithedale Romance* (1852) to take time off from the rigors of a country commune for the intellectual refreshment of Boston. George Tucker, professor of moral philosophy and political economy at Jefferson's University of Virginia, analyzed urban trends in 1843: "The growth of cities commonly marks the progress of intelligence and the arts, measures the sum of social enjoyment, and always implies increased mental activity, which is sometimes healthy and useful, sometimes distempered and pernicious. If these congregations of men diminish some of the common life, they augment others. . . . Whatever may be the good or evil tendencies of populous cities, they are the result to which all countries that are at once fertile, free, and intelligent tend." Even the poet and critic John Crowe Ransom, an avowed spokesman for the traditional agrarian South, had to admit to the obvious—that American cities were not only the drive wheels of modernization but also necessities for the life of the mind.

☆ ☆ ☆ Planning Traditions

The nation's ambivalent attitudes toward the city have been reflected in America's contrasting efforts to design cities that will both fulfill social ideals and encourage national growth. Since the Puritan settlement of New England in the seventeenth century, the desire to control the problem of social change can be seen particularly in the tradition of focused or closed communities. A series of planned communities have used urban design and the physical form of the community to promote broader social aims. Its high self-definition gives the focused community a special appeal. However, it also implies a problem. Whether company towns, religious settlements, or secular utopias, most focused communities have been intended to provide a better life for a carefully defined and limited set of like-minded residents.

Massachusetts towns were the first focused communities. Designed to preserve the strength and purity of the Puritan experiment in the New World, they became closed corporations, freely governed by their "members" but unwelcoming to outsiders. The towns themselves often centered on church, meeting hall, and central square. Mormon settlements in Utah repeated the pattern in the mid-nineteenth century. Salt Lake City was built as a refuge for the converted, with the land allocated by the church and a supervised economy. Each new Mormon town was a carefully planned unit under central control. As late as 1940 Salt Lake City had two downtowns: hotels, stores, and offices for Mormons clustered near their temple at the northern end of the central business district; hotels and stores for "gentiles" at the southern end.

Company towns offered a different version of planning for closed community. The best examples, such as Lowell, Massachusetts (1822), and Pullman, Illinois (1881), were planned as benevolence that paid for itself. The intention was to create a livable environment that protected workers from the worst effects of industrialization. At the same time the beneficiaries of these improved communities were carefully selected and controlled to maintain a stable labor force. Lowell ringed textile mills with dormitories for single women. George Pullman made sure that workers in his railcar factory were sober (by excluding alcoholic drink), serious (by providing a library), and under his control (by renting rather than selling his housing). The community worked well during prosperity and fell apart during depression and labor strife in the 1890s.

A third version of the closed community is the upscale suburb where the upper middle class of professionals and business owners have taken refuge from the cities in which they earn their livings. In the middle decades of the nineteenth century landscape planners responded to the chaos of the booming city with pastoral suburbs of gently curving streets, large lots, and abundant greenery. Llewellyn Park, New Jersey (1853), was a refuge for overburdened New Yorkers. Riverside, Illinois (1869), welcomed harried Chicagoans at the end of a ten-mile train ride from Chicago. The automobile in the 1920s brought a new generation of focused suburbs to house affluent Americans. Shaker Heights (1920), on fourteen hundred acres of land east of Cleveland, rigorously separated houses by price level. The developers supplied tastefully curving residential streets, set aside parks, prohibited duplexes, and imposed strict architectural controls. Palos Verdes Estates (1923), draped over a rocky peninsula that juts into the Pacific Ocean south of Los Angeles, came with schools, golf course, swimming club, riding academy, and an art jury to approve the design of each new house. Kansas City's Country Club District provided the first large shopping center planned for the automobile in 1923. Home owners elected neighborhood boards to police aesthetic standards. The same desire for social segregation has remained an important motivation for suburbanization to the present, as writer John Cheever caught so well in his stories about Shady Hill, whose inhabitants wanted things to stay precisely as they were for fear that "there was a stranger at the gates."

The irony of focused communities was that economic success usually brought pressures to open up to a wider range of residents. Boston began in 1630 as a closed Puritan town, for example, but successful seaports are impossible to isolate from the wider world. The Puritan goal of uniformity quickly broke down in a city that drew its livelihood from contact with the rest of the world. In a later period the growth of Lowell's factories brought Irish immigrants to man the machines and disrupt the social consensus. A city planned for selected segments of society evolved into a normal industrial city.

It always has made more sense in the United States to plan for open communities that mirror the freedom of movement inherent in the American Constitution and the laws of the land. The form of the open city has followed its function, for it has been planned in the expectation of continual growth. Intended to accommodate all comers, open cities are built piece by piece as space is needed. A consequence has been the characteristic use of the infinitely expandable street grid, with city building tied inextricably to land speculation and the private market in real estate. It has always involved a "suburban frontier" as new land is planned and developed on the outskirts of the city in rough proportion to growth.

From the start William Penn defined Philadelphia as a free-labor market open to all. He also chose a plan of perpendicular streets that could be extended indefinitely as the city grew. Having proved its adaptability in Philadelphia, the grid had obvious appeal to New Yorkers, who mapped out streets for the entire island of Manhattan in 1811. Their grid of north-south avenues and lateral streets supported explosive growth in the nineteenth century and redevelopment in the twentieth. New cities throughout the Mississippi Valley also imitated Philadelphia's layout, building types, and even street names. Travelers in Cincinnati, Pittsburgh, Lexington, Nashville, St. Louis, and other western cities found miniature Philadelphias planned for growth. "So dazzling was this plain and staid metropolis to the eyes of Western members and merchants," commented James Parton in 1876, "that, in laying out the cities of the West, they could not but copy Philadelphia, even in the minutest particulars."

The open town was the perfect companion for the railroads that stretched their tracks in straight lines across the prairies and plains between 1840 and 1910. The Illinois Central, the Union Pacific, the Northern Pacific, the Chicago, Burlington, and Quincy, the Minneapolis, St. Paul, and Sault St. Marie, and the Great Northern all staked out right-angled towns at regular intervals alongside their tracks to collect farm produce for shipment and to serve the farming frontier. Even on the hilly shores of the Pacific, settlers laid gridiron plans over the map with little regard for the landscape—up, over, through, but seldom around the steep hills. Seattle washed entire hills into Puget Sound because they got in the way of planning for infinite growth. At the same time cities followed the example of New York's Central Park, designed by Frederick Law Olmsted and Calvert Vaux in 1858, and set aside large tracts of undeveloped land for park and parkway systems.

Formal city planning as a twentieth-century profession has largely preserved the intent of the open city. The so-called "city beautiful" planners at the beginning of the century sought to make the congested industrial city work more efficiently by rearranging its public spaces, streets, and transportation systems. Daniel Burnham prepared his famous plans for San Francisco (1905) and Chicago (1909) for each city's progressive business leaders. The plans were intended to make each city work better as an economic machine. The same motivation lay behind the adoption of land-use zoning after 1916 and urban renewal in the 1950s and 1960s.

☆ ☆ ☆ Livable Cities

Americans had to learn not only to plan their cities but also to live comfortably in the fast-growing communities that they erected. They needed to adapt their lives to the urban pace and to develop institutions to bring order out of the seeming chaos. Industrial workers adjusted to the regularities of factory whistles, time clocks, and foremen. In a city like Philadelphia rates of accidental deaths and homicides began to drop after 1870 as city dwellers learned to control reckless behavior and pay attention on the streets. The end of the century also brought a decline of spontaneous mobs and endemic drunkenness at the same time that the saloon developed as a stable social institution in immigrant neighborhoods.

Cities developed community institutions that linked their people in new ways. Apartment buildings offered a new environment for the middle class. Novelist William Dean Howells reflected contemporary concerns by devoting the first hundred pages of *A Hazard of New Fortunes* (1890) to Basil March's

search for an apartment appropriate for a newly appointed New York magazine editor. Gunther Barth has argued that department stores, penny newspapers, vaudeville theaters, and baseball provided common meeting grounds
and interests for heterogeneous populations. A. T. Stewart's, John Wana-
maker's, Marshall Field's, and the other new department stores of the 1860s,
1870s, and 1880s made emerging central business districts acceptable places
for women as consumers and helped to introduce women into the clerical
labor force. Ballparks and theaters were shared spaces where allegiances and
jokes crossed ethnic lines. Ethnic banks, newspapers, and mutual insurance
societies offered training in American ways at the same time that they preserved group identity.

The openness of the American city to continued growth also brought the
need for professionalism in public services. At the start of the nineteenth
century private companies or amateurs provided everything from drinking
water to police protection. In the wooden cities of colonial times, for example,
the ever-present danger of fire had made fire fighting a community responsibility. Householders were expected to keep buckets in their houses and
respond to calls for help. By the 1820s and 1830s more cities had added
groups of citizens who drilled together as volunteer fire companies, answered
alarms, and fought fires as teams. Problems of timely response and the development of expensive steam-powered pumpers, however, required a move
to paid fire companies in the 1850s and 1860s. Firemen who were city
employees could justify expensive training and be held accountable for effective performance. By 1900 most observers agreed that fire protection in the
United States matched that anywhere in Europe.

Effective fire protection required a pressurized water supply. Residents of
colonial cities had taken their water directly from streams and wells or bought
it from entrepreneurs who carted barrels through the streets. Pressurized
water, however, was necessary for public safety and health, not only to fight
fires but also to wash down the filthy streets. Philadelphia installed the first
system in 1801, building a waterworks that can still be seen in Fairmount Park
along the Schuylkill River. Boston reached twenty miles into the countryside
with an aqueduct in the 1840s. New York surpassed this feat with the Croton
Reservoir and an aqueduct that brought fresh water forty miles from Westchester County to a receiving reservoir in what is now Central Park. Changing
theories of disease and the availability of abundant water for municipal cleaning helped to cut New York's death toll in the 1866 cholera epidemic by 90
percent from the toll of the 1849 epidemic.

The public responsibilities of nineteenth-century cities generally fell into the
three categories of public health and safety (police, sewers, parks), economic

development (street drainage and pavement), and public education. Such expanding responsibilities fueled the municipal progressivism of the early twentieth century and also served to check some of the abuses of utility tycoons like Chicago's Charles Yerkes—depicted as Frank Cowperwood in Theodore Dreiser's novels *The Financier* (1912) and *The Titan* (1914). Led by local business interests, cities implemented civil service employment systems that based hiring and promotion on supposedly objective measures. The city manager system placed the daily operations of government under a professional administrator. As the system has spread since the 1910s, city government has become more and more the realm of engineers, planners, budget analysts, and other trained professionals.

Public intervention came later in other areas like low-income housing. Cities long preferred to regulate the private market rather than to intervene directly. New York pioneered efforts to legislate minimum housing standards with tenement house codes in 1866, 1882, and 1901. However, providing the housing remained a private responsibility until the federal government began to finance public housing during the depression of the 1930s. Even massive investments in public housing after federal legislation in 1937 and 1949, however, failed to reconcile public opinion. Unlike the residents of European cities, American urbanites have usually preferred to believe the worst about public housing and to ignore the viable projects.

A full social agenda for local government waited until the 1960s. Assistance to the poor was the realm of private philanthropy in the nineteenth century, often coordinated through private Charity Organization Societies. The crisis of the 1930s legitimized federal assistance for economically distressed individuals, but city government remained oriented to public safety and economic development. By the start of the 1960s, however, criticisms that the urban renewal programs of the 1950s had benefited real estate developers at the expense of citizens added to an increasing sense that America's multiracial cities were in a state of crisis. In 1964 President Lyndon Johnson declared a nationwide "war on poverty." On the front lines was the Office of Economic Opportunity with its Neighborhood Youth Corps for unemployed teenagers, its Head Start and Upward Bound programs to assist public schools, and its Community Action Agencies to mobilize the poor to work for their own community interests. Two years later the Model Cities program sought to demonstrate that problems of education, child care, health care, housing, and employment could be attacked most effectively by coordinated efforts.

The 1970s and 1980s left American cities with comprehensive social commitments but limited resources. President Richard Nixon simply announced that the urban crisis was over and dismantled programs like Model Cities before they had a chance to prove themselves. Ronald Reagan continued the policy of redirecting federal resources to meet the development needs of politically powerful suburbs. Cities and city people absorbed roughly two-thirds of the budget cuts in the first Reagan budget. To exaggerate only slightly, cities have been left with the expectations of the 1960s and the resources of the 1920s. Or as Mayor Jerome Cavanagh of Detroit complained in 1970, "Some academics now find it stylish to deny that there is an urban crisis at all, let alone one that money can solve. But once—just once—I'd like to try money."

☆ ☆ ☆ Cities and American Society

"I am an American, Chicago born—Chicago, that somber city— and go as I have taught myself, free-style, and will make the record in my own way: first to knock, first admitted; sometimes an innocent knock, sometimes a not so innocent." These opening lines from *The Adventures of Augie March* (1953) capture one of the essential features of the American city. The hero of Saul Bellow's novel about growing up during the 1920s and 1930s knew that cities are the place where things happen. They are centers of opportunity that bring people together to exchange goods, services, ideas, and human company.

At their best American cities are among the most livable environments in the world. We have solved or know how to solve many of their physical problems of traffic, pollution, and deteriorated housing. Failures have come from lack of commitment and political will, not from the inherent nature of cities. The real dilemma in urban areas, of course, is the tendency to use the old centers of metropolitan areas as dumping grounds for social problems. People with limited abilities to help themselves are shunted into cities and then blamed for their ills. The poor are often expected to tax themselves for public services that they can't afford as private citizens. Today, as in the nineteenth century, the centers of our cities display the polarization of society between the very rich and the very poor. As Tom Wolfe's best-selling novel *The Bonfire of the Vanities* (1987) depicts, contemporary New York is a city whose glitzy Manhattan and devastated South Bronx meet only by accident and with no mutual understanding.

The solution is not to abandon public concern but rather to develop cities as centers of opportunity. At the start of the century political reformer Frederic Howe asserted that the city was the "hope of democracy" because it had the ability to assure a fair start to everyone through public education, public health, and social services. Augie March saw his city as a set of possibilities that could "make a nobility of us all."

What cities will continue to do best is to protect diversity. The key to urban vitality is variety in economic activities, people, and neighborhoods. Geographer Brian Berry has argued persuasively that American cities have become mosaics. Their residential neighborhoods range across working-class communities, ghettos, ethnic centers, affluent apartment complexes, family-oriented suburbs, and bohemias for artists and intellectuals. The analysis implies that the multicentered metropolitan area built around automobiles and freeways is a logical expression of American urbanism. In the words of historian Sam B. Warner, Jr., it offers "the potential of a range of personal choices and social freedoms for city dwellers if we would only extend the paths of freedom that our urban system has been creating."

The political expression of the urban mosaic is metropolitan pluralism. Diverse groups defined by ethnicity, social class, or residential location have developed the capacity to pursue their goals through neighborhood organizations, suburban governments, and interest groups. Pluralistic politics has given groups and communities that were previously ignored entrée to public and private decisions about metropolitan growth and services, particularly Hispanics and African Americans. However, cities still need strong area-wide institutions that can facilitate the equitable sharing of problems and resources as well as opportunities. Neighborhood politics and suburban self-sufficiency both require the counterweight of a metropolitan vision that recognizes the value of distinctive communities within a metropolitan framework. Most promising are regional agencies like the Twin Cities Metropolitan Council that have assumed responsibility for planning and delivering specific regional services such as parks and public transportation.

More than fifty years ago a number of the nation's leading specialists on urban growth summed up the promise of urban America in a report to President Franklin Roosevelt. Their comments in *Our Cities: Their Role in the National Economy* (1937) remain valid today:

> The city has seemed at times the despair of America, but at others to be the Nation's hope, the battleground of democracy. Surely in the long run, the Nation's destiny will be profoundly affected by the cities which have two-thirds of its population and its wealth. . . . There is fertility and creation in the rich soil of the broad countryside, but there is also fertility and creativeness in forms of industry, art, personality, emerging even from the city streets and reaching toward the sky. The faults of our cities are not those of decadence and impending decline, but of exuberant

vitality crowding its way forward under tremendous pressure—the flood rather than the drought.

The result is clear. Cities above all else are institutions for storing and communicating messages. Despite urgent economic and social problems, their ability to democratize information and advance the development of ideas will preserve the central role of cities in American life for the coming century.

FURTHER READING

Recent summaries of American urban growth include David Goldfield and Blaine Brownell, *Urban America: A History* (Boston, 1990), and Eric Monkkonen, *America Becomes Urban: The Development of U.S. Cities and Towns, 1780–1980* (Berkeley, Calif., 1988). Monkkonen's periodization can be compared with that in Sam B. Warner, Jr., *The Urban Wilderness: A History of the American City* (New York, 1972). Urbanization as a demographic process is detailed in Adna F. Weber's pioneering *The Growth of Cities in the Nineteenth Century* (1899; reprint, Ithaca, N.Y., 1963), and in Eric Lampard, "Urbanization," in *Encyclopedia of American Economic History*, ed. Glen Porter (New York, 1980).

American attitudes about cities can be judged directly from the sources in Charles N. Glaab, ed., *The American City: A Documentary History* (Homewood, Ill., 1963). Morton White and Lucia White, *The Intellectual Versus the City: From Thomas Jefferson to Frank Lloyd Wright* (Cambridge, Mass., 1962), provides the standard summary of antiurban thought, while Thomas Bender, *New York Intellect* (New York, 1987), offers a contrasting view of cities as centers of intellectual enterprise. For comparative attitudes, see Andrew Lees, *Cities Perceived: Urban Society in European and American Thought, 1820–1940* (New York, 1985), and David Hamer, *New Towns in the New World: Images and Perceptions of the Nineteenth-Century Urban Frontier* (New York, 1990), which compares New Zealand, Australia, Canada, and the United States.

Charles N. Glaab, "The Historian and the American City," in *The Study of Urbanization*, ed. Philip M. Hauser and Leo F. Schnore (New York, 1965), summarizes the first "generation" of studies in urban history. The essays in Howard Gillette, Jr., and Zane L. Miller, eds., *American Urbanism: A Historiographical Review* (Westport, Conn., 1987), bring the trends in urban historiography up to date.

For cities in the colonial period, the detailed starting points are Carl Bridenbaugh, *Cities in the Wilderness: The First Century of Urban Life in America* (New York, 1938), and *Cities in Revolt: Urban Life in America, 1743–1776* (New York, 1955). Also see Darrett B. Rutman, *Winthrop's Boston: Portrait of a Puritan Town,*

1630–1649 (Chapel Hill, N.C., 1965), and Gary Nash, *The Urban Crucible: Social Change, Political Consciousness, and the Origins of the American Revolution* (Cambridge, Mass., 1979).

Comparative studies of urban growth during the nineteenth century include Robert Albion's classic *The Rise of New York Port* (New York, 1939); David T. Gilchrist, ed., *The Growth of the Seaport Cities, 1790–1825* (Charlottesville, Va., 1967); Richard C. Wade, *The Urban Frontier: The Rise of Western Cities, 1790–1830* (Cambridge, Mass., 1959); William H. Pease and Jane H. Pease, *The Web of Progress: Private Values and Public Styles in Boston and Charleston, 1828–1843* (New York, 1985); David Goldfield, *Urban Growth in the Age of Sectionalism: Virginia, 1847–1861* (Baton Rouge, La., 1977); and David Ward, *Cities and Immigrants* (New York, 1971).

For comparative studies in the twentieth century, see Harvey Perloff et al., *Regions, Resources, and Economic Growth* (Baltimore, 1960); Blaine Brownell, *The Urban Ethos in the South, 1920–1930* (Baton Rouge, La., 1975); Carl Abbott, *The New Urban America: Growth and Politics in Sunbelt Cities* (Chapel Hill, N.C., 1987); and Roger Lotchin, "City and Sword in Metropolitan California, 1919–1941," *Urbanism Past and Present* 7 (1982).

John Reps focuses on the physical planning choices of the nineteenth century in *The Making of Urban America* (Princeton, N.J., 1965) and *Cities of the American West: A History of Frontier Urban Planning* (Princeton, N.J., 1979). Stanley Buder, *Pullman: An Experiment in Industrial Order and Community Planning, 1880–1930* (New York, 1967), details the rise and fall of a focused community. William H. Wilson, *The City Beautiful Movement* (Baltimore, 1989), puts early twentieth-century planning into social and political context. Case studies that emphasize political context include Judd Kahn, *Imperial San Francisco: Politics and Planning in an American City, 1897–1906* (Lincoln, Nebr., 1979); Carl Abbott, *Portland: Planning, Politics, and Growth in a Twentieth-Century City* (Lincoln, Nebr., 1983); and Christopher Silver, *Twentieth-Century Richmond: Planning, Politics, and Race* (Knoxville, Tenn., 1984). Harold H. Mayer and Richard C. Wade present the most complete visual chronicle of urban growth in *Chicago: Growth of a Metropolis* (Chicago, 1969).

Suburbanization has become a special subfield. The definitive and insightful summary is Kenneth T. Jackson, *Crabgrass Frontier: The Suburbanization of the United States* (New York, 1985). Also see Sam B. Warner, Jr., *Streetcar Suburbs: The Process of Growth in Boston, 1870–1900* (Cambridge, Mass., 1962); Michael H. Ebner, *Creating Chicago's North Shore: A Suburban History* (Chicago, 1988); and Peter O. Muller, *Contemporary Suburban America* (Englewood Cliffs, N.J., 1981).

Numerous studies examine the ways in which nineteenth-century Americans adjusted their work and private lives to urban environments. Representative are Don H. Doyle, *The Social Order of a Frontier Community: Jacksonville, Illinois,*

1825–70 (Urbana, Ill., 1978); Richard C. Wade, *Slavery in the Cities: The South, 1820–1860* (New York, 1964); Elizabeth Blackmar, *Manhattan for Rent, 1785– 1850* (Ithaca, N.Y., 1989); Roger Lane, *Violent Deaths in the City: Suicide, Accident, and Murder in Nineteenth-Century Philadelphia* (Cambridge, Mass., 1979); Kathleen Conzen, *Immigrant Milwaukee, 1836–1860* (Cambridge, Mass., 1976); Thomas J. Noel, *The City and the Saloon: Denver, 1858–1916* (Lincoln, Nebr., 1982); Gunther Barth, *City People: The Rise of Modern City Culture in Nineteenth-Century America* (New York, 1980); Christine Stansell, *City of Women: Sex and Class in New York, 1789–1860* (New York, 1986); Stephan Thernstrom, *The Other Bostonians: Poverty and Progress in the American Metropolis, 1880–1970* (Cambridge, Mass., 1973); and Theodore Hershberg, ed., *Philadelphia: Work, Space, Family, and Group Experience in the Nineteenth Century* (New York, 1981).

For similar topics in the twentieth century, historians can make good use of such classical sociological studies as Paul Kellogg, ed., *Pittsburgh Survey*, 6 vols. (New York, 1909–14); Robert E. Park, Ernest W. Burgess, and Roderick D. McKenzie, *The City* (Chicago, 1925); Robert S. Lynd and Helen M. Lynd, *Middletown: A Study in Contemporary American Culture* (New York, 1929); St. Clair Drake and Horace R. Cayton, *Black Metropolis* (New York, 1945); Brian J. L. Berry, *The Human Consequences of Urbanization* (New York, 1973); and Herbert Gans, *The Urban Villagers: Group and Class in the Life of Italian-Americans*, rev. ed. (New York, 1982), and *The Levittowners* (New York, 1967). Also important is the literature on racial relations, such as Howard Rabinowitz, *Race Relations in the Urban South, 1865–1890* (New York, 1978); Kenneth Kusmer, *A Ghetto Takes Shape: Black Cleveland, 1870–1930* (Urbana, Ill., 1976); Thomas Philpott, *The Slum and the Ghetto: Neighborhood Deterioration and Middle-Class Reform, Chicago, 1880–1930* (New York, 1978); and James Grossman, *Land of Hope: Chicago, Black Southerners, and the Great Migration* (Chicago, 1989).

Government and public services in nineteenth-century cities are treated in Amy Bridges, *A City in the Republic: Antebellum New York and the Origins of Machine Politics* (New York, 1984); Charles Rosenberg, *The Cholera Years: The United States in 1832, 1849, and 1866* (Chicago, 1962); David Hammack, *Power and Society: Greater New York at the Turn of the Century* (New York, 1982); Jon Teaford, *The Unheralded Triumph: City Government in America, 1870–1900* (Baltimore, 1984); Zane L. Miller, *Boss Cox's Cincinnati: Urban Politics in the Progressive Era* (New York, 1968); and Carl V. Harris, *Political Power in Birmingham, 1871–1921* (Knoxville, Tenn., 1977). For the twentieth century, representative studies include Mark S. Foster, *From Streetcar to Superhighway: American City Planners and Urban Transportation, 1900–1940* (Philadelphia, 1981); Arnold R. Hirsch, *Making the Second Ghetto: Race and Housing in Chicago, 1940–1960* (New York, 1983); and Mark Gelfand, *A Nation of Cities: The Federal Government and Urban America, 1933–1965* (New York, 1975).

Finally, students of the American city will want to go directly to the contrasting ideas expressed by several key commentators and critics: Urbanism Committee of the National Resources Committee, *Our Cities: Their Role in the National Economy* (Washington, D.C., 1937); Frank Lloyd Wright, *The Living City* (New York, 1958); Lewis Mumford, whose work can be represented by *The Culture of Cities* (New York, 1938) and *The Highway and the City* (New York, 1963); Percival Goodman and Paul Goodman, *Communitas: Means of Livelihood and Ways of Life* (New York, 1947); Edward C. Banfield, *The Unheavenly City: The Nature and Future of Our Urban Crisis* (Boston, 1970); and Jane Jacobs, *The Death and Life of Great American Cities* (New York, 1961), and *Cities and the Wealth of Nations* (New York, 1984).

6 ☆ Cultural

☆ Regions of

☆ America

☆ Raymond D. Gastil

Basic Cultural Regions

Almost any generalization about Americans will be true of the members of some groups in the country and as surely not true of the members of others. Since these variations often correspond to differences between the people living in different geographical areas, students of the United States have always divided the country into different regions. Generally these regions are recognized by the people inhabiting them and are bounded by discontinuities in physical geography, historical experience, or the background of the citizens.

Commonly, the United States is divided into four major regions: Northeast, South, Midwest (North Central), and West. This subdivision is used by journalists, the U.S. Census Bureau, and polling organizations searching for variations in attitudes or opinions. The Northeast has its capital in New York City but includes New England and the Middle Atlantic states. The South extends from Virginia to Texas but excludes Missouri. The Midwest centers on Chicago, while everything west of the Great Plains, including Hawaii and Alaska, becomes the West. Clearly these are regions of convenience, as are their further subdivisions into categories such as Far West or Southeast.

There are many other common regionalizations that take off from this beginning. Several attempts have been made to regionalize the country by economic criteria, although with the declining dependence of economic activity on location this approach has been largely limited to agricultural divisions. A popular attempt combining economic and cultural criteria has defined "nine nations," most of which extend outside the limits of the United States to include portions of Canada and Mexico. Internationalizing the regions of the

A. Pacific Northwest
B. Pacific Southwest
C. Rocky Mountain
D. Mormon
E. Interior Southwest
F. Upper Midwest
G. Central Midwest
H. New England
I. Pennsylvanian
J. New York Metropolitan
K. Alaskan (off map)
L. Hawaiian (off map)
M. South

Regions
Sub-regions
Districts
Sub-districts
Non-conforming
metropolitan areas
Lowland
Upland
Mountain

United States is undesirable for several reasons, but the fact that this approach could be developed on a largely nonhistorical basis in the 1980s shows again that real differences will be found across this country by analysts who go beyond the generally accepted subdivisions based on formal or physical criteria.

Historically, one of the most important scholarly approaches to the subdivision of the country was conceived by historian Frederick Jackson Turner, who studied the struggle between the "sections" of America in the nineteenth century. According to his thesis, as the country developed, each section formed interests and traits fitting its particular geography or stage of evolution, and much of the history of the Republic could be seen as struggles of "South" with "North," or "East" with "West." He pointed out that these designations changed as the country grew, so that "West" continually referred to an area further and further from the Atlantic coastline. The distinction between "region" as an area defined by its internal characteristics and "section" as an area defined by its characteristic political interactions with other areas is a distinction that should be kept in mind. Sections need constantly to be redefined according to changing growth patterns and needs, but there are surely still sectional struggles.

Recent interest in regions of America has been primarily concerned with cultural regions, that is, with regions defined by the historical experience and qualities of the people that make up their population. The cultural regions that emerged beyond the Atlantic coast can be seen as developments westward of the original regional organization of the country. In his most recent work, *Albion's Seed*, David Hackett Fischer has advanced the thesis that differences between regional cultures in the United States can be traced primarily to differences between the cultures of the parts of Britain from which the original inhabitants came: eastern England to New England, southern England (particular classes) to Virginia, North Midlands of England and Wales to the Delaware Valley (especially eastern Pennsylvania), and the border of North England and Ulster to the Appalachians (central Pennsylvania and south). Whether or not this thesis is given strong support by the evidence in the eventual judgment of historians, it is certainly true that at the time of its founding the United States was divided culturally into at least three groups of states: New England, Middle Atlantic, and Southern. The majority of people in each area had come from the United Kingdom, although in quite different proportions from the several parts of the "mother country." Whatever the influence of origins, one suspects that subsequent historical experience tended to enhance regional distinctiveness.

Centered on Boston, New England had been established in the early 1600s by deeply religious people anxious to escape the domination and corruption they found in England. Their colonies and their communities were to be an example to the world. Education, work, family, community, and church were central. Of course, later generations strayed far from such ideals, but the tradition has lasted in many ways and, particularly before the twentieth century, made New England very different from the rest of the country. It was more religious, more thickly settled, and more jealous of its independence from British control than the other colonies.

Centering on New York and Philadelphia, the Middle Atlantic states were populated by a much more cosmopolitan mix of peoples. The Dutch had ruled New York for several years from the 1620s to 1664, and the Swedish had even planted a colony in Delaware in the 1630s. German immigrants settled in large numbers near Philadelphia before 1800. While there were many individual farmers in parts of New York and New Jersey, large landed estates had been established in this region before the Revolution, and a capitalist or business class had come to be highly developed in the major cities.

The Southern states, from Virginia south—although Maryland, too, was largely Southern at this time—were also different. Here there were few non-British people and very little urban development. The South contained most of the large agricultural plantations with a labor force of slaves imported from Africa or the West Indies. At the time of the Revolution there were few slaves in New England, relatively few in the Middle Atlantic states, but very large numbers in the South. However, most whites in the South did not own estates. They had come from the British Isles as indentured servants and then obtained small farms. But since they did not come as families and since they adapted to the organization of the country as they found it, they only gradually came to emphasize community and church. The South thus remained at the time of independence relatively undeveloped and sparsely populated.

From the East Coast the original population groups spread westward, generally in parallel lines. The New Englanders tended to go directly west through upper New York State, the Upper Midwest, and on to the Pacific Northwest. Those from the Middle Atlantic states preferred a slightly more southerly strip, and Southerners moved across the Mississippi River into Texas, Missouri, Oklahoma, and the Southwest. After 1800 a new population came to America, so that successive waves of later immigrants fundamentally changed the religious and ethnic nature of the country. However, important distinctions need to be made. The South was affected little if at all by the immigrant waves. Only in recent years has the increasing movement of Latin Americans into the fringe of the South in Texas and Florida begun fundamentally to change the original mixture of largely Anglo-Saxon peoples and blacks that composed the Southern population in 1800. The influence of the immigrants was greatest in the North and particularly in its industrial cities. Here again the movement of new peoples tended to reinforce old patterns. The northern strip of the country tended to receive immigrants from Scandinavia and Germany, while the more central strip had larger numbers from the Mediterranean countries and Central Europe.

Thirteen regions can be distinguished by their cultural or historical particularity, and, within these, further subdivisions should also be distinguished. Although many different origins can be found for the people of every region, each cultural region has been largely defined by the characteristics of the people responsible for its "first effective settlement." Since we are speaking of modern American culture, this means the first effective settlement of white Americans, although in a few areas, particularly the interior Southwest and Hawaii, nonwhites have been an important and continuing factor in regional definition. The basic regions distinguished in modern America are New England, New York Metropolitan, Pennsylvanian, South, Upper Midwest, Central Midwest, Rocky Mountain, Mormon, Interior Southwest, Pacific Southwest, Pacific Northwest, Alaskan, and Hawaiian. The following discussion will attempt briefly to define and describe these cultural regions.

☆ ☆ ☆ The New England Region

The New England region includes the states of Maine, New Hampshire, Vermont, Massachusetts, Rhode Island, nearly all of Connecticut, upstate New York, and a narrow strip of northern Pennsylvania. This is the area occupied by New Englanders in 1800 and stamped with their particular culture. Originally defined by an intense Protestant Christianity, the majority of the people are now Roman Catholics, except in certain rural areas. However, as the immigrant groups came into the region, they were, in a cultural sense, often "converted." As a result the regional emphasis on education and intellectual life has continued to be fostered; today outstanding universities and fine colleges are concentrated in the region. Politics continues to be seen in highly moralistic terms, and the people of this area respond more than the people of others to liberal and internationalist appeals. Its elite continues to have a sense of mission and to represent the idealism of the country. However, the fierce democratic attitudes of its first effective settlement were swept away in the urban culture that succeeded the colonial period. Today all three East Coast regional cultures have a more European or English class system than the other parts of the country.

☆ ☆ ☆ The New York Metropolitan Region

The New York Metropolitan region is restricted to New York City and its environs, but with a population of eighteen million, this small area is larger than many other regions and almost as populous as New England. This is characteristically a society of recent immigrants, as generations of new-comers continue to use New York City as the gateway to America. Because of the density of their numbers, religious and ethnic groups, such as orthodox Jews, Puerto Ricans, and Italians, continue to follow their life-styles with relatively little notice of the general American patterns, unless of course members of such groups wish to "melt" into the larger society. The result of this demographic or ethnic situation is that New York City is in many ways "more European," more varied, and for many Americans more exciting than other regions of the country. It is the center of the communications industry, whether it be newspapers, radio, television, or book publishing, and to an increasing extent movies. It is America's business and financial capital, al-though not of course its political center. New Yorkers have the reputation of being cold and distant, with little sense of community, but their expectations are high, for New Yorkers measure themselves against national and interna-tional rather than regional standards.

☆ ☆ ☆ Pennsylvanian Region

The Pennsylvanian region includes most of Pennsylvania and neighboring portions of New Jersey, Delaware, and Maryland. It was orig-inally a center of immigration, particularly of Germans to its lowlands and Scotch-Irish to the higher interior. Later many people came to work the region's mines. Yet immigration into the area has been slow for a long time. While upstate New York was overrun by New Englanders after the Revolu-tion, the original patterns of large proprietorships were preserved in Pennsyl-vania. In religion, while New England was characteristically Congregational-ist, and later Baptist and Unitarian, the Pennsylvanian region was Presbyterian and Quaker. Pennsylvania was founded as a Quaker colony in the 1680s, and other similar groups such as the Amish soon established settlements. In this early period it was a center of American learning and idealism rivaling New England, yet the preeminence soon faded and the area has since been displaced from its early leadership without finding a definite and positive image of its own.

☆ ☆ ☆ The Southern Region

As a cultural region the South begins in southern Delaware and Maryland. Its hypothetical border moves west over Virginia and West Virginia, crossing southern Ohio into Indiana and southern Illinois. It includes most of Missouri and Oklahoma and nearly all of Texas. The South is thus the largest region geographically in the United States, and it has well over one-fourth of the total population of the country.

In many ways the South is the most distinctive of our regions. Its dialects are more widely recognized than other regional dialects. This is particularly true when we remember that Black English is a Southern dialect, although no longer one defined along geographical lines. The South has produced not only a variety of African American musical forms, such as the "blues," but also several other influential and perennially popular styles, particularly the "country music" known to a previous generation as "mountain" or "hillbilly." The cowboy music of the frontier, too, was in large part derived from the South. Today these separate styles have been largely integrated as "country western." The capital of this development is Nashville, Tennessee. Nashville is also a center of the development of popular religion. However, the capital of the Southern Baptist denomination, the fastest growing of the major Protestant sects in the country, is Dallas, Texas, in the Western South subdivision of the region. In many ways the borders of the South can be determined by noting the boundaries of Southern Baptist predominance in religious affiliation. Incidentally, the South is the only major region without a large Catholic presence.

Among American regions, the South has been noted for its hospitality and friendliness, as well as its relatively relaxed and unhurried way of life. Alongside these traits there has been a peculiarly Southern emphasis on personal honor and valor. These elements may partially explain an emphasis on military service among Southerners, a tendency perhaps reinforced by the location of so many military facilities in the South. Another characteristic of the South is a relatively high homicide rate in comparison to the North; this regional tendency, already reported in the nineteenth century by H. V. Redfield and others, is partly responsible for the high homicide rate of the United States as compared to other developed countries. Relatively severe prison sentences have long characterized the South, as have educational and health levels below the national average. Nevertheless, the region's literary and musical creativity has been outstanding.

Although the South was a distinct region before the Civil War, its regional distinctiveness was enhanced by the war. The racial relations that developed under slavery and postslavery segregation define the South for many Americans, even though there are border areas of the South, for example in Kentucky and West Virginia, that opposed the Civil War and have never had large African American populations. Today, in spite of the history of racial oppression, observers feel that in many areas of the South racial relations are as satisfactory as those in the North. On the local level, African Americans have been elected to many political positions, although this success has largely been confined to areas with black majorities. (Contrary to the image some have of the South, blacks are not a majority in any Southern state.) The recent election of an African American governor in Virginia reflects both improving race relations and the tendency for Virginia to lose much of its historical Southernness under the influence of the Washington metropolitan area.

There are several historically important subdivisions of the South that still have relevance today. The primary division in Southern geography has always been between the lowland and upland South. The lowlands stretched from Maryland south along the coast to northern Florida and then west to the Mississippi Valley and southeast Texas. This was the area of the great cotton plantations with large numbers of slaves. After the Civil War it was the area with the severest racial problems, for the war generally left behind in these sections a very poor, uneducated, but majority black population. The upland South lay inland from this belt. The soil was poorer, farms were smaller, and slaves were few. Further up there were two mountain areas of the South: the Appalachians of the north-central South and the Ozark Mountains of Arkansas to the west. Here life was hard and isolated, and blacks were generally absent. To a considerable degree this area sided with the North in the Civil War, which led to the split of West Virginia from Virginia. It was also an area of very poor farms, and the discovery of coal led to the conversion of much of the Appalachian South into a mining belt that eventually became well known for its industrial violence. The Western South of Texas and Oklahoma developed a more open, aggressive, assertive, and optimistic version of Southern culture based on the riches of livestock and oil. Houston and Dallas now rank alongside Atlanta and Nashville as the leading cities of the South.

Two other very different enclave "Souths" also should be mentioned. Southern Louisiana was originally established as a French colony. As a result the area is largely Catholic in religion, its race relations have been characterized by an attention to "degrees" of racial mixture (more cosmopolitan than the all-or-nothing definition of African Americans that otherwise has been characteristic of America's race relations), and there is still a considerable

French-speaking population in rural areas. Southern Florida is another area that recently has developed along different lines from the rest of the South. Although it still retains many Southern patterns, these have been overlain by recent population movements. First has been the influx of northerners for retirement or recreation. Since these have come largely from New York City, they have imparted a distinctive atmosphere to some areas. More recently a new wave from the Cuban middle class has arrived in the Miami area, followed by an influx of Latin Americans from many countries, mostly of the middle and upper classes. Many observers now consider Miami a major Latin American city.

☆ ☆ ☆ The Midwestern Regions

From a political and social viewpoint the Midwest is centered on Chicago. The section maintains the continuing and special perspective of the interior. However, culturally the area varies so greatly from north to south that it is useful to distinguish between Upper Midwest and Central Midwest cultural regions—even though these are not distinctions commonly made by the residents of the area. The Upper Midwest includes Michigan; the northern edge of Ohio, Illinois, and Iowa; and Wisconsin, Minnesota, and North and South Dakota. It is an area of strong Scandinavian, German, Swiss, Dutch, and New England influence. The "moralistic" attitude toward politics in the region results in liberal voting patterns similar to those of New England and the Pacific Northwest, regions characterized by similar political values. In the Upper Midwest politics is regarded as equally the concern of all. It is felt that ideas and ideals should determine policies rather than the balance of interests that are accepted as policy determinants in most of the country. This region spawned the Farmer-Labor and Progressive parties that added a new dimension to the politics of the first half of the twentieth century. The educational standards and aspirations of the region have been high from the beginning, and the tradition continues today.

The Central Midwest region is a transitional area, with strands of all three East Coast traditions, yet most strongly rooted in that of the Mid-Atlantic area. It has been influenced by the South and New England, and its later immigrant population is a representative mixture of all those European peoples who entered the country after the Civil War. Of course, unlike the entry areas of New York, Miami, or California, the Central Midwest has not attracted large numbers of recent immigrants. It is in many ways a city-dominated area, with the "cultures" of Chicago, St. Louis, and Kansas City determining most of its life. Yet it is quintessentially American, the area to which the news media refer when they speak of the "heartland." It is the only region with significant sections in which the Protestant sects most identified with the country— groups like the Methodists, Presbyterians, northern Baptists, or the Church of God—actually dominate religious affiliation. The region includes central Ohio, Indiana, and Illinois, most of Iowa and Nebraska, northern Missouri, western Colorado, and the state of Kansas.

☆ ☆ ☆ The Rocky Mountain Region

The Rocky Mountain region is the least well defined of the cultural regions. The people of its three states—Colorado, Wyoming, and Montana— are much more interested in their separate identities than in the development of a regional sense. Its population density is the lowest in the continental United States, and the mixture of the peoples that make up the region is as representative of the nation as a whole as that of the Central Midwest. The attitudes of the people in the Rocky Mountain region have always reflected its extreme topography and climate. The attention of the area is focused on its mineral and environmental resources and their exploitation. It is a frontier area, the last area to be settled, the true home of the cowboy and the sheep-herder, the skier, the hiker, and the climber.

☆ ☆ ☆ The Mormon Region

The Mormon region of southeast Idaho and Utah illustrates most vividly the difference between defining regions by physical geography or economic criteria and defining them in cultural terms. Utah was established in the middle of the nineteenth century in the New England tradition as a model state based on a particular religious vision—in this case, the revelations osten-sibly received by Joseph Smith, a young man of New England background. The Mormon community that developed around this faith was driven out of several areas because of its beliefs and practices. The leader of the community finally moved his people to the distant frontier, built the famous Mormon Tabernacle in what is now Salt Lake City, and, through discipline and hard work, laid the foundations for an exemplary society. Aside from the region's overwhelming adherence to the Mormon religion, it is notable for very high educational and health standards. The emphasis on family and community has also led to a high birthrate. Mormons are now prospering in all parts of the country and in many foreign countries, but the heart of the movement remains Salt Lake City and its environs in Utah.

☆ ☆ ☆ The Interior Southwest Region

The Interior Southwest region is confined largely to the states of Arizona and New Mexico. For a long formative period the basic pattern here was one of coexistence among Spanish-Americans, Texans, tourists, and several Native American peoples. Although the inflow of people from all parts of the country has been heavy in recent years, the original patterns are still important, and much of the region remains in the hands of Native American groups that are also rapidly growing in numbers. The climate is harsh but less harsh than to the north. The topography is dramatic, and variations from one part to another may be extreme in temperature, precipitation, elevation, and vegetation. This is a new frontier of settlement for many people, yet the oldest cultures in America, Native American and Spanish, give the region a feeling different from the rest of the West with its more garish newness.

☆ ☆ ☆ The Pacific Southwest Region

The Pacific Southwest region is primarily California; indeed, for many people, "the West" is California. In the peopling of the state, settlers from the Northeast tended to come to the San Francisco area and those from the Midwest to southern California. The especially desirable climate of California's coastal areas, however, has continued to pull in people from the entire country for over a hundred years, including many of the country's most progressive and best educated. The result is that modern movements and modern industries often originate or are fostered in the state. The California system of higher education has long been the envy of the entire country, and California was the first major state to make higher education easily available to all its citizens. With several of the country's leading research universities and private colleges, the region now rivals New England in higher education. The attitude and faith of the people have been highly democratic and optimistic, and its wealth has made it possible to meet the needs of its general citizenry more adequately than elsewhere. California agriculture feeds the country in many specialty crops and provides a large percentage of its fruits and vegetables. The new computer industry is concentrated here, as was the movie industry in its heyday. Like the Interior Southwest, the geography of the region is extremely varied, with very hot and very cold areas within a few miles distance. The region has become a favorite tourist destination for all Americans.

☆ ☆ ☆ The Pacific Northwest Region

The Pacific Northwest is in many respects a continuation and meeting place of the Rocky Mountain and Pacific Southwest regional cultures; however, the environment has produced a different attitude than elsewhere in the country. Only portions of the deep South have as intense a regional identification. The western, coastal part of this region—which comprises the states of Oregon, Washington, and the greater part of Idaho—is more populated and much milder than the interior. The countryside is also more extensively forested, and it enjoys a generally heavier rainfall. East of the Cascade range running parallel to the coast, most of the region is a high, relatively flat and undifferentiated plateau. The Pacific Northwest has a sparse population and has developed slowly. Compared to neighboring regions, its population has received a larger contribution from the people of the Upper Midwest and New England, as well as from Scandinavia, Germany, and Great Britain. It is a Protestant area and one with few recent immigrants. In keeping with these population origins, the politics of the region has tended to be moderate and liberal. The society is homogeneous, largely white, and interested in the environment and wilderness that surrounds it. Because of the weather and the fact that none of its major cities is near the open ocean, the region's beautiful beaches remain uncrowded. One does not find here the beach-and-Hollywood culture of California.

☆ ☆ ☆ The Alaskan Region

The two remaining regions are small in population yet highly distinctive. Alaska is both a state and a region, or group of protoregions. It is still a frontier area with a low percentage of native-born—aside from the Amer-Indians and Eskimos. The latter have profited recently from a settlement in the courts concerning their mineral and oil rights. They now have enough wealth to become a permanent force in the area. Nevertheless, the culture of Alaska is an amalgam of that of the lower forty-eight states of the continental United States. It does not yet have a positive image that goes beyond subsisting in adversity for the exploitation of natural resources. Because of its climate and the high cost of living, it seems unlikely to soon become a stable cultural area.

☆ ☆ ☆ The Hawaiian Region

The Hawaiian region is a particularly desirable place for most Americans. Aside from extreme southern Florida it is the only tropical part of the United States. It is also the only region where nonwhites dominate life. The largest single ethnic group in Hawaii is of Japanese background, but Filipinos, Chinese, Samoans, people of native Hawaiian ancestry, and mainland Americans join in the mixture. The Islands, which were granted statehood only in 1959, were originally settled and brought into the Union as agricultural lands, especially for crops such as sugar and pineapples. Later the Islands became an important American naval base; today the economy is overwhelmingly dominated by tourism. By and large the tourists are mainland Americans and Orientals, particularly Japanese. The Hawaiians traditionally have been characterized as a relaxed people, cut off from the striving that affects much of the country and luxuriating in a beautiful environment. Their life-style appears threatened more than anything else by the shift to tourism and the cutting up of the limited open space for housing.

The Hawaiian region illustrates a point that seems particularly appropriate for concluding this summary. Through the language of cultural regions this chapter has attempted to describe important regional variations in the United States. This is not to suggest, however, that we would not find even more important commonalities among Americans should we compare the people in the cultural regions we have identified with people living in other countries. This was the fundamental mistake of the attempt mentioned above to draw up a list of "nine nations" in North America that cut across political boundaries. For example, the people of Canada's British Columbia share the topography and many of the interests of the people of the Pacific Northwest of the United States, yet as Canadians they are immediately recognizable as different, and as living by different assumptions, from the Americans of the Pacific Northwest. This criticism can be extended to the same author's attempt to define regions that group southern Florida with Cuba or southern California with Mexico ("Mexamerica"). Political boundaries have become cultural boundaries, and the American historical experience has placed an ineradicable imprint on every part of the country. The African Americans in New York, the

Spanish-Americans in Santa Fe, the Japanese-Americans in Hawaii—they are all Americans; and even if they sometimes wish otherwise, all the world recognizes them as Americans.

FURTHER READING

Historically the most influential work on regionalism—actually sectionalism—was Frederick Jackson Turner, *The United States: 1830–1850* (New York, 1935). Important in the further definition of the subject because it took a particularly Southern point of view was Howard Odum and Harry Moore, *American Regionalism: A Cultural-Historical Approach to National Integration* (New York, 1938). This earlier period of regional study culminated in a collection of scholarly analyses edited by Merrill Jensen, *Regionalism in America* (Madison, Wis., 1951). A collection of essays that brings the Jensen discussion up to date, particularly as it applies to the Pacific Northwest, is W. G. Robbins, Robert J. Franks, and Richard E. Ross, eds., *Regionalism and the Pacific Northwest* (Corvallis, Oreg., 1983). See especially the essay by R. M. Brown, "The New Regionalism in America: 1970–1981."

The foregoing discussion is based largely on Raymond D. Gastil, *Cultural Regions of the United States* (Seattle, 1975). Another work with a similar point of view and one more clearly within the mainstream of American geography is Wilbur Zelinsky, *The Cultural Geography of the United States* (Englewood Cliffs, N.J., 1973). A recent historical treatment of the backgrounds to cultural regions is David Hackett Fischer, *Albion's Seed: Four British Folkways in America* (New York, 1989). Illustrative of the new material for such summary works are John F. Rooney, Jr., Wilbur Zelinsky, and Dean R. Louder, eds., *This Remarkable Continent: An Atlas of United States and Canadian Society and Cultures* (College Station, Tex., 1982), and James P. Allen and Eugene J. Turner, *We the People: An Atlas of America's Ethnic Diversity* (New York, 1988). An approach very similar to that of *Cultural Regions* but confined to political attitudes and expectations is Daniel Elazar, *American Federalism: A View from the States* (New York, 1972). Less scholarly but fascinating is Kevin Phillips, *The Emerging Republican Majority* (New Rochelle, N.Y., 1969). The treatment mentioned above that carries the concept of regions beyond the borders of the United States is Joel Garreau, *The Nine Nations of North America* (Boston, 1981). A great deal of information on the regional politics of America from a more journalistic perspective may be found in a series of books produced by Neil R. Peirce, beginning with his *The Megastates of America* (New York, 1972) and including (with Michael Barone) *The Mid-Atlantic States* (New York, 1977).

There are several good analyses of particular regions or subregions or of topics seen in a regional perspective. The best work is probably that of D. W. Meinig, especially his "The Mormon Culture Region: Strategies and Patterns in the Geography of the American West, 1847–1964," *Annals of the Association of American Geographers* 55, no. 2 (June 1965), *Imperial Texas: An Interpretive Essay in Cultural Geography* (Austin, Tex., 1969), and *Southwest: Three Peoples in Geographical Change* (New York, 1971). The latter is a study of the region labeled in this chapter as the Interior Southwest. A different approach comparing the American subcultures that coexist in this region is found in Evon Vogt and Ethel Albert, eds., *People of Rimrock: A Study of Values in Five Cultures* (Cambridge, Mass., 1966), one of the last volumes reporting on a massive study of comparative cultures in one small area of the region. A recent reconsideration of the "midwests" as a single region spiritually is James R. Shortridge, *The Middle West: Its Meaning in American Culture* (Lawrence, Kans., 1989). For the Pacific Southwest, particularly valuable historical studies are those of Kevin Starr, *Americans and the California Dream, 1850–1915* (New York, 1973), *Inventing the Dream: California through the Progressive Era* (New York, 1985), and *Material Dreams: Southern California through the 1920s* (New York, 1990).

The South has probably been analyzed more than any other region. Particularly valuable modern work is that of John Shelton Reed. See his *The Enduring South: Subcultural Persistence in Mass Society* (Lexington, Mass., 1972), *One South: An Ethnic Approach to Regional Culture* (Baton Rouge, La., 1982), and *Southerners: The Social Psychology of Sectionalism* (Chapel Hill, N.C., 1983); and Merle Black and Reed, eds., *Perspectives on the American South* (New York, 1981). For studies of individual Southern traits from a historical perspective, see David Bertelsen, *The Lazy South* (New York, 1967); John Hope Franklin, *The Militant South, 1800–1861* (Cambridge, Mass., 1956); H. V. Redfield, *Homicide, North and South* (Philadelphia, 1880); and Bertram Wyatt-Brown, *Southern Honor: Ethics and Behavior in the Old South* (New York, 1982). The most comprehensive effort to encompass Southern culture is Charles R. Wilson and William Ferris, eds., *Encyclopedia of Southern Culture* (Chapel Hill, N.C., 1989).

Many kinds of basic documentation can be found for regional differences. Perhaps the most valuable are the privately managed religious censuses. These are Edwin Gaustad, *Historical Atlas of Religions in America* (New York, 1962), and Douglas Johnson, Paul Picard, and Bernard Quinn, *Churches and Church Membership in the United States, 1956–1958* (Washington, D.C., 1974). For linguistic variation, the basic reference is the series by Frederic G. Cassidy, *Dictionary of American Regional English (DARE)* (Cambridge, Mass., 1985–). More accessible and directly related to the regional analysis is Craig M. Carver, *American Regional Dialects: A Word Geography* (Ann Arbor, Mich., 1987).

PART

TWO

Expressions

of American

Culture

The Abbé Raynal's remark in 1770 that "America has not yet produced one good poet, one able mathematician, one man of genius in a single art or a single science" was not a superficial challenge. The notion that a people could stand on political institutions alone, without strong cultural foundations, was alien to European observers. Nor was a culture of letters and arts to be brought into existence by mere decree. Rousseau in his famous *Discours sur les sciences et les arts* (1750) and Herder beginning with the *Fragmente* (1767) had argued that culture, arts, and national identity evolve naturally out of the communal experience and expressions of a folk over great stretches of time. What would a nation be without its distinctive manners and cultural achievements? How could such a historically young enterprise as the American colonies lay claim to nationhood?

The poetry of the 1770s and 1780s was nationalistic in rhetoric and revolutionary in fervor but derivative in style. For several more decades the United States would have to satisfy itself with exhorting its poets and artists to invent forms of expression as indigenous as the land and noble as its political institutions, while claiming for the interim that in the New World the rules of cultural evolution need not apply—that here the historical scale was vastly foreshortened by the genius of the Revolution itself. It was still possible for the British critic Sydney Smith to sneer in 1820: "In the four corners of the globe, who reads an American book? or goes to an American play? or looks at an American picture or statue?" And as late as 1858, Nathaniel Hawthorne, struggling with a European romantic conception of art and nationality, observed in his preface to *The Marble Faun*: "No author, without a trial, can conceive of the difficulty of writing a romance about a country where there is no shadow, no antiquity, no mystery, no picturesque and gloomy wrong, nor anything but a commonplace prosperity, in broad and simple day-light, as is happily the case with my dear native land." The challenge to furnish the nation with a native literature and culture preoccupied American artists through the nineteenth century. In some areas cultural independence was not achieved before our own time.

During the age of Hawthorne and the "American Renaissance," however, various American features and themes became well established: an inspiring new landscape, a pantheon of heroes of classical virtue, the Native Americans and folklore of the American frontier, a legacy of colonial and revolutionary life. Throughout the nineteenth century dramatic myths evolved that focused on a new individual poised between society and the wilderness, nature and God, personal will and the "manifest destiny" of the nation. The question that challenges us today is no longer whether there *is* an American culture but *how* the national consciousness expresses itself culturally and what effect the enormous cultural productivity of the United States is having on its own people and other nations. The following chapters will provide some answers.

Neil Harris's "American Manners," Dickran Tashjian's "The Artlessness of American Culture," and Leland Roth's "A New Architecture, Yet Old" illustrate the nation's gradual liberation from cultural colonialism and the adaptation of inherited standards of social deportment, art, and architecture to the always new conditions of the New World. Harris asks, "Do national systems of manners still exist" in international postindustrial society? He then argues that "in the United States the legacies of democratic republicanism, cultural colonialism, ethnic pluralism, and hostility to governmental intervention as well as the power of myths and stereotypes built around the frontier experience and the code of the West are still important." The very architecture of the nation, according to Roth, reflects the dialectic of "a young country with an old mentality" that endeavors continuously "to achieve the optimum balance between the real and the ideal, between the present-day and the timeless."

Nina Baym's chapter "Creating a National Literature" surveys the vast terrain of American writing since independence, from the "self-conscious literary project" of New England to the "numerous groups of formerly silent Americans" who are challenging the canon today. Emphasizing those negotiating institutions and "culturally sanctioned criteria" that determine what comprises "the core of our national literature," Baym points out that aesthetic excellence has never been the chief measure and that American writers long have been preoccupied with the problem of national identity. In "Literature and Values: The American Crusoe and the Idea of the West," Richard Lehan next considers Daniel Defoe's resourceful castaway as a paradigm of national purpose and destiny. Robinson Crusoe heralded the "split consciousness" of the central protagonist in American literature, who has struggled "to reconcile his Puritan sense of God with an empirical state of mind" while establishing mastery over his world—including, unhappily, women, minorities, and the natural environment. By the time "Crusoe Goes to Disneyland," however, exchanging the world of Enlightenment for "the unreal, decentered, unscriptable world of postmodern Los Angeles," the essence that distinguished him from other beings and his environment dissolves in a chaos of signals and the semiotic soup of consumerism, advertising, and mass media.

Chronicling the development of American entertainment and sports, Norman Corwin and Richard Powers illuminate the culture, the values, and the social history of a people who historically have believed that their reason for being lay in work, not play. Today American entertainment, sports, and mass communication are the biggest of businesses. The nation works extraordinarily hard at its play, and the distinctions between amateur and professional have become obscure. Corwin's lament about the passivity of American media and audiences, both here and in his book *Trivializing America* (1983), stands in the prophetic tradition of Walt Whitman's *Democratic Vistas* (1871). But he also detects "signs of reawakened responsibility when it comes to issues of vital import" and offers hope that talent, art, commerce, and politics can unite once again to serve the national well-being.

7 ☆ American Manners

☆ Neil Harris

Like the word *culture*, *manners* possesses both a broad and a narrow meaning. On the one hand, manners can refer to forms representing courtesy and cultivation. On the other, they include ordinary usages, customs, and characteristic ways of doing things. American manners have been the concern of both the dancing master and the ethnographer.

It is the tension between a normative sense of appropriate behavior and a descriptive affirmation of what manners actually are that makes the subject complex. In trying to define the presence of an American way of doing things commentators have invariably sought to discover if that style obeyed established forms—to determine whether, in short, Americans were simultaneously distinctive and polite. The possibility of being both has often seemed improbable.

☆ ☆ ☆ Manners in America

As a problem in American life manners have existed as long as the nation, and even longer, for colonial societies often resemble purified (or decayed) versions of their mother cultures. The communities perched along the Atlantic seaboard in the late seventeenth and early eighteenth centuries were taken to be outposts of civilization, vulnerable to dissolution. Their commitment to European values expressed itself in many ways—religious practices, educational institutions, and the legal system among them—but none more so than by perpetuation of conduct that enshrined gentility as an ideal and deference as a social instrument.

As Norbert Elias has reminded us in his seminal texts, civility was a recent achievement in Europe itself. A pleasing manner, proper dress, refined table habits, careful personal hygiene, disciplined language, repudiation of cruelty, special consideration shown to women, the elderly, and children—these ideals had been nourished by Renaissance courtiers and noblemen and were dispersed as general guides through the rise of an urban and normally commercial middle class. In America, as in Europe, etiquette soon entered religious and civic instruction, its texts devoured by the socially ambitious and the economically mobile. Some of the earliest American printed books addressed the cultivation of good manners.

But if ideals did not change markedly during the colonial period, practices certainly did. Authority about usage and availability of proper models was thousands of miles away. Scarcity of resources made improvisation necessary. A dispersed population valuing social contacts depended on its own resources for amusement and diversion. Curiosity, directness, and simplicity may have been the more valued because of the thin margin on which survival depended.

With time the nondeliberate and almost unconscious shift of manners that evolved during the early years of settlement was supplanted by the self-conscious changes that accompanied independence. Manners became, in the years after 1776, a national problem and, some argued, a national achievement. A rich literature of social analysis and a vast store of anecdotal data developed. Underlining both were some fundamental issues, and from them we select four that can serve as useful illuminants. Although here they are assigned time frames in which they held special importance, these tensions and the models of behavior reflecting them have coexisted for much of the last two hundred years.

☆ ☆ ☆ Equality and Class

The first issue, which dominated social commentary between the Revolution and the Civil War, grew out of the conflict between political democracy and traditional forms of authority. At the heart of the American Revolution was a repudiation of divinely based political sovereignty. This was followed, within a few decades, by a new religion of social egalitarianism as well. Of course it was possible to believe that all men were created equal without believing that all men *were* equal. The persistence of slavery, of legal handicaps for women, and of various kinds of social differentiation demonstrated that fact. Clubs, associations, family alliances, ethnic and religious origins, and ancestral status continued to be important centers of value for many Americans.

Simultaneously, a coexisting ideology insisted that one man's chances and opinions were as good as another's. Many pondered this view's impact on the rich intricacies of address by which people had historically signaled deference to superiority, whether that superiority rested on wealth, office, age, sex, or gentle birth. How would an independent citizenry voluntarily accept any curbs on behavior beyond the constraints that safety and necessity suggested? To answer this question and to see how the new code of sincerity functioned, travelers and natives scrutinized the most mundane experiences. In the first half of the nineteenth century, journalists, novelists, philosophers, and politicians analyzed stagecoach conversations and steamboat romances, behavior in hotel lobbies and at dining tables, the language of parents to children and the treatment of parents by children, the responses made by tradesmen to customers and by servants to masters, the way people gave directions or asked questions or greeted strangers or acknowledged differences of opinion. Almost any act or gesture could be taken as portentous. Harriet Martineau, Frances Trollope, Charles Dickens, James Fenimore Cooper, Alexis de Tocqueville, Michel Chevalier, and Francis Grund helped produce a literature of extraordinary breadth, almost all of them treating manners as a barometer to American democracy.

Evidence and conclusions varied enormously. Those suspicious of the American experiment saw a degenerated social intercourse as a commentary on this radical reshuffling of traditional authority. Biting observers like Frances Trollope published hilarious if embarrassing descriptions of national crudity, including spitting, tobacco chewing, hoggish conduct at table, lack of respect for privacy, animal-like carousing at theaters, boisterousness on holidays, and childish sensitivity to harsh words. Basil Hall, Henry B. Fearon, and many others found further evidence for arguing that American life was long on freedom and short on discipline. The proverbial independence of American children—their insistence upon controlling their own diet and hour of retirement—was presented as endangering the nation's physical health as well as its public spaces. The root of such impertinence was said to lie in the American's universal suspicion of external controls or elaborate rules. Radical democracy could have unsettling effects on unprotected visitors. The Englishwoman Mary Duncan recorded her astonishment when a visitor rang her door to inquire "if the *woman* of the house be at home for I am the *lady* that have come to help her cook." Under such circumstances it was not surprising that a scavenger testifying in court stated that "when he first observed the *gentleman* he was filling the dung-cart." It was not only the social pyramid that had been inverted but the very ordering of language itself.

On the other side of the ledger were those arguing that Americans maintained both civility and social safety without reliance on the characteristic oppressions used elsewhere. If America's social structure had "no fluid Corinthian capital rising into the clear air above," Alexander Mackay wrote in the 1840s, "neither has it a pedestal in the mire beneath." Less picturesque than the inheritance of feudal chivalry, it was nonetheless compact and commodious. America was built less to "attract the eye" than to "accommodate the inmates," Mackay concluded.

Friendly observers admitted that Americans were freer with strangers than European practices permitted but acknowledged that such easy curiosity was different from insolence. Americans did chew and spit almost anywhere, but their respect for women was generally beyond reproach. Indeed American gallantry was claimed as a miraculous intervention of voluntary restraint. Some visitors actually bridled at the deference American women received from uncomplaining men, who gladly gave up everything from seats in crowded horsecars to the best places at the dinner table. A few pointed to the new power women censors seemed to possess; prudery so controlled art and language that even casual reference to the body could excite immediate indignation.

Concern about the feminization of American culture was voiced also by opponents of social democracy, who suggested that egalitarianism produced a herdlike acquiescence in arbitrary social rules and an unnatural fondness for titles, distinctions, and foreign noblemen. Not anarchy but a series of petty social prohibitions could cut the social landscape into a mass of mutually exclusive sectors. The paradoxical coexistence, then, of a belief in radical democracy and an unusual punctiliousness about social codes could be produced by the same cause: reluctance to recognize traditional authority in assigning hierarchies of honor and respect.

With manners and political values so closely linked, it was natural to endow regional differences with special meaning. Northerners and southerners perceived in one another's social forms organic expressions of their respective societies. Manners were crucial symbols in the creation of sectional archetypes. The southerner's hospitality and chivalry, elaborate code of honor and sensitivity to insult; the Yankee's taciturnity, curiosity, and refusal to put on airs; the westerner's casualness, loquaciousness, and independence of manners— these quickly became caricatured in print, on stage, and through political rhetoric. These popular composites reflected a sense that the plantation, the New England town, and the frontier farm, as very different political and social units, would shape the external features that gave the cavalier, the Yankee, and the frontiersman their special characteristics.

☆ ☆ ☆ Parvenus, Aristocrats, and Ordinary Folk

The consuming interest antebellum Americans took in politics, their incessant and forceful sense of patriotism, and their high degree of self-promotion all increased the sense that manners and democracy were intimately related. The ways in which family life, domestic service, and public behavior reflected the political system never ceased to interest social observers. However, as democratic forms congealed in America after the Civil War, and as it became clear that the experiment in collective authority had become a permanent and powerful nation-state, another set of issues shaping national manners developed to complement the first. This involved the growth of wealth in America, the development of an unprecedented level of material profusion, and a corresponding delight in commodity display as the fulfillment of the good life.

The struggle for material success and the presence of considerable affluence had, of course, excited commentary before the Civil War. The label of materialism was employed by many foreigners and also by American political leaders who warned, during the 1840s and 1850s, that consuming absorption with economic advancement and fierce personal competition could produce a melancholy, self-absorbed people, dull, coarse, and insensible to the graces of life. A trading mentality would be bound to affect the level of public behavior and encourage sharp practices and social deceit. Wealth brought luxury in its train, and patriots worried about the loss of civic virtues acquired in the austerity of the young republic.

As the United States developed into an urban-industrial society after the Civil War, the reconciliation of wealth and public virtue became even more difficult. Unheard-of levels of income were attained by individual captains of industry, skillful professionals, innovative merchants, and the fortunate owners of mineral-rich properties. Within a few decades the country was transformed from an underdeveloped backwater to a primary world economy with enormous productive capacity and extensive markets for manufactured goods. Once identified in foreign eyes with political radicalism, Americans could now be associated with wealth and increasing conservatism. Growing contrasts of life-style between rich and poor occasioned a series of harsh debates in the late nineteenth century, but abroad there was a tendency to identify unusual wealth with America as a whole.

Increasing wealth had obvious connections with manners. Focusing upon the coarse behavior of parvenus was one way for traditional elites to respond to challengers. In ancient Rome, in feudal Europe, in the new nation-states of the modern period, the manners of the urban bourgeoisie, rich merchants, and ambitious tradesmen were mocked by those with gentler birth. Tensions between establishments and upstarts formed staple themes for comic literature.

In America these tensions were exacerbated by the scale of the wealth and social crudity and also by the publicity that newspapers and magazines lavished upon the struggles of the new rich to break through older bastions of privilege and proclaim their own gentility. The etiquette of dress, of dining, and of social calling formed a battlefield that developed its own armchair generals and war reporters. Etiquette writers flourished, and disputes developed about nods, bows, handshakes, and curtsies. Social encounters, and sometimes social confrontations, took place in the elaborate hotels and clubhouses of summer resorts like Newport, Saratoga, Long Branch, and Tuxedo Park and at the opera and symphonic associations, the town houses and lavish estates, the churches and athletic clubs, that this wealth supported. Masked balls, debutante cotillions, weddings, and tennis parties were covered for the popular press by artists and writers who serviced curiosity and criticism. Jewelers supplied crests, genealogists devised coats of arms, and hereditary societies flourished.

For those who lay outside the charmed circles of wealth and lineage, the manners of the two groups contending for social primacy provided material for endless entertainment and mordant satire. The frequent faux pas were perfect material for urban journalists like Finley Peter Dunne, who poked fun at the accents, grammar, dress, and aesthetic affectations of new elites. Novelists like Mark Twain, Henry James, William Dean Howells, and Edith Wharton analyzed the impact of wealth and cosmopolitan ambition upon social forms. Typically a small-town businessman who struck it rich would move to the city to advance the social fortunes of his wife and children. There he would encounter complexities undreamt of in the snug security of his native hearth. Comedies of manners like *The Rise of Silas Lapham*, *A Hazard of New Fortunes*, *The Bostonians*, and *The Custom of the Country* examined various aspects of this translation from one world to another and the struggle to develop appropriate social styles.

Wealth exposed American manners to continuing international scrutiny because it underwrote an expansion of tourism abroad. In the late nineteenth century the American abroad symbolized for some the dangers of sudden wealth and became an instrument to expose comparative social codes and standards of morality. Boasting, vulgarity, obsessive acquisitiveness, and insensitivity were soon associated with this early version of the Ugly American. Representing a small portion of the population, the international travelers seemed to stand for the whole country in the eyes of many foreigners, and it was the prodigality of their wealth, the apparently limitless wallets and purses, that seemed most dangerous. American money threatened to loot the Old World of its historic treasures, and aggressive celebrity hunters and relic gatherers threatened to invade European privacy as well.

At home private wealth was charged with corrupting the mutual confidence that once prevailed among citizens at large and replacing it with class controversies. The reputation of American wealth also helped produce another crisis in social relationships. Dreams of financial independence (and personal liberty) lured millions of immigrants to America in the late nineteenth century, many of them from Southern and Eastern Europe. Their physical appearance, religious beliefs, and languages contrasted with American models. Groups of immigrants, particularly the Irish, had earlier aroused complaints by natives centering around national unity and standards of behavior, but American nativism of the later part of the century went deeper. The new immigrants added color, street life, and picturesqueness to American cities, but their deportment and appearance upset purists who thought the perfection of manners lay in strict control of the emotions and subdued personal affect.

According to press reports, urban congestion and commuting, city hotels, restaurants, shopping, and mass transit were also affecting American manners, and not for the better. Middle-class journals at the turn of the century and letters-to-the-editor columns of major newspapers were filled with complaints of rudeness in daily relations, coarse speech, diminishing respect for the needs of women and the elderly, and a broad range of incivilities. As urban services multiplied along with travel opportunities and new entertainment forms, Americans had to solve problems at home they once associated only with foreign settings—tipping, for example. Etiquette writers advised how to behave when on streetcars or crowded sidewalks, how to treat clerks at the new department stores, how to conduct oneself at the theater or in restaurants.

The manners of this population were blamed not so much on expanding democracy as on ethnic heterogeneity, materialism, bitter competition for jobs and status, and the management of "image" in a world where contact was fleeting and often superficial. Technology, too, played a role. Labor costs were high and distances were great, so machines were quickly exploited to save money and time. Automobiles, telephones, and electric lighting all prompted new rules of acceptable usage. The early popularity of many of these innovations in America suggested more than merely a widespread love for novelty and machinery—it indicated also an abiding interest in devices that transcended traditional rankings, releasing individuals from older codes of social expression. Typewriters and dictation permitted executives and secretaries to bypass the slowly acquired courtesies of calligraphic elegance; telephone conversations could replace many written communications entirely; the automobile provided a private setting for the individual occupant to escape the social world of trains and trolleys. American manners seemed to experience the pressures of new inventions earlier than in most other countries, and so, by the early twentieth century, they had acquired some futurist overtones.

☆ ☆ ☆ Mass Culture and American Chauvinism

At about this time the themes of wealth and democracy were reinforced by still another feature of national life that emphasized the role of manners: the expansion of mass communications. As a result of rapid industrialization, innovative advertising, and new distribution methods, Americans had assembled an arsenal of promotional campaigns that promised to "Americanize" the rest of the world. By 1918 European empires, their boundaries redrawn, their economies weakened by war, their political systems challenged by radicalism, could resist less effectively than ever. No American export was better distributed than motion pictures. American actors and actresses, supported by American furniture, dress, automobiles, and mannerisms, flooded Europe in the 1920s. At home as well movies added unprecedented intensity to social representation. Audiences were fascinated by the most ordinary of movements and interpersonal details, and so the first films mixed the fictional and the documentary with remarkable casualness. The absence of a sound track limited the effectiveness of these films in depicting all aspects of daily behavior, but it made them more easily exportable and underlined the functions of gesture and visual expression.

Films and advertising campaigns in magazines and on billboards specified how typical Americans were meant to look and interact. By 1929 image industries had become an American specialty, their managers skillful in projecting values that could appeal to a large constituency. Given the ambivalence with which American manners were viewed historically, suffering from the multiple disadvantages of youth, democracy, materialism, and ethnic heterogeneity, it was ironic that Americans had become the world's pedagogues. Films covered a wide variety of genres—romance, comedy, mystery, western, melodrama, historical romance—but almost all contained scenes that explored fundamental human experiences and the rituals attached to them. Millions of viewers saw how actors walked, dressed, ate, kissed, quarreled, prayed, talked, and traveled—how they entered rooms, paid bills, expressed condolences, behaved at parties. While influences between screen and audience were reciprocal and determining impact is difficult, the detail was breathtaking and riveting. Millions of foreigners were told that this was how Americans acted and interacted.

The mixture of reality that was Hollywood exploited fan magazines and giant publicity machines to encourage a religion of "the stars." Personality cults developed around consumption habits and styles of deportment. These were supplemented by immense advertising campaigns, which used illustration, photography, and words with great imagination. Advertisers were eager to affect manners. Soap and cosmetic manufacturers sought to depict the dangers of poor grooming more effectively than the etiquette manuals of an earlier day. Automakers, food purveyors, and clothing stores all tried to accustom buyers to the symbolic meaning of brand names and model years, arguing that appearance and success were closely linked and could be served best by carefully attending to the advertising message.

American involvement in communications was further extended by forays into mass entertainment that helped shape public manners throughout the world, particularly in the areas of music, dance, and sports. At home and abroad American jazz, social dancing, musical comedy, and athletic events established new forms of sociability. Although these changes were under way well before World War I, it was not until somewhat later that the metropolitan habits of mass spectatorship, social partying, and frequent socializing spread more generally, aided by movies, newspaper coverage, and the spirit of revolt built around (and against) Prohibition. Again, although the origins were older, a franker acceptance of sexuality could be found in some of the dress and behavior codes of the 1920s, as well as a broadening of the boundaries governing emotional expression.

As films and vaudeville and comic strips attracted their patrons, concern about the impact of mass media on traditional moral values surfaced. Simultaneously there were angry attacks on the libidinous tendencies of modern art. In fact, however, mass communications were controlled and ordered without any direct assault on existing morality, and although the authority of traditional manners loosened, Americans continued to devour etiquette manuals. It was during the 1920s and 1930s that Emily Post became synonymous with a standard of deportment, and she was not the only figure to grow wealthy and famous by offering advice on public behavior.

Through the 1940s and even into the 1950s Americans apparently accepted traditional proprieties. Photographs of crowds—on the streets, in theaters, watching parades, in ballparks—reveal men in ties, jackets, and, for a time, even in hats. According to a number of artists and critics, the spirit of "Puritanism" remained powerful. Sexually suggestive materials invited careful scrutiny by those running the publishing, film, and radio industries, and some major works of literature could not be distributed in America because of strict obscenity standards. Complaints about familiarity, lack of deference, and youthful disrespect to elders continued to be heard and were duly noted by social observers. But they merely extended themes of considerable antiquity. If anything, by nationalizing an understanding of manners, mass communications established a tighter sense of limits.

☆ ☆ ☆   Alienation and Revolt

In the America of the 1960s, 1970s, and 1980s, however, the role of manners and civility provoked still another set of controversies. An affluent America dominated world communications systems. The American tourist returned to Europe in the 1960s in greater numbers than ever before and penetrated areas new to mass travel in Asia and Africa. Earlier suggestions of informality were strengthened by colorfully clad tourists—according to tradition, sunglassed, gum-chewing, and camera-holding—wandering through historic shrines with enthusiasm punctuated by fatigue. As television programs were added to the magazines and films as cultural exports, fears of Americanization increased. American slang, fast food, clothing, and social rituals were soon duplicated on practically every continent of the world. Along with these popular modern artifacts came a perceived moral permissiveness, a reshuffling of standards of deportment that had roots throughout the world but was furthered by American politics and by mass media in particular.

These changes resulted from a series of revolts against authority and from revolutions in consciousness. Guilt about national power and wealth, doubt about foreign policy directions, and resentment of social and legal inequities were fed in America by the political assassinations of the 1960s, by riots in urban centers, by rising levels of pollution and disorder, and by challenges to almost every extant social code. Introduction of the birth control pill and improvement of contraceptive devices coincided with doubts about the legitimacy of any form of sexual censorship. The result was a sexual revolution that acted to legalize previously pornographic material and legitimated most types of sexual activity. Courtship patterns and gender manners were revamped, and sexual role models were hastily reexamined. Women demanded legal, economic, and cultural changes to acknowledge their full equality, and this had a powerful if unclear effect on daily manners.

Dress and public behavior mirrored and encouraged these transformations. Once-striking gender-related social differences now blurred. Unisex fashions became popular. Women turned to slacks and pantsuits. Many men abandoned the formality of hats and ties in favor of clothing that was more colorful, revealing, and idiosyncratic. Jewelry and cosmetic aids added to male preening. Both sexes wore jeans, now an international uniform.

Changes in deportment and consumption patterns were partly responses to energetic marketing campaigns and to life-styles popularized in growing areas of the country like California. These changes also appealed to those bent on repudiating the hypocritical garments of a despised respectability. Informality, organic naturalism, and hostility to polluting industry and to modernization in general found expression in a variety of movements; these ranged from potent religious cults to temporary audiences eager for hallucinogenic experiences at transient "happenings." Some adults adopted the new manners and dress because they seemed to be more comfortable than the old or participated in the movement as just one in a long line of fads. Youthful idols—rock performers, folk singers, environmentalists—also encouraged abandonment of traditional forms. Books like *The Greening of America* gained an immense readership in response to their attack on traditional respectability. While the larger movement was international, the large number, available leisure time, and discretionary income of American youth particularly solidified associations between the new permissiveness and the national scene.

Among evidence of changing norms was the spread of a drug culture, no longer confined to the desperately poor and alienated but reaching far across economic categories. Despite (or because of) punitive legislation, enforcement authorities could not control the lucrative market. As in the prohibition of alcohol a generation earlier, the drug trade was linked both to organized crime and to a complex set of political and economic interests. Use patterns helped heighten insecurities about casual encounters in urban areas and produced bewildering, sometimes dangerously disoriented, forms of public behavior.

Expanding drug use increased public discussion of the crime rate. Many factors explained, or seemed to explain, why crime rates had grown. Demographic analysis revealed a young population. Levels of gun ownership had increased. Changes in living and work patterns had produced new levels of vulnerability. In some areas better reporting contributed to greater awareness of crime. But for whatever reasons complaints about crime rates multiplied along with attacks on decisions protecting the rights of prisoners and the accused. Legal permissiveness, to some Americans, seemed as responsible for the problem as anything else. Foreigners had before them the picture of a violent America tolerating, however unhappily, erratic public behavior, crime, dirt, and a general deterioration of the public fabric.

This toleration seemed to be based less on a commitment to diversity as such than on a privatist ethic discouraging involvement in collective discipline. Generational tensions, racial strains, demands for personal fulfillment and sexual freedom, and extensive television viewing with its exaggeration of violence and disorder all produced changes in public interaction. Catching the larger tone, one work of historical sociology published during the 1970s was entitled *The Fall of Public Man*. (Its focus concerned Western Europe as well as America.) Interactive rituals and courtesies once taken for granted and never even classified now came to seem like miracles of human management. Interactionist theories attracted sociologists who, like the travelers of earlier centuries, could use everything from hand signals to yawns as evidence for their arguments.

The apparent corruption of American manners by violence, uncertainty, and a permissive ethic was counterbalanced, however, by other qualities. Trends were not destinies; in many parts of the country the changes seemed small. Foreigners reported that American friendliness and relaxed informality were still impressive. Social voluntarism and sympathy for those in need continued at high levels. Public meetings and political rallies, even amid sectarian bitterness, were orderly and peaceful, with some major exceptions like the 1968 Democratic National Convention. American sports crowds were proverbially more restrained than foreign counterparts. Most American audiences were polite to performers. If anything, spectatorship behavior had improved considerably since the boisterousness of nineteenth-century theater audiences had erupted into mass violence. American tourists, more numerous, diverse, and sophisticated, shed some of the stereotypes that had hounded them since the first era of mass travel. Resurgent traditionalism surfaced in college campus life and in calls for greater authority over daily conduct. Advice columns, however liberalized, still flourished, while the moralizings of television soap operas and situation comedies were often as traditionally sentimental as the most avid nineteenth-century novel reader might wish.

There were also major gains in civility during these years, and transformations of attitude, particularly in the late 1980s. Law and custom were combining to challenge many discriminatory and demeaning social practices. During the 1960s, 1970s, and 1980s, the last vestiges of overt racial discrimination in public places were assailed, along with exclusionary rules for private clubs and associations. During the same period women demanded, more effectively, an end to their unequal treatment. Amid a burgeoning litigiousness that kept legions of lawyers busy, successful attacks were launched on public smoking and on physical arrangements that restricted access for the handicapped. Some of these issues reflected a broadening sense of civil rights and civic responsibilities; others, anxieties about health and sensitivity to disabilities. For whatever reasons, their combined impact helped shape new standards for ordinary behavior and proposed new definitions of rudeness and incivility. Manners and political self-consciousness remained closely tied. If *The Greening of America* reflected the radical mood of the early seventies, Allan Bloom's *The Closing of the American Mind* caught the more conservative temper of the late eighties. Its linkage between intellectual decline and moral permissiveness proved immensely popular.

☆ ☆ ☆ Conclusion

Do national systems of manners still exist? After all, art, entertainment, news, and travel have become internationalized in much of the world. Encounters on streets or highways, at airports or supermarkets, in factories or cinemas or schools or universities, may reflect the logic of the specific institution rather than the national environment. Patterns of contemporary social interaction can be said to mirror the shape of postindustrial society and technology, not simply territorial boundaries.

Nonetheless, interactive rituals do seem to have differing textures; this may be one thing that continues to support international tourism. In the United States the legacies of democratic republicanism, cultural colonialism, ethnic pluralism, and hostility to governmental intervention as well as the power of myths and stereotypes built around the frontier experience and the code of the West are still important. Our ability to map social rituals has been sharpened by the work of semiologists and anthropologists. They propose patterns that differentiate even neighboring societies like Canada and the United States. The persistence of such distinctions may seem both surprising and anachronistic, but it suggests how valuable the ethnologic instincts of the older travel literature remain.

Creating a final balance sheet is difficult. For some, the crudity, boisterousness, and informality of American manners have grown directly out of unsolved problems. For others, the directness and egalitarianism of many of our social forms demonstrate national strengths. Any evaluation of manners, today as in the past, reflects sociopolitical preferences as well as judgments. One effect of democracy, Tocqueville suggested, was "not exactly to give men any particular manners, but to prevent them from having manners at all." In other words, to permit the form and substance of human actions to become identical—"and if the great picture of human life is less embellished, it is more true." Embellishments and social differentiations have multiplied since Tocqueville's day, but many Americans still like to believe in his picture. This aspiration demonstrates as clearly as anything else the persistence of the old republican dreams.

FURTHER READING

For some time the history of American manners has been dominated by semipopular accounts. These include Esther Aresty, *The Best Behavior* (New York, 1970); Gerald Carson, *The Polite Americans* (New York, 1966); and Dixon Wecter, *The Saga of American Society* (New York, 1937). More recently, scholars have begun to concern themselves with the social and psychological issues involved in the history of civility, some of them inspired by Norbert Elias, *The Civilizing Process: The History of Manners* (New York, 1978). Among the more original treatments are Karen Halttunen, *Confidence Men and Painted Women* (New Haven, Conn., 1982), and John F. Kasson, *Rudeness and Civility: Manners in Nineteenth-Century Urban America* (New York, 1990). The burgeoning interest in women's and gender studies has also stimulated volumes of interest to students of American manners. Among them Beth L. Bailey, *From Front Porch to Back Seat: Courtship in Twentieth-Century America* (Baltimore, 1988), and Mary P. Ryan, *Women in Public: Between Banners and Ballets, 1825–1880* (Baltimore, 1990), deserve special attention.

Foreign commentaries are central to the study of national manners; fortunately, many have been extensively read and reprinted. Among the more useful anthologies and secondary studies are John Graham Brooks, *As Others See Us: A Study of Progress in the United States* (New York, 1908); Max Berger, *The British Traveller in America, 1836–1860* (New York, 1943); Henry Steele Commager, ed., *America in Perspective: The United States through Foreign Eyes* (New York, 1947); Peter Conrad, *Imagining America* (New York, 1980); Oscar Handlin, ed., *This Was America* (Cambridge, Mass., 1941); George Harmon Knoles, *The Jazz Age Revisited: British Criticism of American Civilization during the 1920s* (Stanford, Calif., 1955); Frank Monoghan, *French Travellers in the United States, 1765–1932* (New York, 1933); and Richard L. Rapson, *Britons View America: Travel Commentary, 1860–1935* (Seattle, 1971). Some aspects of the Americanization of European mores are covered in C. W. E. Bigsby, ed., *SuperCulture: American Popular Culture and Europe* (Bowling Green, Ohio, 1975).

Among contemporary works focusing attention on the complexity and cultural functions of interactive rituals in modern society are Erving Goffman, *The Presentation of Self in Everyday Life* (Garden City, N.Y., 1959); Edward Hall, *The Hidden Dimension* (Garden City, N.Y., 1969); Lyn H. Lofland, *A World of Strangers* (New York, 1973); and Richard Sennett, *The Fall of Public Man* (New York, 1977). For the crucial role of mass communication, see Daniel J. Czitrom, *Media and the American Mind: From Morse to McLuhan* (Chapel Hill, N.C., 1982); Erik Barnouw, *A History of Broadcasting in the United States*, 3 vols. (New York, 1966–70); and Lary May, *Screening out the Past: The Birth of Mass Culture and the Motion Picture Industry, 1896–1929* (New York, 1980). Important developments in consumption, recreation, entertainment, and aesthetics and their relationships with manners are treated in Elaine S. Abelson, *When Ladies Go A-Thieving: Middle-Class Shoplifters in the Victorian Department Store* (New York, 1989); Elizabeth Kendall, *Where She Danced* (New York, 1979); Lewis A. Erenberg, *Steppin' Out: New York Nightlife and the Transformation of American Culture, 1890–1930* (Westport, Conn., 1981); and Galen Cranz, *The Politics of Park Design: A History of Urban Parks in America* (Cambridge, Mass., 1982).

8 ☆ The

☆ Artlessness

☆ of American

☆ Culture

☆ Dickran Tashjian

"My Dear Portia," John Adams wrote to Abigail in 1780, "I could fill Volumes with Descriptions of Temples and Palaces, Paintings, Sculptures, Tapestry, Porcelains . . . if I could have time. But I could not do this without neglecting my duty. . . . I must study Politicks and War that my sons may have liberty to study Mathematicks and Philosophy, Geography, natural History, Naval Architectures, navigation, Commerce and Agriculture, in order to give their Children a right to study Painting, Poetry, Musick, Architecture, Statuary, Tapestry and Porcelaine."

Adams wrote from Paris, where he was serving as congressional envoy amid the luxuries of Versailles. Faced in 1780 with the crises of an ongoing revolution, he advocated deferred gratification not only for himself but for his progeny. His appreciation for the arts was superseded by the need to exercise practical skills and knowledge to negotiate the affairs of the world. Adams was nothing if not cautious in suggesting that his grandchildren might *study* painting. He did not go so far as to wish that they become artists. At best he lent the arts the aura of an academic project, fit subject for study two generations into the future.

Adams was, however, sufficiently distracted to commission a portrait by John Singleton Copley, a fellow Bostonian who had made his way to London in 1774, when Great Britain and her colonies were on the brink of armed hostilities. For one hundred guineas in 1783 the painter depicted a full-length, life-sized Adams, elegantly clothed in wig, waistcoat, and breeches, standing on the stage of the world, symbolized by curtain and globe: republican virtues ascendant.

Copley had been preceded to London by Benjamin West, an older colleague from Philadelphia, who would eventually become president of the British Royal Academy of Arts in 1790. Copley himself had gained membership upon painting *Watson and the Shark*, commissioned in 1778 by a London merchant who had lost his leg to a shark in the harbor of Havana some thirty years before. Copley's dramatically charged scene enlarged the prestigious category of history painting to include the possibility of individual biography. West, of course, had led the way with his controversial *Death of Wolfe* in 1770, when he updated history painting by selecting an international event from the relatively recent past. King George himself was eventually persuaded of West's view that contemporary heroes might be celebrated in their own garb (rather than Roman togas), as in West's depiction of General Wolfe's death during the British campaign against the French in Quebec.

☆ ☆ ☆ In the Shadow of Europe

With the European success of West and Copley, Adams's prospects for an American art seemed to be confirmed. The two painters had deeply felt the limitations of painting in the provinces. American art had to be pursued in London, then, if it was to exist and prove successful. Other vocations took priority in the colonies. Nearly a century later, Americans were still going to London and Paris. Henry James, writing his novel *The American* in Paris in 1876, followed an established pattern. His American protagonist, Christopher Newman (the symbolism of his name cannot be ignored), is a self-made businessman who in a moment of insight while riding in a hansom cab through Central Park had decided to shuck his commercial life and seek the finer things in Europe. The reader meets him in the opening scene of the novel stretched out on a divan in the main hall of the Louvre, suffering, like every other American on the Grand Tour since, from an "aesthetic headache," having exhausted his Baedeker. For the moment he is bemused by a pretty young copyist, who seems preferable both to the surrounding paintings and to her own pale imitations. If not art, then Newman seeks at least the pretext of art in the American quest of "finer things."

In 1900 Henry Adams, the great-grandson of John and Abigail, visited the international Paris Exposition, the world's fair that eclipsed all other fairs dating back to the Great Exhibition of 1851 at the Crystal Palace in London. Following two presidents in the family and an ambassador to England, Adams thought of himself as something of a failure. He had become a mere professor of history at Harvard. Despite his nostalgia for the past, he was still eager for new knowledge and sought it, he tells us in his *Education of Henry Adams*, among the bewildering array of exhibitions at the fair. He finally solicited the aid of Samuel Langley, a scientist and inventor from the Smithsonian, who knew enough to lead his friend away from the art exhibitions and into the Great Hall of Machines. Standing before the huge dynamos, Adams remained confused. Even Langley, the technocrat-in-the-know, could not explain the mysterious forces at work. For Adams the dynamos became "occult mechanisms," which in their power were akin to the forces of the Virgin that had motivated the construction of Mont-Saint-Michel and Chartres during the Middle Ages. The spiritual energy of the Virgin and the sexual energy of the pagan Venus before her were dissipated or suppressed in American art, which, "like the American language and American education," Adams claimed, "was as far as possible sexless."

Adams argued that even the most prominent American sculptor of his day, Augustus Saint-Gaudens, could not draw upon a comparable energy for his work. While religious feeling, so potent in the past, had been narrowed into a mere "channel of taste," Saint-Gaudens ignored the new force of the dynamo in favor of the horse as a symbol of power. Thus vitiated or cast behind the times, contemporary American art was caught in an impasse, for whatever the impending dominance of the machine, Adams believed that "all the steam in the world could not, like the Virgin, build Chartres." Americans were left with a genteel art that, like Henry Oliver Walker's *Eros et Musa* (1903), suppressed sexual feeling in Latin platitudes and neoclassical stereotypes. Knowledge itself was relegated to a platonic realm inhabited by toga-clad women, as in *The Light of Learning* (1913) by the leading American academician, Kenyon Cox.

Adams's failure to gain from American art an education for the twentieth century was hardly rectified by subsequent developments. In 1913 an international exhibition held in New York City at the Sixty-Ninth Regiment Armory (the now-celebrated "Armory Show") revealed the gap between academic American artists and French avant-garde painting, which had been developing for the previous fifty years. With the onslaught of World War I, some of the European avant-gardists began to migrate to the United States. In 1915 painter Francis Picabia arrived in New York en route to Cuba on a military mission to purchase molasses for the French government. Manhattan became a convenient layover for the duration of the war. Picabia was soon followed by his friend Marcel Duchamp, who had been exempted from the military because of a heart condition. The two painters joined forces with American artists who were attracted to modern art. In 1917 Duchamp helped organize an exhibition of modern art predicated upon the European practice of "independent" exhibitions that showed the work of artists rejected by the state-supported academies. According to the ground rules, any artist would be allowed to exhibit upon payment of a seven-dollar entry fee. There was to be no jury to select the work and thus impose its taste upon the exhibition.

Duchamp decided to test the principles of the organizing committee by submitting to the exhibition a porcelain urinal entitled *Fountain* under the signature of a pseudonymous "R[ichard] Mutt," reputedly a well-known Manhattan plumber. The organizing committee was thrown into an uproar and rejected this *Fountain*. Duchamp immediately resigned from the committee in disgust and issued a brief manifesto in defense of his gesture. He claimed that the urinal was art because an artist had selected the artifact in question. He also overrode objections that the urinal was somehow immoral or obscene. "It is a fixture that you see every day in plumbers' show windows." He concluded that "the only works of art America has given are her plumbing and her bridges."

☆ ☆ ☆ Frontier Necessities

With Duchamp's observation we seem to have returned full circle to John Adams. How can we account for the apparent lack of art in American culture? Two reasons are conventionally offered for this state of affairs. Both can be found in Adams. First, his own argument for deferred gratification placed priority upon a need for the practical arts in a society that had not yet securely established itself. This line of reasoning can be called the *functionalist argument*. Its most succinct statement was articulated in an economic tract published in Boston in 1719: "The *Plow-Man* that raiseth Grain, is more serviceable to Mankind, than the *Painter* who draws only to please the Eye. The *hungry* Man would count fine Pictures but a mean Entertainment. . . . The *Carpenter* who builds a good *House* to defend us from Wind and Weather, is more serviceable than the curious *Carver*, who employs his Art to please the Fancy."

No one would want to deny the harsh conditions facing the early settlers as they established a beachhead first along the coastal areas and then inland as they moved west. An unknown terrain, an increasingly hostile and little-understood native population, a primitive technology, and disease meant that the Europeans had to struggle for survival in the New World. Art could not take priority under such conditions. Yet it is equally clear that the colonists did not banish art completely from their consciousness. Even that early economic tract conceded that a priority for the practical "condemns not Painting or Carving, but only shows, that what is more substantially serviceable to Mankind, is much preferrable to what is less necessary." Moreover, necessity was not narrowly defined: "The studying of *Languages, Arts, Sciences, Divinity, Physick*, &c. and the employing the skill or knowledge obtained by such Study, may greatly promote the *Glory of God*, the *Persons own benefit*, and the good of those he is concerned with."

These qualifications help explain what would otherwise be cultural anomalies. Obviously, by the mid-eighteenth century, urban areas at the very least had established a sufficiently stable economic base to support a number of portrait painters, however tenuously. Both Copley and West were self-taught and possessed sufficient skill to go on to achieve success in Europe. And Adams himself was willing to indulge his wistful yearning for European art by having his own portrait painted in the midst of international crisis. The functionalist argument will go only so far, and then it needs to be expanded to consider the function that art itself plays in a society. At the very least, painting served the wealthy and the well-to-do, precisely that sector of society that many of the founding fathers sought to avoid in the revulsion of the New World toward the decadence of a European aristocracy. As we shall see, art had to conform to republican virtues in order to gain a congenial reception in the New World.

☆ ☆ ☆ The Puritan Legacy

A second reason conventionally offered for the paucity of art in America is based as much in the tone of Adams's admonishments to Abigail as in the very notion of deferred gratification. Adams's rectitude and sense of duty derived from a deep-seated Puritanism. The New England Puritans supposedly proscribed the arts when they strictly espoused the Second Commandment, which prohibits the worship of false idols. The iconoclasm of the Puritans, we have been told time and again, kept art out of New England and—in combination with practical imperatives—almost entirely out of American culture long after Puritanism itself had died.

The notion of Puritan iconoclasm is pernicious, partly because of our stereotypical view of the Puritans, dating back to the nineteenth century. Consider, for example, the grim portrait of the Puritans limned by Nathaniel Hawthorne in his novel *The Scarlet Letter* (1850). Despite Hester Prynne's sin of adultery, we find her vitality and courage far preferable to the repressive authorities of seventeenth-century Boston relentlessly portrayed by Hawthorne. Such stereotypes were renewed as late as the 1920s, when the Puritans were again blamed for the shortcomings of our society. Granting those exaggerations, we still must acknowledge that the Puritans in seventeenth-century England *did* attempt to purify the Anglican church of what they considered Roman Catholic heresies. The eradication of religious art reached its peak during the civil war of the 1640s in England.

Yet it is difficult to conceive of a culture barren of art. Puritan culture is no exception. When we turn to early New England, where the Puritans had the opportunity to build a model Christian commonwealth based on their own precepts, we discover a society that still enjoyed the arts. There were portrait painters (called limners) who eked out a living part-time alongside a variety of craftspersons engaged in needlework, silversmithing, cabinetmaking, and printing. Nor can we dismiss the verbal arts of sermonizing and poetry. Ministers often preached twice-weekly, and elegies were commonly recited at funerals. Finally, there was the proliferation of gravestones, often with elaborate visual designs, throughout New England during the seventeenth and eighteenth centuries.

Even a cursory glance at the material culture of early New England reveals a rich and vital array of the visual arts. Their existence does not indicate a discrepancy between the cultural ideal of iconoclasm and actual practice. A consistency can be found through a closer understanding of the way in which the Puritans chose to interpret the Second Commandment. Both Samuel Mather (uncle of the more famous Cotton) and Samuel Willard, Puritan divines of late seventeenth-century Boston, drew the same conclusion: the Second Commandment, with its prohibition of graven images, applied strictly to the ecclesiastical realm, whereas visual imagery, though not countenanced with great enthusiasm, was permissible in the civil realm. The distinction was consonant with the Puritans' strict though subtle division between church and state. Because Calvinist theology claimed that the spiritual status of a deceased person was predetermined, funerals belonged outside ecclesiastical authority. Therefore gravestones might be carved with visual designs dramatizing death and resurrection, assuaging the grief of the survivors. In fact, most visual imagery throughout New England fell within the civil realm. There were no sanctions against writing poetry, limning portraits, or decorating chests and other domestic articles. The only restrictions were those imposed by community taste and individual conscience. Thus a large common pool of images was available to men and women engaged in the crafts.

By appreciating how the Puritans themselves limited their interpretation of the Second Commandment, American art historians have come to recognize a visual art in New England where little or none was previously seen. At the same time, the application of the Second Commandment within the Puritan church still had important repercussions in restraining the development of

American art. The Protestant sects (unlike the Roman Catholic church) offered little or no support for the visual arts. American painters lost the patronage of what had been in Europe a major source of institutional aid. Thus from the very beginning American artists were constrained to assume the role of entrepreneur in an economy defined by competitive capitalism. As a consequence the distinction between fine art and commerce broke down. American artists not only had to sell their paintings but also had to take other jobs in order to pursue their vocation. In this century, for example, Arthur G. Dove, Marsden Hartley, and Arshile Gorky lived in extreme poverty because they wanted to paint full-time and yet could not sell their work because of their commitment to modern art, which was unpopular for so long with the American public.

Others became Sunday painters or took up their art only in old age after they retired from other work. This was the case among many recently discovered elderly black artists who had been unable to devote themselves completely to painting because of adverse economic circumstances. African Americans faced the added obstacle of racism, which prevented many from entering the art network. Poverty had a direct impact upon the work of both black and white artists. Black artists were constrained to use whatever material was available to them, often creating art out of junk. Gorky was similarly restricted. During the Great Depression he turned to drawing because he could not afford canvas and paint. Others suffered not only the privations of inadequate resources but also the inaccessibility of a congenial working environment. Hartley, for example, managed to paint in Europe for short periods of time only because of the efforts of Alfred Stieglitz, the photographer who championed modern art in America. Hartley was eventually forced into a penurious and lonely existence in his native state of Maine, where he turned to seascapes. The experiences of most American artists belie the charming and picturesque bohemian life fantasized during the nineteenth century.

Faced with these hardships, artists needed to find jobs, preferably in related fields. Winslow Homer began as an illustrator for *Harper's Magazine*. His illustrations of genteel rural vignettes carried over to genre paintings of similar subjects. Not until he spent some time along the rugged coast of Tynemouth, England, and then returned to Maine did he develop his powerful images of men struggling stoically in nature. Many of the painters who came together after the turn of the century in what became known as the Ashcan school (because of their concentration upon the urban scene) initially worked for newspapers in Philadelphia as illustrators of daily events. Other painters, like Charles Sheeler, became professional photographers. In 1927 he was commissioned to photograph the Ford River Rouge Plant in Michigan. Likewise,

Man Ray became a fashion photographer in Paris as a way of supporting his avant-garde experiments. Later, Andy Warhol exploited advertising images largely because of his involvement in commercial art. None of these painters was able to compartmentalize his commercial activities. Their art-for-pay had a fundamental impact on what we like to think of as their more "serious" work.

The absence of the church as a patron of art was accompanied by a lack of government support for artists. This policy was consistent with the prevailing belief in laissez-faire economics. Only with the severe crisis of the Great Depression did the Roosevelt administration offer limited aid to impoverished artists through the federal agency of the Works Progress Administration. Dating back to the early nineteenth century, artists were constrained to seek mutual aid through voluntary associations. Some, like the Pennsylvania Academy of Fine Arts, were locally based, while others, like the National Academy of Design, sought a larger scope. These organizations were predicated upon the European model of the academy but without prestigious state support, as in the instance of the French Ecole des Beaux-Arts. As a consequence, American academies were not so entrenched as those in Europe. A single dissident exhibition such as the 1913 Armory Show was able to undermine the cultural hegemony of American academic artists.

Even so, American academies were not without power, especially in the late nineteenth century, when they became guardians of public morality. This role had its sources in the combined forces of Puritanism and the American Revolution. Moral behavior, predicated upon Christian ethics, was required of the colonial community inasmuch as such behavior was construed as a sign of one's standing among the spiritually elect. Ministers understood their role to be the conscience of the community and logically extended it to the realm of art. The American Revolution drew upon such attitudes in its appeal to universal laws. A republic rested upon the moral character of its people, not upon the mere artifices of government. "Ask the plowman a moral question," Jefferson claimed, "and he will answer it as well as the professor."

This moral element can be seen in American painting from its beginnings down through the twentieth century—from the didacticism of seventeenth-century *memento mori* portraiture to the pietistic fervor of the abstract expressionists, immolating themselves on the altar of art. Nowhere, however, was this moral quality more manifest than in the late nineteenth-century academy. As director of the Pennsylvania Academy of Fine Arts, Thomas Eakins revamped the curriculum to stress the study of the human figure instead of the conventional antique cast. His emphasis upon correct anatomy led not only to mixed classes in the nude but to nude models completely uncovered. His pedagogy caused scandal among the trustees, who gained his resignation in 1886. This episode underscores the power of the academy in its widest range. As an academic instructor, Eakins sought to have a direct impact upon the kind of art his students should undertake. While he cast his naturalistic vision as a moral imperative, he in turn ironically failed to live up to the moral expectations of the trustees. Conflict was inevitable. Those who controlled the institution exercised their power in forcing Eakins to resign.

☆ ☆ ☆ Uniquely American

The hegemony of the American academy was not broken until American artists were attracted to the dissident forces of avant-garde art emanating from Europe. Duchamp was one of the most important influences upon American artists partly because he was close at hand but mostly because of the force of his ideas. If the Frenchman with his *Fountain* came full circle to Adams, he did so ironically and by a different route. Whereas Adams proceeded on culturally defined distinctions between practical and "fine" arts— distinctions that would be promulgated by the British Royal Academy of Arts—Duchamp obliterated such categories with his urinal. He implied that Americans with their commitment to technology were creating art all along but did not know it. And while he would have agreed with Henry Adams's assessment of the insipid character of American art, he was unawed by machine technology and willing to exploit its ironic possibilities.

We have been heir to those aesthetic distinctions that arose in the eighteenth century with the development of the visual artist's professional status out of a medieval guild tradition. Hence we have accepted distinctions between "fine" art and craft, "high" and "low" art, "fine" art and commercial art—the sort of distinctions that in Copley's day elevated history painting above portraiture (which, with its essential client-painter relationship, had the taint of commercialism). Duchamp's *Fountain* radically called such distinctions into question. At the time, the selection of a urinal for an art exhibition was considered scandalous by conservative American artists. Yet Duchamp's gesture was not entirely destructive, for it suggested the possibility that mass-produced objects, products of machine technology, might possess an aesthetic dimension even though such objects had been overlooked as "art." As a consequence, Duchamp's observation about American bridges and plumbing can be construed less as an indictment of American art than a validation of an entire realm of artifacts for their aesthetic qualities previously ignored.

Following Duchamp, then, distinctions between the categories of art, tech-

Fig. 8.1. John Singleton Copley (1738–1815). Portrait of John Adams. 1783. Oil on canvas; 93¾" × 58". (Courtesy the Harvard University Portrait Collection, Cambridge, Mass. Bequest of Ward Nicholas Boylston, 1828.)

Fig. 8.2. John Singleton Copley (1738–1815). Watson and the Shark. *1778. Oil on canvas; 71¾" × 90½". (National Gallery of Art, Washington, D.C. Ferdinand Lammot Belin Fund.)*

Fig. 8.3. Benjamin West (1738–1820). The Death of General Wolfe. *1770. Oil on canvas; 60" × 83⅓". (The National Gallery of Canada, Ottawa. Gift of the Duke of Westminster, 1918.)*

Fig. 8.4. Winslow Homer (1836–1910). Huntsman and Dogs. *1891. Oil on canvas; 28" × 48". (Philadelphia Museum of Art.)*

Fig. 8.5. Lagarde, after Winslow Homer (1836–1910). Raid on a Sand-Swallow Colony—"How Many Eggs?" *Wood-block engraving; 13⅓" × 8⁹⁄₁₀". (National Gallery of Art, Washington, D.C. Print Purchase Fund; Rosenwald Collection.)*

Fig. 8.7. Thomas Eakins (1844–1916). The Agnew Clinic. *1889. Oil on canvas; 74½" × 130½". (University of Pennsylvania School of Medicine, Philadelphia.)*

Fig. 8.8. John Marin (1870–1953). Lower Manhattan (Composing Derived from Top of Woolworth). *1922. Watercolor and charcoal with paper cutout attached with thread on paper; 21⅝" × 26⅞". (Collection of the Museum of Modern Art, New York City. Acquired through the Lillie P. Bliss Bequest.)*

◀

Fig. 8.6. Andy Warhol (1930–87). Campbell's Soup. *1965. Oil silk-screened on canvas; 36⅛" × 24". (Collection of the Museum of Modern Art, New York City. Philip Johnson Fund.)*

Fig. 8.9. Joseph Stella (1877–1946). Brooklyn Bridge. 1917–18. Oil on canvas; 84" × 76". (Yale University Art Gallery, New Haven, Conn. Gift of Collection Société Anonyme.)

Fig. 8.10. Thomas Hart Benton (1889–1975). Cradling Wheat. 1938. Tempera and oil on board; 31" × 38". (The Saint Louis Art Museum, St. Louis, Mo. Museum Purchase.)

Fig. 8.11. Asher B. Durand (1796–1886). Kindred Spirits. *1849. Oil on canvas; 44⅐" × 36¼". (Collection of the New York Public Library, New York City. Astor, Lenox, and Tilden Foundations.)*

Fig. 8.12. David Butler (1898–). Windmill with Man Riding Flying Elephants. *1975. Sculpture; painted tin, wood, and plastic; 47" × 30". (New Orleans Museum of Art. Gift of the artist, Patterson, La.)*

Fig. 8.13. Alfred Stieglitz (1864–1944). The Hand of Man. *1902. Photogravure.
(The Metropolitan Museum of Art, New York City. The Alfred Stieglitz Collection,
1949.)*

▶

*Fig. 8.14. The Shakers. Ladder-back chair suspended from a pinrail. Ca. 18
(Courtesy Shakertown at Pleasant Hill, Harrodsburg, Ky.)*

Fig. 8.15. Charles Demuth (1883–1935). Machinery. *1920. Tempera and pencil on cardboard; 24″ × 19⅞″. (The Metropolitan Museum of Art, New York City. The Alfred Stieglitz Collection, 1949.)*

Fig. 8.16. Charles Sheeler (1883–1965). Untitled (factory slag buggy). 1927. Silver gelatin print; 9½″ × 7½″. (Courtesy the Art Institute of Chicago. Julien Levy Collection. Photograph © 1987 The Art Institute of Chicago. All rights reserved.)

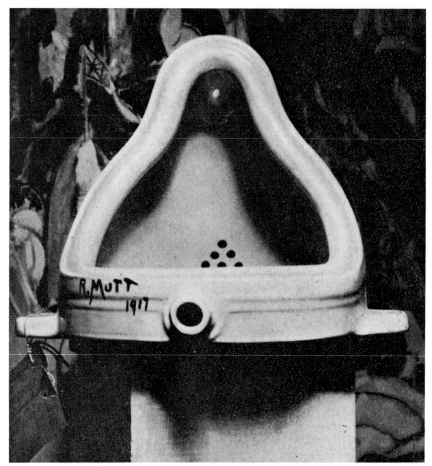

Fig. 8.17. Marcel Duchamp (1887–1968). Fountain. *Reproduced in* The Blind Man, *no. 2 (May 1917). Photograph by Alfred Stieglitz. (Philadelphia Museum of Art. Arensberg Archives.)*

*Fig. 8.18. Henry Oliver Walker (1843–1929). Eros et Musa. 1903. Oil on canvas;
72¼" × 54⅛". (National Museum of American Art, Smithsonian Institution,
Washington, D.C. Gift of William T. Evans.)*

Fig. 8.19. Gravestone of John Foster, Dorchester, Mass. 1861.
(Courtesy American Antiquarian Society, Worcester, Mass.)

nology, and craft have become blurred, and thus we are better able to appreciate vernacular developments in the arts that have affected American painting. "Form follows function"—a dictum of the nineteenth-century sculptor Horatio Greenough—was independently heeded by the Shakers, a religious offshoot of radical Quaker sects in England. The Shakers arrived in the colonies on the eve of the Revolution and established their own communities separate from the corruption of the world. While the most notorious practice of the group involved celibacy, the Shakers were also known for their fine craftsmanship, predicated upon a belief that functionalism manifests spiritual perfection. The simplicity of Shaker design was acknowledged in the 1920s as part of a newfound appreciation for folk art that accompanied a quest for things uniquely American. Charles Sheeler, for example, collected Shaker furniture and developed Shaker motifs in his own painting.

Along with the discovery of folk craft, American painters became fascinated with machine technology, which in its advanced stage in America seemed to distinguish the New World from the Old. Duchamp's ironic play with machines during his stay in New York had been anticipated by John Marin, who as early as 1911 had begun to depict the vital forces of the city in his urban landscapes. Marin, of course, had been supported by Stieglitz, who even before the turn of the century had taken photographs of New York and later would record the various building stages of skyscrapers. Joseph Stella considered the Brooklyn Bridge his favorite subject, and Charles Sheeler explored industrial scenes while Charles Demuth, a friend of Duchamp, painted witty and ironic images of factories and machines. Industrialization and the rise of the skyscraper were perceived as the quintessence of the modern and hence became appropriate subjects for artists interested in the formal innovations of modern painting.

The rise of modernism did not signal the emergence of a uniquely American art in the early twentieth century. If the American academies were simply versions of their European counterparts, modern art had its roots in nineteenth-century French painting. In the 1930s Thomas Hart Benton, with the tacit approval of Grant Wood, attacked Stieglitz for his espousal of a "foreign" modernism and called instead for the development of a regionalism untainted by European "decadence." Yet it is difficult to understand how the exchange of a beret and a cape for a straw hat and coveralls transforms a painter into a truly American original. Nor would cultural uniqueness be derived from exotic subjects alone. While the Hudson River school of landscape painters early in the nineteenth century might be considered the first native group of American painters, their scenes were depicted through a European lens. Landscapes were selected and shaped according to their picturesque or sublime qualities—

visual models derived from a European aesthetic. Nor is uniqueness to be found in form devoid of embellishment. The most radical stripping away of European artifice was achieved by Duchamp in his presentation of the thing itself, a "ready-made" artifact.

Has American art, then, been simply an appendage of Western European culture? Can no claims be made for a uniquely *American* art? As we have seen, the uniqueness of American art has little to do with content or form, even though some American painters—and scholars—have tried to make such claims. The dynamics of American art have hinged upon the tensions between the assertion of European cultural hegemony and the possibilities of an indigenous art with its own tradition. Such arguments are important for the things they tell us concerning what Americans wanted to believe about themselves. In declaring the artlessness of their culture Americans were ambiguously setting themselves apart from Europe. Virtue was equated with simplicity, and plainness thrust against the artful decadence of Europe. But the claim could just as easily be a complaint, a recognition of a defect that required the emulation of Europe for its correction. Finally, artlessness became a way of developing one's own art. A kind of cultural judo was at work in an attempt to gain leverage on European dominance.

These cultural attitudes would have a lasting imprint upon the creation of American art. The American poet William Carlos Williams, who numbered many visual artists among his friends, hit upon the crux of the matter. In an essay entitled "The American Background," written in honor of Stieglitz in 1934, Williams discerned an American culture split between a drive for what the New World had to offer and a reactive fear that sent Americans back to European culture. As an avant-garde poet, Williams preferred the new, but he acknowledged that the new was not to be inevitably associated with America. He was aware of a more profound impulse characterizing American artists. At their best, they were moved by a deep skepticism of intervening authority. Williams simply echoed the credo of an earlier poet, Ralph Waldo Emerson. "We will walk on our own feet; we will work with our own hands; we will speak our own minds."

Emerson's declaration of cultural independence would work not by fiat but through the conviction of an underlying belief in democratic equality and the extension of self-reliance to the arts. On those grounds West and Copley were able to break the conventions of history painting even while in the heart of the academy; Thomas Cole sought the picturesque and the sublime on this continent rather than in Europe and so spearheaded the Hudson River school; Eakins refused to compromise the integrity of his naturalism; Stieglitz and his painters synthesized European modernism with the American scene against the scorn of a conservative American public. Academic or avant-garde, what Williams called painting "in the American grain" would be deeply informed by the same values that drove the colonies to declare themselves a new nation in the New World.

FURTHER READING

An account of American art must begin with Oliver Larkin, *Art and Life in America* (New York, 1964), which is still the best general survey that connects American art to broad cultural trends. See also Joshua C. Taylor, *America as Art* (Washington, D.C., 1976), which clusters paintings around cultural themes of different periods. With the specialization of art history, two further surveys are essential: Barbara Novak, *American Painting of the Nineteenth Century* (New York, 1969), and Barbara Rose, *American Art since 1900* (New York, 1968). These works provide a good point of departure for the more specialized studies of American art and culture indicated below.

For an account of early American limners, see Alan Burroughs, *Limners and Likenesses* (Cambridge, Mass., 1936). Alfred Frankenstein places John Singleton Copley in his social and cultural milieu in *The World of Copley, 1738–1815* (New York, 1970). James Flexner, *America's Old Masters* (New York, 1967), studies Copley, West, Peale, and Stuart. Jules Prown, *John Singleton Copley*, vols. 1 and 2 (Cambridge, Mass., 1966), reveals in superb depth this colonial painter's struggles and his work.

For an extensive survey of the interrelationships of the arts and crafts of early New England, see *New England Begins*, vols. 1–3 (Boston, 1982). For American art and the Revolution, see *American Art: 1750–1800, Towards Independence* (Boston, 1976). For studies of New England gravestones, see Harriette Merrifield Forbes, *Gravestones of Early New England: And the Men Who Made Them, 1653–1800* (New York, 1967), and Allan I. Ludwig, *Graven Images: New England Stonecarving and Its Symbols, 1650–1815* (Middletown, Conn., 1966). In *Memorials for Children of Change: The Art of Early New England Stonecarving* (Middletown, Conn., 1974), Dickran Tashjian and Ann Tashjian discuss in detail the issues of functionalism and Puritan iconoclasm. These and other issues pertaining to nineteenth-century American culture are taken up by Neil Harris, *The Artist in American Society: The Formative Years, 1790–1860* (New York, 1966).

For a view of American art and industrialization, with a stress upon the vernacular, see John Kouwenhoven, *The Arts in Modern American Civilization* (New York, 1967). See also Miles Orvell, *The Real Thing: Imitation and Authenticity in American Culture, 1880–1940* (Chapel Hill, N.C., 1989), and Richard Wilson, Dianne Pilgrim, and Dickran Tashjian, *The Machine Age in America, 1918–1941* (New

174 ☆ DICKRAN TASHJIAN

York, 1986). Vernacular art, variously and inadequately referred to as "folk" or "primitive," has often been thought to be the locus of American values. For example: Jean Lipman and Alice Winchester, *The Flowering of American Folk Art, 1776–1876* (New York, 1974); Lipman and Tom Armstrong, eds., *American Folk Painters of Three Centuries* (New York, 1980); and Sidney Janis, *They Taught Themselves* (New York, 1942). John Vlach, *Plain Painters: Making Sense of American Folk Art* (Washington, D.C., 1988), offers an alternative way to conceptualize folk art.

Scholarship on the Shakers is extensive. One might best begin with Edward Deming Andrews, *The People Called Shakers* (New York, 1963), then proceed to Andrews and Faith Andrews, *Visions of the Heavenly Sphere: A Study in Shaker Religious Art* (Charlottesville, Va., 1969), and their *Work and Worship: The Economic Order of the Shakers* (Greenwich, Conn., 1974). A fascinating study of black artists on the fringes of the art world is Jane Livingston and John Beardsley, *Black Folk Art in America, 1930–1980* (Jackson, Miss., 1982). For a survey of African American artists, see David C. Driskell, *Two Centuries of Black American Art* (New York, 1976). A sense of the process involved for entry into the American art network can be gained from Cynthia Jaffee McCabe, *The Golden Door: Artist-Immigrants of America, 1876–1976* (Washington, D.C., 1976).

The dominant art network in nineteenth-century America is discussed by Lois Marie Fink and Joshua C. Taylor, *Academy: The Academic Tradition in American Art* (Washington, D.C., 1975). For a study of the Hudson River school and the response of American painters generally to the natural environment, see James Flexner, *That Wilder Image* (New York, 1962). John Wilmerding, *American Light: The Luminist Movement, 1850–1875* (New York, 1980), presents artists who defined themselves and their work in response to American light and atmosphere. Another work that makes similar claims for an American art but in terms of physical space is John W. McCoubrey, *The American Tradition in Painting* (New York, 1963).

For individual studies of Thomas Eakins, Winslow Homer, and Albert Pinkham Ryder, the three major American painters of the nineteenth century, see Lloyd Goodrich, *Thomas Eakins*, vols. 1 and 2 (Cambridge, Mass., 1982); Philip C. Beam, *Winslow Homer at Prout's Neck* (Boston, 1966), and *Winslow Homer's Magazine Engravings* (New York, 1979); Goodrich, *Winslow Homer* (New York, 1959); and Elizabeth Brown, *Albert Pinkham Ryder* (Washington, D.C., 1990).

The major European dissident exhibitions in the nineteenth and twentieth centuries are presented by Ian Dunlop, *The Shock of the New* (New York, 1972). The essential source for American responses to the landmark 1913 Armory Show is Milton Brown, *The Story of the Armory Show* (Greenwich, Conn., 1963). For the Ashcan school, see William I. Homer, *Robert Henri and His Circle* (Ithaca, N.Y., 1969); for Stieglitz and his group of modernist painters, Homer, *Stieglitz and the*

American Avant-Garde (Boston, 1977); for Duchamp in New York, Tashjian, *Skyscraper Primitives: Dada and the American Avant-Garde, 1910–1925* (Middletown, Conn., 1975); for the regionalists of the 1920s and 1930s, Matthew Baigell, *The American Scene* (New York, 1974); and for photography in the 1930s, William Stott, *Documentary Expression and Thirties America* (New York, 1973). Finally, for the emergence of the abstract expressionists, see Irving Sandler, *The Triumph of American Painting* (New York, 1970); Michael Auping, ed., *Abstract Expressionism: The Critical Developments* (New York, 1987); and Serge Guilbaut, *How New York Stole the Idea of Modern Art: Abstract Expressionism, Freedom, and the Cold War* (Chicago, 1983).

9 ☆ A New

☆ Architecture,

☆ Yet Old

☆ Leland M. Roth

How might the character of American architecture be defined? In Japan, for example, a traditional wood-framed archetype has served as the basis of a national architecture for centuries—even when it has been modified by contact with the European West. American architecture, in contrast, like American culture, is the amalgamation of many disparate and sometimes contradictory transplanted cultures: from Northern Europe, from Central and Southern Europe, from Africa, from Latin America, and from the Orient. For American architecture there is no Ise Shrine, as in Japan, providing a single ancient model for all subsequent building. Rather, there are many ancestral models, each infused with meaning for a particular transplanted ethnic group. What, then, is the true American architectural character? What constitutes the constructive ideal toward which American architecture strives?

☆ ☆ ☆ The Real and the Ideal

The dilemma permeating the American character and American architecture was sharply defined in 1911 by philosopher George Santayana in an address given at the University of California at Berkeley. The basic conflict, as he perceived it, was that the United States was a young country with an old mentality. For Santayana, it was a country of two mentalities, "one a survival of beliefs and standards of the fathers, the other an expression of the instincts, practice, and discoveries of the younger generations." The result, he suggested, has been that

> one half of the American mind, that not occupied intensely in practical affairs, has remained . . . slightly becalmed; it has floated gently in the

backwater, while alongside, in invention and industry and social organization, the other half of the mind was leaping down a sort of Niagara
Rapids. This division may be found symbolized in American architecture: a neat reproduction of the colonial mansion—with some modern
comforts introduced surreptitiously—stands beside the skyscraper. The
American Will inhabits the skyscraper; the American Intellect inhabits
the colonial mansion. . . . The one is all aggressive enterprise; the other is
all genteel tradition.

From the moment the first European settlers set foot on the North American continent and began to build, they endeavored to achieve the optimum
balance between the real and the ideal, between the present-day and the
timeless. They had to erect the most practical and efficient structures possible,
for their base of capital was small, skilled labor was scarce and costly, and the
demands of frontier life were pressing. Efficiency and pragmatism were absolutely necessary. At the same time, the settlers were displaced Europeans, set
down in a strange land and hungry for the cultural memories that the traditional architecture of their homeland had expressed in its silent language. So
they purposefully built in the accustomed way, trying to make a home away
from home. There evolved, therefore, a duality of thought and a conflict of
desires between pragmatism on the one hand and reassuring architectural
allusions on the other. The result was a compulsion for both pragmatic utility
and symbolic perfection (the real and the ideal), which have been at the root of
American architecture ever since.

Among the first necessities were permanent houses, and these were built to
be decidedly practical. For example, the house constructed in Guilford, Connecticut, in 1639–40 for the Reverend Henry Whitfield by his congregation
had stone walls three feet thick as a protective refuge for the community in the
event of attack (fig. 9.1). But these first homes were also re-creations of the
homes left behind. In the southern colonies, especially, there were a few
versions of the great country houses in England built by those who determined to start afresh in the New World. Thus, for example, the curved Flemish
gables of the brick house built about 1655 by Arthur Allen (later called
Bacon's Castle) in Surrey County, Virginia (fig. 9.2), recall the more elaborate
embellishments of such estates as Montacute House, Somerset, England, built
seventy years earlier.

At the same time in the North, however, the Puritan Separatists perfected a
new building type, drawn from traditional models but ideally suited to their
special demands for a rigorously simple service of worship. Utterly shorn of all

ornament, lest it divert the mind of the elect from the word of the Almighty, the New England meetinghouse was the epitome of adaptation to function. It is exemplified by the Hingham, Massachusetts, meetinghouse (the "Old Ship Meetinghouse") built in 1681, with later additions, and now restored to its original austerity (fig. 9.3). In the New England theocracy of the elect, the meetinghouse served as a house of worship, a place for civil discourse, and a place of refuge in time of trouble, its severe and lean utility serving all of these functions equally well.

The pure functional utility of the transplanted vernaculars of seventeenth-century New England architecture gave way to fashionable aspirations during the eighteenth century in New England and in the colonies to the south. Now the desire was not so much to re-create a version of what had been left behind, but to duplicate—as closely as resources and available crafts skills allowed—the new classically inspired architecture of England. Nonetheless, the desire persisted to economize by retaining what still stood. Isaac Royal, Jr., for example, created his elegant suburban Boston estate at Medford, Massachusetts, by adding upward and outward to a house begun in the seventeenth century by John Usher and later enlarged by Royal's father in 1732. The imposing and balanced west facade, added by Isaac Royal, Jr., in 1747–50, brought to completion a country house that compared most favorably, both in its external and internal ornament, to contemporary work in England (fig. 9.4).

☆ ☆ ☆ Jefferson's Agrarian Classical Dream

For Thomas Jefferson, such adherence to the architectural models of Georgian England served as a sharp reminder of monarchical domination. Jefferson aspired to a more timeless architecture, based at first on the models provided by his favored Italian Renaissance ideal, Andrea Palladio, and then, in turn, on Palladio's own sources in the architecture of ancient Rome. What made Jefferson's buildings especially American was the way they were integrated into the landscape. His beloved home, Monticello, atop a low mountain near Charlottesville, Virginia, built in various stages from 1770 through 1809, is inspired by Palladio's villas but pushed into the hilltop so that its spreading service wings would not obstruct the sweeping panorama of the Blue Ridge Mountains visible from the house (fig. 9.5). It is part of the hill and makes possible "prospects" of what were tilled lowlands to the east and a rugged wilderness stretching to the west.

Just as Monticello was filled with Jefferson's inventions for raising wine bottles from the cellars below or for conserving heat in the winter, so Jefferson's University of Virginia at Charlottesville (1817–26) was planned with a clear view toward utility. Its ten pavilions housed not only the classrooms for the ten departments of instructions but also, in the upper floors, apartments for the professors as well. These pavilions were connected, in turn, by ranges of rooms for the students and fronted by continuous colonnades to permit circulation regardless of the weather. The ranges and pavilions were arranged in facing parallel rows, in descending grassy terraces, framing a view out toward the mountains, embracing the New World landscape. This "academical village," as Jefferson called it, was filled with architectural exemplars, for each pavilion was a lesson in the architectural orders of the classical past (Doric, Ionic, Corinthian), and the whole was focused on a replica of the Pantheon in Rome that housed the library (fig. 9.6).

These architectural "lessons" also showed Jefferson's idealism, already demonstrated in the design he provided on request for the Virginia State Capitol, Richmond, in 1785 (fig. 9.7). So that this new building might serve as an example of good architecture for his countrymen, Jefferson selected as his model the Roman temple called the Maison Carrée in Nîmes, France. Such reference to classical antiquity, to what Jefferson supposed was the architecture of republicanism, clearly served as the inspiration for the Ohio State Capitol, Columbus, 1838–61, a merging of several competition-entry designs worked out by Henry Walters (fig. 9.8). The Ohio capitol was only one of many subsequent temple-form government seats, all inspired by Jefferson's idealism.

The dream of American freedom would be preserved, Jefferson was convinced, only so long as the population was well educated and thus able to carry on a critical civil discourse. He was convinced that the prosperity of the Republic required a yeoman citizenry far removed from the corrupting influence of large cities. But how were these scattered farmers to perfect their architectural sensibilities if they were not exposed to the civilizing influence of good architecture? The solution lay in providing models in engraved plates, in publishing books that illustrated this democratic style and symbol. The Greek model for the freestanding single-family house, in particular, was presented in the books of Minard Lafever. Knowing that skilled wood-carvers able to create Ionic and Corinthian capitals would be rare in the hinterland, Lafever offered a more pragmatic version of the ideal: a classical order that could be built of readily available flat board lumber (fig. 9.9). As a result, in the new Ithacas, Uticas, Athenses, Troys, and the other namesakes of ancient cities, there rose white classical cubes, appropriately embellished in the architectural forms of ancient democracy.

☆ ☆ ☆ Pragmatism, Urbanism, and Prosperity

Jefferson's dream of a yeoman citizenry was not to be. Instead, the growing cities gradually became the controlling force in American life, just as they became the seat of American industry. An alternative that emerged in the middle of the nineteenth century—made feasible, in fact, by the very industrialization that made it desirable—was retreat to the countryside by means of the railroad. For the middle class, this halfway withdrawal to the landscaped pastoral suburb (what historian Leo Marx has called "the middle landscape") meant one could live in romantic rural peace and still commute to the increasingly crowded, noisy, and polluted city to work. One might take the Erie Railroad westward from the shore of the Hudson River, for example, to Llewellyn Park in West Orange, New Jersey. This community was begun by Llewellyn Haskell in 1852 for others who, like himself, preferred the open, landscaped spaces of the country. The streets he laid out generally followed the rolling topography, and numerous trees were planted to create a green canopy. Among the first homes designed there by Alexander Jackson Davis was the Nicholls-McKim house, 1858–59 (fig. 9.10), an almost literal interpretation of the "Cottage in the Rural, or the English Style," which Davis had drawn for publication in Andrew Jackson Downing's manual, *Cottage Residences*, published in 1842.

The United States, pursuing a presumed "manifest destiny" to spread from ocean to ocean during the nineteenth century, grew to be an enormous nation. Hence, an important part of the American character was the impulse to be mobile, to be able to move about the continent, to see what was over the next ridge, to find just a little more elbow room. The steam engine on wheels, riding on iron rails, satisfied this demand for mobility for rich and poor alike, whether one needed to cross the continent or simply move across the city quickly. Thus, at the same time that rails reached out across the landscape, tying together cities separated by hundreds of miles, urban mass-transit lines were also being lifted into the air on metal streets. The developing transportation network of the 1850s and 1860s made possible many things at once: both the concentration of people and services at the urban core and the escape of many to the suburbs at the urban fringe; the consolidation of merchants in the city-center department stores as well as the dissemination of mass-produced goods to buyers scattered across the thinly populated plains.

All of these changes helped spur the rise of a broad middle class that made new building types necessary. At the city center this was well illustrated by such commercial blocks as the Haughwout Building, New York City, 1857, a department store designed by John Gaynor and erected of prefabricated cast-iron modular sections produced by Daniel Badger (fig. 9.11). Here was the quintessential American business building—inexpensive but using modern materials (glass and iron), incorporating the latest conveniences (a steam-powered passenger elevator), devoted to commerce and the sustenance of the middle class. It was an ornate but yet no-nonsense architecture.

As in the 1840s and 1850s when industry first expanded and the American economy grew, in the 1880s, during the next rapid expansion of the economy, there was renewed flight of the well-to-do to an even more idealized landscape farther away from the congested and pulsating sources of their wealth. Seaside retreats became the favored spots for the privileged, and architects such as McKim, Mead, and White, William Ralph Emerson, and John Calvin Stevens experimented there with a new amalgam of architectural sources so dissimilar as to suggest it would have been impossible to create anything coherent. They studied the vernacular *and* the high-style architecture of the seventeenth- and eighteenth-century colonies, traditional Japanese wooden architecture, and the massing of towers in rural French manors of the sixteenth century, together with the contemporary houses of Richard Norman Shaw in England, which were themselves inspired by Elizabethan and Jacobean models. The American architects succeeded in creating out of all this a wondrously free and flexible domestic idiom, the Shingle Style; moreover, in each summer or country house, they fashioned a plan uniquely adapted to site and client, laid out to maximize the relationship to the street or to capture the slightest breeze from the sea. One house that illustrates well the synthesis of all these sources is that by McKim, Mead, and White for Isaac Bell, in Newport, Rhode Island, 1881–83 (fig. 9.12).

When this domestic architecture—open in plan, organized in carefully studied geometries, and wrapped in an even, undulating skin of shingles—was created in the 1880s, it was restricted at first to the privileged few, but the lessons learned, particularly in the new appreciation of the vernacular American architecture of the seventeenth century, were then applied to the housing of workers. Shingled duplexes were built for employees in industrial communities, such as Hopedale, Massachusetts, in 1910 (fig. 9.13). Such housing and the schools, libraries, and social halls that accompanied it in these industrial communities were viewed as important agents in inculcating the American dream in the immigrants who flooded into the United States and operated the machinery of the mills.

During the nineteenth century, as the stylish Greek Revival and, later, the Shingle Style were developed along the East Coast, the nation absorbed wave after wave of new immigrants. Like the new settlers of the seventeenth century, these ethnic groups carried with them the memories of their traditional homes, giving rise to new vernacular traditions as their ancestral forms were merged with available materials and American building techniques. Out of the fashionable Greek Revival house emerged the simpler I-house, the basis for so many farmhouses in the Midwest and Far West (fig. 9.14). From Haitian blacks who moved into Louisiana came the "shotgun" house of the deep South. German immigrants continued to use their accustomed vernacular of heavy wooden frame "fachwerk." The Scandinavians who settled in the Upper Midwest reintroduced their accustomed log construction, already a popular form of frontier building after its first introduction by the Swedish colonists along the Delaware River in the 1630s.

Americans were quick to adopt whatever technical means were available to ease construction. In the 1830s when there was a pressing need to build houses quickly in the Midwest, where the hardwood timbers for traditional heavy frames were not plentiful, Chicago builders George W. Snow and Augustine D. Taylor developed a new method of building using closely spaced small softwood timbers. By the 1860s this technique had been industrialized, with standardized mill-cut two-by-fours and mass-produced soft iron nails. Houses built with these factory-made materials were said to go up as fast as balloons, and the light wooden frame was soon dubbed the "balloon frame" (fig. 9.15). When the broad East River increasingly posed an impediment to movement between New York and Brooklyn, farsighted investors engaged the German-immigrant engineer, John Augustus Roebling, to design a suspension bridge between the two cities using steel wire cables. The result was the Brooklyn Bridge, built in 1869–83 (fig. 9.16).

Even more expressive of the drive to combine pragmatic utility and ideal form was the commercial office skyscraper developed in the 1880s and 1890s in Chicago. Such a commercial office tower, perhaps the most important American contribution to the history of architecture, is well represented by the Guaranty Building in Buffalo, New York, built by Adler and Sullivan in 1895 (fig. 9.17). It reveals its three functional zones clearly: base, with shops and circulation spaces; midsection, with piled-up office cells; and crown, with elevator machinery, water tanks, and other utilitarian facilities. The whole is lifted up on a frame of steel, and its vertical piers are doubled in number to celebrate the decided verticality of the building.

☆ ☆ ☆ Harmony, Unity, and Function

Just as such skyscrapers brought to perfection the ideas barely hinted at in the Haughwout Building, so too did Frank Lloyd Wright's "prairie houses" of the first years of the twentieth century bring to fruition the

Fig. 9.1. Rev. Henry Whitfield house, Guilford, Conn. 1639–40. (Sandak, Inc.)

Fig. 9.2. Arthur Allen house, later Bacon's Castle, Surrey County, Va. ca. 1655. (Sandak, Inc.)

Fig. 9.3. Old Ship Meetinghouse, Hingham, Mass. 1681. (Sandak, Inc.)

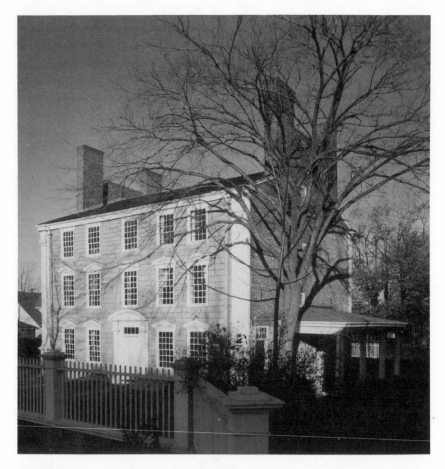

Fig. 9.4. Isaac Royal house, west front, Medford, Mass. 1733–37, 1747–50. (Sandak, Inc.)

*Fig. 9.5. Thomas Jefferson. Monticello, near Charlottesville, Va. 1770–82, 1796–1809.
(Thomas Jefferson Memorial Foundation, Charlottesville, Va.)*

Fig. 9.6. Thomas Jefferson. Library Rotunda, University of Virginia, Charlottesville.
1823–27. (Courtesy University of Virginia, Charlottesville.)

Fig. 9.7. Thomas Jefferson. Virginia State Capitol, Richmond. 1785–89. Plaster model sent from Paris. (Ohio State University Library, Columbus.)

Fig. 9.8. Henry Walters and others. Ohio State Capitol, Columbus. 1838–61. (Ohio State University Library, Columbus.)

Fig. 9.9. Minard Lafever. "Design for Country Villa," The Modern Builder's Guide, *1833.*

Fig. 9.10. Alexander Jackson Davis. Nicholls-McKim house, Llewellyn Park, West Orange, N.J. 1858–59. (© Wayne Andrews/ESTO; Ezra Stoller © ESTO.)

Fig. 9.11. John P. Gaynor, architect; Daniel Badger, manufacturer. Haughwout Building, New York City. 1857. (© Wayne Andrews/ESTO; Ezra Stoller © ESTO.)

Fig. 9.12. McKim, Mead, and White. Isaac Bell house, Newport, R.I. 1881–83. (© Wayne Andrews/ESTO; Ezra Stoller © ESTO.)

Fig. 9.13. Robert A. Cook, architect; with Arthur A. Schurtleff, planner. Lakeside Group, employee housing. Hopedale, Mass. 1910. (Leland M. Roth.)

Fig. 9.14. William Parker house, Parkersville, Marion County, Oreg. ca. 1850. (HABS Collection, Library of Congress, Washington, D.C.)

Fig. 9.15. Diagram of wall framing from William E. Bell, Carpentry Made Easy . . . with Specific Instructions for Building Balloon Frames, *1858.*

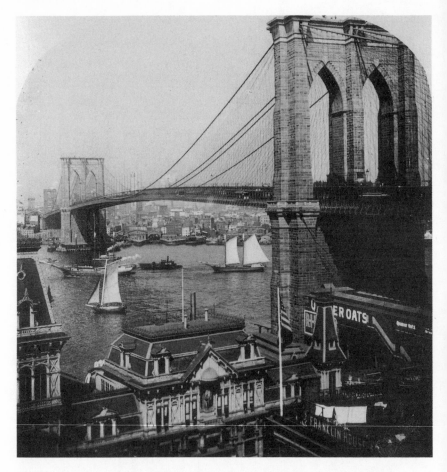

Fig. 9.16. John Augustus Roebling and Washington A. Roebling, assisted by Emily Roebling. The Brooklyn Bridge, New York City. 1869–83. (Brooklyn Historical Society.)

Fig. 9.17. Adler and Sullivan. Guaranty Building, Buffalo, N.Y. 1895. (Northwestern University Department of Art History, Evanston, Ill.)

Fig. 9.18. Frank Lloyd Wright. Frederick C. Robie house, Chicago, Ill. 1906–9. (University of Oregon Library, Eugene.)

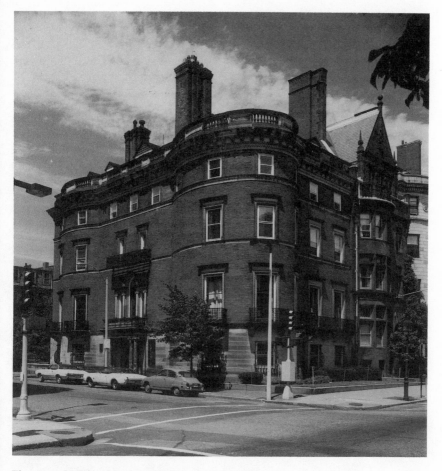

Fig. 9.19. McKim, Mead, and White. John F. Andrew house, Boston, Mass. 1883–86. (Leland M. Roth.)

Fig. 9.20. McKim, Mead, and White. Pennsylvania Station, New York City. 1902–10 (demolished 1963–65). (Avery Library, Columbia University, New York City.)

Fig. 9.21. Albert Kahn. Edsel Ford house, Grosse Pointe, Mich. 1927. (© Wayne Andrews/ESTO; Ezra Stoller © ESTO.)

Fig. 9.22. Albert Kahn. Dodge half-ton truck plant, Detroit, Mich. 1937. (Albert Kahn Associates, Detroit, Mich.)

Fig. 9.23. Frank Lloyd Wright. Edgar J. Kaufmann house, Fallingwater, near Mill Run, Pa. 1936–37. (Hedrich-Blessing, Chicago, Ill.)

Fig. 9.24. Bertram G. Goodhue. Nebraska State Capitol, Lincoln, Nebr. 1919–32. (Leland M. Roth.)

Fig. 9.25. Ludwig Mies van der Rohe. Dr. Edith Farnsworth house, near Plano, Ill. 1945–51. (Photograph by Bill Blessing; Hedrich-Blessing, Chicago, Ill.)

Fig. 9.26. Philip Johnson. Philip Johnson "glass" house, New Canaan, Conn. 1945–49. (Courtesy Philip Johnson.)

Fig. 9.27. Ludwig Mies van der Rohe. Lake Shore Drive apartments, Chicago, Ill. 1948–51. (John Rosenthal/Northwestern University Department of Art History, Evanston, Ill.)

Fig. 9.28. C. F. Murphy Associates with Skidmore, Owings, and Merrill. Daley Center (Chicago Civic Center), Chicago, Ill. 1959–65. (Hedrich-Blessing, Chicago, Ill.)

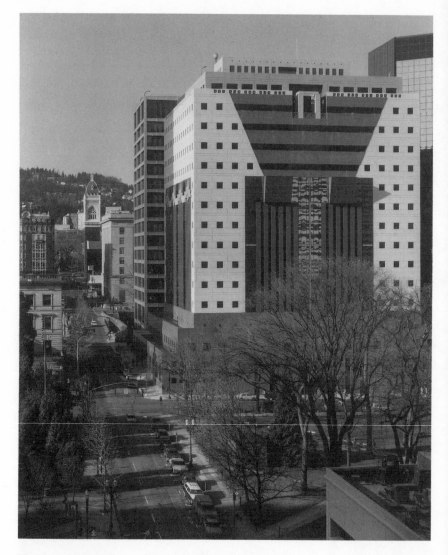

Fig. 9.29. Michael Graves. Portland Building, Portland, Oreg. 1978–82. (City of Portland.)

Fig. 9.30. Robert A. M. Stern. House in Llewellyn Park, West Orange, N.J. 1978–81. (Courtesy R. A. M. Stern.)

ideas expounded by Downing and Davis two generations earlier. Like Sullivan's commercial high-rises, Wright's prairie houses were unified creations, the spinning out of a single germinal idea in brick and stone, wood and stucco, unfolding in interwoven spaces. The best examples are the expansive D. D. Martin house of Buffalo and the Frederick C. Robie house of Chicago (fig. 9.18). Many characteristics set these houses apart from those that came before. There is an easy flow of space—which Wright learned from the Shingle Style—and an integration of ornament, furniture, and utility systems. There is also a pragmatic climatic response. The houses not only reflect the dominant horizontality of the prairie, they are adjusted to the sun. The seemingly weightless cantilevered eaves are proportioned so that summer sun never touches the glass; in the spring and autumn, some light grazes the floor. In the winter, however, long raking beams of sunlight reach into the house to help warm the living room.

Although Wright became a master of the suburban single-family house, like Jefferson he never was completely reconciled to the city. Indeed, during 1932–35 his alternative was to design a kind of landscape that was neither urban nor truly rural—a decentralized, spread-out, automobile-connected pattern of settlement he called Broadacre City. The architects who were more sympathetic to the city and the landscape of the urban street were McKim, Mead, and White. One of their early buildings to demonstrate this was the complex of six town houses they designed for financier Henry Villard on Madison Avenue, New York City, 1882–85. Recessed around a U-shaped court, the complex addressed the street while at the same time creating a semiprivate realm as a transition from the bustle of the street to the quiet of the individual residences.

Even more important, however, was the sense of preserving the ensemble that these architects brought to their work. When building in the new Back Bay area of Boston, for example, they designed the house of John F. Andrew (1883–86) to recall and expand on the image of the bowed-front brick houses of nearby Beacon Hill (fig. 9.19). Similarly, in 1889–99, when confronted with the problem of adding entrance gates around the campus of Harvard University, McKim, Mead, and White chose to base the gates and connecting fence sections on eighteenth-century sources so as to blend with the venerated old Harvard buildings. It pleased Bostonians and Harvard alumni to see traditions thus continued. Echoing the sentiments of Santayana, Boston financier and philanthropist Henry L. Higginson wrote Charles McKim that he thought the gates eminently successful, since they made the campus a "new place and yet old."

Comparable in functional clarity to Sullivan's high-rises was McKim, Mead, and White's immense Pennsylvania Station, New York City, 1902–10, for it perfectly accommodated the functional needs of a large urban rail terminal while providing a suitable image of a gateway to a great city. Its encircling Tuscan colonnade was boldly scaled but was no higher than surrounding buildings. At the center, where the centripetal movement of travelers stopped, the space soared upward in a great waiting room (fig. 9.20), its huge volume marked off into easily perceivable units patterned after the tepidarium of the Baths of Caracalla in Rome. From the waiting room, one passed into the concourse and then to the stairs leading to the trains, which moved through tunnels under the station. The concourse was shaped in a manner recalling the vaulted waiting room but in glass carried in a light frame of steel forms that made a conscious transition from the formal classical waiting room to the utilitarian machinery of the trains below. It was an expensive architecture of openness and grace, scaled to people moving in groups and eminently suited to comings and goings.

Pennsylvania Station, and the other great terminals that arose at the beginning of the twentieth century, marked the culmination of the importance of the passenger railroad and the mode of transportation it offered; but even as that station was being completed, the instrument of its eventual destruction was being developed. The private automobile was to replace the passenger train as a major mover of people, for it offered a degree of freedom never before possible. In making inexpensive automobiles for a public that craved them, a number of manufacturers became extremely wealthy. They spent some of their wealth on elaborate evocations of Renaissance villas or lovingly detailed medieval manor houses, such as the Edsel Ford house in Grosse Pointe, Michigan, outside Detroit, 1927 (fig. 9.21). How curious it seems that these individuals, who were responsible for the greatest social revolution of the nineteenth and twentieth centuries, and who created industries that were to restructure the economy of the world, should also have called into being some of the most archly traditional architecture of the century. What is even more remarkable is that the traditional "period style" Edsel Ford house was designed by Albert Kahn, who also designed the best automobile factories in Detroit, including the Dodge half-ton truck plant in 1937 (fig. 9.22). Albert Kahn worked easily in those two different expressions, one an architecture of symbolic allusion and approbation, the other an architecture of absolute mechanical and pragmatic utility.

During the 1930s, Frank Lloyd Wright enjoyed a renaissance of his career, initiated by a summer house for the Edgar Kaufmann family, Fallingwater, on the little creek of Bear Run in southwestern Pennsylvania, 1936–37 (fig. 9.23). It seemed to show some evidence of the impact of European modernism (or perhaps the functional clarity of Albert Kahn's factories) in its metal sash windows and strikingly cantilevered concrete terraces. Yet it continued to dramatize, even more emphatically than before, the horizontal line of the earth, as if it were organically integrated with and had grown out of its wooded landscape.

One architect of the early twentieth century, in particular, attempted to combine the functional modernity of Sullivan and Wright with the symbolic associationalism of such architects as McKim, Mead, and White. This was Bertram Grosvenor Goodhue. A building that summarizes well his search for a traditional yet modern architecture is his Nebraska State Capitol in Lincoln, 1919–32, a tall beacon in the middle of the wheat fields in the center of the vast continent (fig. 9.24). In this he combined a square Greek cross plan, organizing a hierarchy of spaces both public and private, with a logic of public circulation that was the very essence of Ecole des Beaux-Arts planning (although Goodhue himself never studied at that famous Paris school of architecture). Rising from the center of the cross plan, as a symbol of the building's function and of its period, was not a traditional Renaissance dome but a tower, a skyscraper visible for miles across the Nebraska prairie.

☆ ☆ ☆ The Late Twentieth Century: Stark Utility or Symbolic Expression?

Goodhue sought to combine functional clarity and precision with traditional forms drawn from the legacy of European architecture—the optimum of real and ideal—while most architects chose one or the other. In contrast, the émigré architects who fled totalitarianism in Europe in the 1940s—the creators of the International Style, as it came to be called— advocated an aesthetic functional purism that would be serviceable for all conceivable building types. Their goal was a prototypical architecture that, once crystallized in form, could be used for any function anywhere. One such universal prototype was the weekend house for Dr. Edith Farnsworth at Plano, Illinois, 1945–51 (fig. 9.25), by Ludwig Mies van der Rohe, who had emigrated from Berlin in 1937. The living enclosure was defined by two slabs parallel to the ground and wrapped in a skin of glass. Like the Greek temple, such abstraction wants to stand in distinct contrast with the compromising complexity of the natural world, and so the house is lifted up by eight steel columns. Within is a universal space, deftly subdivided into four sections by the placement of a single utility island. At root, however, the house exists in defiance of the natural world, dismissing the inevitable effects of weatherization and pretending immunity to the effects of solar radiation. The house may do that, but the people inside cannot, and so in the late afternoon they must draw curtains in a futile attempt to keep it from becoming a hothouse.

Even before Mies began the Farnsworth house, his protégé Philip Johnson had built a small glass-walled house in Cambridge, Massachusetts. Then, as the Farnsworth house was started, Johnson built a similar all-glass house for himself in New Canaan, Connecticut, 1945–49 (fig. 9.26). So similar to the Farnsworth house as to seem a copy, it nonetheless has many subtle differences, the most important of which is its relationship to the landscape. Placed at the edge of a podiumlike terrace atop a low rise, the house is shielded by a copse of deciduous trees. In the summer, it is protected under a green umbrella; in the winter, the umbrella drops so the sun can do its work of warming the house.

For commercial high-rises, Mies provided the prototype in his twin apartment towers on Lake Shore Drive, Chicago, 1948–51 (fig. 9.27). He developed a single form that he then repeated, turning it ninety degrees so the two would fit the trapezoidal site. The towers were a latter-day realization of Sullivan's admonition that form must follow function, except that here it seemed that the form was prescribed not so much by the needs and activities of the inhabitants (there was, originally, no air conditioning for these glass-enclosed apartments) as by the structural logic of the steel frame and the mass-produced window units. This and other contemporaneous towers by Mies and architects Skidmore, Owings, and Merrill became the models for all types of urban buildings in the United States and around the world, whether corporate headquarters, speculative office buildings, or apartment complexes. The Chicago Civic Center (now the Daley Center) by C. F. Murphy Associates with Skidmore, Owings, and Merrill, 1959–65 (fig. 9.28), is one example of following the Miesian prototype for a municipal building. In this case, however, because of size requirements for the internal courtrooms, the basic structural module was enlarged to eighteen feet in height with spans of forty-nine by eighty-seven feet.

Within a decade, such buildings began to lose their individual identities as they were endlessly replicated in countless cities. They could, indeed, be anything, anywhere. By 1975, for clients it was no longer enough for a building merely to *do* something—however elegant its structural purity—it was now expected to *say* something, to proclaim and celebrate a particular human intention in a particular place. So in erecting a new municipal office building in 1978–82, the city of Portland, Oregon, selected the competition entry of Michael Graves (fig. 9.29). Not only did it meet the limitations of a stringent budget, it also was ablaze with color and festooned with architectural and sculptural ornament that accomplished several goals. Even though couched in an ornamental language that was rather esoteric and mannered, the color and embellishment nonetheless celebrated the fact that this was a civic building—something clearly distinct from the often-anonymous office towers—and it thus established a civic identity. The ornament also was a gesture toward the Italian Renaissance–style city hall of 1892–95, next door; figuratively, the new building became an extension of it. However the Graves building might be criticized as a design, it made a clear attempt at economy and functionality and at creating a visual and symbolic connection with the neighboring city hall.

At the residential scale, much the same concern can be seen in the work of Robert A. M. Stern beginning about 1970. In a series of houses at Farm Neck, Massachusetts, on the island of Martha's Vineyard in southern Massachusetts, and in suburban Westchester County north of New York City, he endeavored to keep the scale small to reduce cost and choreographed a variety of connected spaces to provide an internal landscape of variety. He accomplished this while also making clear but stylized ornamental references to the Shingle Style of the 1880s. So the houses are part of their own time but also part of a valued tradition. In renovating a Georgian Revival house (built in 1929) in Llewellyn Park in 1978–81, Stern added a glass-covered swimming pool in a recessed terrace (fig. 9.30). Since this might have resulted in a visually weak base for the existing classical house, Stern provided a massive brick and stone wall with overscaled members and boldly modeled courses of masonry to create a strong visual base. As a bonus, the glass roof serves to capture sunlight, heating the pool. Here, too, the reality of fitting the pool into a limited space and having the enclosure serve an economic end is merged with stylized historical references that seek to augment and extend the historical allusions of the original house.

Through comparison, the Portland Building and the house in Llewellyn Park by Stern reveal the dilemma American architecture faces at the end of the twentieth century, for while the suburban house is lavishly constructed of elegant materials and proudly displays its private grandeur, the Portland Building reveals the low budgets that generally made public buildings of the same period mean and shabby. Americans during the Reagan decade were unwilling to reach into their pockets to build public edifices at all comparable to those of a century earlier that they were busily restoring and rehabilitating at the very same time. The question remains what will be left to restore of the cheap late twentieth-century public buildings when our great-grandchildren face the task in another century.

As the twentieth century enters its last decade, American architects continue to explore alternatives to the structural determinism of international modernism. Some have opted for an increasingly historicist classicism, while others have attempted to fuse traditional symbols with modernist form. The most significant failing has been the absence of professional interest and government incentive to provide affordable housing for all of the nation's citizens. The sterile housing towers of the 1950s have clearly demonstrated their failings. The most promising suggestions for the neighborhoods of the future are found in such complexes as the resort village of Seaside, Florida, begun by developer Robert Davis in 1978–83. Even if this experiment is aimed at the uppermost middle class, it demonstrates that in the pedestrian scale and traditional imagery of the nineteenth-century town there resides a model for humane neighborhoods of the twenty-first century.

☆ ☆ ☆ Conclusion

Building is based in the art of compromise, for every building represents the end result of countless adjustments and changes and is a judicious balance between conflicting needs and aspirations on the part of the client, the architect, and the builder. Americans, perhaps more than other builders, have been caught between divergent needs and desires—between the impulse to build pragmatically and efficiently and the simultaneous wish to realize a conceptual ideal. What they want is pragmatic perfection. The pioneers came to the New World in the beginning in search of a measure of perfection and yet found they had to shelter themselves in the most rudimentary of cabins. The conflict between the real and the ideal has continued from that time to the present. Americans continue to build with the goal of achieving maximum performance, but they also have rediscovered the need to attune their architecture more closely to their cultural legacy, their environment, and the land. A people fascinated by speed and change, Americans nonetheless build so as to capture memories and evoke permanence. They still seek a new architecture, yet old.

FURTHER READING

For the comments by George Santayana, see Douglas L. Wilson, *The Genteel Tradition: Nine Essays by George Santayana* (Cambridge, Mass., 1967).

The writing of the history of American architecture is a relatively recent scholarly discipline. One of the first critical assessments was made by James Jackson Jarves in *The Art Idea: Sculpture, Painting and Architecture in America* (New York,

1864). Early critics during the 1880s and 1890s included Russell Sturgis, Montgomery Schuyler, and Mariana Griswold van Rensselaer, whose commentary is reprinted in Roth, *America Builds*, cited below. The first comprehensive summary of American architecture was Lewis Mumford's *Sticks and Stones* (New York, 1924), soon followed by Talbot Hamlin, *The American Spirit in Architecture* (New Haven, Conn., 1926); Thomas E. Tallmadge, *The Story of Architecture in America* (New York, 1927); and Fiske Kimball, *American Architecture* (New York, 1928). Mumford first directed attention to the then-denigrated nineteenth century in his *Brown Decades* (New York, 1931). This lead was followed by Hugh Morrison, *Louis Sullivan: Prophet of Modern Architecture* (New York, 1935), and Henry-Russell Hitchcock, *The Architecture of H. H. Richardson and His Times* (New York, 1936; rev. ed., Cambridge, Mass., 1966). For specialized studies in early American architecture, the trail was blazed by Fiske Kimball in his monograph *Thomas Jefferson, Architect* (Boston, 1916) and his *Domestic Architecture of the American Colonies and of the Early Republic* (New York, 1922).

Since 1945 the historiography of American architecture has come of age with the writing of numerous works, including monographs on individual architects as well as comprehensive interpretive works. Among the most important are John Burchard and Albert Bush-Brown, *The Architecture of America: A Social and Cultural History* (Boston, 1961); James M. Fitch, *American Building: The Historical Forces That Shaped It* (Boston, 1966), and *American Architecture: The Environmental Forces That Shaped It* (Boston, 1966); William H. Jordy, *American Buildings and Their Architects*, vol. 4, *Progressive and Academic Ideals at the Turn of the Twentieth Century*, and vol. 5, *The Impact of European Modernism in the Mid-Twentieth Century* (Garden City, N.Y., 1972); Hugh Morrison, *Early American Architecture from the First Colonial Settlements to the National Period* (New York, 1952); William H. Pierson, *American Buildings and Their Architects*, vol. 1, *The Colonial and Neoclassical Styles*, and vol. 2, *Technology and the Picturesque: The Corporate and Early Gothic Styles* (Garden City, N.Y., 1970, 1978); Vincent Scully, *American Architecture and Urbanism*, 2d ed. (New York, 1988), which has an excellent bibliographic essay; and Marcus Whiffen and Frederick Koeper, *American Architecture, 1607–1976* (Cambridge, Mass., 1981). A particularly perceptive historian of American architecture has been Vincent Scully, whose other major works include *Frank Lloyd Wright* (New York, 1960), *Modern Architecture: The Architecture of Democracy* (New York, 1960), and *The Shingle Style: Architectural Theory and Design from Richardson to the Origins of Wright*, rev. ed. (New Haven, Conn., 1971). A recent comprehensive study is Leland Roth, *Concise History of American Architecture* (New York, 1979), which contains a bibliography. Another recent general study is David P. Handlin, *American Architecture* (London, 1985), which has a detailed bibliography. Most interesting is Gwendolyn Wright, *Building the Dream: A Social History of Housing in America* (New York, 1981).

Since the mid-1970s the study of American vernacular architecture has achieved significant professional status with the founding of the Vernacular Architecture Forum. The association publishes its collections of essays, entitled *Perspectives in Vernacular Architecture*, with the University of Missouri Press. For further work in the field, see Henry Glassie's significant study *Folk Housing in Middle Virginia* (Knoxville, Tenn., 1975); Dell Upton and John Michael Vlach's anthology *Common Places: Readings in American Vernacular Architecture* (Athens, Ga., 1986); and on the buildings of ethnic groups and Native Americans, Dell Upton, ed., *America's Architectural Roots: Ethnic Groups That Built America* (Washington, D.C., 1986), and Peter Nabokov and Robert Easton, *Native American Architecture* (New York, 1989).

The growing popular interest in architecture since 1980 is reflected in Jeffrey Ochsner's comprehensive catalogue *H. H. Richardson: Complete Architectural Works* (Cambridge, Mass., 1982); Leland M. Roth's *McKim, Mead, and White, Architects* (New York, 1982); and the monographs on conservative architects of the early twentieth century that are being published by the Architectural History Foundation in conjunction with the Massachusetts Institute of Technology Press, as well as in two television series during the 1986–87 season—"Pride of Place," hosted by architect Robert Stern, and "American by Design," hosted by historian Spiro Kostof—each accompanied by a sumptuous publication.

Anthologies of source documents in American architecture include Don Gifford, ed., *The Literature of Architecture: The Evolution of Architectural Theory and Practice in Nineteenth-Century America* (New York, 1966), which covers only the nineteenth century; Lewis Mumford, ed., *Roots of Contemporary American Architecture* (New York, 1952), which deals with the modern movement; and Leland Roth, ed., *America Builds: Source Documents in American Architecture and Planning* (New York, 1983), which includes entries from the seventeenth through the late twentieth centuries and covers landscape architecture and planning as well. For landscape architecture, the best introduction is Norman Newton, *Design on the Land: The Development of Landscape Architecture* (Cambridge, Mass., 1971). For Frederick Law Olmsted, one should turn to the various publications of Albert Fein, particularly his *Frederick Law Olmsted and the American Environmental Tradition* (New York, 1972). The most useful anthology on this topic is David Weimer, ed., *City and Country in America* (New York, 1962).

The history of American planning has been written largely by John Reps. Among his many works the most inclusive are *The Making of Urban America* (Princeton, N.J., 1965) and *Cities of the American West* (Princeton, N.J., 1979). See also Christopher Tunnard and Henry Hope Reed, *American Skyline* (Boston, 1955), and Daniel Schaffer, ed., *Two Centuries of American Planning* (Baltimore, 1988). For the history of the planning profession in the twentieth century, see Mel Scott, *American City Planning since 1890* (Berkeley, Calif., 1969). The pervasive antiurban bias in the American character is discussed in Morton White and Lucia White, *The Intellectual Versus the City, from Thomas Jefferson to Frank Lloyd Wright* (Cambridge, Mass., 1962).

Chronicling the development of American building technology has been largely the province of one assiduous scholar, Carl W. Condit. Basic is his *American Building: Materials and Technologies from the First Colonial Settlements to the Present* (Chicago, 1968), adapted from two earlier larger volumes. His special focus has been Chicago, whose early commercial architecture he discussed in *The Chicago School of Architecture* (Chicago, 1964). His sequels to this are *Chicago: 1910–29* and *Chicago: 1930–70* (Chicago, 1973, 1974). A more recent work by Condit deals with the port and railroad facilities of New York City: *The Port of New York*, 2 vols. (Chicago, 1980, 1981).

10 ☆ Creating

☆ a National

☆ Literature

☆ Nina Baym

At least 100,000 original novels and short-story collections have been published in the United States since the convening of the First Continental Congress in 1774. If we add to this number all the original poetry, drama, essays, memoirs, histories, biographies, travel accounts, and other writings with literary aspirations that appeared during the same period, and add to *that* number all similar works published in the 250 years of American colonial existence, it should be obvious that no single narrative can encompass the whole of American literature. At any given time, what we think of as "American literature" must be an extremely narrow selection.

The selection that we meet at any given time is always produced by negotiations among various institutions (like the press and the school) charged with identifying works that deserve to survive—what we call the *canon*—according to culturally sanctioned criteria. In 1900 no critic or teacher would have failed to list James Russell Lowell, Oliver Wendell Holmes, and Henry Wadsworth Longfellow as great American writers. Today these writers are named only to remind us of the quaint taste of a bygone age. Conversely, while in 1900 virtually nobody took the writings of Herman Melville seriously, for the last fifty years *Moby-Dick* has been celebrated as America's greatest literary work. At the turn of the century only scant attention was paid to the posthumously published, carelessly edited verse of Emily Dickinson; her scrupulously edited work now takes its place alongside Walt Whitman's as the best poetry of the nineteenth century. Whitman, in 1900, was scolded and dismissed as a phony democrat; today *Leaves of Grass* is analyzed as an eloquent attempt to articulate the voices of Americans who had been ignored by mainstream culture.

☆ ☆ ☆ The Need for American Literature

Contemporary critical judgments naturally seem much more perceptive than those of 1900, but the lesson of canonical flux is not that judgment improves but that it changes. Moreover, a survey of the reasons given at any time for including or excluding writers from the American canon shows that while criteria change, aesthetic excellence has never been the sole or even the chief measure by which some works and not others are made to comprise the core of our national literature. The point of a national literature is that it *is* national, and pure aestheticism has never been accepted as a component of our national character. Lowell, Holmes, and Longfellow were deemed major in part because they were good writers according to contemporary standards, but even more because their writing was thought to express the highest American ideals. Indeed, critics believed that the excellence of a piece of writing depended on its morality. In the words of a 1903 textbook, the purpose of American literature was "to mirror our American ideals" and to "build up the reader into a worthy citizenship."

American literature was supposed to fulfill these purposes by featuring sterling examples of the national character and rousing expressions of nationalism. The most efficient way to carry out this mission was to take America itself as a literary subject. Inevitably, this is just what many American writers did in the past and what they still continue to do. Unexamined patriotism and uncomplicated depictions of American heroics appear more frequently in American literature today than we might expect, and perhaps a majority of American writers continue to focus deliberately on American topics or infuse their work with allusions to national themes.

Perhaps the chief issue that has preoccupied American writers is that of the national identity. What traits of character distinguish Americans from other peoples? *Who* is an American—and what individuals or peoples in the heterogeneous population actually possess these American traits? American writers seldom have defined "Americanness" as the mere technical consequence of birth or citizenship; rather, they have seen it as an inner state requiring effort to achieve.

From the standpoint of the individualism that Alexis de Tocqueville early identified as America's particular ideology, writers assumed that the truest Americans would also be the most individualistic, the persons least like their neighbors. The plot of many an American story involved the difficulties of becoming oneself, difficulties that were usually represented by the social pressure to conform. The idea of an American identity invested in one's individuality, thus, means that American selfhood cannot be created through group or community membership. And the question of how such a detached self may be representative of a nation remains the unresolved paradox of the American narrative. Its archetypal representation may well be James Fenimore Cooper's frontiersman Natty Bumppo, the hero of five novels written between 1823 and 1841 that came to be known collectively as the Leatherstocking Tales. As society advances across the continent, Natty retreats before it. These tales are the point of origin for that prototypical American hero, the cowboy, as well as his immediate descendant, the outlaw, and his more distant cousins, the hard-boiled detective and the gangster.

Cooper's equation of a particularly American identity with the American wilderness, his suggestion that the development of Americanness was enabled by the nation's open space, proved stimulating to other writers. Henry David Thoreau either imitated or parodied Cooper in his 1854 *Walden*, in which the first-person narrator withdraws to a cabin on the shores of Walden Pond, a full mile and a half from the civilization of Concord, Massachusetts. Thoreau argued—only partly in jest—that he had sufficient distance from his neighbors to "recreate" himself. Thus he spiritualized Cooper's material narrative.

Mark Twain's *Adventures of Huckleberry Finn* (1885) concludes when its boy hero rejects corrupt "sivilization" and takes off for the territory, just like Natty Bumppo. This gesture of withdrawal has been repeated in innumerable American fictions. But other writers have preferred to construct narratives whose protagonists remain uncomfortably within society, the better to represent the tensions between self and the rest of the world. Numerous American authors plead with their readers to keep in mind that a true democracy must respect individuals and encourage the greatest possible degree of personal self-expression in its citizens. Ralph Waldo Emerson was by far the most influential advocate of this position. He wrote in his 1841 essay "Self-Reliance" that "whoso would be a man must be a nonconformist," that the "great man is he who in the midst of the crowd keeps with perfect sweetness the independence of solitude." Community, from this point of view, was nothing but a threat to self-integrity: "Society everywhere is in conspiracy against the manhood of every one of its members."

For another group of writers and thinkers, however, society took precedence over individuals, for if a society failed, its individual citizens would also be destroyed. These conservatives—among whom were such now-forgotten but once-notable names as Edward Everett, Jared Sparks, John Gorham Palfrey, Richard Hildreth, and George Ticknor—did not share their democratically minded compatriots' faith in human nature. They maintained that the triumph of an ethos of extreme individualism would necessarily lead to national suicide: either the nation would degenerate into an anarchy of competing selfish interests that would (so history taught) quickly give way to dictator-ship, or individuals might come together in a shared ethic of material greed that would enable survival at the cost of all moral principle. For these thinkers the challenge of American life involved finding ways to control individualism by an ethic of social obligation. They imagined that a powerful literature, widely disseminated, could be one of those ways.

It was thinkers of this conservative type rather than exponents of individual-ism who initiated the project of creating a national literature that would reflect national ideals as a means of building up a worthy, virtuous citizenry. For those who think of literature as radical in its very essence, it is sobering to realize that these conservatives were at first the *only* people in America who took literature seriously.

☆ ☆ ☆ National Literature as New England Literature

This first group of literary nationalists was comprised entirely of New Englanders, and their program had a strongly regional flavor. Such New England priority was no accident: in 1800 New England had the highest literacy rate and the largest number of schools, colleges, publishers, news-papers, and magazines in the country. Along with their preference for cen-tralized and hierarchical forms of government—a preference that Nathaniel Hawthorne's *The Scarlet Letter* (1850) displays in full to a modern reader—Massachusetts patriots had taken the lead in resisting England. Therefore, members of its elite were able to argue that it was *they*, rather than greedy democratic individualists, who were the "real" Americans. This postrevolu-tionary elite sincerely believed that only wide distribution of New England values throughout the nation could guarantee America a peaceful and pros-perous future.

Chaos theory teaches us that apparently insignificant aspects of an initial situation produce remarkably influential effects. That New England was the first region to develop a self-conscious literary project has had immense implications for American literature. It has meant that a disproportionate amount of the writing in this country has in fact been the work of New Englanders (by birth or adoption) and people of New England ancestry. It has meant that the history and canon of American literature have focused on the New England contribution. And it has meant that writers who wanted to deviate from literary orthodoxy had to invest considerable energy in a struggle against the New England vision of literary value in order to do so. In 1900 every writer who was considered major was a New Englander. Although the canon has been expanded and revised several times in this century, it seems unlikely that any amount of canonical revision will ever remove the New England presence from American literature.

In the program of the New England patriots who attempted to form a self-consciously national literature, two aspects have proven especially consequential. The first was their strong advocacy of the need for a literary establishment to assess, codify, and disseminate literary standards throughout the country. Key activities would be forming critical journals, supporting literary clubs, establishing libraries, encouraging education and learning at all levels and in formal and informal settings. In 1803 a group of prosperous young Bostonians founded a literary club that published a magazine of literary criticism called the *Monthly Anthology*. The *Anthology* undertook to review all American literary productions, attempting both to encourage and control the creation of an American cultural life. This journal, which ceased publication in 1811, was followed by others more enduring: the *Christian Examiner*, founded in 1813, and the *North American Review*, founded in 1815. During the 1840s the Boston publishers Ticknor and Fields embarked on a publicity campaign to present New England authors as the exponents of a truly homegrown high literary culture. In connection with that campaign the house established the *Atlantic Monthly* in 1857. To be sure, there were hundreds of journals and publishers in the United States by the end of the 1850s, and yet the attempt to define New England as the cultural capital of the country succeeded to a striking degree.

The Ohioan William Dean Howells, notwithstanding his strong democratic principles and his commitment to literary realism, could think of no greater bliss than to become (as he did in 1865) an editor for the *Atlantic Monthly*. Mark Twain, for all his backwoods satire of New England self-satisfaction and intellectual pretentiousness, and for all his advocacy of the vernacular, settled happily in Hartford, Connecticut, soon after his marriage in 1870. He sank a considerable proportion of his literary earnings into building a fine mansion there and boasted of having Harriet Beecher Stowe as a neighbor.

The second influential thrust of the New England literary nationalist program was its construction of a chronicle of American history and literature featuring the New England Puritans as the political and cultural progenitors of the entire nation. As elsewhere in their thinking, the early New England literati here combined a parochial boosterism and a spirit of commercial enterprise with deeply held political and ethical convictions. The lawyer and orator Rufus Choate, a second-generation member of this group, put it eloquently: the old Puritan character was "an extraordinary mental and moral phenomenon" that had been raised up by God for the specific purpose of founding a nation. If the Puritans could be made to live in "the heart and memory and affections of all the generations of the people to whom they bequeathed these representative governments and this undefiled religion," then much would be done toward "moulding and fixing the national character." Americans, reminded of their fathers, would remember that they were brothers.

The point is, of course, that the Puritans were *not* the fathers of all American citizens by any means—nor were all Puritans, as Choate's rhetoric implied, of the male gender. The history that was to be installed would achieve unity at the cost of accuracy. In the view of these New Englanders, such pious fictionalizing of early American history would be justified by the results, which would be the production of a uniform and uniformly moral character among diverse Americans. Since the United States lacked the common heritage of rituals, customs, heroes, and history that was thought to underpin a national identity, such a heritage had to be deliberately created.

The only experience that Americans of 1800 seemed to have in common was the participation in the American Revolution, and so the New England nationalists installed the Puritans at the fountain of American history by describing them as the original revolutionaries. The Puritan flight to America for the sacred cause of establishing a polity ruled by their interpretation of God's word was reinterpreted as a migration on behalf of religious and civil liberty for all. Never mind that it was actually the Virginian Thomas Jefferson who wrote the Declaration of Independence; it was John Hancock, a man of Massachusetts, who was the first to sign it.

The initial fruits of this campaign of Puritanizing American life were a proliferation of historical novels, poems, and essays about the Puritans, and the emergence of a strong scholarly interest in the writings of the Puritans themselves. The many early Puritan histories were searched out, recovered, preserved, and published in some cases for the first time. Puritan diaries, letters, and sermons were likewise collected and publicized. William Bradford's *History of Plimouth Plantation* became available as a source for such all-American icons as the arrival of the *Mayflower* in the dead of winter, the disembarkment at Plymouth Rock, and the first Thanksgiving Day. Amid all the religious and political writings of the seventeenth century, New England cultural antiquarians were also able to uncover occasional examples of belles lettres, such as the personal lyrics of Anne Bradstreet about marital happiness, the death of grandchildren, the traumas of her house burning down, illness, and aging. Although the metaphysical religious devotional poems of Edward Taylor were not discovered until the twentieth century, the long-standing interest in all things Puritan made them immediate classics.

Surveying the eighteenth century, the New England nationalists were able to resuscitate the religious writings of Jonathan Edwards, pastor at Northampton from 1729 to 1750, so successfully that he is still considered to be America's finest Calvinist theologian. And although he was obviously no Puritan, Benjamin Franklin, the runaway from Boston who made a name for himself in Philadelphia, could still be claimed as a son of New England. The moderation, industry, honesty, and frugality that he inculcated in his popular *Poor Richard's Almanac* (1733–58) were solid New England virtues, and his belief in the printed word (a printer by trade, he founded the *Pennsylvania Gazette* in 1729) could be perceived as a trait harking back to the Puritans' reverence for the printed Bible. Insofar as Pennsylvania, owing to the pacifism of the Quakers who dominated its politics, tended at first toward neutrality in the Revolution, it was also easy for New Englanders to credit New England for Franklin's revolutionary activism.

☆ ☆ ☆ The Antebellum Era

As New Englanders increasingly lost control of national politics, they turned their attention to cultural matters ever more strongly. Rufus Choate enunciated this fallback position in 1843 when he conceded that New England was no longer politically influential but insisted that "there is an influence which I would rather see Massachusetts exert on her sisters of this Union, than see her furnish a President every twelve years or command a majority of any division in congress; and that is such an influence as Athens exerted on the taste and opinion first of Greece, then of Rome, then of the universal modern world." This influence "would rest on the admiration of the beautiful, the good, the true in art, in poetry, in thought."

Working in the atmosphere of this New England cultural nationalism, New England authors produced a great deal of work that fitted Choate's goals. By 1855 six nationally known authors had emerged who seemed to express the full range of New England literary culture: Ralph Waldo Emerson, Nathaniel Hawthorne, Henry Wadsworth Longfellow, John Greenleaf Whittier, Oliver Wendell Holmes, and James Russell Lowell. Although Emerson's stirring calls for self-reliance and nonconformity could be read as a recipe for individualistic anarchy, they could also be perceived as grounded in a New England certainty that the inner self, directed by the divinity within, would be far more morally demanding than any external authority. Hawthorne's stories and novels were seen to blend the typical New England concern for history with an artistic practice that uncovered the moral significance of material facts. Longfellow, born wealthy and well married, was professor of modern languages at Harvard; he was hailed as an aristocrat who understood the people, a description that the great popularity of poems like *Evangeline* and *Hiawatha* seemed to bear out. Whittier, a Quaker farmer, was a well-known abolitionist poet who represented the reformist idealism of New England; Holmes, a Harvard professor of medicine, composed amusing verse and essays demonstrating the New England aptitude for cultivated wit; and Lowell, an editor and critic (also a professor) from another distinguished family, wrote numerous essays and reviews on behalf of New England literature.

Those celebrated six were by no means the only active writers in antebellum New England. In the 1820s Lydia Maria Child and Catharine Maria Sedgwick contributed to the historical project with novels about the New England Indian Wars and the Revolution. Margaret Fuller began her literary career with philosophical essays and scholarly translations and then left New England to write for Horace Greeley's *New York Tribune*, continuing a trend of New Englandizing journalism that William Cullen Bryant had begun a generation earlier. Fuller authored a feminist treatise, *Woman in the Nineteenth Century*, in 1845. Harriet Beecher Stowe's sensationally successful antislavery novel *Uncle Tom's Cabin* (1852) was one expression of New England idealism; her historical work about the effects of Calvinist theology on everyday New England life—*The Minister's Wooing* (1859) and *Old Town Folks* (1869)—was another. Then, too, though his contemporaries might not have considered him a New Englander, the escaped slave Frederick Douglass settled in Massachusetts and published an autobiography—*Narrative of the Life of Frederick Douglass, an American Slave* (1845)—that applied the New England ethic of responsible liberty to the situation of enslaved African Americans. Indeed the abolitionist movement, which originated in New England, depended much more on an ethos of mutual social obligation than on individualism.

No fewer than four historians from Massachusetts—George Bancroft, Francis Parkman, John Lothrop Motley, and William H. Prescott—began their work before the Civil War; Bancroft's *History of the United States* served as the standard source for American school history texts for generations. Thoreau's *Walden* had to wait until the twentieth century to become an American classic, but with its mixture of nonconforming individualism and intense moralism it was an unmistakable product of this heightened sense of cultural possibility that existed in New England before the Civil War.

The dominant New England presence did not stifle literary activity in other parts of the country, but it certainly diminished its visibility. In New York important work had been done earlier in the century by Washington Irving and James Fenimore Cooper. These men, though they were far less idealistic than the New Englanders, were equally interested in establishing a national literature based on the particulars of American life and history. Irving's *Sketch Book,* published in England in 1819, was the first American work to be favorably received in that country. Two stories in the collection—"Rip Van Winkle" and "The Legend of Sleepy Hollow"—ingeniously adapted German folk motifs to an American setting and made them vehicles of social commentary. Rip, a repudiator of Benjamin Franklin's work ethic who sleeps right through the American Revolution, and Ichabod Crane, the hypocritical psalm-singing schoolmaster from Connecticut, were both good-natured satires on New England mores. Cooper's Leatherstocking Tales with their heroic frontiersmen and their exciting accounts of Indian warfare were translated into numerous languages in every part of the world.

During the 1840s, Edgar Allan Poe, a southerner who edited magazines in Charleston, New York, and Philadelphia, attempted deliberately to counter New England hegemony through an alternative literary practice of gothic fiction, romantic poetry, and severe literary criticism. His premise, that emotional effect not moral uplift was what literature should be written for, was rejected by the establishment. In 1850 Herman Melville—who had scored a popular success in 1846 with *Typee,* a fictionalized account of his adventures in the South Seas—produced a huge book combining sea adventure with metaphysical allegory. Entitled *Moby-Dick,* the work was seen as too difficult for entertainment and too ambiguous for philosophy; yet it was evidently meant to contribute to the dialectic between self-expression and self-control central to New England literature. In 1855 Walt Whitman, a small-time Democratic politician and newspaper editor from Brooklyn, suddenly initiated a program to revolutionize American poetry by printing a book of twelve original poems called *Leaves of Grass.* Written in free verse, and celebrating the body as well as the soul, this poetry was attacked as incompetent and obscene for almost half a century. Over the years, however, Whitman persisted, revising, expanding, and republishing *Leaves of Grass* until, at this death, it contained several hundred poems.

In a quite different vein, an outpouring of novels by, for, and about women attempted to establish a feminine version of American identity. The formulaic plot of these novels showed young women triumphing over obstacles by developing inner strength. Women readers were assured that if they developed themselves as strong and capable individuals, their kind of virtue could balance the effect of a male individualistic ethos that was running amok and destroying any American sense of community. In contrast to Susanna Rowson's *Charlotte Temple* (1791), a sad novel of seduction that became the first American bestseller, these novels—among whose chief practitioners were Susan Warner of

New York and Maria Susanna Cummins of New England—were idealistically upbeat, guaranteeing a place for women in the national polity.

Even as the writings of the Puritans were retrieved from oblivion, the literature of the revolutionary and immediate postrevolutionary periods tended to disappear from view. The eighteenth-century literary forms in which they were written, their intensely partisan rhetoric, and the fact that much of this work had originated outside New England all contributed to their neglect. Among temporarily lost authors was the poet Phillis Wheatley, an African brought to Massachusetts as a slave when she was only seven years old. Her *Poems on Various Subjects, Religious and Moral* (1773) merged Enlightenment rationalism with evangelical Christianity and referred to the author's race only obliquely. Also lost were several lively political satires, a few patriotic epics, and a group of gothic sensationalist novels by Charles Brockden Brown that contained a severe critique of the excesses of American individualism. And— always excepting the Declaration of Independence, which has never lost its position as our greatest political document—the work of numerous southerners also fell out of view. Indeed, the South was progressively marginalized in American cultural life throughout the nineteenth century and had begun to regard itself as an alternative culture well before the onset of the Civil War.

Those who are excluded from a consensus that they cannot ignore have various ways of responding. They may try to refashion themselves in order to be accepted; they may try to modify the consensus to make it more congenial to them; they may try to overturn it; or they may develop alternatives. The New England cultural narrative, though it was intended to be inclusive, eventually provoked all of these responses. Yet every response displayed traces of the consensus it was resisting.

☆ ☆ ☆ After the Civil War

American literature after the Civil War can be summarized as the expression of strategies by which two groups of writers in particular—the regionalists working from the geographical peripheries of the country and the realists (and the spin-off movement of naturalists) located in the cities—broke free of the New England hegemony to develop a literature that they deemed more appropriate for the turbulent social dynamics characteristic of the end of the century. Prose fiction was the chosen genre for all these groups, which saw poetry as the domain of artifice and inflated rhetoric.

At exactly this time, however, the poetry-centered antebellum New England canon was installed in American schools as the heart of national identity, almost certainly as a way of neutralizing the possible disruptive effects of these new literary movements and the swelling polyglot tide of immigrants. The proponents of the old consensus continued to believe that the United States could be unified only if it had a single model of the American type to follow. Thus even as works by realists and naturalists and regionalists proliferated, schoolchildren read works by Emerson, Hawthorne, and Longfellow and learned that these were our national heritage.

The realists, as the name of their movement implies, attempted to portray American life as it was, not as it should be. They were not prepared to recognize that their work could only embody their own perceptions of American life rather than an objective reality. William Dean Howells, who had deserted Boston for New York, took the urban businessman for his particular subject. He studied this new version of the American individualist in novels like *The Rise of Silas Lapham* (1885) and *A Hazard of New Fortunes* (1890). Howells's belief that entrepreneurship should be guided by a sense of social obligation meant that he had not really given up the New England ethos of moral self-discipline. Henry James, who lived in Europe for most of his adult life, critiqued the New England way from the vantage point of an international aestheticism. In such works as *The American* (1877), *Daisy Miller* (1878), and *The Ambassadors* (1903), he conceded that New Englanders were typical Americans only to satirize them as childlike mixtures of innocence, self-assurance, ignorance, and greed. Edith Wharton wrote about rich and powerful New Yorkers, focusing her novels, especially *The House of Mirth* (1905), on the deplorable constriction of women's lives in an atmosphere of empty frivolity and cutthroat business deals. Ellen Glasgow, from Richmond, Virginia, wrote about the oppression of women by a postbellum southern patriarchy committed to outdated codes of chivalry and sentiment; her best-known novel is *Barren Ground* (1925). Since the individualistic ethos had never been fully available to women, it is not surprising that many women writers continued to support and reproduce the New England consensus when many male authors rejected it.

The naturalists dismissed realism for what they saw as its unrealistic belief that human beings could make moral choices. They thought that people were helpless victims of obscure but omnipotent social forces. Their use of extremely powerful individuals as channels for such forces, however, produced characters who looked suspiciously like rampant individualists. Such writers as Frank Norris, Hamlin Garland, Jack London, and Stephen Crane worked from within a naturalist aesthetic. In *Sister Carrie* (1900), Theodore Dreiser meshed the story of Carrie's success with that of her lover Hurstwood's failure to emphasize the randomness of human destiny; in the more moralistic *An*

American Tragedy (1925), he intimated that Americans were victimized by the fraudulent promise of material success.

Regionalism set itself the task of opposing the homogenizing tendencies of late nineteenth-century life. Its depiction of various regional cultures trying to resist modernity made the strongest literary statement before the contemporary era that American identity was an oppressive fiction that denied the fact of American diversity. Yet since its characters were all at odds with the forces of urbanization and technology that became so prominent at the end of the century, and since they were all rural, the movement conceded as much as it claimed. Individuality became part of an agricultural way of life available to fewer and fewer Americans. Their careful attempts to replicate regional dialects centered on the speech of Tennessee mountaineers and Down Eastern folks from Maine, not Poles and Neapolitans. The tone of regional writing varied from nostalgic evocations of golden worlds of female companionship (in Sarah Orne Jewett's *The Country of the Pointed Firs*, 1896) to savage representation of stunted and narrow lives (in Mary Wilkins Freeman's short-story collections *A Humble Romance*, 1887, and *A New England Nun*, 1891). One of these regionalists, Kate Chopin, merged regional writing with a story of the constraints on women's development; her novel *The Awakening* (1899) has become a feminist classic.

Part realist, part naturalist, part regionalist, and all humorist, the most extraordinary writer of the age was Samuel Clemens of Missouri, who, under the pen name Mark Twain, became the most famous author that the United States has ever produced. Twain did more than write about the contradictions of American identity; he embodied them. His down-to-earth, wisecracking, sham-detesting, straight-talking, and infinitely funny persona was the strategic creation of an angry man with a genius for turning vernacular speech into high art. His masterpiece, *Adventures of Huckleberry Finn*, is in every way an affront to New England values of style and substance. Nevertheless, when Huckleberry Finn rejects what he takes to be the voice of conscience and aids the runaway slave Jim, and when the pretensions of the antebellum South are exposed as vicious falsehood, the novel becomes as New Englandish as Thoreau.

☆ ☆ ☆ World War I and After

With the American entrance into World War I came a new cultural sophistication. American literature took a turn toward modernity, cosmopolitanism, and internationalism. Numerous young writers spent time in Europe, simultaneously acquiring a Jamesian scorn for American provinciality while striving to overcome all traces of provinciality in their own writing. Among these expatriates were two antidemocratic poets, Ezra Pound and T. S. Eliot, whose search for order in an increasingly fragmented and violent world led them to reemphasize the importance of poetry and to write poems advocating authoritarian politics (Pound's *Cantos*, written over a period of forty years beginning in 1919) and authoritarian religion (Eliot's *Four Quartets*, 1943). Each had earlier written a stunning denunciation of modern life: "Hugh Selwyn Mauberly" (Pound) and *The Waste Land* (Eliot). *The Waste Land* (1922), with its corrosive pessimism, may well be the most influential poem written in the twentieth century, calling out a host of counterstatements and imitations. The techniques of the poem—complicated syntax, obscurity of reference, fragmentation, multivocality—became hallmarks of the practice known as "modernism," a term designed to suggest that anybody who wrote in any other way was old-fashioned. The difficulty of modernist poetry was meant to alienate the mass audience, whose demands, from the high modernist point of view, had prevented America from developing a high culture.

Other American poets adapted modernism to more romantic, optimistic, idealistic, "American" goals. William Carlos Williams in *Paterson* (1946–50) and Hart Crane in *The Bridge* (1930) attempted to apply modernist techniques to representations of the American landscape, the American present, and American history. Another group, of whom Marianne Moore and Wallace Stevens are the chief exemplars, were more interested in crafting poetry than in denouncing a world that had no use for it; both wrote poems that were simultaneously statements about, and examples of, modernism as aesthetic practice rather than cultural commentary.

Beyond all of these, Gertrude Stein produced the most radical language experiments of her time, anticipating postmodernist discourse in several ways. She was the first writer to develop a literary program from the premise that poetic language and grammatical syntax were male inventions designed for purposes of domination and oppression (see her poem "Patriarchal Poetry"). Thus her experimental writing was an outgrowth of her feminism—and also an outgrowth of her unreconstructed American individualism. It is no accident that her longest work is called *The Making of Americans* (1925). At the furthest extreme from Stein, the programmatic antimodernist Robert Frost tenaciously worked on the project of combining conventional poetic rhyme and meter with the rhythms of ordinary speech, writing poems that eventually made him—after years of obscurity—America's best-known and most popular poet. The voice that he articulated was a self-consciously vernacular version of the old New England consensus.

Many novelists who practiced between the world wars attempted to adapt the modernist aesthetic to prose. F. Scott Fitzgerald became prominent with *The Great Gatsby* (1925), a streamlined, allusive novel that simultaneously glamorized and critiqued American consumerism; there were echoes of Dreiser in its mournful narrative of the destruction of an ambitious young American by the mendacious dream of success. Ernest Hemingway produced two bitter antiwar novels (*The Sun Also Rises*, 1925, and *A Farewell to Arms*, 1929) along with autobiographical short stories about men and war, men and hunting, men and fishing, that inaugurated a powerfully influential cult of hard-boiled sentimentalism projected in a clipped, journalistic style.

The preeminent novelist of the period was William Faulkner, from Oxford, Mississippi, who followed a couple of astonishing experimental novels (*The Sound and the Fury* in 1929 and *As I Lay Dying* in 1930) with a series of romantic, rhetorical, yet sociologically acute novels about the South after the Civil War, of which *Absalom, Absalom!* (1936) is probably the most powerful. Faulkner's work aimed to transform regionalism into universal utterance by recasting it in a modernist idiom. His example inspired numerous southern writers and initiated what has been called the Southern Renaissance. Another writer who built from regionalism was Willa Cather, whose novels about the Nebraska prairie and the Southwest, about women, about artists—including *O Pioneers!* (1913) and *Death Comes for the Archbishop* (1926)—encapsulated a modernist search for stability and value in the American past and American landscape.

During the 1920s the canon of American literature taught in schools began to undergo major modification. Even though Lowell, Holmes, Whittier, and Longfellow were eliminated, the New England consensus was preserved by introducing Thoreau and Emily Dickinson, by bringing in Whitman as an Emersonian idealist, and by attaching Melville and Poe to Hawthorne as investigators of the spiritual meanings of material facts. A sense of the darker side of the human personality, fueled by modernist pessimism, could be given a precedent in the Puritan sense of original sin, and accordingly the study of Puritan literature became newly prominent in college English departments.

It was also in this period that the United States saw the first concerted attempt by African Americans to define a place for themselves in American literary culture. The movement known as the Harlem Renaissance involved such writers as Countee Cullen, Jessie Fauset, Langston Hughes, Nella Larson, James Weldon Johnson, Claude McKay, and Zora Neale Hurston. Surely no other group of Americans faced a more difficult challenge in attempting to negotiate between the consensus idea of American identity, the ideal of individualism, and the claims of their own cultural heritage. The aims of the Harlem writers were complicated by the fact that their readers were almost all white. They hoped that at some future date a black audience would also come into being, partly as a result of their efforts. Some Harlem writers wrote realistically of the experiences of black Americans in a white world; others experimented with importing black folk motifs into literary forms. Probably Hughes, who adapted blues to poetry, and Hurston, who used folklore for plot sequences, were most successful in this latter endeavor.

Apart from these writers stood Richard Wright, whose 1940 novel *Native Son* catches, even in its title, the complex claims of a black literary practice. Bigger Thomas, the novel's murderer-protagonist, was "native" in the condescending anthropological sense of "primitive" and equally in the sense of belonging properly to the nation—both of America and outside it. His character was at once uniquely his own and a product of American racism. Although Wright posed a question specific to African Americans, the implications of his work were basic to the whole question of American identity. Could one ever "really" be an American if one were not white, male, northeastern, upper middle class, and descended from the Englishmen who landed at Plymouth Rock? And if not, wasn't the entire cult of New England literature a strategy of exclusion rather than inclusion?

The stock market crash of 1929 initiated a decade of radical writing that has been neglected because of the political reaction of the Cold War. Actually, a tradition of social radicalism had existed in the United States since the 1880s, but self-consciously radical and revolutionary literary movements flourished with particular strength just before World War I and again in the 1930s. John Dos Passos's trilogy *USA* (1930–36) is probably the best-known product of this movement; however, there were dozens of radical fiction writers and poets, and many writers between the world wars went through a radical phase. Much of this work appeared in periodicals and remains uncollected.

In the years since World War II American literature has pursued a number of initiatives. A group of novelists, chiefly white males, have written novels in which the American dream of self is alternately praised or derided depending on whether it is seen to be attainable or fraudulent. A somewhat younger group of experimental novelists and poets, whom we may loosely describe as postmodernists, have followed Gertrude Stein's lead and rejected the representational claims of language on which novels of human interaction depend, attempting instead to make poetry and prose that constantly gestures toward the self-reflexivity of language. These writers have been joined at times by another group that rejects the notion of personal identity as an outdated fabrication and adapts the postmodern distrust of language to a program of undermining the concept of unitary character.

Parallel with these literary trends is one that may well turn out to be the most important for the future of American literature—the emergence into literary language of numerous groups of formerly silent Americans. American women have written and published since 1640, but they are now writing in greater numbers and with a feminist outspokenness that has not been seen before. Particularly significant has been the development of a powerful tradition among women writers who are black and who have accepted the responsibility of mediating between race and gender. Latin Americans, Asian Americans, and American Indians have all published notable works of literature in the last forty years. It is the sense of exclusion from the canon that has inspired all these voices. These voices do not dismiss the American promise, however, but insist that it must be applied to all Americans, that an American identity that fails to include them is unworthy. The old moral imperative has come full circle; "outsiders" have most fully taken the American message to heart—the message that in America there should be *no* outsiders.

FURTHER READING

Three good one-volume literary histories are Marcus Cunliffe's *The Literature of the United States*, rev. ed. (New York, 1983); Emory Elliott, ed., *The Columbia Literary History of the United States* (New York, 1988); and Peter Conn's *Literature in America: An Illustrated History* (New York, 1989). See also the one-volume *History of Southern Literature*, ed. Louis D. Rubin, Jr. (Baton Rouge, La., 1985). Blyden Jackson has published the first volume of a projected four-volume *History of Afro-American Literature* (Baton Rouge, La., 1990–). *The Oxford Companion to American Literature*, 5th ed. (New York, 1983), is a useful reference tool. Robert B. Stepto, *From Behind the Veil: A Study of Afro-American Narrative* (Urbana, Ill., 1979), is a good general study of its topic, as are Werner Sollers, *Beyond Ethnicity: Consent and Descent in American Culture* (New York, 1986), and Arnold Krupat, *Native American Autobiography* (Berkeley, Calif., 1990).

Kenneth Murdoch's *Literature and Theology in Colonial New England* (Cambridge, Mass., 1949) is still a good book for beginners. Influential statements of the Puritan basis of American literature are Sacvan Bercovitch's *The Puritan Origins of the American Self* (New Haven, Conn., 1975) and *The American Jeremiad* (Madison, Wis., 1978). The eighteenth century is covered in Kenneth Silverman's *A Cultural History of the American Revolution* (New York, 1976) and Emory Elliott's *Revolutionary Writers: Literature and Authority in the New Republic, 1725–1810* (New York, 1982). Lewis P. Simpson's *The Man of Letters in New England and the South* (Baton Rouge, La., 1981) and Robert A. Ferguson's *Law and Letters in American Culture* (Cambridge, Mass., 1984) discuss the formation of a literary establishment. Lawrence Buell's *Literary Transcendentalism* (Ithaca, N.Y., 1973) and *New England Literary Culture: From Revolution to Renaissance* (New York, 1986) are basic reading. Nina Baym's *Woman's Fiction: A Guide to Novels by and about Women in America, 1820–1870* (Ithaca, N.Y., 1978) and Joanne Dobson's *Dickinson and the Strategies of Reticence* (Bloomington, Ind., 1989) discuss literature by women before the Civil War.

For the period between the Civil War and World War I, see the following: Warner Berthoff, *The Ferment of Realism: American Literature, 1884–1919* (New York, 1965); Larzar Ziff, *The American 1890s: Life and Times of a Lost Generation* (New York, 1966); Jay Martin, *Harvests of Change: American Literature, 1865–1914* (Englewood Cliffs, N.J., 1967); Josephine Donovan, *New England Local Color Literature: A Woman's Tradition* (New York, 1983); Donald Pizer, *Realism and Naturalism in Nineteenth-Century American Literature*, rev. ed. (Carbondale, Ill., 1984); and Eric J. Sundquist, ed., *American Realism: New Essays* (Baltimore, 1985).

The period between the two world wars is discussed in Frederick J. Hoffman, *The Twenties: American Writing in the Postwar Decade* (New York, 1955); Walter B. Rideout, *The Radical Novel in the United States, 1900–1954* (Cambridge, Mass., 1956); Daniel Aaron, *Writers on the Left: Episodes in American Literary Communism* (New York, 1961); Roy Harvey Pearce, *The Continuity of American Poetry* (Princeton, N.J., 1961); Marcus Klein, *Foreigners: The Making of American Literature, 1900–1940* (Chicago, 1981); Michael Spindler, *American Literature and Social Change: William Dean Howells to Arthur Miller* (Bloomington, Ind., 1983); Shari Benstock, *Women of the Left Bank: Paris, 1900–1940* (Austin, Tex., 1986); Albert Gelpi, *A Coherent Splendor: The American Poetic Renaissance, 1910–1950* (New York, 1987); and Cary Nelson, *Repression and Recovery: Modern American Poetry and the Politics of Cultural Memory* (Madison, Wis., 1989).

For the Harlem Renaissance, see Nathan Huggins, *Harlem Renaissance* (New York, 1971), and Houston Baker, *Modernism and the Harlem Renaissance* (Chicago, 1987).

For the period since World War II, see Morris Dickstein, *Gates of Eden: American Culture in the Sixties* (New York, 1977); Daniel G. Hoffman, ed., *The Harvard Guide to Contemporary American Writing* (Cambridge, Mass., 1979); Alicia Suskin Ostriker, *Stealing the Language: The Emergence of Women's Poetry in America* (Boston, 1986); and Hazel Carby, *Reconstructing Afro-American Womanhood* (New York, 1988).

11 ☆ Literature

☆ and Values

The American

☆ *Crusoe and*

the Idea of

the West

☆ Richard Lehan

W. H. Auden wrote in his remarkable elegy on William Butler Yeats that "poetry makes nothing happen." In a sense Auden was right. Our national values seem more directly connected to economic and political life than to literature. Literature may reflect those values—but does it create or initiate them? I suggest that there is an inextricable connection between American cultural values and our literature and that at the deepest level of consciousness one reinforces and recycles the other. To the extent that our national identity is revealed in our literature, it is inseparable also from our sense of purpose and destiny. I hope to make these heady ideas a bit more concrete by focusing on an American prototype who embodied our cultural values and whose experiences have become entwined with our sense of national purpose.

He was discontent with his father's life and wanted to test the limits of his own strength and independence. Leaving home and family, he traveled across a sea and settled in a New World colony, then embarked on another adventure that left him shipwrecked on a deserted island where his very survival depended upon his wits and natural intelligence. His name, of course, is Robinson Crusoe, and his creator, Daniel Defoe. Defoe's story in 1719 soon took on an archetypal quality not only because it was inseparable from the tales of com-

236

mercial adventure that characterized his age but also because Crusoe's experience paralleled so closely the experience of the first settlers in North America. Defoe imagined a Crusoe who has turned out to be the father of us all.

☆ ☆ ☆ The Crusoe Legacy: Initiative and Exploitation

Like the early settlers, Robinson Crusoe brought to the New World a split consciousness in which he had to reconcile his Puritan sense of God with an empirical state of mind. Both demanded careful observation of his surroundings—the first for signs from God revealing his spiritual well-being, the second for empirical evidence of the workings of nature. Crusoe survived because he learned to read nature—learned how the tides flowed so that he could get in and out of the harbor to fish without drowning, learned when and when not to plant his corn, learned how to tame and husband his flock. Crusoe ultimately imposed his will upon nature and learned to control his immediate environment. He was helped in this purpose by tools that he brought from the shipwrecked boat as well as his ability to make new ones. As his mechanical ability became greater, he moved to more advanced forms of technology, firing pottery and forging other implements.

His hard work and resourcefulness, his rudimentary understanding of and desire to control his environment, began to pay off. He soon had a surplus of food and a flock of tamed goats and divided his time between a fortresslike home overlooking the crossroads of the ocean and a countrylike estate further inland. As this new world began to give way to his control, he was startled to find that he was not alone on the island—that cannibal tribes used it for occasional barbecues—and so he extended his control over other humans as well as nature itself. His man Friday, in awe of his rifle and other examples of technology, knelt before him and put Crusoe's foot on his head in an act of submission.

As others arrived on the island, Crusoe welcomed them so long as they accepted a contract theory of government with himself as head. Near the end of the novel, as he prepared to leave the island, Crusoe also revealed his beliefs about women. Their role, he insisted, must be subsumed to that of men and justified by breeding (that is, by pragmatic) purposes. Before he left the island, Crusoe laid claim to the land, part of which he gave up for communal use, the rest of which he claimed for himself. When he returned to the island on the last page of the novel, he began to subdivide and sell it as real estate.

If we step back from this novel, we can find the perspective to see Crusoe as our common father. Coming from the Old World to the New, he brought with him both the old religious-mythic consciousness and a new empirical-scientific state of mind. With the help of tools and a rudimentary technology, he imposed his will upon the land, bringing the animals, natives, and eventually women under his control. And before he was through, he had turned this control into wealth.

☆ ☆ ☆ The American Crusoe Conquers the New Land

To probe the origins of the American Crusoe one needs only to turn the pages of our national literature. We see him in William Bradford's *History of the Plimouth Plantation*, where the Puritan is poised to take from the land what it can give and to use the Native Americans to complete that desire. (The episode with Squantum recapitulates the Friday experience.) At the deeper levels of national consciousness, the American Crusoe reflects a value system in which the brightest ideals compete with the most expedient, pragmatic, utilitarian motives—a disposition cogently reflected in the *New Yorker* cartoon that showed two Puritans stepping off the *Mayflower*, one saying to the other: "My immediate desire is religious freedom, but my long-range goal is to get into real estate."

James Fenimore Cooper brought these mixed motives to his Natty Bumppo stories, showing another Crusoe crossing the country from upstate New York to the western prairie. As Natty moves west, he leaves civilization behind. At the end of *The Pioneers* (1823), Cooper writes: "He had gone towards the setting sun—the foremost in that band of pioneers who are opening the way for the march of our nation across the continent." But the achievement is not unalloyed, and in *The Prairie* (1827) Natty castigates the built-in waste that seems inseparable from our desire to conquer the land. Here Leatherstocking condemns the wanton cutting and burning of trees, the slaughter of animals, and the waste of fish caught and left to rot. The trapper concludes: "What the world of America is coming to, and where the . . . inventions of its people are to have an end, the Lord, He only knows. . . . How much has the beauty of the wilderness been deformed."

Herman Melville's fiction also reveals the American Crusoe at work. Melville's own journeys to the Marquesas Islands and Tahiti in *Typee* (1846) and *Omoo* (1847) brought him face-to-face with a primitive world in the process of being corrupted by missionaries and other visitors from the West. In *Mardi* (1849), *Redburn* (1849), and *White Jacket* (1850), he treats the related theme of freedom as a disguise for man's misuse of authority—first in the tyrannical Captain Riga, again with the soulless master-at-arms Bland, and lastly with

Caldwaller Cuticle, M.D., who performs an unnecessary operation and in effect murders a sailor in the name of science. These themes and others come into brilliant focus in *Moby-Dick* (1851), where, in Ahab, Melville combines the American Crusoe with the American Faust. Ahab's indomitable will drives him to demand answers from God and to challenge nature itself, embodied by Moby Dick, the source of his affliction. Like the blasted tree in the forest hit by lightning, Ahab has a scar that runs the length of his body, a symbol of human vulnerability, which he refuses to heed. Ahab will not accept a world of limits, insists upon imposing his will upon all that challenge it, and seems to call from nature itself a rage that finally, and alas destructively, restores us to a more humble position in the order of things. Ahab's desire to impose his will upon the white whale is not really different in kind or degree from Colonel John Moredeck's desire in *The Confidence Man* (1857) to wipe out the Indians, in Melville's brilliant disquisition on the "Metaphysics of Indian Hating." In all of these novels Melville takes on the moral problem of exploitation, of human desire to control and subsume what is wild in nature in the name of our own authority and as monuments to self. Melville has, of course, moved the American Crusoe into a new dimension, making him a little more reckless, a little more wild, and very much more obsessed with a sense of mission.

That sense of mission Melville could have observed in his contemporaries. Judge James Hall, for example, wrote an essay entitled "The Indian Hater," which Melville surely knew, and James Kirke Paulding wrote a long tale, *Westward Ho!* (1832), which includes the following: "The first year of his arrival he was only the lord of a wilderness, the possession of which was disputed equally by the wild animals and the red men who hunted them. By degrees, however, the former had become more rare, and the latter had receded before the irresistible influence of the 'wise white man,' who, wheresoever he goes, to whatever region of the earth, whether east or west, north or south, carries with him his destiny, which is to civilize the world, and rule it afterwards."

These ideals had their origin in Europe with Defoe and his contemporaries like Bishop George Berkeley, who in 1726 wrote, "Westward the course of empire takes its way." The same ideas were later codified by John Fiske (1842–1901), a Darwinian who lectured widely in America and Europe. After one London lecture, he wrote home to his wife: "When I began to speak of the future of the English race in Africa, I became aware of an immense *silence*, a kind of breathlessness, all over the room. All at once, when I came round to the parallel of the English career in America and Africa, there came a stupendous SHOUT, not a common demonstration of approval, but a deafening SHOUT of exultation. Don't you wish you had been there, dearest? It would have been the proudest moment of your life." Fiske retitled this lecture "Manifest Destiny," gave it again at London's Royal Institute in May 1880, and published it in *Harper's* in 1885. The idea of manifest destiny helped to justify the American rush west as well as to justify past history, including the Mexican War.

☆ ☆ ☆ The Counter Response: To a Different Drum

These ideas had not gone unchallenged in our literature. Thoreau had refused to pay taxes that would have financed the Mexican War, and his essay "Resistance to Civil Government" (1849), retitled "Civil Disobedience" after his death, served as an inspiration to Gandhi and later to the protesters against the Vietnam War. Thoreau questioned the assumptions of the American Crusoe, the man who wanted to impose his will upon nature rather than live in harmony with it. He saw what man could lose when he made himself part of the means—that is, the system—of transforming the land, and his own retreat to Walden was an experimental effort to reverse that process. He pointed out that the amount of time it took to walk from Concord to Boston was equal to the amount of work necessary to buy the rail fare, so that now the making of a living took precedence over living itself. Thoreau seriously questioned the "idea" of the West—the need to conquer the land simply because it was there—especially when conquest enslaves people to the monied system that it in turn creates. "We are in great haste to construct a magnetic telegraph from Maine to Texas," he noted, as he pondered whether Maine and Texas had anything to say to each other.

Walt Whitman also had mixed feelings about the American drive west. In *Leaves of Grass* (1855), he celebrated the building of America and the energy he felt inherent in this new experiment called democracy. But after the Civil War, during the corruption of the Grant administration, he had second thoughts that he recorded in *Democratic Vistas* (1871). Whitman was particularly concerned by the growing materialism of America that, he felt, would destroy the possibility of a more spiritual identity, and he challenged Robinson Crusoe's idea of individual exploitation of the land. He called for "a more universal ownership of property, general homesteads, general comfort—a vast, intertwining reticulation of wealth." He felt that a new national spirit could be created through a native literature that better defined our national ideals. Such a literature would come from the writer who went back to nature and lived in harmony rather than in conflict with the land. Such a unity would allow a return of faith that had been "scared away by science."

Mark Twain picked up where Whitman left off. In *A Connecticut Yankee in King Arthur's Court* (1889), Twain gives us his own version of the Robinson Crusoe story. His dream vision, which contrasts the nineteenth to the sixth century, also contrasts two American worlds—North and South. As the feudal world gave way to the commercial-industrial world of Robinson Crusoe, so Hank Morgan, the new technological man, tries to impose his will on the old feudal order. Armed with his knowledge of science and an assortment of tools and gadgets, he not only overpowers the old order but takes the new order to the doorstep of a self-destroying war.

Twain's *Connecticut Yankee* was his answer to Edward Bellamy's *Looking Backward* (1888), a utopian vision of the mechanical society that would supposedly bring world peace and prosperity once the cumulative fruits of the machine were divided up equally in a kind of totalitarian technocracy. What Twain saw so clearly in *Connecticut Yankee*, he had anticipated with Charles Dudley Warner fifteen years earlier in *The Gilded Age* (1873), the novel that gave its name to a post–Civil War era in which exploitation and development of the land were inseparable from the political process itself as an invisible hand of corruption reached out from New York and Washington, D.C.

The Civil War was surely the watershed of American history, a fact that no one saw more clearly than Whitman, Twain, and later William Faulkner. Faulkner also was deeply interested in the Robinson Crusoe legacy and embodied it in *Absalom, Absalom!* (1936). In this novel Henry Sutpen comes out of the backcountry of Virginia and later Haiti into Mississippi intent on cutting his personal empire out of the wilderness, taming the land, and building a mansion as testimony to his own hurt pride. His use of Native Americans, African Americans, and women as agents to this design—a demonic mission that subsumes human to mechanical purposes and ends— reveals a state of mind similar to that of Robinson Crusoe, although far more intent. Such intensity of purpose turned the wilderness into an enemy and led to its destruction, a point that Faulkner makes brilliantly in his novella "The Bear." Faulkner's mythic bear, the very embodiment of the wilderness, is destroyed simultaneously with the forest—"that doomed wilderness whose edges were being constantly . . . gnawed at by men with plows and axes who feared it because it was wilderness." These men precede the lumber company and the railroad, which mark the final end to man's mythic relationship with the land. They are embodied in Boon Hogganbeck, himself a hybrid, a corrupted form of the wilderness and thus appropriately the agent of the bear's death. The novella closes with Hogganbeck hunting squirrels, manifesting a lost sense of the heroic—frantically afraid someone will beat him to his diminished prey. "Get out of here! Don't touch them! Don't touch a one of them! They're mine!" he cries, his last word summarizing the rapaciousness that transformed the wilderness from the beginning.

☆ ☆ ☆ The Apotheosis of the Past

As the American Crusoe crossed the country, a strange phenomenon occurred. He began to locate his most ideal values in the past, even as he exhausted those values in the present in the very process of codifying them.

F. Scott Fitzgerald saw this in *The Great Gatsby* (1925), the last words of which are: "So we beat on, boats against the current, borne back ceaselessly into the past." Gatsby comes out of the West, modeling himself on the old frontier values of a Franklin and a James J. Hill at a time when the frontier had given way to the metropolis. The most immediate model for Gatsby is Dan Cody, whose name encapsulates the beginning and the end of the frontier movement, suggesting Daniel Boone at the beginning, a true American Robinson Crusoe who entered the untamed wilderness, and Buffalo Bill (William Cody) at the end, whose Wild West show made him an immense favorite in Madison Square Garden. At the end of the novel Nick Carraway ponders this historical transformation. He thinks back to what America must have meant to the new settlers, the old Dutch sailors who brought their hopes to the "fresh, green breast of the new world." "Its vanished trees," he goes on, "the trees that had made way for Gatsby's house, had once pandered in whispers to the last and greatest of all human dreams; for a transitory enchanted moment man must have held his breath in the presence of this continent, compelled into an esthetic contemplation he neither understood nor desired, face to face for the last time in history with something commensurate to his capacity for wonder." Gatsby shares this wonder, but, as Nick continues, "he did not know that it was already behind him, somewhere back in that vast obscurity beyond the city [that is, in the lost world of Jefferson and the frontier] where the dark fields of the republic rolled on under the night." Gatsby plays out a former dream in the new city, now dominated by money brokers like Tom Buchanan, who control the land from their boardrooms and no longer from the forest. At this point in American history Crusoe has put on a three-piece suit. The old ideals, now exhausted of possibilities and codified in the *Saturday Evening Post* and *Collier's*, can only create a pathetic sense of false purpose for the new Gatsbys.

In this context we can see the significance of the Rip Van Winkle-like nature of American ideals—that tendency to locate ideals in a world that cannot accommodate them. We have dozens of Rip Van Winkle books—works like Twain's *Life on the Mississippi*, James's *The American Scene*, Dreiser's *Hoosier Holiday*, Pound's *Patria Mia*, Eliot's *After Strange Gods*, Fitzgerald's "My Lost City," and Henry Miller's *Remember to Remember*—in which a writer returns to an American scene, usually after an absence of twenty years, to find that world sadly transformed and the values that he considered so deeply American transformed with it.

Twain's *Life on the Mississippi* (1883) is a perfect example of this model. Twain returned to the Mississippi twenty years after he had left it in order to get firsthand impressions of what was to be the setting for *Huckleberry Finn*. What he saw filled him with nostalgia, particularly for life on the river during the age of the old riverboats that had now been almost totally replaced by the railroad. Such an experience, of course, is in great part subjective, since one man's diminished world becomes the basis for another's ideal. Yet in each case we have a vivid sense of having used up a moment of possibility that will never come again—a sense of having betrayed the promises of our past. The American Crusoe has never functioned with mere impunity, and this phenomenon helps explain the nostalgic quality that we find in so much American literature.

☆ ☆ ☆ Technology: Agent of Progress or Force of Destruction?

In 1893 this sense of conflict was brought into focus in Chicago at the World's Columbian Exposition, a spectacle that drew such important writers as Twain, Adams, and the young Dreiser. Upon seeing the new forms of technology on display, Henry Adams conceived of the essay that he would later entitle "The Virgin and the Dynamo." The American Historical Association also held a meeting on these grounds, and there a University of Wisconsin professor by the name of Frederick Jackson Turner outlined his famous theory of the closing of the frontier and the significance of this event. Gatsby surely would have profited from what Turner had to say. Henry Adams carried the Turner thesis one step further when he insisted that we had entered a new realm—the realm of physical force. The Virgin gave a sense of unity to the Middle Ages by supplying a unifying myth, a sense of common purpose. The Dynamo, in contrast, dominates the modern world, feeding off of natural resources, and has the capacity to change the landscape in a way that takes us beyond the human scale. The terminology of Adams's title is important. The idea of the Virgin involves a mythic construct—the Virgin Mary, to be sure, but also the idea of Woman as a life-giving and sustaining force. The idea of the Dynamo involves a scientific-technological construct—the mechanics of power with the potentiality for cultural disruption. One refers us back to the Middle Ages, the other forward to the modern world, that same division in consciousness that Crusoe brought to the wilderness, albeit his mythic sense had been transformed by his Puritanism.

Twain, as I have already suggested, used this dualism in *A Connecticut Yankee*, where he contrasted the modern mentality of Hank Morgan with that of Merlin and other members of King Arthur's court. While Twain saw both worlds as imperfect, he also saw that one was held together by magic (the power of myth) and the other by science and technology, and that the latter system had substantially increased our capacity to destroy as well as to create. In the religious system, that sense of destruction is conveyed in the mythic terms of apocalypse; in the technological system, it is conveyed through the scientific idea of entropy.

Frank Norris also worked with Adams's duality in his trilogy *The Octopus* (1901), *The Pit* (1903), and the uncompleted *Wolf*, where the forces of nature, embodied by the wheat, clash with the dynamo, embodied by the railroad and its owners. Hart Crane made use of this myth literally in *The Bridge* (1930) when Columbus prays to the Virgin at the beginning of the poem and the airplane falls from the sky near the end. Crane wanted to heal what he called the "iron-dealt cleavage," to suggest the way that mythic and technological-scientific beings could be reconciled. His attempt was a noble one, but the reality went beyond the vision, and the poem finally canceled itself out in muted doubt.

☆ ☆ ☆ Crusoe among the Postmoderns

Embedded in the Crusoe vision are narrative elements that went through a dramatic transformation, and the American Crusoe once again found his values questioned. A primary assault on those values came from Nietzsche, who not only questioned the Puritan legacy that allowed the Apollonian to suppress the Dionysian but also attacked the Enlightenment legacy of reason, science, and technology. Nietzsche wanted to return to the world of Rousseau but did not want Rousseau's creator. What he postulated instead is a universe separate from its creation—human consciousness confronting an unmade universe. In literature this new sense of consciousness took many forms: Henry James's privileged narrators, the Bergsonian consciousness that informs the novels of James Joyce and Virginia Woolf and William Faulkner, the *amor fati* neostoicism of Ernest Hemingway. As diverse as these writers are, all employed forms of consciousness that distance us from the universe and find expression in myth, symbol, the primitive, and a cyclical view of time.

Postmodernism, I believe, begins right here and asks what would happen if we simply postulate a universe that absorbs rather than legitimizes such consciousness, a universe that is intelligible only in terms of the way we choose to talk about it—and the way we talk about it inseparable from the notion of *structure* (or *discourse, episteme, paradigm,* or *systems theory*, depending upon the variant of the postmodern we enlist). We have now moved beyond the externalizing consciousness of Hegel, and the internalizing consciousness of Bergson, to the thoroughly adulterated consciousness of Michel Foucault. Consciousness now becomes part of the system we bring into play rather than something out front, all-directing, like a traffic cop.

In this new context drastic things happen to the world we encounter, whether it be the external world or the world of the literary text. We no longer have a sense of history filtered through a centered and all-powerful subjectivity; we no longer have a platform from which to divide the world into good and evil; we no longer have a perspective that allows us to think of history as the unfolding of destiny or a rational plan. Myths become inseparable from history rather than, as T. S. Eliot had told us, the way of ordering history. Symbolism gives way to metonymy; reality becomes relational in a system that creates and sets its own meaning. We enter the labyrinth—that realm where there is no origin or center, where memory is cut off from repetition, where entanglement dominates.

☆ ☆ ☆ Crusoe in Los Angeles

The modern Crusoe has come a long way. He has moved from one continent across an ocean, then across another continent, before hitting land's end in modern Los Angeles. *The Last Tycoon* (1941), F. Scott Fitzgerald's unfinished novel of Los Angeles, begins near the end of the 1930s with Monroe Stahr flying in from the East. As he looks down from the sky, Stahr thinks of Los Angeles as the end product of a European historical and cultural movement. Impelled by the Enlightenment and the idea of progress, natural rights challenged birth rights; reason and skepticism struggled against blind faith; new forms of technology transformed the landscape; new forms of wealth shifted the center of political power away from a landed aristocracy toward an urban-commercial economy; and rulers came to govern by consent of the governed rather than divine right.

Nathanael West was working with a similar idea in *The Day of the Locust* (1939). Todd Hackett, his spokesman, becomes disturbingly aware of the restlessness of the people who have migrated to Los Angeles in search of some kind of meaning. The Hollywood film industry is the fatal focus for a swarm of dreamers. Hackett comes to realize, though, somewhat sinisterly, that embedded in this frustrated population is a force that can quickly get out of control, as indeed it does at the end of the novel, and that a mass can be used for destructive ends if it is organized and controlled by the wrong kind of master, as West had reason to fear by simply looking at Europe in 1939.

As Fitzgerald and West suggest, the literary image of Los Angeles seems to evoke thoughts of last things, to embody the fear of apocalypse and entropy. The real riot and imagined fire scene at the end of *The Day of the Locust* convey this sense of doom, as do the grunion scene in *The Last Tycoon*, the desert scene at the end of John Gregory Dunne's *True Confessions* (1977), and the marathon dance scene at the end of Horace McCoy's *They Shoot Horses, Don't They?* (1935). Los Angeles, we are told, does not really operate out of a sense of a past (what we have here is pure present), and there is certainly some truth in that. It is a city that raises and razes its buildings. It is not a city that builds monuments to itself or to the past. Yet the sense of an ironic past is embedded in all this. The Pilgrims had come to America in search of a New Jerusalem, moved from Salem (the name is significant) to Boston because they wanted to build their city upon a hill (Beacon), and then moved the dream west. Los Angeles and Jerusalem are both on the thirty-third parallel, but the Holy City has long since given way to the Secular City, not only a contrast Robinson Crusoe would have appreciated but one he contained within himself. Americans played out an East-of-Eden theme as they left their ideals, wasted and corrupted, in the past and moved from east to west across a virgin land.

Raymond Chandler often reminds us of this theme. In *The Big Sleep* (1939), for example, Philip Marlowe describes the oil fields owned by Guy Sternwood and then realizes that the general's millions cannot be separated from the now-polluted land. The landscape becomes a moral mirror, and what it reflects we would rather not see. "The Sternwoods, having moved up the hill, could no longer smell the stale sump water of oil," Marlowe tells us, "but they could still look out of their front windows and see what had made them rich. I don't suppose they want[ed] to," he concludes.

Los Angeles was crafted out of a desert. Without the technology that brings water to it, Los Angeles would never have become more than a parched hamlet. In the late nineteenth century two railroad lines met at the edge of this desert and spawned a winter resort city for wealthy easterners, which soon became a mecca for more ordinary folks from Indiana and Iowa, and then gave way in the 1940s to the technology that makes modern warfare possible. Los Angeles seems to have been born full-blown into the modern world: a city without an origin and without a center; 465 square miles of entangled and labyrinthine space; a city that absorbs other cities—a city that absorbs consciousness.

☆ ☆ ☆ From Pilgrims to Pynchon

The way that such consciousness gets overpowered and collapsed into the landscape seems to be the main element in postmodern literary accounts of Los Angeles. Perhaps the most obvious example of this phenomenon is Thomas Pynchon's *The Crying of Lot 49* (1966). While Pynchon sets his novel in southern California, he does not refer to Los Angeles by name. Instead he calls it San Narcisco, reflecting the way the landscape has absorbed the self. Into this world comes Oedipa Maas—her first name suggesting the woman in mysterious search of the father who pondered the riddle of the infected city, the last name suggesting the maze within which this search goes on. Oedipa's task is to come to terms with the legacy of Pierce Inverarity, a modern Robinson Crusoe and kin to Howard Hughes who has developed the West, that is, has developed America. Pierce's empire, she comes to think, is inseparable from the Tristero system, an underground network that seems to feed off the establishment. The Tristero came into being simultaneously with the rise of capitalism, roughly in the late Renaissance, and then, like capitalism, moved across two continents, attacking the establishment where it was most vulnerable, in its communication system. Thus the Tristero made raids on the Pony Express and established an underground mail delivery system in the modern city. The suggestion here is that the Tristero takes its being from what the establishment entropically throws off; its being is inseparable from the waste and detritus the system itself engenders.

Oedipa is not quite sure, however, that the Tristero exists. She cannot find a perspective totalized enough to give meaning to the landscape of which she is a part. Pynchon had worked with these ideas before. In *V.* (1963) he undid the myth of modernism by rewriting a text like *The Waste Land*. Herbert Stencil goes in search of the last mother the way that characters search for the grail in Eliot's poem. But as he enters history, all he finds is what he brings to it; history simply becomes stencilized. The lost ideal turns out to be not so ideal after all, myth collapses into history, and the mind is powerless either to retrieve a lost past or to create an idealized future.

Pynchon gives us another version of the same process in *Lot 49*. Oedipa discovers that history is not retrievable when she visits Mr. Thoth, whose grandfather had ridden with the Pony Express but who has collapsed the stories his grandfather told him into the Porky Pig cartoons that he watches on television. Oedipa thinks she can verify the meaning of the Tristero since the name is mentioned in the play *The Courier's Tragedy*. But when she goes back to earlier editions for verification, she discovers that there are a number of different editions, each canceling the meaning of the other. All human values in this world become tenuous: friendship and love seem to hover over an abyss; her husband freaks out on drugs; her lover commits suicide; her analyst goes insane.

Near the end of the novel she stands at the edge of the ocean, separated from the land by her rented car, holding a dead phone. She has come to land's end in the machine society, dependent on technological forms of communication that constantly betray her. What she gets back in this computerlike world is what she brings to it. All of Los Angeles has become a kind of Echo Court, the name of the motel in which she is staying. Even her residence is inseparable from the machine.

Pynchon will bring most of these elements to bear in *Gravity's Rainbow* (1973), an excursion through postwar Europe and America that once again ends in Los Angeles. Here Pynchon takes the paradigm one step further to show how modern man has become an extension of the machines he has created. Coming from an ancient family of Puritans, Tyrone Slothrop could, literally, be the great-great-grandson of Robinson Crusoe. Because his father allowed him to be used as the object of a number of psychological experiments at Harvard by the distinguished German scientist Laszlo Jamf, Tyrone has been conditioned to respond to Imipolex G, a substance used by the Germans in the V-1 and V-2 rockets. Thus there is a strange correspondence between Tyrone's sex life and where the rockets are falling in London. One of the fathers of the rocket is named Blicero, or the bleached one, and the novel takes us directly into the Western urge to control nature and bleach it white, even as this literally involves the destruction of colored races. In *Gravity's Rainbow* Pynchon contrasts two states of mind that relate directly to Henry Adams's symbols of the Virgin and the Dynamo. The latter state of mind is masculine, white, involved with systems (corporations like Them), dependent upon science and technology. This is the world of the father, of the North, of Rocket City. The other state of mind is feminine, involved with the colored races, with outcasts from organized systems, caught up in a kind of secular preterit. Here the will is at one with the earth, with others, and with self. This is the world of the South, of love, and of peace.

Pynchon is working here with a deep truth about the American experience.

As George Santayana pointed out in his essay on the end of the genteel era, we have compartmentalized the place of men and women in our society. We have created the world of downtown and uptown, the boardroom and the salon, and these two realms are controlled by very different states of mind. Henry James and T. S. Eliot saw deeply into this divide, and it is no accident that in Eliot's salon "the *women* come and go talking of Michelangelo." It is probably no accident either that modernism as a literary movement led us away from the commercial world, previously described by writers like Norris and Dreiser, toward the world of the salon or studio, where moral and aesthetic sensibility, the awareness of art and high culture, are cut off from more practical matters.

Pynchon brings us face-to-face with this contradiction in our cultural selves. If he oversimplifies by insisting upon polarized states, he at least makes us aware of the forces of life and death that surround us. When he claims that the difference between those states is the difference between Rossini and Beethoven—that after listening to Rossini one wants to make love, after listening to Beethoven one wants to invade Poland—we realize that we are in the world of comic-book realism. But it is a realism that calls attention to our most basic cultural assumptions in a way that few have done since Henry Adams. Indeed the last pages of *Gravity's Rainbow*, where a rocket is about to fall out of the sky onto Los Angeles and end the whole show, have an Adams-like quality.

The riddles that Pynchon has explored take on new dimensions in science fiction novels set in Los Angeles. Most obvious in this context is Philip K. Dick's *Do Androids Dream of Electric Sheep?* (1968), the novel that Hollywood made into the movie *Bladerunner*. Here we are in Los Angeles of the future—a city ethnically diversified (the movie was filmed in Hong Kong)—where cybernetics has gone beyond human consciousness. Not only is consciousness inseparable from the context in which it finds itself; it is now inseparable from the machine that duplicates it. Dick uses this situation to ask the inevitable question: How does one distinguish the human from the nonhuman if the functions of the two are the same? No longer does man have an essence that separates him from the other beings in his environment. Man simply is his environment, and where he begins and ends in relation to that environment are no longer viable questions.

☆ ☆ ☆ Crusoe Goes to Disneyland

The questions these literary texts bring to the surface have been asked in a more discursive way by critics like Fredric Jameson and Jean Baudrillard. Jameson's essay "Postmodernism, or the Cultural Logic of Late

Capitalism" covers a great many facets of postmodernism, but his main argument involves the collapse of modernism into the postmodern. He is interested in the breakdown of categories and distinctions between the two realms. Modernism, Jameson argues, distinguished between high and low culture, believed in tradition (or the uses of the past), and upheld the vitality of language. Postmodernists, finding the monumental past used up, engage only with "dead styles," or literature as pastiche. We have lost the historical referent: "The historical novel can no longer represent the past; it can only 'represent' our ideas and stereotypes about the past."

Jameson argues that we cannot position ourselves in time in a way that gives authority to history or position ourselves in space in a way that will unfold the meaning of place. The example he gives of the city-beyond-knowing is Los Angeles. In his essay Jameson reduces Los Angeles to a kind of architectural trope—his now-famous use of the Bonaventure Hotel. The hotel, as we know, is built out of four conical towers, connected by a fifth conical tower in the middle. Jameson points out that once above the lobby, one enters the labyrinth, a John Portman maze. One tower becomes indistinguishable from another, and points of demarcation are lost. Jameson extends the trope of the Bonaventure Hotel to include all of present-day Los Angeles. To move from the hotel to the city is to move within the same field of force—of space filled but not ordered. The mind, the powers of consciousness, Jameson concludes, ultimately fail us in this hyperspace.

We have fallen into such chaos, Jameson argues, because of multinational or late capitalism, that is, because of a society that takes its mode of being not from a commercial or an industrial order but from the workings of international capitalism, which has created the maze that we cannot untangle. Jean Baudrillard has given us a fairly radical departure from this construction of postmodernism, abandoning the Marxism of his earlier works for a semiotic system that he then applies to an era of consumerism, advertising, and mass media. Baudrillard believes that the sense of difference that we have in most sign systems, the difference that sustains the relational nature of sign and signification, has been broken down by the new consumerism. Advertising works to create a field of desire in which the consumer objects that we see on television and that we see in life lose a sense of relational difference and end up acting like signals (as in traffic signals) rather than as signs—that is, they communicate automatically rather than interpretively. As a result, we really have no way of differentiating fantasy from reality, for each works to surpass the other, and our sense of an original being is replaced by the idea of the *simulacrum* (ungrounded repetition).

Jameson and Baudrillard both maintain that the subject and human consciousness have been seriously undercut, but each for very different reasons. Jameson sees late capitalism as a form of explosion, creating larger and larger concentric rings of conspiratorial activity that make human deciphering impossible. Baudrillard, on the other hand, sees the era of consumerism as a giant kind of implosion, overwhelming the individual in a blitz of media stimulation and fashions until nerve endings fray, reality becomes surreal, and one exists in a sort of hyperspace. For Baudrillard Los Angeles is the supreme embodiment of this implosion, or conflation, of fantasy and reality. Where Jameson sees Los Angeles in the Bonaventure Hotel, Baudrillard turns to Disneyland: "Disneyland is presented as imaginary in order to make us believe that the rest is real, when in fact all of Los Angeles and the America surrounding it are no longer real, but of the order of the hyperreal and of simulation."

We have moved in this chapter from the all too centered, scriptable world of Enlightenment London to the unreal, decentered, unscriptable world of postmodern Los Angeles. Neither construct, of course, is real. Each gives us a way of conceptualizing a city so that it can be retrieved in human terms and brought into intellectual focus. These constructs are convincing insofar as they seem to confirm our sense of history, to help us to arrest and focus the flux of time. Through them we interpret the past, test our sense of the real, and structure the pragmatics of the future. Thus to move from Defoe's Robinson Crusoe to Pynchon's Tyrone Slothrop is to move along an axis of American cultural history from an early version of commercial-technological man to the world city of postmodernism.

Robinson Crusoe has been with us in America for a long time. Over the years he has given up his animal-skin clothes for a three-piece suit and has been transformed from without just as the institutions that he embodies have been transformed from within. But what has not changed is the persistence of the man who conquered the wilderness and turned that triumph into wealth—leaving us fraught, as Baudrillard would have it, with an imploded moment of electric space.

FURTHER READING

Studying the Crusoe legacy in America involves a number of subtopics. Books that treat Defoe's commercialism as part of an expansionist movement are Dominique O. Mannoni, *Prospero and Caliban* (New York, 1964); Martin Green, *Dreams of Adventure, Deeds of Empire* (London, 1980); and Hugh Ridley, *Images of Imperial Rule* (New York, 1983). A book that treats the economic basis of the movement from feudalism to commercialism is Karl Polanyi, *The Great Transformation* (New

York, 1944). A book on literature and the voyage is Philip Gove, *The Imaginary Voyage in Prose Fiction* (New York, 1941).

For a discussion of the frontier thesis, the reader will want to consult Frederick Jackson Turner, *The Frontier in American History* (New York, 1920). Essays and books qualifying or correcting the Turner thesis include Walter Prescott Webb, *The Great Frontier* (Boston, 1952), which argues for a frontier larger than the American West. Howard Lamar and Leonard Thompson extend this point in their edition of essays, *The Frontier in History: North America and Southern Africa Compared* (New Haven, Conn., 1981). Other essays that rework the frontier thesis are Ray Allen Billington, *Westward Expansion: A History of the American Frontier* (New York, 1949); Frederick Merk, *History of the Westward Movement* (New York, 1978); and Howard Lamar, ed., *The Reader's Encyclopedia of the American West* (New York, 1977).

For literary treatments of the frontier thesis, see Henry Nash Smith, *Virgin Land: The American West as Symbol and Myth* (Cambridge, Mass., 1950); Edwin Fussell, *Frontier: American Literature and the American West* (Princeton, N.J., 1965); Richard Slotkin, *Regeneration through Violence: The Mythology of the American Frontier, 1600–1860* (Middletown, Conn., 1973), and *The Fatal Environment: The Myth of the Frontier in the Age of Industrialization, 1800–1890* (New York, 1984); Harold P. Simonson, *The Closed Frontier: Studies in American Literary Tragedy* (New York, 1970); John Cawelti, *The Six-Gun Mystique* (Bowling Green, Ohio, 1971); Stephen Fender, *Plotting the Golden West: American Literature and the Rhetoric of the California Trail* (Cambridge, Mass., 1981); and Richard Drinnon, *Facing West: The Metaphysics of Indian-Hating and Empire Building* (Minneapolis, Minn., 1980).

For an environmentalist approach to the topic of the wilderness in America, see Roderick Nash, *Wilderness and the American Mind*, 3d ed. (New Haven, Conn., 1982). Perry Miller's collection of essays *Errand into the Wilderness* (Cambridge, Mass., 1956) traces the Puritans' notion of mission and its encounter with New World conditions.

For a discussion of literary Puritanism and the American Renaissance, see Vernon L. Parrington's *Main Currents in American Thought*, 3 vols. (New York, 1927–30); Perry Miller's *The New England Mind: The Seventeenth Century* (New York, 1939) and *The New England Mind: From Colony to Province* (Cambridge, Mass., 1953); and F. O. Matthiessen's *American Renaissance* (New York, 1941).

For a critical discussion of literature and the rise of technology, see Leo Marx, *Machine in the Garden: Technology and the Pastoral Ideal in America* (New York, 1967). For a critical discussion of the idea of self as affected by an open frontier, see Walter Allen, *The Urgent West: The American Dream* (New York, 1969), and Quentin Anderson, *The Imperial Self: An Essay in American Literary and Cultural History* (New York, 1971).

R. W. B. Lewis, *The American Adam: Innocence, Tragedy, and Tradition in the Nineteenth Century* (Chicago, 1955), follows a mythic type somewhat similar to the Crusoe figure. In response, see Ernest Earnest, *The American Eve in Fact and Fiction, 1775–1914* (Urbana, Ill., 1974), and Annette Kolodny's two books, *The Lay of the Land: Metaphor as Experience and History in American Life and Letters* (Chapel Hill, N.C., 1975), an analysis of images relating woman to the land, and *The Land before Her: Fantasy and Experience of the American Frontiers, 1630–1860* (Chapel Hill, N.C., 1984), a study of women's complex writings about the frontier.

For two further applications of the Crusoe story to American literature, history, and theory, see Jay Fliegelman, *Prodigals and Pilgrims: The American Revolution against Patriarchal Authority, 1750–1800* (Cambridge, 1982), especially the section "The Prodigal as Pilgrim: *Robinson Crusoe* in America," and, in a more general way, Patrick Brantlinger, *Crusoe's Footprints: Cultural Studies in Britain and America* (New York, 1990).

For a discussion of postmodern consciousness, see Fredric Jameson, "Postmodernism, or the Cultural Logic of Late Capitalism," *New Left Review* 146 (July–August 1984), and Jean Baudrillard, *Simulacres et Simulation* (Paris, 1981), and *Selected Writings*, ed. Mark Poster (Stanford, Calif., 1988).

12 ☆ Entertainment
☆ and the
Mass Media

☆ Norman Corwin

Of forces that have shaped and continue to shape American character and culture, none is broader or less subtle than what we generically call "entertainment." Indeed if a visitor arriving from the solar system of Vegas went looking for clues as to what we are and how we got this way, he (she, it) could do a lot worse than to study American entertainment from colonial days to the satellite dish. As much or more might be learned from such a survey as from studies of our industry, economy, military prowess, communications, education, politics, freeway systems, priorities, plumbing, or jurisprudence.

☆ ☆ ☆ Early Diversions

We have come a long way since the kind of entertainments that distracted America's founding fathers and mothers. Thomas Jefferson, who kept meticulous track of his expenditures, recorded that in 1771 he paid three shillings "for hearing musical glasses," another one shilling, three pence, for a glimpse of an alligator, and two shillings, three pence, for "Dutch dancing and singing." The following year he attended a puppet show and in 1783 bought two tickets to watch a balloon go up. In 1786 he paid a shilling to see "a learn'd pig."

Public fun in those days was almost incredibly ingenuous from the standpoint of today's diversions. The chief excitements came from various bees—husking bees, plowing bees, spelling bees—and from such innocent recreations as barn raisings, quilting parties, skittles (a form of bowling, with nine pins), early versions of golf, tennis, and billiards, and a sport called goose pulling, in which a live greased goose was suspended by a rope high above a stream, while each player stood on a plank in the stern of a rowboat and was rowed swiftly under the goose. The object was to snatch the fowl without losing balance. The contestants usually ended up in the water and the poor goose in a skillet. There was some horse racing, cockfighting, and gambling, but only after the Puritan legacy of hard work and plain living had faded somewhat in the late seventeenth century.

The first American theater was established in Williamsburg in 1716, and it prefigured certain twentieth-century developments by being multimedia— that is, it housed bowling facilities and a dancing school as well as a stage for performances of music and drama. Not all young America was so liberal, for drama was long considered a high road to hell by bluenoses, especially those who thrived in Boston and Philadelphia. A Pennsylvania law of the period imposed a fine of five hundred pounds for anyone presenting or acting in a play. There was little in the way of available spectacles, unless one counts as entertainment such public punishment as that advertised in a broadside of 1767 inviting citizens to attend an event at Charlestown, Massachusetts, where three counterfeiters were to have ears cut off, to be whipped twenty strokes, and to stand in the pillory one hour.

Notwithstanding general strictures on drama, the theater flourished in New York City as early as 1732, when the community, even then eyed as Sodom II by fire-and-brimstone theologians, supported a professional company. Yet the theater did not exactly mushroom after proscriptions were lifted. It was 1820 before Shakespearean plays were produced, and then it took an English star appearing as Richard III to attract enough customers to make a go of it.

The first circus in America came along around the same time, but its thrills were as bland as Jefferson's musical glasses and learned pigs. They included a live elephant imported by one Hackaliah Bailey, which was taken on tour through the length and modest breadth of the country. In 1842 P. T. Barnum exhibited General Tom Thumb, fully grown at fifteen inches and twenty-five pounds, and Joice Heth, a black woman whose age was given as 116 and who was billed as having been a slave of the Washington family when George was born. (After her death an autopsy indicated she was about 80.) Both the midget and old woman were great attractions.

It was decades before America became relaxed about its entertainment. In 1790 the most popular composer of the day was William Billings of Boston, whose *New England Psalm Singer* was a national best-seller. When in 1823 a musical entitled *Cleri, the Maid of Milan* was presented in New York, its hit song was *Home, Sweet Home*, the verses of which indicate the chasm separating the lyrics of our time from those of over a century and a half ago:

> 'Mid pleasures and palaces, though we may roam,
> Be it ever so humble, there's no place like home;

A charm from the skies seems to hallow us there;
Which sought through the world is ne'er met with elsewhere.

In exile from home splendor dazzles in vain,
O give me my lowly thatched cottage again;
The birds singing gaily, that came at my call,
Give me them, and that peace of mind dearer than all.

☆ ☆ ☆ Black Vaudeville

Five years after *Cleri*, two black men, Picayune Butler and a colleague known as Old Corn Meal (because he peddled cereal on the side), introduced a new style of music and patter that led to the development of the minstrel show, with its comic banter, songs, dances, interlocutor, two end men, and a chorus. It was a purely American concoction, in which blacks were personified by whites in blackface, just as a century later the top-rated radio program of the land was "Amos and Andy," in which scores of black characters were played by two Caucasians. The famous minstrel groups that followed included Christy's Minstrels, Primrose and West, and Lew Dockstader's troupe, where singer Al Jolson got his start in show business in 1896.

By 1843, with slavery still being practiced, blacks had become subjects for caricature. In 1857 the U.S. Supreme Court ruled that the race "had no rights which the white man was bound to respect," which meant even lower esteem for blacks in law, politics, education, the arts, and entertainment. Some of the popular songs published late into the century would, if broadcast today, cause a radio or television station to lose its license on grounds of their titles alone: *Gib Me Dat Watermelon* (1882); *All Coons Look Alike to Me* (1896); *Coon, Coon, Coon, I Wish My Color Would Fade* (1900); *Go 'Way Back and Sit Down*; *Coons in Your Class Are Easily Found* (1901); *Little Alabama Coon* (1903). When not scorned as childlike, shiftless, and content with bright baubles, hominy grits, and watermelons, blacks were the subjects of condescension. Even a periodical as sympathetic to their aspirations as the *Billboard* in 1902 referred to blacks patronizingly: "Two old darkies, long years ago (1828), can justly claim to be the originators of Negro minstrelsy. First was an old darky in New Orleans." Stephen Foster, long enshrined in the pantheon of American folk composers, was not indifferent to the condition of slaves, but even he referred to songs based on black subjects as "Ethiopian music" and for a time considered having his own black themes and melodies, like *Camptown Races* and *Massa's in the Cold, Cold Ground*, published under a pseudonym.

☆ ☆ ☆ Simplism in Nineteenth-Century Entertainment

Aside from considerations of race, there existed for decades what seems by today's lights to have been a pervasive innocence, a kind of pandemic provincialism and naïveté that expressed itself in song titles as surely as did the general attitude toward blacks. Between 1892 and 1917 the country was entertained by such songs as: *Let a Smile Be Your Umbrella*; *I Faw Down and Go Boom*; *Look for the Silver Lining*; *The Little Grey Home in the West*; *Maxie, Don't Take a Taxi*; *Love Sends a Little Gift of Roses*; *You Can't Give Your Heart to Someone Else and Still Hold Hands with Me*.

Popular music was only one among many media to reflect social and cultural attitudes. The theater flourished in the middle of the nineteenth century, if not with much greater worldliness than was expressed in popular music, then certainly on occasion with far more penetrating effect. Harriet Beecher Stowe's best-selling novel *Uncle Tom's Cabin*, published in 1852, was dramatized a year later and became, in the course of many versions, one of the most successful plays in the history of world theater. For fifty-seven consecutive years, from ten to twenty *Uncle Tom* companies were on continuous tour of the country. The play, dealing with the evils of slavery, involved archetypal characters (Uncle Tom, Little Eva, Simon Legree) and indulged in melodrama that would be dismissed as bathetic today. From the time it opened, its indictment of slavery infuriated antiabolitionists, even in the North. An editorial in the *New York Herald* warned: "We would advise all concerned to drop the play Uncle Tom's Cabin for once and forever. The thing is in bad taste. . . . It's not according to good faith to the Constitution and is calculated, if persisted in, to become a firebrand of the most dangerous character to the peace of the country." The peace of the country was soon enough disrupted, not by agitprop theater but by the Confederate shelling of Fort Sumter.

Throughout the Civil War theaters remained open and accommodated not only native but imported plays, notably Shakespeare. The English comedy *Our American Cousin*, which Abraham Lincoln was watching when he was shot, survived all the vicissitudes of the rebellion. On the fatal night it was in its seventh year as an American favorite.

Ironically, the grief over Lincoln's death was diluted in some quarters by scorn for his having been shot in a theater. The pastor of Mrs. Lincoln's church, Dr. Philip D. Gurney, who was present in the bedroom when Lincoln died, said later that

it will always be a matter of deep regret that our lamented President fell in the theater. . . . Multitudes of his best friends—I mean Christian friends—would have preferred that he should have fallen in almost any other place. Had he been murdered in his bed, or in his office, or on the street, or on the steps of the Capitol, the tidings of his death would not have struck the Christian heart of the country quite so painfully. . . . The theater is the last place in which his friends would wish him to die . . . a school of vice and corruption through which thousands are constantly passing into the embrace of gaiety and folly, intemperance and lewdness, infamy and ruin.

Following the war, when the anxieties of Reconstruction had abated, rustic theater emerged as a favorite order of entertainment. A play entitled *Among the Breakers* (1872), described at the time as "a simple heart-tugger about a lighthouse keeper and the fifteen-year wait of his wife at the foot of his light," ran up a record almost as astonishing as that of *Uncle Tom's Cabin*. As late as 1956, the encyclopedist Joseph T. Shipley pronounced it "by all odds the most popular drama this country has ever known."

Around the same time bucolic comedy fed a provincialism that carried into the big cities. Merely from the titles of some of these may be inferred the ingenuousness of the playwrights and their audiences. *Aaron Slick from Punkin' Crick* was such a resounding success that it inspired two other works with rhyming titles: *Silas Midge of Turnip Ridge* and *Abba San of Old Japan*. Another farce of this vintage, although not edified by a rhyming title, was *Mrs. Plaster of Paris*.

The same innocent, almost childlike outlook was to be found, again, in popular songs of the era: *Where Did You Get That Hat?* (1888); *Daddy Wouldn't Let Me Buy a Bowwow* (1892); *I Don't Want to Play in Your Yard* (1894). Between 1901 and 1923, America sang songs that often bore outsized titles such as *Hello Central, Get Me Heaven, for My Mamma's There*; *Any Little Girl That's a Nice Girl Is the Right Little Girl for Me*; *Are You Coming out Tonight, Mary Ann?*; *Barney Google with the Goo Goo Googly Eyes*; *Good Morning, Mr. Zip, Zip, Zip*.

☆ ☆ ☆ New Forms of Entertainment

All the while that popular music, legitimate theater, and minstrelsy were producing handsome profits, so were various forms of magic lantern shows. As far back as 1850, mechanical and optical devices broadened the options of the theatergoer. One of the best of these systems was the so-called Panorama, a scrolled cyclorama that moved continuously across a proscenium, unfolding a series of vistas. It quickly took on an educational character and was advertised as "grand moral entertainment." Subjects included the life of Christ, Bunyan's *Pilgrim's Progress*, Milton's *Paradise Lost*, the American Revolution, the Holy Land, and Dr. Kane's Arctic Expedition.

A lesser variation was Panstereorama, in which models of famous cities, buildings, and shrines and tableaux of religious and historic events were projected by "dissolving view" mechanisms. Again, the subjects were usually edifying: models of Jerusalem, Solomon's Temple, St. Peter's Cathedral, Mount Vernon, Windsor Castle; the Raising of Lazarus; the Obsequies of Napoleon; the Ascent of Mt. Blanc. The development of an inexpensive small magic lantern (a Sears model sold for $5.80) was precursor to generations of living-room devices including home movies and television.

In 1905 a new medium was born, one that would become the most gigantic of the entertainment industry until overtaken by the electronic revolution. In that year *The Great Train Robbery* ushered in the motion picture. The nickelodeon, so called because admission was a five-cent piece, proliferated overnight; by 1907 there were five thousand nickelodeons in the country. Demand for pictures increased rapidly; within ten years of the first crude films, D. W. Griffith produced *The Birth of a Nation*. It marked the beginning of modern moviemaking and for the first time brought a socially significant subject to the screen. The story, based on Thomas Dixon's novel *The Clansman*, dealt with antagonisms of the Reconstruction era and was blatantly racial; in it, hooded and robed Ku Klux Klan riders were depicted as heroic. At showings in New York City the movie was picketed—another first—by outraged blacks.

☆ ☆ ☆ Wartime Entertainment, Imports, and the Rise of Jazz

The onset of World War I created few ripples to disturb the flow of entertainment. Out of sixty-four major stage productions in the war years 1914–18, only four dealt with war. One of them, *Out There*, was considered by *Life* magazine's theater critic "a stimulant to patriotism for Americans, coming just at the moment when America needs an incentive to the putting aside of individual gain and individual comfort for the country's good." The rest of the sixty-four were mostly light fare that included *Hitchy-Koo*, *Hello, Broadway*, and a revival of *Our American Cousin*. In 1917 the first Pulitzer Prize for drama was awarded to a frothy comedy, *Why Marry?*

Popular music rallied to the flag. George M. Cohan's sprightly tune *Over There* took on the force of an official war song and stimulated recruitment:

Over there, over there. Send the word, send the word over there,
That the Yanks are coming, the Yanks are coming, the drums rum-
tumming everywhere.
So prepare, say a pray'r. Send the word, send the word to beware,
We'll be over, we're coming over, and we won't come back till it's over
over there.

From the turn of the century to the eve of World War I social concerns
barely surfaced in most of entertainment. Vaudeville had become national,
largely through the entrepreneurship of B. F. Keith and E. F. Albee, who
owned or controlled hundreds of theaters. Their shrewd management and
booking policies enabled vaudeville and variety bills to overtake the legitimate
theater as America's favorite form of mass entertainment.

The first powerful theatrical trust was formed in 1895, when seven leading producer-managers established the firm of Klaw and Erlanger. In 1904
George M. Cohan scored the first of what were to be many hits with the
musical *Little Johnny Jones*, two of whose songs, *I'm a Yankee Doodle Dandy* and
Give My Regards to Broadway, lived far beyond the run of the show and the life
of Cohan and are indeed still heard today. In 1905 David Belasco produced
The Girl of the Golden West, which became the source of Puccini's opera of the
same name. It premiered in Milan in 1910.

Mostly, however, cultural movement went the other way—westward across
the Atlantic. European music was considered more "tasteful" by genteel
patrons of the art, and in the repertoires of so-called social orchestras preference was given to pages of Mozart, Donizetti, Bellini, Boieldieu, Weber,
and Strauss. Americans danced to schottisches, polkas, quadrilles, minuets,
jigs, and gallops. But gradually, toward the end of the 1800s and into the new
century, America began to exploit its own creative instincts, as it had already
done with the minstrel show. Jazz, claimed by its aficionados to be the only
art form truly indigenous to the United States, was born and raised in New
Orleans. Originally it was played by black brass bands at parades and in funeral processions; around 1910 it appeared on phonograph records and
began to take hold around the country. Together with the lively rhythmic
patterns of ragtime came the slow and mournful blues, a genuinely American
idiom. The most famous of the genre, *St. Louis Blues*, was composed as early
as 1914.

Not long afterward musical comedy, already well served by Cohan, asserted
itself. The 1920s produced such solid and enduring shows as *No, No Nanette*,
Hit the Deck, and *Showboat*, with tunes that are still played and enjoyed.

☆ ☆ ☆   Social Issues Emerge

Social drama, which had not moved far since *Uncle Tom's Cabin*, suddenly accelerated in the 1930s and 1940s with the emergence of playwrights like Clifford Odets, Irwin Shaw, Maxwell Anderson, Elmer Rice, Lillian Hellman, and Arthur Miller. Odets's *Waiting for Lefty* dramatized a taxi strike, while Shaw described his *Bury the Dead* as "a play about the war that is to begin tomorrow" (he was only five years off). Marc Blitzstein's *The Cradle Will Rock* dealt with unions and bosses; Paul Peter and George Sklar's *Stevedore* with waterfront workers; Maxwell Anderson's *Winterset* with the aftermath of the Sacco-Vanzetti case; John Wexly's *The Last Mile* with capital punishment; Elmer Rice's *Street Scene* with life in a teeming metropolis; and Arthur Miller's *All My Sons* with war profiteering and his *Death of a Salesman* with the downside aspects of the American dream of success.

Films, too, reflected social concerns, over an even wider spectrum. Among typical major films produced between the world wars and into the late 1950s were *All Quiet on the Western Front*, based on Erich Maria Remarque's powerful novel; *Modern Times*, in which Charlie Chaplin parodied assembly line production; *The Best Years of Our Lives*, concerning the post–World War II adjustment of three veterans; a score of biographical pictures—*Wilson*, *Viva Zapata*, *The Life of Emile Zola*, *The Story of Louis Pasteur*, *Madame Curie*, *Rembrandt*, and *Lust for Life* (Van Gogh); *Gentlemen's Agreement*, on American anti-Semitism; *All the King's Men*, on the rise and fall of a demagogic politician; and *To Kill a Mockingbird*, *Home of the Brave*, and *The Defiant Ones*, all on race relations.

☆ ☆ ☆   Entertainment as Social Barometer

The genre of film that reflects reality most directly is the documentary. Its history in the United States has been one of high distinction, sharing world eminence only with Canada and Britain. Yet the documentary cannot comfortably be classified under entertainment in America, a reservation made not by sociologists or taxonomists but by the public and the film industry itself. Documentary shorts and features have never prospered at the box office. Notwithstanding considerable lip service to the cultural value and influence of the documentary, the producers of motion pictures seldom make, or even attend the showing of, such films. (In 1982, when Oscar-nominated short documentaries were screened competitively for members of the Motion Picture Academy of Arts and Sciences, only 147 of 3,600 eligible voters turned out. Attendance at these screenings has increased since then, but even superior documentaries attract only a fraction of the audience that routinely turns out for all but the drabbest fiction features.)

On the other hand, the electronic media, from the inception of commercial radio in 1920, were far less cautious about crossing lines perceived in Hollywood as separating "reality" from entertainment. While most radio programming, like most of theater and film, concentrated on music, drama, romance, and comedy and avoided serious or controversial subjects, there also were socially significant productions. In 1941 the first four-network broadcast, transmitted by every affiliated radio station in the country, commemorated the 150th anniversary of the ratification of the American Bill of Rights with an hour-long, all-star dramatization to which President Franklin D. Roosevelt, speaking live from the White House, added a postscript. A year later, the four major networks again combined to present thirteen consecutive weekly programs called "This Is War!" dealing with aspects of the ongoing war against the Axis powers.

Television resuscitated the documentary. The major networks, once shy of products that did not present comedy, romance, family situations, sex, guns, chases, or fantasy and spurred by the competition of cable channels, made room for occasional works of social realism. Filmmakers responded with substantial television movies, among them biographies of high quality on subjects like writer James Baldwin, Congressman Adam Clayton Powell, Supreme Court Justice Earl Warren, painter Jack Levine, photographers, athletes, a bookdealer, a composer, a dancer, a demagogue, an evangelist.

Technologically radio reached its zenith during the war years. Television, held back until after Japan surrendered in 1945, expanded with a speed far beyond the expectation of forecasters. It more than kept pace with developments in cinema, whose engineers introduced color in 1922, sound five years later, feature-length animation in 1947, multiple-camera processes and a brief flirtation with 3-D in 1952, and wide-screen dimensions in 1962.

With the proliferation of broadcasting, there developed the activity considered by some to be vital and by others parasitic—the industry of audience measurement. It began with analyses of fan mail and simple telephone surveys and quickly developed complex contrivances that monitored radio listening, calculated power loads at generating plants, and even studied measurements of water pressure at central pumping stations (it was found that pressure fell when listeners left their television sets during commercial breaks to use plumbing facilities).

Later devices included a Poll-O-Meter, mounted on a truck that cruised streets recording oscillations emitted by television sets in operation; a scanning device inside an airplane, which could meter over one million sets per hour; and laboratory-response systems where people were invited to gather in groups and press buttons to indicate progressively their interest in, indifference toward, or distaste for elements of specific programs. Researchers feverishly worked up methods to measure the galvanic skin response, eye movement, muscle pulse, pupil dilation, even brain wave activity of viewers. A dizzying array of gadgets and systems evolved, the names of which index a kind of frantic compulsion to quantify everybody and everything related to broadcasting: Arbitron, Programeter, Centercasting, Instapoll, Electro-Rate, Telerad, Radox, Tanner Scanner, Program Analyzer, Reactocaster, Dyna-Foto-Chron; also acronymized apparatuses called INDAX, QUBE, GSR, ARI, IAMS, and TOCOM. Dyna-Foto-Chron was perhaps the most exotic of these. It featured cameras atop television sets in homes that automatically, at intervals, took still photographs of viewers.

All of this metering, analysis, and cataloging generated social and ethical issues only a little less controversial than the nature and quality of the programming itself. Questions have been raised about the effect of ratings on policy decisions and the potential bias in both content and direction of poll quizzes; about whether early projection of winners in elections is injurious to the electoral system; about whether a "digital democracy" is supplanting the kind intended by America's founders. Many critics and commentators express concern that program pretesting and overnight meter-based ratings are exercising a tyranny over television writers and producers. All of these issues are continually being debated and have in common only the state of being unresolved.

☆ ☆ ☆ Modern Entertainment as a Societal Force

There have been many tributaries to the mainstream of American entertainment, whose recent history is one of teeming invention, steady accretion, and, at frequent intervals, explosive expansion. Progress in almost every phase of industrialized entertainment, including modes, techniques, sizes of audience, production, distribution, promotion, costs, and revenues, has been by geometric leaps, so that today the statistics are astronomical.

Hardly a month passes in which the *Wall Street Journal* or various trade gazettes of the entertainment world do not carry reports or ads announcing or vaunting new bonanzas, box office crests, sales peaks, all-time highs, record-setting revenues. Even in times of recession and depression, the products and by-products of show biz do brisk business—not infallibly and invariably, but often enough to keep the mean gradients steadily rising.

Not a few social critics are convinced that entertainment has developed into an immense and imperious agency that is propelling America toward a dangerous insipidity, a condition in which smash hits and winning teams become major sources of inspiration. A convenient example is the way in which merchandisers and entrepreneurs flourish in the wake of blockbusting movies. Bounties spinning off the success of the film *E.T.* included the sale of fifty thousand life-sized latex masks of the alien E.T., priced from forty-nine cents to fifty-five dollars each. The McCall Pattern Company sold thousands of E.T. Halloween getups for children, at forty-five dollars each. A firm in Pennsylvania sold over a million of another E.T. rig. Hershey Foods, the manufacturer of the candy Reese's Pieces, enjoyed a 65 percent increase in sales after the movie because that confection was used to lure E.T. out of the woods.

Commercial effects of this kind are obvious, but political ramifications are not quite so apparent. "The media," wrote David Clark and William Blankenburg in *You and the Media*, "have become a kind of second government." Recently there has been a marked interface between the second government and the first. A former actor and actress occupied the White House. An actor was appointed ambassador to Mexico. A song-and-dance man was elected U.S. senator. An airport was named after another actor. Shirley Temple was appointed ambassador to the United Nations. Pearl Bailey was assigned to the same body. A newscaster was elected to Congress. A school was named after a first baseman, a highway after a comedian, and a town after a radio program. The star of "Marcus Welby," a television program about doctors, was engaged to make the commencement address at Harvard Medical School; a character actor in "Star Trek" was invited to join NASA's board of directors. When the movie *The Right Stuff* premiered in Washington, D.C., there was, according to the *Los Angeles Times*, "the recurring recognition that the world of Washington and the world of the movies are somehow intertwined . . . an eerie blur of celluloid and reality, an unabashed demonstration that hype can imitate life."

The fusion of entertainment and the press is as solid as that between the other media and government. A sports section running thirty-two pages is not uncommon in a major newspaper. Each issue of the *New Yorker* magazine lists hundreds of diversions in and around Manhattan, by name and title, address and telephone number. Directories like *Cue* are published in most big cities; prosperous periodicals like *Chicago* and *Los Angeles* are encyclopedias of current fare.

"Entertainment," wrote Erik Barnouw, "has become not surcease from daily routine—it *is* daily routine." Whatever the socio-economic-psychological causes, the United States today is the most entertained country in the world. Inexorably new techniques come along—fresh marvels of reproduction and transmission that include cable, satellite, laser, fiber optics, holography, computer constructions, and Buck Rogers paraphernalia that are still in blueprint or incubating in laboratories.

Although already plenteous, the beguilements of Americans seem subject to infinite reincarnations: movies once thought forever buried in vaults, beyond prospect of resurrection, now circulate on television as freely as the commercials that besprinkle them; books long retired are reactivated in paperback editions; the attics of nostalgia are emptied, and antique treasures, along with bric-a-brac, are refurbished and brought to the marketplace—musicals revived, old stage plays dusted off, vintage movies brought up-to-date with new stars, new locales, new contexts, and special effects that were not dreamed of at the time of the original productions. Colorization of old black-and-white films, a practice considered obnoxious by cineasts and most filmmakers, is yet another form of updating.

☆ ☆ ☆ Cultural Democracy

There is much crossbreeding and transmigration between entertainment types: comic strips become Broadway musicals (*Li'l Abner*) and movies (*Popeye, Superman, Batman, Dick Tracy*); novels become operas; operas themselves are transmogrified (*Carmen Jones*); debates and hearings become plays, documentaries, and movies (*The Rivalry, The Case of J. Robert Oppenheimer, Point of Order, The Way We Were, Unfriendly Witness*); historical texts become record albums (*Hear It Now, Churchill, FDR, A Star Is Born*); ponderous best-selling sagas become marathon telecasts ("Roots," "Shogun," "Marco Polo," "The Winds of War").

Sports, and electronic coverage of them, continue to propagate. Not long ago, the football season began in September and ended in November. Now it begins in the summer, gets going full throttle with exhibition games in August, reaches a high pitch on New Year's Day, and ends in the superhype of the Super Bowl. Where once the World Series capped the baseball season, the so-called Fall Classic is now preceded by Summer Classics—divisional play-offs followed by league play-offs before the big payoff.

It is easy to bewail the state of American entertainment, especially when fat returns are brewed from thin soup. The "Beverly Hillbillies" left as indelible a record of triumphant mediocrity in television as *Abie's Irish Rose* did in the theater. The wages of trash are often high. It becomes harder for a good poem or a serious play or a documentary movie to be commercially viable; a worthy new string quartet or a symphony has about as much chance as a banana plantation in Greenland. Nevertheless, if there were a running graph capable of measuring the influence and effects of the entertainment media on American character and culture, the results would not be so lopsided and disheartening as might be indicated by the relative weights, in public consciousness, of Walt Whitman and Walt Disney, *Fahrenheit 451* and "Hawaii Five-O," *The Family of Man* and "Family Feud," Charlie Chaplin and Chevy Chase.

For all their sins, domestic movies, television, print, and advertising have made profound contributions toward redressing some of the grosser inequities of the past, especially in race relations. While discrimination is far from extinct, the changes have been dramatic and swift. Within the lifetime of anyone born before 1947, the owners of fifteen out of sixteen baseball clubs voted to ban Jackie Robinson from playing on their diamonds because he was black (and in the national game, no less). The ugly chauvinism of a search for "the great white hope" to unseat a black heavyweight boxing champion seems today as hard to believe as the barbarism of the *Dred Scott* decision. A good share of the influence toward this altered state must go to the entertainment media. Blacks now appear in movies and television, not as coons or clowns, but as stars; they are conspicuous in news broadcasting and as models in advertising; they win Heisman trophies, Miss America contests, most-valuable-player awards, Oscars, Tonys, Emmys, judgeships, political offices, government posts, and seats on the space shuttle. Portraits of black artists, scientists, and humanists appear in a Black Heritage series of postage stamps; schools, hospitals, and boulevards are named for the martyred black civil rights leader Martin Luther King, Jr., and a legal holiday has been voted by Congress to memorialize him.

The disproportion between blacks and whites in employment and other economic indices continues to be a serious problem, but less so in the entertainment media. The constituency of entertainment was one of the first, not the last, to begin to honor Jefferson's radical premise of 1776 concerning equal birth.

But there have been benefits beyond the improvement of race relations and a fuller awareness of the rights of minorities. Thanks largely to producers like Norman Lear, who persisted against stubborn resistance and repeated rejections, programs of substance dealing with issues of world hunger, bigotry, abortion, the war in Vietnam, violence on television, women's rights, homosexuality—all "controversial" issues feared and evaded by the satrapy of broadcasting—were finally admitted to the air. The overwhelming success of "All in the Family" and programs of like mettle ("The Defenders," "Lou Grant," the

MTM productions) showed that the supposed fourteen-year-old mentality of the average public was a self-serving myth perpetuated largely by executives whose jobs were made easier by formula programs that required no great invention, imagination, or courage—in short, by safely innocuous material.

Another achievement to which electronic entertainment may reasonably lay claim has been that of broadening the base of American culture by making it available to millions of people heretofore without access to great works: masterpieces of music and drama performed by the world's foremost artists; documentaries that would never be shown in movie houses because exhibitors could not turn a profit from them; public events of transcendent character such as moon landings, the funerals of presidents, Sadat setting foot in Israel, tall ships sailing up the Hudson River. People who never in their lives might get to hear, let alone afford to see, a production of *La Bohème, Hamlet, Oedipus Rex, The Iceman Cometh,* who might never be introduced to masterworks of music, now know the names and oeuvres of symphonists and, on occasion, wear portraits of them on sweatshirts.

Cultural democratization with an upward tilt has been made possible by screen and transistor, and although it may be premature to hail the millennium in this respect, considering that audiences interested in such uplift are a small portion of the listening and viewing public, the gains have been substantial. The level of sophistication has risen, however slowly. While hordes still flock to attend slick shockers like *The Exorcist* and stand in long lines to see extrapolated comic strips like *Star Wars, The Empire Strikes Back,* and *The Return of the Jedi,* and while television habitués for whom "the boob tube" was named continue to depend on it for mindless entertainment, there has been a net gain, and an appreciable one.

☆ ☆ ☆ Economic Realities

The same system of free enterprise and some of the same corporate entities that have from time to time been charged with insatiable greed and general philistinism have also, from time to time, given aid and comfort to the arts. Maecenas-minded oil companies and industrial foundations have more than once rescued public broadcasting and community art projects from evisceration by government cutbacks.

The white knights of public programming claim that by federal mandate their product must be of an essentially educational nature, and that in fulfilling their commitment to such programming they cannot address themselves to the same goals of audience size that dominate commercial entertainment. Yet in spite of such disclaimers, public broadcasters count audiences on just as eager an abacus as anyone in the business, the chief difference being that they generally do not lower sights or standards for the sake of numbers, or reduce a rating race to a rat race. The Public Broadcasting System (PBS) as a rule will not cancel a series after two or three episodes simply because the rating is lower than was hoped. They may not renew such a series, but that is something else.

The worst to be said of commercial television is that it too often purveys programs of impoverished quality, matter that is sought, found, budgeted, and produced in the hope that it will attract large numbers. A PBS station brochure on *How Program Underwriting Works* boasted that "commercial broadcasters count households tuned in. Public broadcasters count people turned on." This is not an empty claim, considering that the Mobil Corporation, one of the PBS flock of angels, received seventy-five thousand letters in a single season, all praising "Masterpiece Theater"; and the management of Cyprus Mines was cheered by its assembled stockholders at an annual meeting for having locally underwritten "Wall Street Week."

Indeed the voiced pleasure of corporate sponsors is one of the phenomena of the Medici relationship between the business and public television communities. Often the underwriter himself sounds like a public relations pusher for the carrier. "The corporate satisfaction comes," wrote L. C. Bershon of Atlantic Richfield, "in those private moments when those responsible think and smile, and know that without [their support], millions would have missed Beverly Sills' high C, Baryshnikov's leaps, and Moyers' wit. The returns on investment are impossible to compute. They are all part of a corporation's great social responsibility, the company as part of society." An executive of a pharmaceutical house explained that "underwriting 'Nova' and 'The Boston Symphony in Washington' gives us the opportunity to combine a major public service activity with a subtle but important message—we care."

By the admission of underwriters themselves, it is not all just caring and service and social responsibility. Self-interest is very much in the mix, too, which is not a criticism but a statement of fact. "In public television," the 3M Company advised the Advertising Federation of Minnesota, "additional corporate visibility is available at a fraction of the cost of commercial sponsorship. And the techniques used by 3M and others to reinforce this visibility are available to any company willing to support quality programming."

That such testimonials were not just honeymoon rapture was evident in a study showing that 81 percent of those polled said they admired a company more because it underwrote public television, and 38 percent said such underwriting influenced their choice of product or service. This represents a striking return on investment, especially in light of the point made by 3M that corporate visibility is available at a fraction of the cost of commercial advertising. For example, Exxon's $500,000 grant for 260 half-hour episodes of "The MacNeill-Lehrer Report" would not even buy one minute of Super Bowl commercials.

At the same time, American entertainment is being absorbed increasingly by conglomerates. Not only are the imprimaturs of powerful companies visible on public and commercial television, they are also big on the big screen. Paramount Pictures is a Gulf and Western company; Universal, an MCA company; Warner Brothers, a Warner Communications company; 20th Century-Fox is controlled by an oil man; CBS for a time owned the New York Yankees; General Electric bought NBC.

More and more, entertainment represents massive concentrations of money, resources, and real estate: Disneyland in California and Epcot in Florida; the *Queen Mary* and the *Spruce Goose* (holdings of the Wrather Corporation); Knott's Berry Farm, with its John Wayne theater, Snoopeyville, and a line of jams and jellies; entertainment city-states like Las Vegas, Atlantic City, Six Flags Magic Mountain, Sea World, Raging Waters Park, Great America, King's Island. These are the panstereoramas, the chautauquas, the circuses, the touring companies, the museums, the music halls of today.

☆ ☆ ☆ Mass Entertainment and American Culture

The effect of entertainment upon American culture is discernible to more than scholars undertaking systematic study of it. The public as well is aware. A woman in Santa Barbara wrote a letter to the *Los Angeles Times* concerning details of a nine-day tour of southern California that was arranged for three visitors from New Zealand to include

Queen Mary, tour of Long Beach, Toy and Doll Museum, Wild Animal Park, tour of San Diego, Movieland Wax Museum, Knott's Berry Farm, Buena Park, tour of downtown Los Angeles, Universal Studios, Disneyland for two days, Magic Mountain, Wild, Wild West, Sea World, and Tijuana. . . . Whoever cooked up this tour should be seriously questioned. All that amusement, fantasy, entertainment, for nine days straight? We're spreading a thin image of California and America when we encourage three people, at a cost of $7000 basic, to arrive here and see nothing historical or cultural but (instead) the above. . . . As a native Californian, it hurts to see a nine-day fantasy brought home to us on such an ugly scale.

Some believe American entertainment today amounts to a 365-day fantasy, brought home by vehicles that have the power to come through windows and doors and walls, into our living rooms, our dining rooms, our bedrooms, and ultimately into our culture. However long the queues of clients may be at Disneyland and Universal, they are longer for the entertainments that reach into the parlor. For every thousand pleasure seekers who make their way over the freeways to Sea World and the Movieland Wax Museum, there are millions who stay at home and absorb pleasures by tuning in and turning on.

Yet it would be wrong to conclude that inexorably the spiral is downward and that the American character is in a terminal phase of cultural narcolepsy, notwithstanding protests that "a culture of foaming nonsense now engulfs us" (Robert Osborne); that "the tides of trash rise a little higher by the week" (Barbara W. Tuchman); that "a sleaziness has infected the national culture. . . . There seems to be a fierce competition, especially in the world of entertainment, to find even lower rungs on the ladder of bad taste" (Norman Cousins).

It is too early to conclude that American culture is incurably afflicted. We may be reeling from the effects of what Henry Skornia, critic, calls the "national obsession with celebrity, money and 'things,'" but it must be taken into account that entertainment does not exist in a vacuum, isolated from what is going on in politics, economics, foreign capitals, ministries of war, and councils of supranational cartels. The forces in society that have brought consumers of entertainment to a state of passivity in which they mostly sit back and ingest the familiar are not necessarily fixed and irreversible. Human life expectancy may be short, but culture, like its fair component, art, has longer cycles.

Already there are signs of reawakened responsibility when it comes to issues of vital import—freedom, human rights, justice, tyranny, nuclear hazards, the lessons of history. Motion pictures like *Special Bulletin*, *Norma Rae*, *Missing*, *Friendly Fire*, *Coming Home*, *Testament*, *The Ballad of Gregorio Cortez*, *Hanna K.*, *Under Fire*, *Vietnam: A Television History*, *Gandhi*, *The Day After*, *The Last Temptation of Christ*, *Do the Right Thing*, and *Roger and Me* may be "controversial"—dread word!—but they are at the very least conscionable; and in a world where conscienceless terror and violence have become substitutes for negotiation and instruments of polity, this is not without significance and reason for hope.

FURTHER READING

The literature of entertainment in the mass media is vast and expands daily with every issue of trade journals like *Variety, Billboard,* and the *Hollywood Reporter* and periodicals on the order of *American Film, Sight and Sound, Emmy, Broadcasting, Media Decisions,* and *Radio and Records.*

Compendia, too, are abundant, teeming with facts, figures, chronologies, biographical data, economic annals, reportage, anecdotage, and commentary. Especially attractive to the scholar are Joseph Csida and June Bundy Csida, *American Entertainment: A Unique History of Popular Show Business* (New York, 1978); Margery Longley, Louis Silverstein, and Samuel A. Tower, *America's Taste* (New York, 1960); Mark Sullivan, Jr., *Our Times,* 6 vols. (New York, 1935); and David L. Cohn, *The Good Old Days* (New York, 1940).

A reproduction of the 1767 broadside urging citizens to witness the amputation of ears from the heads of three miscreants, with the added attraction of whipping and pillorying, appears in James Truslow Adams, *Album of American History* (Chicago, 1944), in a section headed "Amusements."

On music in vogue during the period of the social orchestra, see H. Wiley Hitchcock's introduction to a new edition of Stephen Foster, *The Social Orchestra* (New York, 1973), also excerpted as liner text in Columbia Masterworks record album M32577, *Stephen Foster's Social Orchestra* (New York, 1974). On the history of theater and of specific plays, see Joseph T. Shipley, *Guide to Great Plays* (Washington, D.C., 1956). On reaction to the assassination of Lincoln, there is Carl Sandburg, *Abraham Lincoln: The War Years,* vol. 4 (New York, 1939).

On the American documentary film and its difficulties in finding markets and audiences, and also on the interaction of show business and politics, see Norman Corwin, *Trivializing America,* 2d ed. (Secaucus, N.J., 1986). For the history of radio and television, consult Erik Barnouw, *A Tower in Babel* (New York, 1966), *The Golden Web* (New York, 1968), and *The Image Empire* (New York, 1970).

On the character of sponsorship and underwriting of public television, Barbara Isenberg's three-part series in the *Los Angeles Times,* 9–11 December 1979, is useful, as is a brochure published by KCET, the PBS station in Los Angeles, *How Program Underwriting Works* (1979).

Information on radio and television rating systems has been gathered by Mark J. Banks, "Meter Measurement: A Study of the Evolution of Electrical-Mechanical Devices for Measuring Broadcast Audiences," a paper submitted to the Broadcast Education Association History Committee, 1984. See also Hugh Malcolm Beville, *Audience Ratings: Radio, Television, and Cable* (Hillsdale, N.J., 1985), and David F. Poltrack, *Television Marketing: Network, Local, and Cable* (New York, 1982).

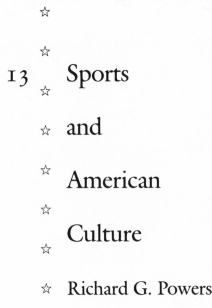

13 Sports

and

American

Culture

Richard G. Powers

"It is quite possible that Americans today care more about sports than about anything else," marveled Jeffrey Hart in a review of a recent book on sports by the late president of Yale University (and commissioner of baseball) A. Bartlett Giamatti. "And it is entirely possible that they are right."

Sports are a mirror of American life, but they are more than just a mirror. They can be viewed as American culture's effort to construct an imaginative alternative to conscious reality, perhaps a fantasy culture, but a culture nonetheless. Sports have their myths, legends, and historical figures; their hierarchy of leaders and followers; their greater and lesser saints and demons; their ethical systems and arcana of mystical discipline. Above all sports culture has its mechanism for helping individuals identify with others, for replacing their loneliness with the security of belonging.

☆ ☆ ☆ The Puritan Legacy

Whatever else sports may be, their present-day prosperity represents a repudiation of the hostility toward games and enjoyment codified in the law books of the first settlers. The colonies' early rulers, North and South, were dedicated to rooting out play and enforcing the discipline of hard work as a moral value in itself and as a frontier necessity, which may help explain today's repression of the play element in professional sports and popular culture's insistence on the moral significance of winning. Sumptuary laws in Massachusetts and Connecticut banned dice, quoits, bowling, shuffleboard, card playing, and dancing. All, however, were prevalent enough to merit prohibition.

The Puritans' war against sports may be traced to their equation of work with prayer or their belief that divine election was accompanied by an easy rejection of idleness. As members of England's rising middle class, the Puritans also had a social bias against the traditional amusements of the aristocracy. Governor William Bradford had to restrain his Pilgrims from playing "stooleball [an ancestor of cricket] and suchlike sports" on Christmas Day, which was supposed to be treated like any other day by these haters of Papist customs.

Nathaniel Hawthorne's "The May-Pole of Merry Mount" describes the triumph of Puritan orthodoxy over the free spirits of old England, but according to Foster Rhea Dulles, "The legislation of early New England forbidding tavern sports, card playing, and dancing throws a penetrating light on how a very considerable number of people were spending such free time as they had. Not the rulers and magistrates, but the everyday people of the Puritan world." Throughout the colonies the old English games seem to have been popular, though cockfighting and horse racing were not permitted in New England. Sledding and ice skating were also popular where the climate permitted; skating remained one form of physical exercise allowed women when the mores of the Victorian era later began to exclude them from sport.

☆ ☆ ☆ Sports and Class in America

The Jacksonian class revolution that changed the rank of gentleman or lady from one of ascription to achievement had a pernicious effect on participation in sports. An eighteenth-century gentleman or lady could hardly lose his or her status by anything short of a major crime, but the kind of gentility that was the goal in the second quarter of the nineteenth century was as easily lost as gained, particularly by women. The new middle class's determination to separate itself from the vulgar meant avoiding anything that had the appearance of physical work, which was enough to rule out strenuous play.

It is not true that there was no American participation in sports during the 1840s and 1850s; these were the years when a primitive form of baseball was evolving. However, these decades were more notable for the rise of spectator sports, early evidence of a taste that would eventually be satisfied by the television sports broadcasts of today. The most popular spectator sport was horse racing, and whole sections, sometimes the whole country, followed rivalries between famous stable owners.

Sailing regattas were another way social leaders could exhibit themselves before the masses in a pastime whose expense insured its exclusivity. Some sailboat races were staged by gamblers for cash purses, but most were sponsored by elite sailing and rowing clubs. The first America's Cup Race in 1851, and the intense interest it aroused, gave the rich an opportunity to pose as defenders of national pride in an arena none but they could afford to enter.

As the nineteenth century progressed, sports seemed to evolve along two diverging paths. On the one hand, sports suitable for general participation tended to be monopolized by elite groups who excluded the working class and immigrants. On the other hand, sports with an ineradicable working-class (and hence professional) character tended to be taken over by commercial interests and run as money-making enterprises. Track exemplifies the first tendency, baseball the second.

Professional track and field, or "pedestrianism," was one of the most popular sports of the nineteenth century, both as recreation and spectacle. Before the Civil War races tended to be promoted by gamblers and often pitted English champions against American favorites; the races were commonly held at horse tracks or on city streets. In 1844 some thirty thousand spectators watched the American runner John Gildersleeve beat the Englishman John Barlow in a ten-mile run for one thousand dollars at a Hoboken racetrack. Forty thousand watched the rematch, which Barlow won with a time of 54:21.

After the Civil War track was enormously popular as a venue for wagering, with the competitors often handicapped with weights or staggered starts to ensure parity. Amusement parks sponsored weekend track meets on an elimination basis with the winners receiving cash awards or readily pawnable trophies. Marathons and long-distance races were also popular.

Probably the most important sponsors of track and field sports in the nineteenth century were the ethnic organizations with their annual "picnics"—mass athletic meets allowing amateurs and professionals to compete both separately and against each other. The Caledonian Games of New York City were the earliest; during the 1880s there were also Irish and German picnics. Picnics were hosted too by military regiments, labor unions, colleges, and wealthy athletic associations like the New York Athletic Club and the Schuylkill Navy Club of Philadelphia.

In the 1870s "gentlemen" began to complain about having to compete against lower-class professionals at track meets. The solution to this genteel dilemma was the doctrine of amateurism, which made it possible for the wellborn to win once in a while and, incidentally, made athletics respectable since social contact with workmen was *infra dig*. In 1888 today's ruling amateur sports organization, the Amateur Athletic Union (AAU), was formed. By strictly enforcing the rules of amateurism, the AAU effectively banished working-class participation from track and field. Not until the 1970s would the rules be relaxed to allow athletes without private means of support to compete.

The professional champions of the "pedestrianism" era set records that still astound. In 1885 a professional runner set a mile record of 4:12.4, a mark that no amateur could match until 1915. The most amazing professional track record of all was set by the outstanding pedestrian Richard Perry Williams, who ran a carefully authenticated nine-second one hundred–yard dash on 2 June 1906. It took nearly seventy years for an amateur to equal that achievement.

☆ ☆ ☆ The "National Pastime" Takes Root

As track evolved into an upper-class preserve, baseball grew from similar beginnings into the earliest, and still the most complete, form of popular sports culture. The roots of the national pastime, or "game" (never the national "sport"), may certainly be traced to the English children's game of rounders, also known as early as 1744 by the name of "baseball," despite A. G. Spalding's effort in 1908 to concoct a myth of purely American origins (the Cooperstown legend). Under the name of "town ball," the game was popular throughout the colonies and absorbed enough of students' time for it to be banned at the College of New Jersey (later called Princeton) in 1787. There was a Rochester Baseball Club in the 1820s, and the senior Oliver Wendell Holmes said that he had played the game at Harvard University in 1829.

Until the Civil War there were really two distinctly different variants of the game. Throughout New England there was the "Boston" game, while the rest of the country played the "New York" game. The critical difference was that the Boston game permitted a base runner to be retired by throwing the ball at him, a practice called "soaking" the runner.

The first baseball clubs of the 1840s and early 1850s were gentlemanly in membership and decorum. Games between status-conscious clubs like the New York Knickerbockers and Brooklyn Excelsiors were friendly preludes to formal dinners with musical entertainment furnished by the host club. These social teams were soon displaced by workingmen's clubs, with memberships drawn from labor organizations (for example, shipyard workers in Brooklyn) or from city government services (the police or the sanitation department) or sponsored by political machines as part of their election strategy. The most successful and longest-lived teams tended to be ones with political support. Political parties could provide city sinecures for the players, allocations for building enclosed stadiums, and permission to play ball on Sunday, the only day a sizable crowd could be attracted. The popularity of Sunday baseball (and the ownership of many teams in the American Association by brewers) made the game a prime target for militant Protestant reformers. The battle over Sunday baseball was probably the most lively survival of the Sabbatarian movement into the latter part of the century.

The less violent character of the New York game (no "soaking") made it more appropriate for play in urban centers between teams that had no neighborly reasons for restraining their killer instincts. In 1858 the National Association of Baseball Clubs was formed with a nucleus of sixteen New York–area teams, and in 1868 Cincinnati organized the first semiprofessional team. It was there also that the first unabashedly professional team was born in 1869, today's Cincinnati Reds.

Full-fledged professional teams first appeared in the Midwest, founded by local boosters eager to publicize their city and to demonstrate its vitality. The Cincinnati Red Stockings of 1869 were financed by the sale of stock in the team corporation; likewise the Chicago White Sox in 1870. In 1870 the National Association of Amateur Base Ball Players tried to expel the Cincinnati and Chicago professionals, and soon afterward, in March 1871, the professional clubs met and established the National Association of Professional Base Ball Players.

☆ ☆ ☆ Baseball Becomes a Business

Organized baseball as we know it today dates from a secret meeting of the owners of the investor-owned teams in 1876. The National Association had been torn by discord between corporately owned teams like the White Sox and the Reds and poorer teams that were essentially player-run cooperatives. The owners of the richer teams were determined to rationalize the business and to combat the public perception of professional ball players as willing accomplices of gamblers in betting coups (known then as "hippodroming"). Led by baseball's first robber baron, William Hulbert of the Chicago White Sox, the owners decided to declare war on the player-owned cooperative clubs. The owners specifically restricted membership in their new National League to clubs that had clarified the role of players as employees. This league, the nucleus of today's major leagues, began with clubs in Philadelphia, Hartford, Boston, Chicago, Cincinnati, Louisville, St. Louis, and New York City. It had to struggle against rival leagues for the next thirty-nine years, vanquishing some (the Players' League and the Federal League) and merging with others (the American Association in 1891 and the Western, later American, League in 1903).

The first few years of the new league were precarious ones, with cutthroat competition between the National League and its rivals. On 29 September 1879, the National League owners met and decided on the strategy that eventually was their salvation, the reserve clause, a contract provision that gave a player's club the right to "reserve" his services for the next season. In effect it transformed a yearly contract into a lifetime indenture. Until 1883 only the top five players on each team were protected by the reserve clause, but these were precisely the players whose salaries were the greatest burden to the owners. As the clubs reserved more and more players, finally covering the entire roster, the players found that their salaries were declining and their working conditions worsening, and so in 1885 John Montgomery Ward, a standout shortstop for the Giants and later a lawyer, organized the Brother-hood of Professional Baseball Players.

Still not satisfied, the owners drew up a player classification system in 1888 to stabilize and reduce salaries according to a standardized evaluation of a player's relative ability (something like today's free-agent compensation pool). Ward was in Egypt on baseball's famous 1888 round-the-world tour when he found out about this. He immediately abandoned the tour and, together with most of the other National League stars, declared war on the owners by organizing their own Players' League. Ward managed to enlist the support of almost all the star players and most of the sporting press, and he and the ball players spent the winter of 1889–90 promoting the new league in union halls, saloons, and wherever fans could be found.

The 1890 season was really a war between the National League led by A. G. Spalding and Ward's Players' League. At the end of the season the Players' League had surpassed the National League in attendance, but the total attendance had been spread too thin for anybody to make money. The players also made some grievous mistakes. They spurned an appeal to join the American Federation of Labor, and they refused to play Sunday ball, which was clearly suicidal. Worst of all, they placed too much power in the hands of their financial backers, counting on the investors to be fair to their ball-player partners.

At the end of the season all of the Players' League teams had shown a profit, while most of the National League teams were on the verge of bankruptcy. It seemed as though the players had won. But when the National League offered to meet with representatives of the American Association (a rival league

organized on the usual investor-controlled basis) and a committee representing the Players' League capitalists, the money men met and sold the players
out. They merged the leagues in a way that left the investors firmly in control.
After dropping some weaker teams, this merger with the American Association created a twelve-team alignment: Baltimore, Washington, Cleveland, and
Louisville, all of which eventually folded, and Boston, Brooklyn, Chicago,
Cincinnati, New York, Philadelphia, Pittsburgh, and St. Louis. In 1892, with
the National League's monopoly once again secure, the most hated features of
the reserve clause were reinstated and salaries again were slashed. The players
had lost all control of their game and would not regain it until the reserve
clause was finally thrown out in 1975. This clause, though grossly unfair to the
players, undoubtedly contributed to the growing popularity of the game by
ensuring the stability of the team rosters and by casting the players in roles
with which blue-collar fans could identify.

The 1890s also saw another development that probably helped ensure the
popularity of baseball—the enforcement of Jim Crow, which turned every
major-league baseball game into a ritual demonstration that America was a
white man's country. During the 1890s blacks had to organize their own
teams, and eventually a two-league system emerged, with a Negro National
League in 1920 and a Negro Eastern League in 1921, both of which collapsed
during the early Depression. A second Negro National League appeared in
the late 1930s, and a Negro American League in 1936. Both leagues died in
1952 when black stars in large numbers began to sign major- and minor-
league contracts after Jackie Robinson's pioneering season with the Brooklyn
Dodgers in 1947.

The National League's 1903 merger with the Western (American) League
created a structure of two eight-team leagues and a World Series. This arrangement remained intact and unchanged until 1953, when the Boston Braves
moved to Milwaukee.

The years after World War I saw baseball mature into America's premier
sports culture, with a full array of mythic underpinnings: an immaculate
conception (the Cooperstown legend of Abner Doubleday's invention of the
game), a myth of the Fall (the fixed 1919 World Series), an Odysseus (Ty
Cobb), an Achilles (Babe Ruth), a Zeus (Judge Landis), an aristocracy (the
Yankees), and a rabble (the Dodgers). More than any other American sport,
baseball lends itself to legend. The statistical records give each game a mythic
dimension as the hits, runs, errors, and strikeouts are melded into the record
books. The mythic power of the game, however, also takes its toll, as even on
the lowest level parents and coaches try to ride the miniature exploits of their
midget performers into the realm of sports fantasy.

☆ ☆ ☆ Basketball and Ethnic Politics

The evolution of basketball exhibits a more complicated mixture of elite uplift and ethnic aspiration. Basketball started as part of the nineteenth-century crusade to Americanize (or Christianize) the immigrants; it was quickly taken over by those targets for genteel uplift as a way ethnics could express their national pride and compete with other immigrants. Along with boxing, basketball is still the most ethnic of contemporary American sports and the most dramatic demonstration of black Americans' domination of the sports they enter, giving rise to the (not wholly unfounded) fear that whites will turn away from the professional game just when black stars like Julius Erving and Michael Jordan have raised the quality of play to a level that was unimaginable a decade or so ago.

Basketball was invented in 1891 at the YMCA's leadership training institute in Springfield, Massachusetts, where one of the physical instructors, James Naismith, developed rules for what he called "a New Sport": tossing a soccer ball into a backboardless peach basket. Naismith evidently intended that the ball be moved only by passing, but players soon discovered other ways to advance the ball without carrying it. At first they juggled the ball overhead (volleyball style) as they ran, but when juggling was outlawed the superior technique of dribbling was developed by players in the South Philadelphia Hebrew Association leagues. Other early improvements included removal of the bottom from the peach basket, fastening the basket to a backboard, and (for a time) surrounding the court with wire fencing to keep the ball in play (hence the term "cagers" for basketball players).

The "New Sport" became particularly popular at YMCAs and urban settlement houses in immigrant neighborhoods. In New York City the University Settlement House fielded championship teams, and by the 1930s there were Jewish Recreational Council Tri-State Championships, Lithuanian Championships, Polish Roman Catholic Championships, a National Federation of Russian Orthodox Clubs, Catholic Youth Organization leagues, B'nai B'rith leagues, and countless other ethnically based leagues and teams.

The first professional teams were also ethnic and had names like the Detroit Pulaskis, the Brooklyn Visitations (Irish), the Newark Turnverein, the Original Celtics (largely Jewish, and based in New York City), the Harlem Renaissance, the Hebrew All-Stars, and the Buffalo Germans. Games were often preliminaries to the dances of the teams' sponsoring organizations. The varnished basketball court comes from basketball's early days on highly polished dance floors.

The ethnic professional teams were succeeded by industrial teams sponsored by factories as part of employee relations programs. This was particularly common among the rubber companies in the Akron, Ohio, area. Industrial teams were the nucleus of the National Basketball League (NBL) when it was organized in 1937. In 1946 the Basketball Association of America (BAA) was organized by the owners of large arenas in major cities; only arena owners were permitted to enter teams. The NBL and the BAA competed until 1949, when the National Basketball Association (NBA) was formed by combining teams from the two leagues. Two years later the color bar came down and the first black players entered the NBA.

The evolution of basketball technique and strategy occurred as innovative players overcame the resistance of a conservative coaching establishment. During basketball's first forty years coaches taught the two-handed set shot that made basketball an intricate pattern of weaves and passes designed to produce two- and three-man picks (human walls between the shooter and the defender) to give a player a chance to attempt this easily blocked shot. In 1937 Hank Luisetti of Stanford University scandalized the coaching fraternity by breaking all scoring records with a one-handed jump shot. Orthodox coaches labeled Luisetti a freak, an exception to the rule, but the more farsighted of them realized that the jump shot was impossible to defend against and that the old patterned-play game was obsolete. Another example of a plausible theory refuted by practice was the coaches' belief that big men were too clumsy to play basketball despite the obvious advantage of their height. Professional basketball today displays several marked characteristics: the most obvious is the appearance of bigger and bigger men at all positions who possess, in addition to extraordinary size and strength, the quickness and ball-handling agility that once seemed the special province of "smaller" players (that is, shorter than six feet six inches).

Another critical aspect of today's game is a team's need for a "dominant" center if it is to have a realistic hope of competing for a professional championship. Dominance at the center position is a complex product of sheer size and strength, quick reactions, a scoring ability that frees other players for easy shots, and mental concentration and physical intensity that intimidate opposing players, preventing them from attempting shots at close range or fighting for rebounds. The most essential of a great center's talents is the employment of all these gifts, which of their nature depend on an unquenchable drive for personal dominance, in a system of team play. It was the demonstration of this equation that made the 1960s battles between Bill Russell of the Boston Celtics and Wilt Chamberlain of Philadelphia, San Francisco, and Los Angeles immortal in the memories of basketball fans.

There is probably nothing as expressive of the impact of blacks on American life as contemporary basketball, and the contrast between the styles of play of whites and blacks on the basketball court might be an important text to be decoded by the imaginative student of American culture. It is quite clear that no team on the professional or college level today can be truly competitive without drawing on the talent of black youths who have honed their basketball skills in the gyms and school yards of the big-city ghettos.

☆ ☆ ☆ Football: An American Spectacle

Football is certainly today's preeminent spectator sport; televised professional football is arguably the preeminent spectacle of any kind in today's American culture. In some parts of the country, high school football is the only religion with no dissenters, and in some areas the state university football team is the community's common bond and proudest boast. It takes a man of stern stuff indeed to resist a televised football game; to steal a phrase from Ronald Reagan, a man who says he doesn't watch the Super Bowl will lie about anything.

Televised football, more than any other game, can be appreciated by the ignorant as well as the informed. The viewer is seduced by the fabulous salaries of the athletes and the virtuosic techniques of the video crews while the colorful pageantry, the spectacular runs and passes, and the soul-satisfying brutality of blocking and tackling make football a stirring experience no matter how little understanding a spectator brings to the contest.

Football is for most Americans their tribal game, and it has always appealed to their herd instinct. The game can be traced back to the annual autumn free-for-all battles at Harvard in the 1820s between the new freshmen and the sophomores. A combination of the old free-for-all, soccer, and rugby survived at Harvard until 1874, when the school played two football games against McGill University of Canada. In the first game Harvard's own peculiar rules were used; the second game followed the rules of McGill's fairly orthodox version of British rugby. The Harvard students decided that the Canadian game was more enjoyable, so they voted to play according to those rules thereafter.

It was at Yale that the game of rugby developed into a game closely resembling today's football. The man behind this evolution was Walter Camp, who played football at Yale from 1875 until 1882, when he began training the team, eventually becoming head coach. During the Camp era Yale established a winning record the likes of which was never seen again. From 1872 until 1909 Yale won 324 games, lost 17, and tied 18, and from 1890 to 1893 Yale outscored its opponents 1,265 to 0! Walter Camp changed rugby into football when he replaced the scrum with a pass from the line of scrimmage. Camp was also responsible for the down-yardage system; he introduced American-style below-the-waist tackling and initiated the annual selection of an all-American team. Camp was a tireless proselytizer for football, speaking, reporting, and even writing novels to promote the game. Under Camp big games became an important link between the Ivy League colleges and elite society, and in 1903 Yale earned a sum equal to one-eighth of its annual budget from its football team.

Almost from the outset American college football was a supremely effective means for binding students, alumni, and community into a cohesive whole. The intensity of alumni and community identification with the football team fostered a win-at-any-cost ethic and placed tremendous pressure on coaches to field winning teams. All this made a sham of amateurism and of the pretense that football was a normal part of student life like panty raids, fraternity hazing, or cheating on exams.

College football had become so corrupt around the turn of the century that faculties made a determined attempt to clean it up, only to discover, as was later said of the city of Chicago, that football wasn't ready for reform. The Western Conference (later the Big 10) was founded in 1895 in an attempt to bring football under faculty control, but the demands of alumni and legislators for winning teams were too strong to resist, so the conference soon fell under the sway of the coaches and alumni.

The ferocious drive to win, the primitive state of the rules, and the rudimentary quality of protective equipment led to an unconscionable number of serious injuries at the turn of the century, although the exaggerated and colorful reporting of the period makes unreliable the often-quoted statistics on the number of gouged eyes, fractured skulls, and broken limbs. The public's perception of football as a brutal upper-class reversion to barbarianism by robber-barons-to-be, however, was strong enough to make Theodore Roosevelt convene his famous White House Conference on football in 1905, attended by representatives of Harvard, Yale, and Princeton. Legend to the contrary, Roosevelt had no intention of abolishing college football; in any case he certainly had no legal or actual power to do so. Had it come down to a test of strength between football and the president, it would have been interesting to see who would have prevailed—or who would prevail today.

In 1910 the rules were amended, supposedly to reduce violence but really to provide a better spectacle for fans by evening the balance between offense and defense and "opening up" the game. The flying wedge was outlawed, the pass rules were liberalized, and the number of chances a team was given to make ten yards before surrendering the ball was increased from three to four. These were the rules that Knute Rockne used at Notre Dame to build the greatest football dynasty since the old Yale teams of the nineteenth century, transforming "Fighting Irish" from an ethnic slur to a badge of pride.

The first professional football players were really semipros, who played more for fun than the pocket money they got by splitting the ticket take. Before 1920 the most famous professional was the Olympic champion Jim Thorpe; Gus Dorais and Knute Rockne of Notre Dame were also professionals of that era. In 1920 the American Football Association (AFA) was founded; two years later it was succeeded by the National Football League (NFL), comprised for the most part of teams from small towns in Ohio. It was the great Illinois tailback, Red Grange, whose publicity changed the professional game from the poor stepchild of the college game into a growth industry with the potential to become the multimillion-dollar business of the sixties. In 1930 the superiority of the professional game was demonstrated when the New York Giants beat Notre Dame in a charity exhibition game. In 1936 the college "draft" system was established, the final step in persuading the public to reverse its perception of college football's relationship to the pro game and to see the universities as minor leagues preparing players for the pro ranks.

Professional football's symbiosis with television began in 1952 when the NFL established its blackout rule for home games. In 1960 Pete Rozelle became the commissioner of the NFL, and under his astute leadership the game achieved a level of popularity that made it America's favorite spectator sport. In 1966 the NFL merged with its new rival, the American Football League (AFL), allowing Rozelle to designate the championship game between the two formerly separate leagues as the "Super Bowl," which immediately became America's premier sports spectacle.

☆ ☆ ☆ The International Perspective

There are those who point with alarm at America's relative lack of interest in the world's most popular game, soccer—a sport many feel has important advantages over football and baseball. Those two popular American sports by their very nature preclude mass participation and so must bear some responsibility for turning America into a nation of spectators. The violence of football makes necessary specialized conditioning and elaborate equipment if injury is to be avoided; even so there are crippling accidents and deaths every year. Baseball (hardball, that is) is so intrinsically difficult that few can participate; pitching demands special talents and training, while batting against good pitching is so difficult that a game with unskillful players is hardly worth the bother. Soccer, on the other hand, is a game anyone can play and enjoy.

Since soccer's superiority in encouraging active participation is so obvious, and since soccer's ability to arouse intense feelings of identification among spectators is at least equal to football's, why has it failed to become a major sport on the professional and college level? Soccer's worldwide popularity may be just what is keeping it from becoming popular. Baseball is also an international sport, played in Canada, Latin America, Japan, Taiwan, Korea, and, in a minor way, Europe. There are professional leagues in the Caribbean, Central and South America, and Japan, but the American public neither knows nor cares about all this. Spectators here are interested only in American teams playing other American teams. Major-league baseball teams from Toronto and Montreal hardly weaken this generalization.

Basketball is another truly international game, and yet here too Americans show little interest in the sport's international aspects. The same is true of hockey. The only time Americans have paid attention to an international sports contest is when the game has had some Cold War significance. (The end to that Cold War may alter America's attitude toward world sports while reshuffling the relative strengths of Eastern and Western European national teams.) While most nations enjoy seeing their countries play a role in the community of nations, Americans see their country as a world unto itself, judging by their attitudes toward sports. Bilateral competition with the Soviets eclipsed all possible relations with other nations.

☆ ☆ ☆ Fitness and the Body Beautiful

Today's physical fitness craze was preceded by similar enthusiasms over the past century and a half. In the 1830s there were theories of physical fitness based on military drill, on the German-derived Jahn system of gymnastics, on manual labor, and on Catharine Beecher's system of female calisthenics. During the 1880s Dr. Dio Lewis's theories of gymnastics eventually led to a gymnasium-building boom. The 1890s witnessed another fitness revival, this one spurred by the resurgence of the German Turner movement that had first come to this country after the European revolutions of 1848.

During the first years of the twentieth century the leading advocates of fitness were President Theodore Roosevelt and publisher Bernarr Macfadden. A wave of interest in physical fitness occurred during World War I and another during the Eisenhower and Kennedy years. The present-day enthusiasm for diets, exercises, and jogging dates from 1968 when Major Kenneth Gordon published his book *Aerobics*.

☆ ☆ ☆ Sports as American Myth

As a full-fledged alternative to workaday America, sports offers what we might call "jock culture": what the professional sports fan knows and admires, what the mass media sportswriter writes, and what the professional sports promoter sells as big-time sports entertainment. It is what "Lazy Boy"–enthroned philosophers of television sports like Michael Novak glorify when they sing hymns to the Super Bowl, the World Series, and the Stanley Cup. It is sports as gospel and moral metaphor.

No game is just a game. According to Howard Cosell and other heralds of jock culture, games are dramas that reveal a team (and its fans) to be a proud band of winners or a pathetic collection of choke-artists.

Jock culture stands in the same relation to actual sports as theology, hagiology, demonology, eschatology, and magic do to organized religion. The legends of the "Great" John L. Sullivan, Jack Dempsey, Joe Louis, Rocky Marciano, and Muhammad Ali are all part of the fabric of jock culture, not so much for their actual lives and deeds as for the web of words laid over them by the sportswriters and commentators who earn their livings by fabricating the illusion that the mythology of sports is true and real. Places like the Cooperstown Hall of Fame and its clones in Canton and Springfield (for football and basketball) are jock culture's shrines for pilgrims intent on personal contact with invisible mysteries. Great sportswriters and publicists like C. C. (Bunion Derby) Pyle, Richard Kyle Fox, Tex Rickard, Grantland Rice, Jimmy Cannon, Howard Cosell, Dick Young, and Red Smith are the means by which talented athletes are transformed into legendary heroes like Babe Ruth, Red Grange, Bronco Nagurski, and Edgar "The Wild Helicopter" Jones.

Just as artists have always turned the superstitions of their tribe into the material of art, so the myths and legends of sports have found their way into the paintings of George Bellows and Thomas Eakins, the poems of Edna St. Vincent Millay, and the novels of Bernard Malamud, Ernest Hemingway, William Faulkner, Jack London, and Philip Roth. Both serious and popular writers use sports to explore moral dilemmas or promote moral lessons: Gilbert Patten and his Frank Merriwell books, John R. Tunis and his series of juveniles, Mark Harris with *Bang the Drum Slowly*, and Bernard Malamud with *The Natural*. The last two books have their defects, Harris's sentimentality and Malamud's inability to master colloquial English, but the larger problem with such "serious" sports art is that seriousness about sports verges on travesty. Perhaps a game is, finally, only a game.

The best use literature can make of sports is to turn it into an excuse for comic extravagance. Popular myths about sport and stereotypes about the habits and character of athletes allow writers to portray ball players as figures of folklore come to life, complete with dialect, grotesque physical characteristics, Rabelaisian appetites, and the propensity for reenacting episodes plagiarized from Mark Twain and Sut Lovingood. Sports have made their most useful contribution to fiction as a spur to comic invention in popular works like Dan Jenkins's *Semi-Tough* or Hunter Thompson's stories about the Super Bowl, Kentucky Derby, and Honolulu Marathon. The best of all is Philip Roth's *Great American Novel*, America's most spectacular piece of sports humor to date.

Today's exercise boom—unlike earlier fitness crazes—has become another province in the jock culture empire. Exercise today is not simply a way to get a workout. It is an entry into a realm of fantasy peopled by cult figures like Jane Fonda and Cher. The early-morning jogger has jogging shoes, jogging suit, jogging watch, and jogging magazine and watches jogging heroes compete on television in the Boston and New York marathons while dreaming the latest version of the American dream: "Oh, that this too too solid flesh would melt."

FURTHER READING

The best single-volume history of American sports is Benjamin G. Rader, *American Sports* (Englewood Cliffs, N.J., 1983). Another well-known history is Foster Rhea Dulles, *A History of Recreation: America Learns to Play* (New York, 1965). For an exemplary combination of scholarship and passion, see Ted Vincent's *Mudville's Revenge: The Rise and Fall of American Sport* (New York, 1981), which traces and decries the "Romanization" of American sports by big business and other elite groups. Other general histories and analyses include John Durant and Otto Bettman's *A Pictorial History of American Sports* (Cranbury, N.J., 1965); Jennie Holliman's *American Sports, 1785–1835* (Durham, N.C., 1935); Donald Chu's *The Character of American Higher Education and Intercollegiate Sport* (Albany, N.Y., 1989); and Allen Guttmann's *From Ritual to Record: The Nature of Modern Sports* (New York, 1978) and *Sports Spectators* (New York, 1986).

Among the many celebrations of big-time televised sports are Michael Novak's *The Joy of Sports* (New York, 1976); Richard Lipsky's *How We Play the Game: Why*

Sports Dominate American Life (Boston, 1981); and A. Bartlett Giamatti's *Take Time for Paradise: Americans and Their Games* (New York, 1989).

For source materials on sports mythmaking, see Gilbert Patten's Frank Merriwell stories (for example, *Frank Merriwell's Loyalty* [New York, 1904]) and Grantland Rice's *The Tumult and the Shouting: My Life in Sport* (New York, 1954). Readers also will be interested in Christian K. Messenger's *Sport and the Spirit of Play in American Fiction: Hawthorne to Faulkner* (New York, 1981) and *Sport and the Spirit of Play in Contemporary American Fiction* (New York, 1990). More critical accounts of commercialized sports include Robert Lipsyte's *Sportsworld: An American Dreamland* (New York, 1975); William O. Johnson's *Super Spectator and the Electric Lilliputians* (Boston, 1971); and Howard Cosell's *Cosell* (New York, 1973).

For sex and race discrimination in sports, see Robert Patterson's *Only the Ball Was White* (Englewood Cliffs, N.J., 1970); Al-Tony Gilmore's *Bad Nigger! The National Impact of Jack Johnson* (Port Washington, N.Y., 1975); Harry Edwards's *The Revolt of the Black Athlete* (New York, 1969); and Stephanie L. Twin, ed., *Out of the Bleachers: Writings on Women and Sport* (New York, 1979).

Nineteenth-century sports newspapers and magazines that should be consulted include the *National Police Gazette*, the *New York Clipper*, *Sporting Life*, *Sporting News*, and *Outing*. Among the more important twentieth-century journals and periodicals are the *Journal of Popular Culture* (see the special issue on sports, Fall 1974), the *Journal of Sport History*, the *Journal of Health, Physical Education, and Recreation*, the *Journal of Social History*, the *Canadian Journal of History of Sport and Physical Education*, *Sports Illustrated*, *Sport*, and *WomenSports*.

Of the major American sports, baseball has received the most literary and scholarly attention. Worth consulting are Harold Seymour's trilogy *Baseball: The Early Years*, *Baseball: The Golden Age*, and *Baseball: The People's Game* (New York, 1960, 1971, 1990); David Q. Voigt's *American Baseball*, 2 vols. (Norman, Okla., 1966, 1970), and *America through Baseball* (Chicago, 1976); Tristram Peter Coffin's *The Old Ball Game in Folklore and Fiction* (New York, 1971); Leverett T. Smith, Jr., *The American Dream and the National Game* (Bowling Green, Ohio, 1975); Robert W. Creamer's *Babe* (New York, 1974); Lawrence S. Ritter's *The Glory of Their Time: The Story of the Early Days of Baseball Told by the Men Who Played It* (New York, 1966); and Warren Goldstein's *Playing for Keeps: A History of Early Baseball* (Ithaca, N.Y., 1989).

More specialized studies of baseball include Jim Brosnan's *The Long Season* (New York, 1960); Eliot Asinof's *Eight Men Out: The Black Sox and the 1919 World Series* (New York, 1963); Bobbie Bouton and Nancy Marshall's *Home Games* (New York, 1982); Jim Bouton's *Ball Four* (New York, 1970); George F. Will's *Men at Work: The Craft of Baseball* (New York, 1990); Kenneth M. Jennings's *Balls and Strikes: The Money Game in Professional Baseball* (New York,

1990); Phil Dixon and Pat Hannigan's *The Negro Baseball Leagues* (Mattituck, N.Y., 1990); and Robert Kemp Adair's *The Physics of Baseball* (New York, 1990). All of Roger Kahn's and Roger Angell's many baseball books are worth reading. On basketball, see Neil D. Isaacs's *All the Moves: A History of College Basketball* (Philadelphia, 1975) and Leonard Koppett's *24 Seconds to Shoot: An Informal History of the National Basketball Association* (New York, 1975). For other sports, see Tom Bennett et al., *The NFL's Official Encyclopedic History of Professional Football* (New York, 1977); Nat Fleischer, *The Heavy-weight Championship* (New York, 1961); Will Grimsley, *Tennis: Its History, People, and Events* (Englewood Cliffs, N.J., 1971); and John Lucas, *The Modern Olympic Games* (South Brunswick, N.J., 1980).

PART

THREE

Society

and Values

Few statements of national purpose have been so succinct and universal as the "self-evident" truths set forth in the Declaration of Independence: "that all men are created equal, that they are endowed by their Creator with certain unalienable Rights, that among these are Life, Liberty, and the pursuit of Happiness." While these ideals might never be realized fully in American society, they have defined the nation's quest for social justice and offer standards by which the unfinished journey can be measured. The six chapters in this section provide historical documentation and models for assessing social values and realities in the United States. They also reveal the unresolved discords left in the wake of our social progress, divisions of race, class, and gender that have survived the social liberation movements of this century, and the specter of poverty in the midst of great affluence.

Nathan Glazer sets theoretical parameters for the chapters that follow by discussing the inherent dilemma of "Individualism and Equality in the United States." American individualism is not unitary, Glazer points out, but two-sided: "the more rugged economic and institutional individualism of the United States, hampered and hobbled by a new kind of individualism devoted to self-realization, to the protection of the environment, to suspicion of big business and big organization." The emergence of the new individualism can be linked to "a dramatic loss in . . . confidence in the old America, from about 1963 on." Concurrently the egalitarian drive, which focuses particularly today on "the great American problem, the race issue," has changed the institutional environment of individualism by "erecting official racial and ethnic categories on the basis of which rights, privileges, and duties are distributed by government."

Addressing what personal experience and the mass media frequently discover to be our most troubled social institution, Tamara Hareven considers "Continuity and Change in American Family Life." The notion of a golden age of the family when three generations once lived happily together in the same household is mythic; in reality, greater longevity in the twentieth century has given opportunity as never before for overlap and stability among the generations. But industrialization and affluence have brought about major changes in the household and family roles, separating the home from the workplace, husbands from wives, parents from children. The major historical change, according to Hareven, has been "from a collective view of the family to one of individualization and sentiment. . . . It has contributed considerably to the liberation of individuals, but it has also eroded the resilience of the family and its ability to withstand crises." Women and children have been particularly affected by the conversion of the home into a "therapeutic refuge from the outside world."

The engagement of women with the outside world in the twentieth century is the subject of William Chafe's chapter "Women and American Society." Without belittling the professional and social opportunities opened by women's liberation or discounting the "success stories" of bright, talented, and economically secure women, Chafe is also concerned about the "millions of other women whose stories represented the direct opposite of the upward mobility and the economic advancement enjoyed by the fortunate minority." The massive increase in female-headed households since the 1960s, induced or complicated by problems of race and class, has "feminized" poverty in the United States.

The cultural approach taken by Waldo Martin in "The Making of Black America" discloses a historical sojourn of African Americans that has been at once progressive and regressive and reveals "ambiguities, contradictions, ironies, and paradoxes" that have implications far beyond the "peculiar institution" of slavery or the quest for freedom and equality. Gullah language, creole communities, black Christian denominations and other organizations, the great urban migration of the early twentieth century—all are stages "in a dialectical struggle with the dominant culture over issues of world view . . . as well as autonomy." Martin concludes with an important reminder that "we need to think seriously about the meaning of our hybrid and composite national culture and the creole quality of its constituent cultures."

The dilemmas of material progress and social inequality exposed by the previous authors are addressed forthrightly in Edward Pessen's chapter "Status and Social Class in America." Power, influence, and access are stratified within American society no less today than in the past, Pessen writes, yet the nation "wears its class system lightly and unobtrusively," and most Americans "seem altogether oblivious to the significance, even to the very existence, of the class distinctions that in fact play so central a part" in their lives. Shared beliefs and institutional commitments to equal opportunity, buttressed by abundant instances of individual mobility, apparently have habituated the people of the United States to consider class less a social force than a matter of personal responsibility.

It is appropriate that John Orr's chapter "The American System of Education" should close this section on society and values and make a transition to the next section on the life of the mind. Since the 1950s no other social or government institution has been charged with greater responsibility for realizing the nation's creed of equality or has been more severely blamed for derelictions in providing for the public literacy and welfare than our schools. Over the three and a half centuries since Massachusetts first passed laws requiring public education, the American education system has been remarkable for the range of religious, civil, cultural, and occupational goals it has served, and especially for its role in the "Americanization" process. Orr represents the educational structure that emerged as universal, decentralized, comprehensive, and professional. While its inadequacies have left us, according to the 1983 report of the National Commission on Excellence in Education, with a "nation at risk," and critics continue to theorize "Why Johnny Can't Read," a third of a million international students attest to the academic prowess of the United States by enrolling in our universities each year. "Mr. Jefferson's university" at Charlottesville, Virginia, and "Mr. Franklin's university" in Philadelphia are just two elements today in the nation's complex plan for "a more general diffusion of knowledge."

14 ☆ Individualism

☆ and Equality

☆ in the

☆ United States

☆ Nathan Glazer

Two values, sometimes seen as in conflict, sometimes seen as complementary, frame discussions of American society: individualism and equality. Each has had, in the course of American history, its defenders and critics. Foreign observers have emphasized first one and then the other as the most marked characteristic of the new society and new polity that arose in the United States.

☆ ☆ ☆ The Double Edge of American Individualism

The distinctively American aspect of individualism is symbolized by the fact that the first use of this term recorded by the *Oxford English Dictionary* is in the English translation of Alexis de Tocqueville's great book, *Democracy in America*. Individualism, Tocqueville argued, was an inevitable consequence of democracy and equality. "I have shown," he wrote, "how it is that in ages of equality every man seeks for his opinions within himself; I am now to show how it is that in the same ages all his feelings are turned to himself alone." He was concerned to distinguish this new form of human behavior from age-old selfishness. In contrast to selfishness, he wrote, "individualism is a mature and calm feeling, which disposes each member of the community to sever himself from the mass of his fellows and to draw apart with his family and his friends, so that after he has thus formed a little circle of his own, he willingly leaves society at large to itself."

He expands upon this bare definition, to give it a social and political meaning: "As social conditions become more equal, the number of persons increases who, although they are neither rich nor powerful enough to exercise any great influence over their fellows, have nevertheless acquired or retained sufficient education and fortune to satisfy their wants. They owe nothing to any man; they acquire the habit of always considering themselves as standing alone, and they are apt to imagine that their whole destiny is in their hands."

It is perhaps already clear that Tocqueville was—as with so many things— of two minds about individualism. A final quotation may suggest the less pleasant face of individualism: "Democratic communities . . . are constantly filled with men who, having entered but yesterday upon their independent condition, are intoxicated with their new power. They entertain a presumptuous confidence in their own strength, and as they do not suppose they can henceforward ever have occasion to claim the assistance of their fellow creatures, they do not scruple to show that they care for nobody but themselves."

This double view of individualism in the United States has persisted ever since. The positive image of individualism has emphasized the American as pioneer, moving out into wilderness and among savages, and making his way alone, with rifle and axe. It emphasized his indifference as pioneer to governmental controls, which on occasion meant taking the law into his own hands as vigilante to impose a minimal order on frontier society. It emphasized his insistence on his rights as an American—his right to challenge government in the courts, through organization and electoral activity and through referendum, initiative, and recall.

Much of American society and landscape is marked by this individualism, such as the pattern of agricultural settlement, with its farm dwelling set alone in the midst of extensive acreage, the nearest neighbor a mile away, the nearest town a day's journey back and forth, so strikingly different from the agricultural villages of Europe. Individualism, too, marked the cities, created with checkerboard patterns so that each individual could select a standard plot and do with it what he wished. Or, in more recent decades, it has been seen in a pattern of haphazard growth, in which each entrepreneur, as individual, managed to acquire some land and, presto, laid out, indifferent to any larger image of metropolitan form or urban design, his own development and sold to anyone who could afford the houses.

We see it, too, in the pattern of American higher education, in which entrepreneurs, individual and group, could without restraint establish institutions they called colleges or universities and provide whatever education they could or felt was necessary. In the course of American history, most of these failed. Perhaps the survivors were sturdier for all that. But we now have three thousand or so institutions of higher education in the United States, and many of them permanently teeter on the edge of bankruptcy. Or consider the pattern of

American religion, in which any church or sect may be founded and in which undoubtedly thousands of expectant prophets and builders of churches have died disappointed. But hundreds more have succeeded, and some markedly. Consider the Church of Jesus Christ of Latter-Day Saints or Christian Science.

I have tried to give a positive picture of American individualism—its opportunity for the individual, its grant of freedom, its encouragement of diversity. But in doing so, I have undoubtedly already suggested its opposite side: the indifference to the preservation of landscape or urban form, as the pioneer—agricultural or urban—moved on from worn-out land and worn-out structures, abandoning them to start up anew on virgin territory; the indifference, too, to those who fell behind in the race. "Rugged individualism," it was called in the earlier twentieth century. "Rampant individualism," answered those who considered the victims of individualists: the industrial workers who were prevented from unionizing, often by armed force; the migrant laborers who made possible the individual farmer sitting in isolated and kingly splendor in the midst of his hundreds of acres. The negative side of individualism has been so well portrayed by American writers and is so well known that it is hardly necessary to add much. One need only read Upton Sinclair and John Steinbeck.

☆ ☆ ☆ Individualism Restrained

In the later 1960s and 1970s, the economic individualism for which the United States was known ran into trouble. The American scene was transformed by a new wave of regulatory legislation reflecting a sharply rising concern for minorities and women, for the environment and the consumer of industrial products, and for the worker in industry and agriculture. The American industrialist and businessman and farmer, still possibly in many respects the freest in the world, began to labor under major new restraints that were unexpected, with consequences that we still cannot foresee. The new age of regulation followed on earlier ages of regulation, stemming from the earlier ages of reform: the late 1880s, when we passed antitrust legislation and created an Interstate Commerce Commission to regulate the railroads; the progressive period of Theodore Roosevelt and the first term of Woodrow Wilson, when these regulatory agencies were strengthened and a Federal Reserve Board and a Federal Trade Commission were created; and the first two terms of Franklin D. Roosevelt, when numerous regulatory agencies were spawned, most significantly a Securities and Exchange Commission and a National Labor Relations Board.

However, I believe future historians will have to record the period between 1964 and 1972—that of the presidential terms of Johnson and Nixon—as the age in which federal regulation of industry, business, education, and state and local governments made its greatest and most decisive strides. In 1964 we created an Equal Employment Opportunity Commission to prevent discrimination against minorities and women in employment; in 1968 we banned discrimination in housing and renting; in 1972 universities and local government came under the control of the Equal Employment Opportunity Commission, and stricter bans on sex discrimination in higher education were imposed. Under the influence of Ralph Nader, and with the rapid rise of consumer and environmental movements, we created agencies for automobile safety, for environmental protection, for occupational safety, for consumer product safety. All of these increased enormously the power of governments to intervene in what were formerly private decisions; they imposed a great burden of paperwork on business and local and state government, which almost every presidential candidate promised to mitigate, promises indeed that helped elect two, in 1976 and 1980.

The new wave of regulations undoubtedly helped us to move in some degree toward their espoused objectives: equality for minorities and women, protection of the environment, protection for workers and consumers. Each also spawned great volumes of regulations, new bodies of law, worked out, as in the nature of government agencies, in pedantic and humorless detail and often to ridiculous extremes. This development raised questions in many minds as to whether it was still reasonable to consider the United States a country in which individualism prevailed, rampant or otherwise.

Thus, to give some examples: Under the ban on discrimination based on sex in education, a boys' choir was considered discriminatory, and so was a mother-daughter event in a school. It was considered discriminatory for an institution of higher education to impose different regulations on men and women. Any sanctions as a result of pregnancy would be considered discriminatory. So might classes in physical education that separated men and women. Requiring short hair for boys and men may be discriminatory, as is requiring that girls wear skirts. Many institutions of higher education in the United States are set up under religious auspices, and in some of these, at least, the upholding of traditional morality is an important part of educational objectives. However, these colleges and universities also fall under the act banning discrimination on account of sex. One, the Mormon Brigham Young University, has gained an exemption on the basis of religion from some of the requirements enforcing the ban on discrimination on grounds of sex.

Rather more significantly, a strong attack was launched on the traditional division of occupational roles between men and women. Major legal cases led to strong requirements to recruit women for skilled manual and mechanical work on telephone lines and skyscraper building sites, traditionally done by males. Congress mandated the entry of women into the military academies. A strong effort was launched, particularly under the Carter administration, to recruit women into all branches of the armed services except those directly involved in combat and to train women together with men. The Department of Justice required local police and fire forces to hire women police officers and fire fighters (the very names of these occupations being changed to remove any implication that they were more suited for men than women). Examinations and tests, public and private, that seemed to favor the male over the female sex were charged with being, and found to be, discriminatory, and every business was put on notice to exercise the most meticulous care to avoid any suspicion of favoring one sex or another for specific jobs.

Much of this legislation and litigation was originally designed to prevent discrimination against blacks and other racial and national-origin minorities; and just as employment and promotion tests that selected different percentages of men and women were found discriminatory, so too were tests that selected different percentages of blacks and whites. In one sense, individualism was being advanced, for hardly any occupation was now closed to women and none was closed to blacks. But in another sense, it was being restricted, for the independence of American employers to hire and promote and fire as they pleased was placed under severe restraint.

☆ ☆ ☆ The Politics of Equality

It is clear that some part of American individualism, whether we consider it "rampant" or "rugged," is now sharply limited. But it is necessary to point out that some kinds of individualism fell under restraint only because another aspect of individualism was doing quite well. This was the political aspect of individualism, in which the single individual or individuals, organized in private groupings, battle for what they conceive to be their rights or a better condition. I have mentioned one name as expressing this rather remarkable aspect of individualism: Ralph Nader. It is hard to imagine a figure of this type having such great influence in any other country. He is without official appointment; he has no membership organization to support him. He wrote a book, *Unsafe at Any Speed* (1965), on the lack of safety in automobiles and was thus almost single-handedly responsible for a great national demand for controls on automobile design, one that has affected the daily life of Americans perhaps more directly and immediately than any other legislation. It is as a result of this legislation that every American who drives a car (and that is almost all adult Americans) will be greeted on entering his vehicle by a buzzer that can be shut off only by putting on a seat belt.

The great civil rights movement, which was responsible for our civil rights legislation, owes much to individual heroes, of whom the most prominent was Martin Luther King, Jr. The women's rights movement, which has forced government agencies implementing civil rights legislation to devote as much attention to women's rights as to the rights of blacks and other minorities for which it was written, flared up, with no official encouragement or awareness, as the result of the actions of individuals and became the most surprising and long-lasting phenomenon of the later 1960s. The women's movement was unexpected, unpredicted, unheralded, but suddenly there, wielding awesome power over government, business, universities, the mass media, and changing the very language we use to talk of women—just as the civil rights movement (or rather, one wing of it) changed the language we use to describe the African American minority. So too with the environmental protection movement, which burgeoned in the later 1960s and developed great power, holding up the Alaskan pipeline and the development of offshore oil resources and curtailing the development of nuclear power. This movement of individuals was able to get significant legislation passed and to intercede in the courts against so many forms of economic development that by 1979 the United States was more subject to the mercy of foreign oil exporters than it was in 1973.

The two faces of individualism are made up of the more rugged economic and institutional individualism of the United States, hampered and hobbled by a new kind of individualism devoted to self-realization, to the protection of the environment, to suspicion of big business and big organization. This latter individualism was still pragmatic enough to have enlisted, often unwillingly, big government on its side, as is possible owing to the openness of the American political process, the power of the press and the media to arouse public opinion, and access to the courts of ordinary people and nonstate organizations, enabling them to affect the very administration of law.

One kind of individualism is hampered by another. Henry Ford hobbled by Ralph Nader. Obviously the two kinds of individualism have different origins, motivations, consequences. Principally, the first kind has contributed to the most marked characteristic of the modern United States, its enormous productivity, while the second clearly places some limits on how this productivity may be realized. Both kinds are suspicious of government, but both are willing to enlist it. The first kind of individualism will enlist government to protect investments overseas, to foster economic growth and profits at home. The second will enlist it to achieve what it feels to be a fairer and more just society and is relatively indifferent to the claims of production.

The second kind of individualism thinks the United States is rich enough. It sees no need to endanger beaches with oil, rivers with nuclear power plants, forests with the axe because wood and newsprint are needed. This kind of individualism is disdainful of the objectives and motivations of the economic individualist. Why do we need more gadgets, or really more of anything? In the 1970s economic individualists, under this assault, lost their former arrogance. Very likely their own children were to be found among the passionate defenders of consumer rights, the environment, women, and minorities. And the economic individualists were hard put to justify themselves. Having praised without questioning the virtues of abundance and continuous growth, they were at a loss when the simple question was put: "Why?" The intelligentsia of the country put this question, ever more sharply, in the schools and universities, in the press and radio and television, in political forums and Congress, and in the courts, which, it seems, routed any other claimant to make the final judgments in American society, moral and political.

☆ ☆ ☆ Disillusionment

The upsurge of the new individualism against the old had many explanations. Basically, there seems to have been a dramatic loss in self-confidence, or, more precisely, in confidence in the old America, from about 1963 on. There was the shock of the assassination of John F. Kennedy, which the American people simply could not explain well enough to themselves. A great tragedy cannot be allowed to remain senseless. The assassination of Abraham Lincoln, for instance, had meaning: he died because he had tried to keep the Union together and free the slaves by conducting a great war against the slaveholding South; he was killed by conspirators who hated him for this. But what meaning could be given to the death of John F. Kennedy? Public opinion—even enlightened public opinion—refuses to accept what seems the most reasonable explanation, as well as by far the best-documented one (indeed, the only one documented), that he was killed by a single malcontent, and insists on finding a greater meaning: he was assassinated by those on the right (Texas millionaires?), or the left (Castro?), or by Castro because the insidious American intelligence establishment, unbeknownst to the president, had tried to assassinate the Cuban leader.

But this was only the beginning of the series of blows to American self-confidence. There was the beginning of student protest on the campus at the

University of California, Berkeley, that best represented America's claim to providing the most advanced higher education to the broadest segments of youth; the riots of blacks in America's leading cities; involvement in a disastrous and unending war. Even that was not the end. There was the wide-spreading Watergate scandal, with all its ramifications. The result was the withdrawal of faith in America's central purposes and underlying virtue by a large part of America's youth, a large part of its mass media, and a substantial part of its intellectuals. The defense of American society, the American political system, American culture, became, for a while, very much a minority and suspect activity, generally conducted under attack, and almost a guerrilla operation.

We lived through a strange period in which two American presidents and their leading advisers seem to have conducted American policy in isolation from, and with the disapproval of, the highly educated public and the elite mass media. But this is not the whole story. Faith in the system seems to have continued, even if shaken and weakened, among the less-educated elements and the political figures representing ordinary people. Thus the United States developed an odd political system. Overlying the more obvious and understandable divisions between the better-off and the worse-off, the businessman and the worker, the minorities and the majority, there emerged in the 1970s a new division: between those who were basically conservative about the American system, who did not want to see rapid change, who felt that despite the traumas of the 1960s and 1970s America had not done so badly; and those who felt quite the opposite, who saw the society, culture, and polity as something like disaster areas and who wanted change. The latter element was better educated and more influential in the media. This created a substantial strain on the American system. A basically conservative populace found its intellectual leadership concentrated in more liberal and to some extent even radical representatives.

☆ ☆ ☆ Reagan and the Older Individualism

The election of Ronald Reagan, which sent a shock through the liberal intelligentsia that was shaped in the 1960s and 1970s from which it has not recovered, represented the victory of that older America of rugged or rampant individualism over the newer individualism of protest—in the streets, the institutions, and the courts. It represented the triumph of those who believed that the productive energies of America could be and should be set free to the benefit of all against those who believed this unleashing of the productive energies would only increase inequality, damage the environment, and flood the society with more gadgets and commercial objects that were unnecessary for the good life. It represented the surprising victory of the religious fundamentalism of the American heartland that had been declining in influence and power for fifty years over the cosmopolitanism of the big metropolitan centers. Despite the fact that he had come out of Hollywood and the movies and was the first divorced president, Reagan became a committed opponent of abortion on demand and a strong supporter of prayer in the schools and of government support for nonstate religious schools. He regularly addressed meetings of conservative fundamentalist and evangelical groups; the access to the White House that the established, liberal churches had enjoyed in the past was radically reduced.

No election in the United States in many years had been so sharply ideological as that in which Reagan contested Carter in 1980; none marked so sharp a shift in the philosophy of government. Liberalism in all its forms was anathema to the new administration. It struck back at the policies hampering individualism and expanding equality that had been instituted in the preceding twenty years, with variable success. Whether economic individualism was unleashed, or whether it was even possible to do so any longer; whether the recovery of 1983 to 1987 could be ascribed to the policies of the Reagan administration, and if so, in what measure—these questions cannot be easily answered. But the philosophy of the new administration was clear, regardless of its success. Many opponents of government regulation who supported the administration were disappointed with the results of its efforts to restore an older economic individualism. When government expands, it is not easy to turn the clock back. However, the attempt was made.

The record of the Reagan administration when it comes to a second great theme of American history, the search for equality, is clearer. Just as this administration fought for the older individualism of free economic activity against the newer individualism that was suspicious of the forces of production, so it fought for an older conception of equality against a newer one that had become dominant in the 1970s. The young individualists fighting for the environment and safety against big business were also fighting for equality, and much of the legislative revolution of the later 1960s and early 1970s dealt directly with equality—for racial minorities, for women, for linguistic minorities, for the handicapped, for the backward student of whatever kind, for the poor and the beneficiaries of government aid.

First there was important legislation—in 1964, 1965, 1968, and 1972—against discrimination on grounds of race, color, religion, or national origin in voting, employment, education, housing, public facilities, or any program receiving federal aid. Great changes took place on the basis of this legislation. Segregation of students by race was finally wiped out in the South; employment practices began to change radically under the impact of the law; blacks began to vote in large numbers in the South in areas where they had been deprived of the franchise and began to elect state legislators, mayors, and other public officials.

Second, there was equally important action, independent of legislation, by the executive department of the federal government, the president, establishing affirmative action requirements for all federal contractors. A "federal contractor" was any business or other institution receiving federal funds—and that meant almost every business or institution. "Affirmative action" meant statistically based programs to hire certain specified groups—blacks, Hispanic Americans, Asian Americans, Native Americans, and women. These programs became powerful tools pressuring business and universities to hire and promote the specified minorities and women.

Third, the federal and state courts mandated quotas on the basis of race and sex in hiring in many businesses and in many local and state governments; more radical desegregation of the schools ("busing"); better treatment for welfare recipients, patients in mental hospitals, prisoners, the handicapped, and children who required special attention in schools.

All of this had substantial impact on daily life. In some cities, one-third or more of the schoolchildren were regularly transported out of their neighborhoods so that each school might have a better mix of races. In many states mental hospital and jail administration fell under the rule of the federal judges, who required heavy expenditures to improve facilities. Almost everywhere, judges required expensive education for children with learning difficulties so that they might have a better chance of attaining education similar to that of other children. This contributed to the financial crises of states and cities. "Due process" expanded to protect the poor and recipients of government funds in many respects; thus families and individuals cannot be cut off from welfare, or tenants evicted from public-housing projects, or children expelled from school without some degree of due process.

We have seen a vast expansion of equal, or more than equal, treatment owing to due process and "equal protection of the laws," but this development has not received universal applause. It makes more difficult the refusal of welfare benefits to those who lie to get it, the expulsion from housing projects of disruptive and criminal tenants, and the suspension from school of undisciplined children who prevent other children from learning. It greatly increases the cost of government, as courts mandate new expenses. And it raises troublesome questions as to whether the basic constitutional division between executive, legislative, and judicial powers has not been transgressed when judges, in pursuit of due process and equal protection, impose changes on local, state, and federal governments.

☆ ☆ ☆ Equality and Individualism: An Enduring Paradox?

The equality revolution in the United States raises a grave question: Has the movement progressed so far that certain aspects of individualism are now in danger? One may ask, how can the expansion of equality threaten individual rights? Of course, observers of democracy have long understood—and once again we can refer to Tocqueville—that there are inherent conflicts between equality and individualism, or, if one will, liberty. Tocqueville was so sharply aware of them because the French Revolution, which swept away the inequalities in law that separated Frenchmen from each other, finally led to Napoleon's despotism. And Napoleon was able to present himself as fulfilling the aims of the French Revolution because, indeed, in the course of his progress through Europe he swept away the distinctions of the old regime and brought legal equality to all men—but an equality in which they were equal under despotic power. Subsequent revolutions have told the same story.

But whatever the long-range threats that equality holds for individualism, the problem in the United States is not that the drive to greater equality is laying the groundwork for the destruction of liberty. The situation that has developed in the conflict between equality and individualism is one that has not been clearly foreshadowed by political philosophers, one that is unique to the United States. The steady push toward equality begins to threaten individualism not because opinion is limited—it has never been freer in the United States; not because access to politics is limited—access has never been easier, as the party structure breaks down; not because access to the mass media to express unpopular opinions is limited—every opinion, even the most outlandish, finds easy access, and indeed the more outlandish the opinion, it often appears, the easier for it to find expression.

The egalitarian drive threatens individualism specifically because it is directed toward the great American problem, the race issue, and in doing so it is erecting official racial and ethnic categories on the basis of which rights, privileges, and duties are distributed by government and by private employers and institutions under governmental pressure. This is a totally unexpected development and one that has created the uneasy feeling that in the United States today the individual is no longer evaluated for purposes of employment or access to education as an individual, without regard for his or her race or ethnic group. Instead, many believe the applicant is regarded precisely as a representative or member of some specific group and receives a particular kind of treatment if falling into one category and a different one if falling into another category.

Of course, this has happened in other democratic societies. In India, for example, reservations for employment and study and political representation are made for groups that have been subject to deep and severe discrimination. In other countries one finds the same reservations, not because one group in particular has suffered discrimination but because a stable political balance in a deeply divided country seems to require it. Such "reservations"—in the United States, "goals" and "quotas"—are not necessarily incompatible with a democratic and just social order. Indeed, they may be necessary to achieve it. But much depends on the nature of the society in which they are introduced. In a society in which two or more groups are clearly defined and are expected to maintain their integrity indefinitely—let us say language groups in such countries as Canada or Belgium or, at dispute today, the national groups in Yugoslavia—justice may require equal representation for each group in many spheres, and this kind of arrangement may be most conducive to internal peace in a society.

☆ ☆ ☆ Public Sanctions versus Private Suasion

But the United States has not defined itself as such a society. It has been a federation of states, not of peoples. Whatever the discrimination to which races and ethnic groups were subjected—and in some cases, particularly blacks, Japanese, and Chinese, this discrimination found expression in public law—it was always the hope of the central body of American public opinion that all Americans would eventually be integrated into a common society without distinction of race, color, or religion. These categories, it was hoped, would become purely private matters, and government would not need to take cognizance of them. This hope was realized in the federal legislation of 1964 and later, according to which these distinctions could not be taken into account by any public body and indeed could not even regulate private behavior when it came to such key areas of life as education, employment, housing, and access to public facilities.

It was the hope of the civil rights movement of the earlier 1960s that we would erect in the United States a color-blind society. But quite rapidly after 1964 that hope was reshaped, and public action increasingly took place on the basis of specific racial and ethnic categories. It is true that this public action sought to undo the discrimination of the past, but it became very difficult to draw a line between the "quotas" that undid the effects of discrimination in the past and the "goals" that demanded employment on the basis of race and ethnic group in the future. Similarly, it became difficult to see the distinction between action to break up segregated schools, which was widely applauded, and action to create a fixed racial proportion in each school, as through busing, which was strongly opposed. The achievement of employment goals and fixed racial proportions in the schools meant that government once again defined people by race and ethnic group, this time, it was explained, not for purposes of discrimination but for purposes of making up for the effects of discrimination.

But of course it is very difficult to distinguish between discrimination against and discrimination for. Indeed, all discrimination for must be against someone. For some time it has been taken for granted by white males, regardless of training and talent, that their chances of getting jobs in universities, against the competition of governmentally favored minority group members and women, are reduced. Undoubtedly there are two sides to this question, and both are really on the side of the angels. Those who call for goals and quotas want to see groups that have had modest or little representation in certain fields of professional work and in certain areas of employment better represented; those who argue against these measures want to see individual effort rewarded. And so we have the conflict between the goals of equality and the age-old individualist thrust in American life, one that has given it so much of its distinctive character.

☆ ☆ ☆ The Tough Questions

The two goals remain in deep conflict. Major constitutional cases mark its progress. In one, a young man, Marco DeFunis, white and Jewish, was denied admission to the University of Washington Law School while others with lower scores were accepted because of their minority membership. He could, of course, have argued that he was a member of a minority too, but his minority, whatever the degree of discrimination against it in the past, was very well represented in the law schools and legal profession. Blacks and Mexican Americans were poorly represented. That was not his argument, however. He did not demand to be numbered among the favored minorities but asserted that no one should be favored on grounds of race and ethnic origin. His case went to the U.S. Supreme Court—which decided to take no action on it. The issue could not be avoided so easily. Another case, that of Allan Bakke, who tried to enter the medical school of the University of

California at Davis, was decided by the Supreme Court, but not in a way that settled the issue, for while the judgment of the court was that Bakke should be admitted to medical school, it also ruled that race could be taken into account in making decisions on admission.

DeFunis and Bakke wanted to be treated as individuals and argued that their race or ethnic group should play no role in whether or not they were granted admission to highly sought places in law and medical schools. The schools in question asserted they had a right, an obligation, to ensure equality of treatment, not of individuals, but of groups, so that poorly represented groups would be better represented. That, they asserted, was what the achievement of equality demanded.

So such questions were raised as the following: Is it not the individual who has the right to fair and nondiscriminatory treatment, and if the individual gets that, must it not follow that the group—simply an aggregation of individuals—is getting fair and nondiscriminatory treatment too? If groups are to be equally represented, in medical schools, in law schools, in university employment, among business executives, in the civil service, must it not follow that individuals will get less than equal treatment? But if we concentrate on individuals alone, and some groups as a result are sparsely represented among important elites, will not the group suffer and therefore be deprived of equal treatment? Does not each group need its own doctors, lawyers, professors, government officials, business executives? How are we to ensure that they get their fair share unless we divide sought-for positions on the basis of population? But if we do that, do we not then give up the hope of an integrated and color-blind America in favor of one in which persons bear the marks of race and ethnicity and are treated on that basis? Will this equal treatment by groups be only temporary, until each group reaches an approved percentage? If we are assured this is temporary, what happens when we turn color-blind and a group begins to fall below its percentage, as a result of the fact that our efforts to recruit, train, and place members of that group have been abandoned? One can add to the questions—they are endless—but they are the questions we must live with in the 1990s and perhaps beyond.

The Reagan administration sharply opposed quotas in employment and education. Its philosophy was clear; its actions were inevitably hampered by the great mass of regulations and court orders that already dictated quotas as the solution to the problems of underrepresentation of blacks and other minorities and women in employment in private and public institutions and in institutions of higher education. It was also hampered by the fact that major government agencies with thousands of employees committed to these policies could not be turned around in any short order. It was also made cautious by political considerations. It could indeed argue that in attacking quotas it was defending one version of equality against another. But to the mass media, dominated by people whose views had been shaped by the civil rights struggles of the 1960s, this was simply turning back the clock.

The Reagan administration was marked by a number of legal battles that attempted to restrict the scale of school busing and the imposition of quotas in employment. It would take us far afield to review these battles, but two points can be made. First, in each case the administration claimed it was protecting the right of the individual to be treated as an individual—"equally." In each case it was attacked by the major civil rights organizations for moving against the recently established rights of minorities and women. Second, on the whole the structure of privilege for minorities and women, insofar as it was established in law, in federal regulation, and in court decisions, stood firm through eight years of criticism by the federal government. Undoubtedly the enforcement of these requirements slackened considerably. But they stood in law ready if and when another administration emerged to push the new interpretation of equality in order to achieve equal status for groups through the differential treatment of individuals on grounds of race, ethnicity, and sex.

We are far past any simple stage in the struggle for equality in the United States. As Tocqueville foresaw, equality was to become the great goal of society. But equality is no simple matter. One can pass the right laws, eliminate acts of overt discrimination, open entry to schools and employment and government and public places. At each stage, however, new questions are raised, questions never dreamed of at the stage before. Those who in the early 1960s thought equality demanded that no person be required to state his or her race or ethnic group in applications for admission to schools and employment now think that it is essential, in order to achieve equality, that every person be required to do so. Troubling and difficult questions have been raised as government, in its effort to achieve a greater equality, begins itself to impose limits on the dreams and aspirations of individuals on the basis of their race or ethnic group. There is only one comfort to be taken from the present situation: we deal with these more complex questions of reconciling individual rights and equality only because, happily, we have already dealt with the simpler ones.

FURTHER READING

The classic work dealing with problems of equality and individualism in the United States is, of course, Alexis de Tocqueville, *Democracy in America* (1835–

40), available in many editions. The discussion has never ended, but one major work instrumental in reviving it and carrying it forward was *The Lonely Crowd: A Study in the Changing American Character*, by David Riesman with Nathan Glazer and Reuel Denney (New Haven, Conn., 1952). Riesman continued the discussion in his *Individualism Reconsidered* (Glencoe, Ill., 1954). The alternation between periods stressing equality and periods stressing liberty (related to individualism) in American history and politics was explored by Seymour Martin Lipset in his *The First New Nation: The United States in Historical and Comparative Perspective* (New York, 1963). A major scholarly analysis of the expansion of equality in the United States is J. R. Pole, *The Pursuit of Equality in American History* (Berkeley, Calif., 1978).

The more recent troubling conflict created by efforts to achieve equality for minority groups has been analyzed in Nathan Glazer, *Affirmative Discrimination: Ethnic Inequality and Public Policy* (New York, 1975; Cambridge, Mass., 1987), and *Ethnic Dilemmas, 1964–1982* (Cambridge, Mass., 1983); Robert M. O'Neil, *Discriminating against Discrimination: Preferential Admissions and the DeFunis Case* (Bloomington, Ind., 1975); Terry Eastland and William J. Bennett, *Counting by Race: Equality from the Founding Fathers to Bakke and Weber* (New York, 1979); and in many other books. Barry R. Gross, ed., *Reverse Discrimination* (Buffalo, N.Y., 1977), is a comprehensive collection of articles on this issue. James Fallows, *More Like Us: Making America Great Again* (Boston, 1989), discusses issues of racial inequality in a stirring call for America to rediscover its distinctive character and reclaim its fading preeminence.

15 ☆ Continuity

☆ and Change

☆ in American

☆ Family Life

☆ Tamara K. Hareven

Through much of the American past the family has been seen as the linchpin of the social order and the basis for stable governance. Even though the family changes more gradually in response to external forces than other institutions, educators and social planners have frequently expressed fear of family breakdown under the pressures of social change. Since the foundation of the American nation every generation has expressed anxiety over the possible disruption of the "traditional" family. More than any other development, however, industrialization and urbanization have been viewed as major threats to traditional family life and as causes of family breakdown.

This perception of change and crisis in the American family today is influenced by commonly held myths about family life in the past. According to these myths three generations lived together happily in the same household, families were intimate and close-knit, and single-parent households were rare. This belief in a lost golden age has led people to depict the present as a period of decline in the family. Nostalgia for a largely nonexistent past has handicapped many commentators in assessing realistically the current changes in family life.

In order to come to grips with the problems of the present, it is essential to examine changes in family life over the past two centuries. A historical consideration of the family places some of these changes in their proper context. It enables us to assess better the uniqueness of present conditions and to distinguish between long-term trends and temporary aberrations. To what extent are these changes part of a continuing historical process, and to what extent do they represent new departures? This chapter examines some of the changes in the American family in relation to the current, seemingly dramatic transitions in the following areas: the structure and organization of the family and kinship groups; functions of the family and values governing family life; and changes in the family over its life course.

☆ ☆ ☆ Changes and Continuity in Family Structure

Recent research on the family in colonial American society has dispelled the myths about the existence of ideal three-generational families in the American past. The historical evidence now shows that there never has been in American society an era when coresidence of three generations in the same household was the dominant pattern. The "great extended families" that became part of the folklore of modern industrial society were rarely in existence. Early American households and families were simple in their structure and not drastically different in their organization from contemporary families. The most typical residential family unit was nuclear—consisting of parents and their children, not extended kin. Three generations seldom lived together in the same household. Given the high mortality rate in preindustrial societies, most parents could not have expected to overlap with their grandchildren. It would thus be futile to argue that industrialization destroyed the great extended family of the past. In reality, such a family type rarely existed.

Family arrangements in the colonial period differed, however, from those in our times. Even though they did not contain extended kin, these households did include unrelated individuals, boarders, lodgers, apprentices, or servants. In this respect the composition of the household in the colonial period was significantly different from that in contemporary society. The tendency of families to include nonrelatives in the household was connected with an entirely different concept of family life. In contrast to the current emphasis on the family home as a private retreat, the household of the past was the site of a broad array of functions and activities that transcended the more restricted circle of the nuclear family. The household was a place of production and served as an abode for servants, apprentices, and dependent members of the community, such as orphaned children and old men or women without relatives.

A considerable number of urban families continued to take in nonrelatives as boarders as late as the 1920s. The practice of young people boarding with other families thus continued even after the practice of masters having apprentices reside in their households had disappeared. Through the nineteenth and into the early twentieth century about one-fourth to one-third of the population either had lived in someone's household as a boarder or had taken boarders or lodgers at some point in their lives. Boarding or lodging with urban families was an important form of exchange between generations. It enabled young men and women in their late teens and twenties who had left their parents' households or who had migrated from other communities to live as boarders in the households of older people whose own children had left home. This practice enabled young people to stay in surrogate family arrangements; at the same time it provided old people with the opportunity to continue heading their own households without being isolated. Boarding and lodging also fulfilled a critical function in providing continuity in urban life and helping new migrants and immigrants adapt to urban living. Its existence suggests great flexibility in families and households, a flexibility that has been lost over the past half century.

Increasing availability of housing since the 1920s and the rise of values of privacy in family life have led to the phasing out of boarding and lodging, except among black families. The practice has virtually disappeared from the larger society. With its disappearance the family has lost some of its major sources of resilience in adapting to urban living. Thus, the most important change in American family life has not been the breakdown of a three-generational family but rather the retreat of the family into its private household and the withdrawal of nonrelatives from the family's abode. Since the beginning of this century the home has become identified as a retreat from the outside world, and the presence of nonrelatives has been considered threatening to the privacy of the family.

Because of the decline in boarding and lodging, the number of households containing only one member has been increasing steadily since the 1920s. While in the nineteenth century solitary residence was almost unheard of, now a major portion of the population resides alone. The disquieting aspect of this pattern is the high percentage of aging widows living by themselves. For a large part of the population, living alone is not a matter of free choice but rather an unavoidable and often painful arrangement. What has been lost over the past two centuries is not the great extended family, but the flexibility of the family that enabled households to expand when necessary and to take people in to live in surrogate family settings rather than in isolation.

☆ ☆ ☆ Kin Relations

Another pervasive myth about family life in the past has been the assumption that industrialization broke up traditional kinship ties and destroyed the organic interdependence between the family and the community. Once again historical research has shown that industrialization, rather than breaking up traditional family structures, has led to the redefinition of family functions. In industrial communities the family continued to function as a work unit. Relatives acted as recruitment, migration, and housing agents for industrial laborers, helping each other to shift from rural to industrial life and work patterns. Families migrated in groups to industrial centers, and relatives were active in the recruitment of workers into the factory system. Often several family members, even distant kin, continued to work in the same place and fulfilled valuable functions in providing mutual assistance and support in the workplace. Migration to industrial communities did not break up traditional kinship ties; rather, families used these ties to facilitate their own transitions into industrial life and to adapt to new living conditions and life-styles.

During the periods of adjustment to migration, to settlement in new places, and to industrial work, reliance on kin persisted as the most basic resource for assistance. Following the early period of industrialization, kin in rural and urban areas continued to engage in mutual assistance and in reciprocal services. Kin performed a crucial role in initiating and organizing migration from rural areas to factory towns locally, and from rural communities abroad to industrial communities in the United States. Thus, although the majority of families lived in nuclear household arrangements, they were still enmeshed in kinship networks outside the household and depended heavily on mutual assistance.

Even in the late nineteenth and early twentieth centuries, workers who migrated from rural areas to the cities in most industrializing communities carried parts of their kinship ties and family traditions into new settings. Young unmarried sons and daughters of working age, or young married couples without their children, tended to migrate first. After they found jobs and housing, they sent for their relatives. Chain migration thus helped maintain ties and continuities between family members in their new communities of settlement.

In factories and other places of employment, newly arrived workers utilized the connections established by relatives who were already working there to facilitate their hiring and adaptation to work. Hiring and placement through kin often continued even in large-scale modern factories. Kinship networks infiltrated formal, bureaucratized industrial organizations and clustered within them. Even when they worked in different locales, kin made collective decisions about each other's work careers.

Kinship networks also formed an important part of the fiber of urban neighborhoods. Relatives tended to settle in proximity to each other, and as immigrants arrived in American cities, they preferred to live close to their kin whenever possible. So kinship ties brought both coherence and mutual support to the urban neighborhood. This pattern has persisted to some extent among ethnic groups but has gradually weakened in the remainder of the population. While major portions of the American population are still in close contact with their kin, the interdependence that was typical of earlier times has eroded considerably as a result of the continuing redefinition of individualism, as well as patterns of migration and the development of mass transportation. Kin have ceased to be the major source of social security, and some of the functions of mutual assistance formerly found among kin have been replaced by public programs.

Even if industrialization did not bring about major changes in the structure of the family, it did produce changes in the functions of the family and in the values governing family life. Since the early nineteenth century the family gradually has surrendered to other social institutions functions previously concentrated within it.

☆ ☆ ☆ Changing Family Functions and Values

During the preindustrial period the family not only reared children but also served as a workshop, a school, a church, and a welfare agency. Preindustrial families meshed closely with the community and carried a variety of public responsibilities within the larger society. "Family and community," John Demos writes, "private and public life, formed part of the same moral equation. The one supported the other and they became in a sense indistinguishable." In preindustrial society most of the work took place in the household. Roles of parenting were therefore congruent with social and economic roles. Children were considered members of the work force and were seen as economic assets. Childhood was treated as a brief preparatory period terminated by apprenticeship and the commencement of work, generally before puberty. Adolescence was virtually unknown as a distinct stage of life. Family members were integrated into common economic activities. The segregation of roles in the family along gender and age lines that characterizes middle-class family life in modern society had not yet appeared. As long as the household functioned as a workshop as well as a family home, family life was not clearly separated from work life.

Even though preindustrial families contained large numbers of children, women invested relatively less time in motherhood than their successors in the nineteenth century and in our time did and still do. Child care was part of a general effort of household production rather than a woman's exclusive preoccupation; children were viewed not merely as objects of nature but as productive members of the family from an early age on. The tasks of child rearing did not fall exclusively on mothers; other relatives living nearby also participated in this function.

The integration of family and work in preindustrial society allowed for an intensive sharing of labor between husbands and wives and between parents and children that was later diminished in industrial society. Housework was inseparable from domestic industries or agricultural work, and it was valued, therefore, as an economic asset. Since children constituted part of the labor force, motherhood, too, was valued for its economic contributions and not only for its nurturing tasks.

Under the impact of industrialization many of these functions were transferred to agencies and institutions outside the family. The workplace was separated from the home, and functions of social welfare were transferred from the family to asylums and reformatories. "The family has become *a more specialized agency than before*," wrote Talcott Parsons, "probably more specialized than it has been in any previously known society . . . but not in any general sense less important, because the society is dependent *more* exclusively on it for the performance of *certain* of its vital functions." These vital functions include childbearing, child rearing, and socialization. The family has ceased to be a work unit and has limited its economic activities primarily to consumption and child care.

The transformation of the household from a busy workplace and social center to a private family abode involved the withdrawal of strangers, such as business associates, partners, journeymen, apprentices, and boarders and lodgers, from the household; it also involved a more rigorous separation of husbands from wives and fathers from children in the course of the workday. Specialization in work schedules significantly altered the daily lives of family members in urban society, since the majority of men worked outside the home while women stayed at home and children went to school. In working-class families this specialization was even more far-reaching, since women also worked outside the home, but often on different schedules than the men in their households.

Under the impact of industrialization, in middle-class families housework lost its economic and productive value. Since it was not paid for, and since it no longer led to the production of visible goods, it lost its place in the occupational hierarchy. Housework continued to be governed by nonstandardized time schedules, thus remaining through the nineteenth century a nonindustrial occupation. This is another reason (in addition to economic ones) why housework has been devalued in modern society—where achievement is measured not only by products but also by systematic time and production schedules.

These changes brought about in family life by industrialization were gradual and varied significantly from class to class as well as among different ethnic groups. While scholars have sometimes generalized for an entire society on the basis of the middle-class experience, it is now becoming clear that preindustrial family patterns persisted over longer time periods in rural and in urban working-class families. Since the process of industrialization was gradual, domestic industries and a variety of small family enterprises were carried over into the industrial system. In most working-class families work was still considered a family enterprise, even when their members were employed in different enterprises and the work did not take place in the home. In such families the work of wives, sons, and daughters was carefully regulated by the collective strategies of the family unit. Much of what we perceive today as individual vocational activity was actually considered in earlier times part of a collective family effort.

With the growth of industrial child labor in the nineteenth century, working-class families continued to recognize the economic value of motherhood, as they had in rural society. Segregation along age groups within working-class families was almost nonexistent. Children were socialized for industrial work from an early age and began to contribute to the family's work effort at a younger age than specified by law. They were considered assets, both for their contribution to the family's economy during their youth and for the prospect of their support during their parents' old age. Parents viewed their efforts in child rearing as investments in future social security.

In working-class families, even though the process of industrialization offered women opportunities for independent work outside their homes, women continued to function as an integral part of the family's productive effort. Even when they worked in factories, single working women were bound by family obligations and contributed most of their earnings to their parents. A woman's work was considered part of the family's economic effort, not an independent career. During periods of large-scale industrial development families continued to function as collective economic units in which husbands, wives, and children were all responsible for the well-being of the family.

☆ ☆ ☆ The Role of Women

This continuity in the function of the family as a collaborative economic unit is significant for understanding the changes in the roles of women that industrialization introduced into working-class life. By introducing changes in the modes of production as well as in the nature and pace of work, industrialization offered women the opportunity to become wage earners outside the household. Industrialization did not, however, bring about immediate changes in the family's corporate identity in the working class—at least not during the early stages of industrialization. Among middle-class families, on the other hand, industrialization had a more dramatic impact on gender roles: the separation between the home and the workplace that followed in the wake of industrialization led to the glorification of the home as a domestic retreat from the outside world. The new ideology of domesticity that developed in the first half of the nineteenth century relegated women to the home and glorified their role as homemakers and mothers.

The emergence of the ideology of domesticity and of full-time motherhood was closely connected with the decline in the average number of children a woman had and with the new attitudes toward childhood that were emerging in the nineteenth century. One of these major changes was the recognition of childhood as a distinct stage of life among urban middle-class families. Children began to be treated as objects of nurture rather than as working members of the family. Stripped of the multiplicity of functions that had been previously concentrated in the family, urban middle-class families developed into private, domestic, and child-centered retreats from the world of work and politics. Children were no longer expected to join the work force until their late teens, a major indication of the growing recognition of childhood as a distinct stage of development. Instead of considering children as potential working members of the family group, parents began to view them as dependent objects of tender nurture and protection.

This marked the emergence of the domestic middle-class family as we know it today. The glorification of motherhood as a full-time career served both to enshrine the family as a domestic retreat from the world of work and to make families child centered. The gradual separation of the home from the workplace that had started with industrialization reached its peak in the designation of the home as a therapeutic refuge from the outside world. As custodians of this retreat, women were expected to concentrate on making the home a perfect place and on child rearing, rather than on being economic partners in the family. Tenderness, gentleness, affection, sweetness, and a comforting demeanor began to emerge as a central value at the base of family relationships.

The ideology of domesticity and the new view of childhood combined to revise expectations of parenthood. The roles of husbands and wives became gradually more separate; a clear division of labor replaced the old economic cooperation, and the wife's efforts concentrated on homemaking and child rearing. With men leaving the home to work elsewhere, time invested in fatherhood was concentrated primarily on leisure hours. Thus the separation of husbands from wives and parents from children for major parts of the day came about. These patterns, which emerged in the early nineteenth century, formed the base of relations characteristic of the contemporary American family. Some of these patterns persist to the present day and are the root of problems and crises in the family.

The cult of domesticity that emerged in the nineteenth century as a major part of the ideology of family life in America has dominated perceptions of women's roles until very recently and has shaped prevailing assumptions governing family life. One of its consequences was the insistence that confinement of women's main activities to the domestic sphere and the misguided assumption that mothers' work in the labor market would be harmful to the family and to society. Only over the past few decades have these values been criticized and partly rejected. Since the prejudices against mothers' labor force participation persevered as long as they did in American society, and have handicapped women's pursuit of occupations outside the home, it is important to understand their origin in the nineteenth-century cult of domesticity.

Although the ideology of domesticity originated in urban middle-class families, it was gradually adopted as the dominant model for family life in the entire society. Second- and third-generation immigrant families, who originally held a more integrated view of the family as a corporate unit, and who had earlier accepted the wife's work outside the home, began to embrace the ideology of domesticity as part of their "Americanization" process. The ideals of urban middle-class life subsequently handicapped the role of women as workers outside the home. As immigrants became "Americanized" in the early part of the twentieth century, they internalized the values of domesticity and began to view women's labor force participation as demeaning, as carrying low status, or as compromising for the husband and dangerous for the children. Consequently, married women entered the labor force only when driven by economic necessity.

Despite the impact of the ideal of domesticity in American culture, working-class and ethnic families to a significant degree continued to adhere to the earlier ways of life and maintained a collective view of the family and its economy. In contrast to the values of individualism that govern much of family life today, traditional values of family collectivity have persisted among various ethnic groups and, to some extent, among black families. In working-class and ethnic families the relationships between husbands and wives, parents and children, and other kin were based upon reciprocal assistance and support. Such relations, often defined as "instrumental," drew their strength from the assumption that family members were all engaged in mutual obligations and in reciprocity. Although obligations were not specifically defined by contract, they rested on the accepted social values as to what family members owed to each other. In the period preceding the welfare state instrumental relationships among family members and more distant kin provided important supports to individuals and families, particularly during critical life situations.

A collective view of familial obligations was the very basis of survival in earlier time periods. From such a perspective marriage and parenthood were not merely love relationships but partnerships governed by family economic and social needs. In this respect the experience of working-class families in the nineteenth century and of ethnic families in the more recent past was drastically different from that of middle-class families, in which sentimentality emerged as the dominant base of family relationships. Among traditional families sentiment was secondary to family needs and survival strategies. Under such conditions childbearing and work were not governed by individual decisions. Mate selection and the timing of marriage were regulated in accordance with collective family considerations rather than directed by strictly individual whim. The transfer of property and work were not regulated strictly according to individual decisions. At times collective family "plans" took priority over individual preferences. For example, parents often tried to delay the marriage of the last child in the household, commonly a daughter, in order to secure continued economic support, especially in later life when they were withdrawing from the labor force.

Thus, the major historical change in family values has been one from a collective view of the family to one of individualization and sentiment. Over the past several decades American families have been experiencing an increasing emphasis on individual priorities and preferences over collective family needs. This individualization of family relations has also led to an exaggerated emphasis on emotional nurture, intimacy, and privacy as the major base of family relations. It has contributed considerably to the liberation of individuals, but it has also eroded the resilience of the family and its ability to withstand crises. Moreover, it has contributed to a greater separation among family members and especially to the isolation of older people.

☆ ☆ ☆ Changes in the Life Course

The full impact of changes in values and functions on the condition of the family today can be best understood in the context of demographic changes affecting the timing of life transitions, such as marriage, parenthood, and the passage to the "empty nest" and to widowhood. Since the end of the nineteenth century important changes have occurred in the family cycle that have affected age configurations within the family and relations between the generations.

Beginning in the early nineteenth century the American population has experienced a steady decline in the birth rate, except for the baby boom in the immediate post–World War II period. This decline has had a profound impact on the life course, especially on the timing of marriage, the birth of the first child and subsequent children, and the spacing of children. It has also considerably affected the meaning of marriage and of parenthood. In traditional society little time elapsed between marriage and parenthood since procreation was a major goal of marriage. In modern society contraception has made possible a time lag between marriage and parenthood. Marriage has become recognized as important in its own right rather than merely as a transition to parenthood.

One widely held myth about the past is that the timing of family transitions was once more orderly and stable than it is today. The complexity that governs family life today and the variations in family roles and in transitions into them are frequently contrasted to this more placid past. The historical experience, however, reveals precisely the opposite condition; patterns of family timing in the past were often more complex, more diverse, and less orderly than they are today. Paradoxically, voluntary and involuntary demographic changes that have come about since the late nineteenth century have resulted in greater uniformity in the timing of transitions along the life course despite greater societal complexity.

The increasing uniformity in timing has been accompanied by a shift from involuntary to voluntary factors affecting crucial demographic events. An increase in life expectancy, the decline in fertility, and earlier marriage age have greatly improved the chances for temporal overlap in the lives of family members. Families are now able to go through a life course much less subject to sudden change than that experienced by the majority of the population in the nineteenth century. This trend toward greater uniformity in the life course has been counteracted only by divorce. Over the past few decades the "typical" life course of modern American families has included early marriage and early commencement of childbearing, with a small number of children closely spaced.

This type of life course experience has been characterized by a compact period of parenthood in the middle years of life, followed by an extended period without children (encompassing one-third of their adult life) and finally often by a period of solitary living after the death of a spouse, most frequently the husband. This life course pattern has had important implications for the composition of the family and for relationships within it in contemporary society. Husbands and wives are spending a relatively longer lifetime together; they invest a shorter segment of their lives in child rearing; and they more commonly survive to grandparenthood. This sequence has been uniform for the majority of the population since the beginning of the twentieth century.

In contrast to past times, most families see their children through to adulthood with both parents still alive. As Peter Uhlenberg has pointed out, the normal family cycle for women—a sequence of leaving home, marriage, childbearing, child rearing, launching of children from the home, and survival at age fifty with the first marriage still intact unless broken by divorce—was not the typical pattern of family timing before the early twentieth century. Prior to 1900 only about 40 percent of the white female population in the United States experienced this ideal family cycle. The remainder either never married, never reached marriageable age, died before childbearing, or were widowed while their offspring were still young children.

In the nineteenth century the combination of a later age at marriage and higher fertility provided little opportunity for a family to experience an "empty nest" stage. Prior to the decline in mortality among the young at the beginning of the twentieth century, marriage was frequently broken by the death of the spouse before the end of the childbearing period. Even when fathers survived the child-rearing years, they rarely lived beyond the marriage of their second child. As a result of higher fertility children were spread over a wide age range; frequently the youngest child was just entering school as the oldest was preparing for marriage. The combination of a later age of marriage, higher fertility, and widely spaced childbearing resulted in a different timing of family transitions. Individuals became parents later but carried child-rearing responsibilities almost until the end of their lives. Consequently the lives of the parents overlapped with those of their children for shorter periods than they do currently.

Under the demographic conditions of the nineteenth century—higher mortality and higher fertility—functions within the family were less specifically tied to age, and members of different age groups were consequently not so completely segregated by the tasks they were required to fulfill. The spread of children over a larger age spectrum within the family had important implications for family relationships as well as for their preparations for adult roles. Children were accustomed to growing up with larger numbers of siblings and were exposed to a greater variety of models from which to choose than they would have been in a small nuclear family. Older children often took charge of their younger siblings. Sisters, in particular, carried a major share of the responsibility for raising the youngest siblings, and they frequently acted as surrogate mothers if the mother worked outside the home or had died.

Another comparison between what is considered the "normal" life course today and its many variants in the nineteenth century reverses one more stereotype about the past, namely that the opportunities for the survival of the family have been diminishing. In reality the major transitions in family roles have been characterized by greater stability and conformity because of greater opportunity for overlap among generations. The opportunity for a meaningful period of overlap in the lives of grandparents and grandchildren is a twentieth-century phenomenon, a surprising fact that runs counter to the popular myth that the typical family of the past consisted of three generations. In earlier times grandparents rarely lived to see their grandchildren as adults.

The significance of various transitions in family roles also differed in the past. In the nineteenth century, when conception was likely to take place very shortly after marriage, the major transition in a woman's life was represented by marriage itself. But as the interval between marriage and first pregnancy has increased in modern society, the transition to parenthood has become a more marked turning point than the transition to marriage. Family limitation has also had an impact on the timing of marriage. Since marriage no longer inevitably leads to parenthood, it is not necessary to postpone marriage in order to control family size. On the other end of the life course, transitions into the empty nest have been more generally experienced and were clearly marked in the twentieth century until a decade ago. (The trend has reversed recently with the tendency of young people to return to the parental home or not to leave.) By contrast, in earlier times parental roles encompassed practically the entire adult life. Transition into the empty nest today often involves changes in residence and changes in work. It brings about a greater separation between the generations while the parents are still in middle age.

The overall historical pattern of family behavior has thus been marked by a shift from involuntary to voluntary forces controlling the timing of family events. It has also been characterized by greater rigidity and uniformity in the time of people's passage from one family role to another over the life course. For example, the transitions into adult roles usually experienced by young people, namely leaving home, getting married, and establishing a separate household, follow a more orderly sequence and are accomplished over a shorter time period in a young person's life today than was the case in the nineteenth century (except for the 1980s, when the rhythms of timing changed again). Prior to the beginning of this century life transitions were timed in accordance with family needs and obligations rather than with specific age requirements. The functional needs of a person's family were considered more important than age norms.

Over the past few decades, on the other hand, age norms have emerged as more important determinants of timing than familial obligations. As John Modell and his associates have remarked: "'Timely' action to 19th century families consisted of helpful response in times of trouble; in the 20th century, timeliness connotes adherence to a socially-sanctioned schedule." The historical changes in the timing of family transitions are mainly twentieth-century phenomena.

The changes in the family cycle discussed above, such as the emergence of the empty nest, extensions of the period of widowhood, and increasing age segregation in the family and the larger society, reflect major discontinuities in the life course. Some of these have resulted in increasing problems in the middle and later years of life. It is precisely in this area that problems of family life and generational relations are lodged today.

☆ ☆ ☆ Implications of Change

One of the major causes of the prevalent anxiety about the future of the family is rooted not so much in actuality as in the tension between idealized expectations for the family in American culture and the reality itself. Nostalgia for a lost family tradition that never existed has prejudiced our understanding of the changes that families are experiencing in contemporary society. Furthermore, the current anxiety over the family's fate reflects not merely problems in the family itself but a variety of other social problems that are eventually projected onto the family. The real problems that American families are facing today are not symptoms of breakdown, as is often suggested. Rather they reflect the difficulties that families face in their adaptation to recent social changes, particularly in the loss of the flexibility in household membership that families had in the past, the reduction of the variety of their functions, and to some extent the weakening of their adaptability.

Current anxieties also reflect the difficulties that American society has been experiencing in accepting alternative family forms and a great diversity in family life. The idealization of the family as a refuge from the outside world has lessened its ability to cope with diversity. The continuous emphasis on the family as a universal private retreat and as an emotional haven is misguided in light of our knowledge of the past. Early American families fulfilled a broad array of functions that went beyond the more restricted emotional functions in the present. Most of the family's roles in the past were intertwined with the larger community. Rather than being the custodian of privacy, the family prepared its members for interaction with the larger society. Family relationships were valued not merely for their emotional contents but for a wide range of services and contributions to the collective family unit.

By contrast, one of the major sources of the crisis of the nuclear family today is its difficulty in adapting to the emotional responsibilities thrust upon it, precisely because some of these functions and expectations represent an artificial boundary between individuals and the larger society. Concentration on the emotional tasks of the family has grown at the expense of another of its much-needed roles in a complex, modern society, namely, preparation of its members for their interaction with bureaucratic institutions. In American society the education and welfare systems have made dramatic inroads into areas that had previously been the private preserve of the family. At the same time, however, the tendency of the family to shelter its members from other social institutions has weakened the family's ability to affect its structure or to influence the programs and legislation that public agencies have directed toward the family.

Attitudes toward family life in America have been governed by the stereotype of the "ideal family," which is based on the middle-class nuclear model. In reality American society has contained great diversities in family types associated with the recurring entrance of new immigrant groups, and ethnic, racial, cultural, and class differences have resulted in a great variety of family behavior. The tension between the ideals of family behavior in the dominant culture and the traditional patterns of the black family and of immigrant families has been a recurring issue in American life.

As part of the "melting pot" process there has been a tendency toward homogenization of American culture and with it an increasing emphasis on uniformity in family behavior. Immigrants, primarily in the second generation, adopted "American" family patterns in several areas, such as limiting their family size, marrying earlier, increasing privatization of the family, withdrawing women and children from the labor force, and changing styles of consumption and taste. However, this ongoing process did not result in a total assimilation of family ways and traditional customs because new waves of immigrants have tended to bring with them traditional family patterns. Thus, contrary to the official creed of the "melting pot," a great many varieties of ethnic family behavior have survived, and new patterns are still being introduced through recent migration. In addition, the increase in alternative family forms in recent years has further diversified the patterns.

It is therefore unrealistic to talk simply about *the* American family. Until very recently the ideal of the private nuclear family has been dominant in American society. Alternative forms of family organization, such as those of the black family or of other ethnic families, were misinterpreted as "family disorganization" because they did not conform to the official stereotype. However, over the past decade the strength and resilience of ethnic and black family ways have been recognized. The traditional resources of family and kinship among blacks and certain ethnic groups have been rediscovered as the middle-class nuclear family, besieged by its own isolation, has proven its limitations in coping with stress.

One of the most distinctive features of families in contemporary America is their cultural and ethnic diversity—a diversity that is in itself an extension of a historical pattern, and which is now being valued as a source of strength and continuity rather than being decried as a manifestation of deviance. Individuals and policymakers today face the challenge of putting these family patterns to creative use in coping with contemporary problems.

☆ ☆ ☆ Looking Ahead

Understanding historical changes over the past century provides a more balanced perspective on family life in modern America. There is no question that American families have been undergoing important transitions. But do those transitions indicate family breakdown—or threaten the disappearance of the family? From a historical perspective, some of these changes represent the continuation of a long evolutionary process. The decline in the birth rate, earlier age at marriage, and change in the timing of life transitions are all part of a process spanning the past century and a half. Similarly, the moratorium from adult responsibilities that teenagers now experience and the increasing isolation of older people on the other end of the cycle are both the result of long-term historical changes.

On the other hand, the increase in divorce rates and the concomitant increase in single-parent households represent a much more dramatic transition in our times. The rise in divorce as such, however, which often has been cited as a symptom of family breakdown, should not be misconstrued. In the nineteenth century people did not resort to divorce so frequently as they do now because divorce was considered socially unacceptable. This does not mean, though, that families were living happily and in harmony. A high rate of desertion and separation of couples took the place of legal divorce. Incompatible couples who did not resort to divorce or separation lived together as strangers or in deep conflict. Thus the increase in divorce statistics by itself is not proof that the family is likely to go out of existence. In some respects it is proof that people care enough about the content and quality of family life and marriage to be willing to dissolve an unsatisfactory marriage (and commonly to replace it with a more successful one).

Much anxiety also has been expressed over the increase in the proportion of unmarried couples cohabiting and over a variety of alternative family forms and life-styles. What we are witnessing in all these varieties of family styles are not new inventions. Many alternative life-styles have now been openly acknowledged because they are being tolerated more than in the past. In short, what we are witnessing is not a fragmentation of traditional family patterns but rather the emergence and increasing acceptance of pluralism in family life.

From a long-range perspective American families confront two major problem areas. One is the high proportion of adolescent pregnancies. While premarital conception was a common phenomenon in the past, it did not occur frequently among teenagers and it was usually followed by marriage. Among some groups in contemporary America adolescent pregnancies are passed on from one generation to the next, often casting women into the roles of grandmothers while they are still in their thirties.

Another problem that deserves serious attention is the potential isolation of the elderly—a major concern that will only grow more severe as we move into the future. The isolation of older people is a result partly of geographic mobility, partly of the decreasing number of kin available, and partly of a general decline in the values of generational assistance. The historical record has demonstrated that there never was a golden age of generational relations in the past. Elderly parents rarely resided with their married children. Older people were able, however, to maintain autonomy and to head their own households by taking in boarders and lodgers and by receiving assistance from their adult children and other kin who were residing nearby. Some of these traditional forms of assistance and support in the later years of life can still be found among ethnic groups today. Historical experience suggests the effectiveness of kinship ties in coping with migration, economic insecurity, and personal family crises, and the affirmation of these ties by certain ethnic groups during times of crisis could suggest a model for the entire society.

Discovering the strength of kinship ties should not lead us, however, to a new myth about the self-reliance of the family. It would be a mistake to assume that the fact that family members are helping each other in times of crisis means that they should be left to take care of their own. The historical record also reflects the high price that family members have had to pay in order to support their kin and help aging parents. The pressures on the nuclear family today, in a context of economic and technological stress, would make it difficult if not impossible for families to sustain continual assistance and support for their kin, especially for aging relatives, without adequate support from the public sector.

FURTHER READING

For general studies on the American family, see Tamara K. Hareven and Andrejs Plakans, eds., *Family History at the Crossroads: A Journal of Family History Reader* (Princeton, N.J., 1987); Carl Degler, *At Odds: Women and the Family in America from the Revolution to the Present* (New York, 1980); and Hareven, *American Family History: A Historical Bibliography* (Santa Barbara, Calif., 1984), *Family Time and Industrial Time: The Relationship between the Family and Work in a New England Industrial Community* (Cambridge, Mass., 1982), and "Family Time and Historical Time," *Daedalus* 106 (Spring 1977).

On the family and women in the colonial period, see John Demos, *A Little Commonwealth: Family Life in Plymouth Colony* (New York, 1970); Philip J. Greven, *Four Generations: Population, Land, and Family in Andover, Massachusetts* (Ithaca, N.Y., 1970); Nancy Cott, *The Bonds of Womanhood: "Woman's Sphere" in New England, 1780–1835* (New Haven, Conn., 1977); and Mary Beth Norton, *Liberty's Daughters: The Revolutionary Experience of American Women, 1750–1800* (Boston, 1980).

On the family in urban society, see Tamara K. Hareven, ed., *Family and Kin in Urban Communities, 1700–1930* (New York, 1977); Theodore Hershberg, ed., *Philadelphia: Work, Space, Family, and Group Experience in the Nineteenth Century* (New York, 1981); Virginia Yans-McLaughlin, *Family and Community: Italian Immigrants in Buffalo, 1880–1930* (Ithaca, N.Y., 1972); Mary P. Ryan, *Cradle of the Middle Class: The Family in Oneida County, New York, 1790–1865* (New York, 1981); and Hareven, "A Complex Relationship: Family Strategies and the Processes of Economic and Social Change," in *Beyond the Marketplace: Rethinking Economy and Society*, ed. Roger Friedland and A. F. Robertson (New York, 1990).

On the family's relation to the process of industrialization, see Talcott Parsons, "The American Family: Its Relations to Personality and to the Social Structure," in Parsons, Robert F. Bales, et al., *Family, Socialization, and Interaction Process* (Glencoe, Ill., 1955); Hareven, *Family Time and Industrial Time* (cited above); Virginia Yans-McLaughlin, "Patterns of Work and Family Organization: Buffalo's Italians," *Journal of Interdisciplinary History* 2 (Autumn 1971); and Louise Tilly and Joan Scott, *Women, Work, and Family* (New York, 1978).

On the black family, see Herbert G. Gutman, *The Black Family in Slavery and Freedom, 1750–1925* (New York, 1976); Robert W. Fogel and Stanley L. Engerman, *Time on the Cross: The Economics of American Negro Slavery* (New York, 1989);

and Jacqueline Jones, *Labor of Love, Labor of Sorrow: Black Women, Work, and the Family from Slavery to the Present* (New York, 1985).

On the relationship between family and demographic patterns, see Robert Wells, *Uncle Sam's Family: Issues in and Perspectives on American Demographic History* (Albany, N.Y., 1985); Tamara K. Hareven and Maris A. Vinovskis, eds., *Family and Population in Nineteenth-Century America* (Princeton, N.J., 1978); Michael R. Haines, *Fertility and Occupation: Population Patterns in Industrialization* (New York, 1979); and Daniel Scott Smith, "Family Limitation, Sexual Control, and Domestic Feminism in Victorian America," in *Clio's Consciousness Raised: New Perspectives on the History of Women*, ed. Mary S. Hartman and Lois Banner (New York, 1974).

On the life course and the family, see Glen H. Elder, Jr., *Children of the Great Depression: Social Change in Life Experience* (Chicago, 1974), and Tamara K. Hareven, ed., *Transitions: The Family and the Life Course in Historical Perspective* (New York, 1978), especially the chapters by Elder, "Family History and the Life Course," and Peter Uhlenberg, "Changing Configurations of the Life Course."

On adolescence and teenage pregnancy, see Joseph F. Kett, *Rites of Passage: Adolescence in America, 1790 to the Present* (New York, 1977); John Modell, *Into One's Own: From Youth to Adulthood in the United States, 1920–1975* (Berkeley, Calif., 1989); and Maris A. Vinovskis, *An "Epidemic" of Adolescent Pregnancy?: Some Historical and Policy Considerations* (New York, 1988).

On divorce, see Andrew Cherlin, *Marriage, Divorce, Remarriage* (Cambridge, Mass., 1981); Elaine Tyler May, *Great Expectations: Marriage and Divorce in Post-Victorian America* (Chicago, 1980); and William L. O'Neill, *Divorce in the Progressive Era* (New Haven, Conn., 1967).

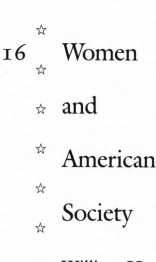

16 Women

and

American

Society

☆ William H. Chafe

The history of women in America serves to highlight the ironies and contradictions of our society. Although women comprise a majority of the population, they nonetheless are often treated like a minority group—assigned a definitive "place" in the social order, denied access to careers and power in the public arena, and viewed as dependent, weak, and submissive by "nature." On the other hand, unlike minority groups, women do not live together in a "ghetto," are distributed through every region, class, and social group, and often share greater proximity and intimacy with their "oppressors" than with each other. Any attempt to understand women's experience, therefore, must inevitably come to grips with both their oneness and their diversity. While, for purposes of social control, women have historically been viewed as "all alike," their individual activities and personal stories are richly various.

Because of these paradoxes women's history offers a distinctive vantage point from which to assess and understand how our society has worked in the past and what changes have—or have not—occurred in recent years. Clearly, any change in behavior that affects the largest single group in America will have a seismic impact on the society. Similarly, any shift in cultural attitudes about male and female "roles" will bespeak significant modifications in the picture of ourselves that we carry around in our heads. Yet examining these changes must not obscure the continuities of women's experience, or what these continuities tell us about how gender interacts with other categories such as race and class to deny individuals and groups the possibility of equal opportunity and treatment.

☆ ☆ ☆ "Women's Place" in American Life

One generalization that most historians of women would probably accept is that cultural prescriptions about women's "proper place" have remained remarkably constant over time. Colonial daughters, like their twentieth-century counterparts, were taught to be moral, pious, devoted, subservient, and nurturant. In the words of one matron quoted in an eighteenth-century newspaper, "I am married, and I have no other concern but to please the man I love; he is the end of every care I have; if I dress, it is for him; if I read a poem, or a play, it is to qualify myself for a conversation agreeable to his taste." Although enormous changes have taken place since then, it would not be stretching the point too far to see Adlai Stevenson's injunction to the Smith College class of 1957—that women's primary role as citizens should be to influence men through their positions as "housewives and mothers"—as a latter-day manifestation of the same cultural worldview that guided colonial America.

Constancy of cultural norms, however, did not necessarily signify that women universally acted to implement such ideals in their daily lives. To begin with, black women, poor women, and new immigrants were never included within the "cult of domesticity" that theoretically assigned white women of the middle and upper classes to a "pedestal." Women of color and women of the working class were always expected to toil in the fields and factories and to accept inferior wages and treatment. Beyond that huge exception, millions of other women from the "respectable" classes also departed substantially from what the dominant culture defined as their proper role. When there were forests to be cleared, crops planted, businesses to be run, and a household economy to be managed, women and men both became indispensable partners in the daily struggle to survive and prosper. Segregated "spheres" were a luxury few could afford, and stereotypes of women as "ornamental" and revered were more honored in the breach than in reality.

During the middle and late nineteenth century, however, reality began to approximate more closely the cultural ideal—at least for the daughters of the white middle and upper classes. As the industrial revolution separated home and workplace, it became a symbol of success for a man to "provide" for his family through his career in the public arena, with women now limited to domestic roles in the home, often aided by servants who were black or recently from Europe. Although some historians have viewed this development as an occasion for women to carve out a new sphere of power over family and home ("domestic feminism"), increasing immersion in the domestic sphere could also become a trap, severely limiting women's capacity to act freely in the public arena or pursue economic aspirations.

Despite such constraints, some middle- and upper-class women still made a significant impact on public policy. Joining together in voluntary associations such as missionary societies or women's clubs, they moved gradually but steadily into the public arena of concern over child labor, juvenile delinquency, alcohol abuse, and factory safety conditions. Frequently they allied with younger women professionals (the first generation of women college graduates) who were inspired to seek careers and transform the world they found around them. Such women founded the profession of social work, started settlement houses, and became increasingly synonymous with the most "progressive" reforms of the Progressive Era—maximum-hour and minimum-wage legislation, the creation of the federal Children's Bureau, and so forth.

☆ ☆ ☆ Suffrage and Other Changes

By the early twentieth century, woman suffrage had become a primary objective of such groups. The vote for women was seen not only as a significant step toward equal legal status but also as an indispensable prerequisite for achieving social reform, cleaning up government and politics, and making morality a priority for public officials. The suffrage, it was believed, would help transform society, even as it promoted women into a larger role of responsibility and equality. In such an atmosphere, and at the conclusion of America's war "to make the world safe for democracy," women received the right to vote in 1920.

Most of the ambitious hopes for the suffrage amendment proved to be in vain, however. Although women reformers continued to work for social welfare reform, and with Eleanor Roosevelt in the New Deal achieved a new measure of political influence, most male politicians had ceased by the mid-1920s to have any fear of a women's "bloc" vote or of a powerful women's party that could act collectively to remove them from power. Even activist women were divided over the meaning of equality, with supporters of the newly proposed Equal Rights Amendment (1923) insisting that there should be no differences in the law between women and men, while most women social welfare reformers insisted that protective legislation designed to guard women's health and safety was still essential to a just and humane society. Such conflicts prevented the kind of cohesion and solidarity that had characterized the suffrage fight and led many people to perceive feminism as a cause that had lost its appeal and relevance.

Nor did the winning of women's suffrage lead to any major changes in the role of women in the workplace. Throughout the early twentieth century the number of women who held paying jobs continued to increase, as did the number of white-collar workers. For the most part, however, these women workers were young, single, and poor, their jobs low paying, sex segregated, and offering little opportunity for advancement. By the end of the 1930s state, local, and national authorities all endorsed discriminatory treatment against married women seeking employment. As one congressional representative declared, a woman's proper place was in the home, not taking a job away from a male breadwinner.

In effect, a married middle-class white woman who wished to work was an anomaly, acting in violation of both her social status and the attitudes of the dominant culture. As the anthropologist Margaret Mead observed in 1935, a young woman contemplating a career had two choices. Either she proclaimed herself "a woman, and therefore less an achieving individual, or an achieving individual, and therefore less a woman." She could not do both, and if she chose to follow the second option, she took the risk of losing forever the chance to be "a loved object, the kind of girl whom men will woo and boast of, toast and marry." Not surprisingly, few women were willing to take such a risk given the norms—and realities—of the society they lived in.

☆ ☆ ☆ World War II and Women at Work

It was World War II that provided the catalyst for most of the changes that have occurred in both behavior and cultural attitudes since the 1930s. Women who a few years before had been told it was a mortal sin to leave the home and take a job were now urged as a matter of patriotic necessity to help win the war by replacing a soldier gone to the front. Between 1941 and 1945 over six million women took jobs for the first time, the majority of them married and over thirty. They performed every kind of work imaginable, from maneuvering giant cranes in steel mills to toppling huge redwoods in the Oregon forest. None received equal pay with men, and very few occupied positions of executive responsibility. Nevertheless, wages were higher than ever before, some of those at the bottom had the opportunity for the first time to make a decent living, and millions of middle-class women discovered that, notwithstanding what the culture had taught them, they were fully capable of running their own lives and playing an active role in the work force as well as in the home. During the war years, the female labor force increased by 57 percent, and the proportion of women who were employed leaped from 25 percent to 36 percent. When the war began, it was expected that virtually all the new workers would return to the home as soon as the war was over. Four years later, more than 80 percent told government pollsters that they wanted to stay on the job. They enjoyed being paid for their work, receiving recognition from society, and having the opportunity to play an active role outside the home.

With the onset of peace, the changes that had taken place during the war came face-to-face with the resurgence of traditional attitudes. A form of cultural schizophrenia occurred, with attitudes going one way and behavior the other. On the surface it appeared that America had reverted totally to a prewar mentality, with the vast majority of middle-class women returning happily to domestic tasks in suburbia. Yet under the surface major shifts were taking place in women's economic and social roles that eventually would create the foundation for a frontal assault upon traditional sex stereotypes.

As soon as the war ended, business leaders, politicians, and social commentators insisted that women must recapture their traditional role as homemakers. A best-seller by Ferdinand Lundberg and Marynia Farnham entitled *Modern Woman: The Lost Sex* (1947) declared that any woman who sought a job must be neurotic. "The independent woman," the book declared, "is a contradiction in terms." Echoing the same theme, Agnes Meyer observed in the *Atlantic* that women served as "the cement of society." "What modern woman has to recapture," she asserted, "is the wisdom that just being a woman is her central task and her greatest honor. . . . Women must boldly announce that no job is more exacting, more necessary, or more rewarding than that of housewife and mother." As more than one million people per year moved to new suburban housing tracts, the ideology that Betty Friedan described so eloquently as the "feminine mystique" was clearly triumphant. The baby boom was sweeping the country. Eisenhower was about to be elected president, and no one seemed interested in questioning the traditional verities of the woman's place in the home.

☆ ☆ ☆ Affluence and the Second Income

Even in the midst of this new cult of domesticity, however, changes were taking place in the work force to make traditional ideas of women's proper role increasingly outdated. Ironically, many of those who joined the move to suburbia could not afford the luxury of a new car or a new home on one income only. From the late 1940s to the present, the most outstanding feature of labor force participation rates has been the rapid increase in the number of women workers. All during the 1950s women's employment rates increased four times faster than that of men. After the initial loss of jobs with postwar demobilization, women returned to the job market at a rapid pace. Significantly, these were the same women—married and over thirty-five—who had dominated the female labor force during the war itself.

At no point did these women see themselves as part of a feminist crusade to secure equality with men. Nor was their work seen by men as a threat to their traditional position of dominance. Rather, these women were taking jobs in order to "help the family"—a traditional female role. For the most part they clustered in sex-segregated jobs such as clerical or sales work. Underpaid, denied promotion opportunities, and treated for the most part as "marginal," these women were not part of any movement toward equality.

Nevertheless, their employment proved crucial to the economy and society. More and more they came from better-educated, more middle-class families. Their employment provided the indispensable precondition for millions of families to achieve a middle-class life-style. Without that second income, owning a home or providing a college education for one's children would have been virtually impossible. A simple statistic tells the story. In 1975 the average income of a one-earner family was $12,000. That of a two-income family was $17,500. The difference, quite simply, was that between a working-class and a middle-class life-style. In all of this there was a clear cultural logic. The crisis of World War II had started the change, providing patriotic legitimacy for women taking jobs. Thereafter, those who led the way into the work force were over thirty-five. Their children were already in school or had left home. As a result, there was no clear-cut conflict with the cultural assumption that women's primary role was to take care of small children. Only after twenty years of change among those least likely to threaten traditional notions of women's proper place did women who were younger, with children still in the home, join the influx to the job market. Moreover, at no time was this shift seen as politically or ideologically motivated.

Still, this transformation of the female labor force eventually undercut the social basis for traditional assumptions about women's proper place. In 1940 only 15 percent of married women were employed. Thirty years later the figure was nearly 50 percent. At the beginning of World War II it was virtually unheard of for mothers with small children to be employed. By 1970 more than 50 percent of those with children six to seventeen years old were in the work force, and by 1980 more than 50 percent of those with children under six were also employed. On Pearl Harbor day, the vast majority of women workers were single, young, and poor. By the 1970s the majority were middle class, over thirty, and married. It was not that those who were least well-off in the society worked any less but that those who had not worked in the past were now taking jobs in great numbers. No longer was it possible to operate on the assumption that most women would spend the majority of their lives tending the home or taking care of children. That experience was now the exception rather than the rule.

☆ ☆ ☆ Women's Liberation in the 1960s

It was against the background of these changes that a strong women's movement challenging traditional sex stereotypes revived during the 1960s. One hundred and thirty years earlier the first feminist movement had developed out of the abolitionist struggle to eliminate slavery. Appropriately, the women's liberation movement of the 1960s also grew out of a massive movement for civil rights. The demand of black Americans that all discrimination based on race be eliminated had direct relevance to discrimination based on sex as well, and when Congress enacted the 1964 Civil Rights Bill, it outlawed discriminatory treatment based on sex as well as race. More importantly, the black and white women who had fought for civil rights on the streets of the South discovered that even within the movement their gender was used as a basis for denying them an equal voice in policy-making councils. Protesting this second-class citizenship, they created their own movement within a movement, and many formed cadres that provided the basis for the women's liberation movement that by the end of the 1960s had spread to cities across the country.

By the end of the 1960s the women's movement had succeeded in challenging nearly all of America's traditional cultural assumptions about women's proper place. The more "established" wing of the movement, typified by the National Organization of Women (NOW), challenged employment discrimination, bias against women in politics, and the antifemale prejudice so dominant in the country's major economic and social institutions. The more radical wing of the movement—the younger women's liberation groups—organized in local communities to build day-care centers, fight for repeal of abortion laws, create women's health collectives, write nonsexist children's books, provide support for alternative life-styles, and, above all, raise the consciousness of women to the cultural bondage of being categorized as a sex object. The movement attacked the whole spectrum of institutions and values that limited women.

Although it was denounced by some and ridiculed by others, the women's movement made an impact that transformed the attitudes of many people in America. A Gallup poll taken in 1962 revealed that less than one out of three American women felt discriminated against. Eight years later, in response to the same question, 50 percent of the women questioned said that they were discriminated against. By 1974 two out of three declared that they were victims of discrimination and that they supported the movement for equality. Although most did not subscribe to the women's liberation movement per se, the vast majority did support feminist programs on day care, abortion, and equal access to professional opportunities.

By the 1970s these trends in behavior and attitude had begun to reinforce each other. College-educated women—those most affected by the rise in feminist consciousness—increasingly declared that a career was just as important a priority as marriage. During the 1970s and 1980s applications from these women to professional schools in medicine, law, and business skyrocketed. During the 1960s the average entering class to medical school or law school had been fewer than 8 percent women. By 1990 those figures had increased to approximately 40 percent of each entering class.

The fastest increase in employment occurred among women in the prime childbearing years, from twenty to thirty-four. By the mid-1970s 61 percent of all women in that age group were employed, and among college-educated women the rate was 86 percent. The fastest rise of all took place among women with young children. From 1959 through 1974 the employment rate of mothers with children under three more than doubled, from 15 to 31 percent, and that among mothers of children three to five years increased from 25 to 39 percent.

As each of these variables interacted with the others, they created a "multiplier effect," with shifting values and changing social and economic conditions building upon each other to produce new patterns of family and work life. By the middle of the 1970s the shape of women's participation in the labor force had come close to matching that of men, and in some age groups, despite a lengthy recession, women's employment had already exceeded the Department of Labor's 1970 projections for the 1990s. The distribution of women in jobs historically defined as exclusively male also showed substantial change. The number of women judges and lawyers climbed from 5 to 14 percent, women architects doubled from 4 to 8 percent, and the number of women Ph.D.'s more than tripled between 1970 and 1990.

☆ ☆ ☆ The Politics of Equality

Political discourse and behavior also reflected the impact of changing gender roles. Although the administration of Ronald Reagan consistently adopted positions that were anathema to feminists (opposition to the Equal

Rights Amendment, withdrawal of federal funding for abortions for poor women, hostility to affirmative action programs designed to assure the hiring of more women and blacks), the same administration appointed the first woman justice of the U.S. Supreme Court, named two women to the cabinet, and claimed to be more committed to women's rights than any previous administration. Both political parties exhibited great sensitivity to the "gender gap"—the finding by political pollsters that women's political preferences differed significantly from men's, especially on issues of war and peace and social welfare. And in 1984 Democratic presidential nominee Walter Mondale broke all political precedent by choosing as his vice-presidential running mate Geraldine Ferraro, congresswoman from New York and a strong feminist.

Partly as an indication of all these social shifts, the typical American family also changed dramatically. As late as the 1950s more than 70 percent of all American families comprised a father who worked and a mother who stayed at home to take care of the children. By 1980 that description applied to only 15 percent of all families. In the same years birth rates declined precipitously. At the height of the baby boom the average family had more than three children. By 1980 that figure had fallen to less than 1.6 children, the reproduction level required for zero population growth. Although there were some signs of a "baby boomlet" by the end of the 1980s, most demographers did not foresee any major reversal of the latter fertility rate.

The shifts in family composition also testified, at least in part, to "new rules" governing attitudes toward sex, self-fulfillment, and gender roles. In an age that emphasized personal happiness and immediate gratification, millions of Americans no longer were willing to sacrifice personal expectations of fulfillment and self-realization in order to maintain marriages or relationships that failed to meet their demands. The divorce rate climbed more than 100 percent in the twenty years after 1960, and by 1980 more than two out of five marriages were expected to end in divorce. The number of individuals living alone in "single households" soared from 10.9 percent in 1964 to 23 percent in 1980. Although there was no provable cause and effect, social scientists noted a direct correlation between the increase in the divorce rate and the number of women entering the labor force.

By the 1980s and 1990s it was clear that for some women—particularly the college-educated young—important breakthroughs had occurred in the realm of personal freedom, self-realization, and autonomy. Informed by changing attitudes toward individual fulfillment, hundreds of thousands of young women had charted a new course for themselves, free of many of the constraints that in the past had assigned women to prescribed roles. It was too early to conclude that dramatic progress toward equality had taken place. The Equal Rights Amendment was not ratified. Most professions were still controlled totally by men; professional women received only 73 percent of the salaries paid to professional men; and while record numbers of women were entering the junior levels of medicine, law, and business, it was by no means assured that they would receive promotions and rewards comparable to those awarded their male counterparts. Nevertheless, massive changes had occurred in female employment, family life, and personal expectations, each shift intersecting with and reinforcing the others. For significant numbers of well-educated individual women, the social struggles of the feminist movement had clearly produced far-reaching and impressive gains.

☆ ☆ ☆ Sex, Race, and Class

Such "success stories," however, described only one aspect of the total picture. If a person were bright, talented, and from an economically secure background, women's liberation could indeed spell a life of unparalleled new opportunity. But there were millions of other women whose stories represented the direct opposite of the upward mobility and the economic advancement enjoyed by the fortunate minority.

For these women, one of the problems was the type of jobs that women workers entered. Over 80 percent of all female workers, for example, were concentrated in only 20 out of the 420 occupations listed by the Census Bureau. Such areas as personal services and clerical work were defined almost exclusively as "women's jobs"; yet it was precisely such occupations that suffered the most dramatic decline in real earnings during the inflationary cycle of the 1970s. Even within such categories, women experienced substantial sex discrimination. Women salesworkers, for example, earned only 52 percent the wages of male salesworkers and tended to be concentrated in those customer areas where commissions were not offered on sales. Thus, although women experienced an employment "boom" in the late 1960s and 1970s, the work they entered in most cases offered no possibility for economic advancement and upward mobility. "We may be approaching a situation like that in some industrializing third world countries," one economist declared, "where there has been a big increase in jobs for women . . . but the jobs don't lead anywhere, they don't lift women out of poverty." Ironically, women's work frequently meant sinking deeper into the quagmire of marginal poverty instead of securing the liberation so much talked about in the media.

Divorce, separation, or desertion further compounded the economic plight suffered by many women. While some gained from liberalized attitudes toward divorce and family breakup, for many more the departure of a male breadwinner spelled disaster. Barbara Ehrenreich estimated that 85 percent of all American women could expect to support themselves at some time in their lives, without the aid of a husband or male jobholder. Although many of these women found work, most frequently the jobs they qualified for paid a minimum wage that left a woman and her children well beneath the poverty line. Approximately 25 percent of all working women heading households with children under eighteen receive incomes beneath the poverty level.

Underlying the rapid "feminization of poverty" was a massive increase in female-headed households from the 1960s through the 1980s. At the end of the 1950s three million Americans received welfare assistance under the Aid to Families with Dependent Children (AFDC) program. By 1980 that figure had soared to eleven million—eight million children, three million women— virtually all in female-headed households. In the 1970s alone the number of women heading families with children increased by 72 percent. The correlation with poverty was direct and startling. A child born into a family with no father present had a one-in-three chance of being poor; if the family was headed by a man alone, the chances improved to one in ten; and if both parents were present, the chances were only one in nineteen.

Perhaps most dramatically, the phenomenon of female-headed households reflected the intersection of race and gender as dual sources of oppression. While the number of white families headed by women increased from 9.4 percent in 1970 to 14 percent in 1980, the number of black families headed by women escalated to 47 percent in the same period, and by 1990 was over 50 percent. Black women also experienced most severely the debilitating consequences of new sexual mores. One out of every three black children was born to a teenage mother, and 55 percent of all black babies were born out of wedlock. (In inner city ghettos the figure often climbed above 70 percent.) The consequences were devastating. "You can't underestimate the stress of raising a child in the ghetto by yourself," Eleanor Holmes Norton, a black lawyer and a civil rights advocate, observed—"without a grandma, without an aunt, with no one you can turn to."

If nothing else, such evidence suggests the difficulty of achieving sex equality simply through opening the top ranks of society to a few individual women. Equality between the sexes has proven to be inextricably connected to problems of race and class as well.

☆ ☆ ☆ Equality and Opportunity: Still a Paradox

Clearly, enormous changes have occurred both in the daily experience of American women and in the cultural norms describing masculinity and femininity in American society. To some the changes appear almost revolutionary in dimension. It is fair to say that a young woman growing up in America today faces a world radically different in both its possibilities and demands from the world that might have faced her grandmother in 1930. Still, the continuities—and the diversity—of women's experience stand out as ongoing reminders of the dangers of overgeneralization. For millions of American women gender continues to be an imposing barrier to full freedom and equality and, together with race or class, remains more a sign of oppression than a symbol of liberation. Now, as throughout American history, women's fate is central to the story of the whole society. Perhaps only when the larger issue of what Americans mean by equality and equal opportunity has been resolved, throughout their ranks, will it be possible for women to be free.

FURTHER READING

Those interested in surveying women's history in America might best begin with the recent, up-to-date overview in Sara M. Evans, *Born for Liberty: A History of Women in America* (New York, 1989). Other important texts include Nancy Woloch, *Women and the American Experience* (New York, 1984), and Mary P. Ryan, *Womanhood in America: From Colonial Times to the Present*, 3d ed. (New York, 1983). For anthologies of material on this entire history, see Nancy Hewitt's *Women, Families, and Communities: Readings in American History*, 2 vols. (Glenville, Ill., 1990), and Linda K. Kerber and Jane Sherron De Hart's *Women's America: Refocusing the Past*, 3d ed. (New York, 1991).

A number of books in American women's history provide a useful backdrop for scholarly work. Gerda Lerner's *The Majority Finds Its Past: Placing Women in History* (New York, 1979) offers an excellent introduction to the conceptual issues of women's history. See also Lerner's *The Creation of Patriarchy* (New York, 1986). Anne Firor Scott's *Making the Invisible Woman Visible* (Chicago, 1984) traces women's contribution to shaping public institutions in America, even during periods when, for the most part, they were denied public roles. Alice Kessler-Harris provides an excellent framework for tracing the evolving economic roles of women in *Out to Work: A History of Wage-Earning Women in the United States* (New York, 1982); John D'Emilio and Estelle Freedman offer a similarly valuable overview of the issue of sexuality in their book *Intimate Matters: A History of*

Sexuality in America (New York, 1988); and Carl Degler does the same for the topic of women and family life in *At Odds: Women and the Family in America from the Revolution to the Present* (New York, 1980).

For those seeking to understand the context out of which nineteenth-century gender roles developed, the best places to start are Mary Beth Norton, *Liberty's Daughters: The Revolutionary Experience of American Women, 1750–1800* (Boston, 1980); Linda K. Kerber, *Women of the Republic: Intellect and Ideology in Revolutionary America* (Chapel Hill, N.C., 1980); and Nancy F. Cott, *The Bonds of Womanhood: "Woman's Sphere" in New England, 1780–1835* (New Haven, Conn., 1977). Each of these books, for the most part, treats white women. For a view of black women's experience in the nineteenth century, see Deborah Gray White, *Ar'n't I a Woman?: Female Slaves in the Plantation South* (New York, 1985); Herbert G. Gutman, *The Black Family in Slavery and Freedom, 1750–1925* (New York, 1976); Jacqueline Jones, *Labor of Love, Labor of Sorrow: Black Women, Work, and the Family from Slavery to the Present* (New York, 1985); and Paula Giddings, *When and Where I Enter: The Impact of Black Women on Race and Sex in America* (New York, 1984).

The linkage of women's reform activities to politics is most clearly framed in Paula Baker's pathbreaking article, "The Domestication of Politics: Women and American Political Society, 1780–1920," *American Historical Review* 89 (June 1984); and in Suzanne Lebsock, "Across the Great Divide: Women and Politics, 1890–1920," in Louise A. Tilly and Patricia Gurin, eds., *Women, Politics, and Change* (New York, 1990). The classic work on woman suffrage remains Eleanor Flexner, *Century of Struggle: The Women's Rights Movement in the United States*, rev. ed. (Cambridge, Mass., 1975). Other important studies of suffrage include Anne F. Scott and Andrew M. Scott, *One Half the People: The Fight for Woman Suffrage* (Urbana, Ill., 1982), and Ellen Carol Du Bois, *Feminism and Suffrage: The Emergence of an Independent Women's Movement in America, 1848–1869* (Ithaca, N.Y., 1978). The issues of continuity, discontinuity, and the Nineteenth Amendment are discussed in Nancy Cott's excellent survey, *The Grounding of Modern Feminism* (New Haven, Conn., 1987).

Historians have done an extraordinary job exploring the issues surrounding women's experience during the World War II decade. See, for example, Karen Anderson, *Wartime Women: Sex Roles, Family Relations, and the Status of Women during World War II* (Westport, Conn., 1981); Susan M. Hartmann, *The Homefront and Beyond: American Women in the 1940s* (Boston, 1982); Ruth Milkman, *Gender at Work: The Dynamics of Job Segregation by Sex during World War II* (Urbana, Ill., 1987); Leila J. Rupp, *Mobilizing Women for War: German and American Propaganda, 1939–1945* (Princeton, N.J., 1978); and D'Ann Campbell, *Women at War with America: Private Lives in a Patriotic Era* (Cambridge, Mass., 1984).

The best overview of the postwar years is Elaine Tyler May, *Homeward Bound: American Families in the Cold War Era* (New York, 1988). See also Eugenia Kaledin, *Mothers and More: American Women in the 1950s* (Boston, 1984). Books that deal with various aspects of women's lives in the 1960s and 1970s include Lillian B. Rubin, *Worlds of Pain: Life in the Working-Class Family* (New York, 1976), and Barbara Ehrenreich, *The Hearts of Men: American Dreams and the Flight from Commitment* (Garden City, N.Y., 1983). For an overview of the years 1920 to 1990, see William H. Chafe, *The Paradox of Change: American Women in the Twentieth Century* (New York, 1991), a revision of his earlier work *The American Woman* (New York, 1972).

The best historical assessment of the women's liberation movement remains Sara M. Evans, *Personal Politics: The Roots of Women's Liberation in the Civil Rights Movement and the New Left* (New York, 1979). Jo Freeman's *The Politics of Women's Liberation* (New York, 1975) deals more with the women's rights segment of the movement and its origins in various state commissions on the status of women. Leila Rupp and Verta Taylor focus on the history of the National Woman's Party in *Survival in the Doldrums: The American Women's Rights Movement, 1945 to the 1960s* (New York, 1987).

Some of the major issues of the 1970s and 1980s were the impact of divorce, the feminization of poverty, labor segmentation by gender, and comparable worth. Winifred D. Wandersee, *On the Move: American Women in the 1970s* (Boston, 1988), is a good overview. See also Lenore J. Wietzman, *The Divorce Revolution: The Unexpected Social Consequences for Women and Children in America* (New York, 1985); Louise Kapp Howe, *Pink Collar Workers: Inside the World of Women's Work* (New York, 1977); Diana Pearce, "The Feminization of Poverty: Women, Work, and Welfare," *Urban and Social Change Review* 11 (February 1978); Karin Stallard, Barbara Ehrenreich, and Holly Sklar, *Poverty in the American Dream: Women and Children First* (Boston, 1983); and Sara M. Evans and Barbara J. Nelson, *Wage Justice: Comparable Worth and the Paradox of Technocratic Reform* (Chicago, 1989). For updates on women's status, see the annual series *The American Woman*, edited by Sara Rix for the Women's Research and Education Institute and published by W. W. Norton (New York), which thus far includes volumes on 1987–88 and 1988–89.

For the perspective of black and poor women, see especially Bell Hooks, *Talking Back: Thinking Feminist, Thinking Black* (Boston, 1989), and *Ain't I a Woman: Black Women and Feminism* (Boston, 1981); Gloria T. Hull et al., eds., *All the Women Are White, All the Blacks Are Men, But Some of Us Are Brave: Black Women's Studies* (New York, 1982); Angela Y. Davis, *Women, Race, and Class* (New York, 1981); Alice Walker, *In Search of Our Mothers' Gardens* (San Diego, Calif., 1983); Michele Wallace, *Black Macho and the Myth of the Superwoman* (New York, 1979); and Toni Cade, ed., *The Black Woman: An Anthology* (New York, 1970).

☆

☆

17 ☆ The

☆ Making of

☆ Black

☆ America
☆

☆ Waldo Martin

The traditional paradigm for conceptualizing the history of black Americans, or African Americans, flows directly *From Slavery to Freedom*, as the title of John Hope Franklin's indispensable study affirms. In a similar vein, August Meier and Elliott Rudwick called their valuable overview of the black experience *From Plantation to Ghetto*. Both texts, reflecting the dominant approach to black history, reveal a linear, progressive vision—an essentially evolutionary model.

As Meier and Rudwick's title suggests, however, upon careful scrutiny the historical sojourn of African Americans might best be characterized in terms at once progressive and regressive. Indeed both works, like the other best work in the field, plainly demonstrate the complexity of the black experience. The problem of unraveling the ambiguities, contradictions, ironies, and paradoxes of that experience persists, and once the complexity is acknowledged, the history itself looks quite different. Rather than mere linearity, we see fluctuation; besides development, even evolution, one also sees devolution.

At the 1989 meeting of the Organization of American Historians in St. Louis, historian Nathan Huggins offered a thoughtful assessment of Franklin's *From Slavery to Freedom* and, after acknowledging the text's many virtues, suggested the possibility of an alternative explanatory model for black America. Arguing that the continuity of struggle and oppression more accurately defines that experience, he boldly questioned the prevailing progressive orthodoxy. He proposed, instead, a conceptual framework built upon the analysis of movement between old and new forms of freedom and dependency alike.

To reconcile the demands of both narrative structure and deconstructed historical reality—encompassing a range of views and experiences—a cultural perspective is fundamental. The history of black Americans and race relations in America must be understood not just in political, economic, and social terms but in broader cultural terms as well. The achievement of Lawrence Levine's classic text *Black Culture and Black Consciousness* is that it so vividly reveals the interior beliefs and practices that profoundly influence the shape, texture, and meaning of historical experience. Joining the "mind of the black folk" with more traditional visions deepens our historical understanding while sharpening our judgments.

☆ ☆ ☆ Creolization

The development of New World systems of black slavery varied according to place, time, and the mix of European, African, and aboriginal peoples. What came to be colonial North America and later the United States experienced its most rapid growth in the African slave population during the eighteenth century. Of approximately 399,000 Africans brought to British North America from the early seventeenth to the nineteenth century, about 348,000 were imported between 1701 and 1808. The essential question is how a variety of enslaved African peoples with different beliefs and practices, speaking a variety of often mutually unintelligible languages, created New World African American societies and cultures. By what processes and with what consequences did enslaved Africans become New World people?

For colonial North America, the African sojourn begins in the early seventeenth century. The first twenty Africans who arrived in Jamestown in late August 1619 aboard a Dutch man-of-war appear to have caused little concern among the English settlers. Over time Africans flowed into other North American colonies, especially those facing acute labor needs like Virginia, South Carolina, and Georgia. The development of distinctive community institutions, however, and a syncretic culture depended upon relatively large plantation units, a predominance of creoles (Africans born in America) within a slave population of some size, and a work routine and social life conducive to strengthening group ties.

That the African American communities and cultures that came about over time were creole, or New World, developments cannot be emphasized too strongly. Neither wholly European nor wholly African, the community institutions and cultural beliefs and practices that emerged reveal a continuing syncretism. The introduction of large numbers of "fresh" Africans in the second third of the eighteenth century, for instance, exacerbated tensions with the creoles. Toward the turn of the century and on into the nineteenth, with the slave population growing more through natural increase than imports, these tensions diminished and the creole quality of the black world intensified. By 1830 the African American world, free and slave alike, had achieved a significant measure of cultural cohesion and integrity.

Notwithstanding the importance of European domination and the New World milieu in shaping African American culture, at bottom its African roots gave that culture its essence. Clearly the nature of cultural contact and interaction between Africans and the English in North America reflected a relationship of power. English domination meant, among other things, suppressing those features of African cultures deemed inimical to control over a servile labor force. Not surprisingly, therefore, African political institutions were not re-created or allowed to be re-created. Likewise the English endeavored to indoctrinate their slaves, in a manner, by forcing their language upon them. This effort to stamp out African tongues and teach the slaves English, the language of the oppressor, was vital to communication between master and slave. It also reinforced English hegemony.

Learning the English language, like much of the acculturation process, proved to be a double-edged sword: a tool for cultural struggle as well as social control. Language acquisition functioned both to help slaves carve out a social niche of their own and to buttress the slave system. The initial stage was the creation of pidgin languages. Transitional, restricted, and lacking native speakers, pidgin languages enabled Africans from diverse linguistic backgrounds to begin forging the bonds of community and culture. A pidgin became a creole language once there were native speakers contributing to intragroup communication as well as group consciousness extending beyond the creoles' ethnic origins. The development of Black English, then, revealed two pivotal mechanisms animating the culture: the persistence of African beliefs and values, even with the adoption of English structures, and the transformation of diverse African peoples into one people.

The early history of the Gullah in the South Carolina and Georgia Sea Islands amply illustrates these mechanisms. The distinctive form of English that developed over time here, known also as Gullah, derived clearly from creolization as at least two language systems melded into a single new language. Principally a spoken language, this tongue largely resulted from symbiosis between an African-derived grammar and the English lexicon. In fact, both African and English linguistic features deeply influenced the speech of whites as well as blacks in the area. This pattern of cultural intermixture was common throughout the New World wherever different peoples—Africans, Europeans, and indigenes—interacted.

The dynamic syncretism can be seen in many areas, most notably the New

World transformation of African beliefs and customs. The development of slave religion, the fundamental expression of the slaves' sacred worldview, demonstrated most vividly the creative fusion of aspects of traditional African religions and Christianity. Gullah folk religion was what historian Margaret Creel refers to as an "African-Christian synthesis," combining traditional spiritual beliefs and practices drawn from various Bantu peoples, especially the Bakongo, and Gullah Christianity.

That creolization cut both ways—English culture influencing the evolving amalgam of African cultures and vice versa—needs to be reiterated. Notwithstanding English dominance, African American culture and English-American culture profoundly influenced each other. That both "black" and "white" cultures are actually creole cultures is the kind of basic historical reality that must be understood fully, in all of its complexity, in order to grapple more thoroughly with the meaning of "American culture." Scholars have been far more willing to acknowledge and to explore the European impact on Africans and indigenous peoples in the New World rather than to consider the reverse. The evidence, regardless, is compelling: Africans and creoles profoundly influenced whites and their culture, particularly in the realms of religion, aesthetics, time, and art. The interpenetration between black and white cultures clearly deserves greater attention.

This cultural interpenetration started with the introduction of large numbers of Africans and Europeans into the South and proceeded apace over time due principally to the mutual dependency that evolved between them. Creolization not only was a reciprocal process but also differed according to variables like time, work routine, and place. In the South Carolina and Georgia low country, where slaves working and living in large units became ever more dominant numerically, the developing culture reflected a pronounced African influence due to its relative isolation from white influence. Two other factors contributed to the distinctiveness of this region. First, the tradition of truck gardening allowed slaves to keep small gardens, as well as some animals, for themselves and to market the surplus. Because slaves refused to give up the practice and the demand for their surplus grew, this tradition was difficult to control and served to enhance slave autonomy. Second, the typical task system of rice production in this area—where one was able to engage in activities of one's own choosing after completing the assigned job for the day—likewise contributed to a significant degree of sociocultural autonomy. While today "freedom" and the inroads of twentieth-century forces, most notably Gullah out-migration and real estate developments, have diminished Gullah landholdings and isolation, the distinctive culture persists in many ways.

In the Chesapeake, especially toward the latter part of the eighteenth century, the tendency of the slave population to grow through natural increase rather than African importation enhanced the creole quality of the society and culture. By the turn of the century the increase in plantation size, the growth in black population density, and the decline in African slave imports contributed to an increasingly stable slave community. Correspondingly, there was greater congruence and convergence between African American and Euro-American cultures in the Chesapeake than in the South Carolina and Georgia low country due to greater interracial contact, larger numbers of whites, smaller plantations or social units, and larger numbers of resident planters exercising more direct supervision over the production of tobacco and other crops.

The comparatively smaller number of Africans and creoles in the Middle Colonies and New England tended to enhance the European impact on black acculturation in these regions. Black and white interaction was not uncommon, especially in urban areas. In many areas without the population size and density necessary to sustain a stable community culture, the African impact on black creolization dwindled relative to that in the Chesapeake and the low country of South Carolina and Georgia. Still, African cultural influence was undeniable, even in New England, where the fewest blacks resided. The culture of black Yankees revealed its African influences in many ways—from folk arts, crafts, and holiday celebrations to religious beliefs and rituals.

The creation of an African American people from a variety of African peoples represented a political as well as a cultural act. It was a crucial step in the construction of both a national identity, or sense of American nationalism, and a viable sense of individual and collective racial identity. Africans and African Americans literally empowered themselves through the very process of transcending and transforming differences among them. The profound significance of reconstituting a singular New World African people out of various African peoples (like Ibo, Fon, Hausa, Ashanti, Bakongo) cannot be overstated. This expansive collective ethos undergirded a Pan-African consciousness—a sense of identity uniting Africans on the continent and throughout the diaspora—and, consequently, has been an important element of the continuing African American liberation struggle.

☆ ☆ ☆ Slavery, Freedom, and Resistance

The American Revolution (1775–83), the Reconstruction era (1863–77), and the civil rights–Black Power revolution (1954–72) promised much to African Americans but delivered far less. At each of these junctures the black liberation struggle mounted the national stage, increasing in significance over time with each dramatic episode. If the strategic dilemma of this freedom struggle has been how best to advance it, the enduring quandary has been what does it all mean. Whether "free" or slave, blacks devised many approaches to resolve both problems. That these seemingly intractable questions continue to haunt us speaks volumes for the ubiquity of racism. That African Americans have "made a way where there was no way" confirms the ultimate triumph of the human spirit.

With the Civil War over in 1865, the Thirteenth Amendment to the Constitution became law. The legal abolition of black chattel slavery completed in part the unfinished business of the American Revolution, which freed the white colonists from oppression at the hands of the British but left intact the shackles on the majority of black slaves. White freedom was forged in the foundry of black slavery, and as historian Edmund Morgan observed in *American Slavery–American Freedom*, this reality has been the central paradox of American history.

During the American Revolution black soldiers, seamen, and laborers fought for both sides. In each case the ostensible goal was liberty, especially for slaves who typically joined the fray upon the condition of their own manumission. It might seem that the American Revolution offered blacks an unparalleled opportunity to exploit wartime conditions and the conflict's libertarian logic to their advantage. Some did, particularly runaways and enlistees; most were unable to do so.

The diplomatic silence of the Declaration of Independence on the issue of slavery, like the compromising slavery clauses of the Constitution, reveal the deep tensions, notably the sectional tensions, that the institution of slavery aroused. In fact, the American Revolution's libertarian and natural-rights logic enhanced the postwar antislavery movement. Less and less economically viable in the northern states, slavery gradually died out there. Legislative, constitutional, and judicial actions outlawed the institution, and moral opposition mounted until in 1830 there were only 3,568 slaves in all the North.

In the South, however, the institution became further entrenched in the nineteenth century. The explosive growth of cotton agriculture in the Lower South, fed by developments like Eli Whitney's cotton gin in 1793, especially deepened the regional commitment to black slave labor. Even as agriculture diversified in the Upper South, moving away from tobacco toward cereals and grains, slave labor remained viable, with the excess in the slave population being siphoned off by a growing domestic slave trade between the Upper South and both the Lower South and the Southwest. The constitutional prohibition of the importation of slaves into the United States beginning in 1808 also contributed to this burgeoning trade. From a slave population of

around 700,000 in 1790—the vast majority of these (around 658,000) residing in the South—the numbers grew to almost four million southern black
slaves in 1860.

Prior to the American Revolution the free-black population was very small,
numbering only 1,800 in Virginia as late as 1782. After the war, though, the
free-black population grew dramatically, from approximately 60,000 in 1790
(27,000 in the North and 33,000 in the South) to 320,000 in 1830 (138,000
in the North, 182,000 in the South). Sources of this growth included those
who gained their freedom through war service, runaways, masters freeing
their offspring from interracial sexual relations, self-purchase, and natural
increase. Another source was the large number of slave manumissions as far
south as the Chesapeake by masters influenced by the revolutionary ideology
of liberty and the rights of man. After 1820 the bulk of the growth was due to
natural increase, especially as the number of manumissions declined. By 1860
the total free-black population had reached 488,000.

The development of free-black communities, North and South, necessitated
independent or separate institutions as an expression of dignity and autonomy, on one hand, and as a reaction against antiblack prejudice and discrimination, on the other. Even in the North, where the black population was quite
small compared to the white population, social, economic, and political proscriptions circumscribed free-black life. In the South free blacks often endured
more severe kinds of proscriptions. Free blacks could not vote in the South
after the 1830s, and by 1860 in the North they could vote only in Maine, New
Hampshire, Vermont, Rhode Island, and Massachusetts, an area accounting
for just 6 percent of the total black population. Things got worse for southern
free blacks in particular after the Nat Turner insurrection in Virginia in 1831.
Southern whites adopted increasingly restrictive measures of social control
against the free blacks lest they undermine the slave system by acting in concert
with their enslaved brothers and sisters.

Free blacks created a plethora of institutions to meet their needs. As a result,
these institutions enhanced their sense of racial consciousness and served to
strengthen the distinctiveness of their ongoing creolization. Pervasive antiblack discrimination and segregation, on the one hand, and more importantly
black pride and self-respect, on the other, buttressed the growth of black
cultural distinctiveness. These forces likewise afforded blacks a vital measure of
cultural autonomy. While adhering to the core values and beliefs of the
American Creed, free blacks ceaselessly denounced the racist oppression they
confronted, focusing their protest energies on both uplifting their own communities and working to free the slaves. As the nineteenth century wore on, it
became increasingly evident that blacks had to rely primarily upon them-

selves—the self-help ethic—in their efforts to free the enslaved, and this awareness in turn promoted racial solidarity and responsibility. Racial consciousness undergirded the sensibility pervading black communities. Throughout these communities, North and South, blacks created mutual aid, benevolent, literary, and male and female societies. They also established schools, institutions to care for the needy, and churches.

As religion and a sacred worldview were pivotal to the Americanization of slaves, so too religion, most notably some variety of Christianity, was central to the Americanization of free blacks. In urban areas especially, independent black churches tended to be the most important institutions, even in the South where these institutions sometimes met stiff opposition from whites concerned about the social control of blacks. The establishment of Bethel African Methodist Episcopal Church in Philadelphia in 1794 by Richard Allen and his followers heralded the development of independent black denominations. While the theology and politics of these churches were forces for both accommodation and resistance, their most important function was to provide an opportunity for collective spiritual renewal, institutional self-determination, and cultural expression. Far more than merely centers for religious worship, these institutions were social, economic, and educational centers as well.

Given the centrality of black churches to black life and the autonomy and confidence they bred, that black ministers became the most important leaders in the community is understandable. Even more important, though, black churches drew black communities together. While promoting unity, these fundamental institutions enhanced individual and group identity and bred pride and self-respect.

As free blacks often found themselves adopting aspects of European cultures to a greater extent than the slaves, notably in urban areas, their cultural lives reflected less obvious African influence. Still, they were an African American people and used Africa in the name of innumerable organizations as a recognition of their origins and a representation of their identity. The first recorded free-black organization, the African Union Society, was established in Newport, Rhode Island, in 1780. Newport's African Union Society contacted Philadelphia's Free African Society in 1789 seeking cooperation with a proposal to emigrate to Africa. While the Philadelphia group rejected the proposal, the two groups stayed in contact. This kind of community of interest spread extensively, blossoming in the nineteenth century. A high point in the expression of black nationalism was the black national convention movement, a series of meetings held in various years at which leaders developed strategies to address their people's plight.

Anomalous, quasi-free, and marginal from the perspective of the larger society, free blacks were deeply ambivalent about their relationship to the United States. Caught in what historian Gary Nash describes in *Forging Freedom* as a "dialectic between oppression and achievement, racism and race consciousness, external structures of power and internal consciousness and experience," free blacks saw the task of freedom as multifaceted. Northern blacks were especially prominent in the antebellum abolition movement that took off in the 1830s. Working in their own groups and with white abolitionists like William Lloyd Garrison, black abolitionists endeavored to prick the nation's moral conscience concerning the awful wrong of slavery. Abolitionists, white and black (particularly ex-slaves), were vital to the movement to end slavery. Indeed free blacks rightly saw their own freedom and elevation as inextricably bound with the effort to free the slaves. If whites were abolitionists by choice, blacks were abolitionists of necessity.

The caste status of free blacks led many to question whether they should stay in the United States. During especially trying times, like the 1850s, this pessimism about black prospects in an antiblack and white-dominated society further deepened. Arguing that blacks would never achieve full equality and acceptance in the United States, a small yet significant number of black leaders encouraged their people to emigrate elsewhere—to points in Africa, Canada, or the Caribbean. An untold number did so on their own, and a few thousand took advantage of organized movements to make the break. Black-led or individual emigration as well as highly suspect white-led efforts to induce blacks to leave the United States revealed powerful and extensive currents of black nationalism in addition to black alienation. The persistence of emigrationism, rhetorical and real, in the nineteenth and twentieth centuries shows something of the depth and persistence of black nationalism and black alienation. Similarly, it illustrates when, why, where, and to what effect these currents relate to each other.

Still, the dominant mood remained a sense of destiny unalterably bound with the American experiment, in spite of oppression and hardship. One way to view the black experience in the United States since the nation's inception is to look at the unceasing black efforts to help "their" country realize its democratic and human promise. The ideological heart of the black liberation struggle is itself creole: a transmuted and generalized, Americanized yet African-based nationalism creatively wed to the revolutionary principles of liberty and human rights. When the great nineteenth-century black leader Frederick Douglass (1818–95) rejected emigration in favor of redoubling the domestic liberation struggle, he spoke not only as an American nationalist, but also and equally importantly as a "race man."

In another sense, the ongoing effort to be African, or black, and American at once has been an extraordinary challenge. At the turn of the nineteenth century the towering black activist-intellectual W. E. B. Du Bois (1868–1963) observed of his people that "one ever feels his twoness,—an American, a Negro; two souls, two thoughts, two unreconciled strivings; two warring ideas in one dark body, whose dogged strength alone keeps it from being torn asunder." Speaking directly to the dilemma of creolization and the role of race in American society, he explained that the African American "would not Africanize America, for America has too much to teach the world and Africa. He would not bleach his Negro soul in a flood of white Americanism, for he knows that Negro blood has a message for the world. He simply wishes to make it possible . . . to be both a Negro and an American."

Essential to African American culture, slave and free, has been the question of the liberation struggle itself. The continuing problem of self-definition, then, has been a psychological and cultural battle, a fundamental strategy of black resistance. In fact, a helpful way to conceptualize and understand the cultural politics of race relations between blacks and whites in the United States is to view black culture in part as a culture of resistance. Clearly the mutual dependency between the races and the resulting ambiguity or situational quality of accommodation and resistance must be fully acknowledged. Still, if one accepts the assumption that liberty and its corollaries have been the basic drives animating the black American experience, it must also be recognized that at bottom the struggle is cultural as well as political. It is a war over the contested terrain of symbols, images, values, beliefs, definitions, and meanings as well as integrally related issues of dominance and control. Like oppressed peoples generally, blacks in particular have been engaged in a dialectical struggle with the dominant culture over issues of worldview, or angle of vision, as well as autonomy.

The issue of slave resistance is far more than the numbers of slave revolts, insurrections, and runaways. While powerful and important, such examples often cloud rather than clarify the problem. As many scholars have shown, organized acts of resistance were not uncommon. That conditions in the United States when compared to those, say, in the Caribbean lessened the likelihood of success of large-scale slave revolts is clear. For instance, in the United States the plantations were typically smaller, areas where blacks far outnumbered whites were fewer, and the environment was far less hospitable to the creation of runaway slave societies or maroon colonies.

To be sure, slave resistance was rife. To see that, however, requires a different lens that enables one to focus on the spectrum of social life and interaction in slave society, from the mundane to the extraordinary. By doing so one begins to get at the complexity of resistance—slapping a mistress, feigning illness, indifferent work, poisoning a master, stealing from the "big house," running away, suicide, abortion. To begin to understand this phenomenon, given the varied and complicated nature of resistance even among free blacks, we must pay more attention to patterns of personal interaction between slaves and their mistresses and masters as well to such traditional topics as the Denmark Vesey plot in Charleston in 1822. In other words, we must begin to take far more seriously than we have in the past "everyday forms of resistance."

The Civil War provided slave and free blacks with the opportunity, in ways ranging from the ordinary to the spectacular, to help abolish slavery as an institution and for the slaves to free themselves. In light of the growing disillusionment of free blacks in the 1850s as slavery seemed to become increasingly impregnable and their own lives were increasingly circumscribed, it is not at all surprising that they saw the war from the beginning in a vastly different light than did whites, North and South. Whereas northern whites saw the war primarily as an effort to preserve the Union, southern whites saw it as a war for the independence of the Confederacy. Blacks, however, saw it as a harbinger and a means of emancipation and racial elevation. Most northern whites had been quite willing to abide by a slave South within the United States provided that the South accept the northern notion of slavery as an institution to be confined within its existing limits. Blacks, though, were against any compromise that left slavery intact. Once the war broke out in April 1861, the die was cast. Alternative explanations notwithstanding, it became increasingly clear over time that this was at its deepest level a contest between slavery and freedom.

Slave and free blacks played indispensable roles in the Union victory and the process of emancipation. President Abraham Lincoln's Emancipation Proclamation on 1 January 1863 and the passage of the Thirteenth Amendment to the Constitution outlawing slavery in 1865 reflected as well as shaped events. That is, even before these official pronouncements, in many areas slaves had seized upon the logic of events to free themselves. In his classic *Black Reconstruction in America: 1860–1880*, W. E. B. Du Bois demonstrated that the slaves played a vital role in their own emancipation and in the success of the Union by withdrawing their labor from the Confederacy. By fleeing to the Union lines when possible, and by serving in various capacities for the Union war effort, from laborer to soldier, the slaves simultaneously ensured their own emancipation and Union victory.

A compelling reason blacks were so critical to the war effort was their numbers. In 1860 there were eight million whites in the South and eighteen and a half million in the North. In addition to the four million slaves in the

South, there were over 713,000 free blacks in the country, around 490,000 of whom lived in the South. Whichever side could attract and mobilize significant black support would obviously have an advantage, particularly in a close military contest. Some slave and free blacks labored for the Confederacy in large measure because they had no choice: many were forced to do so. For slaves in particular it was not certain at first exactly what the war might signal or who the Yankees were. Many masters sought to convince the slaves that the Yankees were their enemies and would woefully mistreat them. Until slaves had solid evidence to the contrary, many remained wary of Yankees as well as Confederates. Yet according to Du Bois,

> as it became clear that the Union armies would not or could not return fugitive slaves, and that the masters with all their fume and fury were uncertain of victory, the slave entered upon a general strike against slavery by the same methods that he had used during the period of the fugitive slave. He ran away to the first place of safety and offered his services to the Federal Army. So that in this way it was really true that he served his former master and served the emancipating army; and it was also true that this withdrawal and bestowal of his labor decided the war.

As slaves contributed to their own liberation as laborers and soldiers in the Union army, free blacks, North and South, helped to free their enslaved sisters and brothers. Initially rejected by President Lincoln and his military advisers, by 1863 black soldiers were being accepted, albeit grudgingly in many quarters. Indeed black soldiers had to fight prejudice and discrimination within the military in addition to that in the outside world. This deeply disturbing reality, typical of black participation in all of America's wars, has only compounded the black military travail. Regardless, black soldiers, sailors, and laborers served well and in innumerable instances with distinction. They struggled for a goal much larger than the Union victory—they sought black emancipation. Their participation went beyond mere wartime service to symbolic duty on behalf of black equality and black manhood. It was imperative that black men fight for their own freedom; this they understood all too well. Approximately 179,000 black men served in the Union's armed forces, 10 percent of the total number of all men who served. That American democracy continued to come up sorely lacking on their behalf and that of their descendants, as it had for their ancestors, only heightened their deep-seated ambivalence toward America.

The emancipation of four million slaves in the United States represented a social revolution of enormous scope and consequences. Southern slave wealth had been obliterated as had the slave-labor system. The necessary economic reconstruction of the South would require infusions of capital in addition to the elaboration of a free-labor system. The freedpeople would play key roles in the latter. Political reconstruction would necessitate rewriting southern constitutions and reconstituting southern legislatures to include blacks. Social reconstruction might suggest more egalitarian modes of interracial public and cultural life.

At the moment of freedom, that point in time when a slave consciously grasped that he or she was a slave no more, the past and the future, while still important, fused. This singular moment defied description and yielded a wide range of efforts to crystallize and signify the immediate meaning of emancipation. Still, far more than a time for joyous celebration—although it was a time for that, too—it was a time for cautious and mature reflection. Beyond the overwhelming now, what did tomorrow promise? A rigid caste and Manichean duality had characterized race relations formerly. Was there really hope for a more egalitarian, democratic, and just society? What did freedom really mean? The uncertainty intensified.

☆ ☆ ☆ Difference, Equality, and Democracy

The First Reconstruction (1863–67), that brief experiment in political democracy where black men in the South participated in the political process, failed primarily because of the white counterrevolution fueled by racist intransigence and not, as some have argued, because of black inability. On the contrary, blacks typically acquitted their political obligations with intelligence and moderation. The problem, then, was not black incompetence—a vicious myth at best. Instead, the problem was black competence and success. In a white-supremacist society, how are those in power to treat these utterly contradictory realities? Intensified segregation and discrimination—all manner of ruthless repression, from legal restrictions to lynching—was the primary response.

The nation's acquiescence in the "defeat" of "Black Reconstruction" meant growing social and economic restrictions in addition to political ones. Violence and intimidation buttressed the solidification of American apartheid, or Jim Crow, in the late nineteenth- and early twentieth-century South. Even without all of the formal racial caste structures of the South, blacks in other areas of the country encountered similar kinds of prejudice and discrimination. The lengths that white supremacists in the South went to separate the races—for example, separate schools, water fountains, courtroom Bibles—attest to the virulence of the racism of the period, which is often seen as the

worst in the history of modern race relations. The constancy of racist discrimination and segregation since 1877 is not merely a telling indictment of our
nation's failure to live up to its ideals; it is also a compelling piece of evidence
for a history of race relations deeply rooted in tragedy and betrayal.

There is a virtual scholarly consensus that the most critical failure of the First
Reconstruction was economic. The collapse of a slave-labor economy and the
consequent development of a "free"-labor economy built upon various highly
exploitative modes of peonage and debt proved devastating for the South, but
especially so for blacks. In many ways there was a remarkable continuity
between the antebellum and postbellum modes of labor organization as well as
social relations. Rural impoverishment was a critical factor leading to urban
migration within and beyond the South. As slaves had represented an oppressed working class, so too did free and freed blacks. Even in the North and
West blacks faced economic discrimination. This century has witnessed significant, if uneven and qualified, black economic progress, notably in the wake of
post–World War II economic growth and, more specifically, the civil rights
revolution (1954–65).

The justly celebrated successes of the civil rights revolution, however, were
legal, constitutional, and political rather than economic. As innumerable
studies since 1965 have made abundantly clear, in spite of the sustained
growth of the black middle class, blacks still earn far less than whites. The
staggering growth of an urban black underclass during these years casts an
ominous pall over the notion of black economic progress. In fact, it suggests
that city life, like the southern plantations of yesteryear, has increasingly
contributed to the impoverishment and economic marginalization of far too
many blacks. If the prospects of cities seemed awesome, the perils have proven
equally awesome. In the city, not unlike the country, racism has diminished the
quality of black life.

A major theme in the twentieth-century experience of African Americans,
urbanization has nationalized the locus of African American life and culture.
In 1890, 90 percent of all blacks lived in the South and 80 percent of all blacks
were rural (85 percent of southern blacks were rural). By 1950, 52 percent
were living in cities. The black central-city population had grown to 15.3
million in 1980, up from 6.1 million in 1950. There were two major waves of
black migration, both driven primarily by the lure of economic opportunity
associated with World Wars I and II. Over a million and a half blacks left the
South between 1910 and 1930, with a large number leaving between 1916
and 1919, the years of the Great Migration. Whereas most of these black
migrants headed to northern cities like New York, Detroit, and Chicago, an
important destination of the World War II–inspired movement were West

Coast cities like Los Angeles, Oakland, Portland, and Seattle. Between 1940 and 1945, for instance, the black population of Los Angeles increased from 75,000 to 150,000.

The growth of black urban populations tended to exacerbate racial tensions. The threat of black economic competition compounded by racist fears and anxieties made for a deadly combination. Interracial flare-ups in many cases led to violence, riots, and death. Obstacles notwithstanding, the quixotic lure of the city persisted as the figures show. Especially important to the romance of black urban life earlier in this century was the hope and propaganda emanating from prominent black urban communities like Chicago's Southside and New York's Harlem. The severe blow of the Depression in the 1930s served to heighten the rural southern black exodus to the city, where hard times often continued. A fascinating cultural expression of the migration phenomenon is the transformation of the Mississippi Delta blues into the urban blues of places like Memphis, Detroit, and most notably Chicago. Black music, like other aspects of black culture, was transformed in the urban context.

The history of the blues in the first half of the twentieth century signifies a shift toward an individualized, solo musical style away from the more traditional communal style. Consonant with mainstream American values—personified by the individualism of leaders like Booker T. Washington at the turn of the century—at first glance this development plainly illustrates the secularization of the traditional cultural ethos. Upon closer inspection, however, it reveals the persistence of various elements from traditional African-based communal music as well. These include polyrhythms, improvisation, and call and response. The persistence of the traditional—the African—amid the modern (and postmodern) in black culture reflects a profound creative tension between the old and the new, the sacred and the secular, that continues to give this culture much of its power and influence. Likewise, the blues is an African American art form with a symbiotic relationship to American culture. Over time the blues has both figured prominently in the evolution of and enjoyed a fertile symbiosis with other musical genres, including jazz, country, pop, rhythm and blues, rock and roll, and soul. This invigorating reciprocity reflects the hybrid reality not only of the blues and black culture but also of American music and American culture generally. The perpetual dynamic of cultural interpenetration represents the continuing vitality of creolization.

Another area where black adaptability has been put to the test in the twentieth century has been the elaboration of separate black institutions within segregated black communities. Needless to say, these churches, schools, hospitals, banks, insurance companies, stores, funeral homes, and the like have performed indispensable functions and continue to do so in many areas in spite of our society's efforts at desegregation and integration. Given the history of racism in this country, it should be expected that the goal of color-blind institutions will be a long-range struggle. Far too much of the black experience is invested in black institutions for blacks simply to quit them for mainstream ones. Rather, the transition to color-blind institutions—provided this is truly what our society wants—must be a reciprocal process, a continuing expression of this nation's ongoing creolization. "Black" institutions, like comparable ethnic/racial ones, must merge more successfully into a mainstream, working to enhance the quality of life in "black" communities.

The civil rights movement produced enormous changes in our national life and culture. The Civil Rights Act of 1964 outlawed Jim Crow segregation in education, voting, and most areas of public accommodation. The Voting Rights Act of 1965 sought to remove all remaining barriers to full black political participation. The locally based, grass roots southern insurgency that brought about these changes represented in a lot of ways the most important social movement of our time. The modern black struggle for freedom—part of the worldwide and domestic freedom struggles of people of color—sent shock waves throughout the world, internationalizing and solidifying that movement's support. While the leadership of those like Martin Luther King, Jr., Fannie Lou Hamer, Ella Baker, and Malcolm X was crucial, even more important were the sacrifices of thousands of ordinary citizens who seized the moment and altered American life and culture forever.

Of course the civil rights movement, and in its wake the Black Power movement, developed out of the ongoing liberation struggle that had experienced ups and downs since the late nineteenth century, the nadir of race relations. In the early twentieth century W. E. B. Du Bois had led the growing black opposition to Booker T. Washington's accommodationist, conciliatory economic nationalism. Harking back to the agitational black political style of the nineteenth century, Du Bois and others like Ida B. Wells argued for a forthright stance against racial injustice. Similarly the appeal of Marcus Garvey's Universal Negro Improvement Association in the 1920s, with roots in both racial pride and alienation from the larger society, revealed the depth of the nationalist strain. The efforts of organizations like the National Association for the Advancement of Colored People (NAACP), founded in 1909 and committed to a legalistic approach, and the National Urban League, founded in 1911 and committed to an economic approach, likewise demonstrated the expanding assault on segregation and discrimination. The global struggle against anti-Semitism, fascism, colonialism, and racism assumed center stage during World War II and established the larger historical framework for Jim Crow's demise.

In addition to traditions of leadership, ideology, and institutions, the modern civil rights movement also built upon traditions of grass roots support. The stunning success of the year-long Montgomery, Alabama, bus boycott (1955–56) in desegregating that city's buses has come to overshadow earlier, less-protracted battles like the successful week-long effort to desegregate the city buses in Baton Rouge, Louisiana, in 1953. Still, in Montgomery and in local communities throughout the South the backbone of the civil rights insurgency was the black church, expanding upon its own resistance traditions. For its organizational efforts, financial backing, mass support, and leadership, the southern black church was pivotal. The emergence of Martin Luther King, Jr., as the movement's key spokesman, from his leadership of the Montgomery bus boycott to his assassination in 1968, personified this critical link.

In the South the boycotts, sit-ins, marches, and similar tactics of civil disobedience ultimately forced the federal government to outlaw Jim Crow segregation and discrimination. The failure of the government to address the grievances of blacks in the North and West, however, in the context of rising expectations fueled by the successes of the southern struggle, contributed to a devastating outbreak of urban riots. After hundreds of deaths and millions of dollars in property damages and losses, a National Advisory Commission on Civil Disorders in 1969 maintained that the United States was fast becoming two societies: black and white, separate and unequal. Fifteen years after the Supreme Court had declared school segregation unconstitutional in the landmark *Brown v. Board of Education of Topeka* (1954), the dilemma of racial segregation and its attendant forms of inequality had been alleviated in some areas but unfortunately, as the commission report made clear, had worsened in others.

The logic of the civil rights movement evolved into the Black Power movement, which comprised a wide variety of efforts to promote black pride and black self-determination. The uncompromising leadership of Malcolm X— with its racialist, nationalist, and internationalist expressions—personified and powerfully influenced this phase of the struggle. After his assassination in 1965, Malcolm X became far more influential as he came to exemplify black militancy. A vital aspect of Black Power, besides the call for black control of black community institutions, was the call for a revitalized cultural awareness. Recalling the militant "New Negro" of the turn of the century and the literary and artistic Harlem Renaissance of the twenties, this rediscovery of self and roots in the late sixties and early seventies both built upon old traditions and endeavored to chart new directions. A most important component of this version of a revitalized black consciousness, as with the civil rights movement, was its grass roots origins and impact.

Any serious exploration of the black experience must get beyond a singular reliance on race as analytically sufficient. As the foregoing suggests, an inclusive concept like culture possesses far greater explanatory power because it captures more accurately the range, diversity, and complexity of that experience. For example, we must begin to reconfigure our understanding and writing of African American history to encompass issues of gender, class, and color. Rather than merely including the contributions of ordinary and extraordinary black women and men, we must begin to think deeply about how the socially constructed categories of female and male have influenced the black historical experience. The fruits of the exciting contemporary scholarship that seeks to conceptualize and analyze the impact of gender relations on the black experience must be more fully integrated into African American history specifically as into American history generally. A broad cultural analysis, then, not only must deal with the politics of inequality but also must confront the gender, class, and racial dimensions of that inequality.

The enduring challenge of American democracy persists. How do we as a nation address the serious contemporary and chronic social, economic, and political problems confronting African Americans? For instance, how do we improve black educational opportunity and achievement? How do we enhance the quality of life for the black poor and the black underclass? How do we deal with the alarming rate of teenage pregnancy or the epidemic of drug abuse and drug-driven violence and crime among blacks? Of course, these problems are evident throughout our society.

As this nation becomes increasingly cognizant of its diverse past, present, and future, the black historical experience—like that of other minority groups and women—must be more fully understood and appreciated, in part for what it can tell us about ourselves as a creole nation. Similarly, we need to think seriously about the meaning of our hybrid and composite national culture and the creole quality of its constituent cultures.

Finally, as a society do we really stand by our commitments to equality and justice? As we increasingly recognize limits to our national bounty, can equality of opportunity ever really be achieved? Realistically, can the idea of the equality of results ever be squared with that of equality of opportunity? The struggle continues.

FURTHER READING

Among the best reference guides are James M. McPherson et al., eds., *Blacks in America: Bibliographical Essays* (Garden City, N.Y., 1971); Richard Newman, *Black Access: A Bibliography of Afro-American Bibliographies* (Westport, Conn., 1984); and Rayford W. Logan and Michael R. Winston, eds., *Dictionary of American Negro Biography* (New York, 1982). A solid series of essays on various aspects of the field is Darlene Clark Hine, ed., *The State of Afro-American History: Past, Present, and Future* (Baton Rouge, La., 1986). Important overviews include John Hope Franklin and Alfred A. Moss, Jr., *From Slavery to Freedom: A History of Negro Americans*, 6th ed. (New York, 1988); August Meier and Elliott Rudwick, *From Plantation to Ghetto* (New York, 1976); Mary F. Berry and John W. Blassingame, *Long Memory: The Black Experience in America* (New York, 1982); Vincent Harding, *There Is a River: The Black Struggle for Freedom in America* (New York, 1981); and Lawrence W. Levine, *Black Culture and Black Consciousness: Afro-American Folk Thought from Slavery to Freedom* (New York, 1977). For family, gender, and women's history, see Herbert G. Gutman, *The Black Family in Slavery and Freedom, 1750–1925* (New York, 1976); Jacqueline Jones, *Labor of Love, Labor of Sorrow: Black Women, Work, and the Family from Slavery to the Present* (New York, 1985); and Paula Giddings, *When and Where I Enter: The Impact of Black Women on Race and Sex in America* (New York, 1984).

For the colonial period, see Peter H. Wood, *Black Majority: Negroes in Colonial South Carolina from 1670 through the Stono Rebellion* (New York, 1974); Margaret W. Creel, *"A Peculiar People": Slave Religion and Community Culture among the Gullah* (New York, 1987); T. H. Breen and Stephen Innes, *"Myne Owne Ground": Race and Freedom on Virginia's Eastern Shore, 1640–1676* (New York, 1980); Gerald W. Mullin, *Flight and Rebellion: Slave Resistance in Eighteenth-Century Virginia* (New York, 1972); Mechal Sobel, *The World They Made Together: Black and White Values in Eighteenth-Century Virginia* (Princeton, N.J., 1987); Edmund S. Morgan, *American Slavery–American Freedom: The Ordeal of Colonial Virginia* (New York, 1975); William D. Pierson, *Black Yankees: The Development of an Afro-American Subculture in Eighteenth-Century New England* (Amherst, Mass., 1988); and Winthrop D. Jordan, *White over Black: American Attitudes toward the Negro, 1550–1812* (Chapel Hill, N.C., 1968).

For the revolutionary period, Benjamin Quarles, *The Negro in the American Revolution* (New York, 1973), and Ira Berlin and Ronald Hoffman, eds., *Slavery and Freedom in the Age of the American Revolution* (Charlottesville, Va., 1983), are crucial.

Outstanding works on slavery, notably in the nineteenth century, are legion and include Sterling Stuckey, *Slave Culture: Nationalist Theory and the Foundations of*

Black America (New York, 1987); John W. Blassingame, *The Slave Community: Plantation Life in the Antebellum South* (New York, 1979); and Eugene D. Genovese, *Roll, Jordan, Roll: The World the Slaves Made* (New York, 1974). More specialized studies of note include Charles Joyner, *Down by the Riverside: A South Carolina Slave Community* (Urbana, Ill., 1984); Albert J. Raboteau, *Slave Religion: The "Invisible Institution" in the Antebellum South* (New York, 1978); and Deborah Gray White, *Ar'n't I a Woman?: Female Slaves in the Plantation South* (New York, 1985).

On the antebellum free-black community, see Gary D. Nash, *Forging Freedom: The Formation of Philadelphia's Black Community, 1720–1840* (Cambridge, Mass., 1988); Leon F. Litwack, *North of Slavery: The Negro in the Free States, 1790–1860* (Chicago, 1961); and Ira Berlin, *Slaves without Masters: The Free Negro in the Antebellum South* (New York, 1974).

Benjamin Quarles's *The Negro in the Civil War* (Boston, 1953); James M. McPherson's *The Negro's Civil War: How American Negroes Felt and Acted during the War for the Union* (Urbana, Ill., 1982); W. E. B. Du Bois's *Black Reconstruction in America: 1860–1880* (New York, 1935); and Eric Foner's *Reconstruction: America's Unfinished Revolution, 1863–1877* (New York, 1988) are valuable commentaries on the great struggle and its sequel. On emancipation, see Leon F. Litwack's *Been in the Storm So Long: The Aftermath of Slavery* (New York, 1979) and Ira Berlin et al., eds., *Freedom: A Documentary History of Emancipation, 1861–1867*, vol. 1, *The Destruction of Slavery* (Cambridge, Mass., 1985).

For the late nineteenth and early twentieth century, see August Meier, *Negro Thought in America, 1880–1915: Racial Ideologies in the Age of Booker T. Washington* (Ann Arbor, Mich., 1963), and Louis R. Harlan, *Booker T. Washington*, 2 vols. (New York, 1972, 1983). C. Vann Woodward's *The Strange Career of Jim Crow*, 3d ed. (New York, 1974), remains sound. W. E. B. Du Bois's *The Souls of Black Folks* (Chicago, 1903) is a classic.

Important works on urbanization include Kenneth L. Kusmer, *A Ghetto Takes Shape: Black Cleveland, 1870–1930* (Urbana, Ill., 1976); James Borchert, *Alley Life in Washington: Family, Community, Religion, and Folklife in the City, 1850–1970* (Urbana, Ill., 1980); and Joseph W. Trotter, Jr., *Black Milwaukee: The Making of an Industrial Proletariat, 1915–1945* (Urbana, Ill., 1985). For black migration, see James R. Grossman, *Land of Hope: Chicago, Black Southerners, and the Great Migration* (Chicago, 1989). Nathan Huggins, *Harlem Renaissance* (New York, 1971), is a significant cultural study.

Gunnar Myrdal, *An American Dilemma: The Negro Problem and Modern Democracy* (New York, 1944), is a classic. Among many works on the modern black freedom struggle are Richard Kluger, *Simple Justice: The History of Brown v. Board of Education and Black America's Struggle for Equality* (New York, 1976); Taylor Branch, *Parting the Waters: America in the King Years, 1954–1963* (New York,

1988); Aldon D. Morris, *The Origins of the Civil Rights Movement: Black Communities Organizing for Change* (New York, 1984); and Manning Marable, *Race, Reform, and Rebellion: The Second Reconstruction in Black America, 1945–1982* (Jackson, Miss., 1984). For recent developments, see two works by William J. Wilson: *The Declining Significance of Race: Blacks and Changing American Institutions* (Chicago, 1978) and *The Truly Disadvantaged: The Inner City, the Underclass, and Public Policy* (Chicago, 1987).

18 ☆ Status and

☆ Social Class

in America

☆ Edward Pessen

One of the most striking features of class in America is the widespread popular disbelief in its existence. Woodrow Wilson in 1912 observed that Americans like to think that "this is the country where there is no distinction of class, no distinction of social status." To judge from Americans' responses to modern sociologists' questionnaires, American attitudes toward class have not changed much during the past two generations. Americans either continue to assert that classes are almost totally nonexistent in this country, with what barriers there are being easily breached, or they insist that they belong to the great middle class. Nor is indifference to class confined to the moderately educated general public. Close scrutiny of the writings of American political historians reveals that most are oblivious to any interconnections between politics and class, while the few who take account of them tend to attribute slight significance to the relationship. Exceptions to this rule are such practitioners of "the new labor history" as David Montgomery, the late Herbert G. Gutman, and Alan Dawley—who, of course, are not political historians. I do not find altogether persuasive the neo-Marxist romanticization of the working class in some of the newer work.

The prevalent scholarly ignoring of class is itself a manifestation of a more inclusive American belief in what scholars call American exceptionalism. Most Americans appear to be convinced that the New World is and always has been different from and more innocent and egalitarian than the Old. The United States is indeed unique in a number of important respects, not the least in its very insistence on its uniqueness. Yet for all the undeniable singularity of American history, the evidence is abundant that classes, class lines, and distinctions of status do exist and have always existed here as elsewhere in the modern world.

☆ ☆ ☆ Definitions of Class

Before launching into a discussion of the changing face of class in America over the course of time, it is, I think, necessary to indicate precisely what is meant by the term. Controversy over the meaning of class is inevitable in view of the abstractness and complexity of the concept, its multidimensional components, the imprecision attending evaluation of such ingredients as status and prestige, and the subjectivity involved in ranking even such objective features as occupation and residence. The number of definitions of class comes close to matching the number of scholars offering definitions.

Not only do different schools of thought present their own definitions, but representatives ostensibly of the same school each tend to present a version that differs in some respects from the versions offered by others. Max Weber differentiated class from status. Marxists define classes as groups having a distinctive relationship to the means of production, discerning in modern industrial society a capitalist class, a working class, and a middle class in flux, whose members are ostensibly ascending to the class above or, supposedly in greater numbers, plummeting down to the class below. The Marxists lay great stress on "class consciousness," or what they regard as the distinctive constellation of values shared by the members of a given class.

In part because American workers seem not to share a common consciousness—divided as they have been by race, ethnicity, religion, income, and type and prestige of occupation—and in part because the American class structure seems far too complex to be captured in a three-class analytical scheme, I do not find the Marxist categories appropriate. Much more sensible, it seems to me, is an eclectic version of class, drawn from the best of what some doctrinaires deride as "mainstream" sociological thought. Not the least of its virtues is its congruence with the usage of informed and sensible Americans themselves when speaking of class and status in the United States.

The families and individuals that constitute a distinctive class are roughly similar in a number of significant respects: their level of wealth; their means of achieving it; the prestige, quality, and relative irksomeness of these means; their style of living, including their uses of leisure; their social repute (resting, among other things, on their racial, ethnic, and religious identity, the kind and the prestige of the schooling they provide their young, the organizations to which they belong, and the role they play in these organizations); the standing of the social circle within which they move and with which they are intimate (and how long they have held such standing); and the influence and power they command in their own and in the larger American community. There are other definitions of class that are no doubt simpler and easier to work with than the one offered here. But the point of a good definition is that it captures the complexity of the phenomenon it purports to describe and explain. I believe my eclectic definition corresponds well to the complex American reality and to how informed persons have perceived and understood that reality.

In differentiating Americans by class, it seems sensible to speak not of capitalists and a working class but rather of upper, middle, and lower classes, with each of these three categories in turn subdivided into an upper and lower segment. There is no suggestion here that the six-level hierarchical structure does the job perfectly; no categorizations can do full justice to the complexities that actually abound in life. But among the virtues of the recommended framework are its usefulness in portraying social differentiation over time, its correspondence both to informed usage and to the actual state of affairs at any moment, and its flexibility. The precise ingredients of upper-upper-class membership were quite different in Thomas Jefferson's America from what they were in J. Pierpont Morgan's a century later. Yet in the one era as in the other, an exclusive, fabulously wealthy, numerically minuscule, and socially and politically powerful class was a significant element of the American social order. A clue to upper-crust standing in the young James Madison's America such as the political office of justice of the peace was no longer appropriate a century later, when that and other marks of status had lost their earlier prestige. The six-level structure is flexible enough to absorb the changes that inevitably overtake the ranking of particular indicators over the course of time, while effectively accounting for the social gulf that separates groups of American families from one another at all times. In view of the dissimilarities in lifestyle and "worldview" of those in the upper and lower levels of the wage-earning category, it seems inappropriate to speak of a single working class in America, let alone of a single working-class outlook.

Sensible people will not be prisoners either to a foolish consistency or to a rigid adherence to any set of prescriptive rules of discourse. Those of us, therefore, who like W. Lloyd Warner and most other American sociologists prefer to think in terms of an evolving social structure that ranges from an upper-upper level down to a lower-lower level will nevertheless refer occasionally to the "working classes"—just as sensible Marxists have been heard to utter the phrases "upper class" and "lower class," for all their adherence to a formula that ostensibly proscribes these rubrics. While defining class is unavoidable in any serious discussion of its operations, good sense suggests that no definition be invariably or strictly applied, that life and its sprawling perverseness not be subordinated to our search for clarity and intellectual order. Class is, after all, only an intellectual construct, designed to promote better understanding of the actual random chaos in any social order. Those intent on doing perfect justice to life's every nuance might insist on twelve— or even twenty-four—levels of classification. The charm of the six-level structure is not that it is correct but that, on the one hand, it is not so unwieldy as more complicated analytical schemes and that, on the other hand, it corresponds to how the human beings who are the raw stuff of class insist on thinking and speaking about their own experiences.

☆ ☆ ☆ Consequences of Class or Social Standing

However defined, class has played a highly significant role in the lives and thinking of Americans. Substantial research on American society from the revolutionary era to the present has established the manifold and powerful effects of class.

Class has controlled the quality and the quantity of the food Americans eat, the clothes they wear, their household furnishings and other possessions, the attractiveness or lack thereof of their homes and neighborhoods, the very air they breathe, the extent of their leisure and the kind of uses to which it is put, whether or not they have to work, and whether their work is fatiguing, demoralizing, and irksome or attractive and fulfilling. It determines their social universe and their sexual behavior, the quality of their marriages, and their fertility. The quality of education and the "socialization experiences" of children have been found to vary by social class, resulting in dissimilar characteristics in children from different social classes and ultimately in different positions in adult society. In the twentieth-century United States the comparatively higher rates of emotional and psychological dysfunction among the poor have been disclosed in a great number of psychiatric studies. Class has much to do with the diseases people are likely to suffer and the remedies they are able to afford, whether medicine, hospitalization, rest cures, or other. The scholarly literature makes clear the positive correlation between crime and social class. Class influences the kind of crimes people commit, the quality of legal defense they can obtain, the severity of the punishments they are likely to receive. Indeed, class has affected not only the quality of people's lives but how long they have lived. A study of early nineteenth-century Philadelphia showed that class strongly affected longevity. One hundred and fifty years later class continues to affect human longevity.

More problematic, though not less important, than the above catalog of what might be called the measurable consequences of class are the intangible and elusive effects of class on the thoughts, feelings, and values of people. The complexity of the matter is suggested by the fact that individuals engaged in the same occupation, living lives that are quite similar in tangible respects, will nevertheless respond quite differently to their similar experiences. Gutman and Montgomery have focused on the radical, in some cases revolutionary, militance of some blue-collar workers over the course of American history. Yet, for reasons that will doubtless continue to be a source of controversy among scholars, the great majority of American working people, although in "the same boat" as their militant colleagues, have not been moved to challenge the social, economic, and political order responsible for their plight.

If class is a significant element in contemporary American life, that is because it always has been a significant element in American life. It is true that the precise ingredients of class have varied from one time to another, and the relative proportions enrolled in the differing classes have changed, as have the gaps between the adjacent classes on the social ladder. But as even a swift glance at American history makes clear, class and status distinctions emerged during the nation's colonial beginnings and have subsequently retained their importance, notwithstanding the modifications inevitably produced by time.

☆ ☆ ☆ Class Structures in Early America

It is a commonplace among historians of colonial America that, despite dissimilarities in the lives and institutions of the people in the three great geographical sections (New England, the Middle Colonies, and the South), society in each area was vitally affected by class and class differences. An upper crust emerged, whatever the topography, the crops, the labor system, or the chief industries of a locale or region. The "better sort," as they liked to describe themselves, were richer and more envied and powerful by far than the "meaner sort" below. Whether their affluence was due to slaves and landownership as was true of the Izards, Drytons, and Middletons in South Carolina and the Byrds, Carters, and Carys in Virginia; to land, livestock, and commerce as was true of the Lloyds, Pembertons, Norrises, and other friends of William Penn in Pennsylvania and the Van Rensselaers, DePeysters, and Beekmans in New York; or to land, fishing, shipbuilding, and commerce as was true of the Jacksons, Cabots, and Crowninshields in New England—the small colonial upper-upper class lived lives dramatically unlike those of the small proprietors and business people, the professionals and clerks, the skilled artisans and small farmers, the laborers, indentured servants, and black slaves who composed the great bulk of American society. In view of the simple and crude, if not primitive, standards of housing, clothing, sustenance, and uses of leisure of the overwhelming majority of colonial Americans, the sybaritic and costly splendor of upper-class life-styles was all the more remarkable. The upper crust came close to monopolizing the positions of influence, whether in the governors' councils or legislative assemblies of the colonies or in the lay groups, such as the vestries in Virginia, that shaped the policies of the then extremely influential church bodies.

No one knows precisely what proportions of the colonial population were "enrolled" in the different social classes, but unquestionably only a tiny fraction composed the higher social orders, commanding inordinate prestige and influence, while the great mass that belonged to the lower rankings had neither admired status nor power. Informed sociologists place about 1 percent of the twentieth-century American population in the upper-upper class; between 1 and 2 percent in the lower-upper (of almost equally great wealth as the upper-upper class, but *nouveau* and of slightly lesser prestige); 9 to 10 percent in the upper-middle (prosperous if not rich businessmen and professionals); 28 to 36 percent in the lower-middle (small proprietors and farmers, clerks and skilled workers); 33 to 35 percent in the upper-lower (semiskilled working people, operatives, and agricultural labor); and 17 to 25 percent in the lower-lower (the unskilled, the unemployable, the marginal types who are the American equivalent of a *lumpenproletariat*). It is highly unlikely that the "social pyramid" in colonial America was very much less skewed, less heavily weighted toward its lower echelons than is the modern sociological model.

The United States, as all the world knows, came into being as an independent nation as a result of a revolution waged against British dominion between 1774 and 1781. Exerting a profound influence on subsequent American thinking about class in America is the fact that as Americans of all classes fought for independence, the political leaders of the society issued a ringing formal justification for the rebellion that proclaimed the equality of all men as a natural or God-given right. During the colonial past, John Locke had written a formal charter for South Carolina's landed elite that attempted to impose a feudal regime and seigneurial class distinctions in America, while throughout the society class distinctions were explicitly manifest in such disparate matters as appropriate dress, forms of address, or seating arrangements in church. In avoiding any mention of class or class distinctions—let alone any reference to the perquisites of an upper class—the Declaration of Independence taught Americans to believe that class was either nonexistent here or not germane to serious political issues.

The Declaration notwithstanding, the leaders of colonial society continued to think, after the Revolution as before, that only the few with a special or large "stake in society" could be counted on to rule responsibly.

Whatever else it accomplished, the American Revolution did not undermine the class system, nor did it weaken the barriers between the classes that had been erected during the colonial era. Indubitably, a new and more democratic political order did emerge on both the national and state levels. Some social amelioration was also introduced, although not nearly so far-reaching nor dramatic as was claimed two generations ago by the historian J. Franklin Jameson (*The American Revolution Considered as a Social Movement*, 1926). Exalted standing and undue influence could no longer be obtained by sycophants of an overseas monarch. Fortunes were carved out in wartime by "new men." And yet, even if voting rights were broadened, the powers of popularly elected legislatures increased, and relatively plebeian men were elected to such bodies more noticeably in the wake of the Revolution, actual political power continued to be largely concentrated in the hands of a small number of individuals, who were themselves of or beholden to the monied men in their states and localities. Insofar as wealth is a clue to class, wealth tended to become more unequally distributed after the Revolution than it had been before. New wealth holders did not supplant so much as they supplemented the accumulators of the earlier time.

☆ ☆ ☆ Class Lines Following the Revolution

In the classic periodizations that most American historians continue to rely on, the two centuries following the end of the Revolution are usually broken up into the early national period, roughly 1783–1820, which I have already briefly described; the Jacksonian era, 1820–50; the era of Civil War and Reconstruction, 1850–77; the "Gilded Age," 1877–1900; the Progressive Era, 1900–1920; normalcy and the Great Depression, 1920 to the mid-1930s; the New Deal and World War II; and the modern or contemporary era. If the Jacksonian era is often described as the "era of the common man" or the "age of egalitarianism," it is because a long-enduring conventional scholarly wisdom held that it was during the pre–Civil War decades that class lines in America were hardest to detect, class barriers most easily surmounted, and upper-crust power most negligible. The chief architect of this intellectual edifice was the brilliant young French visitor Alexis de Tocqueville.

Tocqueville's *Democracy in America*, published in 1835 and 1840, is arguably the single most influential book ever written about American society. Its version of the American social structure, although based more on logic and hearsay than on the factual evidence that its author had little interest in unearthing, was nevertheless long taken as gospel by most students of American society. In Tocqueville's egalitarian social portrait, one American was treated as the equal of another, no matter what their circumstances of birth; wealth was almost equally distributed, at least among native-born whites; and a "tyranny of the majority" over opinion, values, and politics prevailed in a kaleidoscopic milieu where fortunes were regularly made, lost, and regained and where almost all wealthy men had felt in their youth the "sting of want." Alas, this charming canvas of a crude but exhilarating social democracy has been largely demolished by modern research.

In actuality, wealth during the era was distributed perhaps more unequally than at any other time in American history. Nor was age, as some scholars have recently argued, the essential explanation of the maldistribution. Rural and urban working people of whatever age were not in on the good thing. Huge commercial fortunes in the North and landed fortunes in the South, combined with the marginal incomes earned by farmers and artisans, produced a skewed distribution in which the richest one-hundredth of the nation's families owned more than one-third of the wealth, the richest tenth owned more than four-fifths, and most adults owned no property that commanded any market value whatsoever.

The upper crusts lived as though by a strict rule of social endogamy, confining their intimate relationships, their marriages, and their uses of leisure to the rarified elite who moved in their own exclusive social universe. Very few of them appear to have been what Henry Clay at the time called "self-made men." Such well-publicized "rags-to-riches" stories as those of John Jacob Astor, born to a German family of modest standing and circumstances, and his partner Cornelius Heeney, who came to Brooklyn from Ireland with one dollar in his pocket, were taken to be typical when in fact their career lines were most unusual. The great fortunes that were amassed during the era were created not by "new men" but primarily by the sons and relatives of the great wealth holders of an earlier time. It is true that the social and economic elite became increasingly unwilling to participate directly in government; however, a growing volume of studies of local and state politics discloses the great extent to which local and state governments deferred to the presumed interests of the era's large property owners.

For all his possession of the suffrage and the right to hold office, the common man rarely infiltrated the entrenched machines that in most places controlled the major parties and policy-making. Tocqueville had said that in America commoners rule "as does the Deity over the universe." The young

Marx remarked that their possession of the suffrage represented the "political emancipation" of the masses in America—a first step that would soon be followed by their social and economic emancipation. It seems that both pundits misinterpreted the evidence.

☆ ☆ ☆ Social Mobility in the "Gilded Age"

The emergence of a triumphant or mature industrialism in the decades after the Civil War inevitably modified the class order and its operations but did nothing to reduce the gulfs between the classes or the impact of class on American life. At one end of the scale, fortunes of unprecedented magnitude were converted into life-styles, dwellings, and furnishings of almost crass sumptuousness, flaunted in accord with the materialistic values that flourished during what Mark Twain called the "Gilded Age." At the other end of the scale, growing armies of industrial labor, swelled by an influx of non-English-speaking, largely docile, and desperately needy immigrants, settled for conditions both in and out of the shop that rarely met the minimal standards of decent living that the national government for the first time had begun to publicize. Nor did farmers fare well under the "new industrial order," as the "populist revolt" made dramatically clear.

For all the pervasiveness of the view that the era's "tycoons" had risen from humble circumstances here or abroad, the facts were otherwise. Horatio Alger's more than one hundred novels popularized the fiction that the race for economic glory went to plucky, lucky, and hardworking youths of modest origins. The patient empirical research of economic historian William Miller and his students has disclosed that poor boys who became business leaders "have always been more conspicuous in American history books than in American history."

There is, of course, more to social mobility than the leap from the bottom of the scale to the top. Studies of the career paths taken by the sons and daughters and the grandchildren of the poor immigrants who came to America at the turn of the century reveal that a significant amount of upward movement did occur, if primarily confined to what sociologists call "small-distanced" steps. In trying to understand the relative contentment of most Americans and their aversion to radical and socialist doctrines, it is useful to keep in mind that upward movement that may seem slight or barely discernible statistically could nevertheless be of very great significance to the people who experience it. For that matter, census and statistical evidence indicating that many people in the nineteenth century were assessed for no property whatever does not mean that they were down and out. Household possessions that might have no market value could yet be of inestimable importance to the human beings who owned them. We do not live by statistical data alone.

☆ ☆ ☆ Class in the Twentieth Century

The United States in the twentieth century became finally and irreversibly an urban society—a society whose perfected transportation and communication networks, according to sociologist E. Digby Baltzell, paved the way for the creation of a "national upper class." The latter group is neither homogeneous nor monolithic, however. In the late twentieth century "*the* American class structure" remains only a figure of speech. There may be a single structure in the usage of scholarly analysts; but in life, communities of dissimilar age, size, population, resources, wealth, economic activity, and complexity also differ in class and social structures.

Regional and community disparities have disappeared in our time. In the small "Yankeetown" (actually Newburyport, Massachusetts) investigated more than fifty years ago by W. Lloyd Warner and his associates, every informed person might have been able to place every other townsperson in the appropriate social niche. Such rankings, based on the intimate knowledge one might acquire of every family in a small community, are impossible in a great metropolis, most of whose residents are strangers to one another. As for class in what Daniel Bell and others call "post-industrial America," striking changes have occurred, particularly in the balance between blue-collar and white-collar wage earners, but the evidence and its significance remain to be searchingly investigated.

It does seem clear, however, even before the empirical evidence on the late twentieth century is unearthed and its implications are considered, that a number of recent developments have been modifying both the American class structure and some of the traditional indices to the six social levels of which that structure is composed. Higher education, for example, which before 1900 was attainable by perhaps one young person (age eighteen to twenty-four) out of one hundred and as late as 1940 was accessible to less than one out of ten of this age group, was by 1980 available to more than three out of ten. It can be argued that in view of these changes college attendance has lost its former significance as a clue to class standing. The modern sociologists who consign roughly 87 percent of the population to the lower-middle, the upper-lower, and lower-lower classes obviously do not equate enrollment, say, in a publicly financed community college with family membership in either the upper-middle or the upper classes.

☆ ☆ ☆ Contemporary American Attitudes toward Class

These scholars no doubt have a point. Persons at the lower levels of the social hierarchy today may be able to do certain things and enjoy benefits that were once unknown to them, but that does not mean that social stratification has disappeared or that the walls dividing classes from one another have crumbled. Sharp disparities of wealth, life-style, prestige, and influence remain. Yet if the American class structure and the relative contentment of those occupying its lower echelons are to be understood, it is important not to underestimate the significance of *absolute* improvements in living conditions. Certainly a focus on these changes places the American social order in clearer perspective when it is compared to social orders elsewhere.

That young people in the United States attend college in proportions undreamed of elsewhere in the world is a fact of American life that understandably induces relative contentment in Americans and envy in others. That a happy combination of circumstances enables the American economy, for all its problems, to provide even to those near the bottom of the social ladder a level of creature comforts indubitably superior to what their peers enjoyed earlier in American history and seemingly beyond the expectations of the great majority of persons elsewhere may help explain why—for all the disparities that continue to mark the American class structure—criticism of its inequities evokes so slight a response among working people in America. Statistics on wages point to a substantial increase in the real earnings of American workers over the course of the past century. The imbalance between the classes may be continuing, but surely it is an important matter that the material circumstances of those at the lower levels of the social order appear to have improved markedly from one generation to another—at least in this century.

The United States presents a paradoxical scene in which most of its citizens seem altogether oblivious to the significance, even to the very existence, of the class distinctions that in fact play so central a part in American life. The importance of this attitude should not be discounted, for it is by now a commonplace of social thought that what a people think is true constitutes a significant element of the social reality, no matter how inaccurate the thought may be. Nor is the popular perception altogether distorted.

In contrast to many other societies, America wears its class system lightly and unobtrusively. It is not insignificant that Americans experienced no titled aristocracy, that they feel no need formally to defer to a hereditary privileged group in their midst, that they believe that meritocracy rather than aristocracy increasingly determines high place not only in the entertainment fields, the arts, and the professions, but in what might be called worldly affairs as well. No less significant, however, are the continued operations of class in America.

For all the improvements in the material circumstances of those in the lower social order in modern America, influence and power appear to be no more accessible to them now than earlier in American history. At least that is the burden of most of the recent "community studies." With regard to opportunity, the situation is complex. In recently searching out the social backgrounds of the most prolific composers of the great popular songs of the 1920s and 1930s, I discovered that almost all appear to have been uniquely and innately gifted. And yet almost all of them were born to the advantages and opportunities that were available solely to members of the three upper clusters, inhabited by a mere tenth of the population. The rule may turn out to be that success in America is indeed most available to the gifted and creative— but to the gifted and creative who can pursue success on the inside track of unusually fortunate social and economic circumstances. As always in American history, class continues to be significant but also complex, changing, and elusive.

FURTHER READING

A useful recent collection of theoretical and methodological approaches to class is Peter M. Blau, ed., *Approaches to the Study of Social Structure* (New York, 1975). An older but still useful and more comprehensive discussion is Reinhard Bendix and Seymour M. Lipset, eds., *Class, Status, and Power: Social Stratification in Comparative Perspective* (New York, 1966). Dennis Gilbert and Joseph A. Kahl, *The American Class Structure* (Homewood, Ill., 1982), is a balanced introductory text. Robert K. Merton, *Social Theory and Social Structure* (Glencoe, Ill., 1957), contains the insights of one of the most brilliant sociologists. Bernard Barber, *Social Stratification: A Comparative Analysis of Structure and Process* (New York, 1957), is an informed and sensible interpretation. A study that focuses more on conflict is Anthony Giddens, *The Class Structure of the Advanced Societies* (New York, 1973). Richard Sennett and Jonathan Cobb, *The Hidden Injuries of Class* (New York, 1972), is a sensitive discussion of working people's feelings about class.

Classic older studies are the influential W. Lloyd Warner and Paul S. Lunt, *The Social Life of a Modern Community* (New Haven, Conn., 1941); two seminal books by Robert S. Lynd and Helen M. Lynd, *Middletown: A Study in Contemporary American Culture* (New York, 1929), and *Middletown in Transition: A Study in Cultural Conflicts* (New York, 1937); and Thorstein Veblen, *The Theory of the Leisure Class* (New York, 1899), a brilliant satirical critique of the values of the monied classes.

Jackson T. Main, *The Social Structure of Revolutionary America* (Princeton, N.J., 1965), is one of the few studies by a historian of the class structure of an important period. Edward Pessen, *Riches, Class, and Power: America before the Civil War* (New Brunswick, N.J., 1990), examines diverse aspects of upper-class life in the urban Northeast. Stephan Thernstrom, *Poverty and Progress: Social Mobility in a Nineteenth-Century City* (Cambridge, Mass., 1964), is an insightful analysis of working-class opportunity in a small New England port in the post–Civil War decades. Alan Dawley, *Class and Community: The Industrial Revolution in Lynn* (Cambridge, Mass., 1976), is a flawed but imaginative and provocative examination of the effects of technological change on class relationships. John N. Ingham, *The Iron Barons: A Social Analysis of an American Urban Elite, 1874–1921* (Westport, Conn., 1978), takes a quantitative approach supplemented by rich "qualitative data." Stuart M. Blumin, *The Emergence of the Middle Class: Social Experience in the American City, 1760–1900* (New York, 1989), is a historian's treatment of the elusive middle class. E. Digby Baltzell's essay *The Protestant Establishment: Aristocracy and Caste in America* (London, 1965) ranges over the entire American past. A recent comprehensive overview of the interrelationship between class and power in the American past is Edward Pessen, "Social Structure and Politics in American History," *American Historical Review* 87 (December 1982). Influential studies that focus on the class consciousness of the working class are Herbert G. Gutman, *Work, Culture, and Society in Industrializing America: Essays in America's Working Class and Social History* (New York, 1977), and two books by David Montgomery: *Workers' Control in America: Studies in the History of Work, Technology, and Labor Struggles* (New York, 1980) and *The Fall of the House of Labor: The Workplace, the State, and American Labor Activism* (New York, 1987).

Possibly the most influential—certainly the most popular—accounts of social mobility in America are Horatio Alger's more than one hundred novels, dramatizing the roles played by hard work, virtue, pluck, and luck in the rise "from rags to riches." More scholarly treatments of the American cult of success are Irvin G. Wyllie, *The Self-Made Man in America: The Myth of Rags to Riches* (New York, 1966); John G. Cawelti, *Apostles of the Self-Made Man: Changing Concepts of Success in America* (Chicago, 1965); and Moses Rischin, ed., *The American Gospel of Success* (Chicago, 1965). A classic older study that attributed success primarily to genetic factors is Pitirim Sorokin, *Social Mobility* (New York, 1927). The authoritative study on occupations as a measure of social standing and mobility is Peter M. Blau and Otis Dudley Duncan, *The American Occupational Structure* (New York, 1967).

Bendix and Lipset, *Class, Status, and Power* (cited above), contains several valuable studies of social mobility, as does Edward Pessen, ed., *Three Centuries of Social Mobility in America* (Lexington, Mass., 1974).

The most influential community study is probably Robert A. Dahl, *Who Governs?: Democracy and Power in an American City* (New Haven, Conn., 1961), which, while finding power increasingly dispersed or "pluralistic," concludes that the "notables" at the apex of the social structure command inordinate power. Dahl sought to refute Floyd Hunter, *Community Power Structure: A Study of Decision Makers* (Chapel Hill, N.C., 1953), which located power in Atlanta in a "covert elite." G. William Domhoff, *Who Really Rules?: New Haven and Community Power Reexamined* (Santa Monica, Calif., 1978), is a sharp refutation of Dahl's pluralist thesis. Good overviews on this theme are Marvin E. Olson, ed., *Power in Societies* (New York, 1970), and Andrew S. McFarland, *Power and Leadership in Pluralist Systems* (Stanford, Calif., 1969).

For rich entertainment as well as edification on the place of class in America, one should read the novels of James Fenimore Cooper, Edith Wharton, William Dean Howells, Theodore Dreiser, John P. Marquand, and Louis Auchincloss.

19 ☆ The American

☆ System of

☆ Education

☆ John B. Orr

In 1642 Americans took their first steps toward establishing a system of public schools that ultimately would offer educational services to every child in the nation. To be sure, these steps were tentative and limited—the colony of Massachusetts merely passed a law assigning responsibility for the education of children to parents. In 1647, however, Massachusetts extended this commitment to education by passing another, more radical law that required every town to provide its children with schools and schoolmasters. Within forty years virtually all of the American colonies had followed Massachusetts's example. By the end of the seventeenth century it was clear that citizens of the English colonies were to be educated; literacy was to be encouraged in order that children might be exposed to religious truths, that they might be prepared to deal with the uncertainties of colonial frontier life, and that some might develop the skills necessary for conducting the political, economic, and religious affairs of the colonies.

☆ ☆ ☆ Education: Foundation of Democracy

In the years that followed, especially after American independence in 1783, what occurred must be reckoned as a minor miracle of social construction—a feat that is not yet sufficiently acknowledged by the American people. In the space of slightly more than two hundred years Americans liberally taxed themselves to build an elaborate educational system; they created thousands of school districts, reserved public lands for schools, built a vast number of well-equipped school buildings, educated and employed an army of professional educators and educational administrators, and, finally, required American children to spend a large percentage of their childhood hours in public schools. By the mid-twentieth century all states provided free education for children between the ages of six and eighteen, with a number of states extending this right to a public education to include five-year-olds and the first two years of college. In 1990 approximately seventy of every one hundred American youths completed at least twelve years of schooling, with about twelve million moving on to enroll in colleges and universities.

During the early national period, Thomas Jefferson became an aggressive advocate for the need to create this kind of large-scale system of public schools, and his leadership must be regarded as one of the main reasons why a succession of steps toward constructing a comprehensive approach to education was taken. Having been persuaded that the new nation required a citizenry with "a certain degree of instruction," Jefferson urged the Virginia legislature to implement his plan for "a More General Diffusion of Knowledge." Virginia's subsequent ventures into the support of education were replicated in one way or another in other states. Permanent funds were created to support the building of schools and the employment of schoolmasters. In some states lotteries were organized to provide funds; in other places special tax revenues were allocated. In at least one case legislation required able-bodied males to help construct the needed school facilities.

These early efforts were quickly supplemented by the Northwest Ordinance of 1787, which (again with Jefferson's strong support) mandated each township in the nation's Northwest Territory to reserve for educational purposes at least a mile-square section of land in order to nurture the "religion, morality, and knowledge . . . necessary to good government and the happiness of mankind." The ordinance also required each state in the territory to identify townships where publicly supported institutions of higher education could be built. The whole system was designed to build a natural aristocracy in contrast to that of Europe, which emphasized heredity and wealth. This new system would groom men of talent to accept the high responsibilities of self-government in the New World.

A few decades later, under the leadership of Andrew Jackson and others, Jefferson's attempt to build a new aristocracy drew heavy criticism, but there was no decline in the widespread support for public education. Although Jacksonian Democrats viewed colleges and universities as "haunts of dandies," "lairs for condescending foxes," and "protectors of the well-born and stupid," they expected public schools to serve as social equalizers and as places where every child could have access to a solid, basic education. The schools were to be a powerful democratic force, directed toward the cultivation of a nation "wherein every man may be viewed as belonging to a new royalty."

Before the Civil War in the 1860s, there was little taste for laws that coerced children of any age to attend school. Citizens took seriously the principle that government should be limited, and for most people it was sufficient that the laws of the majority of the states held parents legally responsible for the education of their children. Parents alone, Americans often asserted, had the right and responsibility to determine the extent to which children needed formal schooling. Moreover, the limited involvement of American children in schools was comfortably consistent with the needs for child labor in an expansive industrial nation. In this era the so-called right of children to a public education was not yet firmly established; in many cases the claim competed weakly with the needs of the industrial development of the nation and the economic well-being of families.

☆ ☆ ☆ Assimilation through the Public School System

After the Civil War other forces encouraged America to consider compulsory education—especially the rapid rise of cities on the American landscape and the surge of Eastern and Southern European immigrants into these cities. The earlier immigrants to the United States largely had been Western Europeans, and although their arrival had placed strains on the cities, these immigrants had been relatively compatible with America's Anglo-Saxon traditions. The post–Civil War immigrants, however, elicited fears. Their arrival in the cities seemed to promote an urban culture undermining the foundations of democracy. The image of the city child conveyed by church publications, women's journals, and itinerant lecturers implied a national scandal. The urban child was viewed as neglected, unschooled, economically exploited, and—even worse—a potential source of urban disorder and crime.

Consequently, compulsory education laws proliferated at an astonishing rate. In 1870, 6.5 million five-to-sixteen-year-olds were in the public schools; by 1880, that number had grown to 15.5 million. In 1870, only 57 percent of school-age children and youths were in school; in 1880, 72 percent were there.

This unprecedented expansion of the public schools burdened the facilities and staffs that had been built in the period before compulsory education laws. School systems purchased property and erected buildings as rapidly as possible, but for a long period many of the nation's schools had to be housed in shabbily furnished, rented space that was widely regarded as unfit and as a sign of public neglect. Teachers were overloaded. After all, the teaching profession had been recruited to service a system of schools that was considerably smaller—a system whose staff already had been decimated by the flow of male teachers into the Civil War's military service. When compulsory education laws multiplied, a shortage of teachers developed, and school systems found themselves in the difficult position of having to locate new sources of educational professionals to service their expanding population of students. For the time being, the answer to their problem was to transform teaching into a "women's profession" and to support educational expansion by opening up new career opportunities for women.

Although the period of transition elicited by compulsory education laws was marked by strain, it was also a period in which the main lines of the modern American education system were established. It would be an overstatement to claim that the American education system was "set in concrete" during the latter part of the nineteenth century and early part of the twentieth century—that is, that everything that has occurred since then has merely been a variation of an earlier pattern. But it certainly is the case that fundamental assumptions about the American educational system were shaped in that era. Since then, education has often been the focus of politics. Americans have argued about such issues as federal aid to school districts, the appropriateness of prayer and religious instruction in the public schools, the allocation of state resources to private (especially religious) schools, and the utilization of schools to achieve social justice. Still, for over a hundred years there has seldom been a major public reevaluation of the fundamental assumptions about how schools are organized, who they serve, and how they are staffed.

☆ ☆ ☆ Universal

Since the late nineteenth century Americans have been in agreement, for example, that their educational system should be *universal*. To be sure, until well into the 1960s a number of states and districts self-consciously maintained separate schools and colleges for black students, a situation that had been declared unconstitutional in a long series of Supreme Court decisions since the mid-1950s. Nevertheless, even in the most segregated circumstances there was never a doubt that the public at large was obligated to provide some form of educational service for all students of school age. So deep has been this sense of obligation that Americans characteristically have spoken of a "right to education," which belongs to all children and youths who reside within the boundaries of the United States and its territories. Translated into action, this "right to education" has meant that children within an age range that has been legislatively defined can claim educational services that are supported by public taxation.

In some states and districts, the "right to education" begins at age five, when children may (or must) enter kindergarten. In others, it begins at age six. In some areas, most notably in the state of California, the "right to education" extends through the second year of higher education in community colleges, where all high school graduates regardless of the quality of their academic records or the level of their scores on aptitude or achievement tests must be admitted. The "right to education" also has meant that school systems must provide for the needs of exceptional students—the blind, the deaf, and persons with other physical or emotional handicaps. It is not unusual, for example, for school districts to provide instruction for children who are confined to the wards of rehabilitation hospitals or criminal justice facilities.

☆ ☆ ☆ Decentralized

Americans have been in agreement, also, that their education system will be *decentralized*. In the United States there has been no federal ministry of education, established to organize and to oversee a national education system with a uniform sequence of curriculum requirements or a uniform set of standards for the certification of educational administrators and teachers. In the recent past a Department of Education has been organized in Washington, D.C., but its function is sharply limited. In no sense can it be claimed that the Department of Education concretely administers or governs the vast array of educational institutions that provide for the educational needs of the American public. There are no federal elementary or secondary schools other than those that serve particular populations, such as the children of military personnel who are stationed outside the territorial United States.

Indeed, American public education can hardly be considered as a system at all. It is instead an extensive, complex, overlapping patchwork of individual school districts, each governed by a local school board composed of elected or appointed members. Some of these districts are "unified" in the sense that they include all of the elementary and secondary schools that are located in a geographical area. Others are limited to the administration of elementary schools or secondary schools. Still others are limited to the administration of one or more community colleges.

Within bounds defined by the U.S. Constitution, federal and state judicial decisions, and federal and state legislation, school districts have had great freedom in shaping their own programs and personnel policies—a freedom sustained by the fact that, until recently, the major sources of school financing were locally imposed taxes, supplemented only secondarily by state and federal funds. In the past few years, however, school districts have increasingly had to rely on the willingness of state legislatures to allocate money for the support of the schools, and with this trend has come a corresponding increase in state control over such matters as the selection of textbooks, curriculum, graduation requirements, and personnel policies. Still, local boards of education have actively defended their prerogatives. Few would want to surrender the immediacy of their control over the affairs of their communities' schools.

☆ ☆ ☆ Comprehensive

Americans in the past century also have assumed that their schools will be *comprehensive*, especially at the secondary (high school) level. Stated another way, there has been a broad agreement in American society that public education will not follow a strictly defined course of study but instead will offer a variety of options from which students may choose. Comprehensiveness has been a corollary of the American decision to educate the mass of the nation's children and youth, with no procedure for systematically winnowing out the academically less qualified. Providing education for such a heterogeneous group of students has necessarily involved taking account of various levels of intelligence, various career aspirations, various interests, and various levels of social experiences. Thus the typical high school has offered choices: college preparatory sequences that fulfill the entrance requirements of colleges and universities, special-interest courses that can be "elected," courses that are limited to students with demonstrably high or low academic abilities, courses that prepare students for jobs (for example, auto mechanics, drafting, health services), and even courses in which school districts and industries cooperate to provide on-the-job experience.

School districts or state legislatures usually have required as the basis for graduation particular courses (or selections from a prescribed list of options) in such areas as mathematics, science, social studies, and English. Some school districts and state legislatures even have required that students demonstrate a minimal level of competency in such areas as mathematics and the use of the English language. This concentration on required courses and on fundamental learning skills, however, traditionally has been viewed as consistent with America's commitment to comprehensiveness. Comprehensiveness in education has not implied fragmentation in the school's curriculum. Instead, it has affirmed that schools must provide options that reflect the diversity of interests and abilities of their students.

☆ ☆ ☆ Professional

Likewise, in the past century Americans have assumed that their system of public education must be managed and serviced by professional educators and administrators, that is, that education will be *professional*. Such had not always been the case. During the eighteenth and nineteenth centuries the existence of colleges of law, colleges of medicine, and seminaries had witnessed to the fact that there were extremely high expectations for persons who wanted to practice in these fields. Not so in the field of teaching. Until relatively late in the nineteenth century the preparation of teachers, when provided for at all in the academic setting, had proceeded informally within the liberal arts. Teachers had been trained largely on the job, either in an apprenticeship relationship or in an experience of trial and error. Teachers often had received their positions through political patronage and, just as often, were forced to supplement their limited salaries by taking on concurrent jobs.

After the advent of compulsory education laws, however, that situation changed. Education in America became a large-scale enterprise. This enterprise needed professionals who had fulfilled prescribed requirements, who had been awarded credentials, and who had graduated from schools devoted to the preparation of educational professionals. Teachers ceased to be "schoolkeepers" and became "educators." School boards began to expect them to graduate from colleges and universities, to be prepared in the theories of child development, "classroom management," and pedagogy, to demonstrate their adequacy in classroom instruction, and to receive teaching credentials extended under carefully prescribed state regulations. In recent years many school districts have made access to the profession even more difficult by requiring that prospective teachers must pass examinations in basic academic areas.

In short, in a period of a little more than one hundred years, Americans have developed the expectation that they can look to their schools to provide a cluster of experts, duly certified. Although the salaries of teachers and administrators seldom have been competitive with those in business and industry—or often even with salaries in the "trades"—it has been assumed that educational professionals have skills and information that justify the same trust or dependence that one affords to physicians and lawyers.

These high expectations occasionally have bred disillusionment when expectations have not been fulfilled. Indeed, Americans in the past decades have experienced a love-hate relationship with their schools. They have withdrawn tax support; they have complained about "progressive education" and about frills; and they have required teachers to sign political loyalty oaths—a practice not required of other public employees. But this wavering relationship must ultimately be viewed as a sign of the high expectations that Americans hold for educational professionals. Americans, after all, have transferred a significant portion of the nurture of their children to these professionals, and they have insisted that these educator-savants be clothed in the robes of the expert.

Within the system of education created in the United States—a system that is *universal, decentralized, comprehensive,* and *professional*—a number of issues provide the foci for perennial debate. The issues arise out of what is unique to the system itself. While they certainly are to be found in other national settings, four in particular betray their American origins.

☆ ☆ ☆ Issue 1: Curricula and National Priorities

Because education is such a large consumer of tax funds and because it touches such a large percentage of the American public on a sustained, regular basis, Americans inevitably have wondered about the degree to which schools should serve changing public priorities. An astute observer of American public educational institutions, Henry Perkinson, has argued that, from the very beginning, Americans have looked to their schools to provide panaceas for difficult national problems. For example, in the colonial era schools were expected to provide for the moral and spiritual training of the citizenry on the frontier. Later they were used to keep immigrant children off the streets and to provide avenues into the American way of life for generations of immigrant families. They were used to change attitudes toward racial equality in the post–Civil War southern states. More recently they have been used to attack problems of racial and ethnic inequality and especially to provide for a form of integration that contrasted with the segregated suburbs.

As we already have observed, Thomas Jefferson and Andrew Jackson were early American advocates of the idea that public schools exist to fulfill national priorities, particularly to encourage the growth of a national character that would support American democracy. Jefferson and Jackson, however, were not alone. Their vision was widely shared by other public figures such as Timothy Dwight of Yale, who believed that schools should serve as secular churches promoting the values necessary for decent public order, and by Horace Mann, who in nineteenth-century Massachusetts argued that public schools must carry a heavy burden in assimilating immigrant populations into American economic life.

The debate about national priorities and the schools has not been about whether the planning of curricula should somehow be isolated from the concerns of the political sphere. Rather it has been about which political ends should be served. Should the schools serve the immediate needs of the American economy? Should the schools be the front line for efforts to achieve greater racial and ethnic justice? Should the schools emphasize mass education, even at the expense of neglecting the nation's most talented students? Should the schools promote "traditional" values? Should district lines and attendance policies be drawn in such a way as to contribute to the decay of central-city schools and to the rise of high-performance suburban campuses? These are the kinds of issues that educators have discussed during recent decades.

Unfortunately, as Henry Perkinson has commented, America's educational quest for political panaceas nearly always has triggered disappointment. Citizens have wanted their public schools to advance disparate, even contradictory values, and thus, far too regularly, schools have become battlegrounds on which persons have fought with each other concerning their most deeply held beliefs. In recent years Americans have argued about whether schools should provide instruction about sex, whether schools should promote American capitalism, and even whether schools should be able to discuss subjects like evolution. The schools have not been able to be all things to all people, so invariably citizens have become angry when they have believed that their children's education has been biased against their own values. Just as important, when schools have been required to serve national priorities, they often have created other difficult problems. For example, the active use of the schools to promote racial desegregation has contributed to the explosive growth of private schools and, thus, to the possibility that central-city schools may be left as the preserve of minorities and the poor.

For such reasons historians like Diane Ravitch have urged citizens to be more realistic about their schools—to lower their political expectations. America's schools, after all, have succeeded in educating large groups of children and youth—that is, in implementing the nation's commitment to universal education. The public school system has created the needed educational prerequisites for an orderly democratic society, and perhaps, some say, that is all we can reasonably expect.

☆ ☆ ☆ Issue 2: Education and the Labor Movement

During the past decades a second important issue has been the degree to which educators have been willing to identify with the labor movement. To be an educator in the United States has been to think of oneself as a professional—to conceive of teaching as a specialized service to the community, to be trained (especially after the 1920s) in a professional school setting, and to be certified by state credentialing agencies. In spite of the fact that they seldom have received generous salaries, teachers traditionally have been identified with the clergy, physicians, lawyers, and university professors in the "learned professions."

As early as the 1950s, however, the labor movement began to make inroads into the schools, and by 1960 over 750,000 teachers were members of the American Federation of Teachers or of the National Education Association, which by then had assumed an activist, negotiating, lobbying spirit. In 1978 well over two million teachers were in the unions, and by 1980 more than 75 percent of the nation's teachers were members. The reasons for this growth were many and varied: for example, the teachers' low salaries; the proliferation of large, bureaucratic districts that were viewed as impersonal and filled with red tape; the influx of men, who successfully competed with women for high-paying administrative positions; the often-reported feeling that teachers had lost control of the conditions in which they worked; and the need for job security in the face of declining student enrollments.

There was no longer any doubt about the place of the labor movement in American education. It was thoroughly established, as much a part of the educational environment as the red apple.

The unionization of public education, however, has been a puzzling, anxiety-producing event, even for many of the teachers who have joined. Admittedly, the unions have not limited themselves solely to working out salary and security agreements. They have extended negotiations to include such issues as the length of the class day, class size, and time for preparation. That is, they have been concerned about the whole spectrum of professional working conditions. Still, as these issues have been carried to the bargaining table, poll after poll has reported that many teachers have experienced a sense of loss. Many have sensed that their professionalism has been diminished and that the relation of teachers and educational administrators has become modeled too closely after the employee-employer contract.

Especially after the early 1970s, large numbers of American citizens began to believe that teachers' unions were overly concerned about issues related to salaries and job security and not concerned enough about difficulties in the academic performance of students. Pressures mounted to develop systems of accountability that would insure care in the setting of educational goals and in evaluation and would make teachers responsible for the success of their students. By the early 1980s the pressures for reform were even greater, and in several state legislatures explicitly antiunion measures were passed—measures making it easier to dismiss ineffective teachers, limiting the rights and privileges of tenure, and instituting merit pay systems.

It is far too soon to estimate with any confidence the long-term health of the union movement in public education. What *is* clear is that teachers' unions have been in a difficult period and that they have been forced to deal more directly with issues of educational quality and accountability. These are relatively new areas for unions, and their responses to these issues are in a formative stage.

☆ ☆ ☆ Issue 3: Centralization

American educators are often troubled by the educational tradition of decentralization. Notwithstanding the high value Americans historically have placed on local control—the right of citizens to govern, through representatives, their own local schools—this kind of anarchy could not be tolerated endlessly. Citizens who move from one city to another want their children to be able to transfer easily to new classrooms, and they expect at least a relative uniformity in the curricula of school districts. In most cases they are not disappointed.

Much of the credit for the relative agreement about expectations among districts can be given to nineteenth-century publishing companies who, in the early days of the public school movement, spread a series of textbooks across the frontier. In this way publishers encouraged the idea that eastern patterns of education could be replicated in the most primitive of frontier settings and that Americans did not have to fear the educational consequences of their frontier mobility. Americans were on the move, but they carried with them schoolmasters and primers that could teach the same lessons that were available to New England stay-at-homes.

By the middle of the twentieth century most states already had organized agencies or departments of education to provide special services to local school districts and especially to encourage compatibility among the curricula of various school districts. Their primary weapon became the "curricular framework," guidelines that specified academic expectations at various grade levels. The curricular frameworks were not mandates. They did not require the local districts to fall into line with state standards, but they were a powerful force. The product of consultation among experienced educators, these guidelines took into account what was known about educational practices across the nation. The curricular frameworks quickly assumed authority and provided a reasonable counterbalance to the otherwise fragmented discussions about curriculum in the vast array of school district offices.

In the late 1960s and 1970s the states' power over local school district curricula was strengthened by the growth of statewide testing programs designed to insure accountability among teachers and administrators for the instruction they provided. The programs usually took the form of tests that were given to children at various grade levels to measure the progress of individual schools and districts in teaching basic academic skills. In the 1970s a number of states defined standards of performance that could be expected of schools that had particular socioeconomic characteristics, a practice that had the effect of further sharpening instructional goals. Some of the states went even further and specified levels of achievement that would be required for individual students to graduate from secondary schools.

This drift toward greater influence by state agencies became even more pronounced when school districts were forced to rely on state systems of taxation for their support. With the centralization of educational policy-making, doubts sometimes surfaced about whether America's system of local control was still intact.

Other observers have argued that the more fundamental tendency in American education is the movement toward a single *national* system of academic expectations. This movement, they say, is occurring under the influence of large national testing corporations, such as the Educational Testing Service, whose publications encourage citizens to compare performance on achievement and aptitude tests of students in one part of the country with that of students in another part and also to reflect on the effectiveness of the nation's educational system as a whole.

Perhaps in the future there will be a demand for the construction of a national curricular framework or at least for the universal application of a single set of academic achievement examinations. If this demand develops, the American education system will have experienced a major transformation. This system traditionally has attempted to protect the right of citizens to govern their own local schools, but the needs of an economically and technically sophisticated nation have strongly countered this commitment. The construction of a national curricular framework may well be the next step. After that there may be pressures for increasing the activity of the federal Department of Education in defining particular competencies to be taught in specific courses, especially at the secondary level. Whether this kind of centralization will develop is, of course, a matter for speculation. Certainly it is the case, however, that any further movement toward centralization will be a watershed event in the United States.

☆ ☆ ☆ Issue 4: The Quality of American Education

Since 1983 Americans have experienced a period of disillusionment with the quality of their schools, and debate about strategies for "educational reform" has been highly visible in the media, among educators, in the business community, and in state and federal governments. The immediate occasion for this period of debate and reform was the report *A Nation at Risk*, issued by the National Commission on Excellence in Education, chaired by David P. Gardner, who at that time was president-elect of the University of California. *A Nation at Risk* declared that the United States had, in effect, been committing "an act of unthinking, unilateral educational disarmament." With journalistic flair, it concluded that "if an unfriendly foreign power had attempted to impose on America the mediocre educational performance that exists today, we might well have viewed it as an act of war."

Only months after *A Nation at Risk* appeared, another report, *Action for Excellence: A Comprehensive Plan to Improve Our Nation's Schools*, escalated concern about the quality of public schools. This report, issued by the governors group of the Education Commission of the States, concluded that the nation had no "clear, compelling, and widely agreed-upon goals for improving educational performance," and it urged that business leaders, government leaders, and educators cooperate in finding solutions for America's educational deficiencies.

The ensuing debate and educational reforms tended to concentrate in the following areas.

Curriculum. Virtually all states, for example, raised academic requirements, raised entrance requirements for their college and university systems, developed programs in computer education, emphasized the teaching of higher-order reasoning skills, and revised statewide teaching programs.

Teaching preparation. Large numbers of colleges and universities voluntarily reviewed and revised their programs leading to teacher certification, and most state credentialing agencies used their authority to pressure and to reinforce the efforts of these institutions. Most attention was given to upgrading the academic preparation of teachers in the liberal arts, sometimes at the expense of training in teaching techniques and classroom management. Likewise, there were significant efforts to raise standards for admission to teacher educational programs.

The ability of the teaching profession to attract and retain highly qualified persons. In the period after 1983 teachers often received significant salary increases, countering the image of teaching as "the profession of genteel poverty." New, more highly compensated roles for experienced, excellent teachers were created (for example, "mentoring" new teachers) in order to provide opportunities for professional advancement and to create a greater salary differential between new and experienced teachers. A number of school systems began to experiment with salary systems that rewarded teaching excellence and therefore offered incentives for less-effective teachers to improve their skills.

Choice. Especially large, urban systems created "magnet" schools, where particular academic strengths (for example, in the arts, mathematics, science, humanities) were designed to attract students with specialized interests. At the same time, a number of educators and political leaders argued that the academic quality of all schools would be increased if schools were forced to compete with each other, as in American industry, for student "consumers." Following this belief, in a limited number of school districts parents were granted the opportunity to send their children to public schools of their own choice. More extreme proposals argued that families should receive public funds to support choices from the whole spectrum of "certified" public, private, and religious schools that are available in a region.

Participatory management of schools. A few large school districts also have tried to raise the academic performance of students by giving teachers and parents more authority over the curriculum and budgets of local schools. This participative style of management, it is argued, makes teachers and parents accountable for the educational development of their students and grants them the authority that this accountability requires.

Coordination of educational and social services. School districts have become seriously concerned about the large numbers of students who drop out of school programs, particularly at the junior high and senior high levels. Increasingly, these districts are finding ways to provide support services (for example, clothing, food, counseling, health services, employment, babysitting, sexual information) to assist students in meeting the problems that often force them to drop out. At this time, such programs appear to be successful in retaining students who are at risk, and this success suggests that schools may increasingly include social services for children as a regular part of their program.

The American system of education is currently experiencing a period of extreme stress, and many of the proposals for reform that are being advanced raise the possibility of a fundamental restructuring of American schools. Some observers argue that the decline of American educational quality is so severe that there will be an ever-increasing flight from public schools to private schools by more affluent families. Others argue that, as a nation,

America cannot maintain its economic leadership if it allows the academic preparation of its citizens to fall into disrepair. Thus American taxpayers and educators inevitably must find ways to assure educational excellence, and American state and federal governments must find the financial resources necessary for reform.

Stress induces creativity, and the past decade of educational reform has been marked by the coalescing of talented scholars, government leaders, and public school educators on behalf of public education. It has been a period of remarkably fine scholarship in schools of education. In impressive ways, these scholars have been applying what they know about teaching and learning to the creation of new curricula, and they have been working closely with representatives of the public schools. Thus, even while most Americans continue to be concerned about the quality of their public schools, they also are confident that their concern has generated an impressive period of experimentation and creativity.

FURTHER READING

An excellent survey of the development of the American education system is provided by Henry J. Perkinson, *The Imperfect Panacea: American Faith in Education, 1865–1965* (New York, 1968). His general thesis that Americans have expected their schools to provide solutions for vexing national problems is amply documented by other authors, for example, Ernest Moore, *Fifty Years of American Education* (Boston, 1917), and Amy Gutmann, *Democracy and Education* (Princeton, N.J., 1987). Diane Ravitch, *The Great School Wars* (New York, 1974), argues similarly as she describes the early days of the New York City schools, and David Tyack, *The One Best System* (Cambridge, Mass., 1974), extends this thesis to an account of the history of American urban education. David Tyack, Robert Lowe, and Elisabeth Hansot's *Public Schools in Hard Times* (Cambridge, Mass., 1974) brilliantly examines the emergence of reform movements in the period after the 1930s.

Twentieth-century progressivism in American education is the subject of an enormous literature. Undoubtedly the best overall analysis, however, is provided by Lawrence Cremin, *The Transformation of the School: Progressivism in American Education, 1876–1957* (New York, 1961). An excellent example of the large number of books that celebrate the progressivist tradition is J. B. Berkson, *The Ideal and the Community* (New York, 1958). Diane Ravitch, *The Troubled Crusade* (New York, 1983), traces the relatively recent attempts of educators to deal with a declining progressivist heritage and to develop educational programs for a new, politically electric era. Her book is already regarded as a definitive text.

Helpful analyses of the effect of unionism on the teaching profession are provided by Charles Perry and Wesley Wildman, *The Impact of Negotiations in Public Education: The Evidence from the Schools* (Worthington, Ohio, 1970), and by Marshal Donley, Jr., *Power to the Teacher: How America's Educators Became Militant* (Bloomington, Ind., 1976). Lawrence Cremin's *Popular Education and Its Discontents* (New York, 1990) offers an insightful analysis of the post-1983 reform period in American education, an analysis that cuts across political, sociological, philosophical, and historical issues. An alternative, politically radical critique of this same period is provided by Ira Shor, *Culture Wars* (New York, 1987).

☆ PART

☆ FOUR

☆

Varieties of

☆

☆ American Thought

☆

Taking his cue from Voltaire and James Madison, Martin Marty
☆ has pointed out elsewhere that freedom of religion in the United
States was made possible by our very multiplicity of faiths and
☆ sects. Similarly the conscience, the mind, and to a great extent the
political institutions of the United States are rooted in two symbiotic traditions that were firmly in place at the birth of the nation:
☆ the Puritan congregationalism of the seventeenth century and the
Enlightenment thought of the eighteenth, with its natural laws
☆ and natural rights. Following the demographic, cultural, and social
analyses of the previous three sections, this fourth and final part of
☆ *Making America* measures the spiritual and intellectual heartbeats
that have animated the American body for five centuries.

☆ The first three chapters—Martin Marty on "Religion in America," William Goetzmann on "Exploration and the Culture of
☆ Science," and Murray Murphey on "American Philosophy"—
present patterns of sacred and secular thought that were tightly
knotted together for most of the national experience but have
☆ become ever more specialized and alienated in modern times. The
final subheading of Murphey's chapter, "American Philosophy:
☆ From Theology toward Science," nicely states the usual relation of
the three fields today. It is inevitable, however, that this section
☆ should begin with an overview of the religious settlement and life
of America, for the ramifications of Puritan covenant theology run
☆ throughout the chapters, and historians and politicians alike continue to weigh the legacy of individualism, separatism, and com-
☆ munitarianism bequeathed to us by the seventeenth-century Bible
commonwealths.

In a sermon to the Massachusetts Bay Company in 1630, Gov-

☆

ernor John Winthrop gave a now-famous expression of the civil covenant and spiritual purpose that so deeply influenced the contracts later hammered out during the Revolution and embodied in the new federal government. In "A Modell of Christian Charity," Winthrop admonished his cobelievers about the ultimate meaning, for good or evil, of the "city upon a hill" they were to found:

> Thus stands the cause betweene God and us, wee are entered into Covenant with him for this worke, wee have taken out a Commission. . . . Now if the Lord shall please to heare us, and bring us in peace to the place wee desire, then hath hee ratified this Covenant and sealed our Commission, [and] will expect a strickt performance of the Articles contained in it, but if wee shall neglect the observacion of these Articles . . . the Lord will surely breake out in wrathe against us . . . and make us knowe the price of the breache of such a Covenant. . . .
>
> [Let men] say of succeeding plantacions: the lord make it like that of New England; for wee must Consider that wee shall be as a Citty upon a Hill, the Eies of all people are uppon Us.

The religious and the worldly vocations of the early colonists armed them well for the permanent settlement and self-government of the new land, and in 1701 Cotton Mather, the third generation in Massachusetts's most distinguished ecclesiastical line, further synchronized their spiritual with their secular obligations in "A Christian at His Calling":

> Every Christian hath a GENERAL CALLING; which is, to Serve the Lord Jesus Christ, and Save his own Soul, in the Services of *Religion*, that are incumbent on all the Children of Men. . . . But then, every Christian hath also a PERSONAL CALLING; or a certain *Particular Employment*, by which his *Usefulness*, in his Neighborhood, is distinguished. God hath made man a *Sociable* Creature. . . .
>
> A Christian at his *Two Callings*, is a man in a Boat, Rowing for Heaven. . . . If he mind but one of his *Callings*, be it which it will, he pulls the *Oar*, but on *one side* of the Boat, and will make but a poor dispatch to the Shoar of Eternal Blessedness.

From Martin Marty's synopsis of American religion to Robert Walker's final critique on reform, the following chapters remind Americans that their ship of state is propelled by both faith and reason, religion and science, dissent and authority, constitutionalism and social change.

As William Goetzmann demonstrates in "Exploration and the Culture of Science: The Long Good-bye of the Twentieth Century," the same scientific spirit that led Thomas Jefferson to prepare his *Notes on the State of Virginia* also motivated the founding of government institutions and the support of hundreds of explorations of the western lands and the oceanic world during the nineteenth century. The Americans participated as equals in the "second great age of discovery" and, empowered by their pragmatism and the formal separation of church and state, made "the American style" the international style. While Goetzmann closes his chapter unafraid of what the culture of science might yet bring, he also exhibits a strong *fin de siècle* impatience at the sideshows and stunts of twentieth-century exploration and the way the gurus of postmodernism and deconstruction are parodying the confusions of science. His qualified expectations mirror Martin Marty's ambivalences toward the conflicts within American religion today.

In late twentieth-century American philosophy, Murray Murphey writes, "the integration of the worldview is . . . discussed only in terms of the unification of science, and the issues that in another age seemed matters of life and death are now seen as strictly academic." Not until the twentieth century, however, did American philosophy become secular and take the scientist, rather than the minister, for its role model. More typically American was Jonathan Edwards, the "fiercest thinker of his age," who dedicated his life to rebuilding Calvinism upon the bases of Newtonian science and Lockean empiricism. The Enlightenment philosophy of the Revolution enjoyed a brief florescence in the late eighteenth century, but during the 1800s American philosophers returned quickly and completely to their theological, moral, and idealist roots.

The Enlightenment tradition in America is well represented by John Diggins's "Civil Disobedience in American Political Thought" and John Schutz's "The Courts and the Law." Inherent in the American covenant is a tension between civil disobedience and authority, that is, between the dictates of moral law and the requirements of social order. Diggins describes the vital tradition of personal conscience and dissent that has called the nation before the bar of higher principles whenever it threatens to lapse into moral conformity or authoritarianism. His subject favors the Declaration of Independence and individual leaders like Henry David Thoreau and Martin Luther King, Jr.; John Schutz's chapter privileges the Constitution, the Bill of Rights, and the courts. Focusing on the judicial branch of government as the guardian of law, and as an arena where theory meets life, Schutz recounts the Supreme Court's efforts to safeguard and extend to all Americans the fundamental rights of justice, freedom, and equality.

Jane Sherron De Hart and Linda Kerber's chapter "Gender and Equality in the American Experience" raises some of the same issues of social stratification and privilege that are addressed in the third part of this book. Their concern for the "social construction" of gender, however, and for the legal as well as the social and economic problems that must be resolved along the road to equality for all Americans, regardless of sex, suits their treatment to the more theoretical contexts of the chapters in this section. In the final chapter of the book, "Reform and Social Change," Robert Walker seeks a "plausible total perspective" on the multifarious, complex, but continuous reform experience of the United States and proposes a three-mode structure of analysis. Like John Dewey before him, Walker espouses *process* as the American value of highest importance, and he concludes with one last call to pursue the grail of social justice.

20 Religion in America

Martin E. Marty

Almost no one doubts that religion is a major element in shaping character and culture. Not all would go so far as theologian Paul Tillich, who insisted that religion was the *soul* of culture and culture was the *form* of religion. Yet even its enemies pay religion the compliment of having to take an attitude toward it.

☆ ☆ ☆ Religion in National Life

This is especially true on the level of government and national life. Totalitarian nazism did what it could to transform existing religions in support of the Reich. It tried to force upon the people a "German Christian" faith that repudiated the Jewish grounds of Christianity and fused with Nazi symbols. Maoism in China, most sinologists say, devised a quasi-religious set of symbols and in the Cultural Revolution did what it could to transform or stamp out traces of Buddhism, Taoism, and Christianity. One characteristic of the Soviet government in Eastern Europe after the revolution in Russia in 1917 and in other Soviet-bloc nations after 1945 was the restriction of religious observance. In some cases there was nominal religious freedom, but still harassment or persecution of believers was common.

An interesting phrase in the lore of the U.S. Supreme Court describes the view of religion implicit in American culture. The civil society should be "wholesomely neutral" in respect to religion—so the Court has interpreted the First Amendment to the U.S. Constitution. That amendment was designed to keep Congress from doing anything to establish religion by law or to prohibit its free exercise. Yet citizens in general do not read the "no establishment" clause as preserving a neutrality that opposes religion. Poll-takers and politicians alike witness the fact that Americans want to be religious or to think of theirs as a nation "under God." They see religion as somehow utile for civil and personal character and culture.

Both corporate and private sectors have signaled an appreciation of religious power in America. During the mid-century real estate boom it was characteristic of realtors to advertise that new suburbs or subdivisions came equipped not only with schools but with an abundance of churches. While appealing to elements of the population that wanted churches—Catholics, Methodists, and the like—they did not make a statement about the truth of faith or particular faiths. It was generally assumed that a well-churched community would be marked by stability, liveliness, an ennobled spirit, and a concern for forming the character of the young.

That religion is feared or respected in culture, then, is clear. Why it has power to shape culture and character is a bit more complex. Theorists have provided some clues. Sociologist Talcott Parsons once observed that the human in culture cannot tolerate a merely random existence. Things have to mean. People have to be able to endow their joys and their sorrows with meaning. As a French philosopher wrote: "Because we are present to a world, we are condemned to meaning." American anthropologist Clifford Geertz has described religion as a symbol system that acts "to establish powerful, pervasive, and long-lasting moods and motivations in men by formulating conceptions of a general order of existence and clothing these conceptions with such an aura of factuality that the moods and motivations seem uniquely realistic."

Religion includes what Paul Tillich called "ultimate concern"—a symbol system that evokes man's deepest response. Normally it has a social character. When a number of people respond to a common vision or express in common witness, they tend to come together to sustain these through institutions—such as churches and synagogues—or movements. They tell each other a story that promotes "an aura of factuality," until the world of ancient Israel or early Christianity comes to be as real as an Iowa backyard. They have explanations, often of a philosophical character, for an unseen order that stands behind ordinary, mundane life. They observe common rituals and prefer the language of myth and symbol.

Religion is pervasive in culture and will have an impact for better or for worse on individuals and society. American scholars and politicians have learned to reckon with that one-fifth of the world that is Islamic by seeing how Islam shapes Muslim people and peoples. They try to discern patterns of tribal loyalty in Africa. It becomes a matter of foreign policy to see how Catholicism connects with regime and revolution in many Latin American countries. On their own ground Americans are forced to wonder how character is to be formed in a mass society when the old religions break down or give way. Religion has a privileged place in the morals and morale, moods and motivations that go into character development.

☆ ☆ ☆ Religious Pluralism in America

The contributions of religion to American character and culture did not come all at once or all in one form. The most remarkable feature of American religion is its "polypiety"—as one colonial called it—its religious diversity and multiformity. A yearbook lists over 220 recognized denominations, and a recent encyclopedia had no difficulty citing twelve hundred religious groups in America. These are themselves often coalitions of factions and movements, and surrounding them or finding interstices between them are many ephemeral, private, and highly individualized sects. Yet there has been some patterning. There are families of religions, and there are layers of deposit in the sequence of contributions. We do well to sample some of these.

The Native American Situation

Before Europeans reached the Western hemisphere, the native populations had their own religions, though they were not recognized as such or were dismissed as idolatry and superstition by Christian missionaries. It is difficult to generalize about the many different language groups and peoples that made up what the Europeans called the "Indian" population. There was, however, a general sense of awe in the face of a sacred spirit that lay behind the forces of nature. The various peoples developed elaborate rites and ceremonies to celebrate the passages of life, the seasons of the year, and the events that concerned them all.

For four hundred years Christians set out, with varying success, to convert the Native Americans. They killed many and sent others to reservations. Through all the trials, however, Native American ways survived. Periodically Americans of European, African, and Asian descent turn to Native American religion for new resources. Chiefly featured are attitudes of respect to nature and a sense of communality among the people. But the Native Americans were not permitted to live undisturbed after the arrival of Christopher Columbus in 1492, and a new ethos developed with the coming of Europeans.

The Catholic Foundation

Five hundred years after the discovery of America it seems implausible to look back to the era of Catholic reform in Spain and France to find contributions to American character. New Spain lost out in Florida and the Southwest, and New France finally was confined to Canada, while a mélange of Protestantisms formed the American colonies and shaped early national life. The ruins of old Spanish missions or the traceries of French place-names on the landscape do little to shape character today beyond inspiring some reverence for past endeavors.

Yet latter-day American Catholicism builds upon elements of the religion that came with Columbus and his successors, notably the priests and brothers who were chaplains during the conquests of the sixteenth century. We can cite four typical factors.

First, the newcomers from Europe who confronted the Native Americans came with a two- or three-tiered outlook. While the natives dealt with nature head-on, recognizing spirit in or behind it but then generally letting it alone, the conquerors preached that above and beyond this life was a heaven of rewards and below it was a hell of punishments. People became martyrs or crusaders in recognition of the fact that earthly life is only a way station to eternity, that their acts now color their fate in a life to come. Fear of hell may have declined as a motivator of Catholic and Christian character, but some version of "hope of heaven" has long been used to encourage particular patterns of conduct and to discourage others.

Second, the newcomers had a sense of mission not known in what today is called tribal religion. It is the character of tribal religion to be tied to particular places and people. This hill, this tree, this set of people have a story, but there is no need to figure out the meaning of a hill beyond our sight, a tree beyond our ken, a people beyond our acquaintance. We may encounter a people and have peace or war with them. That is all. The Catholic world, however, came in the spirit of a crusade. Columbus, for example, was convinced that he could use wealth from the "Indies" to help Castile stab the infidel Muslim in the back from the east, the other side of a round world. Their sense of mission authorized Spain and France to try to uproot old cultures, to undercut native patterns of character development, and to try to replace them with what was felt to be a superior system. Their mission was to draw Native Americans' souls through the two-tiered system by baptism toward heaven. They strove to educate and "civilize" the natives, particularly the children, into new patterns of conduct and character.

Third, the Catholic contributed a sense of movement in history, a sense that it was building toward a climax. "Millennial" and utopian visions inspired the religious orders of the sixteenth century in their effort to reshape and thus fulfill history.

Fourth, it goes without saying that a vision of heaven and hell, a sense of mission, and a millennial worldview all conspired in creating an imperial outlook in Catholic and later Christian America. Religion was connected with the regime of the conquering nation, and it justified the actions taken by its representatives in founding New Spain and New France. Because the new faith was seen to be superior, the newcomer claimed the right to impose it, to extend not merely Castile or Spain, but Christendom. These attitudes live in much of American culture today.

The Protestant Mainstream

During most of the period from 1492 to 1607, when Spain dominated the New World, and to an extent after 1608, when France began its ventures in northern North America, the agents of Europe were explorers, conquerors, and plunderers of New World wealth. After 1607, however, when the English began coming to the eastern shore of what became the United States, there was much more accent on settlement.

While the Dutch Protestants in New Amsterdam (now New York City) kept the trader's mentality for a while, the English Anglicans in Virginia and the Puritans in New England came to stay. They settled and built colonies. They loved language about the howling wilderness into which they had been sent on an errand. In the face of wolves and "salvages," wild natives, they were to plant gardens, build towns, and form a "citty set upon a hill" for all the world to watch.

New England has left the biggest stamp on American character and myth. Invoking the name of its first settlers, "Puritans," elicits images of very staunch, determined character and intention. These Protestants, being Christian, shared much of the Catholic scheme. They, too, believed in a two-tiered or two-phased existence with a heaven or hell after this life. They, too, had a crusading spirit, directed not against the Muslim infidel but against the Catholic Antichrist to the south and north of them. They brought views of purpose, climax, and the goal of history, millennial patterns that were often revised. And while most of them came for their own religious freedom and economic betterment, they believed in the superiority of England—"God is so much English!," one had scrawled to help inspire colonization—and of the God of the Protestants. They also brought additional elements.

First, more than Spain and in contrast to the Native Americans, they believed in transforming the landscape. Turning wilderness to garden, virgin land to ordered village, raw landscape to tilled soil, water lapping at a shore to commercial harbor, primitive tool to complex invention—the Anglican and Puritan and, later, the Yankee were always puttering and experimenting. This "infatuation with the possible," in the words of maverick Marxist Ernst Bloch, made theirs a restless pilgrimage. They were never satisfied. They were sure that the Lord had called them to "be fruitful and multiply" and especially to "have dominion over the earth." It was theirs to cultivate, not merely to mine or strip, as they thought Catholics had been doing.

Beyond their attitudes toward human transformation of the natural landscape—a religious attitude that still moves in the culture—they brought a
sense of the covenant. This they inherited from the ancient Jews, whose story
they thought they were living out as "the American Zion."

The covenant was a sort of pact or agreement between a reliable God—one
who could be counted on—and a responsive and responsible people. What
they did to the landscape or to commerce, culture, and character was an earthly
acting out of a heavenly destined drama. Their Calvinist's sense of divine
foreknowledge and predestination did not turn them to fatalism or passivity.
They found meaning in the day's toil and went about working out the
meaning of their special election and chosenness.

Some sociologists in the train of Max Weber and R. H. Tawney have noted
the connection between this enterprising spirit and the character and culture
of capitalism. One hesitates even to invoke the connections because to do so
calls forth bibliographies and libraries full of documentation, hedging, and
speculation. Yes, Catholic cultures like Venice in pre-Calvinist times were also
capitalist, and today's capitalist Japan needs no Protestantism or Calvinism to
sustain its ethic. Yes, soon the eternal backdrop disappeared in the American
colonies as other-worldly Puritans became this-worldly Yankees. So maybe the
concept of capitalism need not be introduced at all. Suffice it to say, however,
that the American character is marked, more so than in many cultures, by a
sense of the endowment in the work and doings of each day. One is to be a
good steward of the earth, to make and invent, to earn and save and give,
acting out a pattern of meaning and value that has divine endorsement.

To these ideas of transforming nature and environment—as a sign of
election or chosenness within a covenant—we add a sense of order. Catholic
culture was ordered, of course, around fiesta and siesta and regulated hours of
religious observance in the day. But the Puritan had a special passion for
organizing and being accountable. Richard Sennett has seen this drive fulfilled
in modern times in the preference for "colonial" architecture in suburban
supermarkets and, indeed, in the tidiness of suburban platting and plotting.
Whether the Puritans had a patent on orderliness or not, it is true that they had
a passion for it. They were well poised in the American Northeast to help
spread their plan across the landscape, and they were ready to bring order and
accountability to the process of industrial change.

Finally, there was an urge toward homogeneity. Spain may have evinced this
trait when after the *reconquista* it expelled the Muslims or when it drove the
Jews into exile in 1492 so that there would be one faith for the empire. Yet
when the Anglicans set up a privileged and established faith in all the southern
colonies and the Puritan Congregationalists set up theirs in the New England

colonies, they were expressing an intention to have colonies without taint. No Protestant sectarians or Catholics were welcome. If there was to be character, the timeless pattern of *cuius regio eius religio* (whoever runs the region runs the religion), of territorial faith, was transplanted. Religious freedom in Rhode Island and Pennsylvania and religious diversity in New York were anomalous, distracting, and perhaps subversive of colonial life, thought the homogenizers. The sailor must be restricted to the harbor, the stranger moved along his way, the merchant contained, the dissenter banished—all in the interest of maintaining a single source of character and culture.

Of course, this design was doomed and the pattern fell apart, its last legal vestiges disappearing in Connecticut in 1819 and Massachusetts in 1833. But what the Protestant elect lost through law they tried to win back in ethos. For a century after the new nation was born, superior in numbers and girded by historical precedent and privilege, this group wrote the public school textbooks and worked for "sameness," now by voluntarism rather than coercion.

Given this landscape of religious freedom, two tasks were necessary. The Protestant culture developed both. First, there had to be a form to house the religious impulses; then, there had to be a stimulus in order to fill the forms. People were free, thanks to the voluntary climate, to be members of churches or not and to be members of this church instead of that. Historically, no matter what terms they used, societies had had to distinguish between host churches and guest churches, between privileged bodies and marginal bodies. The Americans instinctively developed the form that began to rise in England— the denomination. It was a deliberately neutral term for an intentionally noncommittal form. Religious bodies were simply "denominated" this or that.

The advantage of this approach to parity in legal status and ethos was obvious. Members of each group were free to regard their own as the true or the best religious body and others to be false or inferior. There could be integrity in the commitment of members to truth as many saw it without a concurrent need to persecute those of lesser quality. The denominations inevitably developed a kind of programmatic form, living between their traditions and their assessment of the needs of a public they served or would serve.

One might cynically say that the invention of the denomination helped Americans drain off conflict into harmless channels. Conflict did remain, and Baptist and Methodist worlds were as far from each other as they were from Presbyterian and Episcopalian outlooks and spheres. Yet bystanders saw no need to get involved in the conflicts, the public could be neutral, and no one was really hurt. This was quite a contrast to the times when the officially true and privileged religious groups would be tempted to persecute the others.

It was on this emergent field of competition that another innovation occurred. To be sure, it also had roots in England and in some ways in Europe,
and it was manifest before full religious freedom appeared. This was revivalism. Churches had often seen renewals of faith, warmings-up, and intensifications. But on the pluralist and competitive religious scene revivalism took a
new form beginning with the first "Great Awakening" of the 1740s. Now one
chose not merely to heat up a faith already held, but to find faith for the first
time or to move by conversion from one religious calling or group to another.

Revivalist preachers and evangelists or awakeners would come to a town, or
rise up in it, and call for repentance and a change in way of life. They asked,
literally and figuratively, "Are you saved? Are you sure that your church
membership guarantees you God's favor? What if your minister is passive? Do
you know Jesus as your personal savior?" This kind of questioning spoke to
the mentalities of frontier people and those in new industrial areas. They were
free to decide, and their decisions affected their own and their communities'
destinies. Soon revivalists were armed with sharp psychological insights and
special rhetorical techniques to help effect repentance, the turn to God, the
choice of churches. At the same time, denominationalism and revivalism
added to competition, diversity, and, to some extent, confusion. In response
to this situation, some people sought to reduce variety and establish unity.

This last element of the Protestant pattern lives on in later American culture
and character, not at all times and in all places but in select and strategic
moments. A kind of envy has moved American conservatives when they see
the social power of coerced homogeneity in Shi'ite Iran: at least *they* have a
creed, an ideology by which to act. *We* need one, too, it is felt. This conviction
lives on both in liberal homogenizing, which relativizes all creeds to an ethic of
"live and let live," and more visibly in rightist religious causes, which seek to
legislate the morals of "the majority," evoking a simpler world of Puritan
village or Baptist town with its steeples and a public school that promotes
mainstream Protestant values.

The Enlightenment Contribution

At a crucial moment when the "American package" was being put together,
Europe began to transform its old Protestantism into a new philosophy with
religious dimensions. This European *Zeitgeist* could not fail to have influenced
people of education, power, and position in the American colonies. Its code
name was the Enlightenment. It was a kind of post-Christian creed that drew
on inherited biblical value systems more than it realized but also set out to
replace them.

In its American form, the Enlightenment was professed by Benjamin Franklin, moderately by George Washington, aggressively by Thomas Jefferson, and in fusion with the older Protestantism by James Madison. Its enemies were particularist claims. The stigmatizing words in Europe, sometimes more genteelly invoked in America, were "superstition" and "priestcraft."

In place of special revelation Enlightenment thinkers sought a general revelation: nature instead of history, science instead of faith, reason instead of creed. Now people spoke of "The Supreme Being" or "The Grand Architect" instead of "The Father of Abraham, Isaac, and Jacob" or "The God of Israel" or "The Father of Jesus Christ." In place of the mysterious deity who was accessible only through precious scriptures or traditions guarded by clerics, divine purpose was available to all thoughtful people.

The Enlightenment leaders like John Adams in New England and most of the founders in Virginia constitutional times did not want to close the churches. Few were so anticlerical as visitor and pamphleteer Thomas Paine or the French Enlightenment "crusaders of the infamy" of Catholicism. Some, like Franklin, were quite respectful of what the churches held in common, and others, like Washington, insisted that "religion and morality" were the twin pillars of society upon which character and culture stood. But they were universalists committed to public virtue and civic character. The churches could support their efforts only insofar as they aspired to universal philosophy and did not rely on private stories about chosenness and election in Old Israel or New Christianity.

The common people did not line up at the salons of enlightened leaders or break down the doors of their libraries. Only a few years after the Enlightenment had made its contributions to religious freedom, separation of church and state, and constitution writing, a new generation of revivalists preaching the Bible, a religion of emotion, and sectarian identity won the hearts of the people on the frontier. Catholic and Jewish and Eastern Orthodox immigrants never felt part of the Enlightenment as they huddled in the poor sections of the great cities. Conservative Protestants repudiated it, letting it live on, chastened and refined, in liberal Congregationalism and Episcopalianism or in small but potent Unitarianism. The enemies of Enlightenment had no difficulty showing that this universalism was also particular and that this antisectarian faith was a sect too.

The Enlightenment did leave many marks on American character and culture thanks to its having come along at the decisive moment and its being propagated by the people who are thought of as the "founding fathers." First of all, it did implant a universalizing dream. The particular faiths had always claimed to be for all people but stressed their differences. Henceforth many Americans began to assert that the divine force behind character and culture could come in varieties of expressions and be grasped by faithful people in different ways: "We are in different ships heading for the same shore."

Second, the Enlightenment's religious ethos had as its corollary the need for tolerance. Thomas Jefferson could lose patience with established churches that would not bend to his will. Benjamin Franklin was anything but equanimitous toward the "Palatine Boors" and other inferiors who spread ignorant religion in his ordered Philadelphia. Yet the intention was strong, and Jefferson put it well. It made no difference whether the neighbor worshipped one god, twenty gods, or no god, so long as there was no civil disruption—no "stealing of my purse." Madison elaborated on the promise of tolerance. He believed that even people holding deep and firm convictions could be forced into tolerance simply because in a diverse society, properly supported by law, no set of them could prevail against all others. Americans have, in the main, believed ever since that the multiplicity of sects and the diversity of interests need not lead to shooting wars but can produce concord. Tolerance can become expensive for character and culture if it is simply the weak virtue of people who believe little and lightly. It can, however, be strong in the form of what Gabriel Marcel calls "counter-intolerance"—that is, the tolerance of people who hold convictions so deeply that they recognize and give warrants for the faith of others.

Third, there is a cherishing of pluralism. The Enlightenment people unwittingly promoted rather simple and homogeneous creeds. Franklin could spell them out in five lines. Yet they also linked up with dissenting sects to write state and federal constitutions and bills of rights and to assure that the courts would guarantee the rights of diverse bodies within a pluralistic society. George Santayana once argued that American liberties came about because of interacting interests. On one hand were the "pensive and rabid apostles of liberty," the sects, who wanted liberty for themselves. On the other were people in the English spirit of compromise who worked out patterns for coexistence and creative coalescences.

Other Influences

To concentrate on the contributions of four groups, the latter three of which are historically privileged, statistically predominant, or strategically poised, is not to exhaust the religious processes by which American character and culture are set and induced toward change. Jews, for instance, make up only 2 to 3 percent of the population, but they have had influence far disproportionate to their numbers. The Christians who used the Bible to enact laws turned chiefly to the Old Testament, or Hebrew Scriptures, which they shared with Jews, a fact that made Judaism more acceptable than it otherwise would have been. The Jewish sense of peoplehood, which allows for both spiritual-political bonds to Israel and an intense loyalty to "the American Zion," overlaps with the Puritanism derived from it but also has its distinctive values.

Religious faith instilled dignity, hope, and pride among black Americans during their time of slavery and has channeled their creative energies for a century thereafter. In modern America black Protestantism has come into its own as a political and spiritual force in the cities of the North as it long had been in the rural and urban South alike. Those not of African American descent frequently have turned to black expressions to enrich their own worship experience.

The "poetic" or "nature" religions of transcendentalism and its kind have softened the harsh Protestant and Enlightenment covenants. Occult and Oriental religions continue to suffuse the old culture or establish new alternatives. There are humanisms and patterns of secularity that by observation of the Supreme Court and the claims of their advocates have a quasi-religious outlook. They are fiercely engaged in shaping character and culture in a "one-tiered" universe in which human endeavors take on a special weight because there is no life to come, no divine signal caller from without, no ritual distraction from ethics. All these have their place in America.

☆ ☆ ☆ Present Trends in American Religious Life

In the preceding paragraphs I have not chosen to deal with history as a remote and finished product. I have tried throughout to show how sediments from the past form the strata of life today or, in a more fluid metaphor, how they can be dipped, stirred, or blended for new mixes. It is valuable to sample several present-day tensions and discontents in the debates over religion, character, and culture to illustrate how the processes continue.

The Natural Landscape and Its Transformation
Whatever else Americans share, they share place, land, landscape, and cityscape. Whether under western skies or in sweatshops, immigrants overwhelmingly have liked it here, have seen value in the land, and have wanted to make something of it. They have always been torn between letting the given landscape dictate the rhythms of life or pursuing present-day economic imperatives and a quick exploitation of natural resources and human invention. Debates over the implications of both sides of this issue will continue, notably among religious groups, and no consistent outcome can be foreseen. The issues of the debate are themselves contributors to character.

Individual and Community

Through most of the five centuries of European, African, and Asian immigration to America, only a minority of settlers have been formally enrolled in religious institutions. The majority have not been irreligious but have welcomed the liberty to practice or not to practice, to believe in a particular way or, putatively, in no way. The modern world has tended strongly toward what sociologist Thomas Luckmann calls "privatism" in religion, taking religion à la carte, as it were, from a menu of choices.

On the other hand are those who stress the inherently communal aspect of vital religion. Some do this by theological argument: God saves peoples and individuals among them. Others do so instrumentally: We need communities and religious institutions to develop schools of moral training and spiritual vision. How else shall we take responsibility for the young and transmit values to a new generation?

America has nurtured both individualism and institutionalism with almost equal power. Citizens are free to strike out on their own and have done so. They also have instinctively looked for, found, or solicited companions for their vision and thus gained power and durability.

The Eternal and the Temporal

Poll-takers find the American majority believing in immortality, or life after death. Implicit in many religious creeds and explicit in some are descriptions of a life beyond, which makes life here and now either tolerable or less significant. Yet whatever the professed beliefs, the overwhelming aim of religion in America has been to endow temporal existence with meaning. Even the "premillennialists" who believe that Jesus is coming again, soon, tend to write religious institutions into their wills so the message can be preached for generations or to support defense budgets to keep America strong for ages.

Churches and synagogues have meddled, say their enemies; have intervened, say their proponents; should intervene, say their prophets—in political, economic, commercial, literary, and aesthetic life. They claim that earthliness and mundane existence are arenas for decisive interests not merely anterooms for what finally matters.

Tradition and Renewal

Almost all observers note the innovative character of Americans as they transformed Old World religions or devised new religions in America. Yet here as elsewhere religion has a conservative or traditional side. Repeatedly the values of time-honored beliefs and practices are recalled. Judaism and Christianity appeal to the traditional in a world of rapid flux, and it is to their enduring values that people turn when considering the national character and culture.

The Cocoon and the Marketplace

Religious, ethnic, cultural, and creedal differences live on in American life. Few are "citizens in general." Most find bases for character and conduct in cocoonlike subcultures that are somehow translucent to the larger world. Thus they are not overwhelmed by pluralism or tempted to starve in a too-rich smorgasbord of choices. The majority of American religionists do not switch religious affiliation in the course of their long lives, despite the advertising of options and the complexities of exogamy. Yet in a world shaped by mass communications and metropolitan interaction they also come into contact with others who successfully shape character and conduct by different means, means they had been taught were "false." So there is an instinctive relativizing of what a person is told to be uniquely true in the cocoon, the tribe, or the ghetto.

☆ ☆ ☆ The Future of American Faith

Religion in America is a dynamic and fluid phenomenon. It experiences periodic revitalizations. For example, during the past quarter century two forces drew a great deal of notice. Many citizens, often young and well educated, turned their backs on majority faiths and were drawn to intense religious groups or, in the mouths of those who despised them, "cults." Others took the impulse to be spiritual but not Judeo-Christian into highly private and personalized beliefs. Some of these went under the code word "New Age," a philosophy positing that humans and all that exists are connected to a sacred energy that pervades the universe.

While such intensifications were occurring, conservative Protestantism, which had been recessive since the 1920s, was resurgent. The 10 percent of the population that characterized itself as "preferring" conservative Protestantism—especially in the forms of fundamentalism, evangelicalism, and Pentecostalism—prospered while the older mainstream churches languished. The evangelicals propagated their faith and life-styles through skillful use of mass media. However, in the course of the 1980s, they overreached in politics and experienced embarrassments in the form of financial and sexual scandals among leaders; consequently televised religion experienced some setbacks.

The debate between religious liberals and conservatives continues. "Liberals," who possess a freer biblical or Enlightenment faith, argue that even a highly diverse society can generate values that will produce an integrated character and culture for the American future. "Reactionaries" bemoan the loss of an old consensus, synthesis, or majority status and point to irreversible changes in the institutions that promote character and culture: the family, the church, the public school, civil life, commerce. They regret the breakdown of the "mediating structures" of life and the moral fabric of the larger society.

Some believe we must repeal the encouragements to pluralism and reconstitute the simpler institutions of homogeneous local communities in order to preserve values and meanings. Others argue that such "tribalism" is the cause of conflicts in societies that it immunizes against tolerance. The conflict may be a sign of lost faith in American resolution and promise. Or it may be merely the current version of a continuing tension from which citizens gain motive and stamina for new outbursts of creativity.

The American blend of landscapes, always new peoples, old and new faiths, and political resolutions looks quite accidental in the light of world history. It may represent a brief experiment, a mere fold in future human memory. Yet in times of reflection and crisis the majority have found reason to celebrate what they have inherited and, after being locked in civil argument, to join in a consensus that inspires them to continue. The outcome is not assured, but the stakes are high and the effort demands the energy of all but the apathetic few who have abandoned the scene of debate.

FURTHER READING

The best recent sourcebook whose readings provide the flavor of American religion is Edwin S. Gaustad, ed., *A Documentary History of Religion in America since 1865*, 2 vols. (Grand Rapids, Mich., 1983). For bibliographic purposes, Ernest R. Sandeen and Frederick Hale, eds., *American Religion and Philosophy: A Guide to Information Sources* (Detroit, 1978), is most convenient.

The standard comprehensive history is Sydney Ahlstrom, *A Religious History of the American People* (New Haven, Conn., 1973), an ambitious and rewarding telling of the American religious story, with excellent bibliographies. See also the shorter Winthrop S. Hudson, *Religion in America* (New York, 1973), the international work by Robert T. Handy, *A History of the Churches in the United States and Canada* (New York, 1976), and a volume that concentrates on the pathfinders, Martin E. Marty, *Pilgrims in Their Own Land: Five Hundred Years of Religion in America* (Boston, 1984). Widely recognized and profound interpretive essays are collected in Sidney E. Mead, *The Lively Experiment: The Shaping of Christianity in America* (New York, 1963). A refreshing chronicle of American religion until

1865 is Jon Butler, *Awash in a Sea of Faith: The Christianization of the American People, 1550–1865* (Cambridge, Mass., 1990). Another original presentation is Nathan O. Hatch, *The Democratization of American Christianity* (New Haven, Conn., 1989).

For fresh angles, see Catherine S. Albanese's pattern-breaking synthetic essay on "oneness" and "manyness," *America: Religions and Religion* (Belmont, Calif., 1981), and Peter W. Williams, *Popular Religion in America* (Englewood Cliffs, N.J., 1980), a discussion of religions that do not fit institutional patterns. Readers will find important suggestions by a variety of scholars in John M. Mulder and John F. Wilson, eds., *Religion in American History: Interpretive Essays* (Englewood Cliffs, N.J., 1978). Helpful maps and three interpretive essays are presented by Jackson W. Carroll, Douglas W. Johnson, and Martin E. Marty, *Religion in America: 1950 to the Present* (New York, 1979).

There has been much discussion of America's "civil religion." Robert N. Bellah's seminal essay, "Civil Religion in America," which first appeared in *Daedalus* 96 (Winter 1967), is reprinted along with controversial counterparts in Russell E. Richey and Donald G. Jones, eds., *American Civil Religion* (New York, 1974). Mary Douglas and Steven M. Tipton, eds., *Religion and America: Spirituality in a Secular Age* (Boston, 1983), updates the discussion, and there are further elaborations in John F. Wilson, *Public Religion in American Culture* (Philadelphia, 1979). A. James Reichley, *Religion in American Public Life* (Washington, D.C., 1985), discusses the impact of church religion in the public sphere. R. Lawrence Moore, *Religious Outsiders and the Making of Americans* (New York, 1986), concentrates on numbers of groups who were not considered part of the mainline. The mainline receives notable attention in Wade Clark Roof and William McKinney, *American Mainline Religion: Its Changing Shape and Future* (New Brunswick, N.J., 1987). Robert Wuthnow, *The Restructuring of American Religion* (Princeton, N.J., 1988), further develops the themes of recent religious change.

Conservative evangelicalism has prospered in recent years. An introduction to its viewpoints and a moderate, balanced overview is Mark A. Noll et al., eds., *Eerdmans' Handbook to Christianity in America* (Grand Rapids, Mich., 1983). The best book surveying the history of fundamentalism is George Marsden, *Fundamentalism and American Culture: The Shaping of Twentieth-Century Evangelicalism, 1870–1925* (New York, 1980). A favored sociological interpretation from 1955 has been reprinted: Will Herberg's *Protestant-Catholic-Jew* (Chicago, 1983). William McLoughlin, *Revivals, Awakenings, and Reform* (Chicago, 1978), is the most convenient summary of revivalist events and theories, by a master in the field.

Chapter 4 of Clifford Geertz, *The Interpretation of Cultures* (New York, 1973), presents this anthropologist's famed definition of religion. Alasdair MacIntyre, *After Virtue* (Notre Dame, Ind., 1981), is a recent pessimistic contribution by a philosopher to the debate over how character and culture are formed.

A number of works introduce huge subcultures. These include Ake Hultkrantz, *Belief and Worship in Native North America* (Syracuse, N.Y., 1981); Albert J. Raboteau, *Slave Religion* (New York, 1978); James J. Hennesey, *American Catholics* (New York, 1981); Jay P. Dolan, *The American Catholic Experience* (Garden City, N.Y., 1985); and Nathan Glazer, *American Judaism* (Chicago, 1972), a sociological comment on American Jewish development. A "mapping" of mainline, evangelical/fundamentalist, Pentecostal/charismatic, "new," ethnic, and civil religion appears in Martin E. Marty, *A Nation of Behavers* (Chicago, 1976). Sources relating women to American religion are available in Rosemary Radford Ruether and Rosemary Skinner Keller, eds., *Women and Religion in America*, 3 vols. (San Francisco, 1981–86).

☆

☆

2 I ☆ Exploration and the

☆ Culture of Science

☆ *The Long Good-bye of the*

☆ *Twentieth Century*

☆

☆ William H. Goetzmann

Because of the West, because of the frontier, because of its vast wilderness domain, America's relationship to the world of science has always seemed centered in exploration. From the days of the Lewis and Clark Expedition (1803–6) onward, throughout the nineteenth century, Americans were considered a somewhat primitive "hunting and gathering" subculture in the world of scientific endeavor. In *Democracy in America* (1835–40), Alexis de Tocqueville declared: "I consider the people of the United States as that portion of the English people who are commissioned to explore the forests of the New World, while the rest of the nation [meaning Britain] . . . may devote their energies to thought and enlarge in all directions the empire of the mind."

Indeed Tocqueville considered the higher reaches of science scarcely possible for a democratic people wholly engaged in subduing a continent. "The social condition and institutions of democracy," he added thoughtfully, "prepare them to seek the immediate and practical results of science." Thus, like most European observers, he failed to see that exploration and practical ingenuity were but two of the many significant ways in which Americans participated in what was a worldwide scientific culture.

☆ ☆ ☆ America and the Culture of Science

I use the term *culture* deliberately because it is important to think of science, not in the traditional sense of accumulated, organized knowledge or solely as a method of arriving at "truth," and certainly not as a European monopoly, but rather as a culture unto itself. It is only by thinking of science as a distinct culture functioning within or transcending national cultures and civilizations that one can clearly see America's contributions to its style, problems, and goals as well as the many ways in which the culture of science has shaped American civilization.

As a culture, science has its own institutions, languages, ideas, values, methods, symbols, and recognizable practitioners. More profoundly, like all cultures, science creates its own reality. It acts as a screen that rejects much of human experience. Science, while it may be "organized curiosity," is not geared to credulity but to critical inquiry. It aims to dispel superstition, myth, fable, old wives' tales, fantasy, hoax, and deliberate falsehood or, in the terminology of the nineteenth century, "trimming," "humbugging," and "quackery." Science, however sophisticated its method, seeks truth—but truth determined by its own practitioners, admitted members of a cultural club or fraternity.

For a long time, America imbibed the spirit of science, but few Americans were considered genuine members of the cultural club. Historically this has resulted in exaggerated claims on behalf of something called "American science." There is no "American science." There are only stages of activity in America that reflect its participation in the culture of science at certain times and in certain places on the continent, the globe, and in outer space. One of the most noteworthy aspects of this American participation in the culture of science is, of course, its exploring activity. But Tocqueville and others like him failed to see the degree to which the United States was literally permeated by the culture of science. Indeed in his travels through Jacksonian America Tocqueville failed to see *any* philosophy, natural or otherwise, at a time when the ideas of the Scottish Enlightenment, in which science stood foursquare in the service of God, had come to dominate American thought. Instead, Tocqueville fastened the practical-minded "Yankee tinkerer" image on all Americans.

I think it is fair to say that the United States was born into the culture of science. Its revolutionary ideals derived from the scientifically inspired philosophies of the Enlightenment, and a number of our early leaders, such as Franklin and Jefferson, were figures of renown in the cosmopolitan culture of science. Franklin, especially, was a world figure because of his experiments in electricity, and his contemporary, John Bartram, was equally renowned for his work in botany. Linnaeus himself called Bartram "the greatest natural botanist in the world." It is misleading to think of early America as isolated and extremely provincial with respect to science. Rather, Americans rapidly accepted the emergent culture of science, adopted its methods, nomenclature, institutions, and philosophies, and, standing on the shoulders of European scientific culture, proceeded in a great leap forward made possible by the lessons learned from abroad.

☆ ☆ ☆ Discovery and Exploration

Americans also participated in critical ways in what I have elsewhere called "The Second Great Age of Discovery"—a worldwide enterprise in which Europeans and Americans together, although sometimes as rivals, explored, mapped, measured, and inventoried the world's oceans and continents in the eighteenth and nineteenth centuries. Such activities stimulated some of the great scientific discoveries of the age, most notably those of Charles Darwin. Darwin's own hypotheses received vital support from the returns of the mid-1850s U.S. Naval Expedition to the North Pacific Ocean and from Yale professor Othniel C. Marsh's reconstruction of the evolutionary development of the fossil horse, a labor derived from his exploring work on the western plains of America.

Moreover, the alacrity with which Americans absorbed the ideas of the scientific Scottish Enlightenment meant that until after the Civil War there was very little conflict between science and religion. Men like Benjamin Rush, Asa Gray, Joseph Henry, and even Louis Agassiz saw science as inevitably providing proof of the existence of God and insight into the Common Sense morality that would make democracy work. Indeed Scottish "Common Sense" clergymen and theologians pursued science and moral science with as much diligence as the self-proclaimed natural historians and philosophers. It was not really until 1874, with the publication of Charles Hodge's *What Is Darwinism?*, that theologians fully realized that the culture of science might well be in conflict with the culture of Christianity since, as Hodge pointed out, Darwinism implied belief in a chance universe—hence, the elimination of Divine Providence and ultimately God himself. But until that point, despite waves of immigration from all parts of Europe, despite great regional diversity, despite even the invasion of European romanticism (itself inspired by a transcendental German science called *Naturphilosophie*), the only unifying factor in pre–Civil War American society was its virtually automatic acceptance of the culture of science.

It is certainly true that Americans of the early Republic differed as to the nature of science, but it is significant that this was a debate that took place *within* the culture of science. The more sophisticated scientific practitioners, such as Nathaniel Bowditch, James Hall, Asa Gray, Louis Agassiz, John Torrey, James Dwight Dana, Matthew Fontaine Maury, and Joseph Henry, however much they disagreed, believed science was most significant when it dealt in theories directly related to the best work of European scientists. A number of others believed that field collection and classification—what has been called "background science"—was of paramount importance. Still others saw no distinction between theory and practical technology. Benjamin Franklin is a good example, but one could certainly find European savants who espoused this position as well, most notably members of the British Lunar Society of Birmingham. By and large, those who demanded *only* "practical" science in America and Europe were not scientists but politicians and keepers of the purse. And even these men did not scorn science as long as it was "practical," leading them to mineral deposits, whale fisheries, and the discovery of commercial products like baking powder, rubber, quinine, steam, and, most recently, oil. Indeed they often invoked the name of science to support their positions and continue to do so today, as evidenced by any energy company television commercial.

I think it highly significant that in the nineteenth century democratic America supported literally hundreds of government-sponsored scientific expeditions into the heart of North America, twenty-five such expeditions to different parts of the oceanic world and to other continents, and the creation of the Smithsonian Institution in 1846 as a national clearinghouse for science and a national museum. These were in addition to agricultural experiment stations across the land, great post–Civil War western scientific surveys like those of John Wesley Powell and Clarence King, the creation of state surveys and scientific academies, and, perhaps most crucial of all, the establishment of land grant colleges in every state after 1862, dedicated primarily to the culture of science. These colleges in turn produced the trained scientists who staffed the large scientific bureaus like the U.S. Geological Survey and the Biological Survey that grew up after the Civil War, parallel to the growth of large business corporations.

The many American exploring expeditions varied widely. In the beginning they represented the multipurpose scientific inquiry exemplified by Alexander von Humboldt. Jefferson's instructions in 1803 to Meriwether Lewis, who had been trained for his mission by the scientists of Philadelphia, are typical. Lewis was ordered to locate "the most direct and practicable water communications across this continent for purposes of commerce." Beyond that Lewis and Clark were required to "fix" geographical positions by astronomical observations so that the whole trans-Mississippi West could be accurately mapped. This required them to master the mysteries of geodesy, one of the key sciences of the age. They were also instructed to study "the soil and face of the country," including its plants, animals, minerals, fossils, evidences of volcanic action, weather, and customs of the Native American tribes—a branch of inquiry now termed anthropology.

Jefferson wanted facts, not myth or hearsay, but he wanted an interrelated ensemble of facts, because the culture of science, which he of course carefully cultivated in his own life, saw nature in the Newtonian way, as a whole, composed of related facts governed by natural laws. Because he was such a prodigious gatherer of facts, and because he could organize these facts into laws, Alexander von Humboldt emerged as the towering figure in the world of science in the early nineteenth century. When the Prussian savant visited Jefferson in Washington in 1811, they had much to talk about since they had the same vision of the world.

The early federal expeditions into the West, beginning with that of Major Stephen H. Long in 1819, were accompanied by naturalists, as well as West Point–trained geodesists. They collected specimens of flora, fauna, and minerals and sent them back home for classification by specialists like the botanists Asa Gray and John Torrey, geologists like James Hall, and zoologists like Spencer F. Baird at the Smithsonian. They measured and mapped the topography and literally incorporated the West into the geodetic domain of science. Men like John Strong Newberry, who in 1857 accompanied Lieutenant Joseph Christmas Ives to the mile-deep floor of the Grand Canyon, were able to penetrate the surface of the earth and, in noting the stratigraphic layers, to begin the scientific reconstruction of the formation of the North American continent. Ferdinand V. Hayden and Fielding B. Meek between 1853 and 1859 traced the cretaceous horizon all across the barren Dakotas and the rugged reaches of the upper Missouri River. These western explorer-scientists linked up their work with that of James Hall of Albany, whose thirteen volumes on the paleontology of New York State constituted the initial North American stratigraphic column.

Geodesy and geology became hallmarks of supreme achievements by Americans working within the culture of science. The one, extremely abstract and mathematical, grew out of the necessity of triangulating the immense width of the continent, a feat not yet possible in other parts of the world. This was conducted by the U.S. Coast and Geodetic Survey in the latter half of the nineteenth century. The other, geology, stemmed from the matchless opportunities afforded American continental explorers to observe exposed landforms and stratigraphic columns, as well as the powerful forces of nature at work in a vast and relatively uninhabited region. This kind of study was brought to a peak by John Wesley Powell, intrepid explorer of the Colorado River in 1869. Fascinated by the river's erosive power and forcibly reminded of evidences of continental uplift, Powell created the field of geomorphology. He worked at times with Clarence Dutton, who made the Grand Canyon his specialty, and Grove Karl Gilbert, whose application of engineering mechanics to landforms that he observed on western expeditions eventually made him the grandfather of modern plate tectonics.

It is not possible here to do more than mention a few of the scientific highlights that resulted from continental exploring expeditions, but in a thousand ways American scientific explorers made noteworthy and accepted contributions to the culture of science, ranging from Joseph Leidy and Othniel Marsh's discovery of the evolution of the horse to the employment of photography in the study of exposed landforms, all of which took place between 1855 and 1880. In this period, too, zoologists like C. Hart Merriam braved the perils of Death Valley and scaled the barren heights of the San Francisco Mountain in Arizona to revolutionize the science of plant and animal geography. The science of ecology, although not born in America, received great impetus from American scientific exploring expeditions and careful study in American laboratories and land grant colleges. In all these examples theory went hand in hand with data collecting, and findings perforce had to withstand the rigors of the scientific test for truth.

At the same time American scientists also took to the sea. Between 1838 and 1842 Lieutenant Charles Wilkes of the U.S. Navy led a floating scientific expedition whose members proved the Antarctic a continent and studied in detail the islands of the Pacific. One member of his scientific cadre, James Dwight Dana, wrote the classic treatise on the formation of coral atolls and his study of volcanic islands was a major clue to plate tectonics, while another, Horatio Hale, anticipated most of the discoveries of modern scientific linguistics. And while Commodore Perry did little more than introduce the camera and American imperialism into the Far East, the Rogers-Ringgold North Pacific Exploring Expedition of 1853–55 provided for the first time conclusive data that proved that species were not immutable. The massive collections from American maritime and continental exploring expeditions occupied much of the time of American scientists back in the growing centers of learning, but they did not preclude the development of sound and fundamental theories or the rapid creation of an institutional infrastructure that made inevitable the dominance of American civilization by the culture of science.

☆ ☆ ☆ Science and Philosophy in America

Eventually American participation in the culture of science engendered a philosophical and religious crisis equal to that which swept over England with the announcement of Darwin's evolutionary hypothesis. In America, however, the outcome of this crisis was not the rejection of science. On one level people went about their business content with the idea that evolution merely demonstrated God working through design. On another level, Spencerian teleological Darwinism merely reinforced ideas of racial and industrial progress in a competitive world. On the most profound level the crisis over Darwin produced a still-newer version of the Scottish philosophy— pragmatism. The American pragmatists, Charles Sanders Peirce, William James, and John Dewey, each in his own way, developed a satisfactory solution to the problems of Darwinism that in one form or another proclaimed the scientific method itself, unfettered by traditional absolutes, as the ideal guide to a public philosophy for the nation.

The pragmatists not only could live with science but positively thrived on the uncertainties of the chance universe. For them the new "open-endedness" of science promised a freedom that was synonymous with the "American dream." This philosophy, based on the culture of science, has continued to be a mainstay of American thought despite all efforts to import substitutes like existentialism or to resurrect old Kantian absolutes. Pragmatism maintains its staying power because it is at once modern and at the same time a new name for old ideas that go back to the birth of the Republic.

☆ ☆ ☆ A "Scientistic" America

Thus one can chart the emergence of a scientific "style" in America. But it seems even clearer that the international scientific style, or cultural ritual of science, was the American style, even to the insistence upon such things as the separation of church and state in the interest of reasoned objectivity.

What of the problems engendered by the governance of American culture by science? For the most part they are problems engendered by the Americans' wholehearted espousal of the culture of science. Most obviously science in its relentless pursuit of truth demands unfettered critical inquiry, which in turn produces a culture in constant change and revision. Rather than producing order, science, like the work of great artists, produces *chaos* as it constantly induces "the shock of the new." The historian Henry Adams in his classic autobiography, *The Education of Henry Adams* (1907), detected this problem when he declared, "Chaos is the law of nature; order is the dream of man," and then in fine *fin de siècle* irony wearily called for "the aid of another Newton." Stability is difficult to achieve in a dedicated scientific society constantly revising the face of its own reality.

As T. S. Eliot noted, "After such knowledge what forgiveness?" Science sometimes discovers things that were perhaps best left undiscovered, most dramatically in our century the atomic bomb, quite possibly in the future the disastrous consequences of gene splicing and the cloning of organisms that threaten to surpass human control. Such a fearsome possibility has been recognized for some time, at least since Mary Shelley wrote her immortal story of Frankenstein's monster.

Most fundamental of all, the culture of science provides no guide to morality. Science is at best neutral, at worst imperial, as it was when an army of explorers mapped and hence forever coopted Native American lands in the West. To suggest, as the pragmatists did, that the more scientific decision makers there are in a democracy, the better the society, begs the question. An ethic of means says nothing about ends, nor does a culture of bewildering and conflicting expertise of the kind described by Christopher Lasch in *Haven in a Heartless World* (1977). In Lasch's rather lurid scenario, science and social science have offered too much advice. They have governed too much in terms of the special interests of the scientific disciplines concerned. His view that everything from child rearing to aging gracefully is by now in the hands of scientists in America has some merit, and one can sympathize with his sense of demoralization through information overload proffered by the lords of science. This is the case, of course, because through science we have found not only "progress" but confusion—that there is not one truth, but many conflicting truths. Bewildered by statistical approximations, we have begun to question whether "probabilistic truth" is moral.

These points by no means exhaust the problems of an America that has now become quite certainly the "creature of science" and perhaps always was. But what of the future? As the people of the globe reach out to the stars in expeditions led by astronauts and complex robots, ambiguity increases and the mysteries of the universe become more profound. Scientists themselves seem currently inclined to uncertainty and even open to relatively mystical approaches to their own work in view of the "uncertainty principle" and the existence of many truths. Meanwhile the scientific establishment itself has grown so large and various that even computer technology cannot keep up with it, nor can the world's resource base support it, nor can the consumer diligently digest its findings. Does this suggest that we are in for a scientific implosion? Or even a fundamental shift in the plate tectonics of world culture whereby science will suddenly lose its authority? Or are we in for a "third wave" of more individualized, and hence better, things through the "miracle of even more modern science," as Alvin Toffler suggests? Will we live happily ever after, dialoguing in computer language and worshiping television set wiring charts like the ignorant post–atomic holocaust monks in that forgotten classic *A Canticle for Liebowitz* (1959)? Or are we even now in a "postmodern" world where science is irrelevant except to induce paranoia and despair? One would think so if one took seriously the works of Thomas Pynchon, John Barth, Ishmael Reed, Robert Coover, and virtually the whole contemporary school of American writers—not to mention the increasing acceptance of mystical Native American approaches to nature or those of Eastern religions.

☆ ☆ ☆ A New Setting for Science

Occasionally there are signs that professional science, in its skepticism even of its own skeptical methods, is prepared to espouse a new sense of accountability—that scientist and humanist, historian and anthropologist might join together in taking a hard look at the culture of science that has spread over the whole globe and beyond to the moon and Mars and Saturn. The global, transnational culture of science constitutes a world problem but also, potentially, a powerful transcending force that could obliterate petty nationalisms and offer new opportunities for peace, prosperity, and ecological cooperation, if only it would come to understand what a very special culture it is and hold itself accountable to the people of the earth. As the 1990–91 Persian Gulf War illustrated, however, this culture is not restricted to the democratic republic of America, conceived in the Enlightenment, an accident or mutation of history. Iraq, too—one of the oldest and most traditional countries in the world, the land of Ur and the fabled cities of Baghdad and Basra—shares in the culture of science, with its nuclear weapons, rockets, supersonic jet fighters, and capacity for biochemical warfare.

I have neither the pages nor the inclination at the end of *this* century to imitate clergyman Samuel Miller's optimistic book, *A Brief Retrospect of the Eighteenth Century* (1803). Too much horror, too many holocausts, too many barbaric global wars have transpired, facilitated by pride, greed, hatred, racism, but also by the culture of science. As Ludwig Wittgenstein once put it, "Science and industry do decide wars." Science, with its callous craving for the general over the humanly specific, especially in its great destructive leaps (regarded by the scientific community as "triumphs"), generated great pessimism in Wittgenstein. It also caused him to dream that perhaps, having caused infinite misery, science and industry might also unite the world. Clearly, however, it has failed to unite peoples and cultures as the world order and nation states, possessed of better and more deadly means of destruction, crumble into multitribalism and ethnic antagonisms.

The imperative that the culture of science develop ways of policing and controlling itself has not been realized. Indeed, the United States, like the most backward of nations, has become "the sorcerer's apprentice," the servant of method, so that one of the most pressing enemies faced by global cultures is the pragmatic, impersonal culture of science. The technological and scientific mysteries confronted in the popular American television series "Star Trek" make this clear for even the most obtuse.

☆ ☆ ☆ Exploration as Stunt

Clearly, American-sponsored exploration did not suddenly stop at the turn of the century. Indeed, propelled by a massive publicity apparatus, of which the National Geographic Society is a conspicuous example, exploration of exotic lands and lately the ocean floor multiplied many times. Often exploration was a mere stunt—for example, the races to the North and South Poles. When Robert Peary proclaimed himself finally the discoverer of the North Pole in 1909, what did it prove? Peary became a recluse while the scientific world then and even now has disputed his claim. Admiral Richard Byrd's "important" first flight over the North Pole in a Fokker airplane, too, is in dispute today, though not his flight over the South Pole, which was meaningless.

Much exploration ended in tragedy. The Italian Umberto Nobile crashed on a remote Arctic island as late as 1928 while trying to float over the pole in a balloon, and an attempt to rescue him cost the life of Norwegian explorer Roald Amundsen, who had negotiated the long-sought Northwest Passage in 1906 and was the first to reach the South Pole in December 1911. British explorers Robert Falcon Scott, who perished on his return from the South Pole, and Ernest Shackleton, who attempted and failed to cross the Antarctic continent in 1914–16, however inconsequential their feats, have been the romantic subjects of continual books and television documentaries. So important was physical exploration, and even reexploration, that the great scientist of plate tectonics Alfred Wegener died in 1930 on an insignificant expedition across Greenland.

Intrepid Roy Chapman Andrews traversed the barren Gobi Desert in search of the remains of the first man, returning with a mere dinosaur egg; self-publicist Lowell Thomas explored seemingly everywhere; husband-and-wife team Martin and Osa Johnson penetrated Africa's jungles, she writing a best-seller about their feats, *I Married Adventure* (1940); exotic animal hunter Frank Buck "brought 'em back alive"—to captivity in the zoos that sprang up in virtually every American city, often built by the Works Progress Administration for "purposes of science education"; and the National Geographic Society made possible the underwater career of Jacques Cousteau, who at least invented the Aqua-lung, which created a new kind of tourism. The National Geographic Society also sponsored Hiram Bingham, "discoverer" of Machu Picchu, Peru, the sky-high "Lost City of the Incas." It did not matter that Bingham's muleteer's family had farmed Machu Picchu's cloud-scraping terraces for generations, or that Bingham, after taking a brief look, headed full-trot for a South American mountain, attempting to beat Annie Peck, "a mere woman," as the first to the top. Bingham suddenly regained his interest in Machu Picchu when he reached the pinnacle and found Peck's pennant fluttering gaily in the wind, especially after his subordinates had cleared, mapped, and surmised the Inca city's very great significance.

One could go on chronicling the multifarious American and European archaeological, geological, botanical, and oceanographic expeditions of the twentieth century. Those that stand out most in our minds today are the manned and unmanned space probes, which involve a complex of imagination and big science displayed before a hundred million television sets. There will perhaps never be another exploring event so dramatic as Neil Armstrong's first footstep on the moon, 20 July 1969. The marvelous feats of later space flights, from Commander Alan Shepard's hitting a golf ball miles through the moon's nonexistent atmosphere to the 1989 *Voyager* flyby of Neptune, then out beyond the solar system itself, clearly could never match the first moon landing in the minds of Americans and those worshipers in the temple of science around the world. The flawed unmanned Hubble telescope, designed to peer into deep space and the profound origins of the universe, seemed an even worse anticlimax, its importance notwithstanding.

None of this was "the right stuff," to use the title of Tom Wolfe's celebrated novel of America's space adventures. The culture of science, in all its complex teamwork, allowed no Promethean heroes, unless it is Russia's Yuri Gagarin, the first man to circle the globe through space and now commemorated by a huge memorial in the heart of Moscow. America's "right stuff" cowboy–test pilot Chuck Yeager—the first man actually to penetrate outer space—now sells auto parts on American television. In late twentieth-century America we have few heroes.

☆ ☆ ☆ Big Science and Cultural Dislocation

Ever since the *New York Times* announced Russia's achievement in launching the world's first earth satellite, *Sputnik*, in the International Geophysical Year 1957–58, big government–sponsored science has moved rapidly to the fore. An emergency space program was assembled, and a generation of schoolchildren were choked to death on "new math" and science and engineering courses. A National Defense Education Act (NDEA) sent more students to college than ever before in American history. It did not, however, produce the mathematics or science geniuses that were envisioned but instead financed the long childhood of leisure that launched the riots and attempted student revolutions of the 1960s and early 1970s. These riots suddenly faded with the canceling of NDEA grants and the end of the Vietnam War draft.

All of this took place during the technological revolution that was television. Science, technology, consumerism, and information distortion by the major "news" programs became an industry so large, so dominant, so fragmenting as to defy control. Its primary cultural value perhaps has become the scapegoat it offers to the "we never watch it" troglodytes and the tool by which local demagogues and foreign tyrants exploit the gullible. On the other hand, it also has played a large role recently in the people's revolution in the former U.S.S.R.

Despite the riots of the 1960s and 1970s, someone was minding the scientific and technological store. The computer revolution, based on ever more complex mathematics and science, swept America, often propelled by the same Japanese ingenuity that threatened to make the American automobile obsolete. This computer revolution was *very big technology*, which, along with the television, produced what some call the "Information Age." While Marshall McLuhan's book *Understanding Media: The Extensions of Man* (1964) was devoured by every college student who could read, only a hardy few could comprehend the gibberish in the computer user manuals. But people who cared about their jobs and an army of "hackers" learned. We now, indeed, are the information culture, which very soon may be all we have to sell in the face of foreign economic competition. The information revolution and cheap foreign goods have perforce turned America into the world's "dream factory."

☆ ☆ ☆ Chaos

In the earlier part of the century time was relativized as Einstein's theory of relativity was gradually absorbed into our culture. What was time anyway but a position? City planner Kevin Lynch typically asked, "What time is your place?" After half a century of paleontology and Darwinist-inspired evolutionary thinking, history appeared to be irrelevant for structuring thought. It seemed, at best, a kind of "noble dream." Taking its cue from developments in modern science, the modernist movement in art and literature stressed the fragmentation of time and the irrelevance of causality and developmentalism in an all-encompassing attack on industrialization in American and European culture. Henry Adams's "chaos theory" found a large audience at last.

The value of the culture of science is in some question as it functions in today's noncommonsense world of chaos. The Darwinist Stephen J. Gould seems almost old-fashioned in holding off the neocreationists. A large coterie of physicists—following in the wake of Ilya Prigogine's Nobel Prize–winning studies of the order of randomness and Benoit Mandelbrot's *The Fractal Geometry of Nature* (1984)—lead us to the inescapable conclusion that the very nature of the universe and everything in it, "all things bright and beautiful," may be forms of chaos.

Self-reference, more than time, was important to the "stream of consciousness" artists and writers exemplified by Thomas Pynchon's masterwork of postmodernism *Gravity's Rainbow* (1973). Space was important to the juxtaposition of scenes in motion pictures that somehow gave the illusion of time. And relative times became important to psychoanalysis, where every man or woman has become his or her own case historian, whose aim it is to presentize his or her personal past.

But if linear history, as we once knew it, is irrelevant, what of the discovery of geological continental drift in 1912 and its general acceptance in America by 1928–30? Easily answered: drift is drift; it has no particular direction and is not caused by a linear hardening of the earth or even a linear softening of the earth or the pull of gravity. It is caused by the perpendicular pendulum motion of isostasy, a system rather than a linear progression. One plate goes down, another comes up and over, and then the reverse is just as likely to happen. But fundamentally, according to chaos theory, the drift of plates is unpredictable.

Biological evolution—the Darwinism that structured so much of the idea of progress in the nineteenth century—is under similar fire in America. While Dr. Stephen Gould mans the Darwinist ramparts with his "flamingo's smile" and his "panda's thumb," the new science offers genetic leaps, uneven and dramatic neocatastrophic paleontological change, mysterious gaps in the genetic and paleontological record, politicized arguments over African or Asian origins of the human species—and creationism, "the white plume" of antiscience fundamentalism. Why not believe in Noah's Ark?

And the "big bang" theory of the origins of the universe? Did that not take place in and strongly suggest linear time? Not necessarily. It involves a conceptual change wherein spatial juxtaposition and lights on a spectrum *become* time, much as in Robert Rauschenberg's strange cataclysmic collages and the serendipitous drips of Jackson Pollock, which stand as the artistic symbols for an age of illogicality in much the same spirit as *Gravity's Rainbow*.

Perhaps progress is visible in medical research—in heart and lung, kidney, bone, and limb transplants, for example. Can we not point to a biochemical revolution as progress? Can the marvels of gene transplants and splicing not provide a measuring stick for progress? No, according to the nation's physicians and surgeons. Dr. Robert M. Centor, representing the sixty-five thousand members of the College of Physicians and Surgeons, recently confessed to Congress that medical science cannot tell which treatment will work best for many common ailments. Dr. John Wennberg of the Dartmouth Medical School added, "Because of [this] . . . uncertainty, medicine is in an 'intellectual' crisis." Robert S. Boyd, after an extensive and devastating survey of the confusion reigning in the medical and scientific establishment, concluded: "Doctors face harsh fact: they don't know what works!"

☆ ☆ ☆ The Language of Babel

This being the case, and American culture a wide-mesh grid that is open to virtually every idea, the chaos theories dominating the scientific and medical communities have found their parallel in the viruslike invasion of our universities and intellectual circles by a whole new set of French philosophies: the creeping *Les Annales* school of social historians who thrive on boredom; the Lévi-Strauss structuralists; the Lacanian psycho-fanaticists; the poststructuralist followers of Michel Foucault; the gullible coterie of "master of the universe" culture critics who troop after Ferdinand de Saussure; the unreadable works of Jacques Derrida, and especially Roland Barthes, who attempt to turn everything into linguistics with themselves in control of the "signifier"; the final chaos of self-referentiality best and most brilliantly exemplified by the mad Jean Baudrillard. These new philosophies, in a sense, parody the confusions of the culture of science. Whereas once we soberly and ridiculously absorbed the clumsy Marxism of Habermas, Gadamer, Wittfogel, and Adorno of the "Frankfurt School," Americans have returned to a new individualism with help from the French—decentered, self-referenced, ideas run amuck. Maxwell's Demon is out of the box.

☆ ☆ ☆ "We Are Not Afraid"

Has American culture today reached the *S curve* of gullibility and trivia overload? Has information become noninformation? Has the biblical Tower of Babel been planted in America? Has the United States, enmeshed in "the uncertainty principle," lost its leadership role? Have techno-bureaucratic, plasticized, industrial organizations and contravening tribalization all over the world demoralized society? It is not hard to answer in the affirmative, and it is difficult to be optimistic as the twentieth century comes to an end, perhaps not with a bang nor even a whimper after all, but rather amid the chaos of billions and billions of humanoids all croaking at once, while nobody is listening—not even God.

Such is one latter-day mood of America, product of exploration and the culture of science and nonsense. Today we live in the land of the looking glass with no commonsense Alice to lead us beyond it. But then, Lewis Carroll knew all this in the nineteenth century. He was a mathematician, and in addition, as the Reverend Charles Dodgson, he knew what was eternal. We Americans must live with the culture of science, unafraid of wherever it takes us in the "long good-bye" of the twentieth century.

FURTHER READING

Exploration, thanks to emphasis on the frontier experience, has always been a major theme in American historiography, although it has not always been so important as it should be to historians of science. I have stressed the centrality of American exploration to both the history of science and American culture in the following works: "Exploration's Nation: The Role of Discovery in American History," in Daniel J. Boorstin, ed., *American Civilization* (London, 1972); "Paradigm Lost," in Nathan Reingold, ed., *The Sciences in the American Context* (Washington, D.C., 1979); *Army Exploration in the American West, 1803–1863* (New Haven, Conn., 1959); *Exploration and Empire: The Explorer and the Scientist in the Winning of the American West* (New York, 1966); and *New Lands, New Men: America and the Second Great Age of Discovery* (New York, 1986).

I have found it interesting to compare the impressions regarding science, religion, and philosophy in Alexis de Tocqueville's *Democracy in America* (1835–40) with the facts unearthed by Herbert Hovencamp in *Science and Religion in America, 1800–1860* (Philadelphia, 1978). Hovencamp's work indicates that Tocqueville, shrewd observer that he was, missed a great deal.

Important works that deal with the theme of this chapter include Henry Steele Commager, *The Empire of Reason: How Europe Imagined and America Realized the Enlightenment* (Garden City, N.Y., 1977); Nathan Reingold, *Science in Nineteenth-Century America* (New York, 1964); Nathan Reingold and Ida H. Reingold, eds., *Science in America: A Documentary History, 1900–1939* (Chicago, 1981); A. Hunter Dupree, *Science in the Federal Government* (Cambridge, Mass., 1957); Joseph Kastner, *A Species of Eternity* (New York, 1977); Cynthia Eagle Russett, *Darwin in America: The Intellectual Response, 1865–1912* (San Francisco, 1976); and Daniel J. Kevles, *The Physicists* (New York, 1977). Robert V. Bruce's *The Launching of Modern American Science, 1846–1876* (New York, 1987) is misleading with respect to the centrality and role of science in America. Bruce neglects the role of science in colonial America and in the founding of the Republic, sees science and society as opposed to one another, and fails to note the critical role of the Scottish philosophy and pragmatism in nineteenth-century America.

One cannot really discuss "the culture of science" in America without referring to the classic works of Henry Adams: *The Education of Henry Adams* (Boston, 1907), "The Rule of Phase Applied to History" (1909), and *A Letter to American Teachers of History* (1910). Christopher Lasch's *Haven in a Heartless World: The Family Besieged* (New York, 1977) gives an interesting critique of our current "scientistic" culture, balancing the overly enthusiastic responses to science espoused by Alvin Toffler in *Future Shock* (New York, 1970) and *The Third Wave* (New York, 1980). Peter Novick's *That Noble Dream: The Objectivity Question and the American Historical Profession* (Cambridge, 1988) shatters the pretensions of historians to having achieved the status of social scientists. For an application of social science to the gender question, see Cynthia Fuchs Epstein, *Deceptive Distinctions: Sex, Gender, and the Social Order* (New Haven, Conn., 1988), which attempts to make scientific sense out of the current sexual confusion in America.

The understanding of culture and the role of the anthropologist exemplified in Clifford Geertz, *The Interpretation of Cultures* (New York, 1973), is most useful; here the anthropologist becomes a congenial humanist. See also Geertz, *Works and Lives: The Anthropologist as Author* (Stanford, Calif., 1988), and Rick Simonson and Scott Walker, *Multi-cultural Literacy* (St. Paul, Minn., 1988). Other works on anthropology relevant to my thinking include George W. Stocking, *Victorian Anthropology* (New York, 1987); Robert E. Bieder, *Science Encounters the Indian, 1820–1880* (Norman, Okla., 1986); Franz Boas, *The Mind of Primitive Man* (New York, 1911); Margaret Caffrey, *Ruth Benedict: Stranger in This Land* (Austin, Tex., 1989); and Benedict's two works, *Patterns of Culture* (Boston, 1934) and especially *The Chrysanthemum and the Sword: Patterns of Japanese Culture* (Boston, 1946).

In the twentieth century, American exploration, indeed exploration in general, has moved toward stunts and "media events." Recent works on the subject include Theon Wright, *The Big Nail: The Story of the Cook-Peary Feud* (New York, 1970); Pierre Berton, *The Arctic Grail: The Quest for the North West Passage and the North Pole, 1818–1909* (New York, 1988); John Edward Weems, *Peary: The Explorer and the Man* (Los Angeles, 1988); Dennis Rawlins, *Peary at the North Pole: Fact or Fiction?* (Washington, D.C., and New York, 1973); and David Roberts, *Great Exploration Hoaxes* (San Francisco, 1982). At present a splendidly irrelevant controversy is raging in journals and newspapers over whether Peary actually reached the North Pole. American polar explorer Wally Herbert is leading the attack on Peary's veracity. Leading Peary's defense are the National Geographic Society and a specially appointed committee of the National Academy of Science, which seems to have proved Herbert, Rawlins, Roberts, and associates wrong through close analysis of the sun angles in Peary's photos.

Herman Viola and Carolyn Margolis's wonderful Smithsonian exhibition on the Great U.S. Exploring Expedition to the Pacific and Antarctica and their book *Magnificent Voyagers: The U.S. Exploring Expedition, 1838–1842* (Washington, D.C., 1985) reveal new facets of the history of American science. John Bierman's *Dark Safari: The Life behind the Legend of Henry Morton Stanley* (New York, 1990) is a long overdue biography of a true "media event" explorer. Alfred Bingham's honest biography of his father, *Portrait of an Explorer: Hiram Bingham, Discoverer of Machu Picchu* (Ames, Iowa, 1989), reveals that Bingham's real intent was climbing mountains, not finding "lost cities," and that it was only after his Peruvian guide had called attention to Machu Picchu, and his assistants had explored it, that Bingham realized its value to his career. Tom Wolfe's *The Right Stuff* (New York, 1979) and the 1983 film of the same name constitute other recent works concerned with accidental and true hero explorers, this time in space.

A most ingenious approach to exploration history as ecological history is that taken by Stephen J. Pyne in two brilliant books: *The Ice: A Journey to Antarctica* (Iowa City, Iowa, 1986) and *Burning Bush: A Fire History of Australia* (New York, 1991). Both bear on the world culture of science.

The literature on space exploration is, like space, virtually infinite. Useful works include Carl Sagan, *Cosmos* (New York, 1980); Walter A. McDougall, *The Heavens and the Earth: A Political History of the Space Age* (New York, 1985); and Bruce Murray, *Journey into Space: The First Thirty Years of Space Exploration* (New York, 1989)—the latter two are especially critical of the U.S. manned space flight program. See also Carl Sagan, Edward Stone, and William Goetzmann, "Voyager Retrospective, a Symposium on Exploration," *Planetary Report* 9 (November/ December, 1989); Thomas R. McDonough, *Space, the Next Twenty-Five Years* (New York, 1987); and Ray Bradbury et al., *Mars and the Mind of Man* (New York, 1973).

The medical and psychiatric literature, as well as that on pharmacology and biochemistry, is a vast, exciting field. Paul Starr's *The Social Transformation of American Medicine* (New York, 1982) is a brilliant, comprehensive book. Serials such as the *New England Journal of Medicine* and the *Journal of the American Medical Association*, the bulletins and reports of the National Institute of Health, the Food and Drug Administration, and the National Institute of Alcohol Abuse, and session reports of the American Association for the Advancement of Science make significant up-to-date reading. One of the most interesting controversies concerns genetic theories as to the cause of alcoholism, wherein the biochemical research community is staunchly opposed by the psychiatric, behaviorist, and sociological fraternities, not to mention the various franchised alcohol-abuse centers. The same kind of controversy exists over the treatment of AIDS and drug abuse.

Another battlefield of science that has existed now for nearly 150 years is that of Darwinism versus creationism. See Stephen J. Gould's articles in *Scientific American* and his *The Flamingo's Smile* (New York, 1985) and *The Panda's Thumb* (New York, 1980). Creationists have their own *Journal of Creationism*.

Randomness in nature is also at the expanding edge of scientific discussion. For a readable popular work, see James Gleick, *Chaos: Making a New Science* (New York, 1987). Benoit Mandelbrot, *The Fractal Geometry of Nature* (New York, 1983), is more complex. The works of Ilya Prigogine are also important. Thomas S. Kuhn, *The Structure of Scientific Revolutions*, 2d ed. (Chicago, 1970), concerning paradigm theory, is still relevant and stimulating, as is Stephen Hawking's *A Brief History of Time: From the Big Bang to Black Holes* (New York, 1988). See also Ray Monk, *Ludwig Wittgenstein: The Duty of Genius* (New York, 1990).

Interesting works on technology include Thomas Hughes, *American Genesis: A Century of Invention and Technological Enthusiasm, 1870–1970* (New York, 1989), and Margaret Cheney, *Tesla, Man out of Time* (Englewood Cliffs, N.J., 1981). There is much current writing on automobile, computer, and electronics technology, often in the context of competition with Japan. Two of many stimulating works presenting the social case against television are Neil Postman, *Amusing Ourselves to Death: Public Discourse in the Age of Show Business* (New York, 1985), and Marie Winn, *The Plug-in Drug: Television, Children, and the Family* (New York, 1977). Daniel Boorstin's *The Image; or, What Happened to the American Dream* (New York, 1962), which criticized the fragmentation of reality in the media and the presentation of television newscasters as experts, has been joined by a host of similar newspaper and magazine treatments but is still worth reading. On the hero, see Joseph Campbell's seminal *The Hero with a Thousand Faces* (New York, 1949) and the Bill Moyers television series and book featuring Campbell, *The Power of Myth* (New York, 1988).

Readers may find Michel Foucault's *The Order of Things* (New York, 1970) and *The Archeology of Knowledge* (New York, 1972) helpful in defining "the culture of science." For claims that linguistics is a science and that it defines reality in our time, see Roland Barthes, *Mythologies* (Paris, 1957); Steven Connor, *Postmodernist Culture: An Introduction to Theories of the Contemporary* (Cambridge, Mass., 1989), a summary of critical theories; Giles Gunn, *The Culture of Criticism and the Criticism of Culture* (New York, 1987); and Jonathan Arac, ed., *After Foucault: Humanistic Knowledge, Postmodern Challenges* (New Brunswick, N.J., 1988). These and the confusing works of Jacques Derrida and Fredric Jameson are but a few examples of the science of "semiology" founded by American philosopher Charles Sanders Peirce in a seminal nineteenth-century essay "How to Make Our Ideas Clear," which is most accessible in Max Fisch, ed., *Classic American Philosophers* (New York, 1951). Peirce's essay marks the beginning of American confusion about the nature of reality. Some cultural critics in the United States are spellbound by the works of the French cultural critic Jean Baudrillard, which include *Simulacres et Simulation* (Paris, 1981), *Forget Foucault* (New York, 1987), and *America* (New York, 1988). Baudrillard argues that nothing is real in the United States, which is a giant imitation of Disneyland—a version of which the French are even now constructing outside of Paris.

22   American Philosophy

☆ Murray G. Murphey

The colonies were settled chiefly by Englishmen, and as provincial Englishmen have done the world over, the colonists looked to the motherland for leadership, intellectual as well as political. There was no need for the colonies to develop original philosophers, or philosophers at all, and few did. In the case of Puritan New England, however, peculiar reasons led to a focus on systematic thought and in due course to original work.

☆ ☆ ☆   Puritan Thought

The Puritan party that came to New England was a distinct faction within English Puritanism and one that subscribed to a special version of Puritan thought. Like all Calvinists, they affirmed the doctrines of the sovereignty of God, original sin, innate depravity, limited atonement, double predestination, irresistible grace, and the perseverance of the saints. Onto this platform they grafted the doctrine of the covenant. (God deals with his people through a series of covenants, of which the covenant of grace in Genesis 17, promising salvation to Abraham and his seed on the condition of faith, is typical.) Despite its historical linkages to the theory of the social contract, Puritan covenant theory was not democratic. What it did was to provide a legalistic terminology in which God's autocratic relation to his people could be described. But the New England Puritans broke with English Calvinists in instituting the doctrine of visible sainthood. That is, they claimed that the reception of grace in conversion so altered a man's nature that other gracious men could tell by visible signs that he was very probably saved. This doctrine permitted the New Englanders to establish an oligarchic rule by the saints, and it bound the explosive individualism of the Protestant doctrine of conversion within a rigid social order, since although conversion was a matter between God and the individual only, the social validation of a man as a saint depended upon acceptance by his peers.

These theological doctrines were combined with logical, rhetorical, and mathematical theories derived from the French Protestant reformer Petrus Ramus (1515–72), with a Neoplatonic theory of conscience derived from

432

Augustine, and with scientific concepts derived from Aristotle and the scholastics. The result was a theory that both viewed nature and history as a symbolic discourse whereby God speaks to his creatures and also emphasized the value of descriptive science. Explanation was to be found in theology, however, and natural causes were viewed either as occasions upon which divine power was exerted or as instruments used by God. The resulting worldview was centered upon God and interpreted human and natural events in terms of his will.

The Restoration in 1660 spelled the end of Calvinist rule in England and therefore left New England an isolated Puritan outpost, grimly clinging to a cause for which Englishmen at home had lost the desire to fight. But cling they did, for in their eyes the fall of Puritanism in England only increased the significance of New England. Reading their Scripture with typological eyes, they saw themselves as the true heirs of Israel, preserving a holy faith against the coming of better times and even believing that it was their mission to lead the armies of light into the millennium. Although Puritan scholars read widely in English and Continental thought throughout this period, their learning was always subordinated to the religious commitment that dominated their lives. Descartes may have staggered orthodoxy in Europe; in America he was warped into its defender.

The Enlightenment of course reached the colonies and was profoundly influential everywhere. In the southern and middle colonies, men such as Benjamin Franklin, Cadwallader Colden, Alexander Garden, and Thomas Jefferson became embodiments of scientific rationalism and, among other pursuits, carried on scientific investigations. If such men became "liberal" in their theological views, they were no more so than their peers in Europe, whose lead they followed. In New England, on the other hand, the new science was drafted to the service of Puritan religion, and men such as Cotton Mather developed a natural theology that would support their traditional creed.

It was not just science and the Enlightenment that posed problems for the Puritans; in the 1740s the colonies were swept by their first major revival, forever after known as the Great Awakening. Revivalism had many roots, and its impact differed from colony to colony, but in New England it was a revolutionary force. It split the churches and the theological leadership so deeply that the divisions could never be erased. As a result the social consensus that had hitherto confined the more anarchic impulses of Calvinist doctrine was destroyed, and the revival was followed by the appearance of one sectarian group after another.

☆ ☆ ☆ Jonathan Edwards: Creating a Synthesis

Out of this crucible arose a liberal antirevivalist wing, headed by Charles Chauncy, which in due course led to such movements as Unitarianism, a conservative Calvinist group that opposed both revivalism and liberalism, and a revivalist wing whose intellectual leader was Jonathan Edwards. The finest American thinker of his age, Edwards (1703–58) devoted his life to rebuilding traditional Calvinism upon a basis provided by Newtonian science, Lockean empiricism, the Platonism of the Cambridge Platonists, especially Henry More, and a subjective idealism that he developed in his critique of Locke. No other thinker in American history has developed so masterful and so finely articulated a metaphysical-theological system as Edwards. Even Europeans who lacked his passionate religious convictions recognized that he was a thinker of great power and subtlety.

Edwards's theology provided a sophisticated justification for an emotional religion of the sort spawned by the revival together with criteria for distinguishing true emotional religion from mere enthusiasm. In his moral doctrines he emphasized "the sense of the heart," meaning an emotional response to the character of an act or object. Edwards was thus thinking along lines also developed by the Earl of Shaftesbury and Francis Hutcheson, but whereas their work led to a secular doctrine of the moral sense, Edwards defined true virtue as the love of God and derived benevolence to one's fellow being as a corollary. Here as elsewhere Edwards resisted the secular effects of the Enlightenment and forced the new learning to serve the ends of Calvinism.

Of all Edwards's works, his defense of predestination was to become the most lasting source of controversy. Defining the freedom of the will as the liberty to do what one wills, Edwards not only denied the Arminian doctrine that only a self-determining will is free but subjected the Arminian position to a withering refutation that was never to be adequately answered. Edwards was an occasionalist in his view of causality, so that God was the only truly efficient cause in the universe, but he also believed in stable natural laws, meaning that on occasions of a given type, God acts in a certain way. Thus a sinful soul has such a nature that it will invariably sin, while a gracious soul has a love of God so powerful that it can act virtuously. That this doctrine left Edwards in the position of being unable to account for Adam's sin without attributing it to God marked a weakness of his system that became a central problem for his followers.

Edwards's influence upon American thought was enormous. He was the founder of a school of thought known as New England theology that continued as a major tradition in American theology and philosophy until the late nineteenth century. Joseph Bellamy, Samuel Hopkins, and Nathaniel Emmons were its great champions in the years after Edwards's death, but Nathaniel Taylor, Timothy Dwight, Charles Hodge, Edwards Amasa Park, and Henry Boynton Smith were all products of this tradition. In depth and subtlety of thought, these theologians must be ranked among the foremost American thinkers of the eighteenth and nineteenth centuries. If they are neglected today, it is because the theological issues that dominated American thought throughout the nineteenth century have ceased to be of central concern to American thinkers of the late twentieth century.

☆ ☆ ☆ The Revolution and Political Thought

The major, and really the only, exception to the predominantly religious cast of early American thought was the extraordinary development of political philosophy in the period from 1763 through the ratification of the Constitution. This remarkable body of thought was created, not by theologians, but by secular men, chiefly lawyers, who confronted the problems of the place of the colonies in the British Empire, the right of revolution, and the framing of new governments. Like other British colonists before them, notably the Anglo-Irish, the Americans found themselves in conflict with the mother country over issues of taxation, commercial regulations, jurisdiction of governing bodies, and imperial relations. Not surprisingly, they drew upon the writings of the Radical Whigs, who had on a number of occasions debated these issues earlier in the century.

The rigid insistence of the English government upon its prerogatives, and its determination to impose its measures by force if necessary, succeeded in forcing an unprecedented unity upon the colonists and led to the Revolution. The Revolution in turn forced the colonists to establish new governments in the thirteen colonies and so led to experiments in state making. The experience of the Americans with these state governments and with the Articles of Confederation (1781) made them recognize the inadequacy of Whig theory while at the same time compelling them to modify it in order to create workable governments. The climax of this process of interaction between theory and experiment was the federal Constitution, a document that departed radically from the earlier Whig theories and that codified the newer ideas that had evolved over twenty-five years. This new political theory, which received its classic expression in the Constitution and in *The Federalist* (1787–88), a series of papers written by James Madison, Alexander Hamilton, and John Jay to promote its ratification, has remained so completely the dominant political philosophy of the United States that, with the exception of Calhoun's writings, there has scarcely been any notable work in political philosophy since.

☆ ☆ ☆ Philosophical Controversies of the Nineteenth Century

From the Revolution to the Civil War, the ministry resumed its dominant role in American intellectual life. In these years, the college and the seminary emerged as the centers of creative work rather than the church pulpit. Since the colleges were almost entirely church controlled, their presidents were chiefly ministers; thus, their primary objective was the creation of Christian character, and academic philosophy was thoroughly religious. Beginning in 1768 when John Witherspoon assumed the presidency of what is now Princeton University (the College of New Jersey at the time), the Scottish philosophy rapidly became the academic orthodoxy in this country. Devised by Thomas Reid, Dugald Stewart, and Francis Hutcheson, the Scottish philosophy combined a realism based upon a sophisticated analysis of sense perception with a moral intuitionism. Designed as a response to David Hume, it traced the origins of his skepticism to Locke's theory of ideas. In its place, the Scots argued for a distinction between sensation, which is subjective, and perception, which is the knowledge of external objects. Sensations are related to external things as signs to their objects, and the laws of signhood are conceived as innate and divinely ordained. The judgments of perceptions rest upon a set of innate principles of "common sense," for example, every event has a cause, so that far from being passive the mind plays an active role in perception.

In the moral realm, the Scots argued for an innate moral sense through which man perceives the moral properties of acts, just as he perceives color through the eye. The concept of conscience is thus assimilated to the empirical psychology of Locke, with the moral sense as a perceptive organ rather than a source of transcendental truth. Variations in moral judgments are then accounted for in terms of conditions of perception, education, and even disease since the moral sense, like the eye, can be affected by illness, leading to what was called "moral insanity."

The Scots also developed a psychological model that viewed the mind as composed of three faculties—the intellect, the feelings, and the will. This model, which dominated American thought until the 1890s, played an important part in the debates within the tradition of New England theology over the freedom of the will. Nathaniel Taylor in particular used it to reinterpret Edwards's views on predestination. Whereas Edwards had identified the affections and the will, so that motives and choices were one, Taylor divided them and saw motives as occasions upon which the will chooses freely. Thus a sinner can choose the path of virtue although he never will unless grace alters his nature—that is, his motives. Hence although Adam was created sinless, he could freely choose evil without thereby making God his accessory. Taylor's work, which became identified with Yale, where he taught, helped to keep the heritage of Edwards a vital and powerful force in the nineteenth century.

There were a few thinkers during this period who achieved significant acclaim while remaining outside the academic institutions. The transcendentalists, led by Ralph Waldo Emerson, Bronson Alcott, George Ripley, and Theodore Parker, were essentially religious thinkers who emerged from the Unitarian fold but for whom Unitarianism was an inadequate answer to their religious needs. They found their answer in romanticism, derived chiefly from Samuel Taylor Coleridge, and fashioned an absolute idealism that achieved its classic expression in Emerson's *Nature* in 1836. Although their idealism was deemed terribly radical in the 1830s, the subsequent growth of the influence of German ideas in America made them appear quite respectable by the 1880s. A second group, or rather set of groups, were the various Hegelian and idealist societies that sprang up in the Midwest around the middle of the century. The St. Louis group, led by William T. Harris and Henry Brokmeyer, was the most influential of these and made a considerable contribution in popularizing German idealism. One should also mention the Hartford minister Horace Bushnell, who became a significant figure within the Congregational church and whose theological radicalism also stemmed from his adoption of German ideas. These figures, whatever their individual merits, are important not for their originality or influence but as signs of the increasing impact of German idealism in nineteenth-century America.

It was the publication of Charles Darwin's *Origin of Species* in 1859 that led to the triumph of German idealism in America. The theory of evolution had shattering implications for orthodox religion, and the publication of Darwin's work led to furious controversies that were all the more traumatic in the United States because of the dominion religion had hitherto held over the nation's intellectual life. While argument raged over issues such as the literal truth of the Bible, the deeper problems posed by evolutionary theory were two. First, Darwin left no place for a spiritual principle in human nature and so called into question the bipartite Christian model of man as a creature part animal and part spirit, a model upon which doctrines like immortality and resurrection were based. Second, Darwinian theory gave no reason to believe that nature was the product of a designing mind and so called into question the prevailing assumption that nature was intelligible to human reason. These problems undercut virtually all preevolutionary philosophy and theology in America and confronted the post-Darwinian generation with an intellectual challenge of great gravity. It was this challenge that brought forth that extraordinary outpouring of intellectual energy that historians have called "the golden age of American philosophy."

☆ ☆ ☆ Charles Peirce: Addressing the Schism

The greatest philosopher of post-Darwinian America was Charles Sanders Peirce (1839–1914). Trained as a mathematician and chemist, Peirce made his career as a physicist with the U.S. Coast and Geodetic Survey and held academic appointments only sporadically. But from his youth Peirce had a consuming interest in philosophy and particularly in logic. Immanuel Kant (1724–1804) was Peirce's early master in philosophy, and it was from Kant that he derived both his passion for an architectonic system and his belief that any such system must be based on logic. Peirce came to the study of logic at a time when mathematical logic was in its formative phase; George Boole, Augustus De Morgan, and their followers were in the process of creating the algebra of logic. Like these men, Peirce was both mathematician and logician, and he was able to develop the new discipline in original and creative ways. It was Peirce who created the modern logic of relations. He also independently discovered quantification (unknown to him, the German mathematician Gottlob Frege had already discovered it) and did important work in proof theory, model logic, three-valued logic, the foundation of mathematics, and logical notation. Peirce was the greatest American logician of the nineteenth century and ranks with Frege and Boole as one of the three greatest logicians of that period in the world.

Peirce was always an idealist. In his early work he sought to develop a theory of inquiry that would be at once adequate for science and for his more metaphysical concerns. He conceived of individual human beings as signs—more exactly, as series of developing signs—in the universal mind. He interpreted the universal mind as the totality of such sign series or, in other words, as a community of minds. The transcendental unity of apperception therefore became for Peirce the logically consistent synthesis of all these sign series.

This synthesis Peirce saw as the result of the process of inquiry; he held that scientific inquiry, if indefinitely continued, will converge to a final consistent set of results. As the transcendental unity of apperception gives us the transcendental object of Kant's philosophy, so Peirce defined the real as what is designated in the final opinion. Thus it was crucial for Peirce to prove that inquiry does converge to a final result, and this led him to a detailed analysis of scientific method, inductive and hypothetical inference, and probability. As part of this investigation, in 1878 he published the famous paper "How to Make Our Ideas Clear," in which the pragmatic theory of meaning received its first published statement.

In his later work Peirce turned to a more fully developed idealism that he called synechism, holding that reality is continuous and that matter is mind whose habits have become so rigid they appear to be physical laws. He elaborated an evolutionary cosmology designed to show that the process of universal evolution is both divinely ordained and moral. Converting evolution into a new form of divine providence, Peirce found in absolute idealism a resolution of the chaos wrought by Darwinian theory.

☆ ☆ ☆ Josiah Royce's Absolute Idealism

Although Peirce had an enormous influence upon his philosophic contemporaries, his position outside the academic world and the difficulty of his writing denied him the public notice that came to thinkers like Josiah Royce, William James, and John Dewey. Royce (1855–1916) too was an absolute idealist and a thinker of real power. From his position at Harvard, he exerted a great influence upon American philosophy in the late nineteenth and early twentieth centuries. Royce followed Peirce in turning to logic as the basis for his system. Although he was not a logician of Peirce's caliber, he was as able a logician as there was in the United States between Peirce and Clarence Irving Lewis.

Royce's argument for absolute idealism was based upon his theory of error. A statement, Royce held, is true or false as it does or does not correspond to its intended object in the intended way. But what is the object spoken of? If it is an object intended by the speaker, then the speaker must already know the object, and his reference to it must be to it as he knows it, that is, to his idea of the object. However, a man's statement can scarcely fail to correspond to his own idea of its object. Therefore, there is no error. But consider the statement, "There is error." If this statement is true, there is error; if it is false, it is in error and there is error. We have a contradiction, therefore, that Royce held is only resolvable by assuming that both object and speaker are ideas in the mind of an absolute knower who can directly compare the speaker's statement with the real object and judge the degree of correspondence. Thus Royce's proof of idealism rests upon dialectical argument, and it is not hard to see why logic should have so attracted him.

Working in the Kantian tradition, Royce sought to establish the basic categories of thought, and he came to the conclusion that these are of two different sorts. The categories of science for him are simply the primitive concepts of the sciences; it is these concepts that make experience describable and shareable. These scientific categories, however, are pragmatic in their justification; they give us a working science but are subject to change and revision as science grows. Furthermore, the categories do not render accurately our inner experience, the appreciative content of consciousness, which is often called subjective. When we talk of other minds, we do not mean physically describable entities but centers of subjective appreciation like our own. The world of scientific description, therefore, cannot be the whole world, for we could not even intend to communicate if we did not believe there were other minds. The world of appreciation, which embraces the world of description too, is the mind of the Absolute, and we can refer to other minds because both they and we are ideas of the Absolute.

Like Peirce, Royce regards the self as a developing series of signs, or ideas, in the Absolute mind. What gives coherence and unity to the self is its teleological organization; a true self is a series of ideas, or life, bound together by a goal-directed plan. The Absolute, too, as a self possesses such a teleological unity, of which we, as its ideas, are constituents. It is clear that Royce is here applying Hegel's notion of the concrete universal, but he was well aware of the problems, raised by Francis Bradley and others, of explaining how human individuals relate to the Absolute. Again following Peirce's lead, Royce turned to the theory of infinite series to explicate this relation. The individual, as an important being, is an infinite series of ideas, but just as the even integers are an infinite subset of the integers so, Royce held, many individuals may be "parts" of the Absolute.

The explication of the logical relation of individual and Absolute, however, did not answer the question of the moral relation. For Royce, like Edwards, true morality consisted in love of God, but in Royce's formulation this takes the form of loyalty. Loyalty at once leads the individual to willing subordination of self to the greater self yet exalts the individual through his service to and sacrifice for the Absolute. Royce's ethics therefore became an ethic requiring all men to seek to increase the amount of loyalty in the world, so that eventually all would be bound together in a voluntary harmony.

In his later work, Royce attempted a daring extension of his logical and mathematical theories into the mind of God. Building on the work of Peirce and A. B. Kempe, he tried to define a very general type of order system from which all types of order systems necessary for the description of the world and the self could be derived. If successful, such a system might be taken as describing the structure of the Absolute mind and would reveal how the worlds of description and appreciation could be consistently combined in the mind of God.

Royce's final major work was an attempt to reconstruct Christianity on the basis of his idealism. Again following Peirce, he redefined the Absolute as a community of selves—in this case, the beloved community that he identified with the Christian church. Of this greater self, Christ was the unifying force and life. Loyalty to the church thus becomes Christian virtue, and disloyalty becomes sin. Royce argues that although a disloyal (that is, sinful) act, once done, can never be undone, it can be atoned for in the sense that it can be made the occasion for a further act so virtuous that on balance one would rather have had the sin and its redeeming act than neither. But Royce is a Calvinist still, as becomes clear in his doctrine of grace, for one cannot simply choose to be loyal; loyalty comes as a call from above that compels the individual will. Thus Royce remained to the end a defender of Christian orthodoxy who sought to rebuild its doctrines upon the basis of absolute idealism.

☆ ☆ ☆ William James and Radical Empiricism

William James (1842–1919) came from a less orthodox but no less intense religious background than Royce. His father was a Swedenborgian theologian, and James's need for a secure basis for his religious faith dominated his intellectual life. James saw very early the implications of Darwinian theory and recognized that only one thoroughly knowledgeable in the biological sciences could meet the challenge. Accordingly, he studied medicine and became an instructor in anatomy at Harvard. For James the central issue of the evolutionary controversy was the nature of the human mind: Was it, as Herbert Spencer and the materialists held, totally determined by physical law, so that freedom was an illusion we are compelled to believe? Or was there some sense in which the mind was genuinely free, so that moral striving represented a meaningful choice? During the 1880s James devoted himself to the study of psychology, and in 1890 he published his monumental *Principles of Psychology*, a work that exerted an enormous influence upon psychology for decades. Writing as a psychologist, James introduced the notion of the stream of consciousness—the ever-changing content of the conscious mind into which the data of the senses are poured in a chaotic torrent. Out of this stream,

James held, our attention selects certain features from which we construct the world around us. It is the selective attention that builds a man's world, and for James the selective attention is the will. In it are reflected our loves and hates, our interests and abilities; but it is still a free will. We choose to attend to what interests us.

The world we construct cannot be a copy of some external reality. Not only are the senses selective organs, but we also build our world by selecting from the data they provide. Truth therefore cannot be a relation between our model of the world and something *out there*; it must be defined in terms of relations *within* our experience. This line of thought led James to develop Peirce's pragmatic theory of meaning into the pragmatic theory of truth. A sentence is true, James held, only if the experiences that it predicts really occur when the stipulated conditions of occurrence are fulfilled. This thesis seems at first glance positivistic, but James gave it a broad interpretation to include not only consequences of the given hypothesis but also consequences of believing the given hypothesis. Thus James was able to argue that the satisfactions of belief can be counted as evidence for a belief.

James used this thesis to justify what he called "the will to believe." A man confronted by two equally probable hypotheses and forced to choose between them may assign utilities to the various outcomes according to different rules. The classic empiricist dictum that one should never believe without adequate evidence amounts to a rule for assigning utilities such that it is more desirable to reject a false proposition than to accept a true one. But James argued that it is just as rational to assign the higher utility to believing the true proposition and the lower utility to rejecting a falsehood. In such cases, the choice of how utilities are to be assigned has to be made in terms of the consequences of believing. Thus James held it to be perfectly rational to believe in God, freedom, and immortality, even though the empirical evidence on either side of the question was equally slim.

James held that the world of experience is not to be differentiated from the "real" world. What there is, he argued, is pure experience. The same experience may stand in different relational contexts. If it always follows the laws of association and can be made to appear and vanish at will, we say it is subjective; but if it stands in invariable causal relations to other experiences and resists our will, we call it objective. In all cases, however, it is the same experience, albeit differently classified. This was James's doctrine of radical empiricism, although the basic idea came from his friend Chauncey Wright.

James could not rest with this sort of neutral empiricism, however, for it left unanswered questions that he knew he could not avoid. If all there is is experience, what becomes of the experience when no one actually experiences it? Further, since all experience is personal and private, as James had shown in his *Psychology*, how can two minds know the same experience? To solve these problems James turned to idealism, but not to the idealism of Royce, which he considered a deterministic system leaving no place for freedom or meaningful striving. James's idealism was a pluralistic panpsychism in which the universe consists of bits of experience that although distinct are continuously connected to each other and so can know each other. This is, of course, Peirce's synechism, albeit a form that Peirce would not have owned. Such universal continuity permits each individual mind to be connected to a wider realm of experience and so to God. There is, therefore, for James genuine religious experience that bespeaks our relation to the divine, although James's God is neither all-determining nor all-embracing. The universe contains a plurality of knowers, God among them, who are genuinely free to act and whose action makes a real difference in the course of history.

☆ ☆ ☆ John Dewey: A Philosophy of Cognition

Born in the year that Darwin published, John Dewey (1859–1952) was younger than Peirce, Royce, and James, but like them he came from a deeply religious background. A native of Vermont reared in a Calvinist household, Dewey imbibed that mixture of New England theology and German idealism that James Marsh had institutionalized at the University of Vermont, from which Dewey graduated in 1879. As a graduate student at Johns Hopkins, he worked under George Sylvester Morris, from whom he learned a full-fledged idealism, and he followed Morris to Michigan as an instructor in philosophy in 1884. In 1894 he moved to the University of Chicago and there rose to national prominence. In 1904 he moved again, this time to Columbia University, and New York remained his stage throughout the remainder of his long, productive life.

Dewey was drawn to Hegel not only by the latter's idealism and historicism, both of which seemed essential to any reconciliation of Darwinian science and Christian theology, but also by his holism. Dewey's early criticisms of such neo-Hegelians as Thomas Hill Green focus on their inability to explain satisfactorily the relation of finite and infinite, science and metaphysics, form and content, spirit and nature. What Dewey wanted was a synthetic idealism that would create a genuine organic unity. By the early 1890s Dewey had begun to work out his solution to these problems. If the infinite (that is, God) is taken as immanent in the world, it is manifested to us as the experienced world, and this guarantees that experience (that is, nature) is inherently meaningful and knowable. The growth of our knowledge is then the transformation of latent meaning into actual meaning, and the method of developing our knowledge, whether called scientific method or psychology, is the means by which the natural is transformed into the spiritual. Since man and nature are really one order of being, there is for Dewey no problem of subject versus object or mind versus matter but only the task of describing the constant interaction among the component parts of a progressively developing system. Thus it really makes little difference whether one sees Dewey as a "naturalist" or an "idealist" because for Dewey there is no such distinction.

Dewey identifies the psychological process of knowing with the process of scientific inquiry. For Dewey the finite organism is a creature, energetic by nature, that seeks goods or satisfactions in its experience. In so doing, it is guided by habits of action, which are energy channeled into a particular mode of behavior to achieve a certain good. Only when the expectation of satisfaction is disappointed do we find ourselves faced with a problem situation, and it is such a problem situation that calls forth reflective thought. Reflection must at once diagnose the situation to discover what the problem is and develop hypotheses concerning possibilities of alternative action that might so reconstruct the situation as to permit its solution. These alternative hypotheses must be elaborated to determine what courses of action they involve and then tested until we find one that works and permits the flow of action into satisfaction to resume. This process of inquiry is for Dewey both the natural history of thought and a self-correcting process of investigation, for we learn from experience better methods of reflection, diagnosis, and testing and thus improve our cognitive skills.

However, to describe this process only from the standpoint of the individual knower is to falsify Dewey's view. Habits are first learned in becoming part of the group, and inquiry is always a social process. Moreover, behavior is inherently moral, both because it is directed to desired goods and because it has social consequences that are constantly appraised by ourselves and others. Morality is for Dewey a way of controlling future action so as to maximize the probability of attaining desired goods. Valuation, appraisal, and moral judgment are as much a part of the "natural" behavior of human beings as eating or sleeping. Man is a moral creature because he is a social creature and because he seeks goods; the problem is not to derive moral judgments from factual ones—ought judgments are facts of human behavior and that is all there is to that—but to correct our methods of moral control so that they are increasingly effective.

Peirce, James, Royce, and Dewey were all idealists, although of different sorts. It was idealism that enabled them to reconstruct the worldview in the wake of the Darwinian devastation and to find a method of harmonizing science and religion that at once seemed to protect the latter while providing a firm foundation for the former. All were meliorists in the sense that they believed human action guided by intelligence could make the world better, all thrilled to the call of muscular Christianity to battle for the Lord, all believed that science would prove a mighty weapon of righteousness, and all were convinced that they fought under the banner of God, freedom, and immortality.

☆ ☆ ☆ George Santayana: Life as a Work of Art

The most radical dissenter from this joyous consensus was George Santayana (1863–1952). Younger than the others, and educated at Harvard, where he was fully exposed to the Cambridge tradition, Santayana did not contract the disease. A Spaniard by birth, Santayana identified with his Catholic background even though he was raised chiefly in Boston, and the Protestant tradition always repelled him. A moralist interested in art and aesthetics, Santayana affected a lack of interest in the issues that so engaged his contemporaries although in fact he was thoroughly knowledgeable about and greatly influenced by Darwinian science and its implications. He delighted in being a self-proclaimed materialist among idealists, a fatalist among activists, and an artist among true believers in science. In 1912 he left America to live in Southern Europe where he had always felt more at home.

Santayana distinguished four realms of being: essence, matter, truth, and spirit. By essence, Santayana meant pure qualities known through sense but considered as universal and static. Such essences he held to be eternal, changeless, and unordered, since two related essences are part of a single simple essence. All that can be known in immediate perception is essences, but by definition essences provide no explanation for change. For that purpose Santayana invoked matter, which is for him the locus of all power, all causality, and therefore all change. It is matter that determines what essences are actualized in what order. But matter itself is irrational and inexplicable, for any explanation of its actions would be a law, or sequence of essences, and that sequence would be just another essence.

Animals, including man, are for Santayana organizations of matter that manifest certain patterns of behavior. The dynamic organization of such patterns in an individual Santayana called psyche. It is an organization dedicated to achieving purely animal aims and satisfying animal needs. But somewhere in the course of evolution, psyche evolved spirit, by which Santayana means the pure light of consciousness. Spirit is a tool of psyche; its function is to provide a wider view of the world and of the possibilities of action than psyche alone had and so to facilitate psyche's search for gratification. Spirit, although an epiphenomenon, is a distinct order of being. It has no power, since it is not material, and it seeks truth and love because these are of use to psyche. Thus spirit is destined forever to seek for goals that psyche prostitutes to its carnal ends and to be a spectator of a passing world it can neither control nor influence.

Truth for Santayana is the complete description of the combination of essences that matter actualizes. Since the essences we perceive are relative to use, our knowledge can be at best a poetic rendition of the world. Nevertheless, the science we create is the only guide we have in action. Perception alone gives us nothing but essence, and to go beyond it we must interpret the essences we know as signs of a material world. We cannot prove that such a world exists—Santayana regarded the skeptic's argument as irrefutable—but we are compelled to make such a leap of faith by our animal needs.

Santayana's view of life stands in dramatic contrast to that of his American contemporaries. They were desperately concerned to rescue religion from science. For all his love of the Catholic tradition, it is not clear that Santayana believed in God at all. They were concerned to prove that man's consciousness was a free and effective agent in the world; Santayana regarded spirit as impotent and bound to psyche's service. They were passionately devoted to the belief that life is a significant moral struggle in which good can triumph over evil; Santayana thought life a tragedy to be endured with resignation and appreciated as a work of art.

☆ ☆ ☆ C. I. Lewis and Pragmatism

The academic philosophers of the late nineteenth century—Royce, James, Dewey, and Santayana—were professional philosophers in the sense that they made their living by doing philosophy (Peirce was not; he was a professional scientist), but they continued to see themselves as public figures whose views on issues were of importance, and they often addressed themselves to lay audiences. The emergence of professional philosophers in the strict sense of those who worked in and for a group of technically competent peers is a phenomenon of the twentieth century. Certainly the leading such figure before World War II was C. I. Lewis. Born in 1883 in Massachusetts, Lewis was trained at Harvard by James and Royce. After a short stint at the University of California he joined the Harvard faculty in 1920 and remained there throughout his career. A prolific writer of great influence within philosophy, his work is unknown outside the academy.

From Royce, Lewis acquired an early appreciation of logic and so was well prepared to appreciate Bertrand Russell and Alfred North Whitehead's great achievement when their *Principia Mathematica* appeared in 1912. But Lewis was distressed by Russell and Whitehead's use of the material conditional to represent implication and was therefore led to construct alternative systems of logic involving what he called "strict implication"—namely, *p* strictly implies *q* if and only if it is impossible that *p* is true and *q* is false. This is, of course, a modal notion designed to avoid the "paradoxes" of material implication (that a false proposition implies every proposition and a true proposition is implied by any proposition), but it creates a curious situation in which we have several alternative logics and are forced to choose among them.

Kant had regarded a priori knowledge as fixed and certain and sense data as arbitrary and variable. Lewis reversed Kant's thesis: it is the given of sensation, Lewis held, that is fixed and certain and the a priori that is arbitrary and variable. By the "given," Lewis means the sensory qualities known in experience—the particular suchness of a sensory impression. Such sensory qualities are certain and indubitable, even though they cannot be precisely rendered in language since no language has a separate term for every experienceable suchness. But the inadequacies of language do not affect the certainty of the experience of such qualities, and it is this certainty that is the foundation of our knowledge.

In Lewis's view, it is the conceptual schemes in which we interpret sense experience that are arbitrary and variable. This arbitrariness applies not only to empirical theories but to logic and the basic categories of thought that Lewis takes to be a priori. A statement like "all swans are white" may be treated either as an empirical statement, refutable by empirical test, or as a definition of "swan," which no empirical test can refute. Our definition of reality is similarly a priori, since whatever does not conform to it is ruled out of order. If this is so, however, how do we choose among alternative definitions of reality or alternative systems of logic?

Lewis's answer is the theory of the pragmatic a priori. We adopt a conceptual scheme, including its a priori elements, because it enables us to deal adequately with experience. If it becomes cumbersome, and if a simpler scheme is available, we may change our conceptual scheme, not because the first is refuted but because the second is more useful. There is indeed no principle, not even the law of noncontradiction, that is not subject to revision in this sense.

Lewis's doctrine involves a sophisticated theory of meaning that underlies his theory of the a priori. To claim that "all swans are white" is a priori is to hold it analytic—to so construe the meaning of "swan" that to be a swan means to be white. Thus in elaborating the consequences of hypotheses to determine what they strictly imply, we are explicating their meaning. A commitment to meaning, synonymy, and analyticity is basic to Lewis's program.

Like the other pragmatists, Lewis sought to expand his theory of scientific knowledge into a theory of valuation. Judgments of value are empirically testable since concrete satisfactions are or are not realized in experiences under stipulated conditions. There is thus for Lewis nothing in the nature of value that makes an empirical and pragmatic theory of valuation impossible, and knowledge of the good may be shown to rest on the same basis as scientific knowledge.

☆ ☆ ☆ Logical Positivism in America

During the 1930s and 1940s American philosophy, like European philosophy, was enormously influenced by the development of modern logic as exemplified by Ludwig Wittgenstein's early work and especially by the logical positivism of the Vienna Circle. The rise of Hitler and the coming of World War II brought many Continental philosophers to the United States, including positivists such as Carl Hempel and Rudolf Carnap. The logical rigor, the scientific precision, and the fierce empiricism of the positivists made them for a time the dominant movement in American philosophy and even led some Americans to see pragmatism as a kind of protopositivism, forgetting its roots in idealism and religious concerns. The sharp distinctions that the positivists drew between a priori analytic knowledge (logic and mathematics), a posteriori synthetic knowledge (empirical science), and noncognitive emotive "knowledge" (everything else) became axiomatic for a generation of American thinkers, despite the opposition of men like Dewey and Lewis who continued to insist that valuation and morality were something more than pleasant poetry.

But what was most inspiring and influential about the positivists was their honesty. They not only claimed that a complete description of the world could be constructed from sensory elements, they attempted to construct it. They not only talked about evidence conferring probability hypotheses, they tried to construct a calculus of confirmation. It was this determination to carry through their program, combined with the extraordinary skills that they brought to the attempt, that so captured the admiration of others, including many American philosophers.

In the post–World War II period, Willard Quine has been the most influential and controversial American philosopher. A student of Lewis and Carnap, Quine has spent his career at Harvard. The best American logician of his generation, Quine's interests were always broad, and over the past thirty years he has written influential works in philosophy of science, epistemology, and philosophy of language. Quine is a staunch antimentalist. Convinced that mental entities such as "ideas" and "meanings" are mythological in character, he began very early to question whether the postulation of such constructs serves any useful function in philosophy. This led him to an attack on the notions of synonymy and analyticity, which he holds to be indefinable except in terms of equally obscure notions, such as modal concepts. At the same time Quine has espoused a holism that maintains that sentences cannot be confirmed or disconfirmed individually but only in sets, so that it is the theory rather than the single hypothesis that is the appropriate unit of test. Since a given theory can accommodate anomalous experiences in various ways, it follows that we need never abandon a particular hypothesis, or even a particular theory; sufficient mulishness fortified by adequate ingenuity can always patch up the theory so as to fit any empirical findings. This thesis has led Quine to view even logic and mathematics as conceptual schemes whose function is making sense of experience and so as being pragmatically justified—a claim that Lewis had also advanced on somewhat different grounds.

Quine's denial of mental entities has led him to identify the meaning of a word with the totality of speech dispositions involving that word. This behaviorism, however, turns out to have a cost, for it calls into question not only interlinguistic translation but also interpersonal communication, not on the traditional practical grounds but on theoretical grounds. In Quine's view, once a matching of linguistic usages has been achieved between two speakers such that each finds the other's linguistic behavior interpretable, there is no point to questioning the correctness of their interpretations. Such questions would only make sense if behind the linguistic usages there lurked mental entities called "meanings," and Quine holds that no such things exist. Since the matching of usages among speakers can be done in different ways, we cannot know that a given speaker of our tongue means what we mean or even that we are referring to the same entity. Thus empiricism without mentalism appears to leave our ontology relative not only to a language but to our private view.

The recovery of American philosophy from the positivist invasion is evident in the works of other philosophers besides Quine. John Rawls's *A Theory of Justice* has stimulated much new work in ethics, while Nelson Goodman's *Languages of Art* has changed the terms of debate in aesthetics. Donald

Davidson and Roderick Chisholm have made important contributions to the theory of action and the philosophy of mind, while Saul Kripke has revitalized modal logic and introduced influential innovations in the philosophy of language. Noam Chomsky's revolutionary impact on linguistics has exerted a major influence on the philosophy of language, while developments in cognitive science and artificial intelligence have had a great impact on the philosophy of mind and language and on epistemology, as evidenced, for example, in the work of Hilary Putnam. At the same time, the philosophy of science has remained a field of vigorous controversy, as Wesley Salmon's recent work shows. Thus American philosophy today is a dynamic field with a broad range of concerns stemming both from philosophic tradition and from the stimulation provided by such disciplines as psychology, linguistics, physics, and computer science.

☆ ☆ ☆ American Philosophy: From Theology toward Science

The story of philosophy in America thus briefly reviewed is of course intimately related to the story of Western philosophy generally. But what has particularly marked philosophy in America is its long identification with Protestant theology. Prior to 1859 there is a very gradual separation of theology and philosophy, chiefly as a result of specialization rather than conflict. With the Darwinian controversy and the emergence of the modern university, professors of philosophy appeared who were not ministers but whose concerns were essentially religious and who continued to model their role on that of the minister. These people turned to idealism as a way of harmonizing science and religion and reintegrating the worldview. Indeed, prior to 1900 it was only in the revolutionary period that a secular group of thinkers achieved leadership in American intellectual life. It is one of the more striking aspects of our intellectual history that this brief florescence of legal and political philosophy led by lawyers and statesmen should have ended so quickly and completely after 1800. Not until the emergence of professional philosophy in the twentieth century does secular leadership assert itself and then only in philosophy that has adopted the social organization of science by specialty as its model. Here the philosopher becomes a technical specialist working within a community of fellow specialists, and his role is modeled on that of the scientist, not the minister. The integration of the worldview is now discussed only in terms of the unification of science, and the issues that in another age seemed matters of life and death are now seen as strictly academic.

FURTHER READING

Among general histories of American philosophy, the standard for many years has been Herbert Schneider, *A History of American Philosophy* (New York, 1963). Recently this has been supplemented by Elizabeth Flower and Murray Murphey, *A History of Philosophy in America*, 2 vols. (New York, 1977). These two works will provide the reader with a general overview of the subject. More specific histories are Bruce Kuklick's *The Rise of American Philosophy* (New Haven, Conn., 1977) and his *Churchmen and Philosophers: From Jonathan Edwards to John Dewey* (New Haven, Conn., 1984). Perry Miller's *The New England Mind: The Seventeenth Century* (New York, 1939) and *The New England Mind: From Colony to Province* (Cambridge, Mass., 1953) are the classic studies of Puritan thought in America in the colonial period. Norman Fiering's *Moral Philosophy at Seventeenth-Century Harvard* (Chapel Hill, N.C., 1981) is an important supplement to Miller's work. On Jonathan Edwards, see Perry Miller, *Jonathan Edwards* (New Haven, Conn., 1948), and Fiering, *Jonathan Edwards' Moral Thought and Its British Context* (Williamsburg, Va., 1981). Bernard Bailyn's *The Ideological Origins of the American Revolution* (Cambridge, Mass., 1967) and Gordon Wood's *The Creation of the American Republic, 1776–1787* (Chapel Hill, N.C., 1969) are the best recent interpretations of the development of American political thought from 1763 through the ratification of the Constitution. See also Garry Wills, *Inventing America: Jefferson's Declaration of Independence* (New York, 1978), and *Explaining America: The Federalist* (New York, 1981). Murray Murphey's *The Development of Peirce's Philosophy* (Cambridge, Mass., 1961) and Bruce Kuklick's *Josiah Royce: An Intellectual Biography* (Indianapolis, Ind., 1972) provide detailed studies of two major figures.

Those who wish to pursue works by the philosophers discussed are advised to consult Jonathan Edwards, *A Treatise Concerning Religious Affections*, ed. John E. Smith (New Haven, Conn., 1959), *Enquiry into the Freedom of the Will*, ed. Paul Ramsey (New Haven, Conn., 1957), and *Scientific and Philosophical Writings*, ed. Wallace E. Anderson (New Haven, Conn., 1980). The papers in *The Federalist* (1787–88) by James Madison, Alexander Hamilton, and John Jay are the finest single exposition of the political thought underlying the U.S. Constitution and are available in multiple editions. Peirce's works are best accessed for the general reader in collections such as Philip Wiener, ed., *Values in a Universe of Chance* (New York, 1966), and Justus Buchler, ed., *Philosophical Writings of Peirce* (New York, 1955). For William James, *Pragmatism*, ed. Bruce Kuklick (Indianapolis, Ind., 1981), and *Essays in Radical Empiricism and a Pluralistic Universe* (Gloucester, Mass., 1967) are recommended. Josiah Royce's works are voluminous. *The Religious Aspect of Philosophy* (New York, 1958) gives the best view of Royce's early thought and *The World and the Individual*, ed. John E. Smith (New York, 1959), of his more developed position. John Dewey's *Human Nature and Conduct: An*

Introduction to Social Psychology, ed. Jo Ann Boydston (Carbondale, Ill., 1983), *Essays in Experimental Logic* (New York, 1953), and *Theory of Valuation* (Chicago, 1966) will provide a good introduction to his thought. George Santayana's *Skepticism and Animal Faith* (New York, 1955) is the best introduction to his system. C. I. Lewis's major works are *Mind and the World Order* (New York, 1956) and *The Analysis of Knowledge and Valuation* (La Salle, Ill., 1947). Willard Quine's writings are usually quite technical, but the determined reader will find "On What There Is" and "Two Dogmas of Empiricism" in *From a Logical Point of View* (Cambridge, Mass., 1980), *Word and Object* (Cambridge, Mass., 1960), and "Ontological Relativity" in *Ontological Relativity and Other Essays* (New York, 1969) the places to start.

The reader may also wish to consult John Rawls, *A Theory of Justice* (Cambridge, Mass., 1971); Nelson Goodman, *Languages of Art* (Indianapolis, Ind., 1968); Donald Davidson, *Essays on Actions and Events* (Oxford, 1980), and *Inquiries into Truth and Interpretation* (Oxford, 1984); Roderick Chisholm, *The First Person* (Minneapolis, 1981); Saul Kripke, *Naming and Necessity* (Cambridge, Mass., 1980); Noam Chomsky, *Aspects of the Theory of Syntax* (Cambridge, Mass., 1965); Hilary Putnam, *Mind, Language, and Reality* (New York, 1975), and *Realism and Reason* (New York, 1983); and Wesley Salmon, *Scientific Explanation and the Causal Structure of the World* (Princeton, N.J., 1984).

23 ☆ Civil Disobedience

☆ in American Political

☆ Thought

☆

☆ John P. Diggins

A common assumption holds that political authority and civil disobedience contradict one another. The first formulation of the problem in classical antiquity seems to dramatize the contradiction. In *The Apology*, Socrates urges civil disobedience to fulfill the demands of moral law; in *The Crito*, he advocates submission to folkways to preserve social order. The conflict between the needs of the state and the right to disobey has remained with us ever since. In American history the writings and actions of Henry David Thoreau and Martin Luther King, Jr., presume that conflict to be the first step in the struggle toward justice. Before examining their thoughts, let us first establish the nature of the problem between authority and disobedience.

☆ ☆ ☆ Ideas of Authority and Civil Disobedience

If we consider the defining characteristics of the two principles, there does indeed appear to be a mutual antagonism. Authority has been defined in various ways: the uncontested acceptance of another's judgment; the ability of an agent or institution to express its will; the capacity to induce compliance either by offering rewards or threatening deprivations; the claims of competence on the part of an expert whose knowledge is put to public service; the aura of "charisma" on the part of an exceptional leader whose qualities inspire admiration and awe; or the existence of established rules that entitle the one or few to represent the many. Whatever the definition, authority is usually distinguished from power because it is based on the voluntary obedience of subjects who have presumably consented to its exercise over themselves.

Civil disobedience, in contrast, often rests on the assumption that the individual is the ultimate source of authority and that the self acts under the sanction of some principle that is "higher" than the state, society, or even the people under a system of democratic government. Its animating ethos is the feeling that one is morally bound to disobey some law or custom, for not to do so would betray the dictates of conscience. Civil disobedience can be either peaceful or violent, although the idea of nonviolent, passive resistance has been the more frequent principle of action. The expression "civil" also implies that the action is of a public political nature, and thus disobedience to family, school, and other authorities does not constitute civil acts of protest. Civil disobedience, furthermore, is not necessarily revolutionary, for in encounters with the state the protester may accept the system of government, however imbecilic he or she regards its institutions. In engaging in openly announced defiance of particular laws or customs, the activist is not so much determined to transform the state as to withhold allegiance from it until its alleged abuses are corrected.

The intellectual roots of civil disobedience can be traced not only to Anglo-American political ideas but also to Judeo-Christian traditions. Jesus expressed the conflict between religious conscience and social customs when he sought to purify the temple by chasing out the money changers. In nineteenth-century America, abolitionists attacked the institution of slavery by refusing to uphold the Fugitive Slave laws. In the twentieth century, Mohandas Gandhi subverted colonial rule in South Africa and India with acts of passive disobedience, a practice later adopted by Europeans resisting Nazi occupation, by American civil rights activists campaigning against segregation, and by students engaging in boycotts and "sit-ins" to protest the Vietnam War.

Such courageous deeds were undertaken in defiance of existing systems of political authority, whether totalitarian or democratic. Yet the idea of political authority and the idea of civil disobedience, rather than contradicting one another, in many ways presuppose one another. The problem of civil authority only arises when recalcitrant subjects question its legitimacy and demand reasons for obeying the laws of the land; and civil disobedience arises when subjects refuse to accept those reasons and instead offer counterarguments designed to undermine them. Thus, although civil disobedience often originates from the inner promptings of conscience, it inevitably expresses itself in a dialogue with external authority, a dialogue that pits the mind against the state.

☆ ☆ ☆ Early American Thought and Civil Disobedience

In American history the relationship between authority and disobedience had its first political manifestation in the conflict between power and liberty at the time of the Revolution. The intellectual forces of that event can be traced to two sources that would continue as the touchstone of resistance politics throughout American history: Protestantism and liberalism, specifically the teachings of John Calvin and of John Locke.

The idea of the "covenant" practiced by seventeenth-century New England Puritans carried both conservative and radical implications. In the first instance the idea called upon the people to submit to their rulers and to obey the laws of the land as the will of God. But inherent in Calvinist political philosophy was also the principle that the people had a right, indeed a duty, to disobey magistrates and rulers when they acted in ways that violated the covenant with God and thus forfeited their authority. If a wayward ruler were allowed to continue in office, the people would be disobeying God and risking his wrath by submitting to a government that had broken the covenant. Historians such as Edmund S. Morgan see the Puritan covenant as the intellectual seed of the American Revolution. To the extent that Americans indicted British rule for its moral leniency as well as political harshness, they believed that the only way America could arrest corruption and backsliding was to resist, oppose, and defy the Stamp Act and other rules and regulations. The English philosopher and statesman Edmund Burke tried vainly to warn Parliament that Americans were, above all, Protestants who loved nothing so much as to protest, question, and deny authority. When the colonists threw tea into Boston harbor, the American Revolution began, at least symbolically, in a dramatic act of civil disobedience.

The second idea spiriting the Revolution derived from Locke. The seventeenth-century English philosopher developed a "social contract" theory of government that made authority and obedience rest on interest and the primacy of self-preservation. The purpose of government was not so much to fulfill God's will as to protect life, liberty, and property as the prerequisites of human happiness. Like the Puritans, however, Locke also emphasized the limited nature of the ruler's power. In Locke we have one of the clearest expressions of what Isaiah Berlin has called "negative liberty," the individual's freedom from government and public authority. Locke offered Americans not only a rationale for the right of resistance but even the right to revolution. To the extent that an existing regime violates the original compact by failing to protect people's rights and safeguard their interests, Americans were entitled to break the "bonds of affection" with their mother country, as Thomas Jefferson wrote in the Declaration of Independence. Thus in early American history one can find the theoretical foundations for civil disobedience to government. The Calvinist covenant and the liberal contract embody both the legitimation of authority and the rationale for its resistance.

☆ ☆ ☆ Thoreau and His Predecessors

But in liberal political philosophy the right of resistance presupposes the will of the majority as the sovereign agency of the people. In Locke's theory there is unanimous agreement that the majority's decision shall be binding on everyone, and thus the decision to either perpetuate or dissolve a government rests on popular consent. Civil disobedience, in contrast, implies that a small minority of citizens have rights that derive from conscience rather than consent.

For Thoreau, as we shall see, dissent could mean even "a minority of one," the solitary individual acting alone against a government that had allegedly abused its authority. Thoreau's theory of civil disobedience also emphasized the right to act morally as well as individually. Here is where Thoreau and the framers of the Constitution posed antithetical views of human nature, that is, in the motives of political conduct. The theory of authority developed by the framers rejected the assumption that people are capable of acting morally as self-contained ethical beings. Instead of practicing virtue, exercising restraint, and working toward the public good, people would be moved by grasping "interests" and undisciplined "passions." Thus the *Federalist* authors believed that the controlling mechanisms of government must be brought to bear on all political conduct. In order to appreciate Thoreau's protest against government as a "machine," we need to examine the idea of authority and obedience in the constitutional theories of the framers. Only then can we understand why Thoreau and the abolitionists turned to the Declaration of Independence, and not the Constitution, to find the political grounds for civil disobedience.

The Declaration had articulated the colonists' grievances against England in order to legitimate their right to overthrow a government that had violated the social contract. The Constitution, however, aimed to do the opposite: to establish the right of a new government to rule and explain the people's obligation to obey. The great promise of the Constitution was that it would preserve liberty by guaranteeing to the people all the rights and powers not explicitly granted to the new federal government. The Constitution would therefore not interfere with the rights that Jefferson had enunciated in the Declaration: life, liberty, and the pursuit of happiness. Yet Jefferson and Thomas Paine remained skeptical of the Constitution, believing that the framers, more preoccupied with citizens' vices than their virtues, concentrated too much on controlling liberty instead of augmenting it. Jefferson and Paine feared the few (aristocracy); the framers feared the many (democracy). The former saw the potential for tyranny in centralized power, the latter in the unruly behavior of aggressive masses. The former demanded a Bill of Rights so that individuals could protect themselves from the actions of government, the latter a system of "auxiliary precautions" so that government could protect itself from the threat of popular majorities. In other words, those who preferred the Declaration feared the actions of the state, and those who valued the Constitution feared the actions of society. Theorists of civil disobedience often feel the threats of both state and society, and thus their protest of the laws of the state provides the means of changing the customs of society. But since civil disobedience activists have more in common with Jefferson and Paine than with the *Federalist* authors, it is worthwhile to distinguish the ideas and values of the Declarationists from those of the Constitutionalists.

The American Revolution had been deeply influenced by the writings of Jefferson and Paine and the Constitution by the writings of John Adams, Alexander Hamilton, and James Madison. Since the Revolution had liberty as its object, and the Constitution had authority, it is not surprising that theorists of civil disobedience often invoke the Declaration and the "spirit of '76." The aim of the Revolution was to reduce the authority of an old government and to restrict and even eliminate its powers; the aim of the Constitution, in contrast, was to enlarge the authority of a new government and to legitimate the exercise of centralized power. The Declaration emphasized such values as individual autonomy and reason, values that came to characterize what we can call *liberal individualism*, the right to pursue one's private concerns independently of government interference. The Constitution focused on the weakness of man and the need for a stronger state to preserve liberty and property by juxtaposing faction with faction, a theory of countervailing power that has come to be called *liberal pluralism*. Paine and Jefferson are the patron saints of the individualist, dissent tradition in American politics. In contrast to the framers, they believed that the problem of power could be resolved to the extent that all authority came directly from the people themselves. Assuming that human beings were essentially good and rational and that the forces of oppression derived mainly from the Old World, they believed they could use mind and pen to speak truth to power and thereby preserve liberty simply by exposing tyranny. Adams and the *Federalist* authors, however, operated from different assumptions. Convinced that the forces of oppression are rooted in the nature of social existence, they believed government was absolutely necessary to prevent individuals from harming one another and that the new Constitution required an elaborate mosaic of mechanisms known as "checks and balances."

☆ ☆ ☆ The Ultimate Individualist

The critique of the American system of politics by Thoreau and the transcendentalists was in part a reaffirmation of Jeffersonian individualism against Madisonian pluralism. But the critique went much deeper. It was not only that Thoreau's call for civil disobedience would transfer authority from the state to the individual or that he rejected the whole system of checks and balances. Thoreau departs from Jefferson as well as from Madison when he questions whether the "pursuit of happiness" must be regarded as a materialist proposition and whether true liberty requires property and the acquisitive impulses that alienate men and lead to "lives of quiet desperation." Thoreau also departs from Locke when he demands that government relate to its subjects as moral rather than political creatures—that government touch the "soul" of citizens and not only their senses. To put it another way, Thoreau was trying to introduce into politics precisely what the founders wanted to purge from it: the rage of moral passion.

The framers believed, as did Paine and Jefferson, that politics and government could be made a science to the extent that the focus was kept on the economic wants and needs of Americans. What they feared was a politics that sprang from "zeal," "passion," and the "pride" of a presumed superior spiritual "conscience." The *Federalist* authors likened political "factions" to religious "sects" in their common tendency to oppress and tyrannize others. Here they followed Machiavelli, Locke, and David Hume in believing that a politics prompted by moral righteousness threatened reason and civility. Adams, for example, appeared to be echoing Hume when he wrote to Benjamin Rush (19 June 1789) to advise him that religion cannot cure the "inveterate evil" of factions, "for parties are always founded on some Principle, and the more conscientious Men are, the more determined they will be in pursuit of their Principle, System and Party." The framers believed that factions arising from "interests" were safer than the fanatical behavior that could often be seen in "parties of principle" composed of zealots hungering after righteousness. What would preserve the American Republic, then, would not be the moral passions of "patriots" but the carefully balanced "machinery of government."

Thoreau would have presented a political nightmare to Adams and the *Federalist* authors. Here was that "conscientious" man they feared, the man who was determined to pursue some "principle" regardless of the consequences, a man who tried to show Americans why politics should be about truth and morality, not power and interests. Ralph Waldo Emerson said of Thoreau that his very presence "embarrassed" Americans. A close look at his now-famous treatise on civil disobedience helps explain why.

☆ ☆ ☆ "Civil Disobedience"

"Civil Disobedience" (1849) was variously titled at different presentations as "The Rights and Duties of the Individual in Relation to Government" and "Resistance to Government." Its immediate historical context was America's war with Mexico. In protest of that war, which Thoreau saw as a pretext for the expansion of slavery into the Southwest, he refused to pay his taxes, a gesture that led to his spending a night in jail. The document, curiously, says very little about the war or about the institution of slavery. Perhaps this is why it has become a classic in the literature of civil resistance. Thoreau used the occasion to write in universal terms about the individual's relation to politics, and "Civil Disobedience" may be one of the first documents in Western political philosophy to suggest that neither genuine freedom nor authentic authority lies in the nature of government.

This is not to suggest, as some scholars have, that "Civil Disobedience" is essentially an anarchist text. Thoreau, it is true, carries Jefferson's suspicions of political power to a radical conclusion that would have made the framers shudder in horror: "That government is best which governs not at all." But Thoreau immediately adds that people are not yet ready for life without a political state, and he openly admits that he himself makes expedient use of some of the services the state provides, such as roads, schools, and libraries. What Thoreau wants to demonstrate is how unimportant government really is in the history of America. It was not the government that created the conditions for liberty, educated the people, settled the frontier, and made possible the beauties of nature. Nor should Americans be so naive as to believe that politics provided the means by which society could be reformed. "It is not a man's duty, as a matter of course, to devote himself to the eradication of any, even the most enormous wrong." The regeneration of society, Thoreau and Emerson insisted again and again, must begin with self-regeneration, not political participation. Thus "Civil Disobedience" advises Americans not to look to political leadership or to rely upon the electoral process. Nor does it advise them to return to the Republic's "first principles," for the Constitution allowed slavery to exist; hence American legislatures cannot follow "the men of '87" and still be moral leaders. Thoreau even departs from Paine and Jefferson by evincing little faith in the will of the people. The majority does not guarantee justice, and although democracy may be based on the consent of the governed, we must recognize that "there is but little virtue in the actions of masses of men."

Although Thoreau, perhaps out of his disgust with the submissive masses, professes to "wash his hands" of political society and "sign off" from all institutions and their problems, he also recognizes that evil and injustice require citizens to act responsibly. Thus he advises all those who oppose slavery to exercise the honored right of revolution and secede from the Union. More immediately, he calls upon the people of Massachusetts to withdraw their allegiance from the national government. On what grounds is the right of resistance justified? Thoreau appeals to individuals not as political citizens but as moral agents: "Must the citizen ever for a moment, or in the least degree, resign his conscience to the legislator? Why has every man a conscience then? I think we should be men first, and subjects afterward. It is not desirable to cultivate a respect for the law, so much as for the right."

The only obligation I have a right to assume is to do any time what I think right. Thoreau makes the individual sovereign unto himself, apart from the state and even the people who compose it. The individual's only obligation is to discern whether an evil like slavery is "in" the political system or "of" it. "If the injustice is part of the necessary friction of the machinery of government, let it go . . . perchance it will wear smooth. . . . But if it is of such a nature that it require you to be an agent of injustice to another, then I say, break the law. Let your life be a counter friction to the machine."

The rhetoric is militant for so meditative a man as Thoreau, the "hermit" of Walden Pond and the "bachelor of nature." When we sufficiently appreciate how militant it is, we are not surprised to find Thoreau later rising to the side of John Brown, the bloody abolitionist who massacred slaveholders in the name of God and freedom. Thus it is not entirely accurate to read "Civil Disobedience" as necessarily advocating nonviolent "passive resistance." As Thoreau grew impatient with Americans' refusal to sabotage the Fugitive Slave laws, his words grew even more burning. In "Slavery in Massachusetts" (1854), he did indeed sound like a fiery anarchist: "My thoughts are murder to the state and involuntarily go plotting against her." This heightened radicalism has been attributed to either Thoreau's unrealistic "romantic sensibility," his concern for his own moral purity rather than social reform, or even his psychological inability to accept authority as a condition of adulthood. Thoreau's motives are less important than his message, however, for "Civil Disobedience" is not really about the citizen's relation to the state. Rather, it was the state's relation to the individual that most troubled him.

In contrast to anarchists and radicals of all persuasions, Thoreau saw the state not as oppressive and tyrannical but as weak and even imbecilic. "I saw," he reflected after leaving jail, "that the State was half-witted, that it was as timid as a lone woman with her silver spoons, and that it did not know its friends from its foes, and I lost all my remaining respect for it, and pitied it." Thoreau would have agreed with the French writer Alexis de Tocqueville, who observed in *Democracy in America* (1835–40) that it was society, and not the state, that posed a danger to individual liberty and freedom of mind. Thoreau's complaint against the state is not that it coerces man but that it does not know how to conceive him. The framers of the Constitution looked to government to control behavior; Thoreau wanted government to elevate behavior by appealing to conscience and ethical sensibility. "Thus the State never intentionally confronts a man's sense, intellectual or moral, but only his body, his senses."

As a moral document, "Civil Disobedience" rings with the truths of the heart; as a practical proposal, it may fail to convince the demands of the mind. Consider the inconsistencies and confusions. Thoreau depicts the masses as lacking in intelligence and virtue, yet he appeals to them to do the right thing. He calls upon abolitionists to oppose slavery more effectively by renouncing their allegiance to the state and demands that Massachusetts secede from the Union, without seeming to recognize that such actions would simply have given the slave states even more power in the federal government. He declares war on the state when his real quarrel is with society, for what stood in the way of the black man's freedom was, as Tocqueville and Abraham Lincoln sadly observed, the white man's prejudice. Yet however questionable as a practical proposal, "Civil Disobedience" did succeed in making a powerful case for conceiving government as an ethical institution and politics as a moral proposition.

In the last half of the nineteenth century the dissent tradition that fructified in Thoreau's writings continued in American politics, if only at its remote margins. The anarchist Benjamin Tucker drew upon the Quakers' ethic of the "inner light" to urge the individual to resist the encroachments of state power. The radical individualism of American Protestantism could even be expressed by thinkers who were unsure of God's existence, not to mention his justice. In Mark Twain's *Adventures of Huckleberry Finn* (1885), the stance of defiance finds a voice when Huck must decide whether he should betray his friend, Nigger Jim, by returning him to slavery as the law dictated. After much soul-searching, Huck decides not to, saying, "All right, then, I'll go to hell." Many of the pacifists of World War I also risked government prosecution, if not religious damnation, by opposing America's intervention.

By the mid-twentieth century the radical wing of American Catholicism joined with Protestant anarcho-individualists to sustain the conscience of civil disobedience. Dorothy Day's Catholic Worker movement offered inspiration to the Jesuits Daniel and Philip Berrigan when they assaulted draft centers in protest against the Vietnam War. Indeed the 1960s witnessed what might be called the "Second Reformation" of the politics of civil disobedience in America. Boycotts, sit-ins, marches, demonstrations, and other acts of civil protest swept through the country. The civil disobedience tactics, in addition to protesting the Vietnam War, were aimed at racial discrimination in the North and institutionalized segregation in the South. Those who participated often went on "freedom rides" deep into the South to expose the tactics that were hampering black voter registration. The hero of the civil rights movement, and the leading theoretician of civil disobedience, was the black Protestant minister Martin Luther King, Jr.

☆ ☆ ☆ Civil Disobedience and the Civil Rights Movement

King's "Letter from Birmingham Jail" (1963) was written after he had been arrested for refusing to halt a large civil disobedience campaign. Although aware of Thoreau's writings, King had been more directly influenced by Mohandas Gandhi and by the theologians Reinhold Niebuhr and Paul Tillich. King's strategy and theory differed from Thoreau's in several respects. Whereas Thoreau called upon Americans to disassociate themselves from the "machine" of government, King called upon them to become more involved in politics in order to secure the voting rights that had been denied to black citizens. Indeed King realized that civil disobedience presupposes recognizing political authority and its processes. Thus he systematically specified the steps to be taken: "Collection of the facts to determine whether injustices exist; negotiation; self-purification; and direct action."

King also possessed a keener sense of power politics than had Thoreau; he conceived civil disobedience as a crisis-heightening tactic that would prod the Birmingham, Alabama, administration into a dialogue that, he hoped, would lead to a solution. He learned from Niebuhr that "freedom is never voluntarily given by the oppressor; it must be demanded by the oppressed." What King and the Southern Christian Leadership Conference had demanded was the fulfillment of racial integration in public institutions as promised by the Supreme Court in 1954 in the now-famous *Brown v. Board of Education of Topeka* decision. In marching to proclaim that demand, King and his followers had violated a court order, a local injunction against demonstrations that King believed deprived him and his black and white supporters of their constitutional right of free assembly. Although King would perhaps have agreed with Thoreau that conscience can be the grounds for breaking the law, he offered several other reasons why a given law could be considered unjust and unmoral.

First of all, a law could be imposed upon a minority that was denied the right to vote and thus played no role in legislating it. Moreover, the law could be unjust if it were not applied universally, and hence a majority compelled a minority to obey what it did not make binding on itself. Above all, a specific law designed to continue segregation resembles "sin" in that it separates man from man. It is thus "out of harmony with the moral laws" of God and with eternal natural law and, as a consequence, "degrades human personality."

Whereas Thoreau's solitary act of defiance failed to end the Mexican War, King's collective movement succeeded in securing black voting rights and integrating schools and other public facilities. Unlike Thoreau and some other New England transcendentalists, King was willing to use the legal and political apparatus of the state. The 1960s, then, one of the most tumultuous decades in American history, legitimized civil disobedience as a tactic on the part of loyal citizens excluded from the conventional channels of power and social change. It would be going too far to say that the 1960s institutionalized that tactic, for King's presence reminds us that successful protest movements require the "charismatic authority" of a great leader. But civil disobedience is a precious resource with roots deep in American history. For American minorities in the modern age, it holds out the possibility that there can be a "long march" through the institutions of power.

FURTHER READING

Not surprisingly, civil disobedience became the center of scholarly and student attention for the 1960s generation, as did the radical dissent tradition in American history. For analysis by political scientists, see Michael Walzer, "Civil Disobedience and Corporate Authority," in *Power and Community: Dissenting Essays in Political Science*, ed. Philip Green and Sanford Levinson (New York, 1970); Elliot M. Zashin, *Civil Disobedience and Democracy* (New York, 1972); and also the useful anthology *Political Obligation and Civil Disobedience: Readings*, ed. Michael P. Smith and Kenneth L. Deutsch (New York, 1972). For the Anglo-American idea of "negative liberty" and its relations to political resistance, see Isaiah Berlin, *Four Essays on Liberty* (New York, 1969). The best work on the radical dissent tradition in American history is Staughton Lynd's *Intellectual Origins of American Radicalism* (New York, 1968); however, for some reservations on Lynd's comparison of Marx and Thoreau, see John Diggins, "Thoreau, Marx, and the 'Riddle' of Alienation," *Social Research* 39 (1972). The anarcho-individualist-libertarian tradition is covered in David DeLeon, *The American as Anarchist* (Baltimore, 1978).

The main currents of early American political thought are dealt with superbly in Edmund S. Morgan's introduction to *Puritan Political Ideas* (Indianapolis, Ind., 1965); Bernard Bailyn's *The Ideological Origins of the American Revolution* (Cambridge, Mass., 1965); and Gordon S. Wood's *The Creation of the American Re-*

public, 1776–1787 (Chapel Hill, N.C., 1969). The inherent tension between Lockean liberalism and political authority is treated in John Diggins, *The Lost Soul of American Politics: Virtue, Self-Interest, and the Foundations of Liberalism* (New York, 1984). A valuable collection of Thoreau's political writings is *Thoreau: People, Principles, and Politics*, ed. Milton Meltzer (New York, 1963). Martin Luther King, Jr.'s "Letter from Birmingham Jail" is found in his *Why We Can't Wait* (New York, 1964). For a comprehensive history of the dissident sixties, see Godfrey Hodgson, *America in Our Time* (New York, 1976).

24 ☆ The
☆
☆ Courts
☆
☆ and the
☆
☆ Law
☆

☆ John A. Schutz

Sometimes Americans forget that their federal government is divided into three branches. Unlike Gaul, which Caesar divided into fairly equal parts, the boundaries of power among the legislative, executive, and judicial branches tend to shift depending upon the issues and personalities of officeholders. But the influence of law (the Constitution) in the daily actions of Americans is ever present, and its interpretation by the three branches is a major aspect of American political life.

In the early years of the Republic until the presidency of Andrew Jackson (1829–37), Congress was undoubtedly the most important branch of government, and in spite of Jackson's impact, Congress continued to be powerful in the two decades after he left office. The opinions and actions of Congressmen Henry Clay, John C. Calhoun, and Stephen A. Douglas often held greater importance for the people than those of presidents of the day. In the early 1860s Abraham Lincoln gave the presidency a personality of compassion, and his leadership diminished some of Congress's importance. However, his successor, Andrew Johnson, contended with a rambunctious Congress that even tried to oust him from office and to pack the Supreme Court. The Court under Salmon P. Chase (1864–73) fought back by voiding ten acts of Congress and asserting in other ways its right to review legislation.

The kind of presidency that has become the preoccupation of president watchers had to await the twentieth century when the term *imperial* was applied to the administrations of Theodore Roosevelt, Woodrow Wilson, Franklin D. Roosevelt, and, in the 1970s, Richard M. Nixon. The reports of their words and actions give the impression that these men were the most persuasive figures in the national government. Their actions, however, often were blunted by the judiciary.

☆ ☆ ☆ The Role of the Supreme Court

The judges of the Supreme Court almost never have been able to arouse the continuous daily attention that people now give the president and had earlier given the Congress. Most of the incumbents, however, have been people of good quality, sometimes possessing fine minds, and a few have possessed warm personalities that would have become better known had they not been constrained by the traditions of the bench. Few men of John Marshall's talent have done more to shape the powers of the federal government than he did. His long incumbency of nearly thirty-five years (1800–1835) surely ranks him among the intellectual founders of the nation. In the twentieth century Earl Warren brilliantly took a quarrelsome, divided Court (1953–69) and directed its energy to civil issues leaving an imprint upon our society that is greater than that of some presidents of the time. His decisions aroused enough feeling to cause opponents to demand his impeachment, often on large billboards, and friends to revere his memory. Even so, Warren, like Marshall, failed to acquire the celebrity status of the presidents who were their contemporaries.

That the habits of most judges are usually reserved does not mean that they were ever a weak group. They have, however, changed their courtroom demeanor since the ratification of the Constitution in 1789, when they often delivered political speeches from the bench, were involved in controversial political issues, and suffered the criticism of politicians and newspaper editors. In the early years of the Republic Congress impeached several judges, threatened more, and removed a few from the bench. Thomas Jefferson spent much time as president (1801–9) worrying about the Supreme Court's announced intention to declare acts of Congress unconstitutional. His reaction to *Marbury v. Madison* (1803), which contained John Marshall's declaration of that power, was surprisingly calm, but he immediately lent his prestige to the impeachment of hated judges and to proposals for a congressional review of judicial opinions. He agreed with Marshall that the Constitution was the supreme law of the land but disagreed with him on who had the primacy of power in interpreting it.

From Jefferson's time to the present, presidents have criticized Supreme Court decisions. The criticism comes more frequently today, however, from a highly professional bar association, law schools, and the U.S. Senate during confirmation hearings on new appointees to the Court. The two judicial systems, federal and state, form layers of courts that evaluate each other and are checked in turn by the law profession and the law schools that study the decisions and create an informed opinion. A judge who offers peculiar or exceptional opinions will in time cause a reaction that may disturb Congress and bring a review of his or her conduct. Congress can, if the issue is not a constitutional one, change laws to satisfy its judgment and reject nominations of prospective judges whose ideas do not meet its favor. While the president nominates the federal court candidates, the Senate must approve or reject them. Congress may impeach and remove judges, and occasionally does, but that power reminds everyone of the distant popular will and is thus used cautiously. Similarly, the governors in the fifty states, the legislatures, and the people of those states often select state judges. California, in an unusual action, recently removed three of its higher-court judges by popular vote because it did not like court opinions on the death penalty. However, the U.S. Supreme Court, with life tenure and the choice of cases to be reviewed, sets the tone of the whole judicial system and has the power to change its mind.

The clash of powerful personalities like Jefferson and Marshall obscured the fact that the legal profession was then in its infancy and most judges had risen in politics from occupations other than the law. Their courtroom demeanor, as well as the popular regard for them, had to mature. Marshall's strategy to win approval of the Court's decisions included putting the Constitution at the apex of the legal system and the Supreme Court in a central position to interpret it. His successor, Roger Taney (1836–64), followed in his footsteps. They had thus to deal with lawyers, state courts, and judges in giving structure to the legal system. Procedures for hearings, appeals, and judgments soon developed in which lawyers argued cases and judges handed down opinions. The semi-independent state courts, interpreting state constitutions and legal systems, were integrated into the national judicial system, and a community of opinion arose in which lawyers debated and challenged prevailing decisions as they confronted new issues. Some distinguished judges like Joseph Story, the associate for many years of Marshall and Taney, even wrote commentaries on the law in an attempt to give direction to their colleagues.

☆ ☆ ☆ The Court Makes Policy: The *Dred Scott* Case

In spite of a successful career as a chief justice, Taney discovered the pitfalls of decision making. He and his associates let their opinions regarding slavery in 1857 warp their judgments, and the Court suffered much public criticism as a result. Their opinions in *Dred Scott v. Sandford* were a notorious example of judicial ineptitude that weakened the Court as an arbitrator of the political issues of the Civil War. The case was taken on a writ of error from the federal circuit court of Missouri. Scott was a black slave who had been taken into free territory and then returned to the slave state of Missouri. Was he a freeman? Years later Scott's friends arranged for his sale to John Sandford so that they could have a test case to answer the question. With the help of antislavery attorneys Scott contested the legality of his sale in federal court. Unsuccessful, they appealed to the Supreme Court, which accepted the case.

Logic would have dictated to the judges that Scott, a slave, could not sue in federal court, leading them to dismiss the case without comment. Or the Court could have cited *Strader v. Graham* (1850), in which it refused to decide whether a slave became free when he entered free territory and left such future cases to state courts for adjudication. They might also have looked into the sale of Scott to Sandford and rejected the case because the defendants had raised a false issue. Instead, the Court, after some months of indecision, took upon itself to discuss broadly the question of slavery in the territories and of slave status but was unable to issue a clear majority statement. Historians have tried to find something good to say about the case but note that one judge broke the honor code of secrecy by feeding information to President-elect James Buchanan so that he could comment on the case in his inaugural address and that the judicial opinions of the Court scanted history and logic in order to make certain political points.

Undoubtedly the Taney Court reached a low point in judicial interpretation, but it is well to remember that other Courts have frequently fallen into similar errors. The appropriate level of political awareness is difficult for the Court to achieve. Judges must be politically sensitive but not too advanced or too reactionary—a fine line to straddle. The Melville Fuller Court in 1895, for example, declared an income tax law unconstitutional, supported President Grover Cleveland in using federal troops to suppress a labor strike, and limited the power of Congress to regulate firms refining sugar (in its exercise of the commerce power). The straitjacket effect of these decisions upon Congress's power to make laws was almost as notorious as the effect of the *Dred Scott* decision upon its rule of the territories. Governor Sylvester Pennoyer of Oregon was rightly irritated by this judicial blundering when he wrote:

> The Supreme Court has not contented itself with its undisputed judicial prerogatives of interpreting the laws of Congress which may be ambiguous, but it has usurped the legislative prerogatives of declaring what the

laws shall not be. Our constitutional government has been supplanted by a judicial holigarchy. The time has now arrived when the government should be restored to its constitutional basis. The duty is plain and the road is clear. If Congress at the next session would impeach the nullifying Judges for the usurpation of legislative power, remove them from office, and instruct the President to enforce the collection of the income tax, the Supreme Court of the United States would never hereafter presume to trench upon the exclusive powers of Congress.

☆ ☆ ☆ The Court Interprets Tax and Commerce

In the life of the Court political crises come and go. Sometimes the crises lead to worthwhile progress by focusing on current evils; at other times the crises create stalemates. In rejecting the income tax, however, the Supreme Court touched a sensitive issue, and the people reacted by approving a constitutional amendment to give Congress the power to tax incomes. The *Dred Scott* decision also brought amendments to the Constitution, but not before the nation was torn apart for a time by civil war. People over the years have been cautious about amending the Constitution and have preferred to let the Supreme Court struggle with current issues of interpretation.

In their days the Marshall and Taney Courts did much creative work establishing rules of law defining commerce, regulating the use of the taxing power, and setting the bounds of legitimate contracts. Other Courts have followed them in creating patterns of interpretation. Since the Constitution made only general statements of federal power, the decisions of the Supreme Court have the effect of writing into the Constitution specific content for these areas of authority. For example, the Constitution grants the national government the authority "to regulate Commerce with foreign Nations, and among the several States, and with the Indian Tribes" (section 8). The case of *Gibbons v. Ogden* in 1824 concerned steamboat navigation on the Hudson River and the validity of a New York law that gave Aaron Ogden exclusive rights to operate boats between New York and New Jersey. Thomas Gibbons challenged this monopoly by securing a license from the federal government under the Coasting Act. When he was prosecuted in the New York State courts, he sought relief in the federal courts and his petition for a hearing was eventually received by the Supreme Court. Marshall spoke for a united Court in a wide-ranging opinion based on four important points. First, he asked, "What is the commerce power?" In answering himself, he rejected the idea that it is merely the selling of goods. No, he said, commerce "is something more; it is intercourse." It includes navigation as well as commercial regulations; it comprehends "every species of commercial intercourse."

Second, he admitted the existence of internal commerce within a state but also that interstate commerce must ordinarily flow across state boundaries and into states. Congress's power to regulate interstate and foreign commerce, "like all others vested in Congress, is complete in itself, may be exercised to its utmost extent, and acknowledges no limitations other than those prescribed in the Constitution." Third, he held that the state governments may exercise power over the interstate commerce incident to the regulation of intrastate commerce. Fourth, he interpreted the power over interstate commerce broadly, rejecting a narrow construction as possibly defeating the purposes of government.

Other decisions soon followed. In *Brown v. Maryland* (1827), Marshall spoke again for the Court by asking: "When does interstate commerce as it flows into a state become intrastate commerce?" Again he answered his own question. He declared that whenever such goods become "mixed up with the mass of property in the country," they become subject to state regulation. The line of definition continued under Taney, whose Court tried to separate the prerogative of government from the rights of the individual, and federal law enforcement from state regulation, refining the law that Marshall's Court had already pronounced.

☆ ☆ ☆ Subtle Interpretation Required Today

While these Courts did their work very well, the problems of commerce for that day seem simplistic when compared with the issues that arose in later years. The Court continued the process of laying down rules, often starting with *Gibbons v. Ogden* in making its initial arguments but moving then to the issues of the moment. In the 168 years since that decision the Court has enlarged beyond belief the Marshall definition of interstate commerce. Commerce today, according to Edward S. Corwin in the 1950s, "covers every species of movement of persons and things, whether for profit or not; every species of communication, every species of transmission of intelligence . . . every species of commercial negotiation." Such rules as the "original package," "reasonableness" of regulation, and the "flow of commerce" have been generally abandoned.

Instead, the Court has cut away old rules and recognized that Congress has power to regulate commerce in almost any way it wishes, even when its regulation affects the powers of the states. It reserves, nonetheless, power for the states to supervise commerce because of the complexity of the economy. Exclusive control of commerce would be obviously too difficult for the federal government to take under its care. Congress thus hands the states large sections of the economy to regulate, often under guidelines set by federal statutes but providing for local standards of health and welfare.

The evolution of such interpretations as those for the commerce clause has not proceeded by straight-line arguments because the opinions of judges and the conditions of the economy must always be taken into account. Even more, there is the prevailing concept of constitutional process that affects judicial interpretation. In the early Republic, for example, the powers of the states and the federal government were thought to be easily separated, especially over commerce. This theory of "dual federalism" held that the powers of the states were sovereign and inviolable—as sovereign as those of the federal government in its own sphere. The Court applied this theory only sporadically after the Civil War, but in the interpretation of the commerce clause it was most evident in the regulation of the insurance industry, child labor, and manufacturing.

In 1869, when *Paul v. Virginia* was decided, the Court excluded insurance from interstate commerce. The issue was, of course, the concept of interstate commerce. Although the business of writing insurance policies may take place only in one area, it may affect incidentally the flow of commerce throughout the United States. From 1869 on, the Supreme Court resisted changes in state control, and it had trouble even in 1944 justifying its arguments in favor of federal regulations. Justice Robert Jackson believed then that the insurance industry was engaged in interstate commerce but felt that the "legal fiction" of excluding such commerce from federal regulation was so well established by rule and practice that it would be foolish to tamper with its legal status. However, his colleagues on the bench voted to overturn the seventy-five-year-old rule by a narrow margin. Tradition had an even greater influence upon the Congress, moreover, than upon the Court, and Congress hastened in 1945 to enact legislation clarifying the powers of the states to regulate the insurance industry and restoring regulations to conditions prior to the 1944 case.

☆ ☆ ☆ The Supreme Court and Social Progress

In combating the evils of child labor, Congress was encouraged by reformers in the Wilson administration to outlaw merchandise manufactured by children. In *Hammer v. Dagenhart* (1918), however, the Court interfered, declaring that the regulation of these products of child labor was not constitutional. The purpose of the law, said Justice William Day, was not to regulate the movement of goods, or the goods themselves, but child labor. "In interpreting the Constitution, it must not be forgotten that the nation is made up of states, to which are entrusted the powers of local government." Then he followed with an *argumentum ad horrendum*: "If Congress can thus regulate matters intrusted to local authority by prohibition of the movement of commodities in interstate commerce, all freedom of commerce will be at an end, and the power of the states over local matters may be eliminated, and thus our system of government will be practically destroyed."

For two decades thereafter the people sought relief from this and similar court decisions by sponsoring a child labor amendment to the Constitution. It gathered much support in the 1930s but not the approval of three-fourths of the states that was needed for its passage into law.

In affirming cases like *Hammer v. Dagenhart* the judges for many years had a decisive influence over social reform. The most troubled period for them and the nation occurred during the Great Depression when the Franklin Roosevelt administrations (1933–45) persuaded Congress to pass sweeping economic and social legislation to pull the country from the crisis. The Court was particularly distressed about the inclusion of production into the concept of interstate commerce, but the judges were also concerned over the vast increase in federal jurisdiction and the social philosophy of the New Deal. For a time in 1935 the Charles Evans Hughes Court struck down most social legislation and all but dismantled the New Deal as a result. When the president struck back in 1937 with plans for Court packing and aroused a public debate, the people opposed his plan but favored his reforms. The Court soon bent under the pressure of change when several judges resigned and others changed their minds. Spectacular reversals of some opinions soon made possible the regulation of labor conditions and of manufacturing, public power generation, and other kinds of production not traditionally regarded as interstate commerce.

Although the causes of this legal revolution have been well commented upon by scholars, the observations of Carl Brent Swisher, in his *American Constitution* (1948), make much sense. He thought the Supreme Court had abandoned in the revolution the concept of a "fixed written document." Once the Court had accepted the possibility of an evolving constitutional system, he believed, its exclusive power to interpret the Constitution was open to question. Certainly the legislative and the executive branches were more appropriately the voice of the people than an appointed Court. This was especially true in 1936, when Roosevelt's first administration was returned to office by a landslide that apparently endorsed the New Deal. If the Constitution was no longer a rigid document, what was it? The question was at first difficult to answer. No one could predict what would happen to the Constitution in the hands of a creative president and Congress. As late as 1954 Edward S. Corwin speculated on the future of the Court. He believed that the revolution had removed most constitutional issues from the review process and henceforth the Court would be hearing contested issues of law enforcement, interpretation, and evidence. Issues of constitutionality thus would become less and less important in its proceedings. The very year, however, when he made these speculations, *Brown v. Board of Education of Topeka* was decided by the new Warren Court (1953–69). This incredible decision reflected Warren's training as governor of California more than any experience he had had in the courts and broke judicial precedents in justifying a decision.

☆ ☆ ☆ Segregation and the Court:
Brown v. Board of Education of Topeka

A group of five school segregation cases reached the Supreme Court in the fall of 1952. All challenged the constitutionality of *Plessy v. Ferguson* (1896), which had affirmed the rule of "separate but equal" in providing education for blacks. The judges seemed troubled by the issues that were raised and questioned first the intent of Congress and the states in passing the Fourteenth Amendment some ninety years before. They also worried about the impact of a ban on segregation should the Court declare *Plessy v. Ferguson* unconstitutional.

Their opinion as written by Warren was remarkable because it avoided legal and historical evidence. It used instead arguments that cited twentieth-century conditions to prove that segregation created feelings of inferiority among blacks. School segregation, in the opinion of the Court, thus violated the "equal protection" clause of the Fourteenth Amendment, which was one of its major and original purposes. The decision was less an interpretation of the amendment than a piece of judicial legislation justified by sociological arguments. In a sense it was judge-made law.

After this breathtaking decision, the Court surprised critics by providing no immediate enforcement for its opinion. Instead, it asked attorneys for arguments on how to implement the decision and heard what amounts to a second case. In separating the enunciation of principle from enforcement, it handed down its order a year later in *Brown v. Board* and asked the several lower courts involved with the five cases to find solutions for segregation that would admit those concerned in the cases "to the public schools on a racially nondiscriminatory basis with all deliberate speed." In short, the lower courts, guided by a rule of law, would find a plan suitable to meet the needs of their areas.

The Court was fully aware of the social revolution that it had caused and chose this unique approach to avoid serious controversy. Yet few people anticipated the massive resistance that was to follow. Most southern legislatures adopted the old doctrine of "interposition," from the Virginia and Kentucky Resolutions of 1798, which had the effect of declaring the *Brown* decisions "null and void." The most significant outbreak of violence occurred in Little Rock, Arkansas. That city's board of education tried to comply with the federal court order and was immediately prevented by an injunction of the Arkansas Chancery Court. A federal judge then countermanded the injunction by issuing a writ of his own that ordered the school board to move ahead with the plans. The writ provoked the Arkansas governor to enter the controversy, and he employed the National Guard to maintain segregation in the schools.

Such defiance of federal law finally aroused President Dwight Eisenhower, who had been reluctant for nearly three years to use force in the South but felt now that the Arkansas governor was creating serious conditions of anarchy. "Mob rule," he said, "cannot be allowed to override the decisions of our courts." When he was accused by U.S. Senator Richard Russell of using Nazi-like tactics in federalizing the National Guard, he replied in great indignation:

> When a state, by seeking to frustrate the orders of the Federal Court, encourages mobs of extremists to flout the orders of a Federal court, and when a State refuses to utilize its police powers to protect against mobs persons who are peaceably exercising their right under the Constitution as defined in such Court order, the oath of the office of the President requires that he take action to give that protection. Failure to act in such a case would be tantamount to acquiescence in anarchy and the dissolution of the union.

The unexpected national notoriety was now too much for the board of education, which successfully asked the federal district court for a stay of the integration order. Appeals to the Supreme Court in *Cooper v. Aaron* (1958) brought a bold rejection of the stay. The Court pointed out almost piously the folly of trying to frustrate the will of the national government. State officials, the Court observed, cannot "war on the Constitution without violating . . . [their] oath to support it . . . else . . . the Constitution becomes a solemn mockery."

Even though all the judges coauthored the opinion, the Arkansas governor proceeded with plans to close the high schools of Little Rock and force the

Court to take other emergency actions. The governor, impressed as he was with the imperial nature of the Court's proceedings, counted on the support of other states. But the local federal district court boldly accepted the challenge by nullifying Arkansas laws withholding funds from the schools, and the Supreme Court backed the district court in *Faubus v. Aaron*. What might have happened if governor and legislature had chosen prison instead of submission is open to speculation. Or if other states had rushed to help the governor, might the outcome have differed? But the people of Arkansas, angry and indignant, had already fought the Civil War and lost.

Only a few weeks later the Supreme Court was confronted with the theory of "interposition." It was used by officials of Louisiana to prevent integration of New Orleans's public schools. The state legislature, in blocking a federal order for integration, challenged the legality of a federal injunction by citing state sovereignty and by passing up to fourteen laws that deprived integrated schools of money and threatened public officials who complied with federal writs. This massive confrontation invited hard action by the federal district court, and its response was no less firm when it declared unconstitutional these force laws of Louisiana. The court even received help from the president and the Supreme Court, which offered another observation, but this time only one terse sentence long—integration in New Orleans, although only on a small scale, must proceed on course.

In the meantime, the Supreme Court accepted cases that challenged the segregation of theaters, restaurants, parks, and buses. The rule of the *Brown* decision was generally applied, with the Court affirming its intention to guarantee equal protection of the law to everyone. Congress and the president soon moved to assure blacks the right to register and vote, and Congress circulated a constitutional amendment to the states which prohibited poll taxes, often used to keep blacks from election booths. By 1961, however, some judges were becoming concerned about invasion of privacy. There was a difference between public and private rights, they said, and selective memberships in private clubs, societies, and fraternities might not necessarily constitute segregation within the meaning of the *Brown* case.

☆ ☆ ☆ Application of the Bill of Rights to State Laws

Probably the most important business of the Supreme Court since World War II has been the application of the federal Bill of Rights to the states. (All of the states have bills of rights, but procedures for enforcement of rights in the states differ sometimes significantly.) The federal power is found in the "due process" clause of the Fourteenth Amendment, perhaps elsewhere in the Constitution, in the Fifth Amendment, and also in the general inclinations of present judges. The result has been the piecemeal incorporation of the Bill of Rights into Court decisions, with the Court scrutinizing an ever-increasing number of civil rights issues in the states and attempting to set procedural rules (due process). By the very nature of the issues the Court has often been unable to draw up precise rules for the state legislatures and courts to follow. One area is capital punishment, which is permitted in the states only after heartbreaking appeals to courts of the state and federal governments. The rules are extremely complex. Often the criminal is not certain of his fate until he has felt the executioner's blow.

The process of incorporating the Bill of Rights into state law began in 1873 with the *Slaughterhouse Cases,* which defined citizenship, but little was done to clarify a position until after World War I when imprisoned radicals sought justice. In *Gitlow v. New York* (1925), the Court reviewed charges against Benjamin Gitlow, who was convicted of violating the New York Criminal Anarchy Act by being business manager of the *Revolutionary Age.* The paper was potentially dangerous to peace and order, but Gitlow was prosecuted in this case for exercising his freedom of speech by being a Socialist. Charged with advocating the overthrow of the government in the Red Scare of 1919, he was convicted in 1920, when a jury took forty-five minutes to find him guilty, and he served time in Sing Sing and other New York prisons. The appeal of his sentence reached the Supreme Court early in 1923, was reargued before new Court appointees later in 1923, and was announced in 1925. On speaking for a divided Court, Judge Edward T. Sanford looked directly at the New York statute as he defined due process of law for Gitlow: "When the legislative body has determined generally, in the constitutional exercise of its discretion, that utterances of a certain kind involve such danger of substantive evil that they may be punished, the question whether any specific utterance coming within the prohibited class is likely, in and of itself, to bring about the substantive evil, is not open to consideration, and that use of the language comes within its prohibition."

The Court did say that freedom of speech and of the press were secured against state action by the due process clause. This admission did not help Gitlow, who was then returned to prison. Frustrated in his appeal to the courts, Gitlow secured help from the American Civil Liberties Union, which soon convinced Governor Alfred E. Smith of New York to pardon him.

In the 1930s a few important cases specifically extended the protection of the Bill of Rights to the states through the due process clause of the Four-teenth Amendment. The extension was made, it should be emphasized, for issues of speech, press, and assembly and not for religious and criminal procedures. Chief Justice Charles Evans Hughes was an important figure of the Court in making this extension into the area of speech, and he was proud of the Court's daring. At one point in Court deliberations he advised an audience: "Let it also be known . . . that with calmness and sanity we propose to maintain the guarantees of free speech, free assembly and the right of representation, and that no one, however poor, friendless or accused, shall be deprived of liberty without due process of law." In spite of his enthusiasm for incorporation of the Bill of Rights, the Court moved cautiously as long as Hughes remained on the bench.

By 1941 the membership of the Hughes Court was nearly completely changed because of resignations and deaths. The new men under the direction of Chief Justice Harlan Stone extended the religious guarantees of the First Amendment to the states, but the extension was only accomplished by split votes. In *Everson v. Board of Education* (1946), Justice Hugo Black stated clearly what the majority regarded as the rule against aiding religion and said that the clause against the establishment of religion was intended to erect "a wall of separation between Church and State. That wall must be kept high and impregnable." Having paid tribute to the tradition, he felt that free bus transportation for parochial school children, the issue of the Everson dispute, was another matter. The bus law, he observed, "does no more than provide a general program to help parents get their children . . . safely and expeditiously to and from accredited schools." Judge Wiley B. Rutledge responded negatively by saying: "First it has been books, now buses, next churches and teachers. . . . Every religious institution in the country will be reaching into [the public] hopper for help if you sustain this [case]." While Justice Rutledge joined the vocal minority, his opinion was significant only because many people opposed bus transportation and hoped to secure a rehearing of the case. Separation of church and state continues to create arguments in the 1990s because the Court has not been able to build the wall.

The most important issue remaining was the incorporation of the criminal procedures of the Bill of Rights into the due process protection of state law. The Court was divided, however, between selective and total incorporation. Justices Hugo Black and Frank Murphy wanted total incorporation of these procedures and of any other right that might become important in the future, but the Court has not even today gone to these lengths. In *Adamson v. California* (1947), Justice Black searched the historical record to make his point for total incorporation. On the bench Justice Felix Frankfurter attacked the position with undisputable logic, while in the press Professor Charles Fairman, in a now well-known essay in the *Stanford Law Review*, agreed with

Frankfurter that "the record of history is overwhelmingly against him [Black]."
The analysis sobered Justice Black but also brought forth a considerable
literature that was often less negative than Fairman's critique.

☆ ☆ ☆ The Court's Work Today

Selective application of the Bill of Rights to state law continued
into the 1960s and culminated for a period in *Benton v. Maryland* (1969). The
case raised the question of a judicial rule for double jeopardy. Congress in the
Criminal Appeals Act of 1970 likewise tried to find a solution for the problem.
The kinds of issues the Court faced arose out of concurrent sentences when
a defendant might have his penalty changed under a state habitual-criminal
statute as evidence of other crimes became known. Can sentences then be
increased without violating the right of a defendant?

The process of hearing cases and finding new frontiers of interpretation will
undoubtedly continue in spite of predictions to the contrary. Logic would
dictate that the Court enters a fenceless field and has to stake out its claim.
Certainly the opinions of Justices Black and Murphy opened vistas for Court
entry that could hardly have been imagined by their predecessors. *Roe v. Wade*
(1973), which guarantees a woman's right to decide for herself whether to
terminate a pregnancy or to bear a child, is the most controversial opinion
of the last two decades. The Court in the 1980s pondered legal limits to this
right by letting the states provide regulation of abortion. Possibly the Ninth
Amendment, which also guarantees privacy, may provide a source for Court
activity for petitions to end life when disease or infirmity has destroyed human
consciousness. The range of decisions could stretch over almost all conditions
of human life. In addition, the Court could struggle with standards of censorship, morality, and capital punishment. Environmentalists also could challenge standards of laws permitting offshore drilling, air pollution, and land
use. Court reviews on such matters presently are occupying more and more
judicial time; perhaps even more can be predicted for the future.

The willingness of the judiciary to interfere with law enforcement is undoubtedly serious. In some areas of litigation the Courts have plainly not
developed clear enough rules for the legislators and interference hurts popular
rights. For example, in legalizing capital punishment the Court has not been
able to set firm rules that can be easily interpreted or applied. Over one period
of study, Justice Stephen Reinhardt of the Ninth Circuit Court of Appeals
found 75 percent of all orders of execution issued by state courts were in
violation of constitutional guarantees. Each case seems to raise again issues of

an earlier one. In the execution of a Florida criminal in 1983, the man served ten years in death row awaiting adjudication of his case. Even minutes before his execution the major courts of state and federal governments again went through the review process. The number of appeals that can be made challenging a death sentence is scandalous, primarily because judges seem incapable of developing rules for legislative guidance. At the present more than two thousand condemned people are waiting on death row in state prisons.

In bringing order and reason to constitutional practices, the Supreme Court usually performs a difficult job very well. Rules of law are easier to formulate in a library than upon the bench, especially in a country crowded with lawyers and clients and associations ready to do battle. The United States is a lawyer's country where the majority of legislators, most judges, and many officials are lawyers. Laws are always finely examined, and someone is usually willing to challenge an interpretation. Nonetheless, the Supreme Court, the federal courts, and the multitude of state courts make the constitutional system survive by being on the firing line of issues and taking the responsibility in many cases for a reluctant Congress and president in handling controversial issues. The dangers of government by judges and lawyers in today's America are that there are too many court reviews that interfere with the prerogatives of the executive and legislative branches and with the rights of the people to have a clear statement of the law by elected officials.

FURTHER READING

Comment on the courts and the law, which is exceedingly wide, includes publications from the scholarly community, the law profession, and politicians. Almost everyone has an opinion on the law. Every year the *American Political Science Review* has a professional commentary on the courts and, in addition, analyzes a dozen or more current books. The reviews of the hundred great law schools also give critiques of current cases. Such important law school journals as those from Harvard, Stanford, Michigan, Yale, Chicago, and California can be readily consulted for expert opinions. One may wish to consult a volume of the annual *United States Reports* or *The Lawyer's Edition*, which give citations for easy reference. Both include statements of the Supreme Court.

Almost all of the important Supreme Court judges, and especially the chiefs of the Court, have been the subjects of biographies or studies of their careers. The unique two volumes of Charles Warren, *The Supreme Court in the United States* (Boston, 1926), is a biography of the Court, with rather full commentaries on the lawyers, judges, and issues. Albert J. Beveridge's *The Life of John Marshall* (New York, 1916–19) is a leisurely account in four volumes. More compact is Robert K.

Faulkner's *The Jurisprudence of John Marshall* (Princeton, N.J., 1968). Earl Warren is now being discovered by biographers. *The Memoirs of Earl Warren* (New York, 1977) and Bernard Schwartz's *Super Chief: Earl Warren and His Supreme Court* (New York, 1983) offer insights into the life of this influential judge. Felix Frankfurter's *The Commerce Clause under Marshall, Taney, and Waite* (Chapel Hill, N.C., 1937) tells much of these judges but more about Frankfurter. His study should be read with Bruce Allen Murphy's *The Brandeis/Frankfurter Connection: The Secret Political Activities of Two Supreme Court Justices* (New York, 1982).

Few commentaries on the Constitution and Court were better known in their day than Edward S. Corwin's. His *The Constitution and What It Means Today* (Princeton, N.J., 1958) and *Court over Constitution: A Study of Judicial Review as an Instrument of Popular Government* (Princeton, N.J., 1938) are good sources of information. One might now wish to read Jesse H. Choper's *Judicial Review and the National Political Process* (Chicago, 1980) and Richard Neely's *How Courts Govern America* (New Haven, Conn., 1981). For the sweep of constitutional history, one should consult Carl Brent Swisher, *American Constitutional Development* (Westport, Conn., 1978). For the views of an important contemporary lawyer, see Archibald Cox, *The Role of the Supreme Court in American Government* (New York, 1976), which is most instructive.

Current issues before the Court are well described by Arthur S. Miller in *The Secret Constitution and the Need for Constitutional Change* (New York, 1987), particularly chapter 5, "Getting There from Here," and by Wallace Mendelson in *Supreme Court Statecraft: The Rule of Law and Men* (Ames, Iowa, 1985). Capital punishment is a major controversial issue of our day. Hugo A. Bedau gathers many opinions in *The Death Penalty in America*, 3d ed. (New York, 1982), which should be read along with R. L. Gardner's "Capital Punishment: The Philosophers and the Court," *Syracuse Law Review* 29 (1978), and Charles Black's *Capital Punishment: The Inevitability of Caprice and Mistake* (New York, 1981). The rights of women have been prominent in Court cases since 1972 and are discussed by many scholars. Naomi B. Lynn, *Women and the Constitution* (Binghamton, N.Y., 1990), and Sarah Slavin, ed., *The Politics and Process of Ratification of the 27th Amendment to the U.S. Constitution* (Binghamton, N.Y., 1982), cover most issues. Gary L. McDowell raises the question of restraint and limits in *Curbing the Courts: The Constitution and the Limits of Judicial Power* (Baton Rouge, La., 1988).

25 ☆ Gender and Equality in

☆ the American Experience

☆

☆ Jane Sherron De Hart and

☆ Linda K. Kerber

Fascinated by the differences that divide the American people and the commonalities that make them one, scholars and commentators have long focused on such centrifugal forces as regional loyalties, geographic mobility, and political dissent. They have also examined the ways in which race, class, and culture bond and divide. Until very recently, however, sexual difference has been largely discounted as a significant factor in the American experience. Whether male or female, members of the same racial, ethnic, and economic groups, experiencing the same great social phenomena, were presumed to share the same historical experience. In many respects, they did. For example, enslavement—primarily of Africans but also, in the early centuries, of Native Americans—was not restricted to one sex; both women and men toiled in the fields together. Similarly, industrialization involved female workers who, like their male counterparts, relied on their wages for their own support and that of their families and, when industrial conditions deteriorated, were at the forefront of working-class protest.

Yet the historical experience of the two sexes, for all its similarities, has proved upon closer examination to be profoundly different in many important ways. Slaves, for example, were assumed to have been provided with at least adequate diets, but new research suggests that for pregnant women and nursing mothers slaves' standard diet meant semistarvation. Differences in life cycles and family responsibilities account for comparable divergence in the experience of factory workers. The employment patterns of white women in the New England textile industry illustrate the point. Young single women at the turn of the century went into the mills to supplement family income, often allowing brothers to improve their job prospects by staying in school; they withdrew after marriage and childbirth but returned to the mills as mothers of small children when the perilous state of family finances required them to do so. As mothers of grown children, they returned to stay. In the work force, the jobs to which women were assigned, the wages they were paid, the opportunities for unionization they encountered, and the relationship they forged with government regulators all reinforced fundamental differences between the sexes.

As scholars begin to incorporate the wealth of new information generated by historians of women into their standard accounts of the American experience, women's distinctive experience has required the modification of old generalizations. It also has become apparent that there is a history of social relations between the sexes, just as there is a history of relations between the races. The differences that derive from sex—in a word, *gender*—have thus become as critical as those deriving from race or class in understanding the complex ways in which American society has remained stratified and the challenges that lie ahead if the ideal of equality is to be realized.

Most people, male and female, particularly if white and middle class, conventionally have understood difference in terms of sex to mean advantage for women. They assumed that women were spared heavy physical labor and fierce competitive pressures. Excused from primary responsibility for family support, wives and daughters could spend most of their adult lives at home rather than in the work force, devoting their time to such congenial tasks as caring for children, doing charitable deeds, and socializing with friends. Those who were employed outside the home were thought to work for "pin money," which they could use to indulge their whims as consumers.

Recent research makes clear that most of these "advantages" were class-specific and chimerical. The notion that the home protected working-class housewives from the competitive pressures of the marketplace, and all housewives from real work, was an illusion. The home always has been less a haven than a workplace. It was the site of housework—heavy physical labor and unremitting toil—work that was no less strenuous for all the denial that it was work at all since it was performed for love of family rather than wages. Even the middle-class housewife who enjoyed the conveniences of nineteenth-century town life and possibly a servant to help with the laundry and cooking struggled with an exhausting array of tasks. For rural women the work load was even heavier. Although twentieth-century technology has lightened the onerous physical burden, the equation of homemaking with leisure remains a fantasy carefully nurtured by the advertising industry. If the nature of housework has changed, the time spent doing it has not. In 1960 nonemployed urban women were spending fifty-five hours per week in housework—three hours more than rural homemakers in the 1920s. Fully employed women in the 1980s each week packed an additional twenty-five hours of work—housework—into evenings and weekends, leading one expert to conclude that their work days were probably longer than their grandmothers'.

☆ ☆ ☆ Gender as a Social Construction

The adverse economic implications for women associated with the old perception that housework was not real work suggest that in this instance, as in many others, difference for women has meant disadvantage. Women's historians not only have documented this disadvantage but also have sought to explain it. The factors involved are very complex and still imperfectly understood. The explanation traditionally offered has been a variant of biological essentialism. As Supreme Court Justice David Brewer put it in his opinion in *Mueller v. Oregon* (1908): "The two sexes differ in the structure of the body, in the functions to be performed by each, in the amount of physical strength, in the capacity for long continuing labor . . . , [in] the self-reliance which enables one to assert full rights, and in the capacity to maintain the struggle for subsistence." Woman's "physical structure and a proper discharge of her maternal functions" place her at a disadvantage in that struggle, he continued, and justify legislation to protect her.

Justice Brewer's statement reveals a common confusion of sex and gender. To the extent that his view of difference is based on anatomical and hormonal features that differentiate males and females biologically, he is talking about *sexual* difference. When, however, he speaks of "the self-reliance that enables . . . [men] to assert full rights," "the capacity [of men] to maintain the struggle for subsistence," and the "proper discharge of [women's] maternal functions," he is referring to *gender* differences. The assumption that men are self-reliant and that women are not, that men struggle for subsistence and women do not, that women nurture their children and men cannot, reflects the ways in which Justice Brewer and most of his generation understood the implications of being male or female.

Sex refers to biological differences that are unchanging; gender involves the meaning that a particular society and culture attaches to sexual difference. Because that meaning varies over time and among cultures, gender differences are both socially constructed and subject to change. Definitions of what is masculine or feminine are learned as each society instructs its members from infancy through adulthood as to what behavior and personality attributes are appropriate for males and females of that generation, class, and social group.

In antebellum America, for example, white southern males, whether members of the downcountry planter class or backcountry working class, identified masculinity with a concept of personal honor, in defense of which fists flew and duels were fought. In the cities of the North, many young working-class males shared their southern counterparts' obsession with physical prowess and bellicosity. So synonymous were masculinity and toughness for those New Yorkers known as Bowery Boys that when the Bowery Boy was represented on stage, he was immediately recognizable by his swaggering gait and aggressive persona. Although the black abolitionist Frederick Douglass would not have been comfortable with the flamboyant aggressiveness and virility flaunted by the Bowery Boys as a badge of working-class masculinity, the identification of force and power with manhood was a concept he well understood. In *Narrative of the Life of Frederick Douglass* (1845), an autobiographical account of his life as a slave and his escape to freedom, the author prefaced a description of his brutal fight with the vicious "slave breaker" Covey in a single sentence: "You have seen how a man was made a slave; you shall see how a slave was made a man."

Not all social groups defined masculinity in this fashion, even in antebellum America. Although aggressiveness, self-reliance, and competitiveness continued to be cultivated in boys because such qualities were needed in the working world of adult males, families whose values were shaped by evangelical Protestantism emphasized that manliness also involved self-restraint, moral self-discipline, and sobriety. These latter qualities became even more important in the new urban bourgeois culture of the late nineteenth century. A bureaucratized corporate capitalism would require of the middle class a different model of masculinity than the rougher ideal characteristic of the frontier. A "real" man, while projecting a virile and, if necessary, tough demeanor, also needed to be a "team player"—an attribute cultivated in boyhood games and team sports. Indeed, competitive sports, virility, and masculinity have become so intertwined in the twentieth century, concludes historian Clyde Griffen in *Meanings for Manhood*, that "the boy or man who dislikes competitive sports or virile postures has little choice but to affect 'manly' interests and behavior and to hope these affections will not be exposed." To behave otherwise is to risk being called a "sissy" or a "queer." Such labels reflect tenacious assumptions that males who desire sexual relations only with males therefore wish to be women and are effeminate.

Because homosexuality has been viewed for most of the twentieth century as a biological deviation from "normal" masculinity or femininity, many Americans fail to appreciate the extent to which sexuality is also socially constructed. Within those boundaries, socially constructed scripts provide cues as to how we respond sexually—what or who arouses our desire. How sexual preference is first determined or chosen, and when, is a matter experts do not fully understand. But here too culture plays a part. It is helpful, historian Carroll Smith-Rosenberg wrote in "The Female World of Love and Ritual" (1975), to "view sexual and emotional impulses as part of a continuum or spectrum. . . . At one end of the continuum lies committed heterosexuality, at the other uncompromising homosexuality; between, a wide latitude of emotions and sexual feelings." Where we place ourselves on that continuum and whether we move within it are affected by cultural norms as well as a strong biological component.

Sexuality has its own history. Conceptions of sexuality, attitudes as to how sexual feelings should be expressed, with whom, and where, have been continually reshaped by the changing nature of the economy and politics. In the seventeenth century, for example, women were believed to be more lustful and carnal than men. Female sexuality was seen as a source of power and corruption to be feared and controlled. By the nineteenth century, when sexual restraints had to be internalized, sexuality was redefined. Women—at least white, native-born, middle- and upper-class women—were viewed as having weaker sexual desires than men. Sensuality was attached to poor or "darker" women—who, by definition, "invited" male advances.

As we begin to uncover the history of sexuality, we can better understand what part sexuality played in women's subordination. We can also see how women tried to devise ways to enhance sexual control and expression. In the nineteenth century, for example, some married women used the concept of women as passionless to reduce the frequency of sexual intercourse so as to reduce the likelihood of pregnancy and enhance sexual pleasure. Women who wished to express themselves sexually as well as emotionally in single-sex relationships constructed life-styles that opened up new realms of freedom. Indeed, we are just beginning to understand the ways in which these private relationships sustained the public activities of women such as Jane Addams or Lillian Wald.

☆ ☆ ☆ Gender and Its Implications

Understanding the difference between sex and gender provides a key to understanding the differences in men's and women's historical experiences. In the workplace, for example, women and men were assigned jobs that reflected the employers' beliefs about the kind of work each sex should do. In a society whose understanding of gender included the conviction that women's primary obligations are familial and their basic talents domestic, female wage earners were persistently channeled into jobs that corresponded with the kind of work done in the domestic sphere or with characteristics long associated with women.

In the preindustrial domestic economy, women did both heavy physical labor (hauling water, slaughtering chickens) and skilled tasks (spinning, weaving, nursing). When women sought new avenues through which to gain economic independence, they followed these chores into the marketplace. As slaves and as "hired help" they toiled on other people's farms; as "mill girls" they tended dangerous spinning machinery for twelve hours a day; as packinghouse workers they labored amid stench and slime.

Upwardly mobile women laid claim to the teaching and nursing professions by emphasizing that the personality characteristics and skills required for such work were precisely those believed to be unique to the female sex. Thus nursing, considered in pre–Civil War years an occupation no respectable woman would enter, was eventually touted as a profession eminently suited to women. Providence, after all, had endowed the fairer sex with what the Raleigh, North Carolina, *News and Observer* called in 1904 that "compassion which penetrate[s] the heart, that instinct which divines and anticipates the wants of the sick, and the patience which pliantly bends to all their caprices." As the economy grew more complex, middle-class women infiltrated the ranks of librarians and secretaries. These occupations had been primarily male but, like teaching and nursing, were redefined so as to emphasize the nurturing, service-oriented qualities ascribed to women—with a corresponding decrease in pay. Newer industries provided new job titles but old work categories. Receptionists and social workers were hired by employers still convinced that the tasks required in these jobs were consistent with the personality characteristics and skills traditionally associated with women. New white-collar jobs were also segregated by race, even in the North where segregation was not officially practiced. White women were overwhelmingly hired as stewardesses on national airlines until after the civil rights legislation of the 1960s.

Because gender rather than individual talent or capability has been the primary consideration, the result of this kind of stereotyping has been to segregate women into certain kinds of work, whether in the professions or in industry. Of the 299 occupations listed by the Bureau of Labor Statistics in 1990, only 56 are thoroughly integrated by sex. Males overwhelmingly dominate 104 occupations. Seventy-nine occupations are predominantly female, and it is into these that over 80 percent of women workers cluster, working as waitresses, salespersons, secretaries, nurses, and teachers.

Once a form of work has been identified with women, it invariably has become associated with low pay and minimal prestige. "Theoretically, the market treats men and women neutrally, judging only the characteristics of their labor," writes historian Alice Kessler-Harris in *A Woman's Wages*. "In the work of economists, the wage is rooted in the play of supply and demand." In practice, she continues, "the wage is neither neutral nor natural, but reveals a set of social constructs . . . that convey messages about the nature of the world, and about . . . men and women and . . . the relations between them." Nowhere are messages about gender relations more clearly revealed than in the demands of nineteenth-century male trade unionists. Higher pay, they argued, was the due of those whose masculinity was measured by work—and by the skill and strength to do it. Receiving a "family wage" enabled a man to be the sole support of his family and confirmed his own and society's idea of manliness. Lower pay, on the other hand, was thought appropriate for those presumably marginal workers whose place really was in the home, protecting purity and virtue and fulfilling family duties.

These gendered assumptions about wages disadvantaged both men and women, especially in working-class families. When the man was cast in the role of sole provider for his family, those men whose wives worked outside the home often felt themselves failures not only as providers but also as men. Women in the work force—whatever their class, whether they worked as a matter of choice or necessity—often received wages that were based more on the sex of the person doing the work than the value of the work itself or the productivity of the worker. In this way, the home subsidized the factory and has continued to do so even in the late twentieth century, when two-paycheck families are the norm and a "working wife" is no longer viewed as a threat to masculinity.

Gender was embedded not only in economic relations but in legal relations as well. In the legal tradition that English colonists brought to America, the husband was understood to be the head of the family and to represent it in its dealings with the world. Upon marriage the woman lost her separate civil identity; it was assumed that she had voluntarily forsworn the claim to make choices at odds with those of her husband. In a powerful legal fiction, man and wife were understood to be one person; the married woman was the *feme covert*, "covered" with her husband's legal identity for virtually all purposes except crime. All personal property that she brought to the marriage became her husband's; he could sell her jewelry, gamble away her money. He could not sell her real estate unless she consented, but he could decide how it was to be used: whether land was to be farmed, rented out, planted in corn or vegetables; whether trees on it were to be cultivated or cut down. Since married women did not own property, they could not make legal contracts affecting it; they could not buy and sell without the husband's consent. A married woman could not decide whether her children were to be kept at home or apprenticed or, if apprenticed, who their masters would be. She could not sign a contract independently; not until she was a widow could she leave a will. So powerful was the fiction that husband and wife are one person that marital rape was inconceivable. Indeed, marital rape was not outlawed anywhere in the world until 1978, when New York passed a statute prohibiting forced sexual intercourse whether by a stranger, an acquaintance, or a spouse. As of 1990, only nine states have followed New York's lead. In most states, for husbands to force sex upon unwilling, even resisting wives is a crime only under certain circumstances. In four states it is not a crime at all.

Gender also defined political relationships. In Anglo-American tradition the right to participate in political activities—voting, officeholding, jury duty— was conditioned on the holding of property. Since married women could not direct the use of their property, it seemed to follow that they could be neither jurors, nor voters, nor officeholders. That politics was considered a male domain, that women were not political beings, is an understanding as old as Western civilization. Aristotle, whose classic work provided the basic terms by which Westerners have understood politics, said that men alone realized themselves as citizens. It is no accident that the civic *virtue* he extolled derives from the same root as the word *virile*. Women, Aristotle maintained, realized themselves only within the confines of the household. Their relationship to the world of politics, like their legal status, was derivative—through fathers, husbands, and sons.

This derivative relationship forced women to carve out a political role that rested upon their ability to influence those who held political power. A time-honored tradition, this use of influence was employed in the interests of a wide range of important social issues and philanthropic causes in the years before 1920, when the Nineteenth Amendment to the Constitution granted female suffrage. Women found that the wielding of influence benefited their communities and enlarged their political skills. The uses of influence continued to be exploited by American women even after they got the vote. As primary adviser to Al Smith, governor of New York and presidential candidate in the 1920s, Belle Moskowitz had enormous impact both on the policies of his administration and on the politics of the Democratic party. But she was uncomfortable claiming power for herself and never ran for political office. Mary McLeod Bethune, a prominent African American educator, was equally adept in the uses of influence. As president of the National Association of Colored Women and the National Council of Negro Women, Bethune met Eleanor Roosevelt. The first lady, admiring the effectiveness with which this forceful, articulate black woman championed the needs of her people, used her own influence to secure for Bethune appointments to a number of positions, notably in the National Youth Administration. From her position within the administration, Bethune in turn organized the Federal Council on Negro Affairs, a group of black leaders who worked effectively to focus the attention of the media as well as the administration on the desperate problems facing blacks in the Great Depression.

The gendering of politics forced women to clothe their political claims in domestic language. Deflecting male hostility to their entry into the political arena, they argued that women should have the vote in order to elect city officials who would see to it that rotting garbage was removed from homes, decaying meat taken out of markets, and polluted water purified; otherwise, the best efforts of mothers to assure their children clean homes and wholesome food would be to no avail. Women in the nuclear disarmament movement also used gendered language, naming their organization "Mothers Strike for Peace."

☆ ☆ ☆ Difficulties of Understanding Gender as a System

Economics, law, politics—each, as we have seen, was permeated by assumptions, practices, and expectations that were deeply gendered. So widely shared were these assumptions, practices, and expectations and so much a part of the ordinary, everyday experience that they acquired an aura of naturalness, rightness, and even inevitability. Common sense dictated that "this is simply the way things are." But "common sense," as anthropologist Clifford Geertz has shrewdly observed in *Local Knowledge* (1983), "is not what the mind cleared of cant spontaneously apprehends; it is what the mind filled with presuppositions . . . concludes." The consequence of comprehending the world in this way—whether in the nineteenth century or in our own times—is that it obscures the workings of a system in which economic, political, and cultural forces interact and reinforce each other in ways that benefit one group and disadvantage the other. Unable to recognize the system, failing to understand that what shapes and defines our lives has been constructed piece by interlocking piece over time by other human beings, we constantly reproduce the world we know believing we have no other choice. As a result the inequities persist, becoming more difficult to challenge because they, too, seem as natural and inevitable as the system that has produced them.

To develop a way of looking that enables one to "see" economic and social relationships that are presumed to be neutral and natural as socially constructed arrangements that in fact benefit one group at the expense of others is always a difficult task. That task is made even more difficult by the fact that language itself is embedded with the values, norms, and assumptions of the dominant group. Consequently it reflects and re-creates reality as it is perceived by that group. Using language that is not one's own to expose unequal relationships or to create an alternative to those relationships challenges the ingenuity and analytical abilities of even the most clearheaded and imaginative thinkers.

Analytical skills, moreover, are not inborn. They are developed slowly and painfully within an educational process that values and encourages those skills as contrasted, for example, with simple memorization or rote learning. Throughout history women have been explicitly excluded from the intellectual community. Prior to the seventeenth century, when most people were illiterate, elite families in which sons learned to read and write rarely provided such opportunities to their daughters. A major literacy gap existed throughout the world until well into the nineteenth century and, in many underdeveloped countries, persists today. At the time of the American Revolution, when it has been estimated that 70 percent of the men in the northern cities could read, only 35 percent of their female counterparts could do so. Slaves were denied by law access to instruction in reading and writing lest they learn about alternatives to slavery.

Not until the second half of the nineteenth century were white women admitted to major state universities. Between 1870 and 1890 a few elite colleges were founded that were designed to provide upper middle-class young women an education equivalent to what their brothers were receiving at Harvard, Yale, and Princeton universities. These new women's colleges reluctantly admitted a few black students. It was left to black women with meager resources in a rigidly segregated society—notably Mary McLeod Bethune and Charlotte Hawkins Brown—to develop their own institutions. Because public schools served black children so badly, these private institutions often began not as colleges but as elementary or secondary schools that later grew into larger and higher-level colleges. Only in recent generations have women in substantial numbers been able to acquire not only a basic education but also the rigorous training that would facilitate their ability to analyze and question the social and cultural arrangements within which they lived.

Another consequence of women's education deprivation was their ignorance of history and, therefore, of an intimate acquaintance with other historical actors, male or female, who had faced challenges that in some way resembled their own. Lacking a history of their own, they had few models, few heroes to emulate or strategies to adopt. The lack of a history in which women were actors made it particularly difficult for even educated women to envision a world other than one in which men—their experiences and needs—were the norm. Marginality in the past thus confirmed and reinforced marginality in the present.

Understanding economic and social relationships that benefit one sex at the expense of another, developing language with which to critique those hierarchical relationships and articulate an alternative vision, and forging the group solidarity necessary to realize that vision have been the tasks of feminism. The term *feminism* came into use in the United States around 1910 at a time when women were engaged in the fight for suffrage as well as a host of other reforms. As historian Nancy Cott has pointed out in *The Grounding of Modern Feminism*, feminism included suffrage and other measures to promote women's welfare that had emerged out of the nineteenth-century women's movement. However, feminism encompassed a wider range of fundamental changes, amounting to a revolution in the relation of the sexes. "As an *ism* (an ideology)," Cott notes, "feminism presupposed a set of principles not necessarily belonging to every woman—nor limited to women." In other words, not all women would oppose a sex hierarchy that privileged men as a group nor would they feel compelled to struggle for sexual equality. On the other hand, some men would, joining feminist women in their efforts to dismantle a system that conferred on one sex the power to define the other. While this system has been partially dismantled—the goal of suffrage was realized in law in 1920—the wider revolution remains to be accomplished.

☆ ☆ ☆ Rethinking the Social Construction of Gender

Embracing the goals of their feminist predecessors and enriched by current scholarship on gender, contemporary feminists seek to reconstruct social relations between the sexes. To do so, they believe, requires change in both public life and private behavior. This double agenda has a long history.

In 1848, when American feminists drafted their first feminist manifesto, the "Declaration of Sentiments," Elizabeth Cady Stanton demanded change in both law and custom. She called for legal change in the form of property rights for married women and voting rights for all women. Recognizing the ways in which women's self-esteem and autonomy were undermined, she also urged women to work for wide-ranging cultural change, such as equal standards of sexual behavior and equal roles in churches.

When twentieth-century feminists began to understand gender as a social construction, they too realized that the feminist revolution had to be waged in personal life as well as public life; in home as well as in workplace; in the most intimate relationships as well as the most remote. "It must be womanly as well as manly to earn your own living, to stand on your own feet," observed the feminist Crystal Eastman in the *Liberator* (December 1920) shortly after the national suffrage amendment was passed. "And it must be manly as well as womanly to know how to cook and sew and clean and take care of yourself in the ordinary exigencies of life. . . . The second part of this revolution will be more passionately resisted than the first. Men will not give up their privilege of helplessness without a struggle. The average man has a carefully cultivated ignorance about household matters . . . a sort of cheerful inefficiency." But it was fifty years before Eastman's insights became an agenda for action.

Feminists of the 1970s captured national attention with bitter criticisms of parents who gave nurses' outfits to their daughters and doctors' bags to their sons and of guidance counselors who urged mathematically talented girls to become bookkeepers and boys to become engineers. Feminists condemned stereotypes that fit children to conventional roles in their adult life and encouraged the publication of books and toys designed to demonstrate to both boys and girls that they need not shape their aspirations to gendered stereotypes. (The popular television show, record, and book *Free to Be You and Me* encapsulated these themes.) Feminists also urged a new set of private decisions in the family, so that both sexes would share more equitably the burdens and pleasures associated with earning a living, maintaining a household, and rearing a family. But gender stereotypes turned out to be more resilient than many had anticipated; socialization is a lifetime process.

Feminists themselves had to wrestle with a culture that maintained a hierarchy of values, reserving strength, competence, independence, and rationality for men and nurture, supportiveness, and empathy for women. Questioning both the hierarchy and the dualisms embedded in this gendering of values, feminists argued that these should be viewed as shared human qualities that are not sex-specific.

Sexual hierarchy was not the only cultural hierarchy that posed problems. There were also hierarchies of race and class. White feminists in the 1970s were criticized for promoting a vision of feminism that ignored black women and assumed that all women who were impatient with contemporary culture were white and middle class. The upwardly mobile vision was a contested vision. The priorities of women of different classes and races did not necessarily converge. Many black women supported elements of the agenda of middle-class white feminists of the 1970s—equal pay for equal work, access to jobs—but they disagreed on priorities. They were skeptical of those who placed the needs of middle-class women ahead of the needs of working women. Middle-class white women, the employers of domestic workers, were markedly more enthusiastic about the elimination of quotas for female students in law and medical schools than they were about the establishment of minimum wage and social security protection for domestic workers. The first generation of white radical feminists fought vigorously for the repeal of all abortion laws and for safe access to birth control; black feminists saw access to abortion as only one of a wide range of medical services for which many black women struggled.

Differences in sexual preference also posed problems for this generation of feminists. Challenges to traditional gender arrangements have always inspired charges of sexual deviance from those seeking to discredit the movement and trivialize grievances. The 1960s were no exception. Concerned about the movement's image, many feminists, rejecting the charge, attempted to push lesbians out of sight. Equality, not sexual preference, was the issue, they insisted. Lesbian feminists disagreed, arguing that autonomy in sexual matters involved more than access to reproductive control. In time, tensions eased as many heterosexual feminists accepted the legitimacy of lesbian involvement and the validity of the contention that straight/gay divisions also constituted a form of cultural hierarchy that reinforced male supremacy.

☆ ☆ ☆ The Complexity of Creating Equality

Recognizing the magnitude of cultural and personal change required for each woman to realize her full human potential, feminists of the 1970s simultaneously challenged the institutions and the laws that denied women equal treatment. They launched a barrage of test cases in state and federal courts challenging practices of unequal responsibility for jury service, unequal benefits for dependents, unequal age requirements for drinking and marriage. In 1971, in the Idaho case *Reed v. Reed*, which tested who was to be the administrator of a will, feminists persuaded the Supreme Court for the first time in American history to treat discrimination on the basis of sex as a denial of equal protection under the law. But the Supreme Court was reluctant to build on this precedent in subsequent cases. The Court's refusal to apply as strict a standard to sex discrimination as to racial discrimination prompted feminists to try to insert a ban on sex discrimination in the Constitution. The Equal Rights Amendment, passed overwhelmingly by Congress in 1972, failed to garner the last three states necessary for the three-fourths majority required for ratification. A contributing factor in its failure was basic disagreement about whether equality under law requires equality of military obligation.

Lobbying vigorously with both Congress and the executive branch, feminists won guarantees of equal pay for equal work, equal employment opportunities, equal access to credit and to education. Building on the tactics and achievements of the civil rights movement, feminists secured major gains in the 1960s and 1970s. In the process, however, they discovered that guarantees of equality in a system structured with men's needs as the norm do not always produce a gender-neutral result. In many professions, for example, there is enormous pressure to demonstrate mastery of one's field in the early stages of a career, precisely when the physical hazards of childbearing are relatively minimal. Although the standard appears to be gender-neutral, it presents young women with excruciating choices that do not confront their male peers.

Nowhere was the challenge of achieving gender-neutrality in the workplace greater than in the matter of pregnancy. Aware of the long history of discrimination against pregnant employees, feminists successfully attacked regulations that prevented women from making their own decisions about whether and how long to work when pregnant. But initial legislative "solutions" raised new complexities that challenged the assumption that equality always requires identical treatment. If employers could no longer fire pregnant women, they still could exclude from the company's disability program those temporarily unable to work during some portion of their pregnancy or at childbirth. Pregnancy, said the Supreme Court in its rulings on *Geduldig v. Aiello* (1974) and *General Electric v. Martha Gilbert* (1976), was not a temporary disability but a "voluntary physical condition." Outraged at the Court's ruling, feminists and their allies demanded congressional action that would require pregnancy and childbirth to be treated as any other physical event that befalls workers. Responding in 1978 with model legislation mandating equal treatment in the workplace, Congress required employers to give physically disabled pregnant workers the same benefits given to other disabled workers. The problem, however, was not yet resolved.

If employers denied disability leave to all employees as a matter of company policy, federal legislation mandating equal treatment for both sexes with respect to pregnancy disability would, in effect, penalize female employees unable to work because of pregnancy-related illness. Equality, in this instance, seemed to require special treatment. Lawmakers in California and a few other states agreed and required employers to provide pregnant workers disability coverage even if no other illnesses were covered. Employers complained that this constituted "preferential treatment" for women. Some feminists, aware of the ways in which legislation designating women as a special class of employees because of their reproductive capacity had penalized female workers in the past, questioned whether such legislation was in the best interests of women. Would it reinforce sexist stereotypes of men as "natural" breadwinners and women as "natural" childbearers and rearers, making employers reluctant to hire married women of childbearing age and further marginalizing women as workers? Wouldn't it be better strategy to concentrate on extending disability benefits to workers of both sexes? Other feminists were untroubled. Pregnancy is unique to women, they argued, and calls for "special treatment" in recognition of that uniqueness. Such legislation, they insisted, acknowledges reality at a time when growing numbers of women become pregnant within one year of their employment.

In a 1987 decision, *California Federal Savings and Loan Association v. Guerra*, in which the Court upheld a controversial California law on pregnancy disability benefits, Justice Thurgood Marshall went to the heart of the equality-and-difference dilemma. Writing for the majority, he noted that "while federal law mandates the same treatment of pregnant and non-pregnant employees, it would be violating the spirit of the law to read it as barring preferential treatment of pregnancy." The California law, he reasoned, "promotes equal employment opportunities because it allows women as well as men to have families without losing their jobs."

The difficulty of determining what is fair treatment for pregnant women dramatically illustrates the complexities involved in reconciling equality and sexual difference. Part of the difficulty has to do with the meaning of equality. Is equality to be thought of, as it has been throughout American history, as equality of opportunity? Or is equality to be defined as equality of results? In either case, do the methods used to achieve equality demand the same treatment or different treatment? The stakes in this debate are high, as the debate over pregnancy in the workplace illustrates, because childbearing impacts so directly on women's struggle for economic independence.

Childbearing is only one aspect of sexual difference that complicates efforts to achieve equality between the sexes. Closely related are other issues surrounding reproduction. In the first half of the twentieth century access to birth control was the contested issue. Feminists argued that the right to choose if and when to bear children was the foundation on which authentic equality between men and women must rest. The debate was intense and emotionally charged because reproductive issues involve sexuality, ethical and religious values, medical technology, and constitutional rights to privacy as well as matters of economic dependence, physical vulnerability, and state power. In the second half of the twentieth century, particularly in the wake of the Supreme Court's decision in *Roe v. Wade* (1973), these issues have been fought out over policies governing access to abortion. Issues of race, class, and gender intersect. For many white middle-class feminists, preserving abortion rights is a top priority. Advocates of birth control, they see abortion as a measure of last resort. Without that option women's efforts to plan their lives, to set priorities and make choices, are severely constrained, and constrained in ways that men's are not. For poor women and minority women who have been the subject of involuntary sterilization and who lack access to a wide range of medical services, abortion is only one among many essential needs, and not necessarily the most pressing one. For many other women, abortion is not an essential need at all. Believing that the fetus is a human being from the moment of conception and that motherhood is woman's key reason for being, they deny any connection between equality and access to abortion. They reject the feminist contention that denying women access to abortion is a way in which men use the power of the state to reinforce their own power over women. Whether the state should permit or fund abortions for teenage victims of incest is the most dramatic of the issues in conflict.

Incest is only one aspect of the larger problem of sexual violence that feminists contend is the ultimate expression of male dominance. Sexual violence, they insist, is violence, not sex, and it is a public, not a private, matter. Rape crisis centers, battered women's shelters, "Take Back the Night" marches—all are expressions of their insistence that government respond to male violence against women. Feminists also attack directly the notion that female victims of violence are in some measure to blame by virtue of provocative dress and behavior or prior sexual experience. In the late 1970s they convinced policymakers that sexual harassment was a form of economic discrimination and that those who maintained workplaces were legally obliged to take action to prevent it.

Feminists also have exposed the link between sexual violence and pornography. Many of them argue that material which objectifies women and equates violence against them with sexual pleasure is an invasion of their civil liberties. This interpretation represents a radical reformulation of traditional civil liberties arguments and a willingness on the part of some feminists to entertain reconsideration of the boundaries of protected speech. The controversial nature of pornography and the complex issues of civil rights and civil liberties raised by efforts to deal with it once again exemplify the challenges involved in creating a society where men and women are equal.

☆ ☆ ☆ The Anguish of Fundamental Change

Reconciling equality and difference, equity and justice, involves feminists in a task as consequential as any in human history. Relationships assumed to be the result of choice, even of love, have been exposed as hierarchical constructs involving power and control. Such exposures are always traumatic. "All the decent drapery of life is . . . rudely torn off," complained the British legislator Edmund Burke in his *Reflections on the Revolution in France* two hundred years ago. "When ancient opinions and rules of life are taken away, the loss cannot possibly be estimated. From that moment we have no compass to govern us; nor can we know distinctly to what port we steer."

Even those in the vanguard of change can appreciate its difficulty; old habits are hard to break even for those determined to break them. For those who are not the initiators, challenges to long-standing beliefs and behaviors, whether issued now or in the past, can be at best unwelcome and at worst profoundly threatening. Feminism is no exception. Demands for equality in terms of power, resources, and prestige are usually seen as redistributive. Giving one party its share of the pie may result in a smaller share for the other. Even individuals who believe in equality in the abstract may find themselves loath to share power and privileges in practice, especially when their own lives are affected intimately. Moreover, new governmental policies designed to provide women equal protection in the law, equity in the workplace, and parity in politics have been only part of what feminists are about. Cultural values as well as social institutions are under scrutiny. Even the definition of family has been tampered with as the 1980 White House Conference on Families made all too clear. Family has always meant that members are related by blood, marriage, or adoption. The term is now being applied to two mothers with children or an unmarried heterosexual couple who are childless. "Anyone living under the same roof that provides support for each other *regardless* of blood, marriage, or adoption" seems to qualify, complained a Reagan administrator. To recognize these arrangements as multiple family forms, which many feminists do, is to legitimate people who, from the viewpoint of traditionalists, are living "illegitimate" life-styles.

From this perspective it is hardly surprising that gender changes which feminists regard as expanding options for women and men alike are seen by traditionalists as rejecting cherished beliefs and practices—as "neuterizing" society. Women who believe they have lived useful and admirable lives by the old rules often regard feminists' attacks on traditional gender roles as an attack on a way of life they have mastered and hence an attack on them personally. In *The Power of the Positive Woman* (1977), Phyllis Schlafly expressed their fear that "a woman who has been a good wife and homemaker for decades" will be "turned out to pasture with impunity" by "a new, militant breed of women's liberationist" prepared to sacrifice justice for equality.

At issue are not just economic security and personal identity of individuals but the larger social order. Convinced that biological differences between the sexes dictate "natural" roles, traditionalists see the maintenance of these roles as socially and morally necessary—a source of stability in a world of flux. Thus feminist insistence that women should be able to seek fulfillment in the public world of work and power as well as in the private world of home and family is viewed by traditionalists as an egocentric demand elevating personal gratification above familial duty. "Feminists praise self-centeredness and call it liberation," observed New Right activist Connie Marshner in *The New Traditional Woman* (1982). By the same token, the demand that women themselves be the ultimate judges of whether and when to bear children is seen by some not as a legitimate desire to insure a good life for those children who are born but as an escape from maternal obligations that threatens the future of the family and ultimately, therefore, of society itself.

To suggest that some Americans find feminism an essential part of their identity and that others define themselves and their lives in terms of traditionalism is not to suggest that the ideological history of woman is bipolar. It embraces many variants. Nor do we suggest that there is nothing on which the two groups agree. Traditionalist women may be as suspicious of male-controlled institutions as feminists. Traditionalists may also be as vocal and publicly active on behalf of their goals. Feminists may be just as dedicated to family as traditionalists. Both groups identify with "sisterhood" and see "women's issues" as special ones, although they do not consistently agree on what they are or how they should be addressed. Partisans of these issues may unite or divide along class, occupational, or political lines. But no matter where they fall on the ideological spectrum, all American women, not merely feminists, are forging a definition of self—and of *gender*—that extends beyond the definitions of the past, illustrating in the process that change in relations between the sexes is an intrinsic part of the complex and diverse history of the United States.

FURTHER READING

For a discussion of gender as a category of analysis in the writing of history, see Joan W. Scott, *Gender and the Politics of History* (New York, 1988). Journals specializing in such analysis include *Signs: A Journal of Women in Culture and Society*, *Gender and History*, the *Journal of Women's History*, and *Feminist Studies*.

That gender relationships have become as important as relations of class and race is evident in recent studies like Carol F. Karlsen, *The Devil in the Shape of a Woman: Witchcraft in Colonial New England* (New York, 1987); Jeanne Boydston, *Home and Work: Housework, Wages, and the Ideology of Labor in the New Republic*

(New York, 1990); Christine Stansell, *City of Women: Sex and Class in New York, 1789–1860* (New York, 1986); Mary H. Blewett, *Men, Women, and Work: Class, Gender, and Protest in the New England Shoe Industry, 1780–1910* (Urbana, Ill., 1988); Deborah Gray White, *Ar'n't I a Woman?: Female Slaves in the Plantation South* (New York, 1987); Elizabeth Fox-Genovese, *Within the Plantation Household: Black and White Women of the Old South* (Chapel Hill, N.C., 1988); Jacqueline Jones, *Labor of Love, Labor of Sorrow: Black Women, Work, and the Family from Slavery to the Present* (New York, 1985); Jacquelyn Dowd Hall et al., *Like a Family: The Making of a Southern Cotton Mill World* (Chapel Hill, N.C., 1987); Carroll Smith-Rosenberg, *Disorderly Conduct: Visions of Gender in Victorian America* (New York, 1985); Mark C. Carnes and Clyde Griffen, eds., *Meanings for Manhood: Constructions of Manhood in Victorian America* (Chicago, 1990); John D'Emilio and Estelle B. Freedman, *Intimate Matters: A History of Sexuality in America* (New York, 1988); and Elaine Tyler May, *Homeward Bound: American Families in the Cold War Era* (New York, 1988).

For further discussion of feminism, contemporary feminist issues, and female opposition to feminism, see Nancy F. Cott, *The Grounding of Modern Feminism* (New Haven, Conn., 1987); Linda Gordon, *Heroes of Their Own Lives: The Politics and History of Family Violence, Boston, 1880–1960* (New York, 1988); Elizabeth H. Pleck, *Domestic Tyranny: The Making of Social Policy against Family Violence from Colonial Times to the Present* (New York, 1987); Alice Kessler-Harris, *A Woman's Wage: Historical Meanings and Social Consequences* (Lexington, Ky., 1990); Rosalind P. Petchesky, *Abortion and Woman's Choice: The State, Sexuality, and Reproductive Freedom*, rev. ed. (Boston, 1990); Kristen Luker, *Abortion and the Politics of Motherhood* (Berkeley, Calif., 1984); Donald G. Mathews and Jane Sherron De Hart, *Sex, Gender, and the Politics of ERA: A State and the Nation* (New York, 1990); and Rebecca E. Klatch, *Women of the New Right* (Philadelphia, 1987).

Issues of equality and difference have been widely explored, especially by feminist legal scholars in law school journals published at Harvard University, the University of Michigan, the University of Wisconsin, George Washington University, New York University, and elsewhere.

26 ☆ Reform and

☆ Social

☆ Change

☆ Robert H. Walker

The title of this book, *Making America*, correctly infers the dynamic character of its subject. The United States is a nation where each generation takes as its birthright the evolutionary task of remaking the culture, where "tradition" means the continuing search for "a better America." No subject illustrates this trait, this America-in-the-Making, so well as reform.

Reform is a mighty force. It splits churches and creates associations. It makes martyrs and binds wounds. It threatens authority and reshapes governments. It occupies the nation's courts. It fills party platforms and the daily press. It inspires memorable protests and major literature. It throws light into dark corners. It furnishes a continuous statement of what citizens think their society ought to be.

Although the study of reform scarcely has been neglected, most treatments of the subject either assume or insist that social change—whether approached as history, biography, or analysis—can only be understood in a limited context. Such studies teach much; it is possible, however, by fusing these elements, to learn even more. It is possible to perform this fusion because, even though the particulars of reform are immensely variable, the general objectives, methods, and rationales are remarkably constant through depression and prosperity, war and peace.

☆ ☆ ☆ The Anatomy of Reform

To arrive at a plausible total perspective requires intermediate steps identifying the major types of reform activity. The primary elements of social change describe three general patterns, each distinguished by its general objectives, its characteristic dynamics, and its affinity for certain forms of expression. The organization of reform into these three large categories is not an end in itself but a means toward the ultimate fusion.

One area of reform is so all-encompassing that it can well be considered the mainstream. Its starting gun was the battle cry that exhorted the patriots of 1776 and defined a principle that was to dominate the following centuries of social action: "Taxation without representation is tyranny!" This watchword translates into the idea that political democracy must be extended in order to remove economic inequity. It is the source of a stream that eventually would broaden the franchise, represent the interests of labor, regulate business, and resolve financial questions in the public interest. The issues are as old as the Constitutional Convention and as new as the debate over home rule for the District of Columbia and the interest rates set by the Federal Reserve.

This mainstream, which for convenience will be called *Mode I (politico-economic reform)*, was prominent in constitutional debates at all levels. The Antifederalists feared an amalgam of wealth with political power just as the Federalists worried about a mob majority threatening private property. Politico-economic reformers focused on suffrage and representation both in the national and state debates. The question of public lands and debates over currency, credit, and banking characterized Mode I during the antebellum days, as did the growing slavery crisis, which must be understood, in part, as an effort to use political means to legislate on a matter of property.

Out of the Civil War came incipient farm and labor organizations that put the greenbacks and the money question at the top of their agenda. The fear of monopoly, an issue since the Republic's earliest days, moved beyond banking and land to engage all large-scale commercial and industrial aggregations and in particular the railroads. Featuring these issues, a congeries of groups and parties marched under the banners of populism, progressivism, the New Deal, the Fair Deal, the New Frontier, and the Great Society. What consistently characterized these movements was their wish to extend and perfect political democracy (through broader suffrage, direct elections, voting rights enactments, election and recall of judges, and similar devices) in order to protect the lowest economic levels of the population from want and exploitation and to forestall the accumulation of unmerited wealth at the top of the heap.

Few Americans, reformers or not, have felt that the American promise included absolute economic equality. From the first, however, there has been the consistent sentiment that special privilege should be eliminated: that exalted status should not bring special justice and that public favors should not bring private wealth. Gradually the other side of the balance has accumulated the weight of social attention until the nation has passed beyond trust-busting and a guaranteed minimum wage to offer assistance to the aged, infirm, unemployed, and destitute.

The connection between the political means and the economic ends is very close. Although the public is sometimes asked to look upon the representative system with its voter guarantees and checks and balances as a thing of self-contained beauty, the reformer has assumed that political democracy was pointless without economic democracy. Even though both may be relative terms, the one without the other lacks social meaning. This sentiment characterizes and defines politico-economic reform.

Mode II (reform on behalf of special groups), it could be argued, is but an extension of the first. If all citizens had been equally affected by the push toward politico-economic melioration, then there would be no category of reform on behalf of special groups. For a multitude of reasons, including their own volition, some groups have stayed outside the mainstream. Some are extremely large groups with prominent reform histories: women, blacks, Native Americans. Some have been set aside by physical or other disabilities, some by occupation or region, some by social mores.

This aspect of social change has produced the most memorable of moments and movements, particularly the abolition of slavery in the nineteenth century and the crusade for civil rights in our own time. No issue has inspired eloquence greater than that of Theodore Dwight Weld, Henry David Thoreau, William Lloyd Garrison, Harriet Beecher Stowe, Booker T. Washington, W. E. B. Du Bois, and Martin Luther King, Jr., on behalf of African Americans. The American Anti-Slavery Society became a prototype for effective voluntarism that is echoed half a century later by the National Association for the Advancement of Colored People. This segment of the reform frontier produced extremes of violence and nonviolence, martyrdom and heroism. It nearly broke the nation in two. It led directly to the most dramatic shift in the history of governmental relationship to social change: the superimposition of civil rights over civil liberties.

In visibility and power the antislavery and civil rights movements know no rivals. But there also have been important and dramatic chapters in the cause of feminism, in Native Americans' search for justice, and in the activity of groups handicapped by disability or public attitude.

Many of these groups have nothing in common but their exclusion from full participation in the politico-economic mainstream. Some, confusing social equity with social conformity, have chosen to remain outside. Virtually none of these groups has failed to attract the attention of reformers who have sought to remove prejudice, to secure minimal social and economic guarantees, and eventually to merge the group into the general polity. So long as there are disadvantaged groups—even though they may be disadvantaged only in the attitudes of outsiders—there will be a Mode II.

Mode III (presentation of alternative social models) is more distinctive. Within it are many who reject one of the prevalent reform assumptions: namely, that gradual change is desirable and appropriate. Reformers in this mode tend to think of their society as sufficiently flawed to require more than modest repairs. Instead of amendments they offer a relatively complete alternative model for society. A few in this category accept a gradual movement toward this model, but most demand a revolutionary rejection of what *is* in favor of what *ought to be*.

In the early days of the Republic many reformers thought that the whole nation could be brought directly into the condition of a model society where all citizens owned debt-free homes on unencumbered land and cast independent votes for altruistic leaders. The first wave of model settlements was rural and remote, reflecting the assumption that the nation would be one of small farms and village crafts. The Rappites and Perfectionists pioneered both in agriculture and in architecture, while the Shakers became justly famous for their furniture and design. Brook Farm and Round Hill experimented with education as did New Harmony. Many sought to redefine the roles of the sexes.

About half these communes were inspired by the French socialist Charles Fourier. The other half were led by religious prophets retreating from the mockery of European and urban settings. The most memorable, John Humphrey Noyes's Oneida, was one of the few to combine both secular and religious ingredients. Communes, according to recent scholarship, have persisted unabated. They left the center of public attention at the time of the Civil War but returned to the limelight in the 1960s when a new wave of settlements protested military conscription and other social controls.

As the nation became urban and industrial, the ideal community was more often described than established. The most famous literary utopia was Edward Bellamy's *Looking Backward, 2000–1887* (1888), an argument for technologically assisted efficiency in the spirit of Christian cooperation. The vogue created by this best-selling romance lasted until about 1910, after which the utopian impulse continued in several shapes.

Closest to the utopian novels is what Isaac Asimov calls "social science fiction," glimpses of a high tech future where social institutions also have evolved. Professional planners took over from the communards with their garden cities and green towns, all of which contained some elements of environmental meliorism. No one ever built Frank Lloyd Wright's "Broadacre City" or Paolo Soleri's megastructures, nor was Buckminster Fuller's geodesic dome ever placed over Manhattan. But the 1930s did witness a giant experiment in regional planning called the Tennessee Valley Authority, and thirty years after the New Deal planned its ninety-nine communities, "new towns" like Columbia, Maryland, began to rise outside the urban beltways.

The dreamers and planners were joined by the advocates of peace and world government. Fuller saw the world as "one town"; all agreed that there was something archaic in planning an ideal community in isolation. Thus Mode III today offers alternative dreams ranging from Clarence Streit's legacy of a world federation; to the shared life of Twin Oaks, Virginia, begun in the spirit of B. F. Skinner; to Arcosanti, Soleri's dream in the Arizona desert.

☆ ☆ ☆ The Dynamics of Change

The most dramatic contrast between the three modes of reform is in their dynamics. If there is a normal sequence of social change, it would open with protest. Protest often begins at random and then develops an organized structure. A crucial moment for many movements comes at the time when negative complaint must be shifted to positive remedy. Many movements fail through their inability either to find an appropriate positive response or to choose among many. The making of an affirmative choice, or the establishment of priorities, gives a movement enough definition so that one may clearly see whether it has failed, succeeded (normally by institutionalizing its cause), or remained in the petitioning stage. Even when the issue has been translated into law, its partisans must retain the vigilance of the watchdog. If the goals are compromised (as, for example, in the first antitrust legislation), then the sequence must begin again: random protest, structured protest; random remedies, structured remedies; and—perhaps for the second or third time— institutionalization.

Most politico-economic issues follow the standard cycle, arising in protest against suffrage restrictions, political corruption, extremes of poverty and wealth. If successful they may result in a broadening of the franchise, a graduated income tax, or a form of unemployment insurance. Mode II exhibits the same sequence, with the important difference that most movements experience this cycle not once but twice. During the first cycle the aim is segregated equality: decent care and facilities even if outside the mainstream, as with segregated education or Indian reservations. As the final stage approaches, however, there is typically a realization that "separate but equal" is a contradiction in terms. This is no less true of the physically and mentally handicapped than of blacks or women. It is perfectly possible for a movement to exist in both cycles simultaneously, divided by factions or geography. But the transition from the Booker T. Washington credo of self-help within the black community (presented in his Atlanta Exposition Address in 1895) to the demands of the Niagara movement (1905) for full integration clearly exemplifies this shift in objectives for blacks. Although several large categories of Americans still await full equality, there are other groups—ethnic and national minorities once reviled and segregated—that have now become an indistinguishable part of the politico-economic pattern. Similarly, new programs seek to "mainstream" persons whose handicaps long appeared to set them inevitably apart.

The third mode, in contrast, has the simplest of all dynamics. To devise an alternative community implies criticism of the contemporary society; however, this kind of reform opens not with protest but with a fully articulated solution. When sponsored by the government (as with planned communities during the New Deal), the alternative is presented to the public only after it has been institutionalized. At the very least the model is offered as a written proposal, as in a utopian romance, or as an actual model, as in the case of the communes. Launched in an advanced stage, the concept either gains acceptance or falls from sight.

☆ ☆ ☆ Actors and Forms

Although all modes attract all types of social actors, and although the government has become increasingly prominent in all modes, there are nonetheless some differences. Mode I is typified by very large associations (national political parties and labor unions). Mode II has followed spectacular individual leadership while also serving as a showcase for voluntarism (the American Anti-Slavery Society, the Woman's Christian Temperance Union, the National Association for the Advancement of Colored People). Within Mode III there has also been a notable tendency to follow strong individual leaders, as in the "intentional" settlements, where the commune becomes a special kind of voluntary association. Utopias are projected by individuals of powerful imagination, such as Edward Bellamy, or by visionary architects like the late Buckminster Fuller.

Advocates of social change use all forms of expression available, and no single mode has monopolized any one form. Within each mode, however, some forms doubtless have been used more memorably. Mode I is associated with conventions, platforms, campaigns, organizational meetings, and political oratory. Ballots, strikes, and boycotts are the particular property of this mode. Labor has its songbook; so does civil rights. Many movements in Mode II seem highlighted by the autobiographies of inspired leaders such as the feminist Elizabeth Cady Stanton, the former slave Frederick Douglass, and the Black Muslim Malcolm X. This mode is also notable for public demonstrations from antislavery parades to Woman's Party trashings to the interracial 1963 March on Washington, where Martin Luther King, Jr., stole the show. Within Mode III there is a natural connection with drawings, plans, and specifications but also with the futuristic romance. All social action in the United States, as has been frequently pointed out, has attracted an unusual degree of involvement from the press (cartoons, muckraking journalism), from the creative imagination (protest fiction, verse, drama, and art), and from voluntarism in many guises.

If there was ever doubt that the three modes were not separate nations but part of a single kingdom, one would only need to look at their underlying arguments. They are virtually identical across modal lines as well as remarkably durable chronologically. The reformers consistently base their appeals on the authority of a higher law, on accord with reason, and on the hard rock of practicality. There are settings and causes that will educe more stress on one or two of these fundamental points, but it is rare indeed when the advocate does not attempt to convince an audience that the proposed change is in tune with moral law, in accord with the best reasoned understanding of nature and society, and within the bounds of feasibility.

The principal points of similarly and contrast between the three reform modes are graphically summarized in table 1.

☆ ☆ ☆ Reform in Historical Perspective

It is important to see the internal contrasts and constants within the body of reform. Once social change is recognized in all its stages and forms, arguments and modes, it can then be reassembled as something more comprehensive, continuous, and consequential than has heretofore been appreciated. To describe its full dimensions would require volumes. Even in outline a narrative summary should open with biblical and classical ages, whence came the concepts governing political philosophy in America, and pass carefully through the Renaissance, where these concepts acquired institutional shape.

Arbitrarily the narrative opens with nationhood and the intense era of self-definition that was as crucial to reform as it was to the development of the nation as a whole. The revision of state constitutions, the ratification of the

TABLE I. *Modes of American Reform*

	Mode I Politico-Economic	Mode II Special Groups	Mode III Alternate Models
Principal actors	Large associations Government: all levels and branches	Individuals Voluntary associations Federal, state, and local governments	Individuals Communal groups Government agencies: all levels
Characteristic forms	Speeches, tracts Campaigns, conventions Strikes, boycotts Cartoons, symbols	Speeches, autobiographies Demonstrations Cartoons, symbols, music	Plans, designs Fiction Model communities Social-impact technology
Dynamics	5-stage cycle moving from random protest through structured protest, from random solutions through structured solutions, and culminating in a legislative act, a court decision, or an executive agency	As with Mode I, except the cycle is typically experienced twice: toward segregated equality, then toward integrated equality Action tends to be interrupted	2-stage sequence moving from a structural solution to institutionalization or rejection
Arguments and assumptions	All modes make the same appeals: to morality, reason, and feasibility		
	Modes I and II assume the inevitability and propriety of gradual change; reliance on progress		Mode III assumes the necessity for drastic change

Constitution of the United States, and the addition of the Bill of Rights (the first ten amendments) combined to impart characteristics to the process of social change that remain enormously consequential. Most of the new constitutions stressed improved suffrage. All of them gave real power to elected assemblies. These twin facts not only put teeth into the idea of a social contract between each generation of the governed and the governors, but they also made inevitable the concentration on elected assemblies as the main forum for institutionalizing social change. The Bill of Rights, with its guarantees of those freedoms essential to protest and partisanship, provided the permanent underpinnings of social change. It would be hard to overestimate the collective impact on reform of the decisions made in the young Republic.

While the basic documents of democracy were being debated, the spirit of independence was generating a euphoria that led many to imagine an imminent utopia, either secular or divine. Some set about to keep the promise of the ages by improving education, conditions of labor, and care for the handicapped. With the fading of hopes for a sweeping millennium came the creation of isolated model societies and the pursuit of more limited issues such as the land question, extension of suffrage, and the regulation of monopolies, including banks.

No later than the 1840s the basic elements of reform were in place. Politico-economic reformers had long been attacking a power elite that they saw as a continuation of British-Tory influence. The two-party system began with this assault on the Federalists and matured into a second party seeking to represent the common man by espousing workers' rights, free land, and currency reform. Reformers interested in special groups had identified not only Indians and women but also victims of alcohol abuse, prisoners, and the insane. A wave of communitarianism, climaxing in the 1840s, exemplified Mode III.

Among social actors there were not only the active-if-unstable young political parties and some spectacularly effective individuals but also the beginnings of the classic voluntarism. A wide range of forms—speeches, pamphlets, cartoons, public demonstrations—was being used. Although the major social issues were characterized more by protest than by resolution, many important political questions had already been settled by adoption in constitutions and charters. Reform's fundamental assumptions and arguments were fully on display.

Just as these patterns were settling into place, however, there arose a set of circumstances that would test the entire system and affect profoundly—as has nothing since Washington's day—the essential nature of social change. These circumstances were the continuation of chattel slavery, the intensification of the campaign against it, and the resulting conflict and its resolution. Of particular consequence to reform was the demonstration that some questions were beyond local solution and that no amount of compromise—however clever—could dissolve true intransigence into the normal process of social change. As a sectional controversy this question showed that the federal government would be the court of last appeal and that this court could not be overruled, even by secession. As a reform controversy the slavery issue showed that a cause with a strong moral appeal would triumph sooner or later. The end of the Civil War in 1865 brought the passage of the Thirteenth, Fourteenth, and Fifteenth Amendments that not only ended slavery but made the federal government the protector of voting rights and due process. These amendments marked a shifting emphasis from civil liberties toward civil rights.

Neither the slavery issue nor the Civil War disrupted the continuing debate on the classic politico-economic issues of tax and tariff, money and banking, labor and property, wealth and poverty. Reformers learned that the success of the Republican party in 1860 was not representative of the usefulness or likely success of third parties. On the other hand, social pressures were slowly demonstrating to the executive and the judiciary that the interests of private property and unrestrained corporate growth were not always to be accorded top billing. While farm and labor movements were developing from negative to positive stages, some issues (civil service, trust regulation) were being institutionalized with mixed success.

☆ ☆ ☆ The Modern Era

With the coming of the twentieth century Modes II and III shifted dramatically; the task of politico-economic reform was to continue the late nineteenth-century struggles between business and labor until the government assumed the role of referee between the large unions and the large corporations. President Herbert Hoover's determined struggle to use private and local sources to cope with the Great Depression of the 1930s dramatized the inevitability of the eventual decision—his and his successor's—to accept central responsibility for nationwide economic problems. In recognizing the inevitable, and in demonstrating this recognition with an unprecedented increase in the scale of the federal government, the New Deal of Franklin D. Roosevelt became a major landmark in reform. Assuming a range of responsibilities beyond the economic, the New Deal meant that the leading edge of social change would be increasingly visible in Washington, D.C.

For partisans of large disadvantaged groups the change in centuries was dramatic. The late nineteenth century, except in women's rights and temperance, had seen little activity; what there was pertained more to segregated accommodation than to integrated equality. The twentieth century brought public recognition to some formerly neglected groups and moved others into the second cycle. Once the impossibility of equality without integration had been accepted, there emerged an increasing number of campaigns on behalf of "mainstreaming" groups previously neglected or kept apart. There were, too, the negative lessons learned from prohibition and suffrage: the futility of trying to legislate in opposition to public attitudes and the hollowness of political victory lacking in social and economic payoff.

The 1920s and 1930s were important years in all three modes. While the politico-economic reformers were extending the lessons of progressivism and accepting the consequences of a new federal power, the civil libertarians were organizing to protect the Bill of Rights from attacks engendered by war and panic. However mixed the ultimate effect, the partisans of special groups were triumphant in the ratification of the Eighteenth (prohibition) and Nineteenth (woman suffrage) Amendments. Although immigration was restricted in the 1920s, the concern for blacks and other minorities showed signs of spreading, especially in the latter days of the New Deal. The fad of the utopian romance, having exhausted itself in the first decade of the century, was replaced in the second and third decades with private and public planning. Promoters of peace and world government, frustrated after World War I, picked up their cudgels in the 1930s and enjoyed some unprecedented successes in the aftermath of World War II, including a United Nations in New York City.

The middle decades of the twentieth century saw the continuation of the reform impulse in ways that, if not predictable, were at least not surprising. The federal government, extending the momentum of the New Deal, approached a Great Society and then, counting the cost, drew back. The worst levels of poverty were alleviated through aid-in-kind, but the unequal distribution of wealth in the higher levels remained resistant to democratization. Efforts to make the system more responsive to citizen participation continued. Campaigns for neglected groups—some of them newly identified—proliferated, while the projection of the model society was manifested in a new wave of communitarianism as well as continuation of visionary planning, futuristic fiction, and world government movements. Achievements, particularly in the area of civil rights and antipoverty, have been notable; but with the reform spectrum more extensive than ever, frustrations also have been numerous.

Even such a drastically condensed summary as the foregoing makes some points that have been by no means universally accepted. One point has to do with scope. To reflect even momentarily on the number and size of groups and movements that have driven social change is to realize that reform is surely one of the major collective activities in America. Another point has to do with chronology. Once reform is recognized in all its conditions, it becomes clear that American history may not be viewed as a flat backdrop of apathy and reaction against which are cast a few frantic decades of passionate hyperactivity. There is no decade that has failed to witness important events in at least one mode, operating in at least one of its stages. American history is one continuous age of reform.

☆ ☆ ☆ Reform and the American Character

If the frontiers of social challenge rival in their impact the frontiers of technology, abundance, and unsettled land, why have they not been more carefully explored for their hidden clues to the national character? Such an exploration might reveal a set of values widely at variance with the picture of an individualistic technocracy driven toward conformity and material comfort.

Cultural values show themselves most directly in the arguments used by reformers to persuade their contemporaries. Three explicit arguments overshadow all others: the appeals to a higher law, to reason, and to a sense of the practical. These three sets of beliefs are not surprising since they arise directly from the worldviews that have shaped this North American extension of Western civilization. The first is attributable to the heavy religious influence everywhere visible during the century of colonial origins; the second is associated with the great Age of Reason that fueled the arguments for independence; and the third attunes itself to the romantic/transcendental/pragmatic chain of ideas.

It is not surprising that these arguments contradict one another, to a degree, but it is surprising to find them offered with nearly equal force in regard to nearly all subjects during all epochs. In a neat chronological world the appeal to higher law would have been succeeded by appeals to reason and then to practical tests. In fact, all causes at all times reflect the substantial and interrelated use of all three arguments, as is poignantly reflected in the titles of two reform classics published forty years apart: *Practical Christian Socialism* (by Adin Ballou, 1854) and *Practical Christian Sociology* (by Wilbur F. Crafts, 1895).

This short list of basic reform arguments omits such frequently mentioned values as progress, equality, freedom, and the sense of special mission. The incongruence is real, although not so blatant as might at first appear. Some values are implicit in either the culture, or the subject, or both. Reformers do not appeal to a faith in progress, but they obviously assume a commitment to social meliorism. Since social protest implies discontent, reformers are likely to appeal to the sense of national mission in a negative way, asking a proud people to show a sense of shame that certain problems exist in a country favored by destiny. Some values might be called "negative values" in the sense that they become evident mainly when threatened or denied. Freedom and equality come under this heading, to judge from the literature of reform.

The great, unresolved conflict is in the way the reform experience denies the primacy of individualism, self-reliance, and the pursuit of material success. In their place this tradition substitutes altruism, a concern for communal well-being, and the commitment to group action. If the study of some frontiers seems to stress the self-aggrandizing individual, surely the frontiers of social change reflect a nearly antithetical value. Walt Whitman, who articulated both sides of this conflict with unmatched eloquence, set down these notes in his journal:

> One of the problems presented in America these times is, how to combine one's duty and policy as a member of associations, societies, brotherhoods or what not, and one's obligations to the State and the Nation, with essential freedom as an individual personality, without which freedom a man cannot grow or expand, or be full, modern, heroic, democratic, American. With all the necessities and benefits of association, (and the world cannot get along without it,) the true nobility and satisfaction of a man consist in his thinking and acting for himself. The problem, I say, is to combine the two so as not to ignore either.

Both individualism and collective action are important; the balance between the two may be more important than either half of the equation in isolation. The study of reform shows that the balance is more nearly level than most students of the national character have imagined.

☆ ☆ ☆ The Preeminence of Process

If there is one supreme corrective that the study of reform applies to the appreciation of national values, it is in the identification of *process* as a value of the highest priority. Process is not a uniquely American value nor a value peculiarly associated with reform. In fact one can hardly study literature or theology, philosophy or social science, without being aware that "process" is not simply a means but an end in itself. It has been singled out by ancient Chinese as well as by contemporary analysts of social dynamics. John Dewey, more uncompromisingly than anyone of his stature, identified process as the supreme moral value. George Santayana labeled it quintessentially American. John Kouwenhoven's *Beer Can by the Highway* finds widely varied evidence of process addiction.

Reformers rely on process almost by second nature. Rare indeed is the individual like William Lloyd Garrison who feels that the slavery question is ended when the Emancipation Proclamation has been issued. His contemporaries knew that the process of social change had but shifted gears and, although they joined Garrison in his toasts and celebrated the vital power of his *Liberator*, they then turned to the Freedmen's Bureau or to the question of wage slavery. The ten-hour day only introduces the battle for the nine-hour day. Woman suffrage is but a prelude to economic and social campaigns. In its most vital sense reform fails only when the process of social change breaks down (as at Haymarket Square or Fort Sumter) and succeeds so long as the process continues.

☆ ☆ ☆ Assessing Social Change

There are ways to measure the success or failure of reform. They occur at levels nearer the surface and may not be so profound as the matter of attitudes and values, but they are of undeniable importance in terms of human lives. While difficult to read, they leave no doubt that the ultimate objectives of reform are far from realization. If voting can be taken as a measure of true democracy, then participation has dropped with each addition to the suffrage. From 1840 through 1900 about 75 percent of qualified voters cast ballots each quadrennium. Since 1904 the average turnout has been close to 60 percent for national elections, less for local ones. Only 50.2 percent of eligible voters participated in the presidential election of 1988. If the distribution of wealth is the target of political democracy, then there is the discouraging news that the spread, measured by quintiles, is about the same in 1990 as it was in 1774. If social justice for minorities is the goal, then one faces a female labor force making 70 percent of its male counterpart's income—while blacks continue to be overrepresented among the poor, the conscripted, and the bottom wage levels. Nor has any fully articulated model community galvanized the nation by its glittering example into a radically improved condition.

A closer look at any of the reform frontiers, however, brings the realization that conditions are more complex and less discouraging than the crude measurements imply. Voting, for example, is not the only form of political participation. As other forms have come under study, it has become apparent that

American citizens, relatively speaking, have a high sense of participation and that the sense of effective political representation is increasing, at least among some groups at some levels. If the end product of political participation is meant to be economic, there too the situation is by no means uniformly discouraging. In the first place, the patterns of inequality have fluctuated throughout most of the nation's history for reasons that no one seems to understand. It is therefore possible to hope that an eventual understanding of inequality may increase the facility for dealing with it. Contrary to some classic theories, there seems to be no "iron law" fixing wealth distribution, at least in the United States. In the second place, there is room to question whether the true target of reform is inequality or poverty.

If the latter, then there are substantial achievements: the virtual elimination of malnutrition and the development of large programs of aid-in-kind. The definition of poverty keeps changing—itself a hopeful sign—and the extreme deprivation historically associated with low income has become increasingly rare in the United States.

The question of measuring economic democracy may be reducible to a matter of attitude: a cup that is half empty or a cup that is half full. Since its founding the United States has enjoyed an enormous increase in wealth, thus giving the opportunity for gross inequality. During most of these years, furthermore, new population tended to enter the system at the lowest levels: most immigrants were not wealthy; proportionately more children were born to the poor. Yet in spite of the acknowledged persistence of wealth, the pattern of distribution has repeatedly reverted to a state no worse than at the nation's origin. Only during its periods of greatest inequality has wealth distribution in America resembled that of Europe. One might indeed ask whether this represents a failure or a triumph for economic democracy.

It is impossible to talk in particular terms about the social progress of groups deemed to have been disadvantaged. Each group demands its own assessment. Yet one can say, at least, that many such groups have been recognized during recent decades and many have been organized for social action for the first time. Except for some of the older national and religious groups from Europe, no one of these minorities has disappeared into the mainstream. Most of them are still vulnerable. In spite of legislation underwriting political and economic equity, disadvantaged groups still suffer most in hard times and advance only when there is enough for all. The two largest of these groups—blacks and women—show the greatest progress when one looks at the level of education and the kind of employment achieved. Progress is most questionable on such fronts as political effectiveness, share of income, and family stability.

Mode III is not susceptible to quantitative measure, and it is obvious that the world has not transformed itself into one green town, populated with harmonious neighbors. It is true, however, that alternative communities have offered some of the best opportunities to experiment with solutions to persistent problems in education and family life. Utopias have led to Garden Cities, Green Towns, and New Towns. Visionary architects and authors of science fiction have imagined forms of technology that would improve societal quality. Without movements for peace and world government it is hard to imagine a League of Nations or a United Nations.

No one said that reform was to have reached all of its objectives by 1990. It may be that the most important thing about reform is that it is alive and well—in all its modes, in all its aspects. Individual leaders replace one another with each generation. Muckraking journalism and protest literature enjoy undiminished readership. The rich tradition of voluntary associationalism becomes newly effective in an age of computers and television. Old targets are struck and fall to be supplanted by new ones. There is no historically important aspect of reform that is not replete with contemporary activity. As Kenneth Boulding has written (in *Quest for Justice*, 1974): "The quest for the Holy Grail is one of the most charming of medieval stories. Its essence is that in the course of looking for it, all sorts of interesting things happened. Social justice is perhaps the modern equivalent. It is something we must continue looking for, even though we all know it can never be found." The quest continues.

FURTHER READING

The perceptions outlined in this essay are fully presented in Robert H. Walker, *Reform in America: The Continuing Frontier* (Lexington, Ky., 1985), and supported by the materials collected in Walker, ed., *The Reform Spirit in America: A Documentation of the Pattern of Reform in the American Republic* (New York, 1976). In the absence of a general history of American reform, this pair of works is the closest approach to organizing the subject historically. They describe a dominant pattern based on objectives, dynamics, and rationales, drawing evidence from major movements and issues.

The most pertinent bibliography is Robert H. Walker, "Reform in America: A Bibliographical Outline," *American Studies International* 24 (April 1986). Other useful bibliographies include Alexander D. Brooks, *Civil Rights and Liberties in the United States: An Annotated Bibliography* (New York, 1962); Dwight L. Dumond, *Bibliography of Antislavery in America* (Ann Arbor, Mich., 1961); Robert S. Fogarty, ed., *Dictionary of American Communal and Utopian History* (Westport,

Conn., 1980); Constance Smith and Anne Freedman, *Voluntary Associations: Perspectives on the Literature* (Cambridge, Mass., 1972); Virginia Terris, ed., *Woman in America: A Guide to Information Sources* (Detroit, 1980). See also the second volume of Donald D. Egbert and Stow Persons, eds., *Socialism and American Life* (Princeton, N.J., 1952), which defines its subject with exceptional breadth, and Clio Bibliography Series 13, *Social Reform and Reaction in America* (Santa Barbara, Calif., 1984), an index to nearly three thousand articles published in 1973–82.

The best way to study reform is to go straight to the sources: legislative debates, party platforms, associational minutes, the press, personal papers of prominent social actors. Document collections can be enormously helpful, and none more so than John R. Commons et al., eds., *A Documentary History of American Industrial Society*, 10 vols. (Cleveland, Ohio, 1910), and Alpheus T. Mason and Gordon E. Baker, *Free Government in the Making*, 4th ed. (New York, 1985). Also of note are Norman Dorsen et al., *Emerson, Haber, and Dorsen's Political and Civil Rights in the United States*, 2 vols. (Boston, 1976, 1979); Donald B. Johnson, ed., *National Party Platforms*, 2 vols. (Urbana, Ill., 1978); Francis L. Broderick and August Meier, eds., *Negro Protest Thought in the Twentieth Century* (Indianapolis, Ind., 1965); Bernard Schwartz, *The Bill of Rights: A Documentary History* (New York, 1971); Upton Sinclair, ed., *Cry for Justice* (Philadelphia, 1915); and William R. Smith, *The Rhetoric of American Politics: A Study of Documents* (Westport, Conn., 1969).

The Encyclopedia of Social Reform, ed. William D. Bliss (New York, 1897), is a unique inventory of reform, made even more useful for understanding the individual social actor by Henry J. Silverman, "American Social Reformers in the Late Nineteenth and Early Twentieth Century," a 1963 doctoral dissertation at the University of Pennsylvania based on Bliss's listings. William A. Gamson's *The Strategy of Social Protest* (Homewood, Ill., 1975) is most useful for understanding collective social actors, even though his focus is not precisely on reform. Sar A. Levitan and Robert Taggert, *The Promise of Greatness* (Cambridge, Mass., 1976), provides a current and useful assessment of the role of the federal government.

For understanding the process and pattern of social change in America, the following works—arranged from the general toward the specific—are especially germane: Kenneth E. Boulding, *A Primer on Social Dynamics* (New York, 1970); Roberta Ash, *Social Movements in America* (Chicago, 1972); Thomas C. Cochran, *Social Change in Industrial Society* (London, 1972); Jo Freeman, *The Politics of Women's Liberation* (New York, 1975); and Ted R. Gurr, *Why Men Rebel* (Princeton, N.J., 1970).

Works helpful in applying quantitative measures and interpretive judgments to politico-economic reform are Sidney Verba and Norman H. Nie, *Participation in America: Political Democracy and Social Equality* (New York, 1972); James D.

Smith, ed., *Modeling the Distribution and Integrational Transmission of Wealth* (Chicago, 1980); and Sar A. Levitan, William B. Johnston, and Robert Taggert, *Minorities in the United States* (Washington, D.C., 1975).

The following works are notable for their coverage of large topics related to reform: Merle Curti, *The Growth of American Thought*, 3d ed. (New York, 1964); Ralph H. Gabriel, *The Course of American Democratic Thought*, 3d ed. (Westport, Conn., 1986); Thomas H. Greer, *American Social Reform Movements* (New York, 1949); John Bach McMaster, *The Acquisition of Political, Social, and Industrial Rights of Man in America* (Cleveland, Ohio, 1903); David J. Rothman, *The Discovery of the Asylum: Social Order and Disorder in the New Republic* (Boston, 1971), and *Conscience and Convenience: The Asylum and Its Alternatives in Progressive America* (Boston, 1980); Charles L. Sanford, *The Quest for Paradise* (Urbana, Ill., 1961); and Arthur M. Schlesinger, *The American as Reformer* (Cambridge, Mass., 1950).

The application of creative imagination to social change can be sampled in Vernon L. Parrington, *Main Currents in American Thought*, 3 vols. (New York, 1927–30); Daniel Aaron, *Writers on the Left: Episodes in American Literary Communism* (New York, 1961); Richard Fitzgerald, *Art and Politics* (Westport, Conn., 1973); Stephen Hess and Milton Kaplan, *The Ungentlemanly Art: A History of American Political Cartoons* (New York, 1968); Alfred Kazin, *On Native Grounds* (New York, 1942), and *An American Procession* (New York, 1984); Ralph E. Shikes, *Indignant Eye* (Boston, 1969); and Robert H. Walker, *The Poet and the Gilded Age* (Philadelphia, 1963).

A true bibliography of reform would be a multivolume enterprise, but the following titles further reflect the categories of discussion in this chapter, favoring works that are accurate and broadly stimulating over studies that compartmentalize the subject.

On politico-economic reform: Bernard Bailyn, *The Ideological Origins of the American Revolution* (Cambridge, Mass., 1967); Robert H. Bremmer, *From the Depths: The Discovery of Poverty in the United States* (New York, 1956); William J. Crotty, *Paths to Political Reform* (Lexington, Mass., 1980); Robert A. Dahl and Charles F. Lindblom, *Politics, Economics, and Welfare* (Chicago, 1953); Chester M. Destler, *American Radicalism, 1865–1901* (New London, Conn., 1946); Eric F. Goldman, *Rendezvous with Destiny* (New York, 1952); Lawrence Goodwyn, *The Populist Moment: A Short History of Agrarian Revolt in America* (New York, 1978); Louis Hartz, *Economic Policy and Democratic Thought* (Cambridge, Mass., 1948); Walter T. K. Nugent, *Money and American Society, 1865–1880* (New York, 1968); Edward Pessen, *Riches, Class, and Power before the Civil War* (Lexington, Mass., 1973); and Sidney Ratner, *American Taxation: Its History as a Social Force in Democracy* (New York, 1942).

On social actors and group behavior: Angus Campbell et al., *The American Voter*

(New York, 1960); Rhodri Jeffreys-Jones, *Violence and Reform in American History* (New York, 1978); Ralph M. Kramer, *Voluntary Agencies in the Welfare State* (Berkeley, Calif., 1981); Charles A. Madison, *American Labor Leaders*, 2d ed. (New York, 1962); Arthur Mann, *Yankee Reformers in the Urban Age* (Cambridge, Mass., 1954); Arthur S. Miller, *Social Change and Fundamental Law: America's Evolving Constitution* (Westport, Conn., 1979); John G. Sproat, *The Best Men: Liberal Reformers in the Gilded Age* (New York, 1968); and Alden Whitman, ed., *American Reformers* (New York, 1985).

On women and minorities: Gilbert Barnes, *The Antislavery Impulse, 1830–1844* (New York, 1933); William H. Chafe, *The Paradox of Change: American Women in the Twentieth Century* (New York, 1991); Charles C. Cole, *The Social Ideas of the Northern Evangelists, 1826–1860* (New York, 1954); Charles F. Kellogg, *NAACP* (Baltimore, 1967); Martin L. King, Jr., *Why We Can't Wait* (New York, 1964); Milton R. Konvitz, *Fundamental Liberties of a Free People* (Ithaca, N.Y., 1957); Aileen S. Kraditor, *The Ideas of the Woman Suffrage Movement, 1890–1920* (New York, 1965); Stanley Lieberson, *A Piece of the Pie: Black and White Immigrants since 1880* (Berkeley, Calif., 1980); Kate Millett, *Sexual Politics* (New York, 1970); Stephen B. Oates, *Let the Trumpet Sound: The Life of Martin Luther King, Jr.* (New York, 1982); and Louise M. Young, *In the Public Interest: The League of Women Voters, 1920–1970* (Westport, Conn., 1989).

On model societies: Isaac Asimov, "Social Science Fiction," in *Modern Science Fiction*, ed. Reginald Bretnor (New York, 1953); Baker Brownell and Frank Lloyd Wright, *Architecture and Modern Life* (New York, 1937); Merle Curti, *Peace or War: The American Struggle, 1626–1936* (New York, 1936); R. Buckminster Fuller, *No More Secondhand God* (Carbondale, Ill., 1963); Hugh Gardner, *The Children of Prosperity: Thirteen Modern American Communes* (New York, 1978); Percival Goodman and Paul Goodman, *Communitas*, 2d ed. (New York, 1960); Rosabeth M. Kanter, *Commitment and Community* (Cambridge, Mass., 1972); Lewis Mumford, *The Story of Utopias* (New York, 1922); John H. Noyes, *History of American Socialisms* (Philadelphia, 1870); Kenneth M. Roemer, ed., *America as Utopia* (New York, 1981); Charles J. Rooney, *Dreams and Visions: A History of American Utopias, 1865–1917* (Westport, Conn., 1985); Helen Rosenau, *The Ideal City*, 3d ed. (New York, 1983); Paolo Soleri, *The Sketchbooks* (Cambridge, Mass., 1971); Clarence S. Stein, *Toward New Towns for America*, 3d ed. (Cambridge, Mass., 1966); Clarence K. Streit, *Union Now* (New York, 1939); and Donald Wall, *Visionary Cities: The Arcology of Paolo Soleri* (New York, 1971).

Works that have placed social change in the largest contexts, and related reform to national values, include Kenneth A. Arrow, *Social Change and Individual Values*, 2d ed. (New York, 1963); Alexander M. Bickel, *Reform and Continuity* (New York, 1971); Thomas C. Cochran, *Challenges to American Values* (New York, 1985); Ralph H. Gabriel, *American Values: Continuity and Change* (Westport,

Conn., 1974); John A. Kouwenhoven, *The Beer Can by the Highway* (New York, 1961); Charles E. Lindblom, *The Policy-Making Process* (Englewood Cliffs, N.J., 1968); Talcott Parsons, *Structure and Process in Modern Societies* (Glencoe, Ill., 1960); David Riesman, *Individualism Reconsidered* (Glencoe, Ill., 1954); George Santayana, *Character and Opinion in the United States* (New York, 1920); and Walt Whitman, *Democratic Vistas* (Washington, D.C., 1871).

Contributors

Carl Abbott is Professor of Urban Studies and Planning at Portland State University, Oregon.

Nina Baym is Professor of English and Jubilee Professor of Liberal Arts and Sciences at the University of Illinois, Urbana–Champaign.

William H. Chafe is Alice Mary Baldwin Professor of History at Duke University.

Norman Corwin, writer-director-producer, is a visiting Professor of Journalism at the University of Southern California.

Jane Sherron De Hart is Professor of History at the University of California, Santa Barbara.

John P. Diggins is Distinguished Professor of History at the Graduate Center, City University of New York.

Raymond D. Gastil is an independent consultant currently residing in Cos Cob, Connecticut.

Nathan Glazer is Professor of Education and Sociology at Harvard University and coeditor of the *Public Interest*.

William H. Goetzmann holds the Jack S. Blanton, Sr., Chair in History and American Studies at the University of Texas, Austin.

Tamara K. Hareven is Unidel Professor of Family Studies and History at the University of Delaware, Adjunct Professor of Population Science at Harvard University, and Editor of the *Journal of Family History*.

Neil Harris is Professor of History at the University of Chicago.

Linda K. Kerber is Professor of History at the University of Chicago.

Richard Lehan is Professor of English at the University of California, Los Angeles.

Peirce Lewis is Professor of Geography at Pennsylvania State University, University Park.

Richard Lingeman is Executive Editor of the *Nation*, New York City.

Luther S. Luedtke is Professor and Director of Graduate Studies in English and American Literature at the University of Southern California.

Arthur Mann is Preston and Sterling Morton Professor Emeritus of American History and Faculty Fellow of the Division of Social Sciences at the University of Chicago.

Waldo Martin is Professor of History at the University of California, Berkeley.

Martin E. Marty is Fairfax M. Cone Distinguished Service Professor of History of Modern Christianity at the University of Chicago and Senior Editor of *Christian Century* magazine.

Murray G. Murphey is Professor of American Civilization at the University of Pennsylvania.

John B. Orr is University Professor of Religion and holds the John R. Tansey Chair of Christian Ethics at the University of Southern California.

Edward Pessen is Distinguished Professor of History at Baruch College and the Graduate Center, City University of New York.

Richard G. Powers is Professor of American Studies and History at the College of Staten Island and the Graduate Center, City University of New York.

Leland M. Roth is Professor of Art and Architectural History at the University of Oregon.

Lillian Schlissel is Professor of English and Director of American Studies at Brooklyn College, City University of New York.

John A. Schutz is Professor of History at the University of Southern California.

Dickran Tashjian is Professor of Comparative Culture at the University of California, Irvine.

Robert H. Walker is Professor of American Civilization at George Washington University.

Index